FILTHY TRUTH

A 'CONOR & STAR' DUET

THE FIVE POINTS' MOB COLLECTION: NINE

SERENA AKEROYD

DEDICATION

TO THOSE WE lost too soon.
May peace taste sweeter on your tongue than life ever could.

FOREWORD & TRIGGER WARNINGS

HELLO DARLINGS,

I know not everyone appreciates long books. But, in this instance, the fact that Filthy Truth is hovering at this page length is not something I'll apologize for. Why? Because this is my love letter to Fecker fans.

This is my last hoorah and my swan song and my final Fecker-shaped farewell.

But I didn't just write this for you, I wrote it for me, too.

I love these people.

They've become family.

While I *will* write about them in the future, in next-gen books, and in upcoming series, it'll never be the same.

So, here we are. Nearly seven-hundred pages later. :)

It's my hope that you enjoy this mahoosive read and that you can tell each word is for those of you who have supported me from the beginning, and who have lovingly waited for each release.

Thank you.

<3

NOW, there are several references to the tragedy that occurred at 19:00 on 21 December 1988 on Pan Am Flight 103 over Lockerbie, Scotland. With a total of 270 fatalities, the terrorist attack became known as the Lockerbie bombing. This event was a tragedy, and I mean no disrespect with my use of this terrible part of my country's history—it remains the deadliest terrorist attack in the history of the United Kingdom, as well as its deadliest aviation disaster.

You can read more about it here: https://en.wikipedia.org/wiki/Pan_Am_Flight_103

If only my characters were real and could bring peace to the families who have lost so much.

To this day, this reprehensible attack remains under investigation.

I ALSO WANTED to clue you into the fact that there's a deleted scene that didn't fit into the timeline of Filthy Lies here: https://dl.bookfunnel.com/sv06kgjd0e

It's dark and has sexual assault in it from Star's time as a sex slave.

IT'S ALSO that time for me to warn you that there are GRAPHIC scenes of violence and several GRAPHIC depictions of death by torture. These are the most violent books yet. Domestic violence—not between Conor and Star!!—is also handled in the story.

DON'T FORGET the second FILTHY TRUTH hits 500 reviews, I'll be dropping a bonus scene in my Diva reader group!

You can join here to read it when it happens: www.facebook.com/groups/SerenaAkeroydsDivas

Perhaps, by this point, there'll also be the bonus scene for FILTHY LIES in Divas so be sure to check that out as well.

I truly hope this makes your heart happy.
Much love,
Serena
xoxo

PLAYLIST

If you'd like to hear a curated soundtrack, with songs that are featured in the book, as well as songs that inspired it, then here's the link:

https://open.spotify.com/playlist/52BfeLC2FqwUyzWPjv9v8r?si=
b319d9e7a592479e&pt=05bbccf8308bf8459c384f2ed5512145

And if you'd like to hear Conor's playlist, then here's the link:

https://open.spotify.com/playlist/2WWftBdPeX3UKBsbNOMCtl?si=
0ff79a8ef2f84a8d&pt=ef0fb2b2b51a390a9e8d33041ecb7cad

THE CROSSOVER READING ORDER
WITH THE SINNERS & VALENTINIS

FILTHY
FILTHY SINNER
NYX
LINK
FILTHY RICH
SIN
STEEL
FILTHY DARK
CRUZ
MAVERICK
FILTHY SEX
HAWK
FILTHY HOT
STORM
THE DON
THE LADY
FILTHY SECRET
REX
RACHEL
FILTHY KING

NAMES OF INTEREST:

NEW WORLD SPARROWS - often abbreviated to NWS. The members are known as Sparrows.

One of three global secret societies of criminals hidden in plain sight, mostly known for sex trafficking. Having infiltrated every aspect of US society, from the government to the courts to law enforcement agencies, they've escaped justice for their heinous crimes for decades.

Old World Sparrows - tied to the New World Sparrows. The oldest organization of the trio. Their territory is Europe.

Eastern Sparrows - the final Sparrow organization. Their territory is Asia.

Éire le chéile go deo - often abbreviated to ECD. The members are known as *cheiles*. An Irish organization dedicated to uniting Northern Ireland with the Republic and removing the British from their land.

Satan's Sinners' MC - a motorcycle club in West Orange, New Jersey. Allied to the Five Points. Led by Rex, the Prez.

Famigghia - Sicilian Mafia. Allied to the Five Points. Led by Luciu Valentini, the Don.

Russian Bratva, newly named The Forgotten Boys - Allied to the Five Points. Led by Maxim Lyanov, the Pakhan/Shukher.

United Brotherhood - An elite Russian version of the Masons. Led by Anton Kuznetsov.

PART 1

If you simply can't understand why someone is grieving so much, for so long, then consider yourself fortunate that you do not understand.
- Joanne Cacciatore

1

CONOR

Conor O'Donnelly

"LOOKS like they're not coming for a friendly chat, Troy," Star, the love of my life, hollered at the woman who we were trying to spare from being murdered as she loaded her SMG with a magazine of bullets. "They're here to *silence* you. And to be honest, I'm not sure I fucking blame them, you pain in the goddamn ass."

With Troy's Range Rover doing a great impression of a burned-out shell, there was no denying the Sparrows had come in guns blazing.

As an Irish mobster who routinely pulled stunts that would give the average citizen nightmares, nothing could've readied me for the intensity that had overtaken the three women once Troy's ride had been hit with an RPG from the highway.

If anyone believed that women were lesser than men, then they needed to see Lodestar, Dead To Me, and Troy gearing up for war while multitasking by bitching at one another.

"I managed to figure that out on my own, Lodestar," Troy snarled back as she packed the holsters she wore on her hip with spare rounds. "Your digging around is probably the only fucking reason they're on their way though. I bet Ovianar is dead and Dagda is under goddamn attack because of you.

"This is why I hated you in training. You were such a digger. You could never leave shit alone. See an unturned stone? Not for long. Star just has to overturn it and unleash Ebola on the world!"

"You managed to get those crosshairs on you all by yourself. I don't think blaming Star when we're here to save you is fair," I growled.

"This isn't helping," was Dead To Me's flat response. Her words were bland but her actions weren't.

Having hauled the duffle bags we'd brought with us from the trunk, she was digging through our gear and kept shoving weapons at the bickering women while checking out the highway for incoming grenades.

Because she was right and because *I* hadn't been handed a semi-automatic, I asked, "Where do I go?"

The bickering stopped, and Star's eyes widened as she turned to me. The deepest welter of regret whispered into being in her expression, so sharp it took me aback, then she stormed over to me, grabbed my shirt, and shook me.

"You get your ass inside. You stay away from windows. You do not leave the building unless I call you. Do you understand?"

Tapping my loaded holster, I frowned at her. "I can shoot, Star. I'm not like you but I can goddamn defend myself and I can help—"

Troy sniffed. "Pretty boy like you ain't got nothin' in him but glittery jizz—"

My brows lifted at that. "Excuse me? What the fuck is glittery jizz?"

"All sparkly like, to make the bitches ooh and aah."

"I've never made a bitch ooh and ahh—"

"I disagree," Star butted in at the same time as Dead To Me snarled:

"We don't have time for this." D strapped a shotgun to her shoulder. "Conor, get your glittery jizz inside the goddamn house. This is our territory. I wouldn't wade into a hacking war. We each have our strengths and there's no shame in that.

"Plus, if Star thinks you're wandering around, it'll distract her and we don't need her distracted. The three of us need to be hot shit."

My mouth tightened but I nodded. I didn't mind admitting that fighting in *sieges* wasn't my strength, but... "I don't have glittery jizz."

The regret in Star's eyes had dimmed some. "We can agree you're a pretty boy, no?"

I sniffed. "If that's supposed to make me feel better, it worked."

She grinned, and that was the best thing I'd done the whole fucking day. If this was the last time—

No.

She wasn't going to die.

I wasn't going to die.

Troy rammed me in the side. I scowled at her as I accepted the SMG she handed me. "Glitter, you think you can handle this?"

"I know how to use it, yeah," I growled. "And it's aCooooig, thank you very much. If you don't want me to call you *Helen* or *The Face*, then I won't, but only if you drop this Glitter bullshit."

It was her turn to sniff. "Don't go G.I. Joe on us. Just head to the second floor. To the east, there's a long corridor that leads to a door at the end of the hall. First on the right, that's where you stand. You stay there. You guard that fucking door with your life, do you hear me?"

"You want me to guard *a door*?" This Australian Shepherd shit was coming back to bite me in the ass.

"I do. Got a problem with that, *Conor*?"

Pointing the gun at the ground, I stated, "No, I don't have a problem with that." Just with her.

Bitch.

She dipped her chin. "Anything happens to us—"

"It won't," Star snapped. "We got shit to do today and dying ain't on the list."

"You two have your EarPods, right?" I inserted quickly, ducking into the trunk to collect my laptop.

"We do," Star confirmed.

"Got them," Dead To Me asserted.

"I'll open up a channel."

"Can you link me in on it?"

Nodding at Troy, I said, "Will do."

Swallowing, Star cupped my face and pressed a hard kiss to my lips. "I love you, Conor O'Donnelly."

My eyes flared wide. "I want to hear that again when you aren't trying to convince us we're not going to die, okay?"

"Okay."

Another hard kiss and I was dumping my shit on the ground and hauling her into me. I only pulled back long enough to growl, "I love you too, Star Sullivan."

Jaw tense, eyes cold, she nodded at me. "We *will* see tomorrow."

Each syllable was like a bullet, settling into my gut with a centripetal force that left me staggered.

"*We* will see tomorrow," I rumbled back, trying to imbue the words with the faith I had in her. A faith that was absolute. A faith that was founded in *us*.

She blew out a breath, then the Star I knew was gone, replaced with one I'd only met in passing.

It wasn't my woman.

It wasn't the love of my life.

It was the soldier.

Thank fuck for the soldier, though, because I needed Lodestar to bring her A-game.

She rushed over to Dead To Me and started loading up even more gear as I headed toward the house without a backward glance because that would *not* be the last time I saw her.

I refused to accept that.

So, I did what I did best.

I obeyed the order on where to position myself and considered it fate that, right beside the goddamn door Troy had described, there was an outlet.

Unpacking my computer from its case, I plugged it in, settled the SMG on the floor and, once I piggybacked onto Troy's Wi-Fi, shot my brothers a warning about Dagda and used the worm Star had given me —*seriously, best gift ever*—to begin the process of hammering into Troy's security so that it unlocked for me.

At the same time, I created a channel that would link us all and, once it opened, demanded, "Check in."

"Here. 1, over." *Star.*

"Here. 2, over." *D.*

"Here. 3, over." *Troy.*

For an answer, I grunted as I focused on my laptop.

With the worm's help, I was inside her system in less than a minute.

Now able to see each of her (impressive) perimeter alarms, I could also shut off that motherfucking noise that was going to drive me crazy.

The lay of the land was spread out like an open book in front of me. It consisted of a bunch of corn fields, then tilled areas that reminded me of my ma's flowerbeds with boxes I assumed were beehives dotted into the formation.

Two sets of gates were blown wide, and once I took note of the vehicles, I briefed them, "Two cars approaching from the front gates, one from a back road. Only the one from the back road is speeding."

"Maybe they do just want to talk?" D asked.

"No. They want answers. If I don't give them to them, then they'll kill me," Troy said, her insipid, bored tone belonging to a Starbucks barista who couldn't spell Sarah and not a woman who was being targeted by a secret society.

"Answers to which questions?"

"Not worth..." Troy cleared her throat then mumbled something that sounded like, "...my life to discuss them."

"That's exactly what's in the cards here, Troy," I snapped. "Your life! So maybe share with the class?"

"You guard that fucking door, Conor. Do you hear me?"

"I do. I hear you, Troy." Hearing the sounds of exerted breathing in my ears and knowing the women were situating themselves in their nests, I peered behind me, wondering what I was guarding. "What am I actually protecting?"

"You don't need to know."

"Are you aware of how annoying you are?" I queried.

"Yeah, douche."

"As long as you are." I rolled my eyes. "Car on the back road is just pulling up. Three men are getting out."

"Have eyes on them," Dead To Me bit off, her regular *laissez-faire* joker self not in attendance.

I knew shit was serious, but that was a massive identifier in and of itself.

"First car contains four guys."

"Yeah, it looks like they want to talk," Star grumbled. "Seven men in two cars for one Troy? Those Sparrow fuckers. I can't wait to tear their world apart."

"There's my girl," I said proudly. "Second car has two men."

"Nine guys total."

"Got eyes on those two cars out front, Troy. If you want to…"

Star didn't get the chance to finish that sentence before bullets were fired. I almost groaned when I saw the gunfire coming from that same fucking tree Troy had stationed herself in before and groaned for real when I saw she'd shot out their goddamn tires.

"You fucking idiot, Troy," D hissed.

"What did she do?"

"She blew out their tires, Star," D snarled.

"You moron. Now they can't tuck tail and run if they want to."

"I've got Lodestar and Dead To Me set up in sniper's nests on my property," was Troy's cool retort. "We're going to slaughter the lot of them."

Star growled under her breath. "You leave us no fucking choice but to do that now, especially when we could have interrogated the one in charge."

As she let off some rounds, D spat, "Idiot, idiot, idiot."

The CCTV footage became a blur of action as men attempted to creep out of their vehicles, guns locked onto targets as they tried to shoot at the nests where the women had established themselves.

Within a matter of five minutes, Star had picked off the guys at the back and had joined D and Troy out front.

The Tarantino fan in me was beyond impressed at how she'd blown one of their heads off and had gone for gut shots that left them incapac-itated on the ground to die a slow, painful death when help didn't come —I felt that.

Actual Sparrows.

In a siege.

What better opportunity than now to burn off past resentments with skillful shots that left the lasting impression of 'til death do us part?

"We just want to talk to you!" a Sparrow shouted.

"Yeah, I bet," Troy roared, taking aim at one of the guys from the second car who'd spent his time crouched behind the vehicle, using it as a shield. "You want to talk to me, but you send in nine guys to make sure I can't get away? I don't think so." She punctuated that by tearing someone's throat apart with a bullet.

With Dead To Me and Star firing as well, the only thing that was slow about this was how the remaining guards were pinned down, only popping up rarely to lessen how often they could get hit.

But, like whack-a-mole, the snipers took them out, and while they were easy prey in the grand scheme of things, that didn't take away from the odds of three against nine.

When the only men remaining were the two from the second car, Star called, "Maybe you should ask your questions now that you're the ones who are outnumbered?"

My lips cocked up in a grin. The nerves of earlier were gone, and it registered then that she hadn't been scared for herself, just for me.

For our tomorrow.

God, I was going to kiss the fuck out of her when I got my hands on her.

Did she even know how hot she was?

"We came here for the girl."

"The girl?" D muttered.

"You can't have the girl," Troy spat. "Not only because I ain't got one, but even if I did, she wouldn't be yours to have."

"She's an active member in an investigation—"

Star hooted. "Because each of you belongs to the Connecticut State Police, don't you?"

"We're satellite officers—"

Three women started cackling in my ear at that.

"Yeah, okay," D shouted. "I'll believe you when thousands wouldn't."

"What investigation?" Star shouted around her giggle-snorts.

"Into her parents' murders."

I zoomed in on the car, trying to see if I could figure out what the pair were doing from behind the shield.

Both cars had been parked at an odd angle, so I attempted to use the reflection from the other vehicle's bodywork to see what was happening.

My eyes flared when, after zooming in, I saw that one of the guys had a hand grenade in his palm.

"They've got more grenades," I snapped.

There was silence on the other end of the line, silence from all quarters.

Then:

"They lob that and one of us could be fucked." D.

"We're fucked if we try to pick them off." Star.

"You got any grenades, Troy?"

"I got a flame thrower, D."

My eyes widened. "You have a fucking flame thrower in your *tree*? You know they're *flammable*."

"I'd prefer to burn than for these pricks to get their hands on me."

"Tell me you're insane without telling me you're insane," I muttered under my breath.

"No, Conor, she's right. She knows what they're capable of. I'd have preferred to burn to death too than deal with what happened to me in Lebanon."

Her words slayed me because Star was a fighter and it…

I released a breath.

"We'll make *them* burn, Star," I vowed.

A soft chuckle sounded in my ear. "I like you, Glitter."

"Don't start, D, and don't use that fucking name or I'll call you Lucinda."

"Children, less bickering," Troy rumbled, but she sounded amused.

These women.

"They're not going to blow us up yet. Not until they think they can get the answers they need," Star mused.

"So we get to them first?" D questioned.

"We need a distraction," I stated. "So that Troy can get down and can use the flame thrower without self-immolating in the process."

This was turning into a game of *Grand Theft Auto* and I wasn't happy about it.

"What kind of magic can you do for us, Conor?" D chirped.

As I riffled through the bag of tricks that was Troy's security, I hummed. "Get ready for your ears to feel like they're going to burst."

Troy cackled so she knew where I was going with this, but she cursed with the rest of us as a high-pitched siren flooded the air, horrific enough to make ears bleed. The noise-canceling feature on our EarPods likely wouldn't protect us for long though.

Into the melee, Star and Dead To Me fired rounds at the car, battering it until it looked like an oversized cheese grater. Into that chaos, I saw Troy climb down from her nest, a flame thrower in her hands.

Studying her position, I watched as she neared their vehicle, and then, and only then, did I disconnect the alarm.

And I watched her roast some Sparrows for dinner.

STAR

PLEASE DON'T SAY YOU LOVE ME -
GABRIELLE ARLIN

Star Sullivan

I'D KNOWN we'd be able to pick them off quickly, but there was always a fear that something could go wrong—it had before—and there was always a fear when you had someone you loved in on the action that they could get hurt.

In this instance, not only was Conor on the ground with me, the only man I'd *ever* loved, but D was too. She was my BFF and the singular person in this world, until Conor, who accepted me—warts, verrucas, zits, and all.

Knowing we were safe for the moment, I sagged with relief against the wall where I was positioned beneath a window. But the relief was quickly replaced with amusement.

From this vantage point, as the men started rolling around on the ground, trying to put out the flames—*seriously, only Troy*—I watched them shriek as the fire tore them apart.

Was there a more satisfying sight than seeing men who'd wanted you dead burning alive?

Nope.

D cackled in my ear, clearly enjoying the show as much as I.

When we had two barbecued Sparrows in the front yard, I asked, "Conor? Visuals?"

"Both sets of gates are blown apart. There's no way of securing them."

"We need out of here then," Troy grumbled. "Fucking serve your country and this is the thanks you goddamn get."

Ignoring her mutterings, because, hell, each of us had served in our own way so she wasn't the only person to have made sacrifices for Uncle Sam, I inquired, "No one else is incoming?"

"Nope. She's got cameras along her perimeter and the only area that's busy is the party out front."

"Good." Acknowledging that we were safe for the moment, I let the news sink in. "Troy? Get your ass in here and pack whatever you need. You're coming with us."

"I'd prefer to go deep undercover."

"I'm sure you would," D said smoothly. "But can you go in deep if you're hauling a kid around with you? Seeing as you apparently have a daughter…"

Technically, you *could.* I'd done it myself but not everyone had an ex in an MC that had severe authority issues. I was just lucky that way, I guessed.

"Fuck, fuck, fuck."

Troy's response told me two things. One, that she *did* indeed have a daughter, which was insane to me. Christ, not just insane, but *impossible.*

Second, that she wouldn't give us any shit about coming with—the woman could bicker at her reflection in the bathroom so I wouldn't have put it past her.

We were allies and had worked together in the past, but she was so far down the rabbit hole that even friends were foes.

I got it.

So, I didn't judge and wanted to help, but you could only help people who wanted it and Troy rarely did.

Stomping into the house like a five-year-old, grumbling with each step, I watched her until she disappeared, then I climbed to my feet and leaned against the wall.

We were safe.

Conor was safe.

Relief made the starch in my knees disappear.

"Come to me, Star."

The words were whispered for me alone, and amid D and Troy's sniping, I heard them and felt them settle in deep.

Straight to my bones.

Etching them with his name.

Giving me the strength to hunt him down.

I strode from the bedroom that I'd selected as my secondary nest and I rushed into the hall. It was a big place, so it took me rounding a few corners before I found him, a gun, and his computer gear scattered on the floor nearby.

Beside him, Troy was knocking on the door to what I assumed was a safe room, and his curiosity had him watching her while also looking down the hallway for me to show up.

When he spotted me, his curiosity faded and he gravitated toward me as quickly as I did him.

We rushed into one another's arms, holding each other tightly, enough that it hurt. Tight enough that I'd bruise. Tight enough that I'd still feel his embrace when he let go.

"We'll see tomorrow," he whispered in my ear.

I closed my eyes and nodded. "I knew we would but…"

"But…," he agreed.

We both knew nothing was guaranteed in this life.

My cell buzzed.

"Mom!"

The pair of us slackened our embrace at the sound of a little girl's voice.

Head whipping around, I watched as Troy, the woman who could lure any mark in like a siren before snapping their necks, sank to her knees and clung to the child as fiercely as the girl clung to her.

"Troy can't have children." It was the only thing I could think to say. Not when she didn't have the computer skills like I did to fake an ID to foster/adopt a kid and definitely not after Beijing.

"Why can't she?" he asked, his gaze on the child who'd come from *somewhere*.

"Accident in Beijing," D stated, stepping up beside us to watch what, I had to admit, was a touching display of affection between a very small, undersized almost, little girl and a woman I considered to be a psychopath.

Yes, that was the kettle calling the pot black, but that was how bad Troy was—she made me look sane.

The kid was sobbing in Troy's embrace, and I winced at the sight because it reminded me too much of Katina.

My sister-in-arms hushed and soothed her, then she shifted back and cupped the girl's cheeks before saying, "You did so good, LyLy. You stayed where I wanted you to stay, and you only came out with the code word."

Shivers rushed down my spine at the nickname.

LyLy—abbreviated for Lyra?

"I was so scared," the little girl whimpered, sniffling as she shuddered with fear.

"I know and I'm so sorry you had to experience that. I told you, no one, *no one*, will ever take you from me, didn't I?"

I got the feeling the words weren't just for LyLy, but for us too.

"You did," she whispered, her bird-like arms scooping around Troy's neck who hauled her into her chest and hefted her up so she was carrying the child.

With a stony glare, she turned to us and stated, "I'm going to assume you have somewhere you want us to stay?"

Us.

"Troy, who is she?" D inquired, her tone calm.

"My daughter." Then, defiantly, she growled, "Lyra."

Conor gently squeezed my hip as we got our confirmation.

"Why did they want the girl?" D continued, her questions gentle.

"You already know why. Don't pretend that you don't know what happened in Ohio," she snapped.

"Why didn't you change her name?" I inquired, perplexed.

"Outside these walls, she's Lee, LyLy to her friends. She's mine now. *Mine*, do you hear me, Star?

"No one will take her from me. Not the goddamn Sparrows, not fucking Jorgmundgander."

Lyra shivered in her arms, hearing the words, her fear becoming a visceral thing—and I needed to ease that.

"I have no intention of taking her from you, Troy. I'm neither with the Sparrows *nor* Jorgmundgander," I told her softly. "But the girl in Ohio, in that car, I *am* her cousin and…"

Troy's mouth firmed into a stark line of rejection. "No."

"Yes, I am. Our grandfather is the reason I'm here. I didn't know about him *or* her until this week."

"He can't have her," she spat, shuffling back a step, but she was hemmed in, and I had to reckon that that only augmented her fear.

"He can't have her," I agreed, watching as some of the tension in her shoulders relaxed. "He only wanted to know if she was being looked after. He was scared that she was in a foster home or something. That she was without a family when family wanted her."

"And he only started searching for her now?" she hissed. "Some fucking grandfather he is. He *cares*, does he?

"Who was the one who held her through the nightmares and who comforted her when she wept? Who got her through her surgeries and who—"

"Her surgeries?" Conor questioned tensely. "She's ill?"

"No. After her… *after*," she said, tone blunt, "she ran into traffic to escape. She got knocked over."

"They tried to find her in the hospitals."

"I have contacts," she muttered, telling us without words that a black-site hospital had been used to help Lyra through her injuries.

Black-site hospitals were only accessible while serving in the CIA actively, which she hadn't been doing because she was working with Jorgmundgander.

I frowned at the news though, asking, "Since when did you have those kinds of contacts?"

She scowled at me. "Since when were you so nosy?"

D tilted her head to the side. "I thought that was bullshit about you being involved with the Çelas."

Troy stiffened. "Don't even think about saying that name under this roof."

"Çela," D taunted, hands plunked on her hips as if she baited a pissed-off lion.

The other woman growled, but I snapped, "Less of the infighting. Who are the Çelas?"

When Conor chuckled, I scowled at being the only one left in the dark. "You *are* Helen, aren't you? Elena Çela?"

I demanded, "Who's that?"

"Albanian Mob. Big in Kentucky and have been for the last twenty or so years."

Kentucky?

He heard my unasked question. "Massive presence in racehorses but small fry in the scheme of things."

"Race fixing?"

"That, but deeper too. They own massive stables and have a stud and everything." I sensed his curiosity at this revelation. "Elena was the daughter of Altin Çela. It was like that whole Shergar situation in Ireland."

"The what with the what now?" I queried.

"Shergar was a horse who got stolen by a gang of armed thieves in County Kildare. Well, the same thing happened here. Only Kelmendi, a prize-winning stallion, got snatched but the daughter did too. The horse was found dead; the daughter was *not* found."

Troy, who'd grown steadily more stony throughout this conversation, ground out, "I don't want to talk about this."

"The things you freakin' learn about people," D muttered, shaking her head in surprise. "Anyway, we need to get going just in case a host of Sparrows come flocking once they realize we're not dead and their dudes are."

"I don't want to go," Lyra wailed, clutching desperately at Troy.

Troy's gaze collided with mine and I appeased, "We wish neither of you any harm, Troy. If anything, we came here to help."

"Sounds like you helped Ovianar," Troy rumbled.

"You don't know what happened there," I spat.

O's passing was going to be an open wound for a very long time and *now,* barely an hour after I got the news, wasn't the moment to be shoving it in my face.

"I know that you left her to fend for herself because if you hadn't, she wouldn't be dead."

The guilt—fuck, the guilt had me leaning back into Conor for support.

As he always seemed to, he gave me that without any question, without any hesitation.

His hand, still on my hip, was a gentle pressure, and I whispered, "I-I didn't think…"

"You don't, do you, Lodestar? That's your problem. You *don't* think."

"That's enough," Conor snapped. "We did let Ovianar down. I accept that. We shouldn't have left her unprotected, and that's on us, but we're trying to do the opposite here and you giving us shit is just wasting time and putting you and your daughter in danger.

"If you can't see that, then you're the one with the problem. Let's stop what happened to Ovianar from happening to you."

Her nostrils flared but she dipped her chin in reluctant agreement.

"Go and get packed," D prompted. "We have no way of knowing when/if you can return."

Lyra started sobbing again at that, keying us into the fact she was absorbing shit she shouldn't be listening to at her age.

Clucking her tongue, Troy soothed her as she escaped to a bedroom. Inside, I heard the sounds of doors opening and drawers rattling and banging as if suitcases were being dropped onto the floor.

Turning to them both, I rasped, "We did let Ovianar down."

Conor graced me with a sharp nod. "We did."

Dead To Me sighed. "Wish I could disagree, but I can't."

My heart hurt. Literally hurt. Ovianar and I hadn't been the best of friends, but she'd been there for me when I needed her and I'd failed to do the same. Failed in the most basic act of friendship.

"Is Minerva in danger?" D asked, watching as Conor squatted down to double-check the cameras on Troy's estate then dug around in his pocket, which rustled with every tweak of his fingers.

Only fuck knew what he kept in there along with the dozen packets of candy he had in storage 'just in case the world tasted too bitter' for me.

At that moment, I could have drowned in sugar and it wouldn't have been enough.

"Could be," I muttered. "We should get someone to help her. She has the Four Horsemen as backup..."

"Once they learn Ovianar is dead, they're going to be pissed and I'm sure they'll help her out," D agreed. "But I think Reggie is there, isn't she?"

I rubbed my brow. "I don't know. I haven't kept in touch with the old crowd as much as you."

"Want me to see if she's in London and if she can help?"

"Thanks, D. I'd appreciate it."

She squeezed my shoulder. "This isn't on you, Star. This BS has been a festering wound since it happened, and you know how it rolls. Just because you survive a job intact, doesn't mean that it won't come and bite you on the ass at some point in the future."

"She had a kid," I whispered miserably.

"And it sucks. But it's not on you. It's on the Sparrows. In the future, we'll work hard to make sure that there's no collateral damage.

"However, in this, Ovianar's been a dead woman for a long time." Her gaze drifted to the open door of the bedroom where Troy was packing up her things. "So's Troy if she won't stop being stubborn and won't let us help her keep those addled brains of hers inside her skull."

Not allowing me to reply, she strode a few steps away, pulled out her cell, and put in a call to Reggie, AKA Regina. Before my forced sabbatical back in Afghanistan, she'd been our CO.

Remembering my cell had buzzed earlier, I checked my notifications.

Savannah: I need you

Fear burrowed into my soul.

Me: What's wrong?

Me: Is it Kat? Is she okay?

Savannah: Sure she is. She's eating with Shay and Victoria.

Thank fuck for that.

Me: Then what's the problem? And don't scare me like that!

Savannah: Didn't mean to. I need you to tell Aidan that you won't get Conor killed.

My brows lifted.

Me: Are you drunk?

Savannah: Maybe a little.

Me: FML

Me: I won't get Conor killed.

Me: He's still alive.

I snapped a shot of him and sent it to her. At Conor's frown, I muttered, "Apparently, Aidan thinks I'm going to get you killed."

"They have such little faith in me," he grumbled.

"I think I'm the problem."

Me: See? Alive.

Savannah: Then why is he telling Aidan that Dagda's been shot?

Me: Because he has been.

Me: But Conor hasn't. Look, I have to go. Sober up or you'll have a killer headache in the morning.

Savannah: I don't know why but I'm glad you're back.

Me: I can feel your love across the state.

Savannah: Good. Bitch. Now, answer my other texts.

Ignoring her last message and turning to Conor, I let loose a heavy exhalation. "Everything okay?"

"No one's incoming. We're still safe."

"Good. That's a relief."

He snagged my hand and, with the other, tucked something into my fingers, saying, "Here."

My lips twitched at the candy corn he'd slipped me. As I eyed the bag that he rattled like a maraca, I asked, "This is to keep me perked up?"

"Fitting considering what just happened." Something slithered into his eyes, something that had me accepting the candy and popping it between my lips.

"I don't want you to say yes or no," he murmured. "I just want you to wear something for me. Would you do that?"

"What is it?" was my wary reply.

Conor snorted. "It's not a gimp suit or anything like that."

I rolled my eyes. "Good to know."

His hand was back in his pocket but this time, he retrieved a small box. A *very* small, very velvet-covered box.

Eyes wide, I watched as he opened it and without any ceremony, took my hand and slipped the ring onto my finger.

My mouth worked as I studied the unusual piece of jewelry, a very unobvious engagement ring, then I whispered, "Why now?"

"Because we'll have a tomorrow and I don't want to spend it with anyone but you."

The words were simple, and in his eyes, there was a warmth that blasted some of the frost settling in my bones that had started to form after learning of O's death.

Heartburn.

Major fucking heartburn.

I rubbed my thumb over the emerald in the setting. "You were just carrying this around? By chance?"

"Not exactly by chance," he dismissed. "Da gave it to me in his will. It's been in the family for a long time."

"It was your ma's?"

"No. My grandmother didn't like Ma." So, she had great taste then. "Normally, she would have given it to Da when he proposed, but she didn't give it to him until she died as part of her estate."

That had my brows lifting. "He gave it to you? Not Aidan Jr.?"

"No. He seemed to think…" His words waned, then he shrugged. "It's mine and I want you to have it."

I stared at the strangely antique setting. It was a cabochon emerald with a woman's face etched into the stone. The cameo was still fresh despite its antiquity, while the yellow gold had scratches from wear and tear.

It wasn't me at all.

Yet… I loved it.

"Who's the woman?" I asked softly.

"There's a story there," he promised, "and one day, I'll tell you. But not yet, okay?"

"Why not? Was she the first highwaywoman in Ireland or something?"

His lips curved. "No, nothing like that."

"That smile says it's exactly like that."

Glee flashed in his eyes but his words were lofty: "You'll find out someday. Will you wear it?"

I could have leveraged the story for a promise to wear the damn thing, but no part of me wanted to hand it back to him.

We both knew what it meant. We both knew that it represented the future. We both knew that I was nowhere near ready for marriage.

Yet, it bound me to him in a way that would cement ties with his family.

"Why didn't you give this to me earlier?" I rumbled, not annoyed, just intrigued.

His brothers' third degree hadn't been painful, had, in fact, made me respect them. Not only because they cared for Conor, but because they were aware of my past and knew that it made me as slippery as an eel.

I appreciated a smart man—Conor was proof of that—but I enjoyed it more when men knew to tread carefully around me. Especially deadly men like the O'Donnellys.

"Because it wasn't the right time."

Frowning, I shot a look at the laptop screen where mangled corpses lay out in Troy's front yard for the whole world to see. "And *this* is the right time?"

He shot me a grin. "I think it sums us up perfectly, don't you?"

"I'll—"

"Some women get fancy meals at restaurants, some get elaborate proposals on bridges over a river in the springtime, but you get a bloodbath, Star," D drawled. "He clearly knows you too well."

My nose crinkled as I elbowed her, but my own smile was sheepish as I admitted, "He does."

She snagged my hand and stared at it. "Who's the broad?"

"An ancient O'Donnelly," was all I said.

"How ancient?"

"The ring's three hundred years old but she's not an O'Donnelly," Conor answered as he started collecting his things and packing them in the case which he shoved at D. "Hold this. I don't want to put my laptop away until we're off this farm."

"Smart thinking," I agreed. "We need to make sure they can't ambush us."

"Fuckers," he rumbled.

"I think this is proof that Garry Smythe and David Foundry know we're onto them," D concurred. "So, what are our next steps?"

"They need to die," I said simply.

D nodded. "Affirmative. What about Dagda?"

"I sent my brothers a message before the siege—"

"I know," I interrupted wryly.

"—I haven't received any updates yet, but I can call once we're on the road."

Troy interrupted our conversation by striding out of the bedroom and heading into a different one. Lyra's hand clutched at hers as she tugged her along with surprising gentleness for a natural-born stomper.

Lyra's chin was tucked into her chest, her face tilted away so that we couldn't see her expression. The only thing I noticed was that her hair was a beautiful golden-caramel color.

My cousin.

My blood.

My fingers curled into fists, nails burrowing into my palms.

Conor's hand cupped my shoulder. "No one will get to her or Katina, Star."

"I know they fucking won't."

Not without losing their brains to my bullet first.

3

———

STAR

Star Sullivan

WE WERE DRIVING BACK to the city when a cell rang. At first, I thought it was the phone D had given me before we split up, the one that Muñoz had been carrying at the time of his death, but it wasn't—it was mine.

Conor was behind the wheel this time, D was with Troy and Lyra—both to make sure they didn't run off *or* get lost on their way to Hell's Kitchen—and I was in the passenger seat, mostly staring at my new ring until that was interrupted by the call.

"Private number," I told Conor.

"When Kuznetsov called me, it was down as that."

I grunted and hit accept. "Hello?"

"Star," he greeted. "You have news?"

My lips quirked because I knew what he was getting at. "You can't expect to work with a spy and not have them evade your guards."

He clucked his tongue. "I told them to let you go at the airport—"

"I just bet you did," I scoffed. "Anyway, we're not in prison, *Grandfather*. We're free to do whatever we want, and right now, our goals align so you know anything that goes down is something that you'll agree with."

"Our goals might align, but I doubt our methods do."

"Don't act innocent when your people are the ones holding Reinier in a shipping container in the Catskills." *Never mind the fact he wanted Troy dead to avenge his son.* "You can't effect change without getting your hands dirty."

"One day," Kuznetsov murmured, his tone wistful, "I wonder if you'll utter that word without contempt."

My brow furrowed. "Which word?"

Conor snorted. "*Grandfather.*"

"Oh. I—" The words 'wouldn't count on it' were on the tip of my tongue yet there was no denying he *had* been helpful in some things, and it wasn't that I thought I'd ever use the label kindly, but rubbing salt into the wound was only my style when I was torturing someone.

Kuznetsov cleared his throat. "Never mind. Where are you?"

"I'm certain you have a trace on our SUV," Conor drawled. "If you're trying to have an open and honest relationship with Star, Anton, then try to be *open and honest.*"

Silence on his end.

On mine, my lips twitched at Conor's retort.

Conor was a family man—it was in his bones. I knew he'd support my grandfather just because he wanted it to be beneficial for me.

Still, nothing in this life came for free, and I was definitely not free and most certainly not cheap.

"Very well." Kuznetsov sighed. "Why are you in Stamford?"

"Because we had to collect someone."

"Someone being…?"

My jaw worked as I rumbled, "Nothing is ever as facile as we believe it to be, Kuznetsov."

"No, it isn't. But I didn't take you for a professor in philosophy, Star. You have found Aleks' killer, I assume, and you know them?"

"I know that her hands were tied."

Once again, silence sounded down the line, but this time, it was loaded.

"Jorgmundgander," he drawled eventually.

"Yes."

"And you know her?"

"She's a massive pain in the ass, but I do know her, and she's good people."

"Jorgmundgander only recruited criminals."

"Most people in the life are half-criminal. Depends on who you ask. You speak with the average citizen, me going around killing people shouldn't be legal, yet here we are."

He grunted. "What happened?"

"It took uncovering the details of Belyaev's death to learn the truth about your son's. Through Belyaev's, the operatives in question told us who worked on Aleks' and we were able to track her down.

"The sniper in question lived in Stamford. We approached her because we had intel that suggested Lyra escaped her father's car after the crash and then waded into traffic. We wanted to know if she had any idea where the child had gone."

"She wasn't in the system?"

"The source of our intel claimed that Jorgmundgander tried to clean house and uncovered nothing."

"They wanted the child dead?" A throb of anger rippled through his words. A throb that gave me hope for the next phase in our plan.

"They did," I confirmed.

A rumble of Russian was snarled into my ear, one that spoke of outrage and grief and disgust.

"No better than animals. Lives mean nothing to the Sparrows. They never have. That is why they are at odds with us—"

Because I didn't need to hear the Union's manifesto, I interrupted, "Jorgmundgander isn't as neutral as you thought."

"No, it would appear not if the Sparrows are using them as a personal army."

"I have a favor to ask."

"A favor when you are already attempting to deny me justice in the form of my son's killer's death?"

My mouth tightened. "This is a form of vengeance. A form of justice."

"What is?"

"Jorgmundgander needs to be shut down."

"On this, we can agree. I will see that it is."

Conor's head whipped to the side and the look he sent me was of pure gratitude.

He knew why I'd done it. Not because of justice. Not even for Kuznetsov's vengeance. But for Eoghan.

"Thank you," he mouthed, the rawness in his eyes making me duck my head away while resting my hand on his lap so our fingers could knot together.

I was coming to realize that that was *our* thing.

We didn't just bridge a connection with one another, we *tied* ourselves together.

"How difficult will it be to unravel the snakes?"

"You can leave it with me," he said grimly. "What of Lyra? Did meeting with the operative in Stamford shed any light on her location?"

There were many things I could have said, many lies I could have told him, but instead of BS, I muttered, "I've met her."

"She lives?" he rasped, his voice loaded with a hope that was borderline painful to hear.

"She's very small, very scared, and very shy."

"Where is she?"

"She lives with the Jorgmundgander operative who treats her as if Lyra is her own flesh and blood."

Kuznetsov demanded, "She is loved?"

I thought about how Troy was acidic and brisk, introverted, and a social misfit. Then, I pictured how Lyra clung to her as if they were symbiotes.

The desperate bond that flared to life between them once they knew they were no longer in any danger from the Sparrows was tangible.

Never mind the fact that my old soldier buddy had a safe room for her daughter, period...

Their love was real and raw and beautiful to behold.

It was, therefore, easy to speak the truth. "Very much so."

"To separate them, Anton," Conor rumbled, "would be to traumatize Lyra again."

He didn't answer that. "She is safe?"

"We're working on that. If I hand you a location, can you send in a clean-up crew?"

"I can if you tell me the whole story."

Though I grimaced, it was a small price to pay as he was being very accommodating in other matters.

Ones that were Eoghan, Troy, and Lyra-shaped.

"I will see that the bodies are cleared away," he confirmed ten minutes later once he knew the full story. "But, child, you *will* keep me in the loop, do you understand? No more running away as if you were an angst-ridden teen.

"I am not your enemy."

He did, I had to admit, keep on proving that.

"No," I agreed slowly, "you aren't."

Kuznetsov released a heavy sigh. "I'm glad you accept this. Now, what's your next plan?"

"To kill David Foundry and Garry Smythe," I confessed without compunction.

Just when I thought he'd argue, instead, he stated, "You might not have known Aleks, Star, but he was your uncle. He was your blood. And more than that, he was a good man. He put himself and his family on the line to uncover your whereabouts and he paid for that with his life.

"Make them hurt for what they did to him, for what they have done to Lyra, and I will consider the first part of our deal to be satisfied."

With that, he cut the call.

4

———

CONOR

Conor O'Donnelly

"WHY'S my place becoming the center of operations?"

I shot Finn a tired half-grin. "Yours is the biggest *plus* you have the house next door."

He grunted as he rocked back in an armchair. "You look like shit."

"I look like an engaged man," I retorted, my weariness fading at the thought of the ring on Star's finger.

His brows lifted. "Only you'd propose in the middle of a siege."

"Technically, it was *after* the siege, and it was a good moment."

Finn shook his head. "I gave Aoife the shittiest courtship in history, but I think I still beat you."

"The shittiest? Has to be better than Da's."

"Thanks for making me feel worse, Conor, because I don't even know now."

My lips curved. "You've got a lifetime to make it better."

"Already fucked up too many times. I know I'm on my last chance," he admitted, "and I don't mind. I deserve that because *she* deserves the world."

"She does." I nodded. "Aoife's the best. I love how she takes everything in stride."

"Had to. Back before we got married, one day, Eoghan comes into the apartment with… Jesus, I don't even remember who it was now. But he'd been stabbed. She offers to start sewing him up because of her training at culinary school. She's a born mob wife. Just didn't realize it."

"Shame we're turning legit then, isn't it?" I mocked.

"That's not guaranteed. Plus, it'll always be there. Buried deep under the rug. Our ties weak. We need a good front and Aoife's bakery will provide that."

"How's it going on convincing her to let us help her expand?"

"She's driving a hard bargain."

"Meaning?"

"Meaning she wants royalties."

"On her recipes?"

"Yup." His eyes twinkled. "So fucking proud of her. I told Aidan that she'll fuck him up the ass and he needs to thank her if he wants Shay in the White House."

"What did he say?" I asked around a yawn.

"He said she'd be gentler than Savannah, so he's good with it."

Lips quirking, I sighed as I took a sip of coffee. "Tell her to add ten percent to whatever her royalties are."

"I did." He smirked again before, concerned, asking, "How did it go today?"

"They had it under control. Pussy patrol for the win." At his snort, I continued, "How about with Dagda?"

"He could be better. He's in one of our 'hospitals.'"

I nodded. "Aoife didn't want to see him?"

"I think she's considering it."

"Life's short…"

"It is. I think she's torn."

"Between?"

"He killed Da and her stepmother. He's her uncle." He sighed. "It's complicated and I don't think she can handle complicated right now."

"Understandable."

"Yeah, I think so. I won't push it but if Dagda codes in the middle of the night or something, I'll tell her and she can make an informed decision."

"Best way."

"What are you working on?"

"Pinning Foundry's and Smythe's locations down."

"You're taking them out?"

"Star wants to and I think it'll give her closure before we pass this to Interpol and let them handle the Sparrows." My phone buzzed and I smiled when I saw it was a text message.

> Star: Be Your Love - Bishop Briggs

> Me: Still talking to Finn. Will listen in a little while.

> Star: Dagda updates?

> Me: Finn says it's looking rough.

"What is it?"

"Star's awake."

"Unsurprising—it's been a hell of a day."

I blew out a breath. "You're not wrong. Getting Troy and Lyra settled next door wasn't easy. Sorry for wrecking Saturday dinner."

"Don't worry about it. Wasn't like you wanted that shit to go down. If it weren't for you, Dagda would be dead."

"That close?"

He hummed.

"Fuck. I'm not sure what to say to that."

"Why?" he inquired.

"He killed Star's mom." Never mind his role in Da's death. "She wanted him dead, but I'm not sure now. She asked about him so maybe she's changed her mind."

"Maybe she wants to question him?"

"Could be. What did Eoghan tell you about Jorgmundgander?"

"Everything."

"Crazy, no?"

"Insane. I thought he was talking about a Marvel movie at first."

"How are you fuckers my brothers and don't watch any of those movies?"

"I've seen a couple. I'm just not a nerd like you." Ignoring my scoff, Finn drawled, "I'm not surprised though. Ever since Eoghan told me he worked for MI6, I knew he was involved in crazy stuff. It explains why his PTSD gets worse even though we thought he was out of action."

"Yeah, I guess it does. The pressure doesn't relent." I blinked. "I wish…"

Finn took a sip of his scotch. "What do you wish, Kid?"

"That he'd had other options. That he'd never gotten into this shit. That he could have been a fucking teacher if he wanted or a goddamn chef."

"That's on Da," he rumbled, his gaze on the amber liquid in his glass.

"It was. What are you going to do about Jake?"

"Give him options."

"The Five Points will die out without an O'Donnelly at the head…"

He snorted. "If you think any offspring of Savannah O'Donnelly isn't going to love the mob as much as she does, you're mistaken."

"Fair point," I agreed with a laugh, and it was so fair that it put an end to that subject. "Thanks for letting Kat and Star stay the night, Finn."

Waving a hand, he dismissed, "Of course. You're welcome to stay longer if you'd like."

"I'm not sure what our next moves are, to be honest. I thought this was a pit stop but now I'm not so sure if she wants to take Foundry and Smythe out."

"The offer's there. You can stay here or at your penthouse. You have choices." He studied me over his glass. "You trust the United Brotherhood, Conor?"

"I don't trust anything that sits in the shadows and has so much control over the world. *But,* I think Kuznetsov means well, even if he makes mistakes."

"What's insane to me is how he let all that happen to Star when she's his granddaughter."

"He was trying to find her. I know that much."

"The Sparrows hid her? Could they have learned of her family ties?"

"There's no way of knowing unless we get one of these bastards to talk." With blurry eyes, I skimmed Smythe's diary for the following week. "Smythe and Foundry are the remaining two at the top of the tree. Reinier is in United Brotherhood custody." I didn't tell him what that entailed. "DeLaCroix was the leader so we have to assume one of those three took over the mantel once his identity was exposed and he was arrested."

He tipped his head to the side. "After everything you've told me, if the end goal is to kill everyone who hurt Star and her uncle's murderer, then DeLaCroix needs to die too."

"He's in jail."

"So? Like that matters."

Silently, I pondered the situation for a moment. "She's okay with them rotting away in a cell."

"She is, but this is different, isn't it? He was actively involved in her and Aleks Kuznetsov's downfall."

"Think Eoghan should handle the situation?"

Finn shrugged. "If you want. It'd be a challenge for him. Nice for The Whistler to stretch his wings for once. I'm thinking he's gotten used to simple hits."

My lips twitched. "I'm sure he'd prefer a different kind of challenge."

"Wouldn't we all?" he mocked.

"True. We go where our skill sets take us."

I let my thoughts wander a touch.

Star had never mentioned slaughtering DeLaCroix, and it wasn't like she didn't have vengeance constantly on her mind…

Narrowing my eyes at my brother, I drawled, "I'll speak with Eoghan."

"Not to be devil's advocate here, but how much longer do you think he has left to live anyway?"

"Not long, I'd imagine. He's bound to have enemies."

"I know he's in protective custody because there have been some attempts on his life," Finn mused.

"Where are you going with this?" I grumbled.

"I'm thinking we let nature take its course." A gleam sparked in his eyes. "And, I'm thinking we make a bet."

"On how long he lives?"

He grinned at me. "Yup. I bet you that Rolex your grandda gave you that he gets killed in jail soon."

Studying him, I asked, "Daily brownies for life."

He started playing with his wedding ring. "You can have that anyway."

"Nah. I always buy 'em. But *you* have to pay Aoife in lieu."

"You have weird priorities, Kid."

"That comes as a surprise, why?"

He shrugged. "Okay."

"How soon?"

"A week."

"I think… five days."

Finn tipped his glass at me. "Five days and Star, Dead To Me, and Troy can't be behind the trigger. Eoghan either."

I grumbled, "You're no fun."

"I'm plenty fun," he retorted. "Anyway, why do I recognize that Troy chick?"

"She was in the news about twenty years ago. She's Altin Çela's daughter."

His brows lifted. "The Kelmendi kidnapping?"

"Yeah."

"I had a hundred thou on Kelmendi winning the Belmont Stakes," he groused. "I was wicked pissed."

"Happened the day before the race, didn't it?"

"Yup. So, she's the daughter?"

"Apparently."

"Huh. You get around, Kid."

My nose crinkled. "I do. But that's it for me today. I need to crash."

"You get what you were looking for?"

"I did, and it was a happy, albeit unsurprising surprise."

"How can a surprise be unsurprising?"

"Because people are always idiots, but you can have faith in their common sense, and then when they prove you were right in the first place, it's an unsurprising surprise."

"Okay, less of the logic. What's unsurprisingly surprising?"

"Foundry has a meeting with Smythe this week in his office here."

Finn's brows rose. "Seriously?"

I smiled. "Seriously."

"Two birds. One stone."

"Exactly. I'm sure Star will be pleased to know they're making it easy for us."

"You still have to get through security," he commented. "The AG and the White House chief of staff? Ain't gonna be easy to get past their guards."

My smirk made an appearance as I logged out of my computer. "Finn, you didn't see them today. They're fucking unstoppable. As a team, no one can hit us and no one would dare get in our way."

It was like being in my personal Bourne movie, but that was between the nerdy kid who still inhabited my soul and me.

Finn, however, shook his head as he got to his feet. "No one's unstoppable. Plan accordingly. I'd hate for you to finally find her only for it to end with your asses getting arrested or worse, killed." With that, he patted my shoulder. "I'll see you in the morning, Kid."

As he left, I stared blindly at my blank computer screen then, with a sigh, switched it back on.

He was fucking right.

As I got to work, my only consolation was that I had the chance to listen to the song Star sent.

And it made me smile.

5

———

STAR

Star Sullivan

I STIRRED when the bedroom door opened, tilting upright on my elbow to make sure it was Conor sliding inside and no one else.

When he spotted me, he yawned. "How come you're awake?"

"On edge. So's Kat."

He paused on his trudge through the room. "She's in here?"

"Nightmare," I said sadly. "But at least she's upgraded to no bed-wetting. That'll save her from feeling embarrassed tomorrow."

"Did she remember any of the dream?"

"No. What do you think happened to her, Conor?" I could hear the hitch in my voice and knew he did too.

Both of us had showered shortly after we'd arrived at the brownstone once my cousin and Troy were settled in next door, so his clean scent gave away his proximity. I held out my hand, knowing he'd take it as he knelt on the side of the mattress next to me.

"Is it okay for me to be on the bed with her in it?"

I blinked. "I'm in the middle."

"Okay. I didn't want to freak her out or anything."

Inside, I melted. Deeper still, I cried for what he'd endured. On the outside, I just tugged him closer to me, wanting his arms around me, hell, *needing* them.

Needing him.

"You won't. She already thinks you're Prince Charming. Why do you think she came to you to save me?"

He snorted. "You'd have saved yourself eventually."

"Your faith in me is too strong. My stubbornness is my downfall."

"It's also a survival mechanism. I thank fuck for your obstinacy because it means you're here, and that means I can do this..." He rubbed his nose down the side of my chin and whispered, "...and this." His lips pressed gently to mine and with a soft breath, I dived into him, escaping this horrible world for those endless moments that he held me.

That he let me be Star.

It was chaste because of Kat, but it meant so much for that reason alone.

This was connection. Pure and simple. This was... *love*.

After a couple moments, we settled together in a spoon formation. I rested against him and he pressed his chin to my shoulder, and for a while, we just stayed that way.

Decompressing, I guessed, was what we were doing.

It took me long enough to realize that I'd still been on edge the whole time he'd been downstairs with Finn, and I finally felt like I could inhale deeply enough to flood my lungs with the oxygen I needed.

With a soft kiss on my cheek, he murmured, "You okay to talk about this?"

"Yes. Kat sleeps as if she's in an iron lung after a nightmare, but she's got earplugs in any way. Aoife was a lifesaver and had some on hand so we can whisper without disturbing her."

He hummed as he slotted our fingers together and bridged them over my belly.

"I think," he said slowly, as if he were thinking out loud, "that the Sparrows believe the kids saw them at this weird meeting they were having where they used their children as pawns to protect themselves, and they think that they can identify them. Which, considering their ages, is a stretch.

"*Or*, they think Reinier or DeLaCroix will ID them to save their own hides, and they're just cleaning up the mess to stay untouchable.

"They're both in positions of power—attorney general and White House chief of staff—so they have a lot to lose."

The rage that churned inside me was a stark contrast to the calm I'd been feeling since he'd wrapped me in his arms.

"I fucking hate them," I hissed, the words bubbling with my vitriol.

"I know. I do too. Tonight, I learned where they'll both be on Wednesday and it's on the island…"

"Which island?"

"This one."

"You're shitting me! They're meeting *here*?" I wriggled around to face him. "Please tell me you're kidding."

"I'm not. They're going to meet at his office. According to Smythe's planner, it's to discuss some law they're trying to hoodwink Congress into, but we both know that's BS."

"Meeting in person is high risk, isn't it?"

"Hardly. It could be passed as work. Foundry's the head of the Justice Department. Smythe could easily justify a meeting."

"We need to grab them," I muttered. "It makes our job a lot easier if they're together and we can contain them simultaneously."

"I had a feeling you'd say that."

"You did? Stop knowing me so well."

He chuckled. "I have an entry and exit strategy, but it needs me on the ground and you, Dead To Me, as well as Troy to get involved."

I shrugged. "They'll be down for it."

"You think Troy will try to make a run for it tonight?"

"I do, but I think she'll end up talking herself out of it. She's hella paranoid, but she's safe here and she loves Lyra and Lyra is undeniably better protected in an Irish Mob stronghold than in a car on the road in the middle of Buttfuck, USA."

"I understand why she's paranoid," he admitted. "Her father's a known psychopath. Just as crazy as Da but without the religion to temper him."

"I don't think religion tempered your da," I drawled with a disbelieving laugh.

"Oh, you'd be surprised." He hummed. "It's interesting that she lost herself in... well, whatever she is."

"Nah. It makes sense. The best way to get rid of your demons is to lose yourself in a cause that's bigger than you."

"What *is* her cause?"

"The CIA recruited Troy while she was with the LVPD. She graduated out of the academy top of her class and walked a beat for a while, but then she made a couple snappy arrests and it green-lit her.

"She's fucking fast with a rifle, not as accurate as Cin, but a quick and solid shot. Plus, it's whacko how many languages she speaks."

"Didn't think they'd have wanted her with her past," he admitted.

"You'd be astonished by what they'll accept if it fits their current agenda."

"I'm surprised you'd know all that but not about her family."

"She isn't exactly the sharing type. Alberto De Laurentiis told me."

He frowned at me. "De Laurentiis? The previous Don of the Camorra?"

I grunted. "I knew him through my dad. He told me he fed her resume to the alphabets."

"Why?"

"He was a clever old coot." A soft laugh escaped me as something hit home after I'd spent years wondering... "Bet he knew about her family and used that as leverage. More than likely bit him in the ass though. Doubt she'd take being blackmailed lying down."

"Did he have anything on you?"

I chuckled. "Photos of bad haircuts when I was a kid? Definitely. Savannah, Camden, and I got wasted too many times to count, and I'd hazard a guess and say that he knew the shit we got up to and could have used it if he wanted, but he didn't. He liked me." I thought back to this past year and how crazy it had been. "I'll miss the old bastard." If my tone was wistful, so be it. "He was so fucking clever. Always ten steps ahead. A bitch to beat at chess."

"Did you ever win?"

I smiled. "Once or twice."

"You have anything to do with his death?"

"Maybe."

He sighed. "Your 'maybes' are starting to give me heartburn."

"At least I'm not the only one dealing with that," I groused.

"You have heartburn?"

"Never mind." I cleared my throat. "He asked me for my help. Who was I to ignore a friend in need?"

"He *asked* for help in dying?"

"He wasn't going to rot in jail for the rest of his days. I couldn't blame him."

Never let it be said the man wasn't smart—he knew I didn't want to talk about this, so he asked, "You accepted the CIA's offer because of your mom?"

"Yeah. Figured I might be able to get some answers into her death if I was on the inside. Ya know, more than, 'She died. Get over it.'"

He squeezed my fingers in commiseration. "Bet you never imagined what you'd be wading into."

"No, but..." I sighed. "I've never been good at keeping my nose out of shit. Always had my own morals and used those as a measure rather than blindly following how the government would like me to be.

"Even if Reinier hadn't used the Sparrows to shut me up when I started making noises about a double agent and the looting of priceless artifacts, I had a feeling it'd get me killed."

"What?!"

"Someone was making a lot of money, Conor. If you make waves when millions are on the line, you end up in a box draped in the stars and stripes.

"Reinier was too much of a businessman to let me go to waste. A reasonably attractive woman with a functioning pussy, asshole, and mouth? Why not put them to good use? Shrewd of him."

"Until you escaped and became a pain in *his* ass."

"I'll be worse than that when I'm done with him." That was a fucking vow. "Same with these other pricks. If they were in on it, which seems hella likely, they'll pay."

Hell, I'd make them pay anyway.

If a fucker thought a person was a piece of meat to be sold as merch, I was doing the world a service in making sure they didn't share oxygen with the rest of us for much longer.

"You got plans?" he asked as he toyed with my fingers.

"I do. Nasty ones."

He snorted.

"It doesn't freak you out?"

"I'm Aidan O'Donnelly Sr.'s son, Star. I've watched him crucify people… You've seen what I put Michael Byrne through too. I think I can cope with whatever you dish out for him."

I had several ideas I was working with but to be on the safe side, I checked, "Can I borrow your electrodes?"

I could feel his excitement. "You can. I messed around with the settings. Made them stronger."

"Excellent."

"You channeled Mr. Burns then. Do not lie to me and spoil my kickass day of watching you be you by telling me you've never seen an episode of *The Simpsons*."

I smiled into the darkness. "Does that make you my Smithers?"

"I want to fuck you as much as he wants to fuck Mr. Burns, but you're cuter than that old bastard and I think I'm hotter than Smithers too."

"You're definitely hotter," I whispered, running my nose along his.

"I'm glad to hear it." He yawned. "Sorry, Star. I'm tired."

"We both are. I was just waiting for your ass to show up before I could get some Zs."

Startled, he blurted out, "Really?"

"Really." I wiggled my ring between my fingers. "Thank you for the cameo."

"It was always supposed to be on your finger." That had me biting my lip, but before I could say anything in my nervous agitation, he whispered, "I told you, you don't need to say yes or no. It can sit there for a year or twenty and it can just mean something to *us*."

I swallowed. "You're too good to me."

He chuckled. "Before you, Star, I was my father's weapon. You gave me purpose even without knowing it. Then, you were *you,* I fell hard, and your cause became my cause. Your fight became my fight. We're in this together, Star. Until the end."

And with those words, I accepted a worryingly beautiful truth—that Conor was the only person alive who had the capacity to raze me to dust, who could destroy me and rebuild me at the same time.

The only person I'd *allow* to do that.

The ring felt like a heavy weight on my hand for that reason alone. Not because I hated jewelry—which I did—but because it represented more than a pretty bauble. Its solid presence was comforting. Exactly like him.

It was timeless.

Forever.

Just like us.

I bit my lip at the thought then whispered, "Did you like that song?"

I didn't realize I'd taken a while to answer until, his tone sleepy, he mumbled, "You knew I would."

Smiling to myself, I calculated it'd take two years for me to broaden his horizons away from *noxxious.*

He'd once told me that only women wanted to change the men in their lives, but he was wrong in this instance.

There was nothing about him that I wanted to change… Nothing apart from his shitty taste in music.

The thought had me settling deeper into him as I turned back around so I could tuck my arm over Katina's waist and, sandwiched between the people I loved the most, I allowed myself to rest.

CONOR
YOURS - ELLA HENDERSON

Conor O'Donnelly

I WOKE up and found that I'd literally died and gone to heaven.

Da was wrong.

There weren't fluffy white clouds and dudes dancing around in togas with their dicks flapping in the breeze as they partied in the sky.

Nor was it Maximus Decimus Meridius's version either—these weren't the Elysian Fields.

"I know I'm out of practice, but if you're too busy mumbling, 'Da's so wrong,' maybe I should stop?" Lodestar huffed as she peered at me from halfway down my chest.

I squinted at her, surprised to see that it was full light outside the windows so that meant I got an even better view of her *there*.

Just, *there*.

"Da *was* wrong," I rasped. "This is heaven."

Her huff of irritation morphed into a softly uttered, "Oh."

She liked hearing that.

Not as much as I enjoyed having her lips on my skin, though.

Star peeped at me. "I-I didn't want to touch you, your..." She sighed. "*You* without your permission but I—"

"You always have permission. I know you'll never hurt me, Star."

Her throat bobbed. "You say that so easily. I've proven that I hurt first and ask questions later."

I reached for her hand. "That was before you wore this." My thumb rubbed over the cameo ring I'd given her. "Everything's changed now, hasn't it?"

A gentle breath whispered from between her lips. "Yes, it has." I cupped her chin, watching as she tilted her head to the side to nuzzle into me. "Conor?"

"Hmm?"

"You always have permission too."

I stilled. "That's big."

"And it wasn't for you?"

"You don't have to say that just because I did," I informed her kindly. "My situation is very different from yours, and yours is also more recent—"

Anger flared in her eyes. "You don't have to downplay it around me. I'm not your brothers, Conor. I'm not your Da. I'm—"

"What are you, Star?" I half-growled, wanting her to say the word. Needing her to say it.

"Yours." Her chin tipped up, the gesture defiant. "If I do something to trigger you, then I won't do it again—"

"I didn't give you permission to trigger me," I pointed out. "I gave you permission to touch me. There's a difference."

Her eyes narrowed. "Are we splitting hairs?"

"No," I said around a laugh, my irritation immediately fading. "We're not. The latter is what happens in an adult relationship. The former is when you're living with a rapist. I'm not your ex-husband."

"You're nothing like him," she ground out, jerking upright as if my words infuriated her. "You'd never do anything that he did."

"Well, then, you know you're in safe hands," I commented with ease, wanting to calm her down when I'd inadvertently agitated her.

She frowned at me, repeating, "You'd never do what he did."

"I wouldn't."

"So never compare yourself in any way to him again. He wasn't my 'ex-husband.' He was my jailor. He was—"

"Where's Kat?" I asked, breaking into her tirade.

"She said she was going to ask Aoife for breakfast. Kat wakes up earlier than the larks. It's a cruel twist of fate seeing as I'm a night owl. Not even the Army broke me out of that habit."

I slid the backs of my fingers across her cheek. "This part of the house is an annex."

"I know. Why do you think I was coming onto you?"

"Just checking that you were comfortable."

She hummed. "I am."

"Did you enjoy killing him?"

What could only be described as malevolent glee exploded into being behind her eyes. I recognized it because I'd seen it often in Da's when he'd been having fun that involved blood spatter and screams.

"Hans?"

I nodded.

"It was satisfying. It was even more satisfying getting away from him. I'd do it again."

"I know you would," I drawled, amused that she felt as if she had to say that. Stroking away a couple locks of hair that tumbled into her face, I tucked them behind her ear. "That's what I can do now you've given permission for me to touch you," I informed her, returning to stroking her cheek with my thumb, watching as, cat-like, she angled her face deeper into the caress. "We learn boundaries as we go, hmm?"

She glanced at me from the corner of her eye then twisted her head so that I wasn't touching her anymore. Before my hand could drop, her lips were around my thumb and my nostrils flared as the hot heat of her mouth collided with it.

I watched as she slid all the way down it then suckled the tip before nipping it.

"That was how I wanted to wake you up," she whispered breathily, her pupils dilated.

Eyes narrowed, I rumbled, "Then I *would* have been in heaven because your lips on my skin is paradise, but around my cock is…" Speechless and without an appropriate word, I hitched a shoulder.

She smirked at me before returning to my abs where she'd been tracing her tongue between the divots upon my waking up.

Maintaining eye contact with me, she continued her original trajectory, her fingers tucking in the waistband of my sweatpants I'd borrowed from Finn and dragging them lower until my dick was free.

"No boxer briefs?" she rasped, on eye level with my cock now.

"Not for bed—" My words cut off with a hiss as she stroked her tongue down my shaft, the tip delving into the nooks and crannies of every vein and artery that wrapped around my length.

Groaning, I closed my eyes to process how fucking good that felt, then they popped open again because watching was half the fun when it came to Star.

With the malevolent glee of earlier having been replaced with a hazy need, I circled my fingers around her lips.

I watched as she tensed a little, knowing she was preparing for me to shove her face into my crotch, and I made sure to keep my movements gentle.

The thumb she'd sucked traced the corner of her mouth as she returned to the glans and started tonguing the slit where pre-cum was already bubbling.

Having relaxed into my touch, I watched as she grabbed me around the base, held me fast, then treated the underside of my dick to the same treatment.

She coated me in spit, getting me wet and messy, then finally, her lips were there, sinking around me.

"Fuck," I groaned, elongating the word as ecstasy sparked inside my veins, boiling my blood until I knew explosion was imminent just as a goddamn safety feature.

I watched when she sank down, and down, and down. Her fingers retreated as she broached the lower inches. I grunted as she flicked her tongue at the base, teasing an area that was rarely touched.

Keeping my hips from bucking seemed to be an impossible task, especially as I watched her stay there, a calmness in her eyes that I didn't share, her amusement tangible as she swallowed around me, her throat doing stuff to my cock that should have been illegal in at least forty states.

I stared at her, feeling tongue-tied when mine wasn't even busy, and then I whispered, "You need to stop."

Some of that glee returned to her gaze. Less sadistic than before but definitely giving me no quarter.

She shook her head as she retreated, moving up and down my length as she continued her ministrations.

I needed to talk, had to speak, but I didn't want to trigger her. Touch was one thing, words were another, and even as overwhelmed as I was right now, I knew—

"My bad girl," I rasped, unable to keep the words back. "So bad for me. That fucking mouth is a sinner's paradise, Star. It's hell not coming down your throat the second those sinful lips are swallowing every inch of me."

The words had her whimpering and I watched as her hand snaked down between us.

Knowing the destination, I rasped, "Let me touch that naughty pussy, Star. You know I won't stop until I make you sing."

This time, when she swallowed around my cock, it had nothing to do with teasing me.

Still, as lust-crazed as I was, I noticed a distinct difference in her reaction between using the word 'bad' and using the word 'naughty.'

As I made a mental note of that, I rumbled a test, "I want you to come on my face, Star. Can you do that for me, my *naughty* girl?"

Her mouth, strained around my shaft, quivered.

"Come on," I crooned. "Sit on my face, my naughty, naughty girl."

Slowly, she retreated, each inch taking a fucking lifetime, making me ball my hands into fists around the sheets at either side of my hips as she tortured me on the way up.

Then, when my dick was missing the heat of her mouth, she jumped off the bed.

I reared upright, wondering what the fuck I'd done as she headed for the door.

"Star!" I called out, but she ignored me. Then, I sank back in relief when she twisted the key in the lock and returned to me, dragging clothes off as she went.

That she hadn't locked the door before starting to kiss her way down my abs told me how spontaneous she'd been this morning, and I was glad for that—glad because I wanted that between us.

We *did* have internal minefields, but the past was in the past, and I didn't want it to affect *this*, us. We deserved to own our futures, to own our pleasures, and for them not to be tainted by the people who hurt us.

When she stood beside the bed, all my thoughts were erased because she wriggled her hips, dropping her sweatpants to the floor, revealing that she, too, had gone commando last night.

My gaze flickered over the myriad scars on her body. Acts of violence that had been perpetrated against her, ones that might have taken her from me. She was a survivor, though, and those scars were proof of that fact.

Fuck, she was hot.

So fucking hot.

Tongue cleaved to the roof of my mouth at the prospect of being able to worship her, of getting to drown myself in her sweet, sweet cunt again, she surprised me by clambering onto my lap and staying there.

Hands settling on her hips, I urged, "I can't wait to taste you, Star."

She bit her lip as she reached for my cock. Shaking her head, she didn't answer, just started rocking her slit against me.

With her tits right goddamn there, I reached up and cupped one, palpating, squeezing, and pinching before I allowed my free hand to give the other the same treatment.

She was drenched around my dick, which made it even easier for her and more torturous for me to be surrounded by slick, hot silk while my palms were filled with her curves.

With her eyes locked on mine, I saw the internal shudder of pleasure every time she nudged her clit.

Fully expecting her to get herself off like she'd done yesterday, I watched her, knowing I was close and that she'd probably need more so I had to hold back.

Her orgasms were slow to burn but fiery in the aftermath, and watching her regain ownership of her pleasure this way was the most satisfying thing I'd ever seen in my fucking life so I'd never short-change her. Not when her satisfaction was half my fun.

Her hands plopped onto my chest as she began to grind into me. Her nostrils flared with every thrust as she worked herself higher, higher, then, as was becoming the standard today, she growled under her breath and jerked onto her knees, making my hands fall to my sides in response.

She quivered above me, frustration teeming from her pores.

With another growl, she snarled, "Why is it so fucking hard?"

I angled my head to the side. "Let me help." It wasn't a question.

"No." Mulishly, she dropped down again and started rocking against my dick. After a couple minutes, she snapped, "I can feel it. It's…" Her expression tensed as she worked herself up—to pleasure or in annoyance, I wasn't sure yet. "It's mine," she rasped. "I wanted this."

Then, she was back to her knees, her entire frame quivering as she hung on the precipice.

Though I knew this was something she wanted to take possession of, I sat up and carefully tumbled her into the sheets so she was lying supine.

I didn't loom above her, just whispered, "This isn't a battle, Star. This isn't something you have to do on your own. Teamwork makes the dream work, no?"

She snorted but didn't answer, just lay there, little sparks of pleasure making her twitch beneath me as if her circuits were starting to short but not enough to lead to the big O.

I let my tongue circle her nipple, but I didn't hang around because she said she didn't have much sensitivity there. Then, I traced her navel before going deeper and nuzzling my face into her mons. Gripping her thighs, I levered them higher so they were together and pinched her labia between them.

Peering around her legs, I informed her, "This isn't a sprint, Star."

"I just want to come," she complained breathily. "I don't want it to be a struggle."

"We'll get there, baby. We'll get there."

Her throat bobbed as she turned her face away from me, but she graced me with a nod.

Reaching down, I pinched her outer pussy lips at the upper apex, watching her squirm as I pinned her clit in place.

Moving my fingertips in a circle, I lowered my other hand and ran a tip through the compressed folds where her juices had gathered.

She tensed but, maintaining the massaging action of my fingers, I asked, "May I?"

Star was quiet for so long that I figured she was going to say no, but instead, the nod she gave me this time was jerky.

"Words, baby."

Her nostrils flared. "Don't hurt me."

My temper surged at that—not at her, but at what had been done to her.

"I will never hurt you. Ever," I murmured, keeping my tone light, hiding my anger at the world from her.

Her throat bobbed as I gently circled her slit and began to thrust a finger into her.

The way she clamped down around me was *not* a good sign.

Needing to change my plans, I kept the finger there, not moving, as I ordered, "Lower your thighs to the bed for me, Star."

She did, letting them fall on either side of me as I bowed my head and started to flutter my tongue around her clit.

Her husky groan was music to my ears, and how her hands immediately fisted around the sheets was a sight for sore eyes.

I flicked my tongue back and forth, sucking on her clit, shaping it with the tip, caressing and teasing, giving her what I thought she needed, and using her pussy as a gauge.

With every moan of pleasure, the intensity of the vice around my finger decreased. Instead, her inner muscles began to pulse around it.

Gently, I began to thrust.

Gently, I began to explore.

All the while, my mouth was busy distracting her.

Her hips started to cant into me, pushing her pussy into my face, proving that she was enjoying the act even if I could feel her tension as the need to come resurfaced.

With my teeth, I nipped her clit. "Tell me how you feel."

"L-Like it's there, within touching distance. I can almost see it. I know how good it will be, but when I try to reach for it," she whimpered, "it slips away." Her sharp cry had me returning to suckling her clit, doubling down on the move until she was writhing against me.

I sensed the shift in her when she tensed again, and I nipped her clit between my lips then retreated to ask, "Why are you struggling today, baby?"

She ground her ass into the sheets. "Because I want you inside me."

Ah.

"You might not be ready for it yet," I said simply, which had her head flying upright so she could properly aim her glower at me.

"I'm *ready*," she growled. "*I* decide, not my body."

My lips almost twitched, but I put them to better use and returned to her clit.

"Fuck," she keened, her body arching against the sheets.

Finger retreating from her slit, I gently circled it with two digits, and as I sucked hard on the small nub, I thrust both into her. She gasped but didn't lock up as much this time.

Keeping the motions nonaggressive, I worked her back toward an orgasm, taking note when she stiffened, when her moans turned frustrated, and adjusting my behavior as a result.

"Conor," she whimpered, sounding more exhausted than ever.

"Yes, baby," I replied even though it hadn't been a question.

Her frustration and fatigue got to me like nothing else could.

Instead of waiting for a reply, I switched moves, and this time, I gave her my weight, settling atop her, sliding my arms beneath her shoulders and holding her close to me.

Her arms came around my neck and her legs cupped my hips, her feet settling against my ass—the toes burrowing in, not her heels.

It was more of an embrace than anything else, and she relaxed into it enough that when she squirmed, it put her cunt and my cock on the path of direct collision.

"You feel good," she whispered before her mouth met mine, our tongues knotting as she found a rhythm she enjoyed, uncaring that my lips were covered in her pussy juices, just needing to kiss me as much as I needed to kiss her.

When the rigidity left her body, I pulled back to whisper, "Put me in you. You control this, Star. You. Not me. You. Take what belongs to you."

Her throat bobbed and I knew she understood what I meant—her orgasm belonged to her, but so did I.

So did my dick.

She didn't reply but her gaze was locked on mine as I levered away from her so that she could reach between us, and that was answer enough.

A hissed breath escaped me when her hand cupped me, and my forehead fell atop hers as she notched the tip of my dick to her slit.

"Are you ready, baby girl?"

She kissed me again, which I took to mean 'no' because she'd have said yes otherwise.

So I stayed there.

I hovered above her, the head of my dick in fucking paradise while the rest was locked out of heaven's gates.

Her tongue thrust against mine and that was a distraction because it encouraged me to do what I wanted—fuck her.

But in this, I just stole her breath, took her kisses, and claimed them for my own.

Then, her hips reared up and I started to sink into her.

Deeper.

One inch.

Two.

Slower.

Three inches.

Four.

I groaned as I hit the halfway point.

Five.

Six inches.

She was still beneath me but not tensed. Her eyes were wide as they remained locked on mine, and her feet on my ass encouraged me to keep going as they burrowed into the muscles there.

Seven.

Eight.

One more half-inch and I was fucking home.

My pubic bone nuzzled hers as I sank in deep and she took me fully.

Jesus.

Mary.

Joseph.

And the twelve disciples.

I'd been wrong before.

This was fucking heaven.

Letting my weight resettle on her, I felt her arms and legs tighten around me as she held me in place.

"You're inside me," she whispered, and that tone of hers, so full of wonder and hope, nearly had me blowing my wad.

"You're perfect, Star. So fucking perfect."

"I didn't… I wasn't sure if I'd be able…" She groaned and her hips bucked. "Thank you," she cried, her mouth colliding with mine again, putting the brake on her words as she fucked me from beneath.

That was Star.

Aggressive, even when she was on the bottom.

She writhed underneath me, thrusting back as I started to rock into her, keeping it deep, not wanting to leave her when it had taken years for me to reach *this* point.

Fuck, I never wanted to leave. I wanted to stay here forever. She was mine. My home. My haven. My fucking everything.

With our tongues thrusting against the other, mimicking what was happening down below, I felt the ripples of her cunt before she did— they were rhythmic, heavy, and deep.

Those taut, inner muscles began to pulse around me, milking me of my cum, tormenting me with the need to fill her, with the urge for her to come around me and for me to share in her bliss.

When her mouth pulled away from mine, I watched as her head ground into the pillows, her hair splaying wide as the peak started to hit.

I chased her lips and kissed her as she whimpered her pleasure, sobbing through it, massive judders in her muscles making her quake beneath me as her body imploded and exploded all at the same time.

There was no way in fuck that I could have survived that—I came.

Her cunt was tight and hot and wet, and it didn't stop clutching at me as I gave her everything I had to give, every drop until we were sealed together.

For-fucking-ever.

When I slumped on her, she didn't shove me away. She clung harder to me, and because I knew she wanted to let go as little as I did, I rolled us over so my weight wasn't heavy on her, and she settled back atop me with a soft, contented sigh.

Covering her with the duvet, knowing that I owed Finn a new guest bed, I held her as she nuzzled into me and both of us fell asleep, our minds unerringly on the same truth—*yesterday had only been our beginning and now, we had a tomorrow.*

7

STAR

Star Sullivan

IT COULD HAVE BEEN AWKWARD, but this was Conor. Nothing was awkward with him.

Which, in itself, had long since told me I was fucked.

Yet, because *it was Conor,* I could handle being fucked.

Literally and figuratively.

That meant when our skin cleaved together from heat and sweat, he chuckled, and that made me grin as we had to pry ourselves apart.

It meant that when I saw the mess we'd made on the sheets, he nudged me under the chin and told me he'd be buying Finn a new bed, ignoring my blush to greet me with another kiss.

It meant that when we showered and he cleaned me down there, I didn't even flinch, just let him tend to me.

It meant that everything was different. That nothing was the same. That the sky was bluer and the sun shone brighter. It meant that Aoife's croissants were delicious, but they tasted so much more scrumptious with the endorphins still whirring around my brain and with Conor's hand on the small of my back.

It didn't even matter that Aoife was blushing as she looked at us and muttered, "You can explain why you were crying to Jake, Conor."

"Crying?" he repeated, bewildered.

"Yes. There were *noises*," she mumbled. "You know? *Noises.*"

"We were that loud?" he retorted, eyes wide.

"No. He wanted to visit his Unka Kid. Thank God you locked the door."

"Jesus." His eyes turned distant. "My bedroom door at home doesn't have a lock on it."

Aoife snorted. "That's the first thing you make sure you get when you have kids."

It had never been an issue for me until today, and I'd only *just* remembered to get up and lock our door before I'd stripped off, but I nodded. "Thanks for the advice, Aoife."

She shrugged. "You're welcome, but you're still explaining why you were crying."

I accepted the dish she offered me and took a deep bite of my second croissant of the day, not needing any jam on it because it was that damn good.

"Where is he?" Conor questioned, scrubbing a hand over his face.

"In the family room with Finn and Katina."

"I guess I should be glad the others are with Ma?"

"Yes, you should be. Expect some proud looks from your brother. I think he's been worried about you."

Conor started to drift out of the kitchen, muttering under his breath about snooping brothers before he froze, twisted around, and asked me, "You'll be okay?"

I smiled at him. "Yes. And I don't think you can judge anyone about snooping…"

He scowled. "Whose side are you on?"

My smile turned into a smirk. "The side of justice."

Aoife chuckled and we shared a grin as Conor stomped off, this time mumbling about only God knew what.

Returning to my croissant, I answered, "Coffee, please. Milky, if possible," when Aoife asked me if I'd like something to drink.

She set a latte in front of me after messing with a fancy espresso machine that would have been comfortable in a bougie restaurant and not a home kitchen.

As if she knew what I was thinking, she said, "Finn's developed a taste for swanky coffee, but he can't use the machine so I had to learn how."

"Why can't he use it?"

She snorted. "I have no idea. I'd think he was faking, but whenever he makes me coffee, it tastes vile. In the interests of not destroying my taste buds, I took over, and now I'm addicted." She wafted a hand at the coffee. "Try it."

"I'm not really an aficionado," I excused, but I took a sip of the brew and my brows lifted. "That tastes great." Well, better than the other disgusting dregs I drank on the regular, at any rate.

"I know. It's the machine, not me. Miracle worker." She tipped her head to the side as she reached for her own coffee. "Cin is next door with your... friends."

I nodded. "I figured as much. Thank you for letting us crash into your lives."

Aoife's chuckle wasn't bitter, more resigned. "Nothing irregular has happened this week."

"Meaning it's crazy every week?"

"You guessed it."

"Does it bother you?" Guilt hit me. "I mean, we've taken over your house... I'm sorry about that."

"It doesn't bother me and you don't have to say sorry. I'm used to it." She took a sip of coffee. "I grew up an only, *lonely* child. There's never any loneliness in the O'Donnelly family if you let them in."

Her words had me biting my lip. "I grew up that way too. I wasn't lonely, though, because of Savannah. Her folks and mine were..." My nose crinkled as I thought about their relationship. I was no prude, but I used to be bitter on my mom's behalf. Now, I didn't have a clue what to think or feel. "I'm not even sure, to be honest," I admitted. "Maybe I'll never understand their friendship unless I ask Lorelei and Dagger.

"I know that when we were in LA, we shared a compound and that in New York, our apartments were in the same building, so we were always close.

"I guess I know what family is, but I also understand that it's nice being able to shut the door in their faces and not let them in when they piss you off."

Aoife's mouth curved at that, and she surprised me by hovering her fist in front of me to bump.

After, I picked up a third croissant, and this one, I loaded down with jam. Screw the saturated fats—I'd had sex for the first time in years and I'd seen the Milky Way.

It was a day for celebration.

"Is everything okay, Aoife?" I asked softly, watching her tear her own pastry apart but not actually eat any of it.

Clearly, I was in a good mood, but she wasn't.

Smiling, she shook her head. "Everything's fine."

"Why do people do that?" I asked.

"Do what?"

"Shake their head in the negative but then speak in the affirmative… I'm thinking that's a lie."

Her eyes narrowed at me but she repeated firmly, "Everything's fine."

"If you say so." I dismissed that as bullshit. "I'm assuming that whatever's *fine* is something you can't share with Finn?"

Her bottom lip got sucked in between her teeth. "You know a man called Dagda."

It wasn't a question.

My hand, in the process of raising the croissant to my mouth, stilled. "Yes."

"He's my uncle. His name's Eamonn—"

"Keegan." I knew her maiden name was that too. "Are you sure you're related?" I tested, trying not to get involved and crack open painful truths when I knew they *were* blood but wasn't sure if she did.

She cleared her throat. "Yes."

"How?"

A few taps on her screen, and she was handing me her cell.

Unknown Sender: Your mom can finally rest in peace now.

"You think Eamonn sent you that?"

"I received it after Aidan Sr. died." Her gaze collided with mine. "I'm assuming it's him."

"Why?" I asked warily. I mean, *I* knew what had happened, but I assumed she didn't.

Her eyes narrowed upon me. "I think you'll be the only woman in the family who the men don't try to keep in the dark."

"I don't think that's something to be envious of," I drawled, but I didn't deny it—*any* of it.

Her hand tapped the table beside mine. "Nice ring."

I hummed as she studied it.

"You said yes?"

"I agreed to wear the ring."

She tipped her head to the side. "Interesting."

"I don't think Conor and I will ever do anything the normal way."

"Probably for the best in this family." She straightened up as she finished her coffee. "He survived the night."

"Dagda?"

"Yes."

"Are you glad about that?"

"I suppose. Not much point being glad about it if you're going to kill him."

I studied her. "I think you know more than you let on, Aoife."

"The men aren't as quiet as they think they are." She sniffed. "Well? *Are* you going to kill him?"

"He murdered my mom," I reasoned. "But my mom wasn't as squeaky clean as I thought she was so I'm of two minds about the whole thing."

Her throat bobbed. "I don't have any family left, Star. Not on my mom's side. And the… What I did have was stolen from me."

"I know," I rasped, my gaze meeting hers. "I'm sorry about that."

"Not your fault and I've made peace with what happened because I love my husband and I understand how this family works. They protect their women. No matter what the women do.

"If I killed Lena, Finn would go to war to make sure I never saw the inside of a jail cell. He'd lose his brothers too because he'd stand by me." She sucked in a breath. "I find comfort in that."

"In knowing you could destroy his whole universe and he'd still stand by your side?"

Slowly, she nodded. "Yes. Not very healthy, but we each find our own coping mechanisms, don't we?"

"We do," I agreed, sharing a measured glance with her. Knowing and accepting that we'd both gone through hell. "Are you asking me not to kill Dagda?"

"I think so. I don't know the man. Maybe he deserves to die? Maybe I'd be better off not knowing him, but…"

"Just in case, hmm?"

"Yes, just in case."

I studied her as I pondered the situation.

Eventually, I queried, "You'll tell me if he treats you poorly?"

The hope in her eyes was painful to behold. "Yes."

"From one sister-in-law to another, I won't target him. I tried to help him yesterday," I remarked. "The only reason Conor knew he was under attack was because *I* got him to call Keegan. So, when I said I was of two minds about the situation, I meant it. His actions don't correlate with what I know of him, and my mom wasn't who I thought she was.

"I have to assume that the O'Donnellys have allowed him to live even though he did what he did to their father for a reason."

"They wanted him to form an alliance with them. Eamonn was the head of the ECD."

"I've heard." That was another reason I didn't think Dagda needed to die. Anyone who went to jail for mass-murdering Sparrows should be a friend of mine. "I won't steal more family from you, Aoife."

"You don't owe me anything," she pointed out.

"You let me into your home. You looked after my daughter." I hitched a shoulder. "I don't forget things like that. Plus…" My nose crinkled. "I have to apologize but I need to buy you a new guest bed."

Aoife rolled her lips inward. "Let Conor pay. He's rich enough."

"I'm not exactly poor," I dismissed.

She wafted a hand. "It's the Catholic in them."

"For nonreligious men, they're religious, aren't they?"

"It's ingrained in them. Do you want another coffee?"

"Please." I studied her as she worked, then I mused, "I heard something myself."

"What?"

"They want to use your bakery as a front?"

She smiled at me over her shoulder. "Yes. Silent investors and royalties on my recipes. I'll be cashing in shortly."

"Do you intend on leaving Finn?"

Her eyes widened in genuine surprise. "Jesus, no."

The tension that had been gathering in my shoulders since I'd overheard Conor and Finn's conversation last night started to disperse.

"What made you think that?"

"Because that's what women do. They squirrel money away and then take off in the middle of the night. What Finn did... I'm not saying he doesn't deserve to be abandoned, but Conor loves you. Like a sister. A *true* sister. I'd hate for him to get hurt."

Aoife's gaze softened. "You love him, don't you?"

"I do." My smile was tight. "I'm still not sure what to do with it, but it's there and it seems to be growing. I'd say it was like cancer, but I don't think you're supposed to classify love as a deadly disease."

Her brows arched. "No, you're not. With your past, though, I suppose it could be forgiven. Conor told me once you were a spy?"

I grunted.

"In that line of work, it's not like love would serve a purpose. If anything, I'd imagine it was an inconvenience."

"Yes," I choked out, taken aback by her understanding.

"You'll come to find it's less of a cancer eventually and more..." She blinked. "Like when you've had a vaccine and it stops you from catching a deadly disease."

"Really?"

"Yeah. Trust me. It grows on you with time." She turned to make me another coffee. "And I won't hurt Conor. Or Finn. I love him.

"Did he let me down? Yes. Did he choose Lena over me? He did.

But…" She sucked in a breath. "She was his mother. His only source of stability in an ever-changing world as a boy where he'd learned that family could and would do heinous things to him.

"She represented hope and love, protection and support. When it came out, he chose me, and in the future, I know he'll keep on choosing me.

"So, using Ellie's Bakery as a front is very fortuitous because I'll make a hell of a lot of money, and if Jake decides he wants nothing to do with the Five Points, I'll be able to bankroll him with my personal funds." She shot me a smile as she set the now-full coffee mug in front of me. "Savannah talks a lot about women having their own bank accounts, and it's always been important to me. Finn has had a joint account for us since the beginning, and I know that I can buy whatever I want—"

"But nothing beats knowing you earned that cash and that it's yours and that no one can question what you do with it," I finished for her.

She nodded. "Exactly. So, no, I'm not going to leave. I just like to have a backup plan because Finn, if he'd had a choice, would never have gone into the Five Points.

"What Jake chooses to do is down to him, and no one will influence his decision."

"From one momma bear to another," I said easily as I raised my mug for her to tap with her own, "I approve this message."

We shared a smile.

Friendship took time, but we'd sowed the foundations of a relationship together.

And not just for Conor's sake, either.

8

CONOR

LATER THAT DAY

LYRA WAS SHY.

Beyond shy.

It was only then that I realized I wasn't used to shy kids. Jake was rowdy, Seamus' confidence was that of a politician in the making, and even Victoria was self-assured. As for Kat, she had the confidence of all three of them, but Lyra was more prone to hiding in corners with her nose buried in a book, a stone's throw from Troy's side, than stepping into the spotlight.

"I've tried," Kat wailed, drawing my attention away from the little girl who wore noise-canceling headphones and was reading a paperback thicker than her waif-like frame.

Star huffed. "Kat, she's my cousin. You can't say 'tried' as if you can't try again. Don't you want her to feel comfortable with us?"

Katina pulled a face. "What if she doesn't want to be comfortable with us? What if she wants to just read her book and I'm disturbing her? It'd be like me trying to yap at you when you're coding. Don't you get mad at me when I do that, huh?"

I hid my smile by pretending to rub my fingers above my upper lip.

Star, of course, noticed and glared at me. "That's a dumb example,

Katina, because you *often* interrupt me, and do I ever not answer one of the million questions you ask on a daily basis?"

Katina's nose crinkled but she mumbled, "She doesn't like me."

"How do you know?"

"She takes ages to talk, and I have no idea if she's being rude or just…" Her small pout spoke of her uncertainty with the situation. "I tried to get her to play *Mario Kart* with me, and last night, I heard her tell Troy that I was annoying and loud-mouthed."

Star grimaced. "I'm sorry she said that, Kat. That was very rude of her."

The little girl wriggled her shoulders. "I *was* being loud, and I figure I kept annoying her because she had to stop reading her book whenever I tried to talk to her."

"How's it feel to be right?"

Kat's eyes widened. "I'm right?"

"Yup," Star agreed with a shrug. "I was wrong for pushing you and I was wrong for not listening. Sorry, kiddo."

She glanced at me. "You heard that, didn't you, Conor? You'll be my witness."

"If it ever goes to court, Kat, you can count on me."

Star shot me a look that had my smile twisting into a grin. "Nice to know whose side you're on."

"I'm on the side of right and wrong," was my pious retort. "Payback's a bitch," I mock-whispered to her in retaliation for earlier.

"I'm on the side of right and wrong too, Conor!" Kat chirped, thankfully not hearing the second half of my declaration. "I'm going to play games now. If you'd like me to whoop your butt, then please feel free to play with me."

With a cascade of giggles, she rushed off, did a cartwheel down the hall, and nearly knocked over one of the vases on a console table in the process before dashing into the family room with the gaming consoles in it.

Star huffed as she sank back into her armchair. "It's a good thing I've got money because I need to fix a lot of the shit she breaks by being clumsy. This past year, she's gotten worse than ever."

"She's going to be tall so she's growing into her arms and legs."

"I did that too and I didn't manage to knock furniture over like a stampede of wildebeest." Though she was huffing at Kat, she was studying her cousin with concern. "She's very…"

"Shy," I agreed.

"Timid, I was going to say, but yes. I'm not used to shy kids."

"Me either. She's just an introvert."

"I don't know how Troy raised an introvert," she mumbled with a shake of her head.

"I'd imagine with a family like hers, she would understand more than most how to give a child what they need." At her arched brow, I continued, "How to let them be themselves, I mean. It was well documented that Elena Çela was forced to attend ballet school and the like when all she wanted to do was ride horses."

"Where was it well documented?" she asked, though her eyes flared at the mention of Troy and ballet.

"I read a book about the case. The cops were stumped—"

"—when aren't they?"

"—and it was a big investigation for a while. I was curious because Da wanted to set up a stable with Çela and he'd set me the task of seeing if the deal was worth it or not."

"What did you decide?"

"I thought that the whole thing stank. I recommended against getting involved with them."

"That must have lost them a lot of money."

"Big time. But it was just before the Belmont Stakes, and it made me wonder what was going on. Turned out the horse wasn't great—they just had mad skills with race-fixing. Their stable was a sham.

"When the horse showed up dead and the daughter was gone and Çela was more grief-stricken about the stallion than his fucking kid, that just settled things in my mind."

She studied me. "How do you know so much random shit?"

I chuckled. "I like to read."

"There's reading and there's reading." She shook her head. "Okay, so where were we before Kat interrupted us?"

"I finished telling you how we can snatch Foundry and Smythe this week. It's where you want to put them that's the problem."

"I was thinking about calling in Kuznetsov for that. He managed to get Reinier to the Catskills. I don't see why he couldn't get them there too."

I watched as she typed out:

> Star: Anton, I need the coordinates for the shipping container in the Catskills.

"Say, 'please,'" I directed.

She huffed.

> Star: Please.

When Anton sent them over, I mused, "And in the aftermath of their disappearances? Why hasn't there been a press release about Reinier's absence, hmm? If Smythe and Foundry go missing, that'll be three high-ranking officials in less than a month that'll have disappeared. It'll trigger a stink."

"Then we make sure the stink is diverted elsewhere."

"Meaning?"

"Meaning I remember Rachel Laker having some meetings with Foundry."

"The Sinners' attorney?"

"And the Valentinis' and countless other people's legal representation."

"She won't be able to tell you anything. Attorney-client privileges."

"I've heard of that before, thank you very much." She shot me an unimpressed look. "But she could point me in the right direction."

Without waiting for an answer from me, she snagged her cell phone off the coffee table and scrolled through her contacts.

A few moments later, the ringtone sang through the speaker, and then:

"What do you want, Lodestar?"

"Sounds like you've left quite the impression as usual."

Her nose crinkled at my observation but to Laker, she mused, "You're mad at me."

"Now, I wonder why. You didn't just take off and leave us wondering if you were okay or if you were even coming back—"

"I had a job to do, Rachel. If anyone should understand that, it's you."

Rachel huffed down the line. "I wouldn't just leave my family in a lurch like you did."

"I left her with people I trust. Not only goddamn that, I left her with a brother-in-fucking-arms. A man I'd go to war for and who'd go to war for me.

"I was heading into hostile territory, Rachel. What would you have preferred me to do? Bring Kat along for the ride? Fuck your judgmental ass!"

"Star," I grumbled. "Flies and honey, not vinegar."

"No, Conor. I'm sick of this bullshit. I left Kat with her sister. I left her with a goddamn war veteran who, even though he's sick, is still deadlier than your average Joe. Hell, he hospitalized your ass and he's half-crippled with his migraines.

"I didn't leave her on the steps of a fucking orphanage. I left her with family. I made promises to her that I kept until I was physically unable to do so because I was being held against my will!

"I'm sick of the Sinners making it out that I'm a piece-of-shit mom because I—"

"I never said you were a piece-of-shit mom. I said you left your family in a lurch," Rachel interrupted, but I didn't think that made it any better from Star's narrow-eyed glare. "You just dumped us, Star. All of us. Rex and I had a baby, for God's sake. I appreciate the flowers. Not."

Because I sensed genuine hurt behind the bitchy statement, I grabbed Star's hand and quickly translated, "She's saying they're your family and you left them behind, Star."

For a second, there was silence, then Star drawled, "If you're saying you missed me, then there are nicer ways to do it."

Rachel scoffed, "I never said that."

My lips twitched.

"What did you call the baby?"

"Sommer."

"First Wynter, now Sommer… You aiming for an Autumn and a Spring next?" Star joked.

"No. Two daughters named after seasons are plenty."

"She okay?" was Star's next question. This time it was uneasy.

"She's beautiful, and Rex is a sucker for her."

"I'd like to see that."

"The compound hasn't moved," she retorted. "You could stop by for a damn visit. I couldn't believe it when Maverick told Rex that you'd had Kat picked up and brought into the city."

More hurt.

I squeezed Star's hand again and translated, "Star, you hurt her feelings."

"Damn straight she did," Rachel groused. "Whoever that is, give him a medal. He deserves it."

"I prefer pies," I retorted with a quick grin.

Rachel sniffed.

"I'm only here on a pit stop. Plus, I… I genuinely didn't think you guys would care."

"Well, we do."

Star's expression was blank—she had no idea what to do with that information—so, Star being Star, she cut shit down to the basics. "If we're family, then you won't have a problem with why I'm calling—I need your help."

"Flies and honey," I muttered with a sigh.

Both women ignored me.

Rachel argued, "I need a massage, a pair of tits that don't leak, and a night off. Some things just aren't possible right now."

"This is important."

"If you think I'm going to let you blackmail some other—"

"I'm not!" Star barked, speaking over Rachel and darting me a guilty look.

"Do I even want to know?" I mumbled to myself.

Star cleared her throat and forged ahead, "I want to ask you about David Foundry."

I'd take that as a no.

"The attorney general? What about him?"

"I'm right, then. Last year, you were in touch with him?"

"Of course. I come into contact with him fairly often. Too frequently in all honesty. The man's a grade-A creep."

"Fits the profile," I muttered.

Star nodded. "We've come to learn that he's a Sparrow."

Rachel's lack of reaction was telling. Then, in the background, I heard the sound of a pen being tapped against a hard surface.

"Does that come as a surprise to you or not?" was Star's brusque retort, and when she received radio silence for her pains, she urged, "It's important, Rachel."

"I'm not an idiot, Lodestar. I managed to figure that out on my own. How do you know he is?"

"We believe he was associated with Justin DeLaCroix. Along with Sheridan Reinier and Garry Smythe. Each is a top-ranking official—"

"Garry Smythe?" she bit off.

"Yes. The White House chief of staff."

Rachel's exhalation was audible. "You didn't hear this from me."

"Of course," Star complied easily.

"Foundry negotiated the purchase of a..." She cleared her throat. "...brothel in Las Vegas."

"A brothel?" My brow furrowed. "Why would the attorney general involve himself in a business like that?"

"Because it's a special kind of brothel. One of my clients used it for a blackmail source."

Star and I glanced at one another. "Don't suppose you'll give us the particulars?" she wheedled.

"No, but I can tell you which company he used to transfer ownership over to him." Another loud exhalation. "I suppose that I should have known."

"What's the name, Rachel?"

"The Bird's Nest LLC."

I choked out a laugh. "*Original*. They take this 'Sparrows' shit too seriously."

"The clientele is highbrow and nearly all politicians. I suppose that's handy when the chief of staff is a friend."

Star's mouth tightened. "Thank you for the information, Rachel."

"You're welcome." She hesitated. "I'm glad you're back, Lodestar. You might be a treacherous pain in the ass, but I wouldn't want you on anyone's side but my own."

When she cut the call without another word, I drawled, "You make friends wherever you go, don't you?"

She shoved me in the side. "Hush."

Grinning, I snatched her hand and kissed her fingertips. "So, the White House has its own internal source of *influence*... Interesting that Davidson isn't a Sparrow but Smythe is, don't you think?"

"Depends. You know how the Capitol works. It's 'you suck my dick, I'll lick your ass.'"

"Think most of the fuckers up there would prefer not to believe they had homosexual tendencies."

"Jackasses," she agreed, her gaze distant. "What's their endgame?"

"World domination," I said lightly.

"Joking aside, we need to make sure that doesn't happen."

"Agreed."

Her mouth turned taut. "Can one of the guards drive Katina back home tonight?"

"Of course." With her fingers still knotted with mine, I squeezed them gently, pulsing them twice in reassurance. "We can end them this week."

"We *will* end them this week," she rumbled, her gaze dark as it locked on mine before it darted away.

As she frowned, I twisted and saw that Aoife had stumbled into the room, her features blanched. "Aoife? What is it? What's wrong?"

She staggered over to the couch and passed her cell to me.

Concerned, I flicked a look between it and her then read the text conversation.

"Need to meet," Star repeated, her confusion clear. "From…?"

Aoife's eyes clenched.

"Your father," I answered for her.

"We've started talking but he…" Her mouth worked. "We *can't* meet. For obvious reasons."

Considering what we'd just been discussing…

"I don't believe in coincidences," I commented.

"Me either. Fuckers," Star agreed grimly. "It stinks of leverage. This is either a trap or they're trying to offset guilt by shifting most of the upcoming news cycle on the president's secret love child than on them."

Aoife blanched at our rundown, sagging back into the couch with wide, scared eyes that made me want to hurt Smythe and Foundry more than I already did.

"That's a grandiose assumption seeing as they kill first, ask questions later," I remarked.

"DeLaCroix was arrested, Reinier's disappeared, and there's an Interpol department being established as we speak… They must think we don't want their blood, just their asses in a jail cell."

There was no arguing with that logic so I shot her a smirk. "How foolish of them."

Her dark eyes turned flat. "Perfect, more like."

9

———

STAR

Star Sullivan

"MR. PRESIDENT, it's an honor to meet you."

Davidson, two steps inside the hotel room, froze at the sound of my voice. "Who are you?"

"I'm here on Aoife's behalf." I arched a brow at him from my seat in one of the suite's armchairs.

"She didn't want to see me?"

"She didn't feel like being at the center of a media storm. Not sure I could blame her."

He narrowed his eyes at me. "And who are you?"

"My name's Star Sullivan."

Davidson rested his hands against the back of an antique sofa and leaned into it. "How do I know this isn't a trap?"

"Call Aoife."

"If it were as easy as that, I wouldn't have asked to meet her." He scrubbed a hand over his face. "I'm cell free at the moment."

"Why?"

He pursed his lips at me. "Give your phone to me and I'll call her. Assuming you have her as a contact?"

"Such little faith, sir," I mocked, but I got to my feet, tapped Aoife's name in my contacts list, and handed him the cell.

With a measured glance, he eyed the phone then accepted it. "Aoife? Who is this person?" His frown darkened at her answer. "Why aren't you here? I need to speak with you." He pinched the bridge of his nose. "I don't want to deal with an intermediary. I want to talk to you, dammit."

A couple minutes later, with gritted teeth, he disconnected the call. I held out my hand, waiting for him to pass it back to me, but he didn't.

He dropped it to the ground then dug his heel into it until it shattered beneath the pressure.

"If you wanted to brick it, you didn't have to go old school," I drawled at the sight of the phone on the expensive carpet beneath us.

"The NSA has gotten their hands on some technology that I'm not even attempting to understand. What I do know is that no phone conversation is safe."

"That tech has been around for years."

"Yes, but the software that…" He rubbed his eyes. "As I said, I don't understand it. I just know that they can listen in to any phone call now and they have a way of both storing and sorting through the conversations."

Why did that sound exactly like the software *and* hardware Conor had adapted to listen in to his brothers' calls so his da couldn't accuse them of mutiny?

"They could piggyback off the TV unit, Mr. President," I pointed out. "Anything with speakers and an internet connection is fair game."

He cocked his finger at me and led me into another room off the suite. "That's why I picked this place. It's supposed to be a retreat. Only a TV and a vintage-era phone in the living room."

As we stepped into the bedroom, I leaned my back against the door and shoved my hands into my pockets.

"Now that we're somewhere more comfortable, sir, I think I should tell you what I know, and then we can figure out how to help you with your little problem."

"How do you know I have a problem?"

My lips curved. "I'm going to put a stupid question like that down to anxiety, sir. You wouldn't need to meet with your love child, a daughter with ties to the Irish Mob, while you're in office and running for reelection if there weren't a situation in need of resolving."

His nostrils flared but he tipped his head forward in assent.

"What you need to understand about what I'm going to share with you, sir, is that it's so off the record, it might as well be saved on microfiche—"

"So, why are you telling me?"

"Because we can stop your career from being destroyed if you facilitate our next actions."

"I'm listening."

"Good. You should know I'm an ex-CIA agent. While I was serving overseas, I started to believe there was a double agent working against us at the same time as I came across the looting of some artifacts, and to shut me up, I was offloaded into the trafficking arm of the New World Sparrows."

"What made you believe there was a double agent?"

"I uncovered the looting first. Then, the double agent. Crates were being released for travel outside of the country and someone was signing off on them. Someone who'd conveniently been blown up in an air raid. That was as much as I uncovered before I was silenced too."

"You were enslaved?" he rasped, his bewilderment clear.

"I was," I confirmed. "I almost died, but I'm a stubborn *daughter* of a bitch." My smile was tight. "I got out and I determined that I'd be their downfall.

"Over the last few years, everything that's been uncovered about the Sparrows has almost single-handedly been orchestrated by me. I've been the architect of their destruction, sir, and I won't rest until they're either dead or locked in a cell… I'll accept either option."

His brow furrowed. "I don't need to hear that."

I chuckled. "Don't be naive, sir, and don't think I don't know about the atrocities you and those from your office have permitted in the hundreds of years of so-called independence.

"You forget, I served my country and I saw firsthand what happened on the ground." I waved a hand. "Now, that isn't to say that I'm not willing to take the legitimate route.

"I've got contacts of my own, contacts that, you will be displeased to hear, hold more power than you, *but* I have two problems. Two problems who are also *your* problems."

President Davidson walked back a few steps and sat down on the foot of the bed. His elbows plunked on his knees as he stared at me.

I expected him to pepper me with questions but he didn't. He said, "Aoife told me you're her sister-in-law."

"She did?" My thumb found the cameo face in the emerald and smoothed over the features. "A little premature, but I suppose she's right."

"How is she?"

"You could ask her yourself."

"She won't answer. She just says she's fine."

"Maybe that's what she is."

His jaw worked. "I made a lot of sacrifices in my life, Ms. Sullivan. Aoife, unfortunately, was one of them."

Unease filtered through me. I wasn't here for a TMI father-daughter sharing session. "You should tell her this. Not me."

"I *intended* on telling her that," he growled. "That's why I invited her here. Not *you*." Davidson scrubbed a hand over his face. "Her mother was the love of my life. Aoife was born of that love. Yet here I am, denying her. Hiding her away like she's the dirty little secret when she's the one *right* thing I've ever done in my life."

"I don't need to hear this."

He surged to his feet. "You can't hold the truth of her identity over me to make me fall in line."

Meaning someone had already tried...

"That wasn't my intention," I told him calmly.

Watching him work himself up over this would have been amusing if he hadn't skipped over his kid to get into the White House.

"Then you just admitted to crimes to the president for fun?" he drawled.

"I admitted to nothing other than doing a better job than your security services at uncovering the Sparrows' identities.

"If anything, that shows incompetence on your government's

behalf, not guilt on mine." With a sniff and a pointed look, I continued, "I'm not trying to make you fall in line. I'm here with a different purpose.

"Let's face it, your approval rating has never been higher. Not only because of your proactive stance on the Sparrows but because of your wife's murder. You'll likely win the reelection."

"Likely means nothing in the end. Especially if Aoife's relationship with me is revealed to the press."

"I assume that you *have* been threatened?"

"Yes. My chief of staff intercepted a letter—" His jaw clenched as the fury in his eyes lit up his whole face. "I don't do well with threats, Ms. Sullivan."

His chief of staff.

Smythe and Foundry were fucking obvious. They had about as much finesse as Kat turning cartwheels down a hallway.

"What did this letter ask you to do?"

"Resign from reelecting in exchange for *discretion* regarding Aoife's parentage."

"Will you comply?"

"No."

"Would your chief of staff have known that?"

"Yes. He knows my stance on these things. I don't do deals with terrorists."

I almost snorted at the irony—his First Lady had been a part of the goddamn ECD.

Unable to stop myself from smiling, my top lip quirked up at the many layers of his ignorance. "What would you do if I told you that Garry Smythe is a top-ranking Sparrow? One of the highest in the land, even."

He stilled. "Garry Smythe… as in my top advisor?" he choked out.

"Yes. The name David Foundry ring a bell?"

"Of course! He's my attorney general—" He rubbed the back of his neck. "The second of your two problems?"

"Yes. As highly ranked in the New World Sparrows as Smythe."

"Garry… Smythe's known about Aoife for years. He found her for me, for God's sake. Why's he leveraging that information now?" He scowled. "You're wrong. Garry can't be a goddamn Sparrow. He's my youngest son's godfather!"

"I'm afraid he is, sir."

"Where's your proof?"

"You don't want to know what proof I have. If you knew, you'd have to act, and you can't."

"Why can't I? I'm the president of the United States!"

"You're a POTUS who's pledged to eradicate the New World Sparrows from his government when his top advisor and his AG are Sparrows! You'd be laughed out of the Capitol.

"They're a problem, sir. They won't go away. They're all pests that are difficult to eradicate but they're due to meet in a day's time. I will be intercepting that meeting and they'll no longer be a problem for either of us. However, I need your help."

"I don't need to know this," he choked out. "If the truth comes out, it comes out. I won't hide her—"

"Don't be selfish," I snapped, my anger genuinely focused on his goddamn ego and his inability to process that this option was *not* beneficial for the daughter he professed to care about. "You might be okay with, how did you phrase it? Your 'dirty little secret' coming out, but Aoife's got a life of her own. Do you think she needs to be dragged into your political battles? Her world torn to shreds by the press because you couldn't keep it rubbered up when you were cheating on your wife nearly thirty years ago?"

His mouth rounded. "She's my daughter. I shouldn't deny her—"

"What you should do is consider her wishes first. If you can protect her from the truth coming out, then that's what you should do.

"She's a businesswoman in her own right, an influencer who's built her reputation on good values. You could destroy everything she's worked so hard for by being reckless."

"Reckless? I'd be ruining my reputation too!"

"Unnecessarily!"

"And what do you propose I do?"

"Let me deal with our mutual problems."

He stared at me. "You mean murder them?"

"I mean 'deal with' them," I said coolly.

"I can't be involved in this," he rasped. "Losing my career is one thing; going to jail for conspiracy to commit murder is another."

"You're not conspiring to do anything," I disregarded. "In the aftermath of their disappearances, it will be revealed that David Foundry owns shares in a brothel in Las Vegas. It's a farm for blackmail as a lot of senior politicians use it.

"I will pass on the information to the press and they will start their hunt into the clients of said brothel and your government will be in a shitstorm that you can ride through with your fancy approval ratings to reelection. Unless you were also a client?" At his rapid headshake, I mused, "There's no point in lying to me. I'll find out soon enough."

"I'm not lying. Whores have never been my vice."

I hummed my disbelief but merely said, "Regardless, amid the maelstrom, Foundry's and Smythe's disappearances can be covered up.

"That's your role in this. *Don't ask questions.* As you said, Smythe has become a part of your family. The president would wade into any investigations on his next-of-kin's behalf. Don't do that. Keep your distance."

"It'll seem strange if I don't!"

"It won't. You should expect a call from Mr. Kuznetsov later." His eyes bugged at Kuznetsov's name. "He permitted me to speak to you before him which I've done as a courtesy to Aoife. This isn't a request, *sir.* It will become an order.

"Much like you helped provide your wife with a pocket of space where she found herself without the Secret Service, you will appear to facilitate the investigations into Foundry's and Smythe's disappearances but you will do no more than you are legally obliged to. Much as you've done with the investigation into the First Lady's death." My top lip quirked into a sneer. "Turning a blind eye is something I think you're good at."

Straightening, I moved from the wall and headed into the living room.

Before I reached the doorway, he rasped, "In our Brothers we trust?"

Frowning, I turned to look at him. "I'm not a Brother."

"Neither am I. My wife was."

I blinked.

Was there anything that skeevy bitch didn't have her nose in?

"Kuznetsov is my grandfather," I shared warily, one victim of a narcissist to another.

"You're Galena's daughter?" he rasped.

It was my turn to freeze. "Galena?"

My surprise appeared to ease his discomposure. "Your mother was a friend."

"What's that supposed to mean? Were you fucking her too?"

He scowled at me. "No. As I said, she was a friend. A good one. Her death was… It was a sad day when we lost her."

"You say that as a…?"

"A friend," he repeated.

My mouth tightened. "How close are you to Kuznetsov?"

"Why do you think I'm the president? I paid a lot of dues to reach this position. The Five Points weren't the only ones who got their pound of flesh when I reached the Oval Office." He hitched a shoulder. "Elizabeth slept with Anton whenever he was in town."

Well, that was more than I bargained for—talk about the whore who kept on whoring. And with Anton's wrinkly raisins too.

Eww.

I studied him longer than I should have, until my words finally formed. "If I were you, sir, I would resign from reelection. You might win, but if the truth comes out about Aoife, then it isn't only your life you'll be ruining—it's hers too. I don't think she deserves that, do you?"

Not looking back, I headed out of the suite and moved toward the elevator. As the doors closed behind me, I delved into my pocket and retrieved another cell phone.

"Did you get all that?"

Conor huffed. "Of course I did."

"How did the NSA get access to your laptop? Do you think they've discovered Maverick's worm? You took that with you when you went into Langley, didn't you?"

"I did, but there was no need to open it." He grunted. "If my checking Eagle's Claw was a front, then maybe the coders were working on remote access…" Silence, then: "No. I'd have known. It's more likely that Riggs broke into my apartment when she knew I was in Langley. Temper collected me from my building. Ordinarily, Riggs would have been the one escorting me wherever I needed to go."

"Your doorman must have let her in. That wouldn't have triggered your alarms, would it?"

"They can enter in an emergency, but I should have seen it on the logs. After everything that happened, I was exhausted and I was starting to freak out about you because of Temper. Maybe I didn't check, but I'm sure that I did." He sighed. "I literally went home to pack my bags and headed to the airport. I didn't give a fuck about anything other than getting to you."

The heartburn was back.

Apparently, admitting that I loved him didn't stop that affliction.

I cleared my throat. "You found me."

"I did. I could ask Denny, but if I do…"

"You'll have to kill him."

He grunted. "Yeah. I'd prefer to get him fired. He just had a kid."

I almost smiled. "That kind heart of yours will bite us in the ass if we're not careful."

"So long as you do the biting, I can deal."

"Of course, you can," I said with an eye roll.

"I'll check the logs once I'm done talking to you."

"Fine. What we know for certain is that your software's rogue. Do you have a kill switch, or is that too much to ask?"

"The storage houses a weakness. The kill switch targets that. If they copied the program from my hard drive, which we can assume they did, then it'll render it unusable. Because half the battle is storing so many files and being able to scan it for keywords."

My brow puckered. "Are you trying to tell me that you don't use a cloud for that?"

"No. I kept running through terabytes of storage too quickly and the SD cards were useless too."

"So you invented something?"

"Yup. I'll show you when you get back if you want?"

"I'd prefer to see your dick."

A soft chuckle sounded in my ear. "I mean, that can also be arranged."

"Make it happen," I growled, turned on beyond reason. "Why the fuck haven't you started mass-producing this solution? You do know how many resources cloud storage drains?"

"I'm still tweaking it."

How was I supposed to function when he was *this* clever?

"We'll tweak it together so we can roll it out faster. I'd like for Katina to live in a world that isn't four degrees hotter than it is now."

"Hey?"

"What?"

"Check your upper jacket pocket and I'll see you later, okay? I'm at my penthouse, don't forget."

I didn't have a chance to answer, but I dug deep into my jacket pocket and...

I sighed. "Damn you, Conor O'Donnelly."

Pulling out a Werther's Original from the pocket I never used, I popped it into my mouth.

I wasn't sure whether it was the toffee or his cuteness that eased the heartburn in my chest, but it definitely had me smiling.

10

CONOR

Conor O'Donnelly

WITH A TIRED YAWN, I checked my cell phone and grunted when I saw one of the crew I barely used anymore, Craig, had delivered Katina safe and sound to Lily Lancaster's home in West Orange.

Not that I needed the notification.

Two minutes later, I had a text from her.

> Katina: Conor, if I'm REALLY good, do you think Star will let me have a cat?

Me: I've heard about kids like you.

> Katina: Whaa. Kids like me? What did I do?

Me: Kids that go behind their mom's backs to get what they want.

Me: ^^ I did that too! Welcome to the club.

> Katina: Eeeeeeeeeeeep. I'm so happy to join!

Me: Thought you might BUT I'm not an idiot, Kat. You think I'm going to say yes to you getting a cat when Star would literally take my computers away from me if we didn't consult her first?

Me: Sorry, little dudette, you're on your own in that fight.

Katina: No fair! But you like cats.

Me: How do you know that?

Katina: I've seen your sparkly one.

Me: Yeah, sparkly one, Kat. It isn't alive. I can't keep things alive.

Katina: Luckily for you, Star can! Me too. I'd be soooooo careful with them.

Me: Wait, THEM? You said one.

Katina: See, it's Amara's fault. You know her, right? She's kinda nuts but her Old Man (he isn't old, but the Sinners call themselves 'old' everything. I've learned just not to ask. They get offended when I ask how old they

I snickered out loud at that.

Me: They, what?

Katina: Sorry, hit send before I finished.

Katina: Anyways, Quin, Amara's Old Man (who is totally younger than her and Hawk. Did Star tell you that Amara has two boyfriends? I don't know how she does it. Boys are so needy, aren't they? Not Shay, though. Shay's different. Do you think Shay likes me?)

When she didn't send a follow-up text, I studied the many questions she'd asked me.

Was I supposed to answer all of them?

> Katina: Conor?

Okay, so she *was* waiting for an answer.

> Me: I did know that Amara has two boyfriends.
>
> Me: Boys are very needy. Best to stay away from them.

I thought about Star dealing with teenage boys who tried to go to second base early and tacked on:

> Me: Wait until you're thirty. They tend to get more interesting then.
>
> Katina: Until I'm THIRTY? That's so long, Conor. They're needy but they're pretty!!
>
> Me: You shouldn't touch things just because they're pretty.

Okay, that was the pot calling the kettle black seeing as I liked touching Star, but I wasn't ten years old either.

> Me: Trust me. Thirty is your year. You can look but don't touch.
>
> Katina: No fair.
>
> Me: You'll thank me when you're thirty.

If I kept on repeating thirty, it'd act like subliminal programming, right?

Me: I'm sure Shay likes you very much. I'm glad you like him too. He's a good kid.

Me: So, where were you going with this conversation?

Not that I wanted to talk about cats, but cats were better than boys. Fuck my life, when had this become a problem I had to handle?

Katina: Amara brought in these kittens. They're so little, Conor, and they're like me.

Me: How?

Katina: Their mom left them. But I want to be their Star!

Hearing the elevator buzzer sound, I slapped a hand over my face. How in the hell was I supposed to say no to that?

Me: Leave it with me. I'll talk to Star.

Katina: Yaaaaayyyyyyy! Thank you, Conor!!!!

Me: You're welcome. But don't get your hopes up. I can't imagine this is the first time you've asked Star for a pet and I'm pretty sure she's always said no.

Katina: Of course! She wasn't happy then. She is now. Though I did hear you make her cry. I don't like it when Star cries, Conor. Please don't do that again.

Katina: I'm going to play with the kitties! Bye, Conor!!

I stared blindly at the screen.
Had she…? Like Jake?
Jesus.
Explaining Star's tears to a toddler while Finn had snickered at me

was a real low point in my life. Justifying it to a preteen wasn't something I needed to deal with in the future.

I needed locks.

And soundproofing.

Stat.

As I dropped maintenance an email, I heard Star call out, "You in your office?"

I peered at her through my fingers as she ducked her head around the door to scope out the room.

"Oh, you are!" Her brow furrowed. "What is it? What's wrong—" Her mouth gaped. "Are those *glasses*?"

Moving my hand aside, I let the frames fall onto my face from where they'd been digging into my forehead. "They are."

"Since when do you wear glasses?"

"When my eyes are tired." I shot her a serious look. "By this point, I'm thinking the whole house heard us because Kat, like my nephew, thinks I made you cry."

Star blinked. "You kind of did. In a good way."

"It's not as if I could tell *her* that," I grumbled.

Her lips twitched. "Are you embarrassed? You need to toughen up. She says worse stuff than that. She once asked me where Tiffany, Sin's Old Lady, got her helium balloons from."

I frowned. "She has big tits?"

"Nope, even better. She's pretty high-pitched when she gets going…"

"And Kat thought she was—"

"Yup. I told her that they had a private stash and that she wasn't to ask if she could have any of them."

"How much do you bet she asked?"

She smirked. "I was there when she did. It was a proud, *proud* moment in my life."

"I'm sure." I snorted.

"Does that mean she made it back to the compound in West Orange safely?"

"It does." Dislodging my glasses, I rubbed my eyes again. "She wants two cats."

"Two?! How the hell did you manage to up the stakes when I was happy with zero?"

I glowered at her. "She said they were like her—they lost their mom and she wanted to be their Star!" Her expression turned pensive so I wafted a hand at her. "Why do you look constipated?"

"Because I'm calculating the odds of her trying to manipulate us *or* if that's just a knee-jerk response after the other day and talking about family."

"Okay. What are the odds?"

"I'm not sure." She pulled a face. "We can't have two cats. I can barely keep her alive."

See, that was why I loved this woman—we were kindred spirits.

"Maybe it'll be different if we work on that together."

A frown settled in her eyes. "You say things like that and it gives me heartburn."

My brows lifted. "I say nice things and it gives you acid reflux?"

She rubbed her chest. "Right here. I'm not used to this." I watched as she staggered over to my desk and plunked her ass on the edge. "You need to only say things that you mean."

"I do."

"Kat's special."

"I know."

"I don't… You can't…" She stopped rubbing. "Could you take off your glasses? They're distracting."

With an eyeroll, I dropped them on the desk and rocked back in my chair. "My lap's more comfortable than the desk. Or did you forget that already?"

Biting her lip, she propelled herself upright and then stumbled over to me. When she settled heavily in my lap and her face instantly burrowed into my throat, I just held her, knowing that I'd inadvertently overwhelmed her and that she needed a moment to process.

I tried to multitask, but without my glasses, the lines on my monitor were blurrier than ever—damn, I needed a nap—so I just rocked back in my seat and closed my eyes, taking the respite where I could grab it.

After at least five minutes of silence, I drawled, "Getting maintenance to install a lock on the bedroom door."

Her chuckle was low. "You've got your priorities straight."

"I like to think so seeing as I also cleared out that desk over there for you," I murmured into her hair.

"Which one? There are several in here."

"You liked the glass one."

"Maybe I like this one."

"You're so fucking contrary. If you like this one, then we'll get you this one."

"I was only pulling your leg."

"You can pull something else. My leg has to remain attached."

"But your dick doesn't?"

"Some things are worth the sacrifice."

"You're lucky I'm not a cannibal," she spluttered around a laugh, but I could hear the easing of tension in her voice and that made me smile—job done. A couple minutes later, she whispered, "I need you to mean that, Conor."

"Mean what? About my legs needing to remain attached?" I teased.

"No." She shoved my other shoulder. "What you said about working on keeping things alive together." She sucked in a breath. "I'm used to everyone leaving me, Conor, so to hear you say that is… I, just, I need you to mean it."

"Some women are too much of everything," I said slowly. "Too intelligent, too strong, too capable. Some men can't deal with that. They think they need to compete. To be more intelligent, stronger, and more capable. But my self-esteem isn't so miserly that I need to put *you* down to feel like a man.

"You've lived in the fakest places on this planet—Hollywood and the CIA—so it makes sense that you don't understand what I am. *Who* I am.

"I'm an O'Donnelly, Star. We cherish our women. We protect them. We kill for them. We don't compete with them because there's no competition between us. We are on the same team, and you've just never experienced that before because for all the crap Da taught us, that was one lesson he rammed home more than any other.

"You are *mine*, Star.

"Whether you accept that or not, whether you run off tomorrow, whether you try to push me away, I'm not going anywhere. I'm by your side. We're in this together and we always will be.

"And that means Kat is too. She's mine as much as you are. We'll keep her and the cats alive because we're a team, and what did I tell you the other day?"

A soft laugh escaped her. "That teamwork makes the dream work?"

"Exactly."

When I felt the tears against my throat, I stopped talking and just continued holding her.

It was a message I knew I'd have to reiterate over the years, but there was joy in that because we had many tomorrows ahead of us.

I closed my eyes again, content to just relax as she settled deeper into my embrace, then when, only God knew how long later, she mumbled, "She can have the damn cats," I just smiled to myself.

Kat owed me big time, and she didn't even know it yet.

STAR

Star Sullivan

ONCE I'D TOLD Katina she could have the kittens and had listened to her squeal with joy amid promises I knew she'd break about looking after the admittedly cute tiny beasts, I watched Conor as he worked.

Though I was busy with a massive to-do list of my own, I couldn't help myself.

I'd already breached The Bird's Nest LLC's management firm and had uncovered the location of the AG's brothel.

I was supposed to be hacking their security so that I could snoop around for blackmail material to feed to the press once Foundry and Smythe were missing. Conor, however, wasn't helping matters.

My concentration was shot because he was a distraction—*the best kind.*

His focus on breaking through the security to the AG's office was absolute, unlike mine.

I knew the plan as well as he did and knew that most of the hacking would be on him while Troy, Dead To Me, and I would be handling the infiltration and evacuation of our marks. I could feel time ticking away as we waited for tomorrow to come.

Maybe that was what made me antsy.

Maybe that was what made me study him more.

You are mine, Star.

He'd said those words so easily, so *fiercely*.

My thumb ran over the cameo ring I wore and I wondered how he had claimed me so utterly while I was undeserving of him and his devotion.

I thought about the candy and the ring and the way he'd flown several times though he hated it and how he'd emptied this desk—for me. My mind skipped over his patience in bed and the way he cherished me even though I'd run away from him, even though I'd hurt him by ghosting him.

No, I didn't deserve him, but that didn't mean I couldn't walk toward it in the future.

"Yes."

The word tripped off my tongue despite there being no context.

He cast me a quick look before his attention reverted to his monitor. "Yes, what? To a steak? God, with those shoestring fries. I'd fucking kill—"

"No."

He stilled. "No to the shoestring fries?"

God, could I screw this up anymore?

I cleared my throat. "No. I mean. Um." I held up my hand. "Yes, to this."

His eyes danced off my expression and onto the ring on my hand. He rocked back in his seat and his grin was dopey as he asked, "Really?"

"I-I don't know when—"

He wafted a hand. "'When' doesn't matter. But an answer is nice."

Speechless, I licked my lips because I knew he meant that. I was coming to learn that he always meant what he said.

Heartburn—this fucking heartburn needed to stop.

Then, he scowled at me. "You're not doing this because you think you're going to get caught tomorrow, are you?"

"No. I mean, it's a possibility, but I know you've got everything under control."

Conor nodded. "Whether or not I was set up at Langley, which makes sense because that code was child's play, my work is better than ever thanks to you."

Thanks to you.

His words from earlier rammed their way home again—*we don't compete because there is no competition.*

I had been dealing with boys my whole life, just waiting for this man to show up.

The thought settled deep in my being, straight in my soul, and I rasped, "Yeah, we've pushed each other to greater heights."

That made him smile. "We have."

"And if you think I didn't know that, you're nuts because I'd have been all over what you're working on, and instead, I'm just watching you do it."

"You trust me."

I swallowed. "I do."

The smile lit up his eyes this time. "How hard was that to say on a scale of one—the Erymanthian Boar—to five—the Kalydonian Boar?"

Snorting, I told him, "You're such a nerd."

"This shouldn't come as a surprise by now," he retorted.

"It was as easy as killing the Erymanthian Boar in *Assassin's Creed*," I mumbled.

"Easy? Hmm. That's what I like to hear." His chair squeaked as he rocked. "I'm almost done if you want to order some food for us?"

"My hero wants steak, then he can have steak. With shoestring fries." He chuckled as I got to my feet. "Did you check your security logs, by the way?"

"I did. I don't have to get Denny fired."

"No break-ins?"

"None."

"So how the fuck did they get your code?"

"I used the bathroom when I was there. It had to be then." He frowned at me. "I pulled the kill switch, though, so it should have deactivated their devices.

"You're the best hacker I've ever met, and I don't think you'd have been able to tear apart the code on Nimue in the amount of time they've had.

"They'll only have been able to duplicate and replicate, not mess around with the inner workings of it."

"How do you know?"

"Because I wrote it in Velato."

My brows lifted at the reference to the obliquely esoteric coding language that was nigh-on impossible to hack unless you knew the key. A key that was personal to each coder.

"That must have been boring as fuck."

"It was but you weren't in my life back then and I was in desperate need of a challenge."

"Fuck, Conor, that's the goofiest coding language—" I groaned. "You wrote it with *noxxious* songs in mind, didn't you?"

I'd just bet one of my dad's songs was the key to decoding it!

"I love that you know I would." He grinned at me. "Hey, the joys of esoteric languages is that few people ever give that much of a fuck about them."

"True."

"Have you heard of an emo kid who's a hacker?"

I pulled a face. "Narrow it down."

"Barely twenty. Her roots were auburn but she dyed her hair black."

"Who is she?" I asked after I shook my head.

"She was the chick who was supposed to replace me as the NSA's go-to cracker."

"You'll always be crackers to me, Conor," I teased when it registered that he was pouting.

"Har-har-har," he groused.

Amused, I just said, "You know that IDs are handles and not faces in our world."

"It was a long shot."

"I'm assuming you think she had something to do with all this?"

He hummed. "Would make sense."

"If they found that, what else could they have uncovered?"

"Nothing major. I always keep that computer clean just in case they haul my ass in. It had the worm on there because I thought I might need to use it, but I had that better secured than Nimue."

"How am I just learning this program's name now?"

"Because I named her today."

"Years later?"

"Better now than never," was his pious retort.

"Why was Nimue on there?"

"Because I always run it when I'm with the NSA. Just in case shit is being said around me that I want to—" His eyes lit up. "I'm a moron, Star. You officially made me a moron."

"Is that supposed to be a compliment?"

"It's to counteract the heartburn I give you," he retorted, hurling his wheeled desk chair over to another desk where he started pounding on the keyboard like he was playing it with the intent to make music.

Unable to stop myself, I smiled. Then, when I realized I was smiling, I stopped. Then, when I realized I was *allowed* to smile around him because he wouldn't view it as a weakness, I went back to it.

Wandering over to him, I watched the streams of code on his monitor but found myself unable to read it because it was in goddamn Velato. Still, he was at ease with it, and then, out of nowhere, a recording played:

"Fuck, what kind of language even is this?"

Conor looked at me over his shoulder.

"Can you open the program or not?"

"I don't know."

"You're running out of time. Do something!"

"I am doing something." A couple moments later, the first woman rasped, *"I'll have to wade through this and see if I can make anything work."*

"Just find something usable on there. I doubt he'll live past tonight so whatever you can find on there is the last of what he'll be able to come up with."

"Bitch," Conor snarled under his breath.

"You recognize the voices?"

"Not the first one, but the second is my handler—Riggs. She knew I was in danger."

I squeezed his shoulder in commiseration but admitted, "She was just doing her job, Conor. I've been in her shoes. It sucks but we don't get a say in any of that."

He didn't answer, but those fingers of his got to working again.

I stood behind him, trying to be supportive even though I was entirely in the dark, then his computer screen changed and a file folder popped up.

My brows lifted at the number of files on there, absentmindedly taking note of how they were arranged in an odd manner.

"This is your storage system?" I asked.

He hummed. "I tried to stop thinking in binary and channeled quantum mechanics instead. I turned files into layers and—" He turned to me. "I can explain another day. My mind isn't on this problem, but the one we're trying to fix right now."

I hummed back, not wanting to disrupt his train of thought, but at least that made sense as to why the file folder was arranged so unusually. It went deeper than files being layers…

As I watched him work, actually *watched* him, not from a distance, not through a webcam, in the flesh and within touching distance, I could feel my heart start to race.

It was in direct response to his intelligence.

Damn, I was in over my head here.

It wasn't in me to *make* shit. I destroyed it. I waded in and rammed through it. Conor was the opposite. It was probably why he felt he'd improved since coming to know me—what he built, I tried to destroy, and he had to get better at building or faster at repairing around me.

But that his mind veered down these channels, that he'd created something so clever and with such little fanfare, impressed me like nothing else could.

And my whole *being* responded to it.

I could feel my pulse start to throb in different areas of my body that shouldn't be reacting right now, not when we had other things to do. But I just knew—I needed him in me.

I needed all that genius inside me.

Filling me.

With no ado, I unfastened my pants and started shoving them down my legs. Toeing out of my boots, I gently nudged them aside then dragged my skinny jeans off so I was standing there in a jacket and tank.

When I dragged his chair away from the desk mid-keystroke, he groused, "Hey! I'm bus—"

I knew his mind was *not* on topic when his eyes flared at the sight of me. I moved around him, put one knee on either side of his on the seat, then straddled him. His gaze dropped down to my pussy, then he reached forward and grabbed the hem of my tank once I'd shrugged out of my jacket.

Within seconds, I was bare and he was not.

Within seconds, I faced a brutal truth—I'd often been naked around dressed men. But this was Conor. And I refused to bring those bastards into this.

So, like I'd classified myself as being earlier, I rammed through those thoughts and instead, I urged myself to find pleasure in his expression, in his eyes, in the curve of his lips, in the feel of his hands.

He was a kid in a candy store.

His fingers dipped here and there, gaze tripping from my breasts and down to my spread pussy lips. Hunger made his jaw clench, and when he ran his fingertips through my slit and I groaned, his feral expression had me arching back and shoving my tits in his face.

His lips found my nipple, and they tugged on it, sucking and licking and nipping it, all while his fingers continued to stroke my clit.

When the digits slipped down to circle my entrance, I focused on how the butt of his wrist put pressure on the nub. I concentrated on the soft groans he made, on the scent of oranges that permeated the space between us. I focused on him rather than on me because I was broken in some parts and Conor was my glue.

I shuddered when his slick fingers retreated and the slippery tips danced around my clit.

My hips started rocking of their own volition and I didn't even care that the chair was starting to creak—shit like that normally took me out of my headspace. No, instead, I could feel the welter of pleasure beginning to form in my core.

It was there, making me wetter, starting to burn, turning my veins molten hot.

When I knew I was wet enough, I jerked away from him and stood in front of his chair. He blinked at me, scowling at my retreat, but the scowl soon disappeared as I reached down and grabbed his zipper. He angled his hips up to facilitate me, and within moments, his dick was in my hand and the mess he made was on my palm, the pre-cum lubing him up as I turned around, presenting him with my ass. He seemed to know what I was doing because he helped me as I leaned back, settling on his lap in reverse.

When his dick was sandwiched between my thighs, I pressed the head against my clit and started working myself on it.

"Go back to what you were doing," I told him around a gasp.

"Are you freakin' kidding me?" he retorted, groaning as his pre-cum lubed his path, making this doubly torturous.

"No, I'm not," I breathed. "You work or I stop."

He stilled. "You can't be serious."

Not a question.

I grunted. "I am."

"Fuck's sake," he mumbled under his breath as he wheeled us closer to his desk and dragged his keyboard nearer to the edge so that he could work around me.

As Velato made an appearance in front of me, the abstract language that he'd learned and the many weird and wonderful ways he'd adapted it for his own use, I registered it was my version of porn.

The lines of code were the theme, the letters and digits were the stars, and the tap of his fingers were the moans of the entertainers.

I rocked my hips from side to side, feeling the hiccup in my breathing as the ride toward pleasure moved faster than usual.

For once, it didn't feel so out of reach. I could sense it. So close. So fucking close.

My pussy leaked onto him, making the whole thing so messy I knew he'd have to change afterward, but I didn't give a fuck.

This was *fun*.

My mind was on my pleasure.

I was watching him work.

He surrounded me, his scent, his heat.

His cock provided me with the slippery lube that kept my clit reeling as it pushed me ever higher toward the peak.

When I thought I'd go mad from it, I wriggled so that his tip was against my slit. As he pierced me, the thick fullness accepted into my channel, his groan was the best sound I'd ever heard as my pussy swallowed him down inch by inch.

As I sat there, stuffed with him, his fingers moved faster on the keyboard, whereas mine clung to the armrests of his seat, nails digging into the soft leather as I breathed through the solid presence inside me.

He was thick—thicker than average, I thought. It meant when I stared down, my labia were spread apart, my clit peeping out of its hood.

For a few moments, I just studied us.

My eyes locked on our union.

But as I looked, my pussy responded in turn, and I clamped around him which made the vein at the base of his dick throb in reaction and his balls draw up.

Reaching down, I ran my fingers over the taut flesh, enjoying his second groan which morphed into a, "If you keep on doing that, I'm going to come."

"Who said that wasn't my end goal?" I breathed, not bothering to ride him just rubbing my clit and letting the clenching of my inner muscles torment him as he worked.

When a shockwave of pleasure rushed through me at my fast-paced fingers, he stunned the hell out of me.

One second, I was on his lap, and the next, he was snapping, "Done," and I was facedown against the desk, my elbows on the glass surface.

His first thrust, he took slow, as if waiting for me to freak out, but I squeezed him tight in greeting, which broke the reins he had on his control and had him bucking into me.

One hand against my stomach, the other he used to shove my fingers away.

As he rubbed my clit, he fucked me.

Hard enough for his monitors to shake, fast enough for his thickness to pound into parts of me that felt untouched.

I screamed again, releasing a sob as he pinched my clit, which had me surging onto my tiptoes and changing the angle entirely.

With each thrust, I felt like he was touching the hand he'd pressed to my stomach, and I writhed beneath him as he carried on.

Over and over.

Hitting that spot that made me want to scream.

His pace quickened even more, and in my ear, his harsh grunting breaths were replaced with, "Come for me, Star. My beautiful, beautiful naughty girl. So fucking tight, so fucking wet. You were born to bring me to my knees, Star. So fucking bad, so fucking good."

A mewling cry keened from me, long and high as I shuddered through an orgasm that almost had me face-planting into the desk— that was how unawares it took me by.

I caught myself, just, as he carried on pounding that same goddamn spot, and I sagged into the desk, the cold chill of the glass sending more shockwaves through me, my feet losing purchase as I allowed my upper body to take my weight.

The next time I screamed, I knew I was going to shut down.

The darkness loomed in my vision and it was speckled red as if the tiny veins at the backs of my eyes were sparking with the electricity generated by my nerves.

When he came, his low, long groan ricocheting in my ears, I swore I could feel him fill me up. I swore that it triggered that endless darkness that had me losing all sensation, that stole me of my very self, only for it to be delivered back to me in a cascade of pleasure that was beyond anything I'd ever known before.

I didn't black out. I was awake but not aware as he somehow

arranged me so that we were back in his seat and he was softening deep inside me.

My nervous system was still sparking as if on overload, so I let him do what he wanted and just rested against him.

Just trusted him.

Just accepted that he was deserving of my faith in him.

Just loved him.

And after a few minutes, when he had his breath under control, he got back to work while I sat on his knee and he proved, yet again, that he did beat the best armchair on the market—I never wanted to leave this spot.

Ever.

12

CONOR

Conor O'Donnelly

I DIDN'T MIND that she spaced out, mostly because I knew why.

If I'd thought I'd triggered her, then it'd be a different matter entirely.

Instead, she was slower than usual. Her eyes dazed. Her mouth was relaxed. Her coordination poor as if she were on a lag.

It meant I got to hold onto her longer, though, so I wasn't going to complain.

She sat on my knee like the good girl she wasn't, exposed and bare in a way I didn't think she'd like, but she didn't seem to be fighting even after gravity did its thing.

When I wondered if I'd made her glitch, I turned her so she lay across me and could cuddle up on my lap.

That was when I had confirmation she was okay—she cuddled into me.

With my chin pressed to her shoulder, I tugged the outer edges of my hoodie around her, and because it was oversized, it provided her with some cover, but mostly, I left her alone as I worked, knowing she was content and not wanting to disturb her.

I thought she dozed because her breathing calmed and she turned her face under my chin as if she needed the darkness to sleep.

I'd never felt as close to anyone in my life.

It was fitting that we shared this, then.

Beautiful, too.

Especially as I hadn't ever associated her with these softer moments. Proof, I guessed, that we *were* supposed to meet.

By the time she was more aware, I was coming to the end of another task on my endless to-do list. Because the NSA had no idea what they were doing with Nimue, it meant that they'd *tried* and failed to cut me off from their source, but instead, they'd just made it easier for me to access it.

Which meant the hundreds of thousands of files they'd already started to collect on people were available for me to listen to, like my very own Audible of their persons of interest.

With a satisfied hum, I set my advanced search engine to work, rifling through the NSA's targets and coming across some interesting names—Maxim Lyanov was on there, as was Misha Babanin… so were Dragon Head Zhao and Custanzu Valentini, plus a hundred other names.

My cell rang, making Star jolt on my lap, and I snatched it quickly so it didn't disturb her.

When I saw 'Ma' on the ID, I sighed, mumbling, "I'd have preferred for it to be Riggs."

"Riggs?" Star muttered back. "Your handler with the NSA?"

"The traitor." I hummed. "It's Ma." At her unsympathetic snort, I rolled my eyes and hit 'connect.' "Ma, what's going on?"

"You'd know if you'd bothered to call me, Conor. I haven't heard from you in over a week!"

"I've been busy."

"Busy? Too busy for your mother?"

"I'm trying to bring down the New World Sparrows, Ma. It doesn't just happen by itself."

"You should be praying to Our Lady is what you should be doing. She'd help bring those horrible men down."

"What about Jesus and Joseph? Can't they get involved too?" I mocked.

"Conor!" she chided. "Your uncle says he hasn't heard from you in a while also."

"No, because I've been working," I repeated blandly. "Are you spending a lot of time with him or something?"

"Not particularly." She cleared her throat. "You *are* coming this Sunday, aren't you?"

Well, that wasn't shady.

"I might not be in the country, Ma."

"Where on earth would you be if you aren't here?" she sputtered. "Since when do you leave America?"

"Since now." I glowered at Star when she started snickering.

"Who's that? I can hear laughing. Is one of your brothers there?"

"No, Ma. It's…" I pursed my lips. "…my fiancée."

Star stopped chuckling at that, her eyes wide as she stared at me, and I shot her a smug smile as I put Ma's call on speaker, just waiting for the explosion.

"You're ENGAGED?" she shrieked. "To whom? This would never have happened if your da were still alive. Where's your head at, Conor? Do I even know this woman?"

"You don't know her, and it would have happened if Da were still alive because she's it for me, and my head is firmly on my neck—I haven't lost it in the five minutes since this conversation began."

"How could you do this to me?"

"I haven't done anything to you," was my calm retort. "This isn't about you, Ma."

"Who is she?"

"Her name's Star Sullivan."

"That's not an Irish first name. Who's her father? Harry Sullivan?"

"We don't live in Ireland," I grumbled. "And no, her father isn't Harry Sullivan. She isn't tied to the mob. She's…" Inspiration struck. "Savannah's best friend."

"Aidan's Savannah?"

"Yes. She's the daughter of one of Dagger's bandmates."

"Who?"

"The lead singer."

"The one who shouted through all those songs you used to listen to?"

"He didn't shout," I groused. "But yes."

"Is that how you met? Through Savannah?"

"No."

"Then, how?"

I huffed. "Is this twenty questions?"

"No, but it can be if you want."

"I don't. Want, that is." I frowned when Star snorted. "I met her through work."

"You said she isn't tied to the mob."

"She isn't!" I reached up and dug my fingers into my eyes. When I scented Star's pussy on them, I smirked and let my hand fall to her belly which she immediately slapped away, seeming to know where I was taking this. I pouted at her glower and said, "She's an ex-soldier."

"Does Eoghan know her?"

"Does Eoghan know every soldier who ever served in the US Army, Ma? Christ Almighty," I retorted even though I knew Eoghan *had* met her during his service.

"Don't be blaspheming in front of me, Conor!"

"I'm not in front of you."

"You know exactly what I mean."

"Da was the religious whack job, not you. What's going on? Paddy isn't practicing, is he? Giving you bad ideas?"

"Yes, bad ideas like good and evil, son," she tutted. "I had an epiphany."

"Between the last time I ate Sunday dinner with you and today?"

She sniffed. "Yes."

"What was it?" I retorted.

"That I've not been leading a blameless life."

My eyes flared wide at that. "No, Ma, you definitely haven't."

She ignored me, continuing, "And I've decided that I'm going to spend my remaining years doing what's right by my sons.

"Inessa told me she thought she was pregnant, and it made me realize that those girls need me to stick around to help them."

"Aoife can help them too," I pointed out gently. "I understand you want to be there for them, but you don't need to be putting too much pressure on yourself, Ma."

"Aoife asked me for a lot of advice. When you pop out as many children as I have, you learn a few things." She sighed. "You also learn what not to do. Aoife's a good mother, but she's a busy woman. Camille and Inessa would need advice, and don't get me started on Savannah. If she doesn't forget her baby in a restaurant sometime, I'd be stunned."

"Aela did a great job with Shay."

"She did, and she did it on her own, but they don't have to do it on their own now, do they? They've got me." She blew out a breath. "I was going to tell you this on Sunday, son, but if you can't even take the time to come and eat roasted chicken with us, I'd best tell you now."

"What?" I asked warily, ignoring the side dish of guilt trip.

"I've decided to sell the estate and move back to Manhattan."

"I told you you should do that."

"Paddy's staying at Finn's place, but I don't think Aoife would appreciate me moving in with him there. I was wondering if you could find me someplace I might like."

"Sure. I can send you brochures over if you want."

"Would you come with me to visit them?"

I pulled a face. "Ma, I can try, but I'm going to be tied up for a while with this Sparrows' BS."

"Do you think you can eradicate them, son?"

"I do."

She tutted. "Then I can wait to move. Does eradication involve pain?"

"No. It involves long jail sentences."

"Or," Star chimed in for the first time. "If their case falls apart and they think they got away with it, then there will be pain."

Silence throbbed at the end of the line.

"Is that your fiancée, Conor?"

I rolled my eyes at my 'fiancée.' "It is."

"She can hear us talk?"

"She can."

"Isn't it polite to tell people when you're putting them on speaker?"

"It is, but we're among family, aren't we?"

Ma scoffed. "You're rude. I'm sure I didn't raise you to be this rude."

"I think you'll find you did," I mocked. "Anyway, Ma, meet Star. Star meet Lena."

"Pleasure to meet you, Lena," Star drawled, crossing her eyes at me as she said the words.

"Yes, a pleasure to meet you too, Star. Is that a nickname?"

"No. It's on my birth certificate."

"Interesting."

She made it sound like her father had called her Morticia.

"Anyway, Ma, I'll get looking for some properties that I think you'll like in the city. You want to be in Hell's Kitchen, right?"

"Yes." She hesitated, and I knew she was embarrassed because she thought Star could listen in. "Maybe somewhere in one of your buildings?"

"We have all the penthouses," I pointed out. "Apart from Aidan."

"Your father handed those out like they were play toys. I'm fine with a floor in the middle of the building."

"You'd be downsizing by a lot. Wouldn't you want some outdoor space?"

"I can manage, son," she drawled.

"How many bedrooms? Or will you be sharing with Uncle Paddy?"

"Conor Nathan O'Donnelly!" she gasped as I rocked my chair back and laughed silently. "How could you ask me such a thing with your father so recently passed?"

"Just figured you two were getting cozy."

"Cozy is one thing—he's very like your father in some things but far more relaxed."

I pulled a face. "I didn't need to know about your and Da's sex life."

When she released a second, sharper gasp, I half-expected her to hang up the phone on me. "Conor, you should wash your mouth out with soap."

"Nah, that would taste bad."

Ma huffed. "I apologize, Star. I wish I could say that he isn't always like this, but I'm sure if you agreed to marry him, you know that's a lie, and Our Lady wouldn't approve of that."

"She wouldn't approve of you getting with Uncle Paddy either. Out of wedlock, that is," I said, tongue-in-cheek.

"I'm going before you manage to blaspheme St. Anthony too."

"St. Anthony? What did you lose?"

"Your father, of course!"

"Wasn't he the patron saint of lost *things*?"

"What's your father if not that!" She harrumphed. "Hopefully I don't see you on Sunday and it'll give you a few weeks to *grow up!*"

I snorted as she disconnected the call and turned to Star with a grin. "I think that first meeting went very well, don't you?"

Star sighed. "Only you, Conor."

I just winked at her.

13

STAR

Star Sullivan

"PA IS OFFICIALLY LOCKED in the bathroom stall with an explosive case of diarrhea."

"Good," I muttered at Dead To Me, gently tugging on the blonde wig I wore as I strolled through David Foundry's office with all the confidence of someone who belonged there.

"Should be inconvenienced for at least forty minutes."

"Jesus, how much ex-lax did you put in her coffee order?"

D chuckled in my ear. "You don't want to know."

Grimacing, I said, "You should have just dosed Foundry and Smythe with that. It would have helped—"

"Ew, I'm not dealing with two hostages who have the shits!"

I forced myself not to smile but it was damn hard.

I continued as if D hadn't interrupted, "—but I looked at her schedule and I don't think she knew Smythe was in the building anyway. She was supposed to be having lunch with her son."

"I saw that," Conor chimed in. "But I thought it was best for her to be incapacitated too just in case she decided she needed to come back early.

"Be grateful they're corrupt motherfuckers who evade their guards. Otherwise, they'd be shitting their pants as well."

"Right," I muttered, "shut up now. I'm heading in."

"I'm shutting up. But Troy and I are waiting around the corner so don't worry, we'll be there the second you hit 911."

"Conor, you ready to reroute the emergency call?"

"Yup."

I smiled at the sound of his calm confidence, feeling absurdly content because he was in on the job with us when this half of my life had always been a secret from any relationships I'd had—even Maverick.

"Is this the wrong time to tell you that blonde hair suits you?"

Lips twitching, I didn't answer him, but with a gentle knock on the door, I waited to be granted entry to the AG's office.

"Come in," Foundry called out. As I stepped inside, I watched his head tilt to the side as he peered at me. "You're new. Where's Anna?"

"She had to step out, sir. Stomach troubles."

His mouth curved down at the corners as he glanced at his guest, obviously unhappy with that PG version of Anna's current digestive issues.

With one hand in the file folder I was holding, I moved over to his side and pretended to drop it onto the desk. A cascade of documents tumbled toward the surface, making Foundry jump in surprise and Smythe glower at me.

"I'm so sorry, sir!" I said breathily. "I didn't mean—"

"Just get out," Foundry grumbled as I started collecting the papers with one hand, and with the other, I jabbed him with the hypodermic needle in his nape. He yelped and twisted around to scowl at me, but my hands were loaded with documents.

I held them to my chest and began scurrying out as he spat, "You useless bitch. Get me Anna! Where the hell is Anna?"

By the last half of his sentence, his words were slurring and Smythe cried, "David! Are you okay? What's wrong?" To me, he snapped, "He's having some kind of seizure!"

I hurried back to the desk.

When David started seizing in earnest, I reached for the phone and started jabbing the buttons for 911.

That was when Smythe caught my wrist. "What are you doing?"

"I'm calling for an ambulance!"

His fingers tightened around the fragile bones of the joint he was trying to restrain me with.

Pretending to be in pain, I moaned and struggled against his hold. "What are you doing, sir?"

"Who are you?" Smythe snarled.

"I'm Star, sir," I cried. "I'm just a temp!"

"You did this." He waved his other hand at Foundry who was starting to vomit over the papers I'd spilled and which I'd failed to collect.

"No! I-I just needed a signature. Please, let me call for an ambulance!"

He dragged me over to him and shook me. "More like the cops. You're a murderer."

"He's not dead yet," I shrieked, but I knew the face of greed too well to register his satisfaction at the situation.

That was when I let the remaining papers in my hand fall to the floor and with them, the charade. As quick as death, I delved into my pocket and reached for the second syringe.

He fought hard, I had to give him that. When he saw what was in my hand, he spat, "You bitch."

I winked at him. "You've no idea."

Smythe went for my throat, but I blocked him and kicked him between the legs before I grabbed his balls in my fist and made a eunuch out of him.

As he proved he had the singing range of a mezzo-soprano, I broke free of his grip on my wrist and thrust the needle into his throat.

Staggering to his knees, I watched as the same symptoms afflicted him.

"Fucking…," he slurred. "…cunt."

"My favorite label," I drawled with a smug smirk before I rounded the desk again and picked up the phone. "Dialing 911 now."

"Redirecting," Conor rumbled. "And recording."

"I need an ambulance!" I cried out like I was panicked.

Troy, on the other end, sounding bored as fuck, went through the rigmarole with me and, a few moments later, declared, "An ambulance has been dispatched, ma'am."

The outer office wasn't bustling because Foundry had *two*. One where his PA sat and the other was loaded with secondary staff.

Retreating to Anna's desk, I pulled out a black body bag that I'd stored there after she'd darted to the restroom and returned to the office where I hauled Smythe into the covering first.

Huffing at his weight, I muttered, "It's a good thing I started training for this shit again."

Conor snorted. "Is there a 'haul a dead body around' program at the gym that I missed?"

"Technically, they're not dead, just a deadweight," I panted. "Okay, Smythe's in the bag, D." I pulled his body away from the door and tucked him into the corner. "Tell me when you're about to leave the elevator."

"Will do," D agreed. "We're just pulling up now."

"Good." Calmly, I studied the outer door, just waiting for someone to burst in and uncover what I was doing. *But* it seemed Anna had everyone suitably terrified of trespassing because no one even knocked.

"Exiting elevator in three, two, one…"

Nodding to myself, I rushed over to the second door and pulled it open, shrieking, "Where are the EMTs?"

Most of the ten-strong team were out on their lunch break, but two turned to stare at me just as D called, "We're here, ma'am. Please, step aside!"

As they bustled forward into the office, I started sobbing when the first woman approached me.

"What happened?" she cried, standing on her tiptoes to peer over my shoulder as I blockaded the door.

I hurled myself into her chest and started wailing like I was traumatized.

"Jesus, you should have gone into acting," Conor muttered in my ear, but I ignored him, too engrossed in the role that would keep the front office distracted as the 'EMTs' worked on Foundry.

Within twenty minutes, Foundry was declared dead, his 'corpse' was carefully loaded into the body bag with Smythe, and they were both on the stretcher that D and Troy wheeled out of the building.

In the time that it took for the staff to make it back from their lunch break, their boss had died and he had been taken to the morgue.

Amid the chaos, I slipped out of the office and reverted to my regular brown hair in the restroom which, courtesy of Anna, stank like the pit of hell.

Tucked away in a stall, I removed my makeup and changed my clothes quickly. Not just because I needed out of there, stat, but because that ex-lax and its results were potent as fuck.

By the time I was in the elevator, I was relieved to be inhaling non-tainted air, and I was smiling to myself at a job well done.

14

STAR

UNDISCLOSED LOCATION, CATSKILLS MOUNTAINS

Star Sullivan

"HELLO, SHERIDAN," I called out, waiting, ear hovering against the shipping container for him to reply.

He didn't disappoint. "LET ME OUT OF HERE!"

I smirked at no one in particular. "Where would the fun be in that?"

"FUN? You sick bitch! Let me out of here. Who the fuck are you? Do you know who I am?"

"Unfortunately for you, she does," Conor said with a chuckle.

"You need to keep away from the door, Sheridan, or I'll make you regret the day you were born," was my amicable retort as I leaned one of Conor's toys against my leg.

Conor dipped his head to whisper in my ear, "It'll take a cow down if you're not careful."

"Isn't that the point of a cattle prod?"

"How the fuck do you have such good hearing, D?" Conor grumbled.

Ignoring them, I tapped the shipping container. "Sheridan, are you standing near the door?"

Silence.

"I bet he's by the door," D mumbled. "Never did have any sense."

"I agree." Bracing myself, I turned to them, nodded, and watched as the three stood behind me like a barricade in case Sheridan managed to get the drop on me.

Unlikely, but we tried to plan for all eventualities.

I reached for the padlock, turned the key I'd slipped into the barrel, and waited for the loud click.

I turned on Conor's toy, nodded, and that was their cue.

Troy leaned forward, unfastened the padlock, then D opened the door.

He was there.

Ragged, filthy, eyes wild.

Desperate.

All I could think as I stuck him with the metal prongs was, *He knows how I felt now.*

There was no pity in me, no remorse, no guilt.

Not an ounce.

If that made me as bad as him then I didn't have a problem with that.

If it made me evil when his body started to steam from the force of the electricity ramming its way through his muscles, then I'd take that too.

"He'll die if you don't stop," Conor informed me, his voice calm.

I released my rigid hold on the cattle prod, aware that Conor hadn't undersold the strength of the weapon in my hands.

Little judders ricocheted through Reinier's body in the aftermath, as if his nervous system were still responding to the surcharge of energy.

Picking up the flashlight I'd laid on the ground by our feet as we set this place up, I took a step into the shipping container, turned around to face my peeps, and said, "I'll see you on the other side."

Conor frowned. "I still think this is a bad idea."

D clapped him on the shoulder. "That's because you still ascribe to the patriarchal belief that men need to fight women's battles for them—"

As Troy slammed the door closed behind me, a whistle of wind drifted into the space, sharp and bitter as I flicked on the flashlight.

It was powerful, another of Conor's designs, and it lit up the disgusting pit that had been Reinier's home for the last few weeks.

"The sweet smell of piss and shit," I drawled, unsure if he could even hear me, uncaring if he couldn't. "How well I remember it."

I moved to Reinier's side and levered a foot beneath him to turn him over so that he was facing down in case he started seizing and choked on his fool tongue.

Retreating to the door, I leaned against it. "I never imagined when I enlisted that was something I'd acclimate to."

And that was the sorry truth.

It hadn't been the sex slave part of my past that had made me adapt to the most perturbing of sights *and* smells.

Nah, that had been on Uncle Sam's dime.

And the best lesson they'd taught me?

Swipe Vaporub on your top lip.

Helpful, right?

For a good twenty minutes, we stayed there like that. Me leaning on the door, him face down, all while outside, I could hear Troy, Dead To Me, and Conor arguing as they prepared for Foundry's and Smythe's punishments.

Working as a team on this was strange, awkward almost. But good. Ordinarily, I'd be in here and there'd be no one out there. I was used to that, well at ease with the solitude of working alone, yet that didn't mean *this* didn't feel right.

"Who are you?" The words were slurred. Weak.

I didn't believe the fragility of his tone. He was running on adrenaline. Reinier knew what this had been—his only chance of escape.

"That you don't recognize me hurts my feelings, Sheridan. I mean, you went to so much effort to eradicate me, you'd think you could remember who you tried to destroy."

If my voice was bland, free from emotion, then so be it. If I lost control now, I'd just watch him fry on the floor of the shipping container like a piece of human bacon.

I had that in me. That rage. That hatred. And Conor had armed me with the tool to make it happen.

God, I needed to kiss him for that later—I had the best boyfriend ever.

Okay, *fiancé*.

Reinier finally flopped onto his back then peered at me with heavy-lidded eyes. "Star Sullivan," he said after a long time of just staring at me.

"That's right, Sheridan. Do you want points for remembering?"

He dragged himself onto his elbows. "I think that's only fair," he retorted, as snarky as ever.

"I knew you were high up the hierarchy," I mused.

"You just didn't know I *was* the hierarchy." He released a soft chuckle that, to me, sounded nervous. "Few ever did. Until now. What do you want?"

"You to die. Horribly," I said pleasantly.

"I can give you whatever you want, Star. I have uncapped resources at my disposal."

"Your world is tumbling down around you, Sheridan. You don't have dick at your disposal anymore." I smiled at him. "How does it feel to know that one of your sex slaves is holding the bonds to your freedom, hmm? Bittersweet? Annoying?"

"I knew I should have harvested your organs instead. I just preferred the prospect of you suffering more," he growled.

Harvesting my organs?

I didn't, not for a moment, let my expression falter.

"Sounds like this got personal a long time before I served under your directorship, Sheridan. Sharing is caring. Want to tell me when you started hating my guts?"

"In our Brothers we trust," he mockingly sang.

"You thought I was a Brother?" I sneered.

"No. I knew who your family was though. Even if you didn't."

My mouth tightened. "How did you know that?"

He just scoffed. "What are you going to do with me? The director of the CIA can't go missing. There are repercussions—"

"I wasn't a Brother before, but I'm not against using every option open to me when the time comes."

"That old bastard—more faces than Janus himself." He turned a stony look my way. "If you trust him, then you're a fool."

"I trust no one."

It was only when I uttered the words that I realized that was a lie.

And that was *not* a conversation I needed to have with myself right now.

Chuckles sounded outside, and his shoulders hunched as he whipped around as if he could see with his own two eyes what was happening. "What is that?"

"Don't you mean who? Got some of your friends here, Sheridan. It's going to be one big party."

For the first time, his stoicism ruptured—his jaw quivered. "I can give you anything you want."

"I don't want anything."

"Power, money—"

"How about, after years of being raped, can you delete the memories? Can you give me back nights where I sleep through without being plagued with nightmares? No? Didn't think so."

"I have connections!"

"What connections could *you* give me that would put you in a position to bargain?" I crowed.

"There must be some reason you're here," he shouted, sounding more and more desperate by the minute. "You must want something or you'd have just killed me weeks ago!"

I smiled at him. "You know, at my core, I've always been a hater. It's just in me. It's just who I am. And you, my dear Sheridan, have gotten on the wrong side of all that hate."

I strode forward, letting the metallic tip of the cattle prod shriek as I trailed a path into the metal wall.

At my approach, with the last of his waning adrenaline, he tried to kick out, to take me down, but I just clipped him around the head with the tool in my hand, using its bulk to aid me, then I dug the prongs into his cheek.

"The question is, do you want to live, Sheridan? I could kill you right now. Take you away from this with just a couple of pulses from this device. But then that robs you of what you're still hoping—that you'll be saved. That someone from your world will come and rescue you and you can eke out another decade of getting rich on other people's misery." I dug the tip into his cheek harder, until blood bloomed on the flesh and it was scraping against his teeth. "What'll it be? Life or death?"

I wasn't waiting for an answer, not really, but he snapped, "Kuznetsov is just using you."

"As far as I can see, he's giving me everything I could have hoped and dreamed for. Unlike you."

I let the prongs trail down his chest and buried them against his dick. As he yowled in pain, I watched with sweet satisfaction, feeling the switch being pressed in my brain as the indoctrination this man had overseen during my training began to kick in.

Pain = answers.

Answers = mission success.

At some point, it didn't even matter about promotions. They just had you so fucking hooked that mission success became equated with your country's safety, even if you were pulling stunts you knew that no American would dream you were doing in their name.

"Come on, beg. You might as well. You don't know what I'm going to do, so you should try to bargain with me." I retreated at the last moment before I zapped him in the crotch. "Once upon a time, I used to be able to make grown men weep without even touching them. Now, I have this."

He tried to shove the cattle prod away from his junk, but I kicked my leg out and pressed my booted foot to his throat. He gasped as I added extra pressure to his trachea.

"I'm not—" He spat. "Going to—" He groaned. "—waste my breath."

I dug the prod harder into his balls. "Yeah, you are. You're going to sing for me. You're right in that it won't affect my judgment, but you have to try, don't you? Just like I had to try and accept *my* fate." I smiled as I borrowed Dead To Me's catchphrase. "Sucks to be you, Sheridan."

"I-I can give you information."

I tried to pretend I wasn't interested. "About?"

"Your grandfather."

"I can find that myself."

"You can't! He's not as—"

"I'm bored. I think I'll play with some nuts," I snarled, watching his eyes flare wide in horror and a high-pitch screech escape him as he wheezed:

"I have files, records, at my estate in Florida. Blackmail material. Worth billions of dollars in the right hands!"

"On whom?"

"Clients," he rasped. "Friends. Politicians. Everyone I came into contact with."

"You don't have an estate in Florida," I disregarded.

"S'a secret," he cried as I added to the pressure of my hold on him, making it almost impossible for him to speak. But then, there was nothing he could say that would halt this. Nothing he could promise that would stop me.

"A secret. So secret it doesn't exist?" I laughed. "If you're going to lie to me, Sheridan, at least make it entertaining."

"No! I'm not lying! Please! No—"

But his pleas were too late in coming.

It was time for vengeance.

Time for *me* to take back what had been stolen from me in the only way people like Reinier and I understood—blood.

15

CONOR

Conor O'Donnelly

THE BODY BAGS on the ground started shuffling.

It'd have been amusing if it weren't creepy as fuck.

"That antidote worked fast," Troy muttered.

"Updated version," D answered. "Good shit, right?"

Troy grunted. "I wish I'd had that in Mombasa."

"That little issue with the US ambassador over there was you?" D inquired.

She sniffed.

D and I took that as an answer.

"I think I need to address the fact that you're all my heroes," I drawled.

"Heroines, dude. Get it right," D corrected, kicking Foundry when, screaming, his hands scrabbled against the fastener from the inside out. "Shut the fuck up, you piece of diarrhea splatter."

"Love the imagery," Troy slotted in.

"I thought it was fitting," D agreed with another kick when Foundry's hysteria was shoved up another notch. "If you don't shut up, we'll just never let you out of the fucking bag, prick."

His heaving breaths slowed down, but there was a whine behind them as if, in the next couple minutes, he'd be sobbing for his momma.

Smythe, by comparison to Foundry, was still, but he was talking to himself. Low mumbles that, I assumed, were supposed to calm him down.

I jerked in surprise when, from the shipping container, a scream echoed around the clearing.

Troy chuckled. "She's still got it."

D shot her a smug look. "I told you." To me, she muttered, "You didn't break her."

I blinked. "She's cracking his nuts?"

D cackled. "That's a euphemism."

"I'm not sure I want to know," I mumbled, barely refraining from cupping myself because I knew if I did, these two would find that hilarious.

"You probably don't," Troy confirmed. "Lots of ways to torture people without spilling a drop of blood. Star used to—"

As if Star wanted to make it known that she agreed with her, Reinier screeched out his agony at whatever she was doing to him, stopping Troy from finishing her sentence.

For once, I wasn't altogether desperate for an answer.

"On the positive side," D mused, "it's shut these two fuckers' traps. Guess they know it's best to stay off the radar before they're dished up for the entrée and dessert."

The body bags *were* still now. Smythe wasn't even mumbling anymore. Not that staying small and quiet, no matter D's spiel, would save them from their fates.

They'd signed and sealed that deal years ago—it was being delivered to them today.

Justice was mighty fucking sweet sometimes.

Their eternal resting places had been dug out after Star had locked herself in with Reinier.

We'd gotten confirmation that this place was a dead drop because Troy had uncovered a small lean-to that housed a mechanical digger.

That meant we'd been able to adjust our plans for maximum hurt.

And thank God for machines because the soil was still frozen and it'd have been a real bastard to dig as deep as we had otherwise.

"The beauty of being in the middle of nowhere," Troy mused as Reinier started sobbing, the howling noises echoing around the clearing, "is that the only creatures who can hear you scream are mostly hibernating, and you wouldn't want to disturb their sleep. We are the lesser of two evils."

Both women started chuckling at that, and it triggered a discussion on whether bobcats would eat through the vinyl of the body bags or if they were too discerning about getting plastic stuck between their fangs.

Troy had been relatively quiet up to now, but I found her to be an odd mixture of D and Star. D's sense of humor was undeniably dark, and the more you knew her, the more it came out to party. At first, she'd been stilted around me, but that had broken down quickly because of how glued Star and I were to each other.

The same went with Troy—there was a certain level of comfort there that made D relax and her whacko idea of what was funny or not surfaced.

As for Troy, she was more serious than Star but found humor in these situations too. I didn't think Star did. Not particularly, at any rate. If she did, it was founded in satisfaction.

Depending on who you asked, though, I'd guess that made it worse. Star's pleasure was sadistic but after what she'd endured, who the fuck could blame her?

Another hoarse scream from the shipping container had me glancing its way and prompted the women to bump fists.

When Reinier started entwining a shriek with a sob on an endless loop, the noise echoing around the clearing because of his intermittent cries, there came the sound of beeping.

A few moments later, Star slipped out of the container, her cell to her ear.

As the door creaked open, both Troy and D moved to stand guard as they'd done earlier where all four of us had tackled the CIA director who'd been fighting for his life. This time, he didn't rush out, but his sobs were even louder than before.

"Who is it?" I mouthed as she strode over to me.

"Kuznetsov."

Nodding, I turned back to the still body bags. Behind them, two open graves had been dug, and I watched as D and Troy shuffled over to Foundry after replacing the padlock on the shipping container door, proceeded to pick him up between them, and, despite his wriggles, pushed him into the thin pit.

With his arms and legs bound, he was stuck upright in the narrow aperture. I moved over to their side, picked up a shovel, and started helping to pack Foundry in place.

With three of us working, as well as Star when she was done 'talking' to Kuznetsov, it didn't take much work to bury him alive.

Next came Smythe.

He struggled more as, I assumed, he'd figured out what our plans for him were. It was no use—he was restrained and contained and his only destination was the afterlife.

Once we'd buried him too, and when both men were packed in deep to their shoulders, Star squatted in front of Foundry and tugged on the zipper.

Exposing his face to the elements, his terrified eyes darted around the clearing as he took us all in.

"Who are you?" he garbled out from behind his gag.

"Your worst nightmare," Star replied, her tone as calm as anything. Hell, I'd heard her be less calm when talking to Kat about which Pokémon was her least favorite.

"I'll pay anything," he burst out as she shoved his gag aside. "Anything!"

"You could offer me a billion dollars," she assured him, "and I'd still tell you to go suck your own dick."

"His dick or his stump?" I questioned dryly.

Star winked at me but, to Foundry, as she replaced his gag, tugging on his hair to hold him in place, she drawled, "You're going to die, David. But it's going to be deliciously slow and it'll hurt." She shot D a look, who tossed her one of those honey bottles shaped like a bear. "It's cold out, David. Very cold. Lots of predators hunting for food.

"Aren't they lucky that you're just lying around..." She opened the bottle, grabbed his hair, used it to tip his head back, and squirted the oozing amber liquid over his face. "I hope they eat your eyes. All the soft shit first." He screamed, face whipping from side to side as she worked, but it wouldn't dislodge her and just made the syrup slip and slide over his features. "You're going to feel yourself being eaten alive," she promised. "And I can tell you now, it's nothing to what you've done to the millions of women who you've pimped out, that you've enslaved, that you've turned into fucking animals.

"You, you soft, white asswipe, who sat in your ivory tower and made money off of women's misery, women like me..." Her smile was as vicious as could be. "So, no, you could offer me the earth, and it wouldn't be enough."

She kicked her boot into his face, not stopping until he was yowling and blood spurted from his nose.

"I hope it hurts. Just like *I* hurt as I was raped, over and fucking over. No one cared if I said no. No one gave a shit if I was bleeding or if I was hurting. I was a piece of meat, but you're the one who's about to be something's dinner."

When Foundry was a mess, she moved over to Smythe and anointed him with another bottle of honey and a kick to the face.

Just as she had with Foundry, she shared her own truths with him, truths that made me glad this would be their deaths.

Truths that hurt my fucking soul, knowing that she'd endured what she had. But there was pride in the mix too—she *had* survived, and together, fuck, *together*, we'd live. We'd bring these assholes down, but that would only be the start of our story.

There'd be so much more to our future than destroying the lives of these pieces of shit.

Smythe, unlike Foundry who'd sobbed and snotted his way through Star's 'makeup' process, garbled something as she made to move away.

Whatever it was clearly held her interest because she froze in place and pulled out his gag to let him speak.

"You wanted to talk so badly," she rumbled, a warning in her tone that he'd be a fool to ignore. "Then talk."

"I know who you are."

"I'm sure you do," she agreed. "I'm sure I'm on a lot of watch lists, and I'm doubly sure that ever since I escaped the prison you fuckers slammed me in, that you all learned my resume from front to back.

"I'm certain you'll know my weaknesses and that you're strategizing about how to bargain your way out of this situation.

"But that's the joy of living, Smythe. People change."

"Not this much," he snapped, sounding remarkably cool and calm for a man in his position. "Fundamental parts of your core self don't change. Like how you only got into this life because of your mother."

A soft smile curved her lips, one that surprised me because it was so discordant with the situation.

I watched her.

Warily.

"Are you going to tell me who plotted her demise? Are you going to tell me some hard truths but *only* if I let you go?

"See, I know who killed her. Maybe I don't know the why, but I can figure out a semblance of the truth, and even if you *did* know exactly what happened, how the fuck can I be sure that it isn't a fairy tale that you're trying to sell me—"

"Nobody killed her," Smythe rasped. "She didn't die. She's alive and well and I can take you to her."

16

STAR

Star Sullivan

CIN HAD DONE plenty of weird shit in her life, plenty of gross shit too, so I felt comfortable leaving her in the clearing as she lived out of a tent to make sure that no one approached the men while they were in their 'appetizer' phase.

I had to figure that having their faces gnawed off would induce exsanguination, but I hoped it didn't. I hoped they suffered for days. I hoped that it lingered and that they had to endure an abbreviated but still living hell before they were delivered to the real deal.

Maybe someday, we'd be neighbors down below and we'd have to enjoy Conor-inspired spiky-butt stuff from Satan himself, but that wasn't my today or my tomorrow—unlike them.

"You were put through the wringer, weren't you?"

I blinked at Troy's remark, thoughts of what had just happened stalling at her question. "You think I started all of this for shits and giggles?" My gaze turned distant as I watched Conor fulfill the plebeian task of loading our SUV with gas.

How did the man make that hot?

"Never know with you, Star, never know why you do the things that you do."

"Like you can judge," I retorted, preferring to watch Conor's butt than deal with this conversation.

"Not judging. Just… I'd probably have been nicer to you when you showed up at my house if I didn't think you were staging some kind of intervention."

I had to laugh. "You need more than an intervention, Troy."

"Don't we fucking all," she grumbled.

"I don't show up to interventions with SMGs either."

She rubbed tiredly at her eyes. "You think he was lying about your mom?"

"Of course he was. Saw her body. They can make deep fakes now, but not back then."

"Deep fake corpses… a new low."

"In a century that challenges new lows," I concurred.

"Still. Has to hurt."

"You grow a heart while you were raising my cousin, Troy?"

"Apparently. There *are* ways to tamper with bodies," she said hesitantly.

"I was always a maudlin kid. When she died, Dad didn't want me to see her. He tried to keep me away from the funeral home—"

"But your stubborn ass didn't listen."

I shook my head. "Of course not. Savannah…" I paused. "You don't know her. But she's the daughter of—"

"Star, I'm pretty sure you think that I live under a rock, but I don't. I know who your folks are, and I know *noxxious.* Ergo Savannah Daniels is on my radar.

"Plus, I was impressed by that TVGM shitshow she orchestrated. The second I saw her deal with that asswipe on breakfast TV, I figured that she grew up with you."

God, I hated how open my past was.

Fucking fame.

Still, I had to smirk.

Some days, I wasn't sure if Savannah had rubbed off on me or if it was the opposite.

"Guessing you know Camden then," I mocked.

"Lyra's a big fan."

The smile that curved my lips was painful in how large it was. "She and Kat have something in common then. She considers him her soul mate."

"Weird kid."

Proud, I nodded. "The weirdest. She's mine."

"How did that happen anyway?"

"Same way you got yours."

She stilled. "Katina is Bogdan Belyaev's daughter?"

"She is. That's why I get what you're going through with Lyra and I'll never let my grandfather take her away from you, because I'd make what I did to Smythe and Foundry back there seem like child's play if someone even *thought* about taking Kat away from me."

"Funny how two women who should never have been mothers are so protective of the cubs in their fold," she mused, but her tone was loaded with her approval at my idea of punishment.

"I think it makes perfect sense. Who better to know how shit the world is and with the skill set to keep them safe from it?"

"True."

"I'd do anything to make sure she never goes through even an inch of what I have."

"Same." She cleared her throat. "I appreciate you saying that though. It… concerns me."

"Understandable." With my eyes locked on Conor's ass, I asked, "Who was your partner?"

"In Ohio? Useless piece of shit. Shot him myself afterward. Was worth getting an extra year added to my sentence."

Typical Troy. "Who was he? A hacker?"

"I could hack better than him. His name was Dazzy."

My brow puckered. "Never heard of him."

"Not surprised. He was useless. I swear, half the trouble I got into in Ohio was his fault. Still, when I picked up Lyra, she stole my heart. Dazzy had to die. Didn't matter if he was hot shit at hacking or a pile of crap. To save her, he had to go."

If I'd needed proof of how much Troy loved her daughter, I had it. "How did you get out of Jorgmundgander?" was all I said.

"You don't. You finish your time, know that they could call you up at any moment, and you deal with it. It helps that I'm not as good of a shot as I used to be because of my eye." She grunted. "You can tell he doesn't do this often, can't you?"

I had to laugh.

Conor *was* taking an inordinately long time in filling up the SUV's tank.

"Hates driving."

"That's why you made him take the wheel?"

My lips twitched. "It's good to do things you hate sometimes."

She snickered. "Life lessons according to Mrs. Lodestar."

"I should have been a teacher," I agreed.

A scoff was her only answer to that. Then... "You know who Belyaev was?"

I cast her a glance. Her expression was hidden by the depths of the backseat, but her tone was ominous, to say the least. "Conor looked into him. Said he was a front. You know differently?"

"He was a front. In a sense."

"Meaning?"

"Remember the Romanovs?"

"I have a preteen daughter, Troy. I've seen *Anastasia*."

"Yeah, well, good thing, seeing as Belyaev believed he was a direct descendant of the Romanovs."

I hooted out a laugh. "So, he was a stoner, then?"

She chuckled with me. "Whatever *we* think, he believed it and he had others believing it too. He was a nasty fucker though. I wished I'd gotten his hit. Your..." Her tone sobered. "Your uncle seemed decent. It didn't make sense that he was a Sparrow in all honesty."

"Because he wasn't. He was there for me. My grandfather told me that he was friends with Belyaev. Aleks knew that Belyaev had killed his wife and used that as a bargaining chip to further his ties with the Sparrows so they could find me."

"Interesting."

"Fascinating," I drawled.

She hitched a shoulder. "Sorry."

"Thanks for lying," I mocked, but I was smiling. 'Adapt and overcome.' I hadn't been a Marine, but I lived by their motto.

"Weird that they'd be friends though," she mumbled out loud.

"No weirder than you and me being friends." I grabbed the bottle of juice Conor had brought with him and took a sip. "So, who was Belyaev and how do *you* know when Conor could barely find anything about him?"

"Because Jorgmundgander gave us his profile but in the aftermath, they tended to wipe their targets' slates clean."

"Why?"

"Easier to pretend they never existed that way. Jorgmundgander's MO is skeevy as fuck. They make the CIA appear friendly. They don't just kill someone; they eradicate them. Every part of their lives."

At her long pause, I frowned. "Wait… Are you saying what I think you're saying?"

"That you were probably dumped into the sex slave business because of your ties to your mother? Yeah. That your dad probably got dealt some shitty coke or something to kill him, yup. They go in and they clean up after themselves.

"You probably only lived as long as you did without interacting with them because of your dad's status."

"Fuck."

"About sums it up," she agreed. "If your grandfather and uncle *were* looking for you, that's probably why you were impossible to find. That you were a commodity the Sparrows could use undoubtedly worked in your favor and stopped them from killing you outright. If you consider living to be a benefit, that is."

We shared a glance. Snorted. Returned to staring straight ahead.

"Until Kat, I didn't. After, *now*, with Conor, I'm even gladder to be alive."

She hummed. "Never took you for a fool in love."

"It gets us all," I mocked. "So, Belyaev…"

"He was the key player in sourcing the women in the Baltics."

"Didn't stop them from having a steady stream once he was dead."

"Course not. They shoved his younger sister's husband in the hole he left behind, but he had a lot of power and his replacement didn't.

"As I said, he had others believing he was a Romanov too. Where he was from, at any rate. It was why they took their daughters to him— they thought he'd give them a better life."

"Bastard."

"Yup. The dream career of most women in Russia is prostitution."

"Bullshit."

"Nope. You ask around on the ground, and it is. That's what poverty and years under a communist dictatorship do to you. The families would pay *him* to help their daughters find work if you can believe that."

"Didn't they question shit if they never heard from their kid again?"

"The ones with families became brides. The ones who were on their own became slaves.

"The brides went with average middle-class Americans, and to people in the Baltics, that's practically luxury living. Why wouldn't they spread the news that Belyaev had the means of giving their children better lives?"

My brain whirred with the new information that wasn't *new*. Alessa, Kat's sister, had been on her own when she'd become a slave, whereas her mom, who'd left Alessa and her own mother behind, had become a bride.

I thought about Amara, another victim of this heinous market Belyaev and his ilk had exploited. "Why were some kidnapped?"

"Easy marks, of course." The *duh* was silent.

"Belyaev must have had an empire by the time he died."

"I think that's why they wanted him gone. Ya know, stop him before he got too big for his britches. If he *was* feeding Kuznetsov intel, that probably didn't help matters." She sniffed. "All supposition though. Finding out why these bastards do what they do is next to impossible."

"Understatement."

"Yup."

The driver's door opened and Conor hopped in behind the wheel, bringing with him the scent of oranges.

It was refreshing.

Freeing, almost.

It took me away from the truth of the moment and made me think, instead, of good times.

Better times.

"It's colder than a witch's tit out there."

"How do you know witches have cold tits?"

"On the behalf of all witches, I'm annoyed," Troy concurred.

Conor grunted. "It's a saying."

"In which part of the world?"

"My world. Witches can be men too. Now, who's being sexist?"

"They're warlocks. Wizards if you're a *Harry Potter* fan. Which," I tacked on before he could speak, "knowing you, you are."

"I prefer *Star Wars*."

"What does one have to do with the other?"

"If you know, you know," he taunted. "Anyway, witch, warlock, or wizard, ever heard of man boobs?"

"I've heard of them. Surprised you have." Especially when I thought of his pecs.

"I was chubby as a kid."

"No way."

"I lived on my computer and hacked into NASA for fun, Star," he drawled. "I didn't play outside much because I knew what the boogeyman looked like and I was addicted to video games. What about that sounded healthy?"

"Why did you hack into NASA?" Troy queried. "They have none of the good stuff."

"Everyone's a fucking critic. I was curious, okay? And it got me into more shit than it was worth," he groused.

"He's on a watch list," I explained to Troy.

"Aren't we all?"

"In this car, sure," I demurred.

"Which agency?"

"NSA," Conor grumbled.

"Hardcore." She sounded impressed. "Takes a lot to get them involved. Normally, it's the Feds. What happened?"

As he started the engine, he tossed something in my lap. I hid a smile when I felt the shape of a couple Pixy Stix.

"What's with him and feeding you candy all the damn time? And aren't you going to offer me one?"

"None of your business and no."

Conor chuckled, but once he'd pulled out of the gas station, he headed onto the highway, explaining, "The first time was for kudos. The second time was to access a satellite."

"Moronic move."

"He knows it was."

"Been paying for it ever since," he mumbled. "Heading to Russia was my first trip out of the States in years."

"Once the Sparrows are dealt with, we'll get my grandfather to negotiate on your behalf with the NSA. Might as well use his influence while we can."

"While he's still alive, you mean?"

I hitched a shoulder. "People die around me."

"You have to make everything about you," Troy grumbled. "People die. Period. It's not always about us."

"Fuck off. Are you trying to tell me that people don't have a higher likelihood of dying in our vicinity?"

"Sure, but that's usually because they're marks!"

"*Ergo*," I mocked, "people die around us. It's not about ego, just statistics."

Conor chuckled. "You have a plenty big ego."

I elbowed him in the side as I tore open a Pixy Stix and sank back the hit of pure glucose. "Like you don't."

"I'm proud of mine. Nothing to be ashamed of when I have you around to keep it in check. We just need to get yours back under control. Ya know, so you don't run off thinking the whole world will stop turning if you're not involved."

I took the hit, but when Troy hooted at his comment, I rolled my eyes. "It wasn't that funny, *Elena*."

Pulling a face and opening up another Pixy Stix, I nearly choked on the dust when Troy slapped me on the shoulder, joking, "More like hilarious because it's fucking true. You never could delegate. Wasn't that nearly always on your reports?"

As I coughed my guts out on a hit of glucose, Conor peered at Troy. "Seriously?"

"Seriously. She's always been shit at sharing jobs. I used to think it was that ego of hers, but it's more that she's a control freak."

"I have high standards," I said with a sniff.

"The highest," Troy agreed. "Even if it fucks you over."

Ugh. "True."

"Remember that job in Bangladesh?"

"Yeah," I mumbled.

"Which job?" Conor inquired. And I just knew he was regretting starting our journey at the prospect of story time.

"Lodestar had to get in and out of a privatized hospital that was specifically for high-ranking officials of the government. She needed to move fast. Snag this computer and pass it onto—"

When she faltered, I mumbled, "Grail."

She clicked her fingers. "That's it. Grail."

"Like the Holy Grail?"

"Yup," I said with a sigh. "She'd watched the third *Indiana Jones* movie so many times, she knew the script front to back. She got obsessed with Grail lore, had her own freakin' diary like Sean Connery did in the movie as well."

"Past tense?" Conor asked quietly.

"She's not dead," Troy answered. "Just crazy, changed her surname to Jones. Officially. Crazy. So Peyton *Jones* is an archaeologist now. Private."

"She became a merc after she left the army, didn't she?" I asked Troy.

"Yeah. She funds her own digs. Anyway, Star, here, was supposed to hand off this computer to Grail. Instead, she decides Grail's no good—"

"That's not fair. She'd just lost her fucking dog and was crying all the time!"

"Yeah, but she was fit for work," Troy argued. "Stop interrupting. I'm getting to the good shit. So, because Star thinks she's an all-knowing, all-seeing benevolent being, she doesn't hand it off and as she leaves, she gets caught with the computer on her person."

"Triggered a diplomatic incident until Dead To Me managed to put two bullets in the guards holding her."

"Wow," Conor breathed. "You do have control issues."

My nose crinkled. "You knew that already."

"Maybe. But not to that extent. I mean, I figured it was thanks to everything that happened with the Sparrows. But it's not. It was *before* them. At work."

"That's just *one* job, Conor. If she weren't so fucking good, they'd have fired her ass. Plus, our team was one of the best."

"Your team was all women?"

She chuckled. "We had a few guys along for the ride from time to time."

"Remember Chad?" I asked with a smile.

"Yeah. He had it hard for Dead To Me."

"She had it harder," I retorted. "I know she has feelers out on him."

"Why?"

"He went missing after he came back Stateside. You know how the sandbox fucks with people's heads."

"It's criminal how we treat our veterans," she stated grimly.

"True dat," Conor concurred.

"The guys never stuck around for long. Creed did though. He was with us for a year."

"Dead To Me liked him too, didn't she?"

"They got caught fucking in a tank, Troy," I retorted. "What do you think?"

"Hate fucking is totally a thing," Troy retorted around a cackle, one that petered out into a long sigh. "They weren't all shit times, were they? We had some laughs too."

"We did," I agreed. "It was only when Reggie left that things went to the dogs."

"Regina was your CO, right?"

"She was," I confirmed, answering Conor's question. "She left and we started falling apart, got split up, and then I got captured. If I couldn't trust my girls with half of the missions we were sent on, there was no way in fuck I could trust strangers."

A soft, sad silence settled among us. It sank into my marrow—*regrets*. So many of them. Some days, I felt like I was drowning in them.

Conor cleared his throat, asking, "What's our next step, then? Dagda?"

I frowned. "Why? I promised Aoife I wouldn't kill him."

"So kind of you," he teased, lips curving into a wide grin. "I just thought you'd want him to confirm his involvement in your mother's death.

"It's not like he's going anywhere while he's tied to a hospital bed. He can't run away from you, can he?"

"You think a man with his rep stays still for long?"

"He's old, Star."

"The only old spies are dead spies," Troy intoned, but she was right.

You had to be reactionary in this life, no matter your age, or you'd end up in a coffin earlier than anticipated.

Unless the PTSD was bad like Maverick's, you cared about dying ahead of time.

"Anyway," Troy continued, "Star thinks Smythe was bullshitting."

"He'd have told me that my dad was alive if he thought it would spare him." I crumpled the Pixy Stix wrapper in my hand. "I should have fucked his face up even more for his audacity."

Conor hitched a shoulder. "Wouldn't you prefer to have confirmation from the guy who allegedly killed her?"

Perplexed by his blasé tone, I turned to him and queried, "Conor, how can you stand to be around him after everything? How don't you want to strangle him?"

"That's a dangerous question, Star."

"Why?" Troy broke in to ask.

"Star… maneuvered things so that my father and another enemy of Dagda's were at the same place at the same time. I'm sure you can imagine how that ended."

Troy, never a jar short of cookies when it came to this stuff, snorted. "Cold, Star. Cold."

"Which is why it's a dangerous question." Conor sighed. "My da had ALS. You'd have to know him to understand that a man like him could never be seen to be sick."

"That's very ableist of him," was her pious retort.

"You can add it to the tons of other -ists that described him," I mumbled under my breath.

Though Conor had to have heard me, he answered Troy, "It sounds as if it is, but it was more a survival mechanism.

"Think about it—he was the head of the Irish Mob. If he looked sick *ever*, someone would come for him. Then, they'd likely come for Ma and, when we were younger, his sons. The mafia underbelly is Darwinian bullshit at its finest."

"That's why you're okay with Star arranging for him to be in a coffin?"

"Nice, Troy," I spat, inwardly cringing at her wording.

"I'm not okay with it, but we're working through it."

"What is this? An episode of *Dr. Phil*? I thought you said you didn't do interventions, Star?"

"I never said I didn't," I retorted. "I just said that I don't show up to them with SMGs!"

"I don't even want to know," Conor muttered as he switched on a radio station and set it on low. "Dagda did my da a favor. A debt is paid and he doesn't have to suffer and be used as target practice by another faction who wouldn't be as noble as a sniper in ending his life. *That's* why I can be in the same room as him.

"If you'd asked me when he died, I wouldn't have said that. I grieved him and you hard. But I wouldn't have wanted him to suffer, and I've got you back."

"God, pass me a barf bag," Troy said, faking gagging.

Conor huffed but turned up the music even more.

When silence settled between us, a song filled in the gaps that conversations normally took. It gave me time to think about my situation, and that skewed guilt filtered through me as I reflected on what I'd done over the years.

I didn't like Aidan Sr. I certainly didn't like what he'd done to his son. Nor did I like how he treated his family, but my guilt wasn't for the man—it was for Conor.

For what I'd done to *his* father.

Tentatively, half expecting him to shrug my hand off his lap, I let my fingers rest on his thigh.

When he cupped them, knotting our digits together, I breathed a little easier, finding comfort in anchoring myself to him.

Still, my voice was rough as I rasped, "I'm surprised your brothers haven't set The Whistler on me."

He arched a brow I only saw because of the gleam from the dash. "Someone had to die that day. The sins of the fathers can't always be passed onto the sons."

"What the hell's that supposed to mean?" Troy grumbled. "Are you purposely speaking in tongues?"

"Da gave Dagda his vengeance. He got him off our backs."

"Why does Dagda have a hard-on for the Irish Mob?" Troy queried.

"Because they had his sister killed," I muttered tiredly.

Troy whistled under her breath. "This is better than an episode of *A Day of Our Lives*."

"Shut up," I groused. "And I think you mean *Days of Our Lives*. If you're going to bitch at me, get it right."

She harrumphed. "This is prime-time TV shit here."

"Not sure they'd air men getting their faces eaten off by animals before eight PM," Conor drawled.

I had to snicker at his droll retort. "Yeah, we've become desensitized to violence but not by that much."

"Not yet anyway," Conor agreed with a chuckle.

"Okay, so, your da had Dagda's—" She paused. "Wait. Lyra told me that Aoife is related to Dagda."

"What? When? She doesn't even talk." I spluttered.

"She *can* talk," Troy snapped. "It's just easier for her to listen."

I was quiet for a moment. "Let's hope she becomes a teacher and not another spy. With that talent, she's a shoo-in for the family firm."

"So, Dagda *is* Aoife's uncle, right?" Troy asked, otherwise ignoring me.

"Yeah," Conor confirmed.

"Awkward."

I grimaced. "Very awkward."

"And your da killed Aoife's mom, why?"

Before I could correct her, Conor cleared his throat. "To keep her quiet."

Well, that was a lie.

Interesting.

"About?" Troy peppered.

Curious about where he was taking this when his ma was the one who'd killed Michelle Keegan, not his father, I waited for him to explain.

"Does it matter?" he grumbled. "This has nothing to do with our current situation."

"That's where you're wrong. Whatever led each of us to this point is pertinent to our current situation."

He huffed. "Dagda is the head of the ECD."

"Those IRA psychos that take extremism to the nth degree?"

"Those are the ones," I confirmed.

"Now you get involved," he groused at me. "When Dagda was in prison, he maintained his position in the ECD, but a Five Pointer, a guy we trusted, wanted to take over the group. Da helped him."

"And they used his sister as leverage?"

"Yeah," Conor lied.

"Huh. You know, the first family get-together needs to be televised because I have to watch this showdown."

"Shut up, Troy," I retorted, uncomfortable with her mockery because I'd had a part in causing this chaos and it was only coming to light because of my meddling.

Plus, I'd inadvertently shit in my own bed because they were my family now.

Conor had opened his arms to me no matter what I'd done in the past and he'd offered me acceptance.

I already knew that I was a moron—this just confirmed it.

She heaved a sigh, but thank God she stayed quiet because, suddenly, his lies made sense.

For whatever reason, Dagda believed that Aidan Sr. was behind his sister's murder, not Lena O'Donnelly, and seeing as his da was dead and his ma wasn't, Conor obviously wanted to perpetuate the lie.

As silence fell among us again, I let my mind drift onto the topic of the moment—not by one iota did I believe that my mother was alive, but maybe Conor was right. Talking with Dagda might be the one thing I'd never had until now.

Closure.

I'd never found any justification for her death, and that made sense. If it was a Jorgmundgander operation and her identity was as wiped as the snakes could make it, the only person with some answers was the man who pulled the trigger.

Maybe closure was why Conor could forgive me?

He had that with his da's passing.

His father, never a man to accept anyone controlling his fate, had died on his own terms…

"Okay." When Conor shot me a quick look, I stated, "I'll see Dagda."

"I'll let Finn know you want to speak with him."

"Why Finn?"

"He'll tell us when Dagda wakes up and is able to talk." He laid his hand on my knee this time.

The gesture went deeper than he could imagine.

I didn't know if I'd have been able to forgive me for *my* trespasses against his family, but maybe that was just proof Conor was a better person than I was.

When he squeezed me there, pulsing his fingers twice, gently, I slipped my hand over his, a welter of gratitude filling me.

He was too generous with himself. Too kind and loving with those he considered his own.

I'd let him down so badly, his family, the only people who mattered to him, too, and…

I gritted my teeth.

I couldn't control the past. I couldn't change it. But I could make a difference going forward.

I'd be the best 'insert label' that Conor could ever have.

Unaware of my thoughts, mistaking my internal tension and assuming it revolved around the situation with my mother, he murmured, "Dagda might have nothing to add to the narrative you've got in your head, but it's better to know, isn't it?"

That was the thing—the 'narrative' I had on my mother's death was riddled with plot holes.

I guessed it was time to fill in the gaps.

17

CONOR

AFTER DROPPING Troy off at the brownstone next to Finn and Aoife's place, we headed inside to ask Finn to loop us in on updates about Dagda.

Aoife had brownies fresh out of the oven so, of course, we had to eat those after she offered us the guest shower to clean up thanks to the grimy work of a makeshift undertaker.

With me borrowing some of Finn's sweats and a hoodie and Star doing the same with Aoife's clothes, we left our gear with my brother so he could see to them being incinerated.

Afterward, we talked about Dagda's current status, ate some of their leftovers too, and it was while we were eating that Star received a text that immediately soured her mood.

She didn't exactly turn sullen, just went quiet.

Knowing how private she was, I didn't push the conversation but wound things with my brother and sister down and got us out of there.

After she settled in the passenger seat and I was backing up the tank of a car that felt *and* maneuvered like it weighed a thousand tons, I asked, "Who texted you?"

I half expected her not to answer, but she mumbled, "Reggie."

Concern hit me because I knew her ex-CO was currently on guard duty. "Is Minerva hurt?"

"No. Not aside from being heartbroken." She pinched the bridge of her nose. "The funeral's on Tuesday."

I whistled under my breath. "That's fast."

"That's the Four Horsemen for you. They look after their people. Reggie just told me she was asked to stand down. That the Four will be watching over her from now on." She heaved a sigh. "I want to attend."

"Then we'll attend," I replied, even as I tried to catalog what I knew of the Four Horsemen.

"You don't think it's a bad idea?"

"Probably, but you want to see her off, don't you? Say goodbye?

"We don't have to stand at the front, Star. We can be at the back. It's not about making waves but saying goodbye to a person who supported you when you were in trouble."

"Minnie won't see it that way."

"Then she won't see it that way. She'll curse at you and shout, and maybe that's what she needs to feel better. I think you can handle an argument."

She snorted. "Maybe."

"More than maybe. More like definitely."

"If it makes her feel better."

I grunted. "It would. I'd have liked to shout at you a few times during Da's funeral."

Her swallow was audible. "I'm sorry, Conor."

For the first time, I felt like she actually meant it. Maybe not because of what she'd done, but because it had affected me.

"Thank you, Star," I said, accepting the apology and not dismissing it. "Call your grandfather and ask to use his jet. I'm still technically on the NSA's leash."

She didn't call him but sent an email and received confirmation of the flight by the time we parked in the garage at my building.

I was used to having an in with people, what with Da's ties to the head of the FBI—even if that link had been no help with my NSA situation—but I had to admit that Kuznetsov was on a whole other level.

His fingers dipped into Interpol? Shady NATO operations? Homeland Security?

He was seriously becoming my favorite person after Star.

When we made it home, I started toward our office, but in the doorway, she grabbed my hand and tugged me to a halt.

I stared down at her with an arched brow.

"What am I to you?"

That had me frowning. "Aside from a pain in my ass?"

Her lips quirked. "You know I can put you on that pained ass in less than two moves, don't you?"

"I like to live dangerously," was my retort.

"Evidently." A spark had come to life in her eyes though. "You know what I mean."

"I guess," I drawled. "But it isn't what you are to me; it's what you think you are to me."

"What the hell does that mean?"

"It means you're my penguin."

"We're not back to penguins, are we? I keep expecting Benedict Cumberbatch to start narrating our lives whenever you bring them up."

I grinned. "I could probably arrange for that to happen."

"You're rich, but are you *that* rich?"

"Everyone has a price."

"Benedict Cumberbatch doesn't," she mocked.

"Anyway, of course, we're back to penguins. That's what it boils down to, isn't it?" My lips twitched. "Though I guess in that phrase, you should be glad I don't call you 'my lobster.'"

Her eyeroll was borderline painful. "So, on official documents, you'd put Star Sullivan down as 'your penguin?'"

"Not sure the government is that forward-thinking yet. But between you and me? Sure. If you want to make things more simple by calling me your boyfriend or your fiancé, then that's boring, but I'll accept those adjectives."

"They're labels, not adjectives. And I'm a boring person."

"You are when it comes to *labels*." My grin deepened. "What am I to you, then?"

Her eyes were back to twinkling. "That's for me to know and for you not to find out."

"Hey! That's not fair," I grumbled, but I used her hold on my hand to drag her into me. In one of my smoother moves, I twisted her around so that I could loom over her. "Fair's fair, Star Sullivan."

Her grin was pure arrogance. "Thought nothing was fair in love and war?"

"Which are we in?"

"Love, of course. We did the war part already."

"I guess we did. And we did it damn well." I tipped my head forward and ran my lips along the high curve of her cheekbone. "Did you imagine when you rammed into my code that you'd end up here?"

"Pinned between a door and a coat rack? Nope."

I reared back to point at my tree. "It's a tree. Not a coat rack."

"Can't it be both?"

"No. If you hang coats on it, you won't see the branches."

"So passionate."

"I'm a passionate person," I retorted.

"I'd never have guessed." She angled onto her tiptoes, reminding me again that this was the only way in which Star was diminutive in comparison to me—I had a good four inches on her—and she let our lips brush. "You have weird taste, Conor O'Donnelly."

"I have great taste," I retorted. "In women and interior design."

She snorted but rocked back and forth until my lips parted. As her tongue speared a path into my mouth, I let her take the lead, knowing that was her comfort zone.

She kissed me with a gentleness that took me by surprise. Not pouncing on me, just tasting. Just… savoring.

The notion had me retreating as I pressed my forehead against hers. "What's wrong?"

Her brow furrowed. "Nothing." She tried to kiss me again but I held my position and kept my mouth at a distance from hers.

"You've been weird since we drove back from the Catskills and I know it has nothing to do with torture."

She pouted. "It could. I have a conscience."

"Do you?" I smirked. "Could have fooled me."

Star shoved my shoulder. "Shut up."

"Why? You like my mouth when it moves, don't you?"

"Yeah, and I don't know why."

"Because it keeps you in line?"

"Ha. Right. You believe that if it makes you feel better."

I grinned. "It makes me feel incredible."

She rolled her eyes. "I just… I realized I was lucky."

"Why?" It kind of boggled my mind that she considered herself lucky, what with everything that had happened to her in the past.

"Because if I were you, I'd hate me, but you don't." Her voice was small. "I-I don't want to lose you, Conor."

Whatever I'd expected her to say, it wasn't that. "Everything I talked about on the ride over, it wasn't to make you feel bad."

"The truth hurts," was her only comment.

"It does," I agreed. "But it wasn't to make you feel shitty. You know that, don't you?"

"I do. I think that's what brought me to that realization though. If I were you, I'd have me in your crosshairs by now. I wouldn't be kissing you."

"Then we're fortunate that I'm a more generous person than you, aren't we?"

She huffed and angled her head to the side, disconnecting us. "Stop joking around."

"I'm not," I countered calmly.

"I-I think I know what you want when you talk about atonement." She bit her lip. "And it makes me feel weird."

I let our foreheads kiss again. "What makes you feel weird?"

"I know that I could have lost you." Her chin trembled and that vulnerable gesture paved a path directly to my heart. Star wasn't one for emotional displays like that, small as it might be. "I-I never want to lose you, Conor," she repeated, and I believed her.

I really, genuinely did.

I fought the urge to make everything better, to soft-soap this so she didn't worry, and, instead, went with the truth. "Why didn't you just come to me, Star? We could have worked things out together."

She released a heavy breath and I knew, *knew*, that she truly did understand what I meant when I talked about atonement.

It wasn't something as simple as her saying 'I'm sorry.' Nor was it a matter of time healing all wounds.

It was an attitude shift for her.

That was the only apology I'd accept.

No more acting like she was an island. No more making decisions on her own without conferring with me.

We were a team.

Nothing less would do.

"I needed to draw Dagda out. Only prime bait would work. I knew you'd make me choose a different path and I..." She scrunched up her eyes. "God, I wanted him gone, Conor. I had blinders on.

"My to-kill list is a mile long, and no matter what happened to me, once I knew he was behind her death, he was always at the top of my most-wanted list.

"After you killed Michael, I realized what part the First Lady played in everything and I knew I had an in. Your father was collateral damage, I guess.

"I didn't like him, didn't like what he did to you, didn't even approve of how he treated your brothers, so I guess I just reasoned it in my head that none of you would care that much." She swallowed. "Then I saw you in the graveyard."

I tensed. "You were still watching?"

"Cin tried to get me to leave, but... I just couldn't." She closed her eyes. "I didn't know if I'd ever see you again and I couldn't go, not when..."

I thought back to that day and the memory alone was enough to make me lock down.

I'd been the one to alert my brothers to a meeting between the First Lady and our da in Green-Wood Cemetery. I'd been in Jersey, West

Orange to be precise, trying to find more intel on Star's disappearance, but even though I'd raced to Brooklyn, I'd been too late.

He'd died with my brothers around him, but *I* had been too fucking late.

"I'll never understand why you do the things you do," I rasped. "But I got an insight into it today because of Troy."

After what her soldier buddy had shared, I believed I knew her better. Understood her more than ever before.

Her jaw worked. "If you rely on yourself, the only person who can let you down is you, and the only person to blame is you. I prefer..." She paused. "*Preferred* that."

"Nice catch," I praised, which made her shoot me an apologetic smile.

"Old habits die hard but you're right, Conor. There's no point in doing this if I act as if I'm on my own still." She sucked in a breath. "Do you want to know something terrible?"

"Hit me with it." Then I braced myself for what she considered terrible...

"When I saw how I'd hurt you, that was when I knew how much I loved you because I hurt *with* you. I was the reason for the pain, and..." Misery flashed over her expression. "It was another reason to cut myself out of your life.

"I'm cancer, Conor. I wanted to save you from that. Spare you from me. Maybe Kat too. By that point, I didn't even know if I'd make it back alive, and a part of me hoped that for your sakes, I didn't."

"Do you want to know why I don't hate you?"

Her brow furrowed but her answer was simple. "Yes."

"Because I couldn't hate you any more than you hate yourself."

A sharp breath escaped her, one that was so raw, so deep, so filled with agony that I knew it came from her soul—not her lungs. Her very soul.

Tears flooded her eyes and as she closed them, shielding those beautiful crystalline orbs from me, they dripped tracks down her cheeks.

"My relationship with my father was unusual. My grief for him was too. Does it hurt that you were behind his death? Yes. But it took me a while to realize that he's been trying to die for a while." My gaze was unfocused as my thumb slipped along the tear track on her silken skin. "When they set fire to the cathedral two Christmases ago, he and Ma tried to kill themselves."

"What?!"

"They'd just found out what happened to me. I didn't uncover this until later when I overheard a conversation between Aidan and Da." My thumb continued its soft movements along the arc of her cheek. "They'd tortured the archbishop and his ultimate punishment was being burned to death in his own parish." My mouth twisted. "They were going to end it too, though."

"Hardened Catholics willing to kill themselves?"

"Easier to end it than deal with me, I guess."

She shoved my shoulder. "Don't you dare say that."

"What am I supposed to think? Aidan and Finn had to drag them out of the cathedral, Star. Physically lift them out. Aidan's knee was fucked back then too. I'm not sure how all their asses weren't cremated." I shook my head. "I should have known that I..."

"That you, what?" she whispered.

"It wouldn't just be guilt over what happened to me that'd be the reason he wanted to end things. It made sense once I found out he had ALS." I tucked my chin into my chest. "It's not that I wanted him to feel so devastated over what happened to me that he'd kill himself, but I just... I knew it'd be about him. It always was.

"He wasn't a normal father, and we weren't normal sons. At the graveyard, the son in me mourned the loss of his father, but then I remembered what he was."

"Your general," she whispered.

That hurt to hear. It hurt, even more, to admit, "Yes. We were just soldiers to him."

"Do you feel the same way about your ma?"

"No. She loves us. She's weak, but aren't all humans?"

"True."

"I had proof of that love when I saw what happened after Aoife cut her off. It hurts her. Physically hurts her."

"Maybe that's a wound time will heal?"

"I doubt it. Aoife's angry. Rightfully so. Why do you think my brothers have rallied around her? Because of their wives?" I scoffed. "They're whipped, but not that whipped.

"They know what Ma did was wrong, they know that they'd do exactly the same as Da did for their women, so they made adjustments…"

She reached up and slipped her hand around my nape. Using that as a support, she pulled me down until our foreheads could touch again. "Why did you lie to Troy about that tonight?"

"No one else outside of the inner circle knows the truth."

"I'm in the inner circle?"

"You sound surprised."

"I am. I'm…"

"*Cancer*. I remember. Luckily for you, we have great treatments out there nowadays." I hummed. "Of course, you're inner circle. You wear my ring, don't you?"

"I do."

I wanted to hear her say those words in front of a priest.

Until then...

"Don't cut me out, Star. Don't make plans on your own. Don't act like you're a team of one. I'm with you on this. One hundred percent.

"Whether it's regarding the Sparrows or things that come up in the course of a long life together—"

"Teamwork makes the dream work?"

My lips twitched. "Exactly."

She angled her head and this time, I let our mouths collide. When she slipped her tongue around the soft lines of mine, I permitted her entry and didn't even tense when her fingers slipped through my hair.

They were her fingers.

This was my Star.

I'd been waiting for her for fucking years—now that I had her, not even *she* would keep us apart.

I didn't fuck around, didn't want this to be slow. I wanted us to reconnect and that wasn't gentle—it was power. *We* were power. Together, we could make the world burn or we could douse the flames.

I shoved at the waistband of her borrowed sweats, sliding my hand beneath the elastic so that I could delve between her legs.

She sighed into my mouth as I found her slit and started to trace my fingertips over her clit. She was warm but dry, so I was careful as I stroked the nub, my mouth doing most of the legwork to get her hot.

Her moan as I took over the kiss was *everything*. Each of my nerve endings felt the aftermath of it as I thrust into her mouth, taking her there like I'd take her later.

As her nails dug into my scalp, the tips, short but not blunt, shaped into a slight tip, were a reminder of who exactly was touching me.

Star.

Mine.

They dragged over the sensitive flesh, making goose bumps run down my spine.

As I dove into her, giving her my all, knowing she shared that with me in return, I groaned when she hooked one of her legs on my hips.

With my other hand, I angled it around my waist so that I had better access to her.

She released a soft sob as I dipped deeper, finding her core. Not dry, but not wet. For Star, that was drenched.

Sliding a finger into her, I waited for her reaction. Her breath stalled and she stilled, but when I thrust it into her carefully, a shudder came from her.

The butt of my hand rubbed against her clit now, and as she squirmed, hips rocking in a circle for maximum sensation, I smiled into the kiss.

"You take your pleasure, Star. You own it. No one else."

A hiss escaped her and she reared up to nip my bottom lip. "We own each other," she rumbled.

I froze.

"Teamwork makes the dream work," she repeated with a gasp.

She had no idea what that meant to me at a moment like this, and I didn't make a thing out of it, just grinned as I tore into her mouth with my lips, teeth, and tongue, knowing she was as into this as I was when her pussy clamped down around me.

Star ripped her mouth away from mine as she let loose a growl, head arching back against the wall as I moved faster now that I knew she was into this.

With her getting wetter, I pressed a kiss to her throat, tracing the sinews before I nipped her and started suckling the sensitive skin.

When she tugged on my hair, my focus wavered a touch, but I brought it back under control, refusing to let that fucking bastard and what he'd done to me spoil this moment.

I slipped another finger inside her, scissoring them as I nipped at her throat some more, unwilling to stop until she bore my mark.

I wanted to hear her whine at me about having to cover it with foundation—just the thought of that conversation made me double down until she was clutching at my fingers, harder than ever.

"Conor, please, I want you. Your cock. *Now.*"

Her request had me rasping, "How could I refuse?"

She released a breathy chuckle. "Then don't."

"You want it, you take it," I informed her, pleased when, barely a second later, her hands scrabbled at the waistband of my sweats.

When her fingers slid around my cock, I growled under my breath as she stroked me once, twice. I bit her throat, rougher than I would have if I were in my right mind, but she didn't freeze up on me, just tightened her hand around my shaft in retaliation.

I slipped my fingers out of her pussy then used my now spare hand to shove the leg she had wrapped around me to the ground. Then, I pulled the sweats further down her thighs, dropping to my knees to drag them to her ankles. Unhooking one around her shoe, I freed her from their constraints then jerked upright and hauled her into me.

She hooked both around my hips this time, then hissed when my dick rubbed up against her slit. I let the tip collide with her clit, rocking slightly so she could feel the pressure, but she took control of things by pressing the glans to her gate and allowing me inside her.

I didn't thrust into her, just let her adapt to the new fullness. Inch by inch, slowly, she opened up to me and rewarded me for my patience. Gravity and her relaxing allowed her to sink onto me. Her nails dug into my shoulders this time as she released a soft wail that had me clenching my eyes closed.

For a moment, I just pressed my forehead to the wall beside her as she took all of me.

I breathed in her ear, "This will never not be my home, Star."

When she sobbed, I nipped at her earlobe and slowly made my retreat.

After a couple thrusts, she adapted to the position, and that was when I slipped a hand between us so I could rub her clit.

"I can feel how fucking hot you are around me, Star. It's heaven. Fucking heaven."

"You fill me so good," she whimpered. "Should be too much, but it's not. It's just... perfect."

I didn't associate Star with softness, but this was a newer side of her, one that I couldn't wait to uncover fully.

"That's us together—perfect," I confirmed.

She bucked against the wall then demanded, "Faster, Conor. Faster."

I complied, groaning as she tightened around me, her pussy muscles urging me to come, but I fought back by frigging her clit faster too.

"I-I—" Then, she screamed. Only, it wasn't pleasure-filled. "Why is this so fucking impossible?"

I nipped at her earlobe again. "Because you're thinking too much. Stop it. Just relax. Naughty girl."

She shivered.

I sucked on the tender flesh. "Such a naughty girl. So impatient. Pleasure requires patience."

"You feel so good, Conor," she whispered thickly. "It hurts how good it feels."

"Then just roll with it," I murmured, slowing my thrusts so she could feel every inch. "This isn't a race."

A soft breath soughed from her. "You're right."

I pulled back to grin at her. "Why does that come as a surprise?" When she barked out a laugh, my grin widened. "This isn't a fight, Star."

"It used to be easier."

"That means every time you come, I earned it," I replied, my lips rubbing against hers. "Let me earn your pleasure, Star."

Her face crumpled. "How do you..." I saw her tears. Felt each of them in my heart. Her mouth found mine and she whispered, "I love you, Conor O'Donnelly."

"And I love you, Star Sullivan."

Slowly, I started back up again.

It was only then I realized how tension had been thrumming through her.

She was more relaxed than before so each time I filled her, I felt the soft tremors inside and they packed a hell of a punch.

Stroking her clit, I whispered, "You're so fucking beautiful, Star. Such a naughty girl, trying to run before you can walk, but so good too. So fucking good. I want you to come around my cock. Can you do that for me?"

Her head lolled against the wall. "I-I think so." She started to thrust into me, snapping her hips back so that we were in sync. She whimpered, "God, you feel so... so..." This time, when she cried out, it came from a deeper place than before. "Oh, God. Fuck. Conor, there. *There.*" She shuddered. "Faster. Please. H-Harder."

I gave her exactly what she asked for and she rewarded me. When she screamed, it wasn't about frustration or anger—it was about release.

As those delicate inner muscles began pummeling my cock, I stopped holding back and came too.

As she took all I had to give, she clung to me, holding on tight, so tight that I knew she never wanted to let go.

And I was *more* than okay with that.

18

______

TEXT CHAT

ACUIG

LODESTAR: *Got news. You won't believe me if I tell you, but you need to know I wouldn't mess around with this.*

Maverick: *Stop burying the lede.*

Alessa: *Is Kati in danger?*

Lodestar: *Not anymore.*

Maverick: *Mission accomplished?*

Alessa: *Thank God.*

Lodestar: *Did you notice her nightmares, Alessa?*

Maverick: *No missing them.*

Alessa: *Yes. Every night, sometimes two, three times.*

Maverick: *My poor Old Lady. It's a wonder she hasn't gone insane. What with me and Kati. I'm sorry, Alessa. I wish things were easier for you.*

Alessa: *Maverick, things are what they are and I'm blessed to have you both in my life.*

Lodestar: *Less of the pity party, Maverick. She loves you. You're lucky. Just treat her like the queen she is (or else).*

Maverick: *I feel the threat over in Jersey.*

Lodestar: *So you should.*

Maverick: *And I will. Hopefully, I already do?*

Alessa: *He does. He's helping me go to school, Star.*

Lodestar: *Which school?*

Maverick: *Like, getting her GED, you know? So she can go to college.*

Alessa: *I want to be a nurse.*

Lodestar: *You do?*

Maverick: *Yeah, I told her she kinda is already. :/*

Alessa: *Shut up. I know it's been a bad couple of days, Maverick, but we're in this together. Forever.*

Maverick: *Forever, baby girl.*

Alessa: *:**

Lodestar: *So, to cut up the mushy stuff, and it's not because I'm allergic to mush or anything, but Katina's family isn't exactly 'ideal.'*

Maverick: *In what way?*

Alessa: *On her father's side? My mother was a farmer's daughter.*

Maverick: *She is related to you, isn't she?*

Lodestar: *Fuck off.*

Maverick: *:P*

Alessa: *This isn't the time for joking, Maverick.*

Lodestar: *She's not my cousin. But we found out who her father is. His name was Bogdan Belyaev. Have you heard of him, Alessa?*

Alessa: *Belyaev was her father? That's impossible.*

Lodestar: *It isn't, sweetheart.*

Alessa: *He can't be.*

Lodestar: *He is.*

Alessa: *I don't understand.*

Maverick: *Who the hell is Bogdan Belyaev?*

Alessa: *He's the man who you go to in Ukraine to get help to come to the US.*

Maverick: *You went to him?*

Alessa: *Not him personally. He has a, I suppose you'd call it a network? They have small offices in big cities, even. It's all legitimate. Until you get involved and realize what it is.*

Lodestar: *He's her father, Alessa.*

Alessa: *They say he's a Romanov.*

Maverick: *Highly unlikely. No matter what Disney says on the matter. O.o*

Lodestar: *Conor's sure he's a front. So, hell, maybe he IS a Romanov.*

Lodestar: *And if you're not holding her hand, Maverick, I'll shoot you myself.*

Maverick: *She's sitting on my knee.*

Alessa: *I'm okay, Star. Really. I have to be.*

Alessa: *My sister's father is the man who sold me into slavery.*

Alessa: *It's not Kati's fault. It doesn't change how much I love her.*

Lodestar: *I know. I wish I had better news.*

Alessa: *What is a front? Like a door?*

Lodestar: *No, it's a name someone uses to hide their real identity.*

Alessa: *Like Maverick?*

Lodestar: *Sort of.*

Alessa: *You think he operated under Belyaev but his name was different?*

Lodestar: *No, Conor does.*

Lodestar: *I don't care lol. We have bigger fish to fry right now.*

Maverick: *Who killed him?*

Lodestar: *Remember I told you about Jorgmundgander?*

Maverick: *I do. They handled him?*

Lodestar: *Yeah. It was a power grab by the highest of the high in the Sparrows.*

Maverick: *You sure you dealt with them? You don't need help?*

Lodestar: *Lol. I didn't need help. I was working with Troy and Dead To Me.*

Maverick: *TROY? She's still alive? Fuck me. I didn't think she'd make it when she was so fucking paranoid.*

Lodestar: *Still alive and kicking. Rocking an eye patch.*

Maverick: *Bet it suits her.*

Lodestar: *It does actually lol. She's as terrifying as ever.*

Maverick: *I'll bet. How's Cin?*

Lodestar: *Horny.*

Maverick: ***Snorts.***

Lodestar: *You doing okay, Alessa?*

Alessa: *I'm fine, Star. I'm home. Some things have to happen for us to find our way. I know I'm where I'm supposed to be.*

Lodestar: *You're a lot more accepting than I am.*

Maverick: *She is.*

Alessa: *I learned that wishing for things that are outside of my control is futile. But I know that you are different, Star.*

Alessa: *I know that very little is outside of your control and I think that makes it easier on me.*

Lodestar: *Because you know I'm handling it?*

Alessa: *Tak.*

Lodestar: *You got that right, sweetheart. I'm handling it. Hell, the leaders are handled. As for the rest, they're going to get theirs from Interpol itself. We found how they communicate and now that we're in, there's no escaping us.*

Maverick: **whistles* Interpol? You brought in the big dogs?*

Lodestar: *My grandfather, Anton Kuznetsov, did.*

Alessa: *Your grandfather is a Kuznetsov?!*

Lodestar: *You've heard of him?*

Alessa: *In our part of the world, we have sayings about the Kuznetsovs.*

Maverick: *What kind of sayings?*

Alessa: *It says a lot about why you are who you are now that I think about it.*

Maverick: *Hit us with the sayings, Alessa! I'm curious.*

Alessa: *The translations aren't easy.*

Alessa: *In Ukraine, they say that the Kuznetsovs are spiders. They have webs in every corner of your house.*

Maverick: *Lol, definitely fitting for you, Star. You little spider, you.*

Lodestar: *Charming.*

Maverick: *;)*

Alessa: *In Russia, it is more sinister. Less about spiders and more about saying their name out loud and it coming at a risk.*

Maverick: *Sort of like Candyman, Bloody Mary, or Beetlejuice, I guess.*

Lodestar: *I can believe that. I'd never heard of them though. I spoke with Russians about them too.*

Alessa: *They would not say anything. It is too ingrained in them to stay quiet.*

Lodestar: *Huh. I was working with Maxim Lyanov while I was over there. He never said dick about the name BUT afterward, when I got into shit, he tried to get me out of Anton's clutches. I guess I owe him more than I already thought I did lol.*

Alessa: *He tried to take you? Physically? Or did I misunderstand?*

Lodestar: *It was a misunderstanding all round so I'm not surprised that it makes no sense. Anton, kind of, imprisoned me.*

Maverick: *What?!*

Lodestar: *I was trying to kill him at the time.*

Maverick: *Ah. Burying the lede again. The only way to stop you is to lock you up. And I say that knowing your past. :/*

Lodestar: *Mhm.*

Maverick: *So, Maxim tried to help rescue you from Kuznetsov's clutches?*

Lodestar: *Yeah.*

Maverick: *Alessa just gasped like she'd seen the boogeyman lol. So I'm going to assume that was a baller move from Lyanov.*

Alessa: *It was!*

Maverick: *Wait, is that why the Bratva in New York is now called 'The Forgotten Boys?'*

Lodestar: *Yeah. Conor said Moscow cut ties with Lyanov, but the men on the street over here backed him so they created this new faction.*

Maverick: *Interesting.*

Alessa: *He must be a good man, or a crazy one, to take on Kuznetsov.*

Maverick: *Or both.*

Lodestar: *Both, I'm thinking.*

Maverick: *So, Alessa and Kati are safe?*

Lodestar: *They are.*

Alessa: *Thank you, Star. For everything.*

Maverick: *Yeah, thank you. I'm fucking sorry about letting you down with Kati, Star. Especially when I knew what you were doing.*

Lodestar: *I'd say don't worry about it, but if it happens again, you know you need to.*

Maverick: *It won't happen again. That's a fucking promise.*

Alessa: *Star, you will have to come to a house party we're having soon. Bring Conor?*

Lodestar: *You sure?*

Maverick: *I need to apologize to him anyway.*

Alessa: *Yes, you do.*

Lodestar: *When is it?*

Maverick: *We got a few coming up.*

Lodestar: *I'm heading to the UK for a funeral but once I'm back, I'll come. Thanks for thinking of me.*

Alessa: *You are a Sinner lol. I didn't think of you. I just know you're busy.*

Lodestar: *I'm not a Sinner.*

Maverick: *You are. Maybe our first girl too.*

Alessa: *Don't tell Giulia that.*

Lodestar: *LOL. Or if you do, tell her when I'm there?*

Maverick: *Hahaha.*

Maverick: *Who died?*

Lodestar: *You don't know her. Just her handle. Ovianar.*

Maverick: *Shame. She was a hot-shit cracker.*

Alessa: *Like a Saltine?*

Lodestar: *No. Crackers crack code lol.*

Alessa: *Oh! Oops.*

Lodestar: *Let me know when the dates of the house parties are and we'll head over.*

Maverick: *Take care at the funeral.*

Alessa: *Much love to you for your loss. <3*

Lodestar: *Thanks, guys.*

TEXT CHAT

DEAD TO ME: *Foundry hasn't got a nose anymore. Want a pic?*

aCooooig: *No.*

Troy: *I do. Send it to me privately.*

Lodestar: *What else hasn't he got?*

Dead To Me: *No ears either. There's a lot of gore, Star. It's going to attract a cougar or a bobcat soon. It's a miracle we haven't already.*

aCooooig: *Bet it stinks.*

Troy: *It's a good stink when it's an enemy.*

Lodestar: *Hate to agree, but it is lol.*

aCooooig: *You're gross.*

Troy: *We just have high nausea tolerances lmao.*

Dead To Me: *>.<*

aCooooig: *Great.*

Troy: *You safe if the wildlife is starting to encroach? They're in hibernation though. Surely?*

Dead To Me: *That's how bad the stink is lol. It'll wake everything up in the vicinity soon.*

aCooooig: *Christ, are you safe?*

Troy: *Don't insult her.*

Lodestar: *Of course she's safe. It's Dead To Me!*

Dead To Me: *I'd take a bow, but the only person who can see me is Foundry. Smythe's eyes got eaten yesterday.*

aCooooig: *Oh Christ. I'm about to eat. I don't need that imagery even if they fucking deserve it.*

Troy: *Don't be a wimp.*

aCooooig: *I think I'll accept that title for this conversation.*

****aCooooig changes name to Wimp****

****Lodestar changes Wimp's name to aCooooig****

Lodestar: *You're not a wimp. It's not a bad thing to be intolerant to people's faces being eaten by wild animals lol.*

Lodestar: *D, they're dead, right?*

Dead To Me: *Foundry's got a couple hours left in him. Max. Not surprised this happened so fast tbh. They were literally open wounds. But the temperatures are frigid so I think they're gonna freeze before the local animals get to enjoy a good meal.*

Dead To Me: *It's a shame we couldn't invite a scientist to this party to monitor what killed them first. There's probably some kind of life lesson here.*

aCooooig: *Don't piss off spies?*

Lodestar: *Hahahaha.*

Lodestar: *Right, we're heading for Sunday dinner. So fuck off.*

Dead To Me: *I expect details.*

Lodestar: *You'll get 'em.*

Lodestar: *Stand by for evacuation, D.*

Dead To Me: *Copy that.*

Troy: *Later, fuckers.*

Star Sullivan

AFTER JUMPING out of the Mini Cooper, I stretched with no small amount of relief even as I stared at the O'Donnelly 'homestead.'

Sunday dinner—a sacrosanct affair amid the O'Donnellys.

So sacrosanct, in fact, that Aoife's first declaration of rebellion against the patriarchs of the family was to skip this meal permanently.

Funny how a family's traditions could be so different.

The Sullivans didn't have a similar tradition. Was that a weakness I'd never spotted before? Were a family's traditions what set them apart and what bound them together?

"Why so pensive?"

I blinked at Conor over the roof of his Mini Cooper. "No reason."

He snorted. "Yeah, keep telling yourself that."

Shoving my hands in my pockets, I studied him with a measured glance. "No one calls me out like you. Do you know that?"

"Nope, but I figure it's one of the reasons you keep me around."

Smiling at that, I mused, "One of many."

"Good to know." He rounded the car even though he was nearer to the door than I was and slipped his hand inside my pocket so he could knot our fingers together. Which, of course, was when I felt the prickle of plastic—more candy. Could he rock any harder?

Pulling out the Payday he'd burrowed in there, I groaned. "I love these."

His smile was smug. "I know."

"You nervous?" he asked as I did a quick shuffle, passed the candy bar to my other hand, grabbed his again, then tore into the packet with my teeth before I started chowing down.

"Not really. Just thinking how we never did anything like this."

"When you were kids?"

"At no point. Savannah doesn't do this with her folks."

"Probably because they're not always in the same state."

"Even if they were, I don't think they'd do it."

"Don't blame them. Having to drive upstate every fucking weekend is a pain in the ass."

"Not for long. She'll be moving to the city as soon as you set her up somewhere, won't she?"

"We'll see. There's time for her to change her mind."

"Is she changeable?"

"Not particularly. But who knows right now? After... everything, she's acting oddly."

I thought about how many *everythings* the O'Donnellys had gone through lately. "All the 'Our Ladies?'"

He grunted then scanned the cars in the yard. It was like an ad for SUVs/tanks, apart from an Aston Martin which stuck out like a sore thumb. "All my brothers are here."

"And their wives."

"You met them already."

"Barely," I grumbled. "A 'hello' and 'bye' doesn't count for much of a meeting."

"The worst of the bunch is Savannah and you got her back on your side, didn't you?"

"Sort of. As much as you can get Savannah Daniels on your side."

"Savannah O'Donnelly," he corrected. "Don't let Aidan hear you use her maiden name."

"Pissing on her would be quicker."

"Not as clean though. Plus, Ma made it a rule a long time ago—no whipping out our dicks in public."

I let loose a laugh. "Thank fuck for that."

Amusement gleamed in his eyes as he tugged my hand from my pocket so our knotted fingers could swing between us. "Seriously, though, you doing okay?"

"I'll be better when we're in London and the funeral is almost over."

He grimaced his understanding. "Makes sense. Until then, whatever Aoife can say about Ma, she can't argue that her roasted chicken isn't the best in the tristate area."

Though I snickered, as we stepped toward the house, him flicking the alarm on his ride over his shoulder, I drawled, "Aoife said very little about your mother."

"That's because she's too kind for her own good."

"Probably for the best in a family like yours."

"*Ours*," he corrected, which made me bite my lip.

"Ours," I repeated though I cleared my throat before *and* after I said it. "Next time, I'll bring Kat, yeah?"

He nodded. "Of course."

"I'd have brought her with us today if it weren't for the fact it'd disrupt her schedule, seeing as we're leaving for the UK tomorrow."

"You don't have to explain—"

I sucked in a breath. "Sure I do. We're a team. We make decisions together."

His smile made the concession worth it. "Then I agree that you made the right decision. Though I think she'll enjoy our meals."

"Why? Because Seamus is here?"

It was his turn to snicker. "Yes."

The door opened to reveal an ever-dramatic Savannah standing in the doorway.

I watched as my sister/friend strode toward me in too-high heels. "She should have been on the stage."

"She does channel *Glee* energy, doesn't she?" he teased.

"Is there a reason you haven't answered my texts yet?" Vana shrieked.

My brow furrowed. "You haven't texted."

"My *old* texts."

I rolled my eyes. "Who the fuck has the time to answer old messages, Savannah O'Donnelly?"

"*You* do. If you want me to send you any in the future."

"Are you being serious?"

"Uh, *yes*. I want a reply to each one."

"Can they be emojis?"

"Sure but hurry it the hell up. I have a backlog of TikToks to send you."

I gaped at her. "Then I won't hurry up. You think I have time for TikTok?"

"You need to make time. I swear I posted a video on there yesterday and it went *viral*, Star. That shit about Congressman Tully's foot fetish has been liked by nearly eighteen *million* people. The conversation is happening and we're not even steering the press."

"I'm sure Tully's grateful about that."

"His wife has feet too. He could worship them instead of a hooker's in Nevada."

"Your logic, Vana," I grumbled.

"What's illogical about that? You can't be elected into office with kinks. They're just weaknesses waiting for some reporter to hold against you."

"Some reporter, in this instance, being you?"

She smirked, her bright red-lips a slash on her pretty face. "Yes. I swear, I shit news at this point and people love it."

"Lovely image, Savvie," Conor mocked, earning her attention.

Her smirk faded and she scowled at him before she prodded him in the shoulder. "Don't think I'm not mad at you too."

"What have I done now?"

"I called you. Twice. What is it with the people in this family ignoring me?"

"You know that's a lie, Savannah. I never ignore you."

Aidan's cool drawl had me chuckling when it made her cheeks bloom with heat. She stopped pouting when her husband's hand settled on her waist and he drew her against his chest.

I studied the move with interest, having never seen her intimate interactions with her spouse before.

Figured that it took an O'Donnelly to tame this particular shrew.

"Why are you giving Conor and Star shit, little one?"

The blush deepened, but I thought that was a combination of the words 'little one' and the way she darted a look at me, as if she were nervous that I'd tease her for letting him call her that.

But who the fuck was I to judge?

Conor called me 'naughty girl' and I creamed harder than I did when I fingered myself.

"Star didn't answer my messages and Conor ignored my call."

"I'm sure there's a reason for that, Kid?"

There was a warning in Aidan's tone that had me hiding a smile. Anyone who could see beneath Vana's cocky facade and knew to protect her sensitive side was someone I could grow to like.

"It's not as if I've been killing time watching Knicks' games," he retorted with a huff. "Anyway, if you wanted to talk to me, you could have come up."

"And invade your privacy? You're in the honeymoon phase," Savannah grouched.

"By the way, the purchase went through, Conor. I'll need you to extend the security settings to the whole floor."

Conor arched a brow. "Is this a memo I missed?"

"No. You know I don't like sharing, so I gave the other apartment owners an offer they couldn't refuse."

"Very Don Corleone," I mocked.

"There were two other apartments on the floor below me, Aidan."

He shrugged. "So?"

Conor huffed. "I don't have time right now."

"We can work on it together," I said calmly. "But it's not a priority, is it? You'll be modifying the other apartments first?"

Aidan folded his arms across his chest. "Security modifications need to be taken into account before the reno starts."

"Then it'll just have to wait," I countered sweetly. "We have other things on our plate, and Conor isn't your indentured servant."

Aidan frowned at that. "I never said he was."

"No? You just drop the fact that he needs to amend your security on him when he comes by for Sunday dinner?"

Flicking a glance at his younger brother, Aidan's tone was wary. "Kid—"

"I'll see to it," Conor said with a huff.

"On *our* time," I argued, squeezing his fingers with mine.

"No, I'll—"

"You won't figure something out, Conor. Your brothers need to accept that you have a goddamn life and you need boundaries as much as they do."

He smirked down at me. "You're cute when you're pissed."

"I'll be even more pissed," I warned, "if you take on extra work when you're already pushing your limits."

Savannah waded in, "I'm not sure there's anyone worse to talk about boundaries than you."

"I'm turning over a new leaf." And I'd turn it over a few million times if it meant sparing Conor from his family.

"Since when?" Vana queried, but she was studying me with as much interest as I'd had in her when taking note of her reactions to Aidan's touch and his gentle terms of endearment.

"Since right now. It's not like we're sitting at home twirling our fucking thumbs, Vana."

She shrugged. "It can wait, can't it, Aidan?"

The eldest O'Donnelly son wasn't scowling, not entirely, but he was bemused by this conversation. "I guess it can."

With a satisfied nod, I drawled, "Good."

Conor preened as he tugged an arm around my shoulder. "Is it the wrong time to tell you it's hot as fuck when you stand up for me?"

"Yes, seeing as I have a future mother-in-law to meet."

Savannah grinned. "To be honest, I've been looking forward to this all week."

"Only you," I grumbled.

When she grabbed my hand and started tugging on it, I let go of Conor's only after we shared a glance. There was definitely heat there—he hadn't been bullshitting about liking it when I stood up for him.

As we departed, Aidan informed him, "Paddy wants to talk to us later."

His gaze still on me as I continued staring at him over my shoulder, relying on Vana to guide me into the house, he asked, "About?"

"Liam."

"Liam's their cousin."

My head whipped around so I was facing forward this time. "I know who Liam is, Vana."

"Did you know he plays for the Mounties, smart ass?"

"Of course. What's that about?" I asked, motioning behind me.

"What's what about? Conor's brothers treating him like he's Ask Jeeves or why Paddy's dancing around like a leprechaun with itching powder down his pants?"

I snorted. "Both?"

"Old habits are hard to break," was all she said. "His da treated him that way so they did too. Guess that's changing now that you're insisting on boundaries?"

"You have a problem with that?" I growled.

"No," she said slowly. "I'll be glad for Conor if anything. They put too much on him and I know he's been tired lately."

"How do you know that?"

"I have eyes. Plus, he just seems weary. That could be your fault—"

"Charming."

"—because he looks the brightest I've seen him since I met him, but it's more than likely to do with his workload.

"Which is where the kettle and the pot clash because your workload can't be classified as light."

I hitched a shoulder. "Maybe not, but we start as we mean to go on."

She hummed. "I suppose."

"You suppose, what?"

"Just wondering what brought this on."

"Conor and I are a team," was my staunch retort. "You watch out for your teammate. You have their six when they don't protect themselves. You don't let others take advantage of them."

"I know how teams work, Star," she drawled.

"Do you?" I mocked. "I'd never have guessed seeing as you're as much of a lone wolf as I am."

"We're a team in our own way," she disregarded. "You just prefer to think of yourself as a solitary alpha female when you know full well you can call on me any time, any place."

Unease settled inside me because this was too much like my recent conversations with Conor.

I didn't answer, just squeezed her arm with my own. She wasn't to know that I was trying to change that part of my nature and that that change came with making sure Conor's generosity wasn't used or abused.

"Are you nervous?" she queried, surprising me by allowing the previous subject to drop.

"Why would I be?"

"You're about to meet the matriarch."

"Thought I already met her." Her bewildered frown prompted me to add, "Aoife."

Her lips twitched. "Not me?"

I snorted. "No. You're not matriarch material."

"You're so great for my ego."

"I try. But don't make it out like you're miffed when we both know you're not."

She shrugged. "You could at least pretend to make me feel better about myself."

"That's Aidan's job. Not mine."

"Why did I miss you again?"

"Because no one tells you the truth like me," I teased, laughing at her huff. "But no, I'm not nervous about meeting Lena. I'm surprised you were."

"You know how I am about the mafia."

"Actually, I'd forgotten," I admitted.

"That's probably because you were in boarding school when that shit show went down."

My nose crinkled. "One of my many interventions. I should have been there for you back then."

"It's fine."

"It's the opposite of fine when you have a crush on the mafia—"

"Oh, shut up." She shoved me in the side. "Lena's okay."

"Whether she is or isn't is no concern of mine."

"They all rally around her."

"I figured that out on my own," I retorted. "Is this a warning? Don't get on her bad side or Conor will dump me? Because, Vana, I can tell you now—I've done worse shit to that man than piss his ma off and he hasn't thrown me to the curb. I think I'm set for life with him."

"You want to be set for life with him?" she inquired softly.

"That's what you picked up on?" I groused. "And yes. I do. Like I told Aidan—I'm keeping him."

"He isn't a puppy you were gifted for Christmas."

"Thank fuck he isn't. Do you remember what happened to that dog Dad got me?"

"Didn't he end up giving him to one of the roadies?"

"Yeah, because I kept forgetting to walk it and Dad got sick of standing in dog shit on the tour bus." I chuckled at the memory. "You don't need to walk cats, do you?"

"No. You can, but you don't have to."

"Did you walk Teabag?"

"Surprised you remember Teabag."

"You loved her," was all I said. "And only you'd name a cat after a sex act."

She sighed. "I did. And it wasn't after the sex act, you heathen. It was after a tea. Bag. You know. A bag. Filled with tea?"

"That's more boring than my version."

"I have a new cat now."

"You do? Let me guess, it's from the same source as my new kittens?"

"You have kittens?"

"I don't. Katina does. She's got Conor wrapped around her pinkie already."

"Yeah, he doesn't look like he'd be a sucker for kids but he is. So, Amara, right?"

I grimaced at the mention of the Sinners' Old Lady. "Yes, *her*."

"Mine's a teenager, but I still have some of the kitten stuff if you want me to bring it up?"

"You could do that. Or if you could order whatever shit I'll need when you have the chance and have it sent to us, I'll love you forever."

"Sure thing," she said easily as she guided me into a room that was loaded with photo frames.

I tugged her to a halt as I stared at the pictures, smiling at the sight of Conor wherever I could see him.

There was his graduation ceremony, another of him at the beach with Eoghan and Declan and he had the cutest chubby cheeks.

In another, Aidan had him in a noogie but they both posed for the camera with big grins while maintaining the hold on each other—that one made me laugh.

Another was of him and Brennan eating donuts in a park. I could see that he was plumper than the others until he hit his teen years, and then he shot up like a beanstalk.

There were hundreds of family shots—the six boys together, a motley crew who'd been forced to wear suits when they were kids, not yet men.

When I'd picked out every photo of Conor, I found one of Lena and Aidan Sr. standing together on their wedding day.

She looked hella young and he was hella proud.

"I didn't realize I was into silver foxes until I realized Aidan would be the spitting image of his da when he gets older."

Savannah's wry comment had me shaking my head at her. "Sex on the brain, Vana."

"With men like ours, where else could it be?"

Though I smirked, I let her tug me into a kitchen where the woman herself was standing.

She hadn't changed much from her wedding day in all honesty. Sure, she was a touch rounder and her face was crinkled in the usual spots from age, but she was as straight-up as back then, as… commanding.

Yes, even back then, undoubtedly coerced into a marriage with Aidan O'Donnelly, she'd had a presence.

At the moment, that presence was focused on the chicken she was basting.

As Conor's sisters-in-law ceased their chatter when they saw there was fresh meat in the room, she peered away from the bird and stared at me.

"Star Sullivan?"

"Magdalena O'Donnelly?"

Her eyes narrowed as she slipped the oven mitts on then opened the door to shove one of three chickens I realized she was roasting into the heat.

When that was done, she asked, "Would you like something to drink?"

"Water will be fine, thank you."

"It's good to see you again, Star," Camille greeted. "We didn't get the chance to talk last week."

That was being polite. 'Hello' and 'goodbye' weren't my idea of sterling conversation.

Inessa straightened up from her seat and moved toward me. She placed her hands on my shoulders and air-kissed my cheeks. Because I wasn't expecting it, I allowed her to follow through with it.

As for Aela, she just dipped her chin at me while she nursed baby Cameron.

"You know Savannah, Conor tells me," Lena stated as she passed me a glass of water.

"Practically in the biblical sense."

Savannah, who'd been on the brink of drinking some coffee, sprayed out what she'd swallowed.

Inessa, Camille, and Aela gaped at me while I just smiled as I sipped my own drink.

"Shut up," Vana rasped.

"I saw plenty on those tour buses." I whistled under my breath. "Wild times."

"What kind of wild times?"

"Shut up," Vana hissed at me this time when she saw I was going to answer Aidan's question.

Her hand clapped over my mouth as I studied the brothers who either made a habit of joining their spouses in the kitchen or who were coming to watch me and Lena meet.

"It's a rumor, but they say *noxxed up* was inspired by the parties on the tour buses during the late nineties," Conor drawled.

"Is that an album?" Inessa asked him, and he immediately groaned.

"I need to do something about your music education, Inessa, but yes. It's one of their most renowned albums."

"Triple platinum before the year was out," I agreed. "Only God knows what it is now, and it *is* a rumor, but it's definitely true."

Brennan cleared his throat. "I'm not as big a fan as Conor but I remember that one song, "Disgusted"? It was about someone doing coke…"

I cut Lena a look and hid a smirk. "They used to pour it down the groupies' ass cracks and they'd either lick it up or sniff it up."

Inessa eeeewed while everyone else chuckled. Apart from Lena who'd gone beet red.

"Where is everyone?"

"In here, Paddy," Aidan called out.

Ah, the prodigal brother returned.

He was, I saw, a diluted Aidan Sr. and I didn't mean that as an insult either.

Though plump around the middle, his suit worked wonders for hiding it. He was clean-shaven, a little sparse on top, but his eyes were kind and his smile was genuine as he bustled inside the massive kitchen.

"What's everyone doing in here?" he questioned as Savannah hissed at me:

"I'll get you back for that."

I just drank my water.

"We're watching the showdown—"

Aidan butted in before Eoghan could finish that sentence, "We thought we'd hang out here while Ma and Star were introduced."

Paddy's eyes widened but he peered around the room on the hunt for me. When he found the only person in the room he didn't know, he beamed a grin at me and held out his hand as he crossed the space to reach my side.

"It's a pleasure to meet you, Star."

"The pleasure's mine," I chirped. "Any man who can clean up a crime scene in a church is my kind of guy."

"Star," Conor groaned.

"What? It's true! How you deal with a crisis says a lot about a person." My grip was strong as I shook his hand. "I'm hoping you—"

Before I could finish that sentence, Paddy blurted out, "Conor, did Aidan tell you I need to speak with you?"

Well, that was fucking rude.

Conor sighed. "He did."

"It's important, son. I wouldn't ask otherwise."

When Conor made to stand and he headed toward a door off the kitchen, I had no compunction in traipsing after him once Paddy followed him too.

"Uh, Star?" Vana called.

"Later, babe."

"This is Points' business, Star," Aidan drawled, to which Eoghan chuckled.

I shot him a polite smile over my shoulder. "If it's Conor's business, then it's my business. You just entertain yourselves while Conor fixes all your problems as usual."

That shut them up.

Apart from Eoghan whose chuckle morphed into outright laughter.

"What?" I heard him mutter. "I like her."

Paddy stared at me oddly when I opened the door he'd just closed, but he was polite as he murmured, "This is private, Star."

"Anything you say to me, you can say to Star," Conor said tiredly as he leaned against a desk I figured was his da's. I moved beside him, close enough that our arms touched as I mimicked him and folded mine too. "What's going on with Liam, Paddy?"

"Your cousin—"

I rolled my eyes. "Only manipulate people who are dumber than you, Paddy. Conor knows who Liam is without you trying to guilt trip him into acting because of family ties."

The older man narrowed his eyes at me. "I'd unsheathe your claws if I were you."

"You're not me." I drummed my fingers on my biceps. "This is supposed to be a family day, a rest day, so get on with your tale of woe before it ruins our appetite."

Conor scratched his jaw, but I knew he did so to hide a grin—I saw it when I peered at him.

Hell, *he* was the one who told me it was a turn-on.

You couldn't say that to someone and not expect them to react.

"She's not wrong, Paddy. What's going on with Liam?"

"You heard of the Rabid Wolves?"

"Of course I have. We work with them across the border."

"They're threatening him."

"Liam? Why?"

"They want him to throw his next match against the Maple Leafs."

"What do they have on him?" I queried.

Paddy huffed. "Nothing."

"Bullshit," I countered. "People only pull these kinds of stunts if they have leverage."

I thought back to what I knew of Liam Donnghal—not much, really. Not as a person.

Mostly, I remembered his stats as a player. I also recalled that said stats had plummeted after he was kidnapped last year.

Matter of fact, I was the reason the guy was still playing lackluster in the rink rather than fertilizing roses—I'd found his ass and had helped bring him home.

"Liam's a good boy—"

"Sure he is," I drawled. "He's a professional athlete. They never get into *any* trouble."

Conor chuckled. "She has a point. The Rabid Wolves deal drugs. Has Liam started using?"

Paddy's Adam's apple bobbed. "No."

"Convincing," I mocked.

"After the kidnapping, he's gotten paranoid. Understandable but... he bought a gun from them and they're holding that over him."

Conor heaved a sigh. "Why didn't he ask us to procure one for him?"

"He doesn't like talking to me. You know that."

Even as I wondered what had triggered a falling out between father and son, I scoffed, "He talked to you about this."

Paddy conceded that with a grimace. "Desperate times. His words, not mine."

Ouch.

"He could have bought a gun the legal way. Why go to some shady MC when you have a legitimate reason to be paranoid?"

"Not this type of gun," he muttered. "Gun laws are stricter across the border."

"Rightfully so," I sniped.

"Didn't think you'd have that opinion," was Conor's surprised retort.

"I'm full of contradictions."

"You said it, not me," he said with a snort. To his uncle, he asked, "What does Liam think I can do?"

"Make up a gun permit for him for the weapon. *Or* get the Rabid Wolves off his back."

"I can do that," I offered. "They do runs with the Sinners. I've got plenty of dirty laundry of theirs I can air. You'll deal with the permit?"

Conor nodded. "The Mounties face the Maple Leafs next week if memory serves?"

"Yeah. Thursday," Paddy answered.

"We'll sort it."

Paddy flicked a glance between Conor and me. "Thank you. I know he'll appreciate it. He offered to come down himself but figured it was best to stay on the down-low."

I grunted. "Tell him he owes Conor a fruit basket."

"A fruit basket?"

"As a 'thank you.'"

He blinked. "Oh. Sure. Wouldn't you prefer cake, Conor? I know how much you love sweet treats, and I don't mean fruit."

"Candy would be great. I have to share mine now," he said, the teasing tone for me alone.

I nudged him with my elbow then watched as Paddy split another look between us. "She the one, Con? That's why she's wearing my ma's cameo?"

"She's the one," he agreed, sliding his arm around my shoulders.

"That's why I'm wearing the cameo *and* why I'm defending his ass from his family. There are only so many pieces he has to give, and I'm not going to let you steal each of them away from him."

Paddy's brows arched. "It's for the family."

"Don't give a fuck if it is or isn't. Family are the ones who'll drain you the quickest if you let them." I sniffed as I slipped my arm around his waist, holding him as tightly as he held me. "Figure you'd know that seeing as you ran away from yours decades ago."

Though he stiffened, he took the hit on the chin. "Thank you for helping Liam, Conor." He cleared his throat. "Star."

I bowed my head at the acknowledgment and watched as he left the office.

"You setting yourself up as my guard dog, Star?" Conor asked as he pressed his cheek to the top of my head.

"Someone has to before they dry you up and turn you into a shriveled prune."

"Wouldn't you still love me if I were a shriveled prune?" he teased.

"Sure. I'd just soak you in syrup. Rehydrate the wrinkles."

"Good thing I like sugar then, huh?"

Snickering, I concurred, "It is."

"And don't worry about me. I get my kicks out of them."

"You do?"

"They have a thing for fucking in elevators that are under my purview. Or talking about shit they wouldn't want any of us to hear within reach of one of my mikes."

I mock-gagged. "You watch them fuck?"

"Nope. But I still know they did it." He tapped his nose. "Who knows when I'll need to blackmail them into doing something?"

I cackled. "This is why we're good together."

He winked. "One of just many reasons."

Heartburn.

Goddamn heartburn.

But this was the kind not even a Tums could fix.

21

CONOR

A THOUSAND YEARS - CHRISTINA PERRI

Conor O'Donnelly

"SO, Star, what is it that you actually do?"

Pausing as I spooned potatoes onto my dish, I flicked a look between my mother and my partner.

Star, in the process of loading her plate with broccoli, didn't skip a beat as she answered, "I'm like Conor. A little bit of this, a lot of that."

"You work on computers, then?"

"You could say that, yes," she replied politely, handing the dish to Brennan who was seated beside her.

"Ma," I said, a warning in my tone once I saw her fold her hands together and place them beneath her chin.

"What? I'm entitled to ask, aren't I? It's not as if you've ever brought a girlfriend home before."

"You're supposed to be eating," I countered.

"I'm not stopping you from eating yours now, am I?" she grumbled.

"No, but I don't feel like listening to you grilling my girlfriend over roasted chicken."

"Hardly your girlfriend. Did you think I wouldn't see the cameo?"

"What cameo?" Aela inquired.

"You got the cameo?" Eoghan asked, surprised.

"Da left it to me in his will."

Brennan's brows lifted. "You always were his favorite."

"Your father didn't have favorites."

Aidan, sitting in Da's place, hooted. "Since when?"

She scowled at him. "It's disrespectful to talk ill of the dead."

"Why? Not like they care," Star reasoned. "Plus, your husband wasn't perfect, Mrs. O'Donnelly. You, more than anyone, should know that."

Though she'd been given leave to call her 'Lena,' I knew it was a strategic move that she didn't use Ma's first name.

A silence fell among the family, but no one stood up to defend Da. What would be the point? Defending him would mean lying and he'd been the one who taught us that lying was a cardinal sin.

The logic was beyond satisfying.

"No one's perfect," Ma drawled. "My husband never claimed to be. And while you're under my roof, I'll kindly ask you to refrain from speaking badly about him."

Star hitched a shoulder as she asked, "Could you pass me the gravy please, Brennan?"

Bren complied, and the cabochon emerald seemed to gleam in the light of the dining room, brighter than ever. Enough that I knew almost everyone was looking at it apart from Star.

"You're wearing hundreds of years of history," Ma informed her coolly. "I wonder if you know that."

"Conor told me it was stolen from a noble."

Ma smiled but it was Paddy who explained, "Quite literally. Back in the old country, the Donnghals were Robin Hoods of what's now County Kilkenny." He raised his wine glass to his lips and took a deep sip. "That comes from the hand of some English noblewoman that our ancestors held up on the road to Dublin."

Star grinned. "So I'm wearing stolen loot? Why does that make it a hundred times better?"

"Because you're weird," I told her with a wink.

"So, the cameo isn't an O'Donnelly?"

"Nope. One of our victims," I mocked.

"Aidan made our family as rich as it is, but we always had good jewels from those days. It's how our great-grandfather started the property empire. He sold them off as collateral for loans until we started being able to pay them in… other ways."

"What you're saying is you've always been crooks?"

Aidan agreed with a chuckle, "I think that's what Paddy's saying, Star."

"The question is whether you're okay with that," Brennan rumbled, his voice deep with suspicion. "Seeing as you were an alphabet."

"I *am* an alphabet," Eoghan retorted, stabbing his fork into a piece of chicken with more force than was necessary for a breast as succulent as what Ma roasted. "You got a problem with my loyalties, *dearthair*?"

Brennan narrowed his eyes. "That's different."

"Is it?"

As Eoghan and Brennan engaged in a battle of wills, Ma murmured, "Which agency were you with, dear?"

I grimaced at the term of endearment but Star merely replied, "I was with the CIA. Recruited from the Army and sold into slavery by the same alphabet agency, so you can rest assured that I owe them no loyalties."

Ma's mouth gaped a little, but it was Brennan who cut her a look. "This could be a double-blind."

"Would you like to see my scars, Brennan?" Star quipped, and warily, I studied the fork in her hand.

"Brennan," I warned, but it was too late.

The fork was there, buried in the antique mahogany between Brennan's pointer and middle finger. The metal quivered in place from the kinetic energy thrumming through it.

Eoghan chuckled. "You deserved that."

Victoria croaked, "Did you miss on purpose?"

"Star rarely does things without purpose," I informed her with a smile that I hoped was soothing.

"Is that supposed to reassure me that you're trustworthy?" Brennan drawled, moving his fingers out of the way of the makeshift weapon.

"It is actually. You should see what she did to her grandfather."

Ma released a shocked gasp that morphed into a bark of laughter. She slapped a hand to her mouth to cover it up, but it was too late for that—I'd already seen *and* heard it.

"You did that to your grandfather?"

Inessa's question was drowned out by Savannah's, "Who the fuck is your grandfather and why have I never met him?"

Somehow, that set the tone for the rest of the meal.

Brennan, less suspicious than before but still wary, had even laughed a few times at Savannah and Star's bickering.

Later, when we were leaving—everyone apart from Paddy, of course—Ma grabbed my hand. "I like her."

"I could tell."

"Did she stab her grandfather?"

"She did."

"Did he deserve it?"

I pulled a face because the jury was still out in my mind. "Star thought so."

"She's strong, son. Very strong. That's a weakness in itself sometimes."

Curious at her insight, I pressed a kiss to her cheek. "We're working on it."

"Your father didn't rely on me until it was too late and our paths were set, Conor. Even then, he didn't trust me with his illness, didn't trust me with his plans. Start as you mean to go on or it'll taint what you build together." She swallowed. "I think your grandmother would approve that she's the one wearing her cameo. Maybe she knew, right from the beginning, that I wasn't good enough for it."

My brow furrowed at that. "I'm sure that's not true."

"And I'm sure it is," she quipped. "You go on now. Declan let it slip earlier that you're traveling to England?"

"I am. Tomorrow. For a funeral."

She sighed. "I'm so tired of death."

"You should go on that cruise you were talking about at Thanksgiving."

"Maybe I will." She angled her head to the side. "What did Paddy want to talk to you about?"

"Are you sure you want to know?"

"I'm sure."

"Liam, his son—"

"I know who he is, Conor," she clucked.

"Someone's blackmailing him to throw a match."

She blinked. "Funny how your father never got into that racket. I never understood why he didn't. I used to watch my brothers gambling on the horses and thought it was a fool's game."

"We have bookies," I countered.

Ma hitched a shoulder. "Shay's been talking to me about his plans for the future."

I leaned against the door and folded my arms across my chest, well aware that Savannah and Star were arguing in the driveway about TikTok so were occupied for the moment. "He's still having nightmares?"

"Of course he is. It helps, him talking to me. Aela might not like it, but I failed as a mother and I won't as a grandmother."

"You didn't fail us," I rasped uneasily.

"I did. I let Aidan whip you into shape because that was all I knew. That was what my da did, what my grandfather did. But I should have been the instrument of change. I should—" She swallowed. "Less of that. The past is done. I can't change what I did but I can make sure I'm better with the next generation.

"As for Shay, he's told me his father's been speaking to him about his grades, making noise about him applying for Harvard?"

I shrugged. "So?"

"So... you think I'm deaf to what Seamus has been spouting? About wanting to be a politician?"

"Where are you going with this, Ma?"

She shrugged but patted my chest. "Food and sports—no truer way to get to an American's heart."

My brow puckered as she leaned up and I automatically ducked down to let her kiss my cheek.

"Just something to think about, son. You drive safely back to the city, hmm?"

Still frowning, I stated, "I'll look into getting you that apartment when I'm back from the UK. Okay?"

"Sounds good to me."

As she drifted away to the kitchen, something about her seemed so frail, so alone that it hit me on the raw. Then, Paddy appeared. He said something I didn't catch and it made her chuckle, and she seemed a touch less alone. A little less sad.

After decades of marriage to my father, I figured that was the least she deserved.

Even if my brothers didn't.

22

———

STAR

Star Sullivan

"FINN SAYS DAGDA'S AWAKE."

Moving the pillow off my shoulder, I squinted at him as I yawned. "Talking? Or just awake?"

"Finn knows what your intentions are. He wouldn't have texted me with the update otherwise."

Rubbing my hands over my face, I mumbled, "Did you catch any sleep?"

"Some. Worked on securing the gun permit for Liam. Did you manage to put any pressure on the Rabid Wolves before you crashed?"

That was when I remembered where I was—one of Conor's desks. Well, *my* desk now.

That was why my back hurt like fuck, and he must have been the reason for the pillow.

Stretching my arms wide open, I wriggled to right some of the cricks in my spine, mumbling, "I asked Nyx for any recent intel and informed the Canada Revenue Agency that they hadn't been declaring all their income on one of their more popular bars."

He chuckled. "Remind me never to get on your bad side."

I winked at him. "I'll do worse to you if you do. That's the cost of being loved by me."

"Hey, that's not fair," he argued.

"It's plenty fair. I love you, ergo you have the power to hurt me more."

"True." His nose crinkled. "Okay, Dagda. We going?"

"What time's our flight?"

"We still have four hours before we need to be at the private airfield."

"Oh, plenty of time then." I yawned again then stretched some.

"You're not as eager as I thought you'd be to meet him. Haven't you been waiting for this for years?"

I shrugged. "I'm not the same woman as back then."

"Why? Because you're still pissed at your mom?"

"That plays a part in it, but not all. I'm just… *different.*"

He made no comment other than to dip down and pull out an energy drink from the fridge he kept under my desk.

Frowning at the sight, I drawled, "That won't make up for good sleep."

"Like you can judge," he teased as he tossed me a can too.

I settled it on the desk. "I sleep *some*. That's more than you. You do too much, Conor. I did half of what I had to do tonight because of you. So thank you for that."

His yawn cracked his jaw. "Come on, let's get this shit with Dagda over with."

I took the can with me as we headed downstairs and opened the tab when I thought it wouldn't blow up in my face.

Conor set the GPS to our location and I jumped behind the wheel of a more fitting Mob ride—an SUV tank that would have served us well in the sandbox.

Thanks to it being four in the morning, traffic was quieter than usual. We got to the building in short order and there was a Pointer waiting to get behind the wheel so he could park it for us.

Oddly enough, the building was in the center of the city, not on the outskirts, and it appeared to be a now-defunct mall.

We were quiet as we headed inside, and I grimaced at the black-site hospital which was located next to a water feature and between two non-functioning escalators.

The ward's walls were made of thick, heavy-duty plastic that was shaped like a cube so Dagda was enclosed in a sterile environment.

Because it was transparent, I could see him sitting up in his hospital bed, his chest covered in blood-stained bandages, which told me his wounds were still leaking.

"Infection?" I inquired.

Conor hummed.

I cut him a look, saw the exhaustion in his eyes, and silently promised him we'd sleep on the flight over the Atlantic. No way in fuck was I letting him head to the funeral tomorrow as tired as he was now.

It was a weird feeling caring about his well-being. Not because he didn't deserve it, but because I'd never felt that way about a man before. I guessed I had with Maverick; however, it wasn't like *this*.

I wanted to cup Conor's cheek and press a kiss to his eyelids.

I wanted to get into bed with him, to make sure that he slept.

I wanted mushy shit. Mushy when I'd never let myself get like that before.

I didn't know if it was a weakness or a strength, which put me on edge, but I had to trust that it'd work itself out in the end.

Loving Conor was the simplest thing I'd ever done, but that didn't mean complications wouldn't arise from it as a result.

I was prepared for those complications, and that was all I could do.

"You're staring."

I hitched a shoulder. "You look tired."

"I am." He rubbed his eyes. "Ma mentioned something that got my mind racing and it made getting into the Canadian gun registry harder than it should have been."

"What did she mention?"

"Match-fixing."

When he gave me no other context, I rubbed his arm. "I need sleep too. We'll get some rest on the plane."

Quickening my pace because I wanted this interview over with, I made my way to the makeshift ward in the abandoned mall with him at my back.

A nurse in scrubs opened a zipper from inside the cube and shot us both disapproving glowers before she took her leave.

Dagda wasn't wearing an oxygen mask, but he had it piped up his nose. His face wasn't cut up any, but his chest was a maze of gunshot wounds.

"You're lucky to be alive," I drawled unsympathetically.

His eyes flickered open, and there was curiosity there. No fear. *Intriguing*. "Lodestar," he greeted.

"My reputation precedes me?"

"No, you're too much like your mother." Eyes drooping, he chuckled under his breath. "You mean to tell me that I survived that fucking mess only to meet my end in this hellhole?"

I knew what he meant—black-site hospitals were the worst. The security vulnerabilities made it hard to rest and recuperate which was a vicious cycle because that was the only way you'd get out of the ward.

"I made a deal with your niece. I'm not going to kill you, Dagda. But I want answers."

His expression was disbelieving. "What kind of answers do you think I have?"

"My mother was a Jorgmundgander hit?"

He tensed. "She was."

"And she died?"

That had his brow puckering. "What kind of question is that?"

Conor cleared his throat. "Someone led us to believe that Star's mother might be alive."

Dagda frowned. "Impossible."

"How do you know?" I insisted.

"You want the details?"

"I want whatever you, as an ally of the Five Points, can give me."

Dagda flicked a look at Conor. "She's yours?"

Conor merely dipped his chin.

Though the question pissed me off, I knew why he asked.

"Got her in the throat." He sighed. "Watched her die through my scope."

I thought back to that traumatic day at the funeral home. It had started with an argument because Dad hadn't wanted me there. Then, I'd seen her and I'd understood why he'd tried to protect me.

Mom didn't have it in her to be still. But she was.

Her skin was faintly clammy when I'd pressed my lips to her forehead, with a smooth, porcelain-like texture that had felt fake. There'd been no color on her cheeks aside from an unnatural blush.

I remembered Dad had the undertakers put her in her favorite sweater and jeans. He'd said she'd be more comfortable like that.

Had they dressed her in a turtleneck to hide her wounds?

It made more sense than using reconstructive makeup.

Mind stuck in the past, I loomed above Dagda, stuck a thumb over the bloodied spot on one of his bandages, and pressed down.

His heart rate increased to the point that the machine started beeping, but he only clenched his jaw.

"No way she could have survived."

"You sure about that?"

He gritted his teeth when I didn't let up, but he didn't shove my hand away, didn't try to stop me. "I'm positive. 100%. I watched her pass."

The nurse from earlier tried to rush in, but Conor blocked her as he reasoned softly, "Star."

Disregarding his warning, I maintained my stare into Dagda's eyes. Not relenting until I was certain he wasn't bullshitting me.

Only then did I pull back.

"You've no idea why Jorgmundgander targeted her?"

"I wasn't in on the decision-making process," he rasped, gaze darting to his blanket-covered knees. "I was a tool. Nothing more."

Blood-stained hand held high, I retreated. I grabbed the corner of his bedsheet as the nurse busied herself around him, glowering at me as she ministered to her patient while I wiped the blood onto his coverings.

"Though I promised your niece that I wouldn't kill you—" The nurse gasped but I ignored her. "—if I leave this room and find out you *have* lied to me, I won't be afraid to break that promise. Understood?"

His nostrils flared, further exposing the tubes that supplied him with oxygen. "Understood," he croaked. "I'm an ally now. We're on the same goddamn side."

"So long as you remember that, we're good."

He dipped his chin as I made my way to the cube's point of entry.

Once I left the sterile environment, I breathed a little easier, turning on my heel to study the mall and its many, *many* security risks.

"You didn't have a better place to hospitalize him?"

Conor shrugged at my question. "No idea. Finn tends to be the one who deals with this."

"Why Finn?"

"He's the money man. You think this shit comes cheap?"

I thought about the equipment they used, never mind the medical care they'd require. "True." I studied a movie poster from two years ago. "You didn't approve of my methods."

He arched a brow. "Killing him at that point would have served no purpose. I was just warning you to pull back before you took it too far."

I shoved my hands into my pockets as I twisted around to look at him. "You're a spy's perfect boyfriend, aren't you?"

A sparkle lit up his tired eyes. "I've been called many things in my time, but not that."

"Remind me to get you a mug made up with it for Christmas then, hmm?"

His grin hit me in all the good places, places that only existed because of him.

When he pressed his lips to mine in a quick peck, I laughed as he mumbled against my mouth, "I'll remind you. Don't worry."

23

STAR

THE FOLLOWING DAY

Star Sullivan

"GOOD JOB, VANA," I muttered under my breath as I took in the selection of headlines in front of me.

Peering over my shoulder, Conor picked up one of the papers that declared:

Nevada senator claims leaked footage is a deep fake.

"I wish it didn't smack of kink shaming."

"We're not kink shaming."

"The US public is. That's what we're relying on—a bunch of prudes."

"It's our Puritan souls. We can't handle foot fetishes."

"It's not even that big a deal."

"You got something you want to tell me?"

His grin was a wicked slash that tempted me to kiss him. "That I like you in heels and boots?"

"Good to know," I teased. "Shall I let Vana drag me to a salon for a pedicure?"

He hitched a shoulder. "Sure. Go for bright red."

"Blood red?"

"Like I need the reminder you're more of an assassin than anything the developers of *Assassin's Creed* could come up with."

Snickering, I shoved him in the side then picked up another paper.

Boston congresswoman claims terrorists are behind recent influx of headlines that are 'destabilizing the nation.'

"How right she is," I crooned, skewering her in the face with my fingernail.

"How many more reveals?"

"At least ten."

"On top of these six?"

"Yup. Vana's helped me stagger them. We're keeping the cops plenty busy, and if the politicians start whining about these privacy infractions being a terrorist attack, then that's where the alphabets will shift their focus."

"A job well done?"

"Uh huh. Aoife hasn't heard from her dad?"

"Finn didn't say anything to indicate Davidson had been in touch. That he isn't photographed on any of the front pages is telling in itself."

"He's keeping his head down," I agreed. "Smart man."

"Ish. He dumped Aoife for a chance at the White House. That was a dumb move."

"Men rarely appreciate something until they've lost it. He was cut up about meeting with me and not her."

He cupped my shoulder. "It's between them. Don't meddle."

I arched a brow at him. "Who said I was going to meddle?"

"I can hear it in your voice."

I sniffed.

"That only confirms it," he retorted. "Anyway, the car will be here in five. Are you good to go?"

Though I nodded, I released a yawn. We'd arrived late last night and though our alarm call had been for ten AM, my circadian rhythms didn't agree.

Dumping the paper I'd been reading on the dinner table, I stretched. "I'll be glad when this is over with."

He curved an arm around my waist and I let him haul me into him. "It's a good thing you're doing."

"Being Minnie's target practice?"

"Yeah. She needs someone to blame, and she can't blame Ovianar yet even if, in the grand scheme of things, Minerva knows she was living on borrowed time."

"How do you always cut to the heart of the matter?" I grumbled, turning away from the windows that showed London's cityscape to bury my face in his chest.

"Because neither of us appreciates bullshit?"

"Katina speaks fluent bullshit."

"We'll cure her of it."

"Nah. It's a good skill to have in this fucked-up world we live in. Imagine her in PR?"

He whistled under his breath. "You make a good argument."

"It's how I roll." I smiled as I tugged on his jacket. "You look smart."

"You don't," he teased.

"Hey! I resent that."

"You're wearing shitkickers, Star. To a funeral."

"It's my uniform." I shrugged. "I won't apologize for it."

"Never asked you to. I'm only saying it's against the law to wear jeans to a funeral."

"They're black! So's my tee!"

His lips twitched. "Come on, G.I. Star. Let's get this show on the road, hmm?"

Huffing, I let him lead me out of the suite we were staying in and toward the elevators. As the doors opened, my brows arched when I came across Tryn Bowen.

Conor froze then did the sweetest thing—attempted to shove me behind him. When that didn't work, he stepped ahead, growling, "This is a private elevator."

Bowen merely smiled. "I own the hotel. Nothing is private to me." He held out a hand. "A pleasure as always, Star."

"You know this guy?" Conor demanded, twisting around to study my expression as I shook Tryn's hand.

"You do too. By name, at any rate. This is Tryn Bowen."

Conor frowned but when Bowen kept his hand out for him to shake as well, he accepted it. "Four Horsemen, right?"

Bowen smirked. "One and only."

"Which are you?" Conor mocked. "Death, pestilence, war, or famine?"

"Oh, I'm pestilence," Bowen retorted, amusement lighting his eyes. "Harder than VD to get rid of."

"I'm sure."

"Irish Mob, no?"

Conor hummed. "That's me."

"I always make a point of meeting any factions who wish to stay at one of my hotels." He eyed me. "Even more so when they come with an intriguing entourage."

"I was in and out of London," I argued. "There wasn't time to meet with you first."

"You make time, Star. You know I don't like being kept out of the loop. See what happens when you do—Ovianar is dead. If I'd known—"

"If you'd known, there was dick you could do. She could have contacted you but she didn't. Why is that?"

"Because she thought her involvement with Jorgmundgander was unknown to my cousins and me." He made a dismissive gesture with his hand as his gaze trickled over me. "You're attending the funeral? I'm not sure Minerva invited you."

"She didn't, but I'm showing up anyway."

A gleam appeared in his eye that had Conor settling a possessive hand around my waist. "Crashing a funeral," he tutted.

"I aim low," was my bitter reply. "Is there a reason you're here, Tryn? Just to piss around your hotel like a dog marking his territory or…"

"I was curious when you didn't arrange to speak with me."

"I didn't think I needed to. I'm literally just here for a funeral."

"You're never 'just' anything." His gaze flickered between Conor and me and because he was a Bowen, I knew that he didn't miss a damn thing. Something he confirmed when his focus drifted to my hips where I'd planted my left hand. "You're getting into bed with the Five Points?"

"She's already *in* the bed," Conor growled, which made me shoot him a perplexed glance. "And she's going nowhere."

Bowen clucked his tongue. "Star's a viper. I hope you have plenty of antivenom on hand for when she strikes."

"I've built up an immunity over the years," Conor drawled.

"Interesting." He tilted his head to the side. "We can ride down together."

It wasn't a request.

I glanced warily at Conor whose mouth was a taut line, but he graced me with the slightest of nods.

"Sounds good," I answered.

When the doors to the elevator closed behind us, Bowen asked, "When do you leave?"

"You want to get rid of me already?" I mocked.

"Where you go, trouble follows," he retorted, wrapping both hands against the rail at the back of the elevator. Body language alone told me he was in full-on 'I own London' mode.

Rolling my eyes at him, I mused, "And trouble leaves London alone when I'm out of the city?"

"For the most part." He pursed his lips as the elevator stopped on the first floor. "I want to speak with you before you leave. I'll leave the details at the reception desk."

I scowled. "We're flying out tomorrow."

"Is that the truth I hear?"

"It is. We're leaving in the early hours."

"Then we can speak this evening." He dipped his chin at me then Conor. "Until later."

When he left, Conor demanded, "Did you have a relationship with him?"

My brows lifted. "No."

"He wants you."

I snorted. "Is this you being jealous? If it is, it's cute."

His glower faded. "That's not funny, Star."

"Sure, it is." With that glower still aimed at me, I mused out loud, "You do realize you're the only guy I'll allow to touch me, Conor?"

"What does that mean?"

"It means that *now*, never mind years ago when I first came across Tryn, the notion of a guy touching me sexually makes me heave." I fought the urge to retch at just the possibility. "As for the past, I used men, Conor. Every one of them I came across was a fool waiting for me to lead them around by their dicks."

"And I'm not a fool?"

"And you're not," I said easily, reaching up to run my hand along the sharp edge of his jaw, hoping that would soothe him rather than incite. "Got your ring on my finger," I reminded him.

"You do. What happened with him?"

Sad that he didn't feel secure enough to let go of this, I hitched a shoulder. "He doesn't like my methods. Can't blame him. The guy thinks he walks on water. He was just asking to be pulled off his pedestal."

For the first time since Bowen had interrupted us, amusement gleamed in Conor's eyes. "Why does he want to speak with you later?"

"He's full of his own importance," I dismissed then checked my watch. "We're going to be late if we don't get going now."

Though he nodded, when I stepped away, he grabbed my hand and tugged me into him. When I barreled into his chest, he stared into my eyes. "No secrets between us, Star."

"No secrets. But I'm not going to detail who I've fucked and when, Conor, just like I don't expect you to share that information with me. Especially as both of us have admitted that we always fucked and ran in the past."

He grunted.

I took that to mean he agreed but didn't want to verbalize it.

I smirked at him as I hovered my mouth above his. "I love you, Conor."

He grunted again. "Love you too, Star."

More amused than ever by his begrudging tone, I dragged him into the foyer and the concierge drifted alongside to guide us toward the door where a car was waiting.

Upon seeing us, the driver moved to the back seat and opened the door so we could slip inside.

The ride to the cemetery was short but not exactly sweet thanks to the usual traffic that riddled the streets. I pressed my hand to the window, watching my body heat steam up around my digits as we drove through Kensington toward the outskirts of Central London.

It was a good thing we'd elected to avoid the church service and intended only to watch the coffin be interred because we were later than anticipated when the driver, apologizing all the way, pulled up outside the cemetery.

By the time we were walking down the gravel path toward Ovianar's plot, it had started to rain.

"Fucking England," I muttered. "Always raining."

Conor tipped his head back. "Nothing wrong with rain."

"They've said we can't drink the rain now. It's too acidic."

"Since when do you drink rainwater?"

"Hey, don't judge. Sometimes rain is the only water source for miles around."

He hauled his arm over my shoulders and dragged me into his side. "If we ever get stuck in the wilderness, you'll totally save our asses, won't you?"

"Yeah. I'm good in dire situations," was my dry retort, but my words faltered when I saw the people gathered around the grave.

He squeezed me, murmuring, "It'll be over soon."

"I know. I'm just—"

"What the hell are you doing here?!"

"Jesus," I muttered under my breath at Minerva's shriek.

"Has she got eyes in the back of her head?" Conor queried in surprise.

"Sixth sense, more like," I groused, shrugging off his arm so I could catch his hand as we made our way toward the plot. "I've come to pay my last respects," I called out, well aware that I hadn't just knotted our fingers together—mine were practically superglued via sweat to his.

"Last respects? You're the reason she's dead," Minerva spat. "She wouldn't want you here and I sure as hell don't!"

With a glance around the crowd, who were gawking at us, I happened to see Tryn Bowen standing at Minnie's side, his hand firmly fixed on the shoulder of a young boy, his cousins like his personal bookends hovering around him.

Wondering if he had a magic wand that let him attend the funeral on time, unlike us, I narrowed my eyes at the humor in his expression before pinning her in my focus.

"I made a mistake," I said calmly. "I'm sorry, Minnie."

"Don't you dare call me that."

"I'm sorry," I repeated, then, deciding to go for broke with the truth, I admitted rawly, "If I'd known she was in danger, I'd have made sure that she was secured. I'll regret it until the day I die that I let you both down."

My honest words earned me a sneer. "I'll regret the fact that you knew each other until the day *I* die."

I flinched but Conor was the one who stated, "We'll stand here until the service is over and we'll pay our respects then."

That seemed to infuriate her even more because she shoved off a woman's arm who'd been holding her back and stormed forward. Hair flickering around her face, she snarled, "You're not wanted here."

Bowen surprised me by stepping toward her and pressing his hand to her arm.

Head whipping to the side, she snapped, "Leave me the fuck alone. It's my right to throw out unwanted guests."

Bowen's touch gentled, but to us, he directed, "I think it's best if you return to the hotel."

"You knew she was in the city?" Minnie cried, shooting him a look of betrayal to which he heaved a sigh.

"Of course I did. Ovianar and her were close at one time, Minerva. It's only natural that she'd—"

"Get her killed? Everyone around you dies, Star," Minnie spat. "You're fucking poison. I hope to God I never see you again. Get away from my family. O's the only one you can't hurt anymore and I'm not willing to risk having you around the rest. Go. GO!"

I staggered back at her dismissal. Her vitriol came as no surprise, but it didn't stop the tears from pricking my eyes as I tugged on Conor's arm and prompted him to retreat with me.

He was silent on the walk back to the car, and the silence continued on the drive to the hotel because I wasn't about to take more of a verbal beating from Minnie for sticking around to pay respects that only needed to be given for a miscalculation on my part.

I was relieved about the quiet because I didn't feel like talking, not even when Conor tucked a Jolly Rancher in my hand.

Minnie's words had hit a sore spot. Hell, the sorest of spots.

"You're not poison. Nor are you cancer."

That was the first thing he said to me once we were back in the suite, and I shot him a tired look. I didn't bother arguing with him though. Just patted his chest and returned to the dinner table where this morning's papers were still spread out.

He ordered coffee for us, two club sandwiches showed up at the same time, and he pulled out his laptop and did some work while I read through the headlines.

It was a testament to how the papers were flooded with dirty gossip from the Capitol that the article was barely more than a couple inches long.

Disgraced ex-Chief Justice DeLaCroix found dead in his cell.

My brows lifted as I read the rest of the column before I told Conor, "DeLaCroix's dead."

He smirked. "Finn owes me brownies for life."

That had me blinking. "What does the one-time head of the Sparrows dying have to do with you getting brownies for life from Finn?"

"We had a bet on when he'd die."

"You should have said. I'd have asked Troy—"

"Nah. We agreed we wouldn't manipulate the outcome." He stretched his arms out in front of him. "Feels good knowing that the bastard's dead?"

I hummed. "Someone gave him a cyanide capsule. Wonder who was behind that."

"How very Nazi Germany of them."

My lips twitched at his dry humor. "You'd be surprised how many spies still carry them around."

"Death before dishonor?"

"No. More like death before waterboarding. I didn't mind waterboarding. Not my idea of a good time but—"

He gaped at me. "You've been waterboarded?"

"Of course."

"Of course?" he screeched.

"Part of training," I tried to appease, seeing his distress was real.

"*We* did that to you?"

"Prepares you for the worst."

"Yeah, sounds like it if agents are still carrying cyanide pills around with them." He rolled his eyes. "I swear you're going to give me a heart attack before we're done."

"When will that be?" I half-teased, but a wariness had filtered into the words which was a direct result of today's interactions with Minerva.

Everyone left me, after all.

Why should he be any different?

"'Til death do us part," he murmured, the saying purposeful. *Meaningful.*

I swallowed. "I think I can handle that."

"Good."

And that was the end of that conversation.

24

CONOR

GETTING NOWHERE - JOHN LEGEND

A QUICK INVESTIGATION into Tryn Bowen let me know his poison of choice—guns.

In the Four Horsemen hierarchy, a gang that I'd heard of but had never bothered to learn more about as our ties weren't UK-based, he was the Declan of the Four Horsemen family.

Azrael Shaw dealt drugs, Edwin Carsten handled their prostitutes, and Cole Flyn managed the protection racket.

Each 'owned' a quarter of London, separating the boroughs between them, though their umbrella corps—the guns, drugs, prostitutes, and protection racket—spanned the city.

What fascinated me the most, however, was how the Four Horsemen had run the capital in this way for almost *two* centuries with a Cole, Azriel, Edwin, and Tryn each heading the group since the Four Horsemen came into being.

The growth of the city had been cultivated by the gang itself, its power slipping through the roots and into the body until their rule was more pervasive than whichever government was in charge.

It came as no surprise, then, when we were guided into the Harrods Tea Room and it was empty apart from Tryn.

He was seated in the center, illuminated by the overhead glass ceiling, while a pianist played swing music.

To "Fly Me To The Moon," Bowen dolloped what appeared to be a thick type of cream on a scone as he watched us slip toward his table. The maitre d' held out the chair for Star, who sank gracefully onto it, and she immediately reached for one of the sandwiches on the stands without waiting for an invitation to do so. As she ate, a server appeared and poured us tea.

It was the most British thing I'd ever seen in my life.

Bowen remained silent until the staff disappeared.

"Didn't take you for the kind of guy who ate finger sandwiches," Star mocked.

Bowen arched a brow. "Why was Ovianar killed?"

"Minerva didn't tell you?"

"Her doctors have her sedated—"

"That was her *sedated*?" I muttered.

"She hasn't taken O's passing well," Bowen concurred, neatly pressing the edge of a napkin to the corner of his mouth. "Brady isn't either. I hope your business was worth the destruction of their lives."

"Now, listen here, bud, you think we wanted shit to go down how it did?" I growled, my hand seeking Star's beneath the table. Her fingers clutched at mine, reminding me of nothing less than a little girl hunting redemption and coming up blank.

"I wouldn't know," he rumbled. "Seeing as I'm in the dark as to your true intentions." His gaze fixed on Star. "If you ever want to step foot in this city again, you will clue me into what's going on. I let it pass that you came to London without an audience that first time, but you've used up any clemency you earned in the past, Star. Understood?"

Nostrils flaring, she snapped, "If you think I wished any ill will on Ovianar—"

"Whether you did or not, she ended up dead, and Minerva..." His jaw worked. Something sparked to life in his eyes. Something *personal.*

A shudder wracked Star, making her frame tremble and drawing my attention her way. "I know she did. I managed to figure that out on my own." Chin tipping upward, she rasped, "In the future, I'll let you know when I'm heading into London."

My brow puckered. "Are you an unofficial ICE agent or something?"

Bowen's lips twitched. "If you're a criminal, sure."

It was clear to me she wanted to get this over with because she stated, "The New World Sparrows were behind O's death. I never imagined they'd come after her or I'd have stayed with her, made sure her family was safe. You know me, Tryn. You fucking know how I work.

"She got involved with Jorgmundgander to spare Minnie. *That's* why she hates my guts. Because she wants to blame me but her own actions led to O's death as much as mine did."

The gaze he scrutinized her with was more thorough than one of the scanners at the airport. I figured she passed muster, though, because he got to his feet, buttoning his sports coat as he did so. "Feel free to enjoy the rest of your evening here. Do try the scones, they're not to be missed."

With Star's agreement, he left, and I mimicked, "Do try the scones."

Star shoved me in the side. "Hush."

"Could he sound any more English?"

"No. But he *is* English."

Glumly, she reached for a sandwich on the small Art-Deco-style tea tray.

A small legion of servers seemed to take that as a cue because a fresh one was brought out, filled with different pastries as well as finger sandwiches.

A new teapot was planted on the snowy linens next, and scones—our biscuits, only sweet—were replenished on thin china dishes while silver pots loaded with a thick type of whipped cream and two kinds of jam were placed in front of us.

"At least he knows how to treat his guests right?" I muttered as I reached for a thin sandwich the length of my middle finger and without crusts. My nose crinkled. "Why is this cucumber not with cream cheese and chives?"

"British tradition."

"The Brits ruin everything."

Her lips twitched as she drank her tea then, on a sorry exhalation, mumbled, "Years of living outside the UK, and I still prefer tea."

"Never see you drinking it."

"Coffee's easier to prepare."

"Is it?"

She shrugged. "Filter coffee is always warm. Plus, we're heathens in the US and we microwave the water, not boil it. Then there's the fact coffee doesn't taste vile in travel mugs like tea does."

I snatched a mini croissant that was split in half and loaded with what looked like tuna salad but was, in fact, some kind of crab concoction. Whichever, it tasted damn good.

"Didn't take you for a nervous eater."

Her remark had me shrugging. "I'm not nervous."

"I am," was her flat response.

"Why?"

"Everything's changing. I can feel it."

"Changing for the worst?"

"I've burned bridges. I didn't intend on doing that. You don't make enemies of the Four Horsemen."

"Do they usually treat their enemies to afternoon tea at Harrods? Because I can guarantee Da's enemies wish they'd gotten the star treatment like this."

Her lips curved. "True. It's not exactly torture, is it?"

"No. So, what's the problem?"

"Change is… hard to cope with for someone like me."

"A control freak?"

"Yes," she admitted.

I placed my hand on her shoulder. "You're not alone now, though."

"No," she whispered, gaze clashing with mine.

"Your enemies are mine and vice versa."

"Yes."

"So, what's the problem?" I repeated.

She swallowed, nodded more to herself than to me, then reached for a sandwich. "No problem."

25

STAR

Star Sullivan

THERE WAS a surprise waiting for us on the jet that would take us back to the US—my grandfather had perched himself on one of the bucket seats, a paper in his hands, one of several he had discarded on the table beside him.

"You have the subtlety of a jackhammer, Star, but in some instances, it's to our benefit," was his greeting. He didn't even look up from the article he was reading.

"The nation is distracted," I agreed.

"Which is why I said it's to our benefit, but it won't last forever. Three important men have gone missing within the space of a month," he pointed out.

"Isn't that what you're for? To deal with any repercussions?"

He sniffed. "It's fortunate for you that I have the power I do."

Though I squinted at him, I only asked, "Is that supposed to be an olive branch?"

"I didn't know we were in need of one. Interpol is awaiting the influx of your files and they have already commenced their investigation now that they have the means of accessing the Sparrows' communication app via DeLaCroix's account. Is that not enough of an olive branch?" The paper crunched as he peered at us over it. "Conor," he greeted, his tone more cordial than it had been with me.

"Anton." Conor seated himself with a weary sigh as he sank into the bucket seat.

A quick scan revealed to me that he was less tired than the other day but that jet lag had worked its wiles on him.

Something he confirmed by rocking his head back against the rest and closing his eyes.

"Did you see DeLaCroix is dead?" I inquired.

"See?" Anton chuckled. "My dear girl, I made it happen."

My brows lifted at that. "Interesting."

"Some pigs just can't be allowed to live," he stated, retreating behind his paper.

I didn't disagree, but it was still curious when his Brotherhood was so pious.

"This Interpol department... How did you pick the officers manning it?"

He heaved a sigh. "I hand-selected them but, by all means, I will have the list of officers sent over to you for vetting."

Surprised by the easy concession, I murmured, "I'd appreciate that."

"There are no skeletons in the officers' closets as far as my *Pauks* could uncover, but a second set of eyes, especially when they're yours, is always a wise decision."

I had no idea why but my mind shifted to something Sheridan Reinier had said: 'If you trust him, then you're a fool.'

As a result, my question came out more abruptly than I'd have liked:

"Was my mother's real name Galena?"

His hand tightened around the paper, making it crunch in his hand.

"I'll take that as confirmation."

"Her name was Galena, *da*." He folded the newspaper in his lap. "Why do you ask?"

"President Davidson implied they were friends."

"They met when he visited Moscow in his role as an emissary to the defense secretary in the late eighties."

"And a friendship was born?" I queried.

"It was. Your mother could be persuasive when she tried."

"Was it romantic?"

"She never said. I didn't task her with seducing him if that's your question."

"Good to know you didn't pimp her out on that occasion," I mocked.

His eyes narrowed upon me, the papery skin crinkling between his brows, but he stayed silent.

"I spoke with Eamonn Keegan, *Dagda*, before we flew to England. He confirmed that Mom's death was related to Jorgmundgander." When he didn't say anything, I demanded, "Well?"

"I wasn't aware that you asked me a question."

"Why have you gone to such lengths to avenge your son but not your daughter?"

"Isn't that obvious?"

"Not to me. I'm not a child and I deserve to know what happened to her, dammit."

"She does, Anton," Conor rumbled softly. "She only went down this path and ended up where she did because she needed to understand what happened to her mom."

Anton appeared to ponder that before, eventually, conceding, "The reason I don't need to avenge her is because she's already avenged."

"Dagda's living and breathing in New York City."

"And you yourself told me that Troy should not be erased for killing Aleks."

"Who was behind her death?"

"He's currently sitting in a shipping container in the Catskills listening to his colleagues being eaten by the local fauna."

"Sheridan Reinier was behind my mom's death?" I cried, digging my nails into the leather armrests to hold me back. Conor's hand slipped over mine, and I knotted my fingers with his, clenching down so hard that it undoubtedly hurt us both.

Anton rubbed the bridge of his nose. "Your mother was a beautiful woman. She was memorable. Too memorable. Reinier met her when he and Davidson came to Moscow. When she was a part of my guard," he clarified.

I swallowed. "He recognized her."

"Yes. And used it as a hold on her." His mouth tightened. "I suspected for many years that she was… that she'd turned. Had become a Sparrow. It was one of the reasons why I kept my distance. Not just from the investigation into her passing but from you too. I only waded in once I knew what they'd done to you, and like always, I was too late."

"I wondered what prompted your involvement," Conor mused. "Now, and not back then, I mean. What changed?"

Anton shot me a pointed look. "My granddaughter waded into the fray and began killing my colleagues then targeted me."

"Don't expect an apology out of me."

"I expect nothing from you apart from a bad attitude," he sniped.

I grunted.

"*Was* she a Sparrow?" Conor asked.

"Temperance Black has spoken with Reinier while under our custody. I've been assured that Galena wasn't a Sparrow, nor a double agent."

"So why kill her?"

"Because Reinier spoke with her personally. She had to die because she could implicate him as a Sparrow." He rubbed his chin. "As long as there are Sparrows, there will be Brothers. I like to think we are better, but in this, I'm as bad as one of them—my satisfaction in knowing of their suffering knows no bounds. Those men killed my children. I'm glad their pain will be excruciating before they are robbed of their lives, just as they did with my Aleks and Galena." His gaze was measured as he leveled me with a verbal blow: "Your mother does not deserve to be hated."

"You acted as if she—"

"Do you know the pain of losing two children, Star?"

There was such agony in his voice that even I, in all my selfish, childish rage at a mother who'd abandoned me too soon, quieted.

"It is the nature of life for a child to lose a parent but to suffer the reverse? Twice?" He shook his head. "Their sacrifice wasn't in vain, but that makes it no less of a sacrifice."

"I-I thought you resented her," I rasped.

"I did. For dying. I lead a double life, child. There are few who know all of me and your mother was one such person. Aleks was younger than her and there were... There were things he didn't know about me."

"Things Mom did?"

He dipped his chin. "Weaknesses of mine, strengths. She was a good girl. The best daughter. Yes, Reinier deserves his suffering. It is not in me to be needlessly cruel, but I see nothing needless about his end."

"Why was she with my dad? Was it love?" I braced myself. "Or was it a mission?"

"It started as a mission, an easy means of traveling the globe, hitting the major cities without suspicion—travel back then wasn't as *laissez-faire* as it is now. Then, over time, it became love. She wouldn't have stayed with him, wouldn't have given birth to you if that weren't the case."

"How do you know? Why did I never meet you?"

He sighed. "Because of one of my weaknesses."

"What do you mean?"

"Your grandmother was a difficult woman. Ours was not a marriage of love nor was it a mission. It was a union. A way of creating tighter binds between myself and another on my council."

"Your council?" Conor peppered.

"The men Star killed to reach me." His lips quirked. "I hated most of them so it is no waste to me, but you must curb your homicidal tendencies once this situation with the Sparrows is complete, child. I can keep you out of jail only as long as I'm alive."

"I only kill people who deserve it."

"I'm not sure the police would agree with such a mindset."

"Liberalism gone mad," I grumbled under my breath, making Conor snicker tiredly.

"Your grandmother was royalty—Edward of Midlothian's eldest daughter. We did not like each other. Most of the time, we despised each other, but we played too good a role for Galena and Aleks.

"Both of us had been raised with miserable parents in miserable households and we'd vowed to be different with our children."

"She caught you cheating, didn't she?" Conor questioned, his voice low.

"She did," he confirmed. "And never forgave me for it."

"Ever?"

"Not before she died. It undoubtedly played a part in keeping her away when she always called Russia home."

The words pained me—that Russia was 'home' when I remembered spending every Fourth of July at a massive party *she* organized to celebrate the occasion because she loved her country.

That she was capable of being as childish as me—judging our parents with the mindset of betrayed children rather than that of an adult—was oddly comforting.

But her life with us hadn't been a total lie, and his admission enabled me to admit to a solid, undeniable, indefatigable truth—hating her was harder than loving her.

"I loved her," I whispered brokenly, swiping at my cheeks like the child I was at that moment. A child who'd lost her parents.

"I did too," Anton rasped, reaching over to pat my hand.

"I didn't want to lose her."

"Nor did I."

"How did it happen? Dad would never tell me and when I was old enough to go looking for details, I was stonewalled."

He tipped up his chin. "That was my doing."

Around us, the flight attendants prompted us to prepare for take-off, but even the flight's departure didn't stop our discussion.

"Why?"

"It was a file filled with lies. I'd rather there be a question mark over her death if anyone went hunting for answers than those miserable falsehoods marking the so-called truth of her passing."

"What happened?"

He rubbed his forehead. "You know of Dagda's skill. It was fast. It was lethal. It was from a distance. One minute she was strolling down a street, the next she was bleeding out on it. Simple. Tragic. It happens to too many in your country and, that day, my daughter became another statistic." He released a sharp breath. "I attended her funeral, as did Aleks. We did not make ourselves known."

"Why not? Did you not think I needed you?"

"What could we bring to you but more death and intrigue? If we withdrew, you had the chance at a normal childhood. We had no way of knowing that you'd seek answers until it led you down the rabbit hole we inhabit." He studied me. "Your father *never* told you the details of her passing?"

"No. He wouldn't talk about it. At all. Would just say she died of 'shortness of breath.'"

His brow furrowed. "An unusual turn of phrase."

"Dad thought he was a poet."

"He was in the music industry," Conor rumbled.

Though my eyes were red from crying, his words had me rolling them. "If you say so."

"Did he know who she was?"

"He knew she was in the CIA. I don't think he knew about the Brothers. He wouldn't have been able to keep it out of his music." I arched a brow at Conor. "We have our resident *noxxious* expert in the house. Any mention of secret societies in his lyrics?"

"No. He did refer to the CIA and your mom though. '*In the shadows, she hides, alphabets keeping me safe, but no one can save me from her.*' That was in 'Fractious.'"

"Before she died?" At his nod, I mumbled, "See? He couldn't keep anything a secret."

"But he kept the truth of her death from you," Anton pointed out.

"He was heartbroken. For the next year, he was either stoned or drunk. Everything changed when she died. Everything."

"I'm sorry, child."

I sucked in a breath. "Me too."

"Is that why Temperance was on me when Riggs called me into Langley?" Conor asked softly.

The abruptness of the question had me blinking, but Anton merely drawled, "You're talking about Reinier's kidnapping?"

"Yes."

"Operation: Eagle's Claw is a genuine project, but I learned of a leak that led Reinier to suspect you were friendly with Star. I've been waiting for a long time for his tangled webs to strangle him."

Conor frowned. "I'd like a name."

"Priestley O'Reilly."

When his lips pursed, Anton asked, "You know who that is?"

"The wife of a Five Pointer who was turned by the Sparrows. We were close friends once upon a time."

"Why would she be speaking with the CIA about you?" I questioned.

"I don't think she was speaking to Reinier in his capacity of CIA director."

Fury flashed inside me as Conor winced then blew out a breath. "This is a mess."

"Tangled webs often are," Anton intoned. "However, we are coming to the end of this web. You will be relieved to know that Jorgmundgander is now defunct.

"Upon my arrival in the States, I will be interceding with the FBI to make sure Reinier, Smythe, and Foundry become statistical anomalies. And Interpol will make their moves and rid the world of the trash heap that are the Sparrows. The only thing left to do is to help their victims return home."

The words settled so deeply inside of me that they became a part of my DNA.

I stared at him a little blankly, unable to accept the truth of what he was saying yet feeling a relief so virulent that I sagged in my seat, knowing he was right.

This was dusk for the Sparrows but the dawn of a new day for Conor and me.

What was that saying?

The sun shines on the righteous?

For the first time, I felt as if that could apply to me too.

PART 2

Nobody noticed until all my pain turned into anger
and now I'm the bad guy.
   - Unknown

26

TEXT CHAT

Lodestar: You won't fucking believe it.

Dead To Me: Give me a hint.

Lodestar: I shot him in the ass.

Dead To Me: Ah, Muñoz. I shot him in the head. Does that mean I beat you?

Lodestar: Technicalities. That piece of shit was a goddamn Sparrow.

Lodestar: Now I'm just pissed that you had the kill shot and not me.

Dead To Me: How do you know he was?

Lodestar: He has the app on his phone. The one they use to communicate.

Dead To Me: Jesus. You're lucky Temper warned me. God knows what their endgame was.

Lodestar: Nah, he's always been a shit shot. He missed me the first time in Dubrovnik. And don't talk to me about Temper and her treacherous ass.

Dead To Me: Hmm.

Lodestar: What are you doing?

Dead To Me: Stuffing hair into a small space.

Lodestar: I don't want to know.

Dead To Me: Conor told me you're down.

Lodestar: Jesus, are you two talking about me behind my back?

Dead To Me: Nah. I told him to give you hot chocolate in the morning instead of coffee. I think he thought I'd have another top tip on all things Star.

Lodestar: What did you tell him?

Dead To Me: To get creative in the sack.

Lodestar: LOL.

Dead To Me: Did it work?

Lodestar: Conor's always creative.

Dead To Me: Lucky bitch. Those pilots were a dead end.

Lodestar: Shame.

Dead To Me: More interested in me than in each other. *pouts*

Lodestar: *rolls eyes*

Lodestar: Go back to your stuffing, Cin.

Dead To Me: I will.

Lodestar: And don't kill anyone I wouldn't.

Dead To Me: ;)

27

CONOR

Conor O'Donnelly

"WHERE ARE YOU TAKING ME?"

When she laughed, relief filled me.

It was genuine this time. Happy. Free from the sorrow of grief that had plagued her since our return flight to the US.

Not even vetting Anton's list of officers for the Interpol department or getting some tossed off the team had cheered her up.

I'd known I had to do something when hot chocolate hadn't worked and neither had us cracking Muñoz's phone with Maverick's worm and shooting over the first few clusters of file drops to the new Interpol department.

'Doing something' had involved asking Dead To Me for advice. I'd made several mental notes not to do so in the future.

Still, I'd come up with the idea of another date night and had been happy when she'd grown excited by the notion and had offered to organize it.

"You know full well where we're heading," she teased.

"I mean, I can read the road signs like anyone but I'm not sure why we're heading to the New York Saturns' stadium."

"Because there's a game tonight."

"Why didn't we bring Katina?"

"It's a school night."

"So?"

"So, this is for us. Before I bring her…" She hesitated. Swallowed. "…*home* this weekend."

I could forgive her anything when she called my apartment home.

Grinning at her, I said, "That looked painful to say."

"It wasn't," she denied with a snort. "Just, I haven't had a home for a long time and it's only home because you're in it."

I whistled under my breath. "Jesus, are you trying to lead up to telling me you broke my rig or something?"

This time, she outright laughed as she shoved my knee with her hand. "No, dumbass. I'm being nice."

"It's weird. Stop it."

Her lips were still curved wide though. "I'm going to drown you in mush tonight."

"Why?"

"Because it's date night with a *purpose*. Don't ask what purpose because I won't tell you until we get there."

"Intriguing."

"Don't lie. I'm always intriguing."

"I figured it was all that time as a spy."

"Sure. Makes a person shifty and, apparently, you like shifty."

"You know it. Did you get Kat enrolled at Shay's school? Or is she having a vacation before the next semester starts?"

"Got her enrolled, yup. Straight into the frying pan for her. She'll love it. They have a gymnastics team and everything."

"Feel like making a bet?"

"On what?"

"The likelihood of her being a cheerleader."

She groaned.

"You're only groaning because you know I'm right." I chuckled as she pulled up at a stop light and shot me a pleading glance.

"What are we placing as stakes? Cash?"

I scoffed. "Nothing so boring."

"As disturbed as I am at the prospect of her being a cheerleader, I'm interested."

"Thought you might be. I bet you an orange that it'll happen this year."

"An orange?!"

"You'd prefer an apple?" At her disgusted look, I laughed harder. "A banana?"

"I was hoping for six months of you writing code for me or me promising not to hack your code for a year."

"Well, if you'd prefer those to be the stakes…"

"You jackass! You totally walked me into that."

I grinned. "Guilty. Okay, so six months of writing code and my code's safe for a year."

"Yeah, but I bet that she gets the offer and turns it down."

I held out my hand to accept the bet. As she shook it, cars honked their horns behind us as the red light flickered to green.

She took her sweet time about setting off, mostly because she was an ornery PITA, but that was probably why I loved her as much as I fucking did. Ornery was interesting, and Star had fascinated me for years.

As we pulled into the parking lot of the stadium, I let her take the lead because she knew where we were heading.

My brows lifted once or twice at the amount of security we had to bypass, and they were nearly touching my hairline by the time we were in the owner's box.

This would have made sense if we were heading to a Knicks' game, a sport I actually enjoyed, but we weren't so I knew she was up to something.

A half-hour before kick-off, the owner himself showed up.

"Jordan Maloney," he introduced, a wide snake oil salesman's grin on his chops as he held out a hand for us to shake.

"Conor O'Donnelly," I greeted, watching Star as he leaned in to air kiss her.

When she reacted like a normal person and air-kissed him in return, my curiosity was piqued even more.

Star was… *behaving.*

That was more fascinating than anything else that was going to happen in the stadium tonight.

"Your better half told me you're interested in investing in the club," Maloney announced after a couple minutes of small talk.

When I felt the nudge of her elbow in my side, I smiled at him. "Soccer's always…" *Bored the ever-loving shit out of me.* "… intrigued me."

"That's great to hear. It's such an underrated sport in the US, and I've never understood why. But, because it is *so* underrated, I think that's why we have a brilliant fan culture. The Saturns, in particular, have the Saturns' Explorers, as well as countless other supporter groups—"

I shot Star a wide-eyed look.

Did he think dedicated fan groups would make me buy a damn soccer club?

As much as I loathed the sport, even I knew the Saturns were the city's dirty secret.

"It's why our games sell out, too," he enthused, seeming to disregard the half-empty stands. "And that, in turn, leads to the highest-grossing concession stands in the MLS."

Star coughed, but I thought that was more about hiding her smirk than anything else.

Not that Maloney seemed to care. He was into his spiel and going a hundred miles an hour without a care in the world.

"Our boxes are very popular as well—"

Maloney continued discussing his boring-ass team for the remaining time until the game kicked off.

Because I had zero interest in the match, I flicked a glance around the owner's box. The glass was reflective—I knew that because it cut out some of the sun from outside—but rays still shone through the panes, lighting Star, rather fancifully I thought, in a ring of light that made the reds in her hair dance like they were a living flame.

The comfortable leather easy chairs were staggered a few feet apart, and in between, there were small tables that had been prestocked with a couple different types of beers. The snacks held more of my attention than the game, but I did notice the Arizona Panteras scored three goals in the first twenty minutes.

For all that Maloney had tried to tell me they were sold out, I had to admit the meager crowd was active, cheering and booing in the right places.

Unfortunately, the team never actually gave them the gift of a goal. They tried to push them over the boulder, but cheers didn't make up for a piece-of-shit team.

As the Panteras continued whooping the crap out of the Saturns throughout the first half, Maloney disappeared five minutes before half-time with the excuse of using the bathroom, and when he didn't return for the second half and we were left alone, I had to figure he'd escaped from sheer embarrassment.

Thank fuck.

"You bring me to this torture," I complained, holding out a hand for her, "then the least you can do is make it worth my while."

She snorted but levered herself out of her seat and plunked her ass on my lap.

"We've rarely discussed sports, but I'm pretty sure you know I loathe soccer," I whispered as I hooked my arm around her waist and drew her deeper into my hold. "Ya know, seeing as I never, ever, ever talk about it."

"I do, but you mentioned match-fixing at the mall the other day and it inspired me."

I thought back to the mall but had no memories of a conversation about match-fixing. "I did?"

"Yup. You were tired though. That's probably why you don't remember."

I clicked my fingers. "I was talking about how it was more difficult than it should have been to get into the Canadian gun registry. Okay, so what about match-fixing?"

"You haven't thought about it since we got back from the UK?"

"In all honesty, cleaning up the evidence we have on the Sparrows so it doesn't reflect badly on either of us has taken precedence over

Five Points' business. I thought that was what you were working on too."

She tweaked my chin. "It takes a woman—I multitasked. Helps that I know the shit Bear sent us through and through. I knew what to remove and where to go for it in my half. In between, I did some scouring."

"For?"

"The Saturns."

"Your research brought you to a middle-of-the-road soccer team?" I sputtered. "One where the proudest thing the owner had to say about his team was that the stadium has the same groundskeeper as the Yankees…"

She snickered. "That was a particular low point, for sure.

"So, I admit that I let my imagination run away with me. But you also said that your ma made you think about match-fixing and I reasoned that you're searching for ways to legitimize the O'Donnelly fortune." She looked at me from the corner of her devious eye. "You should speak with Anton about your plans too. Davidson told me he was practically a shoo-in for the Oval Office because of him."

My brow furrowed. "It probably helped that his father was a senator."

She shrugged. "The United Brotherhood has their fingers in many pies. Maybe it's not enough to be a legacy politician in the upcoming years. The Sparrows have changed the political landscape. Trust in the household names is at an all-time low—"

"That was mostly facilitated by you and spreading the news of their foot fetishes to the masses."

"They should practice what they preach. Still blows my mind that some states teach 'abstinence only' as sex-ed." Her grin was unapologetic. "Anyway, MLS is easier pickings in my opinion. Not as popular as the other sports in the US, but still impressive enough that if the O'Donnellys tied themselves to a winning brand and brought home the CONCACAF Champions League title, the association would be priceless."

Intrigued by her thought process, I asked, "So why the Saturns? That guy is an asswipe."

She patted my chest. "Maloney's got money problems. I'll show you the file I made on him yesterday. He's ripe for the picking. Plus, I've got something to blackmail him with if you're interested."

For a couple moments, all I could do was study her. Entranced, I slipped my hand around her nape and tipped her chin so that I was in a better position to press my lips to hers. Her pleased hum made my lips tingle, and once I savored her, I pulled back to ask, "Blackmail and business is your idea of a date night?"

She smiled and I had to taste it. I kissed her again, hunger and need starting to entwine with the appreciation I felt for her uniqueness.

Slipping my tongue between her lips, I dove into her, sliding my hands through her hair to keep her there, *right there*, where I could better hold her.

When she moaned, I nipped at her bottom lip, pulling back before things got too out of hand.

She surprised me by cupping my wrist, sliding her fingers around it, and adjusting my hold on her so that she could angle it where and how she wanted.

When she rested it against her lower abdomen, I groaned and let my fingers trickle downwards, moving slowly in case her intent changed.

It didn't.

I rubbed the tips along the inseam of her pants, grunting when her head angled back onto my shoulder and she tore her mouth from mine to swallow down air.

"Touch me, Conor. Please."

"Will Maloney return—"

"No. I arranged for him to go. He was supposed to stay until half-time though. The Saturns did us a favor and had him leaving earlier with how badly they're doing."

Arching a brow at her, I asked, "You prepared for this?"

Her hold on my wrist tightened and she rocked her hips against my fingers. "Yes."

I gave her the pressure she needed, just as I trailed my tongue along the line of her throat.

As she quivered, I rasped, "Tell me what you want, Star."

"Y-You," she breathed, releasing a keening sound that shot straight to my dick.

"Here? In public?"

"I-I want to do something crazy, Conor."

"Something crazy?" Her eyes were wild as she dropped her hands to the fly of her pants. As she opened them, fingers fumbling, I repeated, "Something crazy?"

"Spontaneous. Me and you."

Spontaneous when she'd planned it?

I knew she was going somewhere with this and as it seemed important to her, I didn't push the issue because I thought she was buzzing on her nerves.

When she wriggled her pants down over her upper thighs, she slipped her legs forward so her bare ass was on my lap.

My fingers dug into the gently muscled flesh. "There could be cameras."

"Brought that toy of yours along. It's in my purse."

Relief sank into me, though I should have known she'd have brought a purse for a reason—she wasn't exactly the type to worry about shit like that.

"The one that fucks with cameras and radio signals?"

The second she nodded, I slipped my fingers around her upper thigh to touch her pussy.

She was wet.

That alone had my brows lifting.

When I slipped a single digit along her cleft, she released that keening sound again and I growled in her ear. "I didn't know you were into exhibitionism."

"I'm not," she rasped, parting her legs slightly so I had better access to her.

As I rubbed her clit, I demanded, "Then why are you so into this?"

"Because I'm taking *me* back."

With all her wriggling, my dick was hard. Hell, it usually was when she was close by. But something in her words niggled at me.

"Talk to me, Star," I rumbled, trailing my nose over hers. "Where's your mind at?"

"Maybe I *am* into public sex," she whispered.

I arched a brow at her. "Doubtful." Then I moved my hand back to rest on her thigh. "Please, Star. Talk to me."

She clenched her teeth, swiped her head to the side, then muttered, "He brought me to a soccer match in Düsseldorf. When I found out about it, I was excited. I've always enjoyed soccer. I should have known he'd find a way to ruin that for me too."

Hans.

"What happened?" I demanded.

"It was a box like this." She trailed her hand over the mahogany armrest. "When we walked in, I knew that we weren't here to watch the game. Most of the women were naked; a couple guys were too. The owners were the only ones dressed. The second we were through the door, he had me strip." Her jaw worked. "It was the first time he put a collar on me and fucking used it."

Angry for her, I rasped, "I'm sorry."

"Not your fault." She blinked up at me. "I want to replace those bad memories with good ones, Conor." Her tongue peeped out as she swiped it along her lips. "In Dubrovnik, I owned what happened between us. I had so many bad oral experiences but I took back ownership and I enjoyed it. It was me and you. No one else. Does that make sense?"

"I don't think it has to make sense so long as it makes you feel better." I pressed a kiss to the end of her nose. "We'll do whatever you need to do, Star, understood? Just… warn me?"

"I'll try to. Thank you, Conor."

"Oh, baby, you don't have to thank me for that."

"I-I want you, Conor. That's so new for me. *Wanting*. But I do. I want you. I want your cock. Inside me. Filling me full. Please," she whispered, and I closed my eyes, enjoying those words spilling from *her* lips.

"God, you've no idea how fucking long I've waited to hear you say that."

She moaned then whimpered when I stopped touching her clit so that I could release my dick from the cage of my jeans.

I grabbed her hips and toppled her forward. Her legs were trapped by her pants, and her hands gripped the sides of the chair as she hovered in place as I helped seat her on my dick.

It took a few tries to get it right, but her already tight pussy, tighter than ever thanks to how her pants locked her legs together, clutched at me as she sank, inch by torturous inch, until I was acting as her chair.

She sat there, prim and proper from the waist up as the Saturns finally scored a goal that had the meager audience cheering while, from below the waist, she was sin incarnate.

With my hands on her ass and hers still on the armrests, we did a better workout than at the gym as we got her working her way down my dick.

"So fucking wet for me, Star. Is that who this is for? All for me?"

"Always," she moaned. "I'm yours, Conor. I'm yours."

"My favorite words in the whole of the English language," I growled, moving one hand around us and drifting my fingers along her core from her drenched slit up to her clit. A sharp, startled cry escaped her as I demanded, "Tell me again who this pussy belongs to."

"You! You, Conor. Always you," she breathed, the words frantic as her cunt clutched at me, pulsing in time to the strumming of my fingertips.

After she released a soft sob, I knew she was close. It was the quickest and easiest route to orgasm we'd ever experienced together when, with the shadows of her past haunting us here, I figured it'd take a lot longer.

Because I needed to reclaim this moment, to brand it with *us*, I made sure to give her clit extra attention.

Even as she raced toward her orgasm, I didn't let up. Just carried on teasing the nub with one hand, and with the other, I tilted her chin so that our mouths were connected.

I didn't fuck her there, just forged a link that went deeper than sex. That went deeper than healing scars.

It was us.

Pure.

Simple.

Us.

She groaned into my mouth, small whimpers drifting from her as she ground into me, her hips rocking from side to side as she worked herself on me.

Cock aching like a fucker, I kept the focus on her, dipping my fingers down to the beautiful mess we made together and coating the tips with the juices I found there.

"Feel how fucking wet for me you are, Star," I rumbled against her mouth.

A mewl escaped her.

"So fucking wet, and so fucking tight, and so fucking perfect. This cunt was made for me, do you know that? No place else I want to be than right here. Even if it means being in the goddamn Saturns' stadium."

Her groan combined with a chuckle as her breath hitched when my slick fingers found her clit once more.

Now slippery, it let me move faster and with little friction. Her thrusting slowed and her frame tensed.

"I-I'm going to—"

"Good. Give it to me, baby. Give it to me. I want it. I want you. All of you. Don't stop," I rasped, scissoring my fingers down so that I was touching more of her sex.

She cried out, head arching back as her orgasm hit. This time, she locked up, her pussy clamping down around me so that I had no alternative but to be tugged along with her.

She sagged into me, her pussy milking me even as her body thrummed with her satisfaction. Heart pounding as she pulled every ounce of cum from me, I wrapped my arms around her and held her, uncaring that gravity would be shortly working against us, just needing to maintain this close contact.

As I nuzzled my face in her throat, I heard the gentle soughs of air puffing from her lips and whispered, "I'll be whatever you need, Star. You know that, don't you?"

She rubbed her forehead against my chin, showering me with a tenderness I didn't think she'd have been capable of before. "I need to be that for you too."

I turned her face to the side so that I could anoint her lips with a kiss, then, against her mouth, I whispered, "Baby, you do that by breathing," and she melted into me.

We spent the rest of the game like that.

The Saturns lost 5-1, and somehow, the O'Donnellys had found their next project, and Star and I had uncovered the next phase in our relationship.

Not bad for our second date.

28

CONOR

Conor O'Donnelly

"CONOR!"

Though I winced at the high pitch, I smiled as Katina came bursting through the doors to our office, screeching until she found her way to my desk, arms outstretched so when she barreled into me, she could immediately wrap me up in a hug.

That was when I heard a snarl from the hall.

"Goddamn cats!"

Katina grinned at me before she planted a sticky kiss on my cheek. "Star hates them now but they're so cute, Conor. Thank you, thank you, thank you! I know you convinced her for me—"

"Ow! You bast—"

Katina's grin turned into a laugh. "They keep scratching her."

"Why?"

"She called them Ren and Stimpy."

I chuckled. "So they're offended?"

"I think so. I don't know who they are—"

"Gross cartoon characters from when we grew up."

"I didn't know they had cartoons when you guys were young."

"Katina, exactly how old do you think we are?" I grumbled, pulling back at her in offense.

"Don't ask her that question or you're begging to be insulted," Star growled from the doorway, one kitten dangling from her shirt by its claws and the other hissing and swiping at her with every step she took. "Katina, they're your kittens. Why am I the one carrying them?"

"Seems like they're doing most of the heavy lifting."

She glowered at me. "Shut up. This is your fault."

Katina skipped away from me and started cooing at her pets. Within a couple moments, she had them purring in her arms, both tucked together against her chest as they relaxed.

Star gaped at her. "Why didn't you do that earlier when Stimpy tried to bite me?"

"Her name isn't Stimpy. It's Suzette."

"Stimpy's a better name," was Star's bland retort as she rubbed her arm where the kitten had scratched her by the look of things.

"What's the other cat's name?"

Star grimaced. "Wait for it…"

"Crepe."

"As in… Crepe Suzette?"

"Lily served it for dessert and it was so yummy. They're the color of it too! Yellow and cream."

"I agree that Ren and Stimpy are much better names."

Star sniffed. "I have superlative skills at picking names."

"You do," I concurred. To Katina, I shook my head. "You don't."

She huffed. "They're my kittens."

"And you can call them Crepe and Suzette and we'll call them Ren and Stimpy because after a few weeks of changing that litter box, I can guaran-damn-tee that's going to be a chore you 'accidentally' forget to do," Star grumbled, but she sounded more resigned than annoyed.

Still, Katina didn't seem nervous at being in what was her new home. That was a bonus that came from the cats breaking the ice when she put them down on the floor and they immediately took off toward the door.

As she ran toward them, Star called out, "Make sure they use the couch in the living room as a scratching post!"

"Hey!" I argued.

"That couch is miserably uncomfortable. It's like Captain America's uniform—overpadded and too good to be true."

"I thought Katina was supposed to be the queen of insults."

"She is but she came by it honestly—*me*."

Grinning, I asked, "How did it go in West Orange?"

"It went."

"That bad?"

"No, just..." She cleared her throat. "I should have mentioned it before but they want us to come to a party."

"Okay. We can do that. A family one?"

"It'll probably be a house party."

"Thank God. Their last BBQ ended with Savvie and Aidan getting kidnapped."

"Yeah, well, they'll be tucked up safe and sound in Hell's Kitchen so that won't happen again."

"You know what I mean."

She rolled her eyes. "I do."

"When is it?"

"Couple weeks' time. After everything's calmed down."

"How's Alessa taking the move?"

"Think she's ready for a break. She's only a young kid herself and she has to deal with Maverick's illness. Throw in Kat and two kittens and she needs a vacation."

"She knows she's welcome to visit us anytime, right?"

Her smile was sheepish. "You're too good, you know that?"

"Makes up for how naughty you are."

A gleam appeared in her eyes. "You like me when I'm naughty."

"Bet your sweet ass—"

"STAR! Suzette peed on the rug!"

She growled under her breath. "I showed you the litter box! And since when do cats pee on rugs? That's for dogs!"

When she stormed off after her, both of their shouts breaking up the still silence of only moments before, a dopey smile quirked along my lips as I rocked back in my chair.

I wasn't meant for silence.

I'd been the middle child in a large family—chaos was in my bloodstream.

That didn't stop me from wincing when a loud crash sounded in the living room and Kat yelled, "Sorry, Conor!"

Despite the fact I'd curated everything in my apartment, I had to smile at the sounds of life both women brought to it.

God, it was good to have them home.

29

STAR

Star Sullivan

TROY HELD out a hand for Anton to shake. "Pleasure to meet you, sir."

My lips curved at her unusually polite tone. "Troy was in my unit with me, Anton. Same as Dead To Me. Before everything went to shit."

"For both of us," Troy retorted.

"Oh, I know," I countered easily, tumbling back onto the couch so I was eye-level with Lyra who was hiding at Troy's side. "Are you going to meet, Anton, Lyra?" I asked, tone kind. "He's been waiting a long time to meet you."

Troy patted her head. "She's nervous."

"I am also nervous, Lyra." Anton heaved a heavy breath as he sank onto the couch beside me.

A couch that had taken D, Troy, and me to edge into place yesterday when we'd helped move her in.

As he settled on the seat, his suit jacket rode up, revealing a large scar on his wrist that appeared to run vertically along his forearm.

Suicide?

Perhaps.

The thick rope of pink flesh was old and slightly faded, but still raised.

Like always, there was the faintest delay before Lyra carefully enunciated, "Why are you nervous?"

"Because I think if I say anything to upset you, Troy will make me regret the day I was born."

Lyra peeped out from behind Troy's fatigues. "When were you born?"

"A very long time ago."

"I can count to five hundred."

"Are you that old, Anton?"

He shot me a dour look. "No, Star. I'm not five hundred. Not yet."

My lips twitched. "He's ancient, but not that ancient, Lyra. You don't have to be frightened of him. He'll crumble to dust if he scares you."

"Charming, Star," was Anton's droll retort. Then, he reached into his pocket. "I knew your father, Lyra."

"You did?" she asked slowly.

"His name was Aleks."

Lyra moved her face away from Troy's pants entirely and her lips formed the name before she repeated it aloud. "Aleks."

"Do you remember him?"

She hid behind Troy again, leaving her to answer, "She was only a toddler when he passed away."

Anton held out a picture. I studied it from the corner of my eye, taken aback to see Aleks and a much younger version of my mom, though she was definitely the older sibling. It was only then that I realized a bizarre truth.

"When was Mom born?"

Anton frowned at me, clearly startled by the question. "1957."

My mouth rounded as I learned about yet another of her lies—her age. Slow to process that, I didn't realize the conversation had changed course until Troy growled, "I don't need your charity."

Cutting her a look, I asked, "What's wrong?"

Just as Lyra tugged on Troy's pants, querulously asking, "Mom?"

"Nothing, sweetheart," she said to my cousin. To me, she bit off, "Your grandfather says this apartment is for me and Lyra to live in full-time."

I arched a brow at this news but shrugged. "I live in this building with Kat and Conor."

"Then I will have one of two guest rooms in which to stay when I visit New York, *da*?" was Anton's placid retort.

"Don't push your luck," I said with a sniff.

"I don't need your charity," Troy repeated.

"You lost your sanctuary because of the Sparrows because you saved my granddaughter for the *second* time in her short life. If you think that doesn't deserve gratitude—"

"She saved her three times."

Anton frowned. "What do you mean?"

"Lyra was injured in the car accident that…" My gaze clashed with his. He nodded his understanding of precisely which car accident I was talking about without needing to say it in front of the traumatized little girl. "…and she needed medical care."

"The only way I can show you the depth of my gratitude, Troy, is to help you now. This is not charity. This is thanks."

"I did it for neither. You can thank me by letting me raise her the way I have been doing—"

"Have I not promised you this already?"

"You have," Troy groused.

"And are you not in need of somewhere to live?"

"I suppose," was her glum retort. "My bees are in more need than we are."

"Rest assured, they're safe. I asked a friend who dabbles in honey to care for them until you can make more permanent arrangements."

She appeared unconvinced. "Dabbles in honey?"

"Harrow's Bees."

Recognition flared to life in her expression. "They're good people."

"Indeed," he drawled. "Anyway, would you not like to be close to Star?"

She sniffed. "Not particularly." When I rolled my eyes and Anton hid a laugh, she grumbled, "I guess we could stay here until I make other arrangements."

"That would please me greatly." To Lyra, Anton asked, "Would you like to stay close to Star too?"

She gave him a timid nod and peeked at me, her shyness returning.

"Then it's settled," I said, a note of finality to my words. "Lyra's going to Velcro herself to me so that she can stay close at all times."

When she giggled, Anton's face lit up with a smile. Once he inquired after the book she had tucked against her chest and Lyra, in her slow and cautious manner, explained what it was about, Troy and I shared a glance—just like I'd told her, I'd kept my promise.

Lyra was, and always would be, *her* kid.

30

CONOR
YOU - TWO FEET

Conor O'Donnelly

"I'M TELLING you this will work," I drawled as I read the message Star had just sent me.

Star: I want to kill Stimpy.

Me: She'll never forgive you if you do.

Me: Leave the damn cat alone. At least it's cute.

Star: Lucifer was supposed to be beautiful.

Me: You can't compare a cat to Satan.

Star: Sure I can. Cats are spawns of Satan.

Star: You ever heard anything about the Sparrows harvesting organs?

Me: Where the hell did that topic come from?

Star: I just remembered something Reinier told me.

Me: Jesus. We never actually talked about what you two discussed. Maybe we should?

Star: No. He said nothing important.

Me: That's a lie. But no. I've never heard anything about organ harvesting. Though I've read it's becoming a trafficker's idea of a smart business choice. Body parts have a high street value for people in need of organ donations.

Star: Creepy.

Me: Agreed. Reinier said they were into that?

Star: He said he wished he'd harvested my organs instead of putting me into the sex slave market.

"Are you listening?"

I arched a brow at my eldest brother. "Of course."

Me: And you genuinely don't think we need to talk about what you discussed?

Star: Not really. He was lying. I know he was.

Me: How?

Star: He talked about a secret property he owned in Florida where he had a bunch of blackmail material on clients. I've already scoured his tax returns and the bank accounts he used to filter his dirty money through. He doesn't have a property in Florida.

Me: Do I want to know how you got access to them lol?

Star: Probably not.

Me: Could it be in his wife's name? A child?

> Star: Maybe. But I already checked. It doesn't matter. Was just something that came to me when Ren and Stimpy double-teamed me and scratched the shit out of my arm.

> Me: Doesn't sound like nothing to me.

> Star: I'm just being open.

> Me: Ahh, teamwork makes the dream work?

> Star: Sharing (mostly) is caring.

> Me: Lol. I can look when I get back?

> Star: If you want. It isn't necessary though.

> Me: If you say so. Speak later xo

> Star: Course <3

"Where did you come up with this idea again?"

> Star: Oh, before I forget. You - Two Feet

"Conor, dammit. Are you listening?"

I blinked at Aidan. "It was something Ma said combined with Liam's current problems."

"Not so current seeing as the Rabid Wolves are off licking their wounds," Brennan muttered darkly, glowering at my phone like he had a personal vendetta against it.

"What the fuck is going on with you?" I demanded, all thoughts of Star, Ren, Stimpy, and Reinier fading as irritation with my brother took up the full blast of my attention span. "I'm well-adapted to your grouchy ass but Jesus Christ, you're more miserable than usual."

He pinned me with a disapproving glare. "I'm not miserable. I'm cautious."

"More like overcautious," Eoghan grumbled behind a Knicks' travel mug I wasn't totally convinced didn't contain whiskey.

Finn, who'd been doodling on the notepad in front of him, mused, "Ever thought he misses your… our Da."

"Still having trouble with those possessive pronouns, Finn?"

"Yes, Conor. It's a lifetime's habit I'm breaking and it's not easy."

"Well, Bren?" Aidan peppered.

"Well, what?"

"Do you miss Da?"

Brennan's nostrils flared but he bowed his head. "What's to miss?"

"Fair point," Declan chimed in. "I don't miss getting my ass kicked or being accused of trying to make my son gay because I took him to the ballet."

Finn's brows lifted. "He gave you shit for that?"

Aidan snorted. "Of course he did. It's Da. You know, it's a wonder we're not all homophobic asswipes."

"More like a miracle," Brennan mumbled, but he hitched a shoulder. "It's weird to miss someone you hated more than you liked."

"Emotions *are* weird," I said carefully, knowing that 'feelings' and Brennan weren't a comfortable combination. Seeing as he was the bruiser of the family, it was only fitting that he'd find it hard to deal with losing Da. "We're coming out of a toxic relationship where the only escape was death. How was that *not* supposed to fuck us up?"

Brennan grunted. "Ma's finding it easy enough."

"Are you mad at her for finding some peace with Paddy?" I questioned.

"It's early days, wouldn't you say?"

"How early is too early? They ain't getting any younger, Bren," Declan stated.

"He has a point," Eoghan drawled.

Brennan scrubbed a hand over his face. "Do you guys miss him?"

A silence settled over the dinner table. Because Aoife's kitchen was constantly packed with experimental versions of her recipes, we'd taken to meeting in Finn's house—whether he approved or not.

"You know when you pull a hamstring?" Finn asked as he doodled. "And the pain is there for goddamn ages and you want the ache to go away but it won't and you know it'll take however long it takes to heal?"

"And then, one day, it's not there, and you forget about the ache until you remember it's not there anymore?" I added, nodding.

"Yeah, it's like that," was Finn's gruff retort.

"Like a toothache that's gone after years of misery, but you still miss the tooth because hell, those fuckers don't grow back," Aidan rumbled.

Declan scratched his chin. "I don't miss toothaches or hamstring aches."

"That's because he treated you like shit," I murmured. "He never had a kind word for you, never gave you any approval. You can't kick a dog and expect it, at some point, to like you."

Declan reached for the creamer as he dosed his coffee. "I guess."

"I don't miss being fined."

Aidan chuckled. "I can keep that arrangement going if you want?"

My lips twisted. "Nah. I'm good."

"Thought you might be."

Brennan cleared his throat. "Da blamed me for what happened to Ma for so long that every time he looked at me, I knew he was thinking about *that*. About my fuckup. It's strange not having to deal with that residual guilt."

Because that was about as open as Brennan got, the five of us stayed quiet. I figured we were waiting to see if he had more to say. Then, when the silence grew weird, I broke it because Brennan and Aidan had been around Da's toxic bullshit longer than any of us and getting them to talk about this stuff was next to impossible.

"You know you had no reason to feel guilty, don't you?"

"I let Ma down."

"You didn't." Aidan cracked his knuckles. "You were a boy. Just because he treated us like men doesn't change the years on the clock."

"He blamed *you* when he was blaming himself. He was the reason she got taken. The Aryans had beef with him and he fucked up by not being prepared for every eventuality.

"Ma should never have been kidnapped. That's why we've got our wives locked and loaded with more guards than the president. Especially after what happened with Aidan and Savannah, which only went down anyway because we trusted those asswipes," Eoghan rumbled. Then, to Brennan, he continued, "There's nothing wrong with missing the old bastard. It's like Stockholm syndrome. There ain't an instant cure."

Brennan chuckled. "Stockholm syndrome. Never thought of it that way."

Eoghan took a sip of his drink. "I think Kid's idea is a great one."

None of us were surprised by the change of subject, but I still corrected, "It was Ma's idea. Star perpetuated it."

"Yeah, but you put in the work. Does it have to be soccer?"

"Start small. You know it's the league with the least interest in the States, *but* it can have a global impact with the international tournaments."

"What's the aim, Conor?" Aidan tapped his pen against the table. "Match-fixing?"

I shrugged. "I figure we have several routes we can take. Match-fixing, *eventually*. But we need to be associated with wins.

"I think we take the Saturns, for example, a team that regularly underperforms, and make our mark by sending them soaring to the top of the league.

"It's the next phase of 'Shay for the Oval Office.'"

"You know, if he knew he was a phase, we'd never get him out of his room because of his fat head."

"Don't lie, Dec. You never get him out of his room anyway," Aidan retorted. "I remember that age. He doesn't have a girlfriend, does he?"

"No."

"So his left fist is—"

Declan groaned. "Do we have to talk about this?"

Aidan grinned. "Like you don't know he's doing it."

"Aela's glad she's not the housekeeper. Let's put it that way." He smiled sheepishly. "I told her he can't knock up a sock. Shay overheard and now, he won't maintain eye contact with either of us."

I chuckled. "Ah, the joys of youth."

"Youth, my ass. It's ten times harder now than it was for us. At least the only thing Da cared about was us becoming a Five Pointer. You should see the crap you need to do to get into Harvard. I don't think even you'd cope, Kid."

"I foresee a wager," Eoghan drawled.

I rubbed my hands together. "Can't be that difficult being a mature student, can it?"

Aidan chuckled. "You're about to find out. But before you become Harvard's next MVP, can we get on with this conversation, please? What can we hold over Maloney's head to make the purchase?"

"Nothing. We just buy it." At their blank looks, I snickered. "Your faces. Honestly, did you think we could go into this by blackmailing him? Legitimacy has to start somewhere."

Brennan frowned. "That's going to be expensive—"

"And a presidential election campaign isn't?"

He conceded that with a grunt.

"I'm telling you this is the way forward. We formulate a Super PAC with O'Grady subsidiaries as major cash cows for the election campaign, funds that come from legitimate income streams like Ellie's Bakery, and then we get the O'Donnellys linked with sports."

"I've started checking out locations for new branches of the bakery," Finn said. "Aoife's being difficult, but it's her baby so she can be."

I hummed. "So long as we start the expansion soon, she can be as difficult as she wants." To my younger brother, I informed, "Declan, you'd have to be the one who approaches Maloney."

"Me?!" He groaned. "I hate fucking soccer."

"We all do," Brennan pointed out.

"I hate it more than most. Can't we buy out a ballet company or something?"

"So we can look more elite than our bank balances allow?" I arched a brow at him. "Sports unite, Dec. Ballet doesn't."

"He's right, Dec," Finn stated.

"He is," Brennan agreed.

When Aidan and Eoghan nodded, he grumbled, "Fine. But if I have to suffer, one of you can too. I'm not doing this shit alone."

"Need us to hold your hand, Dec?" Eoghan mocked. "I'll suffer with you. I don't hate it as much as you fuckers."

"I hate the sport, but I'll come with. Wouldn't be a bad thing to get friendly with Maloney. His fiancée's father owns Puritan Oats. Ya know, what our nation was founded on."

Brennan whistled. "Those and Cornflakes."

"Okay, so while the youngest are keeping out of trouble," Aidan mocked, "we focus on…?"

"We need to make strategic purchases of players. Nothing major at first, a slow build. But we need to make an impact over the next two seasons. Splash our names about. While that's happening, Aidan, I've got a connection I need you to... encourage."

"Who?"

"Star's grandfather. Anton Kuznetsov."

"The head of the United Brotherhood?" Eoghan queried.

"More secret society bullshit," Brennan complained.

"Not bullshit," I corrected. "More like *useful*. Have you seen what that Interpol department he built has accomplished since its inauguration?"

I tossed a newspaper at him, one whose headline declared:

Interpol confirms two dozen arrests of previously unknown
*   Sparrow agents via DGSI, Scotland Yard, and Guardia*
*   Civil.*

He sniffed as he read it, but I ignored him to continue, "Plus, he's a kingmaker. We want to think that we are, but we're not where the legitimate side of things comes into play. *He* is.

"Aidan, you get on his side, and he can lay the path for Shay."

"Does Shay know what we're doing for him?" Eoghan demanded. "You were joking earlier, but he could knock up a girl and ruin everything we're working toward. Is he on board? Shouldn't we talk to him before we go further down this path?

"The soccer route is smart. Match-fixing and gambling—they're all great revenue streams. But getting involved with the Union is heavy shit. We don't want to owe them dick if we're going to fall through—"

"He's right. We'll come early on Saturday, Finn. We'll talk to him before we eat," Aidan instructed.

"That'll work wonders for our digestion," Declan muttered. "I'm not even sure if I want this for him. It's a lot of pressure."

"It's what he wanted."

"When I was his age, I wanted to be a fucking artist," Declan sniped at Aidan. "We change our minds more than we change our underpants as teenagers."

"Shay's less like you and more like me," I remarked. "I knew what I wanted when I was thirteen and I went for it."

"What did you want?" Brennan asked.

"I wanted to know everything."

Aidan frowned. "You mean that literally, don't you?"

I hitched a shoulder. "I don't like closed doors." People whispered behind them. "I wanted to open as many as I could and I have. To this day, I work on the same tasks. Nothing's changed. I don't think it will with Shay, either. Politics is as much of a vocation as being a doctor is."

"Less of a God complex with a politician than a doctor though," Aidan drawled.

Finn grunted. "True that."

"We'll talk with Shay on Saturday, Conor, and once we learn if he's ready for what we've got planned, then I'll talk to Kuznetsov."

"He's in the city until next week," I confirmed. "Star's with him now."

"Is that why she isn't here?" Finn queried.

My lips twitched. "Probably."

"She shouldn't be here anyway," Brennan grouched.

"Star's not like the other women," Finn remarked. "Her insight would—"

"Come at too high a price," Brennan snapped. "We can't trust her yet."

I slapped my hand against the table. "Yes, we fucking can. What's she got to do to prove herself to you, Brennan?"

"She's not an O'Donnelly."

"That's all it takes? A wedding ring?"

"It'd help if the Feds wanted her to testify against you," he retorted.

My brow furrowed. "This is about her ratting us out?"

"Conor undoubtedly has as much shit on her as she has on him, Brennan," was Eoghan's lazy retort. There was definitely whiskey in his coffee mug because his words were starting to slur. "If she betrays him, I figure he can take care of himself."

"She wouldn't betray me. We're in this for the long haul." I stabbed a finger in the air at him. "I get that you're mourning and that you're so emotionally repressed because Da was a shit father that you can't cope with your grief, but don't take any of this out on Star.

"You want Cammie. I want Star. You married Cammie. I put a ring on Star's finger and *we* will decide when we're ready to marry. It'll have nothing to do with pressure from the Feds and most certainly not from you! Understood?"

"Understood, but I don't want her at these meetings. Whether you like it or not, my concerns are valid."

I got to my feet. "Star is the one who's helped me work out a solid plan to bring the Saturns around—"

"Star likes soccer?"

I barely flicked a glance at Aidan. "She spent a few years in London. Says she got hooked on it then. Whatever, she's as invested in this as I am. If she has something to bring to the table, then I'm not going to pay her back for her help by telling her she can't come.

"Whatever problems you have with her, Brennan, you need to get over them fast. Because if she isn't welcome here, then *I'm* not welcome here."

My words sent a shockwave around the table, but I strode off and allowed them to settle like nuclear fallout because I meant each and every one of them.

It was time Brennan accepted that.

NEW YORK SATURNS PURCHASED BY ACUIG CORP.

REAL-ESTATE MOGUL ACUIG CORP acquires New York Saturns in shock move.

Declan O'Donnelly to be named president of the club.

31

STAR

Star Sullivan

"Vana." I arched a brow at her as she loomed in the doorway, fidgeting with her hands. "Thank you for all the cat shit by the way. I didn't even know kittens needed that much crap."

"You're welcome," she mumbled, peering over my shoulder.

I peered over my shoulder too. "What's wrong?"

"Nothing!" she declared brightly. Then, her eyes narrowed. "What the hell are you wearing?"

I looked down at my usual skinny jeans, shitkickers, wife beater, and leather jacket. "Clothes?"

"You need to dress the part."

"What part?"

"The part of Conor O'Donnelly's fiancée."

My nose crinkled. "Will you do it for me? The shopping and…"

Her smile turned devious. "Gladly."

Ah, crap. That smile meant I was getting new bras too. Fuck, and I'd just gotten this one how I liked it.

As if she knew what I was thinking, she asked, "Bra size?"

I grumbled out my measurements. On her front stoop no less.

"Come in."

"You were holding me hostage before you got me to agree to that?"

"*You* made the suggestion. Not me."

Bullshit. "What's going on?" I countered, knowing her too well to trust her on word alone.

"Nothing!" She peered around me once again and saw Kat with a Switch in her hand, headphones tucked firmly on her head as she played a game. "Why's she wearing headphones?"

I shrugged. "She likes the game noises. I hate them so she wears them."

Vana made a 'huh' sound then mumbled, "Okay, I guess it doesn't matter if you drop an F-bomb then."

"Why would I?" I demanded, on high alert now.

"Because it's time you met my best friend. She'll help me with your atrocious wardrobe."

I ignored that. "Oh. I already know Jennifer Valentini."

"How do you know her?"

"Duh. I know everyone."

"You're such a bullshitter," she sniped as she finally dragged me into her apartment.

"I mean, I try." I peered around the open-plan living area. "This is massive. Why do you need more space?"

"I don't. Aidan doesn't like sharing. Plus, I think it's a dude thing. God forbid Conor has more square feet than him."

My lips twitched. "Seriously?"

"I think so. I mean, he didn't come out and say it was a dick-measuring contest but I read between the lines. Plus..." She gulped. "I think it's his response to me maybe being pregnant."

"Maybe? It's a kind of yes or no situation, Sav."

"I did some tests."

I smiled. "How many?"

"Six."

"Were they all positive?"

"No. Three were positive and three were negative."

I had to laugh. "Only you would break the laws of false positives, Vana. When are you going to the doctor?"

"I'm not. I don't want to know. If I know, I'll worry, and if I worry, I'll think about how unsuitable I am to be a mom."

"You're right. You're pretty unsuitable."

"Hey!"

Chuckling, I grabbed her arm and hauled her into a hug. "I'm joking. I'm the most unsuitable mom in the world and Katina's alive, isn't she? You don't have to be technically good at being a mom to be good technically at being a mom."

"Remind me not to come to you again for support," she groused, but her arms were like tentacles around me as she pretty much strangled me in her hug. Her goddamn cat was just as bad, winding itself around my feet so I was surrounded.

"Have you told anyone else?"

"No," she whispered. "I don't dare. They might get their hopes up and I couldn't deal with disappointing them."

"Surprised you told Aidan."

"He was the one who asked me why I hadn't gotten my period."

"You didn't figure that out yourself?"

"I don't need to. He keeps better tabs on me than any app—"

I held up a hand. "What you two get up to is on you."

Though she pouted, I could see the fragile combination of fear, anxiety, and hope in her gaze. Whether she wanted to admit it to herself or not, she was excited.

"Want me to come to the doctor with you?"

She released a shaky breath. "I forgot how good you are in a crisis."

"This is hardly a crisis, Sav. This is a nice thing. Right?" I patted her arm.

Vana grabbed my hand and squeezed my fingers. "You're not going to run off again, are you?"

My lips quirked. "If I did, I think Conor would come after me so I wouldn't be away for long."

She sighed. "You're right. He's the same kind of whacko as you."

It amused me that she found that reassuring.

"Anyway, you going to introduce me to Jennifer or what?"

"She's in the bedroom. She's got a kid too. Saverina—" She paused to preen, "—drinks a lot."

"Named after you? Christ, did they want her to be a Diva?"

Vana huffed. "Like you're not a diva too."

"You're a capitalized Diva. I'm not." I snagged Kat by the shoulder and steered her inside the living room with me. As the door closed, I asked, "Why are you so nervous now that you've told me about maybe being pregnant?"

"I'm not nervous," she said nervously, hands still toying with one another as she glanced at her watch.

"You so are. What have you done?" I demanded, directing Kat over to a table.

When she took a seat, she scanned her surroundings, shrugged, then said, "Hi, Aunt Savvie. Oh, Star, I forgot to tell you. I gave her that laptop you wanted me to."

My lips twitched as I shrugged off her words. "Better late than never told. Thanks, brat."

She hummed and returned to her game. Last night hadn't been good—two nightmares—so I wasn't going to be hard on her about not being sociable.

"She means last year, right? At the Sinners' BBQ?"

I smirked at Vana. "Yeah, she means last year. Unless she's given you another laptop since then?"

"Nah." Savannah blew out a breath but her anxiety was too high for her to pepper me with more questions. Handy, really.

I didn't want her to know that I'd given Conor access to a worm via that laptop I'd smuggled off the Sinners' compound through her.

"What's with you?" I demanded.

"IinvitedPaddyheretoo," she said in a rush.

"Paddy? As in Conor's uncle? Good at clearing up the corpses of Catholic perverts? You invited *him* here?"

"Yeah. That one. He's Jen's biological dad."

Because that wasn't news to me, I hummed. "Did she ask you to arrange this meeting?"

"No."

I groaned. "So why did you?"

"Because they met at our wedding—which you didn't attend, so fuck you—"

"You know I hate weddings."

"—and it was strained and it made me feel sad. Paddy's a granddad now as well. It seemed… mean to exclude—"

"That was none of your business, Savannah," I said with a sigh. "I mean, she knew who her father was and she didn't prompt you to make an introduction."

She bit her lip. "That's why I'm nervous."

"Because you fucked up?"

"Because it seemed like a great idea at the time and now I'm thinking it isn't," she mumbled as she dragged me into the kitchen with her. "Why didn't I keep my nose out of this?"

"You can't help yourself. It's the journalist in you." I huffed. "Want me to pretend that I brought him with me?"

Her eyes lit up. Then immediately dimmed. "I couldn't ask that of you."

"I offered. I got no skin in this game."

"I want her to like you."

The doorbell buzzed.

Savannah released a high, fretful noise that was totally unlike her. I bit the bullet, taking the decision out of her hands by electing to be the responsible adult in this situation.

"Leave it with me," I drawled, heading into the living room. I moved over to Kat and tousled her hair just because I knew it'd piss her off.

She growled under her breath. "You spent ages making it look like this."

"I made it, I can break it," I teased.

Her glower would have curdled milk. "I bet Conor can do French braids better than you."

"What makes you think that? The guy's never been around little girls in his life. He's from a family of boys, remember?"

"He gave me his cell number so I'm going to ask him if he can do it."

I grinned at how proud she sounded. "Do you know how many people have that number?"

"He told me that only his family had it." Her smile turned shy. "That means I'm his family now, doesn't it?"

"It does." I tugged on her ponytail. "Ask him about the braids in person. Always corner people face-to-face when you want them to do something for you that they won't like. Life lesson there, kiddo.

"Plus, we want him to do them for when you start taking part in competitions. He can be the one who handles that. It'll stop you caterwauling at me when the braid drops out when you're doing a jump."

Her gaze flickered as if she were making a mental note of my life lesson, then the door buzzed again. "Who's that?"

"Conor's godfather."

"More family!"

"You've got it coming out of your ears now, haven't you?"

Her smile turned un-Katina-ly shy. "*We* do, don't we?"

Her correction had me squeezing her shoulder. "We do." Ducking down to bump my lips to the crown of her head, I mumbled, "I'm glad you're happy about it, sweetheart."

"I just want them to like me."

"Why wouldn't they?"

"Lyra doesn't."

The doorbell rang for the third time. Impatient, much?

"One minute!" I called out. To her, I said, "She doesn't like that you talk so much, but that doesn't mean she doesn't like *you*. It means talking is hard for her. It means she's shy. It means that it's not as easy for her to formulate words as it is for you.

"Her challenges are not your challenges," I reminded her softly.

Though she bit her lip, she repeated, "Her challenges are not my challenges. It's okay, Star. You can get the door."

"You sure?"

"Yeah. I'm sure."

Another squeeze to her shoulder was my parting farewell, but her sweaty fingers caught my hand, though, and she patted it.

"Thank you, Star."

I smirked at her. "For being sick?"

Her nose crinkled. "You can't call yourself that."

"Sure, I can. I'm the sickest thing in New York."

Her laughter warmed my heart but it was only compounded when she said, "Sometimes, you can be."

Chucking her under the chin, I headed over to the door, feeling a little better after last night's nightmares, and tugged it open to reveal the washed-up version of Aidan Sr.

"Padraig," I greeted smoothly.

He frowned. "Did I get the wrong apartment?"

"You're not on the top floor," I said blandly. "This is Aidan and Savannah's apartment. You're here by my invitation though."

"By your invitation? Savannah—"

"Savannah asked you for me," I lied.

"She did? Why?"

I hitched a shoulder. "Wanted to get to know you. You're close to Conor, aren't you?"

"Getting there," he agreed. "We were closer before I left."

"A nearly three-decade-long absence doesn't make for enduring friendships," I pointed out.

"Is this going to be about you getting in my face?"

"About abandoning him? Nah." My lips curved, though, as I thought about the shit he was going to get dealt from Jennifer Valentini.

I stepped back so he could enter the apartment, and he glanced around the space then asked, "Where's Savannah?"

"In the kitchen."

"Savvie! I swear she just said her first word!" Jennifer shrieked from the other side of the apartment.

Savannah came skidding out of the kitchen. "No way! Was it 'Savvie?'"

"No. Just because you've been training her to say that didn't mean she was going to say it," Jennifer retorted, but she was laughing as she swept out of the hall into the open-plan space.

Her happy gaze darted around the room, then it faded as she saw the guy standing at my side.

She clutched at the baby in her arms who was propped against a burgeoning stomach that told me Luciu Valentini, her husband, had a breeding kink, then like a wall had come down between her and the rest of us, she tipped up her chin. "I have to go and tell Luc. He'll be pissed that he missed her first word."

"You don't have to leave," Savannah warbled.

"Did you arrange this?" she hissed at the woman who was practically my sister.

"He's here for me," I said calmly.

"For you?" Jennifer frowned. "Who are you?"

"She's Conor's girlfriend, Jen," Savannah rasped, her hands pleating together.

God, didn't she know that was a dead giveaway?

I understood she wanted to mend fences here, but you didn't get that by burning bridges.

Huffing, I muttered, "I'm his fiancée, actually."

Jennifer's brows lifted. "He proposed?"

I waggled my hand. "Got a ring and everything." Swaggering deeper into the room, I settled my ass on the couch and was immediately joined by the cat. "Come on, Paddy." I flicked the other woman a look. "Tell me something about Conor that'll embarrass him later. Something that only a godfather would know."

Paddy's chuckle was wary, but he peered between the three women in the room and, seeming to sense that I was his best chance of survival, edged toward me and planted himself at my side.

I knew the whole story about how Jennifer was Paddy's kid with some two-buck whore, and when he'd done his disappearing act, he'd left his daughter in a lurch.

Savannah claimed Paddy didn't know about Jennifer, but who the fuck knew with *that* generation of O'Donnellys?

I wasn't sure why, but Kat had removed her headphones and was studying us with interest as Paddy reasoned, "I don't go around embarrassing the boys unless they deserve it."

That made me snort. "Katina, you won't be so lucky. I'll tell your boyfriends about the embarrassing shit you do."

"Hey! That's not fair."

I winked at her. "More reason to behave like an angel at all times."

"Where's the fun in that?"

The twinkle in her eyes made me glad she still needed adult supervision.

Behind us, I heard Savannah and Jennifer whispering furiously at each other. I didn't know if they were angry words, but when Jennifer didn't storm out, I figured that was phase one of Savannah's plan underway.

"I won't use whatever you tell me as ammunition in a fight," I vowed.

Paddy's brows rose. "Ammunition in a fight? Jesus, poor Kid. He's got himself a handful with you."

I showed him my teeth. "I'm sure that aligns with what you've heard about me."

"True, it does." He cleared his throat, and his chest rattled—he was a smoker. "Okay, well, Conor wasn't the brother with the most embarrassing stories."

Interest pricked, I asked, "Which was?"

"Aidan."

That was all he had to say for Savannah to swoop in. "Oh?"

Paddy flashed another glance between us, then, cautiously, he stared at his daughter. Her focus was entirely on her baby, but she was there. That had to be enough.

"We knew Aidan was into girls because they kept popping up in the apartment they were living in back then. His da was proud, of course. Especially as Declan was into art—"

My scowl made an instant appearance. "What is it with this family and assuming that art can trigger homosexuality?" To Kat, I stated, "Kat, that's utter bull so don't you let anyone tell you otherwise. Sexuality is simple for some and complicated for others. The only thing I *ever* want from you is to be yourself. Whether you wanna kiss Harry or Harriet, I don't care. Understood?"

In response, she just snorted.

"She's right, Katina," Savannah assured her. "The older O'Donnellys have antiquated beliefs on this subject."

"I already know I like boys."

To be fair, I'd known too. What, with her crushes. But that didn't mean she wasn't free to be with whomever the fuck she wanted. I'd fought in wars to defend my people's rights. That was the whole goddamn point of freedom.

"The magazines say my boy is bisexual."

"And you got a problem with that?" I demanded.

"Why is he in magazines?" Kat inquired.

"He's a hockey player."

Her eyes rounded. "He's famous?" She cut Savannah a look. "More famous than Camden?"

"Camden who?" Paddy queried.

"You don't know who Camden is?!" she shrieked.

Savannah chuckled. "He's a singer, Paddy."

"Oh. I never heard of him. Liam's popular."

"You don't know him well?"

Even Kat quieted at Jennifer's question.

Maybe she'd overheard more of our conversations than I'd anticipated, but none of us spoke as Paddy rumbled, "Been blessed with two kids but was never blessed with the sense to be a good father. Not sure if it's something that's a case of 'better late than never' but…"

When his words waned, Jennifer didn't rush in, just mumbled, "You shouldn't have children unless you know you can bring them into the world with love." She pressed a kiss to her daughter's forehead.

"That's a very wise sentiment," Paddy rasped, twisting to study her over his shoulder. "I wish I'd been so wise when I was your age."

"I do too," she agreed.

He cleared his throat. "That's a beautiful baby you've got there."

"Her name's Saverina."

"I-I heard you say that she's spoken her first word?"

Jennifer's smile was more open this time, warmer. "She did."

"What was it?" I asked when no one else seemed brave enough to broach the topic.

The smile turned lopsided as she cut her sperm donor a quick look before staring down at the floor. "Dada."

Savannah broke the ice by covering Saverina in kisses, which the baby received with happy giggles. I just took in Padraig's pink cheeks, wondered how deep his regret was at that moment, and vowed to myself that I'd never, ever let Katina down by disappearing on her.

She'd forgiven me because I'd somehow managed to raise her to have faith in me, but if I did it again, that fragile balance would be forever ruptured.

Nothing was more important than family. That was a core value Conor and I shared, even if it was only now that I registered how much of a priority it was to me too.

32

CONOR
COVER ME IN SUNSHINE - P!NK, WILLOW SAGE HART

Conor O'Donnelly

"MAVERICK!" Katina screeched.

She seemed to do things at three volume levels—shouting, screeching, and shrieking. Sometimes, she broke shit up by mumbling, but that was only before bed and after waking up.

What surprised me was that I didn't mind it. Had it made me jump at first? Sure. I was a bachelor who lived alone. Having a kid racing around that made more noise than a jumbo jet was definitely a change of pace. But after ten days of living together, I was adapting.

I was also acclimating to my sofa being used as a scratching post, my decorative tree doubling up as a coat stand, and the second bathroom down the hall smelling of weird perfume thanks to the litter boxes we stored there.

Maverick winced at the screech, but when Katina approached him, she slowed, and her hug was gentle, as if she thought he was fragile. My experiences with the man said he was anything but, and when I neared, I waited for him to stick out his hand first.

We shook on it, mostly because Lodestar had threatened me on the ride over, and he grimaced. "I'm sorry about—"

"The concussion?" I prompted.

His grimace deepened. "Yeah. That. But this little shit had freaked me out."

Katina oohed. "Wait until I tell Alessa you swore in front of me."

She raced off, giggling, maneuvering through the crowds that were *her* people—she was a Sinners' brat. For the moment. I'd make her a Fecker before she was done with childhood.

Maverick grunted at her departure. "Thanks for bringing Star home."

"I wasn't about to accept any other alternative."

"She needs someone like you. Smart enough to keep her on her toes, quick enough to chase after her when she lets herself get caught up in other people's problems." Maverick lifted his can of Bud Lite to his mouth. The sight was incongruous, what with the ink and the leather cut, but I figured he probably wasn't even supposed to be drinking that with all the meds he was on. "Saw that ring on her finger. You wifing her?"

"Was I supposed to ask the Sinners for permission first?" I drawled, tone smooth as I looked onto the gardens where a couple guys were smoking.

Maverick's mouth quirked into a smirk. "You could ask, and we'd have said no. That wouldn't have stopped her though."

"Not much does."

"Sure as fuck not the law, and definitely no Sinners' bylaws either." He pulled a face. "Crazy not having her around, can't deny it. And the peace is fucking weird now that Kat's gone too. I'm used to tripping over her shit wherever I go. Didn't think I'd miss it, miss *them*, but I do."

"I was relieved when Alessa didn't stop Star from moving out of Jersey," I admitted.

"She knows who Kat's mom is. She also knows that I'd rip you both a new one if you tried to tear Kat and her apart and didn't allow her to visit."

I lifted my own can of beer to my mouth. "Does this mean I'm part of the family if you're only offering to ream me and not kill me?"

"It does," he groused.

"We have plenty of space in our apartment," I offered. "You can come and stay whenever you like."

"Same goes here. Lily won't mind. This place is a secondary clubhouse anyway."

'This place' was a billionaire's mansion.

"Does that mean the Sinners have gone bougie?"

Maverick snorted as he tipped his beer at me. "I think we have."

I grinned at him then, when I saw a bunch of women clustered around Star, asked, "They giving her shit?"

"Yup," he said placidly. "They're our Old Ladies. She cut and run without warning them and they're not happy about it."

"I'm glad she's got people who care about her."

"She thinks she doesn't, but she does."

We were definitely on the same page about *that*.

Maverick chuckled. "Just wait until Rex and the rest of the council get a hold of her."

"They're pissed at her too?"

"Wicked pissed." His grin was lightning-fast and malevolent with it. "I'm surprised she came today, to be honest. Shit's still fresh."

"She mentioned something about ripping off a Band-Aid quickly…"

"Yeah, she never let nerves hold her back. I'd be impressed if I weren't pissed at her myself." He cut me a look I didn't spot because I was watching Kat do some cartwheels next to a table loaded with—

Well, it was loaded with drinks *before*.

The table tipped as she kicked it with her toes. Somehow, she landed neatly on her feet, but that didn't mean the room survived unscathed.

"They're only cans. We learned at her first barbecue not to have glass bottles out when she's around," Maverick assured me as the women stopped haranguing Star and clucked around Kat, checking on her, while some other bikers, Sin being the only one I recognized, started gathering the cans and restocking them on the table they'd just laid out again.

"Bet you don't miss her knocking everything over," I joked.

He smirked his agreement. "Anyway, you don't want to stick around with me. I'll have to go in for a fucking nap soon."

I frowned. "You're feeling ill?"

"No. But sleep keeps the migraines at bay, and it makes me feel fucking ancient to say it but it'll make tomorrow less miserable."

"I'm okay with sticking around until you need to go in?" I asked hesitantly, knowing that Star had loved this man at one time and that she still cared for him as a friend.

"Yeah?" He shot me a sheepish grin. "I thought I'd give you an out. Alessa told me to play nice and I figured Star did the same thing…"

"Oh, she did," I retorted, "but that doesn't mean we don't have a lot in common."

Maverick shrugged. "Guess we do, at that." He held out his can. When I stared at it, he made a show of tapping his against mine. "You can call me Maverick."

"I'm Conor."

"Pleased to meet you, Conor."

"Pleased to meet you too, Maverick."

He chuckled. "There, we appeased the women."

"For the moment."

"True dat." He arched a brow at me. "Is what I've been hearing about you and the NSA real or bullshit?"

I pulled a face. "Why does she keep telling people about that?"

"It's impressive. Very niche."

"Niche isn't good. I'd have preferred the fucking Feds. My da was close friends with the director."

"That's why it's impressive. The NSA are a bunch of robots."

Thinking about Riggs made me grimace. "I can't argue with that." I cleared my throat. "Star's given me access to your worm."

Maverick snorted. "She likes that bit of kit."

"Can't blame her. It's fucking effective."

His lips twitched. "Not totally useless."

"Useless?" I choked. "It's the most destructive malware I've come across in years!"

Maverick went inside after ninety or so minutes of me praising his beautiful piece of coding and sharing the various ways in which I'd used it.

Afterward, I was left hovering around the edges of Lily Lancaster's living room. I didn't mind, not when Kat was enjoying herself and Star was having fun too—arguing with Rex's Old Lady Rachel about only the fuck knew what.

As I stood there, looking over the house that had been bought and paid for with Sparrow blood money and ancestral funds from Lily's mother's family who was an American blue blood, I had to chuckle to myself at how full circle things had become.

The Sinners had only cropped up on the Five Points' radar when Mary Catherine, my cousin and Sin's half-sister, had fled her dipshit father's notions of an arranged marriage with an older Pointer.

When her father had declared the Sinners had 'kidnapped' his daughter, Da had waded into the fray and had promised to bring her back.

That was when he'd learned she was married to a brother already—Digger.

They both lived in Ohio now, but they'd been the start of the ties that bound the Irish Mob to Jersey's most notorious MC.

It seemed fitting that Star and I would tie all that shit together with a fancy bow.

"Star says only crazy people talk to themselves."

I blinked down at Kat. "She talks to herself all the time."

"She says she *is* crazy and that the best kinds of folk are." *That sounded like her variation of logic.* She entwined a strand of hair around her finger. "Conor?"

"Yeah?"

"Would you braid my hair, please?"

Though I stared at the rat's nest on her head, I only answered, "I've never done anything like that before, Kat."

"Would you learn how to do it?"

Ah, Jesus Christ. "Now?"

"Star's fell out already. One little cartwheel and it was in my face." She leaned into me. "I don't want to hurt her feelings though."

"Since when?" I teased, knowing that bickering was their love language.

She giggled, and that sound warmed up a part of my heart that I didn't even know was stone cold until she came along.

Inwardly wincing, I curved my arm around her shoulders. "I'll learn but not to—"

"Yay! I'll go and borrow Alessa's hairbrush!"

Before I could finish the 'tonight' part of that sentence, I heaved a sigh as she raced off to steal a hairbrush from her sister.

Sitting down on one of the benches in the hallway, I waited there, picking up my cell to find a 'how to' on YouTube.

As I watched, I inadvertently overheard a conversation between Star and Rachel, the MC's First Lady.

"...I think it would be a great idea, Star."

"Not yet. It's too soon."

"How is it too soon? Charities don't just pop into existence overnight," Rachel retorted. "It takes time and planning to organize this kind of foundation."

"I don't want to cause extra work for you. Not now that you've got Sommer."

"I've got Sommer, yes, and having a baby is tough with my job, but Rex has stepped up like crazy and I have two assistants and I can always hire more if need be.

"This is important to all of us, Star, not just you. But I wanted you to be on board. Hell, on *the* board. If anyone should be, it's you, Alessa, and Amara."

Star choked, "Amara? You want her on a charity board?"

"Why not? Sure, she's deranged, but have you seen her offload all the animals that follow Quin around? She's the perfect kind of person to ask for money—"

"From fancy socialites?"

"Sure. She'll get cash off them and they'll leave the party full of salad leaves and with a cat or dog—whichever she has a surplus of hanging around the clubhouse."

Kat appeared in front of me like one of the moles in a whack-a-mole game. I jolted in surprise then ducked out of the way when the hairbrush she was brandishing in her hand almost collided with my nose.

Grabbing it before she could inadvertently grace me with a second concussion on Sinners' territory, I asked, "You okay with kneeling on the ground?"

She hitched a shoulder but had dropped to the carpeted floor before she finished saying, "Sure!"

With one ear on Katina's chatter about how many cats Amara had now, and then Rachel and Star's discussion about the charity, my focus switching between them *and* the YouTube video, I was amazed when, after thirty minutes, there was something resembling a braid on her head.

Some of the pleats were a little loose so, knowing partly what I was supposed to do now, I untucked the braid and set to doing a better job than with my first attempt.

"What are they talking about?"

With the thin brush between my teeth, and the odd silver stick that acted as a handle dangling out of my mouth, I mumbled, "Rachel wants Star to help her with a charity."

"What kind of charity?"

"To help people like her."

"Why does she need help?"

My lips twitched. "She doesn't now. But she did."

"Star's awesome."

"She is."

"How awesome?"

"Very awesome."

"Do you like us living with you?"

"I do."

"Why?"

"You ask a lot of questions."

"Star told you that already."

"She didn't tell me. I think I inferred—"

"Why do you like us living with you?"

Pondering the question, I hummed as I tucked the pleats tighter on her head, making sure the line followed her parting. "Because you bring the apartment to life."

She giggled, and because it was a full-body giggle, she wriggled on her knees. "You're weird, Conor."

"I thought Star told you only the best people were weird."

"Nah, she said *crazy*."

"Who's taking my name in vain?"

With my hands full of thick, blonde hair, I groused, "*Now* you decide to come over."

Star peered at us both. "She was right."

"Who was?"

"I was," Kat crowed. "I said you'd be able to do it."

"Do… braiding?"

"Yup. I just knew you could."

"Why?"

"I don't know. I just did."

"Why?" I teased. "I can ask questions too, you know?"

She harrumphed, then, with more earnestness than I expected, she murmured, "I think I knew you'd care enough to learn."

Star's mouth rounded and the hand she placed on my shoulder was shaky. The kiss she pressed to my head was shakier. Then, she whispered in my ear, "*Thank you.*"

Taken aback by both my girls' responses, I just cleared my throat as I twisted the hair tie around the last inch of hair that I couldn't braid.

"There," I declared. "That should stay—"

Back to her giggling self, Kat exploded into movement. Two cartwheels later, the French braid still in place, she crowed louder than before, "Told you so, Star!"

"I guess she did," was Star's tremulous retort as she plunked herself on my lap and clutched at me like I'd disappear if she didn't.

I was going nowhere, but I wasn't about to argue with the hold she had on me.

33

STAR

Star Sullivan

THERE'S KNOWING you love someone, and then there's feeling it vibrate through your whole fucking nervous system as if you're a tuning fork that's just been struck.

It rattled along my nerve endings like a bolt of electricity that needed to escape and the only outlet was him—so I wrapped my arms around him after I settled on his lap and held him tight.

This overwhelming surge of love was partly to do with finding him braiding my kid's hair at an MC's house party, a look of utter concentration on his face as he tried to get it right.

Then, there was a part that revolved around her confidence in him, which had nearly fucking broken me.

Then, there was that conversation I'd left behind with Rachel—my past, so ugly, head-butting the beautiful present I existed in.

Conor pressed his chin to the top of my head and held me. Just held me. No words were needed.

Amid the music from the party, three different types depending on where you were standing, the clatter around several tables holding various potluck dishes, and the chatter and laughter from over a hundred people, I eventually whispered, "If this had happened last year, I'd never have allowed myself to attend."

"What do you mean?"

"Too much to do. Too many things to juggle. It's been a long time since I've done something…" I chuckled as I selected the word. "…frivolous."

"Dubrovnik wasn't frivolous?"

"The pizza and the ice cream, sure, but the shooting in between, not so much." Now, Muñoz being a fucking Sparrow made our first date night even *more* memorable.

"What about the soccer game?"

"Again, partly frivolous." I hid a smile. "I like partly frivolous. But this is totally frivolous."

"All work and no play makes Star a dull girl."

"We already established you're the dull one, Con."

He snickered as he pressed his lips to my forehead. Together, we stared out onto the living room where the Sinners were congregated, some eating, others drinking, most of them talking and if not talking, then arguing.

"I-I think," I whispered, "these guys might have been my family and I didn't realize it."

"What gave it away?" he whispered back.

"They missed me."

"Of course they did."

"No, I didn't think they would." I released a breath. "I didn't even think Savannah would."

"You were wrong about that too, weren't you?"

"I was and I'm glad I was wrong. But don't tell Kat that."

His chuckle came from the heart. "I won't share your dirty secrets with anyone."

"Enough of the filthy secrets and the filthy lies, hmm?"

"Only the filthy truth for us," he agreed with a gentle squeeze of his arms.

"Do you want to do something crazy?"

"Something crazier than a house party on a Wednesday?"

"They're an MC. They don't work regular schedules."

"Apparently."

"Don't be a product of a capitalist society, Conor." I tutted.

"God forbid," he mocked. "Okay, something crazy. Hit me with it."

"Have you met Indy?"

"Yeah." He quieted. "Ah. You want to get inked?"

I swallowed. "I'm wearing your brand."

He reached around us and rubbed his fingers over the cameo on my hand. "You are. You want me to wear yours?"

Tilting my head back against his shoulder, I whispered, "Property of Star."

He chuckled. "Where do you want it?"

My nose crinkled. "I'd say your ass cheek but then Indy would have to see it and your tush is mine."

"Where then?"

"Somewhere your brothers won't see it if you work out together."

"I don't care if they take a jab at me—"

"*I* care. I don't want anyone to mock you for it."

"If they don't see it, how will they know who I belong to?" he drawled, but his tone was dark, deep. Like hot silk that poured over my skin, making goosebumps pop up and sending whispers of sensation coursing through my nervous system.

"Where, then?" I choked out.

"Ribs."

"I'd like that." I pressed my mouth to his throat. "You know what this means, don't you?"

"What?"

"That I'll be yours forever."

"Oh, sweetheart," he breathed. "You already were that anyway."

34

STAR

Star Sullivan

AS CONOR GOT HIS INK, I found myself being dragged outside by Quin and was shortly surrounded by the Sinners' council. Well, *sans* Rex and Maverick.

That meant I had Nyx, the VP, Link, the Road Captain, Sin, the Enforcer, Steel, the Secretary, Cruz, the newly-patched Reaper, as well as Hawk and Quin who were hovering around because the latter worked at his sister's ink studio.

It was a lot of leather-wearing man meat to be surrounded by, but that didn't stop me from scowling up at them and demanding, "Why did you leave the party?"

Nyx cracked his knuckles. "What the fuck were you thinking just taking off like that?"

"Who are you? My dad?"

"If we *had* been, you'd probably have been better behaved," Link joked, sliding his arm around my shoulder as he tugged me into his side.

I peered at him. "I've already spoken to you since I got back so why are you a part of the delegation?"

"Just in case you need backup."

Oh. That was sweet. But—

"I don't need backup."

He winked. "They're wicked pissed."

Folding his arms across his chest, Steel growled, "Star, you can't just take off like that—"

I sniffed at him. "I know."

He paused halfway through what appeared to be the beginning of a diatribe then muttered, "Excuse me?"

"You heard me. I know I can't just take off like that. But I did. I went, I saw, I got captured, then I conquered. I won't be doing it again."

Nyx's gaze, always dour, grumpy, and semi-insane, sharpened upon me. "We ride together or not at all."

"I'm not a Sinner," I denied, even though his statement made me feel… weird.

"You are by proxy."

My brow furrowed. "Then you should have patched me in."

"You lived with the fucking Road Captain, treated the clubhouse like it was your home, and sniped at our Prez without getting your tongue cut out—what more of a memo could we have given you?"

"When you put it like that…"

"Yeah, I'm putting it like that," Nyx snapped. "What happened? Maverick's told us some shit but he claims there's another goddamn secret society out there. But they're good cops where the Sparrows are bad cops?"

I grimaced. "That's one way of describing them."

"And your grandfather is the head, right?" Cruz queried.

"Yeah."

"What happened in Russia?"

"Tried to kill him."

Link chuckled. "Because he was your grandpa or the head of the United Brotherhood?"

"The latter. I only found out the former when I met him."

"With a view to a kill." Hawk whistled. "You're more entertaining than a Bond movie."

The guys, apart from Nyx of course, laughed.

Steel scratched his jaw. "You didn't kill him though?"

"No. But his guards held me captive until Conor showed up."

"Don't talk to me about that fucker." Nyx grunted. "Now I find out you've gotten with a Five fucking Pointer!"

"This is getting weird," I complained. "I don't need to ask permission for dick."

"Literally," Link teased, cackling until I elbowed him in the side to shut him up.

"Look, I know I shouldn't have cut out how I did and I won't do it again. But if you want a pinkie promise outta me, then you can screw off," I declared with a sneer. "I'm pretty sure you didn't ask permission to brand any of your women. Why the hell would I ask you if I could date a Five Pointer?"

"That ring on your finger says you're doing more than dating him," Sin drawled. "And I know the O'Donnellys, don't forget." His mom— a shitty one at that—was related to them and was married to a high-ranking Pointer. "They don't stick rings on fingers if they don't mean it and now he's getting ink? Are you branding each other?"

Link chuckled. "You picked up on Sinners' traditions, Star, for someone who claims she ain't a Sinner." When I just glowered at him, his brow furrowed. "You became family, Star. Surely, as big as that brain in your head is, you figured that out?"

"I mean, I... No?" Uneasily, I fiddled with my engagement ring. "I wasn't invited here. I-I stormed my way in and usually stuck my nose where it wasn't wanted."

"True. Then you fucking left. Without a word to anyone but your kid." Nyx scowled at me. "Who does that?"

"Me, apparently."

"What's going on now? With the Sparrows, I mean?" Cruz inquired. "We've all seen the headlines. Figured you'd have clued us in by now."

Ouch. The guilt trip was real.

Grimacing, I muttered, "I should have stopped by and attended a council meeting. It's been busy since I got back."

"Understandable," Sin reasoned. "There's such a thing as a cellphone though? You know, they're this nifty invention that means you can talk across long distances."

My nose crinkled. "You think you're funny."

"I am funny. You're the one who has to eat humble pie."

I huffed. "My grandfather created this Interpol department that's geared in its entirety to decimating the Sparrows. Conor and I figured out how the Sparrows communicate with one another, and from there, we've found evidence that annihilates key people from not just the New World Sparrows, but the European and Asian operations too, while also letting us infest the network so we can identify who's who. This is going global. They're all going down."

"Knew they were making so many arrests because of you," Nyx crowed, for the first time sounding anything but pissed off.

"Conor and me." I shoved my hands in my pockets. "He's a good man."

Nyx scoffed, "He's a mobster."

"You're a biker. In the hierarchy of the criminal underworld, I think he outranks you."

"No one outranks me apart from Rex," he rumbled.

I sniffed. "You never thanked me for that pedophile I sent you."

"I didn't deal with him. Priest did."

"He's dead?"

Link cleared his throat. "It went wrong before it went right. He's dead now though."

My mind whirred with the possibilities. "He fucked up? Lost his mettle?"

Sin pulled a face. "Neither. If he lost anything, it was his sanity for a while."

"You're saying he channeled Giulia, then?" I drawled.

Nyx chuckled. "Yeah. My little terrorist." Then, his chuckle faded. "I might be out of the 'hunting' game because of Samael, but I swear to fuck, if that prick hurts you, I'll boil his blood, do you hear me?"

Quin muttered to me, "The big brother act gets fucking old fast, doesn't it?"

I stopped gaping at Nyx to cut his younger brother a look.

Is that what this was?

Studying the men who had most of Jersey under their control, who were all, to a one, studying me with no small amount of disgruntlement, I had to accept that they were mad at me.

For leaving.

Without a word.

For leaving *them*.

Without a word.

"I…"

"I think she's speechless," Cruz rumbled, but his stormy gaze pinned me in place. "If anyone understands, it's me. Sometimes, your family chooses you before you can choose it."

Nyx sniped, "Just don't fucking leave without telling us. You got me? Katina heading off to Manhattan to bring in a goddamn hacker is bad for our rep."

"Yeah," Link said with a wink. "Because that was what mattered."

I blinked a couple times, still feeling like this was an out-of-body experience or something. "I won't leave again without clueing you in," I assured each of them.

"You getting yourself an Old Man?" Steel asked, his voice softer than before.

"I mean, yeah."

"So you do know you're a Sinner," Sin pointed out.

"Do you see me wearing a cut?"

"Like you'd wear one. You might think you're a lone wolf, Star, but you ain't." Nyx grunted. "I got a woman and a kid who are more terrifying than you waiting for me. I have to get back." His eyes narrowed. "Stay safe in New York. You hear me?"

"Yes, Dad," I mocked because it was easier to do that than to freak out about what was happening here.

Quin was right. This *was* a big brother showdown. Even if I wasn't their blood, they'd still drawn me into the circle as if I were…

Link hauled me in for a hug, as did Sin, Steel, and Quin. Cruz dipped his chin at me and so did Hawk. Most of them retreated to their hogs, but a strange thought whispered into my mind.

"Hey," I called out before any of them had the chance to kick their legs over their bikes. When they turned to me, each wearing various expressions of inquiry, I asked, "You heard anything about organ harvesting?"

Nyx's brows lifted. "You in the market for a new heart, Lodestar?"

I flipped him the bird. "I'm being serious."

"Figured as much," Nyx quipped, still smirking. "And no. Never heard much about that kind of shit. Least, not around these parts."

"You think it's tied to the Sparrows?" Cruz demanded, his scowl dark.

I didn't have an answer for that. I wished that I did.

"No," I said slowly.

"Then, why ask?"

Studying Link, I sighed. "I heard a whisper. Nothing more. But I can't let it go."

"If you infested the Sparrows' network, surely there'd be something on there?"

"There would," I agreed with Sin.

"So, what's the problem?"

"Bad feeling."

"Want us to put some feelers out?"

Did I?

Or was it a waste of time and favors? 'Feelers' usually came *quid pro quo.*

"Star?"

With my eyes locked on Nyx, I nodded.

Though his brow furrowed, he agreed, "Consider it done."

That was the cue for them to get on their bikes.

As they raced out of Verona, where Indy's tattoo studio was based, they left a cloud of noise in their wake as they returned to Lily's place. Only Quin stayed back, his gaze where mine was—on the dust storm that settled once they'd gone.

"You ready for your ink?" Quin prompted, his tone kind.

"Yeah." I cleared my throat. "What the hell just happened?"

He snorted. "I told you—the big brother experience. You're lucky that O'Donnelly is an ally. They'd probably tie him to a lamppost and let cougars bite his balls off or something if he weren't."

"I'd kill them if they did," I growled. "Those balls belong to me!"

"That wouldn't deter them," he drawled with a laugh.

"I didn't…" I hesitated. "That was unexpected."

"Really?"

Warily, I nodded.

"Why? The club doesn't need blood to bond. We're all brothers, whether or not we share parents. And guys have been patched in who haven't been around as long as you."

"You calling me a brother, Quin?" I asked, aware my voice was hoarse. Unaware of how badly I needed him to say yes.

He hitched a shoulder then clapped me on mine. "You shouldn't need me to tell you that you are, Star."

With that, he walked into the ink studio, leaving me hovering there until Conor called out:

"Indy, if you stick that in me one more time, I'll hack into your—"

"No hacking!" I called out, storming inside before he could finish his threat. "Definitely no hacking into the Sinners."

They were family now, after all, and family got a free pass.

35

STAR

Star Sullivan

WHEN EOGHAN SLIPPED OFF his flat cap and tossed it on the side, Camille asked, "Inessa bought that for you, didn't she?"

He frowned. "What?"

"The hat. Inessa."

"Yeah?"

"Thought so." She shot him a pleasant smile as she kissed his cheek. "You look brighter."

He glanced at me. "I feel better."

My brows lifted but I said nothing as he wandered out of the kitchen to find his brothers.

I was curious, mostly, as to why his glance and his words had been directed at me.

Deciding to follow him down the hall, I wasn't altogether surprised to note that he was staring at an original Ansel Adams, waiting for me to catch up.

"I'm still assigned to MI6 but it's better than the ticking time bomb of Jorgmundgander. Conor told me I have you to thank for that?"

I stared at the picture too. "Do you let family stay stuck in a living hell if you can think of a way to get them out of it?"

His attention turned to me. "Is that what I am to you? Family?"

"Related to Conor, yes."

"I'm like you, Lodestar."

So, it was gonna be that way. "Whistler, we can switch off."

"You're inactive."

"Not by choice," I retorted.

"I'm active and that's not by choice," he countered.

"We make a pair, don't we?"

He grunted. "A pair of morons. What the fuck were we thinking of? Playing at goddamn life when we were kids. I remember you back then. You were so fucking young."

"And you weren't? You're, what? Four years younger than me? We were babies with weapons. That's how the world works."

"It shouldn't," he snapped. "It shouldn't be this way." Tension rippled through him. "Sorry. I didn't mean to lose my temper."

"You don't have to apologize." I cleared my throat. "You ever need to talk about those times, Eoghan, I'm here. We went through some of those shitshows together."

"Kembesh," he said with a shudder.

"Yeah." I released a breath. "I thought that was going to be the low point of my life. I didn't realize worse was yet to come."

"That happened when…?"

"A year before I was taken." My grimace said it all. "We both watched as a unit was skewered in place and left to fend for themselves then witnessed our government try to cover it up. That's the kind of crazy that sticks with you."

"I have nightmares about it," he admitted.

"Kembesh stars in some of mine too." My gaze tripped over the scene in Yosemite National Park as I cast him a look. "How did you get involved in MI6?"

He hitched a shoulder. "Seemed like my only opportunity to get out. Didn't realize—"

"It'd be more of a trap than ever? No one knew about Jorgmundgander?"

"Hell, I don't think my handler in MI6 knows about those snakes."

Because I could believe that, I hesitantly touched his arm. "Conor worries about you."

"He's right to."

"There are things you can—"

"Take?" His laugh was bitter.

"Might help."

"Did it help you?"

"No," I admitted, returning my focus to the mountain range and the play of contrasting light that made a beautiful panoramic scene so much more evocative. "Doesn't mean drugs won't work for you and if they don't, then maybe we can talk about the shit that keeps us awake at night, hmm?"

Eoghan's jaw worked. "You ever wonder why you?"

"Why me?"

"Why do some people come out of it free and clear and some don't?"

"No one comes out of it free and clear, Eoghan." I patted his arm. "They're just damn good at faking it."

I drifted back to the kitchen, leaving him to look at the picture.

Of anyone under this roof, I was the only person who got where his head was at.

The shit that our government asked of its soldiers was reprehensible, but there was no change there—war, in and of itself, was inhumane.

The subject matter in the kitchen couldn't have been more different than out in the hall.

Much like Inessa, Savannah had found out that she wasn't pregnant and both of them were sitting together, mourning children they didn't think they wanted but ended up wishing they were carrying.

Aoife was doing something indecent to a turkey, Camille was trying not to puke at the sight, and Aela was nursing Cameron—not feeling the need to tuck into a bedroom for privacy as Jennifer had with Saverina.

Upon my entry, most eyes turned to me, but it was Inessa who asked, "How is he?"

"Who?"

Savannah huffed. "Eoghan. Duh. I told Inessa you'd sort him out."

"Did you expect me to beat the crap out of him in Aoife's hallway? I've already taken advantage of her hospitality too much this month—"

Aoife's smile said otherwise. "You're in my good graces since Finn told me you met with my uncle and he came out of it alive."

"That's the first time anyone's ever liked me for not killing someone," I drawled, hitching my hip against the counter as I folded my arms across my chest. "Eoghan isn't a bag of laundry that needs to be sorted into whites and colors, Savannah."

"You talked to him though?" Inessa peppered, seeming quite urgent.

"I did."

"He's been so down since we found out I wasn't pregnant." She bit her lip. "It's strange because we both agree that I'm too young for any of that."

"If wishes were horses, beggars would ride."

Inessa blinked at me. "Eoghan isn't a beggar."

"You couldn't tell with what you've got him wearing. Been binge-watching *Peaky Blinders*, Inessa?" Camille taunted, watching her sister blush with a grin.

"Shut up!" she hissed in Russian.

"But it's so fun to tease you," Camille retorted in their mother tongue.

"And I can totally eavesdrop and let everyone know what you're saying."

Both women gaped at me as I spoke to them in fluent Russian.

"God, you spies never let anyone have *any* fun," Inessa grumbled, making me snort.

Savannah, Aela, and Aoife cast each other confused glances, but I merely shrugged and said, "You're all boring. I'm going to talk to the boys. At least they talk about murder and guns."

"You're such a tomboy," Savannah called out, but I ignored her and wandered over to the room Aoife called Finn's 'man cave.'

If that was a cave, the Neanderthals were more evolved than we thought.

I didn't bother knocking on the door because if I did, they could always toss me out. Instead, I waltzed in and saw them glance at me before they looked away. Even Brennan who I knew had a hard-on for me. And not in the way Conor did, either.

Speaking of, Con held out his hand for me and I moved over to his armchair and took a seat on the armrest. "What are you plotting?"

Brennan grunted under his breath, but Declan kicked him.

I just mocked, "Conor, I think your brother has low blood sugar. Give him some candy."

He snickered and tossed him a Jolly Rancher from the treasure trove of candy that was his pocket, which Brennan batted away with a scowl. Then, he answered, "The types of questions we should ask Shay so it doesn't seem like we're interviewing him for the most important job in the world."

I chuckled. "Most important job in the world? Doesn't meeting my grandfather put that into perspective?"

Conor grimaced. "True. Hell, even that fucker Sheridan Reinier had more power than Davidson."

My moue of distaste didn't go unnoticed by him and he grabbed my hand and pressed his lips to my knuckles.

Surprised by the tender, affectionate act in front of his siblings, I stroked my thumb over the fingers that still held on tight to mine.

"Is he in debate club?" I asked Declan.

"Sure is." He sipped his scotch. "And the little fecker can run rings around me already."

"That's because you weren't made for debating," Aidan retorted. "That's Brennan's specialty."

Brennan gaped at him. "What?"

"It is. You're great at arguing. You listen and let people fall into the belief that you're not interested then you trap them with some insane bullshit that always proves them wrong."

Conor's nod came slowly but it came. "He's right. I never thought of it that way. I'm used to you always keeping quiet because of Da."

My sniff said it all.

"You have a problem?"

"Yeah, I do. I know exactly what you did when you were a teenager, Brennan." His tension flooded the room at my words. "And that's baloney. Your da blaming you like you were a foot soldier for what happened to your mother says more about *him* than you."

He scowled at me. But that was it. No comeback.

Aidan's gaze darted between the pair of us. "You know what happened?"

"Of course I do."

Conor shrugged when he found himself at the center of his brothers' attention. "She'd have found out anyway."

"Not if you didn't tell her," Aidan retorted.

"Since when was it a family secret?"

"Since forever." Declan rolled his eyes.

"I don't see why it's so bad that she knows that dipshit over there is only a dipshit because he's emotionally stunted."

"I think you mean repressed," I corrected.

Conor snorted. "Same difference."

"If we've finished psychoanalyzing me," Brennan growled. "Can we return to the topic at hand?" When everyone stared blankly at him, he prompted, "Shay? And whether he wants to be the goddamn president of the United States before we go to the trouble of handing the position to him on a platter?"

Eoghan grumbled, "Whatever you do, don't phrase it like that. He's too fair for his own good."

"Eoghan's right. He'll want to win the race fair and square," Declan said uneasily.

"There's no reason he can't win on his policies," I tossed down. When they peered at me like I'd started talking in Latin, I sighed. "My grandfather might be a kingmaker, but he believes that he's a righteous man. It's bullshit to me, but it's not to him. He believes in the Brothers. He believes their cause is a noble one."

"You mean he doesn't like to be tarred with the same brush as the Sparrows?"

"Got it in one, Eoghan."

Conor frowned. "She's right."

"Naturally," I purred, earning myself a quick grin from him.

"Anton won't help for the sake of helping," Conor reasoned. "Shay will have to be a good candidate."

"The best," I corrected.

"And if your intentions aren't pure, Aidan, then he won't help us either. Let's face it, he's not going to be around to see Shay's election, but that doesn't mean he can't set things into play for us."

Aidan rested his chin on his fist as he settled his focus on me. "My intentions aren't pure, though."

"Doubt that. It's not every day that an Irish mobster wants his nephew to sit in the Oval Office," I retorted. "Anyone who gets a boner for politics knows that without Congress on his side, a president can't do dick. And that's with legitimate policies, never mind illegitimate ones.

"What power are you going to get by Shay becoming president? Never mind that he can't run until he's thirty-five, so you're all going to be using walkers by that point—"

"We're not that goddamn old," Aidan argued.

"Speak for yourself, Grandpa," Eoghan retorted, making me chuckle and prompting a huff out of Aidan.

He studied me though. Long and hard. Another woman would probably have been nervous, but I just arched a brow at him and stared right back.

"Is this a staring contest anyone can join?" Declan inserted.

Aidan's voice was a croak as he admitted, "I want to right old wrongs."

"What kind of old wrongs?" I prodded.

"The church is corrupt. Our governments are corrupt. If we can't rely on the church or the fucking state, who can we call upon?"

"The Irish Mob?" Eoghan drawled.

Just as Conor mocked, "Batman?"

Though the others snickered, I didn't. I just nodded. "You believe Shay has a vision for a better future?"

"He's a kid. He's busy fucking his socks so he doesn't get spunk everywhere—"

"Jesus, Aidan," Declan spluttered, spraying scotch in every direction.

"But he's got more about him than we did as kids," Aidan continued like Declan hadn't interrupted. "He cares. About so much shit. The climate, the state of the country, racial injustices, women's rights…

"You ask him about something that's going on in the papers, and he's in there, ready to debate, caring so fucking much about this godforsaken world that it makes me hurt just to look at him.

"I don't think I've ever given that much of a damn about anything outside of Savvie and my family, but he's feeling all that about—"

A knock sounded at the door.

Each of our heads whipped to the side.

"Who is it?" Finn called out, proving that Aidan might be Manhattan's filthy king, but he didn't rule this particular roost.

The door popped open. "It's me." Shay grinned as he peered through the gap he made. When he saw the serious expressions, he blinked. "I-I… Sorry. I'll come back later—"

"Seamus, is Kat okay?"

"Yeah, she's watching a movie about pants that these girls share." His nose crinkled. "I don't know why they just don't buy their own."

Hiding a smile, I explained, "It's a coming-of-age story."

If anything, that perplexed him even more. "Okay," he drawled, extending the 'ay' sound.

"Son, come on in," Declan invited, patting the cushion on the couch next to him.

Shay frowned. "Am I in trouble? I only came in because Aunt Aoife wanted me to tell you dinner will be ready soon."

"Thanks, son. We just, we wanted to talk to you about things."

"Things? If it's about my grade in gym class, the coach has it in for me—"

"He still giving you shit because he wants you on the track team and you keep refusing?"

Grimacing, Shay nodded at Brennan's question. "I don't have time with my other extracurriculars."

"Understandable," Aidan conceded.

Shay's gaze flickered around the circle we made, not landing for long on his uncles until he came to a halt on mine. "What's going on?"

"Nothing," I appeased with a gentle smile. Somehow, that deepened his frown.

Apparently, I didn't have Aoife's skill of soothing with a smile.

"You ever thought about the future, bud?" Brennan asked.

"Sure, Uncle Bren, most of the time. Stops me wanting to beat the crap out of kids in my class who piss me off."

Brennan chuckled, but Declan queried, "What do you think about? College?"

Shay snorted. "No. But I've had to think about it more since the guidance counselor looped me in on the extra credit I'll need to get into Harvard.

"It'll suck but it's a good launch pad. I can make the right connections, especially if I make it into a fraternity."

Aidan scratched his chin. "You'll make it into a fraternity."

Shay's frown was stark. "You don't know that."

"You're a wealthy man, Shay. Not just because of your dad, but because of your mom. She's a famous artist. You think they're going to blackball you?"

"Anything's possible. I'm not exactly popular in my school now."

"You have time to iron out the creases, and what you can't iron out, we can help you with."

"The question is," I inserted before Aidan could bury himself in his own grave. "How much are you willing to sacrifice to get where you want?"

The question floored him. "Sacrifice?"

I nodded. "Sacrifice. Everything's a sacrifice, Shay. You don't know me well, and to be frank, you don't know anyone in this room as well as your mom. *But* think about it. To raise you right, she had to make a sacrifice. Love is a sacrifice; honor's a sacrifice.

"You can play dirty, or you can play straight. Either way, it'll cost you. You're the one who decides how expensive something is and whether or not you're willing to pay the price to achieve your goals."

As he studied me, I noticed that the others faded out of the conversation. I wasn't sure if that was smart, but no one said a word, letting him formulate his own answer because that was what mattered here.

At this moment, Shay had a choice that few sixteen-year-olds would be capable of making. That few teens would ever get either.

"What are we talking about here?" was what he eventually said.

Clever kid—he knew something deeper was going on, just didn't know the minutiae and wasn't willing to kick himself in the ass by speaking out of turn.

"Your future," I told him calmly.

"Why isn't Victoria in here too?"

"Because Victoria isn't an O'Donnelly. Victoria isn't you."

"She's family," was his stout retort.

"She is, but she has her own path."

"Will Camille and Inessa talk to her about it?"

Brennan stirred long enough to say, "They will when she's ready."

"What makes you think I'm ready?"

Declan cleared his throat. "Do you remember last year when I gave you a choice?"

His mouth worked. "The gun or the pen?"

Declan ignored us all to say, "This is like that. You can choose whichever path you want, but you have to choose."

"Now? That's not fair. I've got two years left at school!"

"Circumstances dictate that we make a move immediately, Shay," Conor inserted, his expression reassuring as he looked at his nephew. "You should know by now that our world isn't predictable."

Shay huffed but queried, "What are my options?"

"You join Acuig Corp, work your way up, and eventually become an executive. A little like Finn," Aidan stated.

Eoghan, still staring into his glass, drawled, "Or you become a Five Pointer, and don't pretend like you don't know what the Five Points do, kiddo."

Though Shay flushed, he didn't argue.

"Or, you go your own way," Declan continued. "You go into politics and you let us set you up to win."

Nervously, Shay flicked a glance between his uncles. "To win what?"

"The biggest election of them all," I added.

His brow furrowed, but before he could answer, Brennan said, "You still want to go into politics, Shay?"

"You know I do, Uncle Bren. Was just arguing this week with you about that bullshit law in Georgia and how it's a goddamn disgrace that more isn't being done to stop it from being passed."

I didn't need to ask *which* law. It had been plastered all over the papers, taking up column inches Savannah and I were trying to dominate with blackmail fodder on dirty politicians.

"Think you can do better?" Brennan asked quietly.

Slowly, his eyes widened. "You mean it?"

"What are we offering, Seamus?" Aidan inquired.

"To help me become president."

It sounded ridiculous coming out of a kid's mouth because that was what Shay was. Whether they liked it or not, they were doing as their da had done—forcing a kid to make a man's decision.

Declan nodded. "Do you want that, Shay? We can make it happen."

"That's not how it's supposed to work," he argued. "It's supposed to be about democratic choices—"

"Democracy hasn't been a part of our *republic* for a long time, Shay," I said quietly. "You just need to read the news to see that." As he bit his lip, gaze flickering once more between us, I continued, "Do you want to change that? Do you want the chance to make this country a better place?"

He swallowed, his still-forming Adam's apple bobbing with the move, but his answer was definitive, sure, *confident*. "I do."

Declan squeezed his son's shoulder. "So be it."

36

———

CONOR

Conor O'Donnelly

"ANTON," I greeted. "This is my brother Aidan. Aidan, this is Anton."

As both men shook hands, Anton stated, "It's a pleasure to meet you, Aidan. I have heard plenty about you."

"Plenty? From Conor?"

"No. From the city itself." Anton's eyes, for the first time since our initial meeting, were cold. "There are plenty of whispers about you."

"Brothers have infiltrated the Points?"

"No, but even I know the impossibility of keeping hundreds, if not thousands, of tongues still." He sat back in the armchair in the whiskey club where he'd asked to meet with us. "I've heard you're an aficionado of whiskey."

"Aren't most rich men?" Aidan mocked, in full self-deprecating mode.

Studying them both, I mused on how strange it was to see Aidan cornered. It happened so rarely now that Da was gone that it was unusual.

Apparently, his vice for whiskey was becoming infamous if both Star and her grandfather were using it against him—I'd need to guard against that.

As I made a mental note of my brother's Achilles' heel, Anton argued, "Not unsurprisingly, my vice is vodka." He clicked his tongue. "Though I can appreciate a nice single malt."

As if on cue, a waiter appeared out of nowhere with three empty glasses and a bottle on a tray.

As he served us, setting a small dish of dates stuffed with salted pistachios in the center of the table before departing, Anton explained, "The Glenlivet. From 1965."

"Beautiful vintage," Aidan agreed, twisting the cap on the fresh bottle and then pouring the three of us a couple fingers.

Raising the glass to his nose, he took a deep inhalation. His eyes closed as he savored the notes, and curious as always to see what was so damn good about it when it might as well have been air freshener to me, I lifted the glass to my nose too but failed to be impressed by the top notes of alcohol, alcohol, and alcohol.

Anton chuckled at my grimace. "You're not a connoisseur, Conor?"

"Alcohol's never tempted me."

Aidan's eyes popped open. "Conor's biggest temptation is work."

"Hardly," I scoffed.

"You're a workaholic. No matter what Star says about us cracking the whip on you—you *choose* to work. Sure, you bore the burden without asking for it, but you thrive on it now."

I scowled. "I don't thrive on work."

"When did you last do nothing for Acuig or the Five Points in a twenty-four-hour period?"

Scratching my nose with my middle finger and making sure he knew it was directed at him, I retorted, "Last Wednesday."

After he took a sip that he clearly savored, he asked, "At no time on Wednesday you worked?" When my mouth tightened, he clicked his fingers. "Of course you did."

I ignored his smug look.

"I'm not sure the leader of the Irish Mob spends much time resting on his laurels," Anton mused, staring down into the amber liquid in his glass. "I'm well aware that you collect information on people—"

"Conor is the best and the worst of us all," Aidan dismissed before Anton could finish.

"You love your family, don't you, Mr. O'Donnelly?"

He frowned. "Aidan."

"It's strange to me to call you that when I've met your father…"

"You met Da?" I blurted out with none of the formality of Aidan's tone.

"I'm sorry to say that I have. A few times over the years."

"You never said."

"It never came up."

Even Aidan was startled by this news. "Why did you… I mean, *how?*"

Anton merely raised a wizened brow. "He ran New York, son. Of course, I dealt with him. Just as I'm speaking to you now. To be sure, this is on a different, far more pleasant matter, but your father and I were acquainted."

"You didn't like him," I stated.

Amusement gleamed in Anton's eyes. "I did not. Your father was… fractious."

"Fractious is too kind an adjective. Volatile is the word you're looking for."

He merely bowed his head, politer than I was on the subject of Da.

"I do love my family, Anton," Aidan said, bringing us back to the topic at hand. "Why do you ask?"

"Conor has given me some insights into why he called this meeting but I must ask… Do you understand the scrutiny you're inviting? The risks involved?

"What are your motives for putting an O'Donnelly in the Oval Office? These are the things I must know before I can make an informed decision."

Eyes locked on Anton, Aidan raised the glass to his nose and gently swirled the whiskey around the base.

Inhaling deeply, he explained, "If you asked any of my brothers if we liked our father, I think we'd all say that Da was not a man who needed to be liked. He was a powerhouse. Mostly, in a negative sense.

"We're dealing with the repercussions of his parenting skills, or the lack thereof, because none of us intend to raise our own children in that way, and Seamus, my nephew, spent most of his life outside of his influence. I'm not certain I'd be making this suggestion if Da had played a major role in his childhood."

Gently, Anton inquired, "This 'suggestion' is out of ego?"

"I'll be honest and say that it started as a last hoorah for Da." His smile was sorrowful. "Liking Da is one thing, dealing with the aftermath of him is another, and despite it all, we loved him. I thought about how none of us, not a single goddamn one of us, wanted to come into this life, and we weren't given an option either. We had no choice.

"If Da had lived, he'd have probably forced my brother Declan into pressuring Seamus into this life, and the notion of perpetuating..." He blew out a breath. "It's one thing to want to be a Five Pointer. There's a cost—the risk of jail—but there are advantages too. A community— tight-knit, loyal. It comes with cash and power and respect. You don't get that working in an office from nine to five.

"But Seamus has a vocation. Who am I to stop that, especially when he could be exactly what this country needs?

"He's a rich kid, but he isn't spoiled. He's charismatic but kind. He's already seen the worst of mankind, but he cares about the underdog.

"Is it hubris to suggest, at sixteen, he's the right man for the job? Yes. But you tell me which president didn't have a helping hand and wasn't steered from a young age onto this path."

Anton conceded that with, "Alan Davidson certainly was. Every move he made from middle school onward brought him to this point in his life."

"Exactly. It's naive to think future presidents aren't being groomed as we speak. While crusty old white guys fill our most hallowed political halls, that doesn't mean it'll always be that way."

"Not with how they're resigning like rats escaping a sinking ship," I mocked.

"Yes, the papers have definitely been interesting lately. Scandalous if you're innocently inclined." Anton nodded. "You have spoken with him about his future?"

"This past weekend. He wants to make a difference."

Anton's laugh was wistful. "Ah, to be young again."

I grimaced because I knew exactly what he meant even though I was more than half his age. "His naivety is painful," I admitted. "But he's a good boy, Anton."

"He is *now*. When he's nineteen, I'll meet with him," was Anton's decisive retort. "Six months into his first year of college to be precise."

To see if being away from home turned him into a party animal.

I got it.

What was the point in investing in someone who might change his mind when freedom from Mom and Dad turned his head? But…

"At the risk of being impolite, Anton, you're an old man."

Anton chuckled. "This is why you and Star get along so well, Conor. You're both blunt enough to be disarming."

"You'd think it would trigger arguments, but it doesn't," Aidan agreed. "They do have a good rapport."

"Your approval means the world to me," I mocked, rolling my eyes at my older brother who, shaking his head, chuckled at me.

"Whether I die or not, there will be… *plans* put in place. He might meet with me or he might meet with my successor. Either way, he'll meet with the United Brotherhood before we endorse him. Six months into his degree, not a moment sooner," he pledged.

Hearing the note of finality in his tone, I knew that was as much of a concession as he'd grant us.

And to be frank, with him having influenced the current president's elections when the man was as imperfect as he was, with as many secrets as Davidson had, that was a green light if ever I'd heard one.

"Elizabeth Davidson had ties to the *Éire le chéile go deo*."

Anton cut me a look. "Her husband was in the dark, but that was important to keep his nose clean."

I had to wonder if Davidson *did* know about her ties because he sure as hell knew about Anton fucking her.

"So, you must know about Aoife too?"

"Naturally."

"And still you endorsed him?" I spluttered.

"You better than anyone know the importance of a bargaining

chip." Anton shrugged. "Anyway, a malfunctioning Ireland keeps Britain at odds with the rest of the world."

"And that's in the Brotherhood's favor?" Aidan questioned warily.

"Now that you're the head of the ECD," he mused, taking a sip of his whiskey and definitely *not* answering Aidan's question, "you might find there are other means of being of service to your country before your nephew is a sitting president. Would that interest you, Aidan?"

My brother straightened in his seat. "Of course."

Anton's smile was cool but pleased. "I'm glad to hear that."

37

STAR

WHAT THE WATER GAVE ME - FLORENCE AND THE MACHINE

Star Sullivan

CONOR STOPPED HUMMING to the song I'd sent him earlier, Florence and the Machine's "What the Water Gave Me," to ask, "Where's Katina tonight? With Lyra and Troy?"

"Nah. Troy said Lyra needed some space after Kat got too noisy yesterday. I can't blame her. Kat was more hyper than usual. The damn kittens didn't help, what with their yowling." My nose crinkled at the memory—getting to know my cousin wasn't easy when Kat and she didn't get along. "Kiddo is the direct opposite of Lyra so she's with Savannah who shares a noise and energy level with her."

"Not that I want to argue about spending time together, but why?"

"This is date night number three," I explained as I chowed down on a watermelon Airheads he'd given me as I jumped behind the wheel.

He arched a brow as he rested his boot on the dash and propped his elbow on his knee. "Date *numero tres*. You can't get enough of me, can you? Admit it."

My lips twitched. "If we crash, you'll shatter your femur if you stay in that position."

"That's not a sexy way to start date night," he grumbled, but he moved his foot back into the footwell.

I did like a man who *listened.*

Combined with how, on nights like tonight when he was extra play-ful, he was practically a vibrator with how goddamn *giddy* he made me.

"It's definitely not sexy. But I don't intend on spending the night in the ER."

"If we're not going there, where *are* we going?"

"Jennifer Valentini told me about *Russu*."

"The Valentini front?"

"Yep."

"You want to go to a nightclub?"

"Yep."

"Why?"

"Because."

"Helpful."

"I try."

"You hate clubs. At least, I thought you did."

"I didn't always hate them."

My words had him falling silent. Then, quietly, he asked, "Another scar?"

Scars were what we'd started to call these little blips in my past that I needed help overcoming.

"Uh-huh. *But* I asked Jennifer if she could arrange with the club to play the music I like. I even asked her to throw in some *noxxious* remixes later on in the evening. Though I'm not fucking you while my dad's singing."

"Fuck, no." He shuddered. "That's creepy."

"I'm glad we both agree," I retorted.

"Wait—" Conor twisted in his seat. "You want to fuck in the club?"

"I do." I motioned at my skirt. "Why do you think I'm not wearing jeans?"

"I didn't think about it. I saw your knees and suddenly knew there *is* a God."

I snickered, but my cheeks bloomed with heat. "They're just regular knees."

"Star Sullivan, you take that back."

"Take what back?"

"Nothing, and I mean *nothing,* is regular about you."

Grinning, I shoved him in the side. "You're already going to get lucky tonight. You don't need to amp up the charm."

"That's just how I roll, baby."

Because it was, I didn't scoff, just shoved him again, but there was a wide smile on my lips, one that ate into any anxiety I was feeling about being back in a nightclub.

My last memory of one involved a collar, a leash, and being strangled by both as Hans had to stop me from jumping—

I started to veer away from the recollection, not wanting it to diminish the excitement that filled me whenever I was around Conor, but I owed him an explanation.

That was our deal, after all.

Clearing my throat, I admitted, "You might not like what I need to do tonight."

His hand clamped down around my knee. "Whatever it takes to help you heal, Star."

There was that heartburn again.

Tears pricked my eyes at how easy it was for him to say that.

It made it easier to admit, "He liked to push my limits. Liked to offer me freedom so that it was more fun for him to take it away from me. To prove that he owned me, that I was his. That my wants didn't matter. That *I* didn't matter."

"Bastard."

My lips quirked up. "Agreed."

"He liked to humiliate you, didn't he? Taking you to these public places?"

"It was a whole subculture. Rich motherfuckers who bought humans and who liked to hang out with others just like them. I spent way too much time being degraded in front of other people."

"Thank you for telling me."

I huffed. "There are better things I could have shared."

"This is a piece of your past. It helps me unlock every part of you."

"Most of those parts aren't pretty."

He hummed. "Maybe not, but it all makes up the magic that is you."

Biting the inside of my cheek at his words, I let my mind tick away.

Magic.

Did he think that was me?

That I was magic, not toxic?

Amazing how that made me feel lighter. More in control. Less directed by an urge I had to heal this sliver of my past…

"I'm surprised Savannah agreed to babysit," he drawled as we approached the club where traffic grew thicker.

His words broke into my heavy thoughts.

"Kat's got that project to finish," I told him. "I just said she had to supervise and make sure she didn't play on her Switch or go to bed past two AM."

He chuckled. "I think she can cope with that. If not, Aidan can."

"Agreed," I said with a grin.

"How's it going with Lyra? Is she opening up?"

"Not really. It's only been a short while since we met, though, so I'm not rushing anything."

"That's for the best. She'll just get used to you hanging around."

"Like a bad smell?"

"You said it. Not me."

"Oh, by the way, I'm dealing with Temper."

His head swiveled to the side. "You don't have a temper. Actually, you're pretty zen for—"

I snorted. "I appreciate the upvote but nah, I meant Temper Black."

He grunted. "I don't like her."

"We're in agreement there. I'm making sure she knows how I feel about her being a double agent."

A chuckle escaped him. "What have you done?"

"Set Eagle Eyes on her."

His chuckle morphed into a belly laugh. "You set a sniper on her?"

"Yup. Anyway, I told him to make it obvious that he's hunting her too. Let's skewer the bitch's nerves."

"You're gaslighting her? Or is the endgame to shoot her?"

"I would if she weren't Dead To Me's cousin. But she is, so I have to dial it down a touch."

"'Dial it down,'" he repeated softly. "Not sure if I'm bewildered or impressed that that's your idea of dialing it down."

My lips twitched. "I'll settle for a mixture of both. Especially as the bitch is the shoo-in for the deputy director's job. You watch her soar to the top of the food chain over the next few years."

"It's not what you know, it's *who* you know," he said gruffly.

I sniffed. "I fucking hate how true that is."

When we finally breached the traffic and made it outside of *Russu* and a valet popped up to park Conor's SUV/tank, he murmured in my ear, "What did you offer as payment for controlling the playlist?"

"Nothing. She was being nice."

"Why?"

"We were trying to be kind to each other for Savannah's sake."

"You're more than Savannah's best friend."

"I know. We don't have that kind of relationship. We're more like sisters, I guess, but Jennifer wanted to make a good impression and so did I."

"Curious."

"What is?" I queried as we made it down the long red carpet toward the club's entrance.

"That two ornery women decided to get along because of a third ornery woman."

Chuckling, I retorted, "A match made in hell."

"Seems like it. Aoife's the odd man out in the bunch."

"Why?"

"She's best friends with Jennifer."

"She is?" My brows rose. "Why didn't Savannah invite her the other week?"

"Aoife doesn't particularly like Savannah. They get along okay, but they're not each other's favorite people."

Offended on her behalf, I asked, "Why?"

"Because of how Savannah became friends with Jen. You know,

that whole pretending to be a client of her accounting firm so she could grab some of her DNA to check if she was an O'Donnelly love child?"

My nose crinkled. "Yeah, there are better meet-cutes."

"Right?"

"Savannah always makes life difficult for herself."

"Like you don't."

"I'm not saying I don't," I argued. "Just saying she does things the hard way. When I arrived, she was panicking because she'd invited Paddy along so he and Jennifer could get to know one another."

"Why would she do that?" he shouted over the music as a hostess appeared from behind a bouncer as we made it into *Russu's* atrium and were guided up to the VIP section.

"She was trying to be kind but it never works out for her," I called back.

The hostess swept open a door and led us onto a private balcony that was ours for the night.

Not unsurprisingly, the balconies around us were in the dark, while the nightclub itself was awash with red lights. It wasn't particularly to my taste, seeing as it looked like Bram Stoker's idea of great interior design, but the music was heavy techno and it reminded me of when I'd spent six months undercover in Berlin—great times—so I was already hopped-up.

As Conor tipped the hostess, I rushed to the balcony and peered over it.

Jennifer had gotten us onto the highest floor—I owed her one as I'd have wanted to kill people if I'd been stuffed into that crowd.

From below, I could see a massive fountain that pulsed to the beat of the music while somehow simultaneously resembling a pool of blood.

Creepy but cool.

Maybe I just had the personality for it?

When arms slid around my waist, I didn't jump or startle because the scent of oranges hit me first.

I sighed into his embrace, stopping the faint bounce on my toes as he held me tighter. His chin settled on my shoulder as we looked over to the chaos of the dance floor.

I had no desire to wade into the fray, was more than happy up here even if it was a little too close for comfort to another time, another place, and another man.

When he pressed his mouth to my shoulder, I smiled as I slipped my hands over his.

For the first time in my life, I didn't mind that a guy was taller than me. Not when he smelled of oranges and had floppy brown hair that tickled my cheek.

Tilting my face to the side, I waited for him to work his way up my throat. Sensations shot down my spine from that simple touch, reminding me of what it felt like to be *alive*. Something that was happening with such frequency that, soon it would become the norm, but I knew I'd never forget what a gift he was.

As his mouth brushed along my jawline, I sighed as, finally, we came together.

Soft at first, maybe because he sensed my mood, then the beat of the music worked against him.

Techno wasn't his vibe, but that didn't mean it didn't get into his blood. It *had* to.

Parting my lips, I sighed again as he slipped me some tongue. Stroking it with mine, I leaned into that kiss, nourished it, and fed it until his dick was grinding into my ass and his hand was on my stomach, pinning me tighter into him.

I groaned into his lips as I twisted around, wrapping my arms around his neck as his hands shifted down to my ass. This time, the thick length against my belly felt like a brand.

It scorched me.

Made my core burn in a matching heat.

I could feel that tingle—the one that was becoming less and less elusive as time with him passed—and I reached for it. I didn't clutch at it desperately like I did when we first got together. I rocked toward it as each of his fingers dug into my glutes and he tugged me into him, making me feel his searing, burning need for me.

"I love you, Conor."

Warm words, but he didn't respond with warmth. He responded with *fire*.

His growl lit me up from the inside out and I ate up his snarl as if it were a pint of Ben & Jerry's finest. He tongue-fucked me. No kinder way to describe it, and I fought the flames of his need with my own.

When he ducked down and dragged me against him, I was very glad about my skirt, more so when he tore at the slit to make it higher. A move that enabled me to cup him with my legs.

As my heels dug into his ass, he maneuvered me to the side of the balcony and that was the first time I pulled back.

"No. Put my ass on the balcony railing."

He frowned. "What?"

"Put my ass on the balcony railing," I rasped.

I watched the cogs working behind his eyes and saw the sweetest glimmer of pain flicker to life as he came to terms with *what* I was asking and *why*.

Grateful that he didn't say anything, just moved back so that my butt was against the cool metal, I sighed with relief when his mouth returned to mine.

We were back to soft and gentle—apologetic. I didn't want that. I wanted *him*.

That fire was what I craved because it was only through that fire that I could be burned and reborn from the ashes.

I tugged on the deep V of my blouse, revealing the small brand that Indy had inked onto me.

The phoenix, formed in her iconic Mandala strokes with Conor's name tangled amid those flowing lines, sat pride of place on the curve of my breast.

When he saw it, he dipped down and pressed his lips to it. As he tongued the outer edges, shaping its form, my head tipped back.

My hair was loose so I felt it flowing against my spine. It was an illusion but I felt like Rapunzel with a mile of hair dangling over the balcony, long enough to hit the floor.

I could feel gravity's pull much as I had years ago, but this was different.

Death wasn't calling me now. The urge to fall was gone.

Life was what beckoned me.

A future.

And I knew, point blank, that Conor would never, ever, *ever* let go of me.

I groaned when he nuzzled the neckline of my shirt away, nipping and sucking a path along tender skin until he reached my nipple.

When he nipped, hard enough to sting, my fingers knotted in his hair, my nails scoring his scalp.

For a couple moments, I reveled in his touch.

How he savored me sent liquid pleasure coursing through my veins, but then his hips rocked forward against my core and that was all I could think about.

His hands were a solid presence at my waist, and I knew they'd stay there so I helped by reaching between us.

To get a hold of him, I had to wriggle away, but he snatched me to him, jerking upright, his arms sliding around my back as he dragged me into his chest as if he thought I was going to jump.

"Jesus, Star!" he snapped, and because we were plastered to one another, I felt the heavy pounding of his heart.

Was it stupid to think it beat in time with mine?

"I was just reaching for your cock," I said apologetically. "I didn't mean to scare you."

He blew out a breath as he held me close, so close, and amid the tight clutch of his arms, I angled my head so that I was kissing his throat this time, sipping and nipping and tasting and teasing.

Thanking him with loving kisses and explorative strokes.

My tongue found his pulse and I palpated the flesh there, feeling it slow down from the adrenaline-based fear and shift into arousal.

His groan rumbled in my ear, the vibrations sending shivers down my spine, especially as his teeth found my earlobe and he nibbled it before sucking hard, reminding me of the pressure of those lips around my clit.

"I need you alive and kicking," he whispered then, the words only audible because of how close we were.

I squeezed him, trying to imbue the embrace with my apology. "I just need *you*," I whispered back.

He groaned as I squeezed my hands between us and finally shaped his cock with one. The other was aimed at finding his fly. As I dragged the zipper down, I sighed when I found him in my palm. Hot, thick, heavy.

My pussy clutched at nothing, already eager for what was becoming its BFF.

Digging my feet into his butt, I repeated, "I need you, Conor, now. Please, *now*."

He groaned, the sound tortured as his head rocked back like it was too heavy for his neck to support. I took advantage and worked on leaving him a hickey as I started to jerk his cock, using his pre-cum as lube until the emptiness inside me was just too goddamn much.

When his hands clutched at my waist, rough enough to hurt, I nipped my way up to his ear and murmured, "I'm so fucking wet for you, Conor. I wish you could feel it." His fingers tore at my blouse. "I am. It's all for you. No one else. No one makes me feel this way. Only you. Only you."

As he snarled, I let his dick experience the gift I'd had waiting for him—no panties.

"Jesus Christ, Star. Were you walking around like this?" He hissed as he dragged his cock back and forth. Then surprise whispered through his words. "You *are* wet." He groaned as my juices coated his shaft. "God, you're perfect, Star. So fucking perfect. Never let anyone tell you otherwise."

I urged our mouths to collide so he could taste my smile, my thanks, my *love*.

He hissed again as his tip found my slit, and slowly, so fucking slowly it was painful, he rocked into me.

Then, when I crossed my heels so I had more support, I used that to urge him deeper into me, not stopping until I was full of him. So goddamn full that I choked out a breath that he swallowed in his kiss.

The shocked breath morphed into a moan at how perfect *he* was.

The only dick I'd ever wanted *this* much.

The only man I'd ever *needed.*

I had no idea why the thought made me cry. Maybe it was because the last time I'd been in this position, I'd been a toy. No choice, no free will, no say.

Now, I had it all.

And I had him.

I was blessed.

I cried and didn't care if he felt the liquid emotion raining down my cheeks as I sank into his kiss, absorbing that like I took him in.

When he felt my tears, he slowed down and tried to draw away from me, but I didn't let him. I chased his mouth and started to rub my clit with the one hand that had still been trapped between us.

As my pussy clutched and fluttered around his dick, I knew that pleasure was close. Surprisingly so. It loomed on the horizon like the dawn of a new day, and *that* thought was so appropriate that I let it flood me.

Maybe he knew I was letting go because his hold on me tightened in reaction and he sped up.

Behind me, the crowd roared and surged to the music.

Beneath me, I could feel gravity's call just as I had years ago.

But, *before* me was him.

"Mine," I groaned into his mouth.

"Yours," he ceded easily, but his tone was rough. Gruff.

As we climbed toward release, the tingles started in my core, spreading out, surging down my legs, through my stomach, and pricking my fingers as they waved along my arms.

When I shouted out my climax, nobody knew.

It was just one of many cries amid the noisy crowd, but to Conor, it was a signal.

He stopped holding back, moving faster, faster, *faster* until he roared in my ear, hips pumping as he chased every ounce of his release and I milked him dry, knowing from experience that it only enhanced the delirium he alone could make me feel.

The fire stopped licking at my heels and instead surged through my veins, sending flames roaring through my system until I was encompassed in the inferno.

Hearts racing toward one another, I slumped into him, but as he started to relax, he stiffened, jerking me away from the railing as if he only just remembered where I was propped.

When he drew me over to a leather couch, I didn't argue when he fell back into it with me in his lap.

Nuzzling my face into his throat, I murmured, "Thank you."

I had no idea how he heard me, but he knew what I was thanking him for. Conor pressed a kiss to the tip of my nose, whispering, "In the future, when you tell me I won't like something, I want specifics."

I'd felt his fear as if it were my own so I replied, "Okay."

"Never again, Star."

Knowing what he meant, I nodded, content.

That scar had been healed.

I'd never *need* to do this again.

38

CONOR

TIME IN A BOTTLE - ROB LANE

Conor O'Donnelly

"DO you want to take the ferry into Jersey, Kat? Do something different for our visit today?"

There was no logical reason for that blank look to make an appearance in Kat's eyes at Star's cheerful offer, but it slithered into being like a veil passing over her irises.

It wasn't *Exorcist*-esque, but it was creepy nonetheless.

The second it happened, Star dropped Alessa a message in the group chat we shared, explaining why we wouldn't be coming to West Orange today, then carefully hustled her into the living room, ensconcing her on the couch in a pile of blankets, where she put on a Disney movie.

Over the next couple hours, I worked in there with them both, wondering when my edgy interior design had been replaced with fluffy pink throws and myriad picture frames of a little girl I'd never known I'd be fathering in various stages of maturity—Kat beaming at me with a gap-toothed smile in one, her mid-flight as she practiced a somersault, her scowling at a teacher at an end-of-year recital…

I could say, hand on heart, I never thought I'd have kids. Too many trust issues. Too many issues, period. But watching the slow thaw as Kat returned to her usual bubbly self, the rightness of it all hit me.

Not that she was suffering, not that a simple question could trigger dissociation, but the parts of her adults had broken, maybe they were something I was uniquely placed to fix?

Hadn't adults broken me?

Who else could understand her better?

"What happened, sweetheart?" Star asked her an hour later when Kat decided to do an impromptu midair somersault during some movie about a frog.

Gymnastics were clearly a coping mechanism, but they were also something Star was using as Kat's baseline—the more chaos she was wreaking midair, the more Star thought Kat was back to her usual self.

Kat's beaming grin dampened some. "What happened when, Star?"

"You went away." She shot her a gentle smile which was bound to freak Kat out because Star wasn't gentle often. If ever. That wasn't her parenting style. "Here." She motioned to her eyes.

"I did?" Kat swallowed.

"You did," I agreed, gently popping into the conversation.

"I-I don't know why."

"Do you not like boats?" Star questioned.

Her head whipped to the side. "I don't."

"Do you know why? We've never been on a boat together so it must have happened... before."

Kat blinked a couple times. "I just don't like boats."

"But you love swimming," Star pointed out.

"Swimming is different. Swimming is in a pool." She shuddered. "The ocean..."

"Technically, the Hudson is a river. If that helps any," I remarked.

Star snorted. "He's right."

Kat giggled. "It's not the same as a pool, Conor!"

"Don't you want to see the Statue of Liberty, Kat?" I questioned carefully.

"I've seen her."

"From a distance. On a boat, you can get up close and personal. Always so much to do on the water," I peppered.

She shivered. "I don't want to get wet."

"That's what a boat is for," Star murmured. "So you won't get wet. Do you feel like trying? It's still light enough."

Kat licked her lips. "You promise that I won't get wet?"

"Nope."

"We could take the Staten Island Ferry. The terminal's two blocks away," I said easily.

"It's also free. Conor's such a cheapskate, Kat," Star teased.

I didn't mind being poked fun at, not when it made Kat chuckle. When I started tickling her and she shrieked in joy, I declared, "I'm not a cheapskate! Say it, Kat, say it!"

"Conor's a cheapskate, Star!" She cackled when I made a mock growl and dangled her by her calves.

Star, staring at the pair of us, shook her head. "If she's sick, you get to clean it up."

"I'm not going to be sick!" Kat screeched then whooped when I hovered her gently above the floor.

"You gonna do a handstand for us?"

She pressed her hands to the floor. "Okay, let go, Conor!"

When she walked a few paces on her hands then did some flip thing, Star and I shared a smile—she was back.

For the moment.

That was how I ended up on the Staten Island Ferry just so I could glance at the statue I'd seen almost every day I'd been alive up close and personal.

On the walk to the terminal, Kat was her usual bustling self, over-sharing about school and her fellow classmates. She bitched about her math teacher and jabbered away in Italian when Star prompted her to, earning an impressed look from a hot dog vendor who stopped trying to sell us pretzels long enough to chatter with her.

When we approached the waterside, her conversation faded, however. She was quiet as we stepped on board the vessel, quieter still as we rode to Staten Island and back again because the return journey had the best views of the statue.

When we approached Lady Liberty, that was the first time she let out a shaky sigh. "She's so pretty. She's what you fought for, isn't she, Star?"

"I can't say that I had her in my mind when I was in the sandbox, kiddo, but what she stands for? Sure. Liberty. Been fighting for that and justice my whole life."

Kat swallowed. "The bad people who hurt you, they've gone away, haven't they?"

"They're in the process of going away," she corrected.

Kat fell silent, her eyes big and round as she peered at the statue. A hat was tugged over her forehead and her scarf covered her from the nose down, so they were all that was visible. Then, she whispered, "My daddy's name was Bogdan, wasn't it?"

I stilled. It wasn't exactly quiet on board, but the whisper had been so faint I could have misheard.

"You remembered that?" Star questioned, twisting on the faux-wood bench to study Kat.

She swallowed. "I did."

Floating a theory, I asked, "You know when you go away, Kat, is that when you remember something?"

The little girl bit her bottom lip. "Yes."

"Is that what you remembered today? Your dad's name?"

She nodded.

"What else have you remembered?"

"My daddy used to make my mommy cry." Her voice was so small, so fucking small that it made me want to break something. "He used to hurt her. Why did he do that, Conor?"

Christ.

"Because some men are very weak, Kat. They think it makes them 'strong' to scare someone, to hurt them, but it just makes them smaller." Those big eyes of hers peered at me and I knew what she was asking. "I'll never hurt Star, sweetheart. Or you. I promise."

Slowly, she nodded, and her gloved hand reached for mine. As she knotted our fingers together, I didn't think I'd ever been shown such a sign of faith, of trust, than I had at that moment.

I stared at Star over Kat's head and saw the gratitude and the love beaming back at me and returned it with a smile.

Though it was a total tourist move, I let Star take a picture of us with NYC's most famous lady in the background, mostly because I knew that shot would end up on my desk…

The rest of the journey took place in silence, most of us just staring out onto the river, each of us processing what we'd learned.

We picked up burgers for dinner, watched a movie, and headed to bed. Star fell asleep quickly, which didn't surprise me, to be honest, because the day had been an emotional pit of stress, but by contrast, I *couldn't* sleep.

I ended up heading to our office.

Running some programs, I started a search on child shrinks because I figured that it was time we went with some professional help if Kat was remembering her father 'hurting' her mother.

Considering the bastard had ended up murdering her, the last thing we needed was Kat remembering that in a dissociative state without having some outside help close by.

Around two AM, I heard Kat scream from a nightmare.

I always woke before Star did when that happened, which spoke of how bad my sleep was, but today was different. *Tonight* was a new night.

Kat remembered a father who hurt her mother. I needed to replace that memory, needed to do something to make *that* better.

So I didn't go and wake Star up. Instead, I cautiously opened Kat's bedroom door and from the doorway, called, "Katina, you can wake up now. You're safe."

She didn't stir, just kept on crying, and those tears fucking broke me. They wrecked something inside me that had never been touched before, and I knew this was the moment where I had to step up—no longer was I just the man dating her foster mom, I was more than that.

Because I wasn't simply dating Star—I was engaged to her.

Star was my forever. My fucking everything. And that meant Kat was too.

Feeling awkward about entering her bedroom, I shuffled over to the bed and cleared my throat.

That didn't work.

I reached down and gently cupped her shoulder which was trembling. Ren meowed at me, but I ignored the kitten to whisper, "Kat. You're safe, sweetheart. You need to wake up because you're dreaming. Whatever you're seeing isn't real. It's just a dream."

I crooned the words to her, hoping she'd hear them, but if she did, she merged from sleeping to waking in increments.

Taking a seat at her bedside, I gently stroked her hair, doing what I guessed I wished Ma had done to me when I'd had nightmares.

When Da had stopped her from comforting me because I needed to man up.

The thought had a frown puckering my mouth as I did what I could to soothe her until, out of nowhere, her arms were sliding around my waist and she was sobbing, "Why won't they stop, Conor? Why won't they stop?"

My throat felt thick with emotions I didn't know how to express, probably *couldn't* express because I'd been stunted in that sense when I was her age.

"I wish I knew why, sweetheart. I wish I knew." I sucked in a breath. "What did you dream of? Do you want to talk about it?"

"He was hurting her again."

"Is this the first time you remembered?"

"No," she whispered as if it were a secret.

"You remembered before but didn't tell Star?"

"I didn't want to upset her." She sniffled. "She's worried about me."

"I am too," I reassured.

"I know but you're different."

"I am?"

She hitched a shoulder. "I don't know why, but you are."

Deciding to take that as a positive if it meant she'd open up to someone, I said, "I used to have bad dreams when I was your age."

"What did you dream of?"

"A man who used to hurt me."

"Why did he hurt you?"

"Because he could." My throat bobbed. "Did your father hurt you, Kat?"

"No." She had no idea how goddamn relieved I was. "He used to hurt Leo though. His daddy didn't protect him. He said he needed to make him into a man but he was only little. How could he make him into a man by hurting him, Conor?"

Leo.

Her cousin.

"My da used to think like that, Kat. When I was your age and I had nightmares, my ma wasn't allowed to come and help me get back to sleep."

"That's horrible."

"It is," I agreed. "My brothers used to try to help but if they didn't hear me then how could they?"

"They couldn't. Which brother?"

"The older ones. Declan, when he understood, used to crawl into bed with me." I swallowed.

"Did your da stop the man who used to hurt you?"

"No. My brothers did."

"Which ones?"

"Aidan and Finn. They stopped him."

I could still remember that day as if it had happened last week.

They'd burst into the church like superheroes to save me. Aidan and Finn, until my dying day, would know my endless gratitude and loyalty for doing what they did.

"How did they stop him?"

"They hurt him," I said simply, "until he could never hurt me again." It hit me what I'd said too late. "I probably shouldn't have told you that—"

"The Sinners used to think I wasn't listening but I did. I know they used to hurt people, that they used to kill them," she whispered, turning onto her side in her PJs that were covered in flying pigs, with her wispy blonde hair floating around her face, both of which were visible because of a nightlight she needed to sleep.

Christ, she was too young to know this shit.

Furious with myself, I scrubbed a hand over my jaw. "You shouldn't have listened, Kat. If you ever hear anything like that, you should walk away and keep your ears closed."

"How do you close your ears?"

"You hum to cover up the other people's conversation."

"Wouldn't they know I was listening then?"

"They would." Unless… "Were you eavesdropping?"

"No one tells me anything," she grumbled with a pout.

"And what you learned, does it feed your bad dreams?"

She tucked her chin into her chest. "Maybe."

I sighed. "That's why you shouldn't listen into conversations that are for adults, Kat. Stay a kid for as long as you can. Being a grown-up sucks."

"Conor?"

"Yes, Kat."

"Didn't your da know about the man who hurt you?"

"Not until recently."

"Why didn't you want him to know?"

Christ, that was the real question, wasn't it?

I cleared my throat. "My answer isn't a nice one, Kat."

"I won't tell anyone," she whispered. "Pinkie swear."

Her pinkie made an appearance in front of me—so close that it almost went up my nose. I lowered it a little, hiding a smile, then curled mine around hers.

"I didn't think he'd believe me." I hesitated. "No, that's not true. I knew he wouldn't."

"Why not?"

"Because the man who hurt me was a man he trusted implicitly."

"What does implicitly mean?"

"In this instance, it means Da trusted him one hundred percent."

"He was wrong to, wasn't he?"

I choked out a bitter laugh. "Yeah, he was."

Ren, supremely unconcerned by our distress, started washing himself on her pillow.

"Conor?"

"Yes, Kat."

"I'm glad your brothers hurt the man," she whispered in a rush, petting Stimpy when she jumped onto her bed and snuggled into her side.

"Me too."

"I like them more than the others now."

That had me snorting. "You can have favorite uncles, but you can't make them your favorite because of something they did for me. It should be because of something they did for you."

"You're my family now, aren't you? And if they'd do that for you, then maybe if anyone hurt me too, they'd do the same for me."

"That isn't a question you need to ask yourself, Kat. If anyone *dared* hurt you, and trust me, they won't because you're an O'Donnelly now, every single one of us would make that person wish they'd never been born."

She shivered. "I like knowing that."

"Good. When you have bad dreams, you should remember that. You have a family that even the boogeyman is frightened of."

"I do?"

"You do," I confirmed, leaning over to brush a kiss on the crown of her head. "Are you ready to get some sleep?"

"Conor?"

Unexpectedly ragged from this conversation, I sighed. "Yes, Kat."

"I want to call Star 'Mom.' Do you think she'd let me?"

"I don't see why she wouldn't love that."

"If she's my mom, does that mean, eventually, you'll be my dad?"

My eyes flared in surprise but with an ease I wasn't feeling, I said, "It does."

She hummed happily. "I'll let you know when I'm ready to call you that, okay?"

"You do that, kiddo. Get some good sleep and remember that no one is allowed to hurt you. Not even your dreams."

Her smile was sleepy but content, and it filled me with a contentment of my own knowing that I'd given her that ease.

My parents had never done that for me so it put me in the perfect position of understanding what Kat needed and when.

There could be some good from them letting me down. *My* family would never know what it was to feel isolated and afraid.

That was what being called a father meant.

I'd earn the title of 'Dad' if it was the last thing I ever did.

39

CONOR

PRAY FOR ME - THE WEEKND, KENDRICK LAMAR

Conor O'Donnelly

NOON THE FOLLOWING DAY

KNOWING that Star had taken Kat downstairs to visit with Troy and Lyra, I started a group call with my brothers—it was time to come clean. Especially as I knew what was happening later this afternoon and wanted in.

Declan was the first to accept the call. "You heard anything from Luis Albarez?"

My nose crinkled. "Do we have to talk about soccer? I am so goddamn sick of that game."

"Uh, *yeah.* Seeing as I didn't want the team in the fucking first place but if I have to own one, then they're not going to suck ass. Plus, for some weird reason, Shay is actually enjoying talking about it."

"Thought he liked American football." That was Aidan who'd just jumped into the conversation.

"He does. But I think all the time spent overseas has given him a preference for fucking soccer. I blamed Aela but she just laughed at me."

Eoghan popped up, scoffing, "You're lucky she only laughed at you. Seeing as it's your fault he was overseas in the first place."

My eyes widened. "Jesus, Eoghan. You woke up and chose war today, huh?" I cut Declan a look, but his expression had locked down.

Guilt.

Nothing better for the soul than that.

Aela and Declan had only recently gotten back together, after all. She'd kept Shay a secret for fifteen years…

"That was harsh, Eoghan," Finn, who'd joined silently but in time to hear *that*, agreed.

Eoghan just shrugged, unapologetic to the last.

"If you didn't call about soccer, what did you call about?" Declan rumbled, his expression still stony.

"More secrets."

Brennan grunted. "What a welcome."

Aidan pinched the bridge of his nose. "I thought we'd laid everything out in the open."

"I mean, most things, sure," I concurred, not even bothering to look at Eoghan who'd been hiding his role as an agent in a super-secret NATO organization, then there was the fact Declan had a thing for pilfering the goods from art heists, and never mind that Finn had been approached by the United freakin' Brotherhood to become a member…

"What is it, Kid?" Brennan rasped, straightening his shoulders as if preparing for the blow.

"I kind of hacked NASA when I was a teenager—"

Declan groaned. "We know. Da was beyond proud—"

"Let me finish. The first time, I got in and out. But the second time, I got caught."

"The *second* time?" Aidan demanded, jerking to his feet. "What the fuck did you go in a second time for? In and out!" He clicked his fingers. "In and goddamn out, Conor. Did having Padraig as a godfather teach you nothing?!"

"It taught me plenty," I snapped. "But I wanted to gain access to a satellite."

"Did you?" Eoghan inquired, his tone as calm as ever. Even when he dealt blows, he sounded calm—it was starting to get annoying.

"I did, but it's now defunct." That still pissed me off.

"What were the repercussions?" my youngest brother asked.

"The NSA swooped in and made me an offer I couldn't refuse."

As one, my brothers sucked in a breath. Shocking them like that would have been impressive at another time, but this was bad. I knew it —they did too.

"What kind of offer?" Finn rasped.

"They wanted me to work for them. Test their software and ensure their hardware was impenetrable. Eventually," I admitted after clearing my throat, "I got to be important. No one else on their staff could do what I could."

"It gave you power?" Aidan murmured, his eyes still wide but respect creeping into them now.

"It did. I used it to leverage our family's safety."

This time, they didn't suck in a breath; they just gaped at me.

For a full minute.

Okay, now *I* was impressed with how impressed *they* were.

When they carried on staring, I sheepishly rubbed my nape. "It's why we've been so untouchable."

"Not Da…?" Declan whispered.

"No."

"Jesus fuck, that's how important you are to the NSA?" Eoghan rumbled, the sound of his hand slapping the desk loud amid the echoing silence from my other brothers.

"Used to be. That usefulness wore out recently."

"And that's why you're telling us? You're warning us?" Aidan asked carefully.

"No. Maybe? I'm not sure. I guess it might be for the best that we're trying to behave outwardly." I paused, reflecting on Anton and how he'd probably protect us if Star asked nicely. "I'm telling you because…" Though I'd spent last night sleepless, trying to figure out how to explain this to them in the fewest words possible, I was still coming up dry. "Okay, so…" I hesitated. "Right, I mean…" I coughed. "It started…" I sighed.

"Just spit it out, Conor, for fuck's sake."

Brennan's use of my real name had me cringing. Not that I appreciated my nickname, but that meant he was pissed. I didn't have a problem with annoying my siblings, but I kind of needed them on my side if today was going to end how I wanted it to.

"I'm just trying to explain how this particular 'situation' happened," I defended before blurting out, "You know how I can listen in to your calls and texts?"

"No, we forgot," Declan drawled, but unlike Brennan, he appeared amused rather than annoyed with me.

My lips twitched. "It's a clever piece of tech. It's adaptable for any device with an internet connection—"

"Fuck," Eoghan rasped, four steps ahead. "They got their hands on it? They've been gathering intel on us?"

"They did have it in their possession. For a short while. But they weren't collecting data on us.

"Anyway, the clever part isn't accessing any device. Long story short, collating *that* much information requires a lot of storage so I developed a new method of storing all that data.

"We were thinking of cloud storage in a strictly binary way, but I was like, what if I think in quantum…" When they stared at me blankly, I grunted. "Never mind. It's unique. It's what makes the system work because there's too much to store and not enough time to trawl through what's saved.

"It's not something that can be replicated. So I got access to that and have seen what they've used my program for. We're not featured on there, *but* the Valentini Capo is, so's the new Pakhan of The Forgotten Boys, and then Dragon Head Zhao is too."

"Why are you telling us this if we're not in danger?" Aidan rumbled.

"I want to attend the Summit today." A Summit that had only been called because of the recent revelations in the press.

"Why?" Brennan growled.

"In the spirit of cooperation, I think it'd be wise to give the Russians, the Sicilians, and the Chinese what the NSA gathered. There's no guarantee that they didn't copy what they found."

"And, I repeat, why? They couldn't use any information they gathered, not when it was collected illegally, and I'm no criminal attorney, but it's likely entrapment too, no?"

I scowled at him. "You might be a bruiser, Brennan, but I know you're smarter than that."

He narrowed his eyes at me. "Is this about Star?"

"I think it'd be wise if the other factions learned she was with us now."

Declan chuckled, but it was Aidan who smirked at me. "This isn't 'take your girlfriend to work' day, Kid."

"I never said it was," I grumbled.

"She'd get a kick out of it," Eoghan answered for me.

Aidan heaved a heavy sigh. "I can't disagree that it's a wise move to share this information with the factions. What do you think, Finn?"

"I think it'll make us look benevolent."

"Benevolent equals weak," Brennan argued.

"No. They're not idiots. They, like we do, know that they're on watch lists the country over. This appears benevolent but is giving them nothing. That's my kind of deal," Finn retorted. "I also think it's wise for them to know Star is with Conor."

I knew he was my favorite brother for a reason.

"You fucking would," Brennan sniped.

"Hear me out." Finn surged forward in his seat, pissed enough to startle even Brennan. "You need to back the fuck off Star, Brennan. I understand that her past is colorful, but your fear she'll betray us to the alphabets is insane when *they* turned on *her*. You need to get over this goddamn paranoia—it's tainting your every judgment in regard to her.

"There's no denying that our brother is smart. That the factions themselves are aware of this too is indubitable. But the only person who has ever broken his code, who has ever breached his security, is *Star* fucking *Sullivan*.

"She's built herself a reputation as much as he has, and for the other factions to be aware that they're now a couple, that she's with the Irish, is akin to bragging rights that *we* have them and they don't.

"They're a fucking powerhouse, Brennan, and if you don't recognize it's wise for the other factions to know that powerhouse belongs to the Five Points, to be frank, your judgment is skewed to such a degree that it makes me question if you should be Aidan's second."

For a moment, dead silence fell.

Even more so than when I'd made my confession.

Brennan's line abruptly cut.

The rest of us blew out a breath.

"I wasn't the only one who woke up and chose war this morning, was I?" Eoghan stated, a small espresso cup in his hand—where the fuck he'd gotten that from, I had no idea.

"It needed to be said. He's being illogical and childish," Finn reasoned unapologetically.

Aidan rocked back, his chair squeaking with the move. He made no comment on Finn's argument or on his threat to Brennan, just said, "See you at the warehouse. Star, too."

When he cut the call, Eoghan and Declan did as well, though they shot me a smirk apiece, which left Finn on the line.

"Thank you for that, *dearthái r*."

"You've done more for me," Finn dismissed. "But I meant it. It might not wake him up to the nonsensical attitude he has toward her, but it might make him cut her some slack."

"I appreciate that." I hunched my shoulders. "I really fucking do."

His lips quirked to the side. "See you at the warehouse. I hope the kick she gets out of it was worth that confession."

I grinned. "I know it will be."

He winked then ended the call which turned out to be perfect timing because Star suddenly ambled into the room, *sans* Katina, Ren and Stimpy in her arms.

For once, they weren't trying to bite her and she was muttering soft sounds at them and—was the world ending?—nuzzling them against her cheek.

"You drugged them?" I asked warily.

She sniffed. "No. They're sick."

"They are?"

Nodding, she moved toward her desk and dragged their bed beside it.

As she placed them inside and tucked them between the blankets, she explained, "Just went into the kitchen and saw they'd had a feast of the chicken skin we threw in the trash last night. You need to get the waste disposal repaired."

"I'll contact the super now," I said immediately, pulling up my emails and shooting off a message right then and there.

With that done, I rocked back in my seat and watched as she fussed around the kittens she professed to dislike, but those cooing noises of hers made a liar out of her.

When they were snoozing, she retreated with a sigh to her computer.

I pulled a small box from my desk drawer and called out, "Heads-up."

That drew her attention. A second later, the rattling box landed in her hand and she smirked as she tore open the Boston Baked Beans.

"Thanks, Conor," she sang as she started snacking before plunking her ass into her chair.

Working with someone in here was new, and I was surprised by how much I enjoyed it. I'd thought I might need some space, what with how I'd lived before, but I appreciated her presence.

She broke up the silence I hadn't realized was infesting my life.

She filled the spaces that had been expanding with time.

The thought had me sighing with contentment as I cracked on with my own work too.

An hour later, when an email came through confirming a train of thought I'd had the other night, I broke into the silence to state, "Belyaev's sister, Yelizaveta, is still alive."

She frowned at me over her monitor. "I never thought she'd be dead."

"Why not?"

"Umm…" Her nose crinkled. "I genuinely forgot to tell you."

"You mean this isn't you holding intel back from me?"

"I promise."

"Yeah, yeah," I teased, deciding that giving her shit was important for keeping her ego in check.

"Troy told me that Belyaev's brother-in-law took his place in the organization."

"Fuck, Star. He's a leader we missed?!"

"No, he wasn't as powerful as his brother-in-law. The heads kept that from him. Doesn't mean his ass won't be in jail soon."

I watched as she started pummeling her keyboard with some quick keystrokes. "Kat seemed to like her aunt."

"She barely remembered her. She hasn't brought her up since. Or her cousin."

"She had a nightmare last night. She mentioned 'Leo' too."

Star shot me a concerned look. "She did? Why didn't you wake me?"

"I handled it."

"You did?" A strained smile danced around her lips. "Thank you for that."

"For what… being a father figure? I never thought you were anything other than a package deal, Star. You know that, don't you?"

"I do. You keep on showing me though, and it's always a nice surprise."

Nodding my understanding, I posited, "Maybe the nightmares are her brain's way of manifesting her memories?"

Her gaze drifted over my arm and the mostly healed tattoo as she changed the subject. "Why did you go for that? And why there when you wanted it on your chest?"

I stared down at the only ink I had on my body. Indy, the Sinners' resident tattoo artist, had designed it so that the letters were stylized to fit into the shaft of an exclamation mark. Instead of the dot, there was a star.

"You know why."

"I don't. Your handle is *aCooooig*. Not *aCoooooig*. Four 'O's, not five."

"Each 'O' is a brother."

She blinked.

"Uh huh."

"But you'll never show Finn."

"You don't know that. We work out together sometimes."

"Sometimes. How about never." She snorted. "Maybe with Brennan. The jackass."

"Why do I think you like him the most?"

A smile danced on her lips. "I like awkward things."

"Brennan is definitely awkward," I retorted, folding my arms across my chest. "Since when am I?"

"Since always." The smile was out in full force. "I bet you were born breech."

"Nah, that was Brennan." I winked at her. "I just took forty hours to come out."

"Your ma told you?"

"Many times when she was wailing about how I hacked into our school computers to change our report cards so we wouldn't get shit from her."

"Not your da?"

"Da didn't give a fuck about education until he realized that I had unusual smarts." Her eyes gleamed at my use of the word 'unusual.' Proof I was awkward. Damn, I'd walked myself into that one. "He put us in the best schools because that was what was expected of a man in his position. Plus, the law wouldn't have liked his kids not being educated."

"Finn's smart too."

"He is. Da didn't realize it until later. Hired tutors for his final years before graduation and after." I folded my arms against my chest. "What are you going to do about Kat and her aunt?"

"What do you want me to do? Get her to come over for a pool party?"

"No. But you can't keep this from her. You need to take her to a shrink like you said you were going to. I know you tried to handle this on your own, but I don't think you can if her father was hurting her and she remembers that."

"I've been researching therapists too," she sniped. "You think I'd just google 'kid shrink?'"

I hit send on an email I'd been waiting to share with her. "Best child psychiatrists in the tristate area just dropped in your inbox."

She stared down at the list and scowled. "Why ask if you'd already made a list? And why make a list? You knew I was on it."

"You're not the only control freak in the house. You think I was going to let Kat near anyone unless they'd been thoroughly vetted by both of us? This way, you can screen the list too and pick the best of the best."

Her brows lifted. "Vetted how?"

"FBI. Cross-referenced with the NSA's database."

"I *had* started looking, Conor. I don't want you to think I hadn't."

"I never thought that. But I know you're wary and that always slows things down."

She didn't deny being wary. "The NSA... You asked your handler? Or did you snoop?"

"I asked Riggs."

"Thought you didn't trust her anymore after Nimue."

I sniffed. "I don't, but you said it yourself. She was doing her job.

"Anyway, I asked her because I liked traveling outside of the continental US and didn't want to piss her off."

"Thought Anton had dealt with that for you?"

"He has. But if I piss her off then she'll find a way to rescind my passport and travel permission."

"If I hadn't already sucked you off this morning, I'd do it now."

I flashed a grin at her. "For future reference, there's no wait time on another round. *But,* I have a gift for you."

"Another one? Better than this?"

I hummed. "Want to come to a Summit?" When her eyes widened, I knew I was in for a blow job later. "Yeah, I'm not teasing."

"A Summit? Why would they let me come? Brennan barely lets me into Finn's man cave without giving me sass." When I chuckled at the idea of my bruiser of a brother 'sassing' my woman, she winked at me. "You can tell him I said that too."

"Oh, I will. Don't worry. And yeah, *the* Summit. Mostly because we need to share that Dragon Head Zhao, Custanzu Valentini, and Maxim Lyanov are persons of interest to the NSA."

"Didn't they know that already?"

"Yeah, I mean, they *are* who they are," I drawled. "It's not like it comes without a warning from the Justice Department. But there's a difference between being a regular person of interest and then being targeted by my 'radical' bugs."

"Who called them radical?"

"Me."

She rolled her eyes. "I'm not the only one with a big ego."

"Big everything according to you, *darling*."

"See? Even your dick's awkward. Couldn't be a little smaller so it'd fit easier."

"Is that a complaint?"

"Just confirmation that you're difficult. That's why I like you. The best things in life are always difficult. Look at Kat. It's why she's the perfect child."

"You didn't say that last week when she broke your computer."

"That computer was kidproof until she dropped a bottle of cream soda on it." At my snort, she grumbled, "You sure they'll let me come?"

"Told them I needed you there."

"Why? Not like you need backup."

I shrugged. "If they think I want you to hold my hand, they can. Mostly, I just knew you'd think it was cool."

She bit her lip before she burst out of her seat, startling Ren into a surprised *meow*, raced across the office, then hurled herself at me with enough force to shove my chair back a few feet.

As she choked me in a hug that I wasn't entirely sure was *loving*, she squealed as loud as Kat which keyed me into the fact that she was happy.

She only confirmed it with: "You're the best boyfriend ever."

"Boyfriend? Hey, what's with the demotion?" I teased, even though I loved her excitement.

"Fiancé! Mine! You get to choose whichever you want."

I tutted. "Then you know what I'll go with."

"You're not going to kill my buzz, Conor O'Donnelly!" she crowed. "You. Are. Officially. My. Penguin."

Beaming at her, I smacked a kiss on her cheek. "If that's the only thing I had to do to get you to admit to that then hell, I'm a moron for not thinking of this sooner!"

She dismissed that to demand, "When is it?"

I checked the clock on my monitor. "Couple hours."

Her eyes flared. "A couple hours?! I have to get ready."

When she took off with the same speed as she barreled into me, I didn't have the chance to ask her what the hell she thought you wore to a Summit, but ninety minutes later, showered and changed too, I got my answer.

She wore a black, sleeveless, knit turtleneck that displayed her strong shoulders, her hair was back in a bun that was librarian chic, and she wore dark-gray tailored pants that swirled around black, patent-leather heels. Over her arm, she'd draped a black trench coat.

"Since when do you wear heels?"

Arching a brow at me, she demanded, "Do you have a problem with my shitkickers?"

"No, but…" I whistled under my breath. "Dear God, you're hot. Where did this outfit come from?"

"Savannah, of course." She sniffed. "She said I needed to have a wardrobe that fit my position as penguin to an O'Donnelly."

I smirked. "She's smart."

"She's a pain, but hell, I didn't have to shop and she did so we were both happy."

"How many more outfits did she pick?" I queried, brows high. "Do I have more surprises in my future?"

Her lips twisted. "That would be telling. Now, is the car here for us?"

"Yeah, it's downstairs."

She peered at me, raking her eyes over my form before she graced me with my own wolf whistle. "We look like mobsters."

"No, *I* look like Clyde. You look like Bonnie."

"Hmm. I'm not sure I mind that. I definitely don't mind *this*." She took in the dark-navy suit with a slimline pinstripe that Finn had insisted upon the last time I was at his tailor. I'd gone the whole nine yards and even wore a vest. "Is that a pocket watch?"

I smiled as I slipped it from the purpose-made pocket. "My great-grandfather's."

"Who gave it to you?"

"Da."

She frowned. "He did love you in his own way, didn't he?"

"'His own way' sounds about right."

"What else did he give to you?"

"Jewelry wise? Just the ring and the watch."

"Was your great-grandfather a mobster?"

"Of course. Not as successful as the Valentinis who were behind Capone getting, well, Caponed.

"On the O'Donnelly side, that is. The other one was neck-deep in the IRA and the ECD."

"Your roots would horrify the average woman."

I swooped her down into a kiss that would have had the 'average' woman shrieking. She just moved with me, hovering over my arm as I murmured against her lips, "Since when are you average? If I'm awkward, you're atypical."

She smacked a kiss on my mouth. "We're just full of compliments today."

"Expect more when you go around looking like that. You know Brennan will be there?"

"Don't worry. I won't make him fall at my feet."

"That's my job."

"I love that you know I meant I wouldn't kick him." She grabbed my ass. "More reasons for blow jobs."

When she started to drop to her knees, I gaped at her, then at my pocket watch, and rasped, "Fuck it."

40

STAR

Star Sullivan

THE SUMMIT WAS something I'd been curious about ever since Rex, the Prez of the Satan's Sinners' MC, had gone in one time, guns blazing, his end goal to shed Italian blood.

Of course, I'd known about the Summit for years.

While the CIA was confined to international affairs, I had plenty of acquaintances who dealt with things on a national level.

I'd even heard about there being after-parties between the alphabet agencies on surveillance once the seldom-held meeting was done and the evidence had been collated.

"You know the alphabets are watching, don't you?" I inquired, infinitely curious about this side of Conor's life.

My fiancé, who still wore a happy smile from earlier, drawled, "Why are you trying to ruin my day by suggesting I'm an idiot?"

I snorted. "I find it ironic that despite the shit they must collect on you, no one gets arrested. Ever. And none of the transcripts turn up in sting operations."

"It's easier *now* because I just scramble their devices. The only person who has the true transcript is me."

"It's hot how easy illegal stuff is for you."

His lips quirked. "Feel free to give me another blow job."

"Three in a day is excessive."

"Excessive smexcessive. We have *years* to make up for."

I snickered as we reached the doorway of the warehouse where three different guards patted us down and the fourth nodded at Conor before pointing us in the right direction.

"One guard for each faction?"

"Of course."

"Before you made the 'scrambler,' what did you do?" I asked, curious. Having seen the worktable he had at the back of his office behind Japanese screens, I knew that was where he invented his 'toys.'

Including, I thought with a small whisper of excitement, my long-awaited Christmas gift.

"It varied but I came up with the prototype early on," he answered, unaware of where my thoughts had taken me. "Mostly I delayed the feed and would make sure that they got dead air if there was anything that incriminated the Five Points."

"Not the other factions?"

His look said it all.

"How did they cope without you when you were a kid?" I muttered, shaking my head.

"They had a lot more men in jail," he said simply. "You heard of the Old Wives' Club?"

"Yeah?"

"We had a lot more deaths too. There are fewer 'younger' members of that club."

When his jaw clenched at that, I touched his arm. "Is everything okay?"

"Unfinished business. Priestley O'Reilly is one of the newest members."

"She's…" I blinked. Slowly. "Callum O'Reilly was her husband. Anton told us that she was feeding information to Reinier."

"He did."

My brow puckered. "What are you going to do about her?"

"She has a kid, Star."

"So?"

"Her husband's dead. Because of us."

"And I repeat, *so*? He was a traitor! You told me that he's the reason Finn and Aoife's wedding ended up like that dragon show you made me watch." I clicked my fingers. "Game of Rings."

"*Game of Thrones*," he groaned, grabbing my hand and shoving it to my side. "How do you know so much shit but have zero pop culture references in your life unless I introduced it to you? *And* keep your voice down."

"Conor, she betrayed you. *Us*."

"I know, Star."

When I frowned up at him, it clicked in my head. Just like he'd made that list of shrinks for Kat, I'd need to do this.

"Leave it with me," I told him softly.

"No, I—"

"Leave it with me," I repeated, brushing my fingertips over his jaw. "This is women's business."

Was I surprised when he blew out a breath and nodded? Not entirely. Some things were just too hard to face. I knew Callum had been a close friend. Someone on his 'crew.' Not that I'd seen much evidence of this so-called crew. At least, not for Conor.

I'd met Finn's when Troy and Lyra were staying in the brownstone next door to his. Aidan's were around too, those cutie Frasier brothers, and so were Brennan's, now that I thought about it.

Seemed like the younger brothers didn't have as much use for extra men as the older ones did.

"Don't—" He bit off whatever he was going to say, then grated out, "She has a baby."

"You ready to look after one?"

He swallowed. "The kid has a grandmother."

"Then she'll be the one raising him and if she dies because she's a treacherous cunt, then we'll take him in."

"You mean that, don't you?"

"Kids shouldn't suffer because their parents are pieces of shit."

He tucked his arm around my waist and squeezed me against his side. That squeeze told me he agreed but I'd robbed him of words—I liked doing that to him.

I could hear talking at the other end of the warehouse, so I knew he had to hear it too.

I was half-expecting him to drop his hold on me as we neared them, but instead he pressed a kiss to my temple. "If you were any other woman, I'd let go of you because some asswipes will use someone's beloved as a weapon to hurt men like me."

My lips curved. "I appreciate your faith in me."

"Always."

So, that was how we strolled into a Summit.

And it garnered attention.

Mostly from the Triads who were the staunchest and most 'traditional' faction going.

What with the Valentini Don being obsessed with his wife and Aidan being all loved up for Savannah—neither of them could judge. As for Maxim Lyanov, he knew not to fuck with me anyway.

"Conor," Aidan greeted. "Star."

Brennan looked as dour as ever—the dude was a dick but he grew on you like skin cancer.

Finn's smile was more in his eyes than on his lips, but I figured that was from our current location.

The Valentinis and The Forgotten Boys—ex-Bratva—just peered at me like I was a Martian who'd stopped by for coffee. As for the Triads, I could see the calculations being made in their eyes.

Felt them, even.

When one of their guards just happened to drift by, fuck only knew his intent, so I grabbed his arm, dragged it behind his back, kicked his feet out from under him, drew his gun from his shoulder holster, and pressed it between his brows.

By this point, Conor had let go of his hold on me, but his amusement was as much in his eyes as it was in Finn's.

Brennan heaved a sigh as the Dragon Head jumped to his feet and snarled, "What is the meaning of this?"

In Mandarin, I retorted, "I am here to advise you, Zhao. Do *not* piss me off."

"Star? Maybe put the guard down?" Finn drawled.

"Not like a dog. Just let him go," Brennan clarified, his eyes flaring wide at any potential misunderstanding.

I flicked the gun around in my hand, released the magazine, and as it clattered on the concrete floor, I threw the Glock to the Dragon Head who fumbled the catch and ended up having to splatter it against his chest to hold it.

Holding in my smirk, *barely*, I looked around the table at the usual suspects.

"Lyanov," I greeted in Russian. "Heard you tried to rescue me in Moscow. I do *not* forget favors and I haven't forgotten that the situation with the *Krestniy Otets* is worse than ever as a result of your actions. I'm on hand to help with whatever you need in the future as compensation."

Though his stony features didn't exactly relax, he drawled, "I appreciate the offer and accept it."

"How goes it in The Forgotten Boys? Still the Pakhan?"

"Everything's the same but the name," he retorted. "I'm no longer Pakhan, but the Shukher."

I hid a grin but nodded at him before I turned to the Sicilians. It was prudent to speak with Luciu Valentini first even though my inner feminist longed to deal with his sister foremost.

In Italian, because I hadn't picked up Sicilian yet, I murmured, "Your wife and Savannah bought me these shoes, Valentini."

"Great shoes," Custanzu replied.

Valentini merely smiled. "She has the best taste."

"Apparently." I motioned between us. "We're still okay?"

Aurora chimed in, "Yes, Luciu, are we still okay after she arranged to have Alberto De Laurentiis murdered?"

My brow furrowed with annoyance. Though something niggled at me, I was too pissed not to snap, "If anyone has an axe to grind then it's me because *you* fucked up my plan. And Hunter too. But he should know that I don't do things for shits and giggles."

"I only fucked it up because *you* didn't key me into the plan in the first place," she snarled.

"Of course, I didn't. You had to appear innocent if the cops talked to you."

She sniffed at me. "As if they had the chance to do that when I am who I am. They dealt with our attorneys."

"Hate to break it to you, lady, but the reason you weren't in the know was Alberto's idea. Not mine. And, to be completely honest, after years of getting Hunter to chase after you, was it any wonder that he didn't know what your endgame was?"

Aurora's expression didn't give me much hope of us getting friendly, but that was fine with me.

I didn't need to make friends, only had to stop making enemies.

Hunter was the one I missed anyway.

I'd have just liked it if two smart-as-fuck women in positions of power in NYC's underbelly had gotten along.

"Aurora?" Luciu drawled then switched into Sicilian—the exact goddamn reason that was at the top of my list of priorities.

I fucking loathed it when people thought they could talk around me.

Aurora glowered at me throughout whatever the hell it was Luciu was saying because, *damn*, Sicilian was entirely different than Italian —a whole other language in and of itself.

Eventually, she huffed. "Fine." In Italian.

Then Conor spoke.

In Sicilian.

Goddammit, this man. He was so fucking hot with all the shit he knew. I didn't even care that I had no idea what he said.

Luciu's nostrils flared but he replied in English. "You learned Sicilian?"

Conor smirked. "The moment you became a faction worthy of my attention."

Custanzu arched a brow. "Is that high praise or low?"

"The highest with Conor," Finn retorted, leaning back in his seat with all the ease of a man who was comfortable with his power.

And *power* they had.

Despite losing their father, Aidan Jr. had picked up the mantle and he dominated this arena.

It wasn't as simple as him staring down the length of the room *at* the others, but in how the others looked at him as if he were in charge.

To be fair, with the Russians and Sicilians so fresh on the scene, only the Triads were a potential threat, but how could they be when the Sicilians and Russians had such close ties to the O'Donnellys?

Check. Mate.

Oddly aroused by how much power Conor had, I waited for direction because Brennan already had his panties in a bunch from how I'd managed to dictate things since I'd shown up.

Aidan, mimicking Finn by leaning back in his seat, stated, "Conor and Star are here to help."

"How could they help us?" the Dragon Head sneered.

Aidan waved a hand. "I'll let Conor explain."

"While it would be moronic to think that you're not aware you're on watch lists, the NSA recently had some software come under their purview."

"Illegal software," I muttered. "And definitely unconstitutional. The whole nine yards.

"Whichever way you swing it, the alphabets had *no* right to use it for their own gain."

"That bad?"

"Yeah, Aurora, that bad," I replied, shooting her a cool glance. "To the point where you, in your role as D—"

Her eyes flared wide, then in Italian, she snarled, "They know nothing about my past."

"Of course, they *know* who you are. They just don't bring it up," I retorted. "Don't be a fool. A different haircut doesn't change your identity."

"We don't speak of it here," Luciu confirmed. "She was the DA but only to further our gains—"

"I grow tired of this multilingual meeting," Zhao snapped. "It's *rude* to speak in other languages, even if it is an attempt at a power play from you, Ms. Sullivan." His eyes narrowed. "I assume you're the reason we found my son? Lodestar's skills are infamous."

"They probably are but I don't refer to myself in the third person yet." I hitched a shoulder, though I noticed the Valentini siblings peer among each other in surprise—they hadn't realized the Dragon Head knew I'd worked for them. "The Valentinis asked me to look into a laptop and I happened to find him. I don't deserve—"

"You do." He rapped his fingers against the table. "You speak of this software as if you know it well."

"I made it," was Conor's answer. "That means I know what it could have picked up."

"It would be inadmissible in court," Aurora pointed out.

"It would, but that doesn't mean it can't lead to other investigations," Finn answered. "That's all it needs, isn't it?

"With as much as we stonewall them, something like this gives them an avenue to wander down that was closed to them before."

"And therein lies the danger," I agreed.

"How did they gain access to this software?"

Conor cast Custanzu a glance. "They had it in their hands for a very short while. I locked them out the moment I knew they were using it."

"That's a relief," Aurora mocked.

Conor's brothers suddenly appeared grouchy. Ah, so he'd told them. He cleared his throat. "I had an arrangement with the NSA."

As outrage moved around the factions like a tidal wave, I called out, "It wasn't by choice, and it was from when he wasn't as experienced."

"Meaning?" Custanzu demanded.

"I'd lessen the sass, Custanzu, considering your actions when you were a teenager."

His cheeks blanched. "I beg your pardon?"

"I think we both know what happened—"

"Enough," Luciu barked, studying his brother concernedly. "We are friends, Star. Do not let us part from this meeting as enemies."

I pursed my lips as Conor placed a calming hand on my shoulder.

"I was caught hacking into a government database when I was a kid. They knew I'd serve them better out in the open rather than in a jail cell."

Luciu frowned but, to Aurora, asked, "Does the NSA frequently make deals like this?"

"You'd be surprised how prisoners can be mobilized," I muttered, "for their government's gain."

"If anyone would know," Aurora said simply, "it would be you, Sullivan."

We shared a look and nodded at one another.

"As I've grown older, I've become better—"

"One of the best hackers in the world," I interrupted, elbowing him in the side. "This isn't the time for being humble, Conor."

"If you'd stop interrupting him, Star," Brennan snapped, "maybe we could get this part of the meeting over with."

I scowled at him but zipped up.

Conor admitted, "Star is one of the best too. For her to compliment me tells you everything. As I *improved*, my worth to them did as well. It meant I had as much bartering power with them as they did with me."

"You negotiated your family's safety with the NSA?" Maxim questioned, sounding impressed.

"I did. The deal is no longer in place. The NSA were recently in need of my skills and at the same time, members of the CIA tried to dispose of me—"

I glanced at his brothers and saw from their stoniness that he hadn't shared that piece of news.

Making a mental note to get Eagle Eyes to frazzle Temper Black's ass for betraying me—but also to send her a fruit basket for saving Conor's behind while I wasn't around to do it—I tuned back into the conversation.

"—it was on this occasion that my software was taken. As I said, it wasn't used for long and I have access to what they uncovered." He reached into his pockets and pulled out microchips. That seemed to be a signal because he turned to the guards lining the walls. "I'll hand them to one of your men."

A guard from each faction drifted forward after receiving nods from their leaders, but before Conor could pass them out, I barely hid my gasp as I recognized one of the men.

Chadwick.

Wait, he was with the Sicilians?

I frowned at him but he cut his eyes to the right as if telling me to keep our connection quiet.

As Conor passed him the chip, I felt something being slipped into my pocket, and I didn't react, knowing he'd have left a card for me there.

"Everything they had on us is here?" Luciu questioned once the chip was in his hand.

"Yes." Conor hitched a shoulder. "It might be nothing; it could be everything. Regardless, this is a measure of the trust and respect we have in our Summit factions."

Maxim studied the chip in his hand. "Why didn't you try to use this as leverage?"

"Because the power balance in New York has just reached an equilibrium that we're all content with, wouldn't you agree?" Aidan queried, bringing the dialogue back to him. "We're allies."

"And this tightens our ties," the Dragon Head groused, sounding more querulous than ever, but there was also something resigned about his words. As if he knew he was locked into being the second most powerful faction on the East Coast.

Aidan shot Conor a look, and Conor dipped his chin.

That was our cue to leave, I figured.

This was definitely my idea of a surprise—I had the best penguin ever.

41

TEXT CHAT

ANTON: *I heard you attended a Summit.*

Star: *How did you hear that?*

Anton: *Have ears in many places.*

Star: *You do, hmm? Should I warn Conor?*

Anton: *No. They're friendly to us both.*

Star: *Intriguing.*

Anton: *Hardly.*

Star: *Do you want to know what was said?*

Anton: *No. I wanted to talk to you.*

Star: *About?*

Anton: *Anything. Everything.*

Star: *Huh.*

Anton: *If you wish to talk to me in return, that is.*

Star: *I don't not want to talk to you.*

Anton: *I suppose that's something.*

Star: *It's a lot of somethings. I don't want to talk to many people.*

Anton: *Then I'm honored.*

Star: *Yes.*

Star: *I'm meeting up with an old soldier buddy of mine tomorrow.*

Anton: *That's nice. You served together?*

Star: *We did. We play chess together. He always beats me.*

Anton: *The next time we meet, I shall teach you some tricks. Chess is my sport of choice.*

Star: *I'd like that. We could teach Kat? She doesn't have much patience.*

Anton: *Yes, I should meet her.*

Star: *Troy says Lyra's settling in, by the way.*

Anton: *She told me this too. You haven't seen her?*

Star: *Not really. Been busy, plus Troy dances to the beat of her own drum.*

Anton: *Your daughter is well?*

Star: *She's been having nightmares. Conor gave me a list of shrinks to look up but I'm wary about choosing one.*

Anton: *Why?*

Star: *I don't trust them with her. I certainly don't trust her past with them.*

Anton: *Understandable, I suppose. When I was a child, we didn't have such things. That isn't to say that the world isn't a better place for having them, but perhaps you could talk to her? Get her to open up?*

Star: *I'm scared to make things worse.*

Anton: *Then don't pressure her and, in a pinch, you have a list of someones you can call on if things do not turn out right.*

Star: *True. I could try, at least.*

Anton: *That is all any of us can do.*

Star: *Have you heard of Rachel Laker?*

Anton: *The attorney, of course.*

Star: *She and I and a few other women are starting a foundation.*

Anton: *I know. I saw the paperwork. Helped push it through.*

Star: *You and your 'eyes.' Now I know where I get it from.*

Anton: *You're far more impressive. What you do, you do on your own. I have a collective working on my behalf.*

Anton: *It is good what you're trying to do.*

Star: *I want to trust the department you've put together. I want to step back.*

Anton: *I'm surprised to hear this.*

Star: *I can't let go entirely, but I can let go some. I need to live, Anton. I didn't realize until Conor came and got me that what I was doing wasn't living.*

Anton: *You've lost many years because of the Sparrows. I applaud you for making such a healthy decision for yourself.*

Star: *This way, I can help the people who matter—the victims. I was one of them.*

Anton: *You'll never be one of them again.*

Star: *No. I won't.*

Anton: *You are happy with Conor?*

Star: *I am.*

Anton: *You wear his ring.*

Star: *I do.*

Anton: *I'd like to attend your wedding whenever it may be. Do you think that would be possible?*

Star: *Yeah.*

Anton: *I'm glad to hear it. :)*

Star: *Conor told me that you asked Aidan to mobilize the ECD.*

Anton: *Not that I'm surprised he did, but he shouldn't have told you that.*

Star: *What are your plans?*

Anton: *A weaker Britain.*

Star: *Why?*

Anton: *We all have our pet plans, don't we?*

Star: *Hmm. That's not an answer.*

Anton: *It is time for a revolution, my dear.*

Star: *Ah, crap. You don't have illusions of grandeur, do you?*

Anton: *No, just a dream that Lyra's and Katina's grandchildren will still be able to inhabit this planet. I'm an old man but even I can see the writing on the wall.*

Star: *And dissembling, what, the old guard will do it?*

Anton: *No. Capitalism. But that's a conversation for another day. Now that I'm without a council, thanks to you, I have more power than ever.*

Anton: *Time to use it for good.*

Star: *Just don't turn into Stalin.*

Anton: *Your great-grandfather severely regretted not being able to assassinate him.*

Star: *He tried?*

Anton: *Many times. How do you think the Great Purge happened?*

Star: *;/*

Anton: *And communism fell because he and I worked together to ensure that it did.*

Anton: *You may not like to hear it, but your family has always made kings and slayed them. Perhaps when it's time, you'd be interested in helping me…*

Star: *I wouldn't say no. Just not yet.*

Anton: *Fine. I understand you need closure. We shall work on that, and then we shall close that chapter of your past and focus on the future, da?*

Star: *Da.*

Star: *Have you heard anything about the Sparrows harvesting organs?*

Anton: *How grim. No, I haven't. You have?*

Star: *A whisper. From an untrustworthy source. But I had to ask.*

Anton: *Stepping back lasted all of 2 minutes?*

Star: *Curiosity killed the cat and only the answer brought it back. :)*

Star: *That aside, I need your help.*

Anton: *With?*

Star: *Katina.*

Anton: *You need help with the fact she's a missing person in Ohio?*

Star: *I shouldn't be surprised that you looked into us, should I?*

Anton: *No. You shouldn't be surprised. You're lucky that you're not in a federal jail though.*

Star: *Nah. I was living on an MC compound lol. I was pretty damn safe.*

Anton: *What do you want? The kidnapping charge or her file in the social services' registry to disappear?*

Star: *Could make the file disappear. Could probably make the* *kidnapping charge go away if I tried, but I'd prefer for things to be legal…*

Anton: *You wish to adopt her?*

Star: *Yeah.*

Anton: *I'll make it happen. It will take time. These things do when you follow the rules…*

Star: *That's why I rarely follow them lol.*

Anton: *I can see that. I'll make it work.*

Star: *Is this your rebellious phase?*

Anton: *It's my 'I'm an old man and I want to know my grand-daughter' phase. That means I'll bend the rules for you.*

Star: *Not for the world?*

Anton: *Maybe. As Peter Parker's uncle once told him, "With great power comes great responsibility."*

Star: *That quote would impress Conor but I'm not a comic book nerd. Still, you get some points on his behalf.*

Anton: *Glad to hear it. I suffered through that movie.*

Star: *Why?*

Anton: *I helped a Brother make it happen.*

Star: *You're into movies?*

Anton: *I'm into everything, dear. Most of which I wish I were in the dark about.*

Anton: *Okay, I shall speak with you when I have news on the adoption.*

Star: *Thank you, Anton. I can't tell you how much I appreciate that.*

Anton: *If anyone understands the pull of family, Star, it is I. Now, try not to get into any trouble until we speak again, da?*

Star: *Da.*

TYCOON'S MEGA YACHT SEIZED IN NICE

FRANCE'S DGSI, under the guidance of Interpol's Special Trafficking Unit, seizes the mega yacht of George Bailey-Smith, British tech tycoon, in Nice as 'crime scene' in the ongoing investigation into the 'Sparrows' organization.

Several women described as 'sex slaves' are currently being treated. Many are in critical condition.

PART 3

Watch carefully,
the magic that occurs,
when you give a person,
just enough comfort,
to be themselves.
- atticus

42

STAR

Star Sullivan

"WHAT DID you want to meet here for?" I grouched. "We could have done this in a coffee shop."

Chadwick peered at me from the bench he was sitting on. "You stop playing or something?"

Grimacing as I stared at the unusually blue sky, I muttered, "No. But chessboards are mobile. Anyway, you're just pissed I beat you during our last game."

Didn't matter that was around seven years ago… Soldiers bore the worst grudges.

He hitched a shoulder. "Let's see if you got better or worse."

Heaving a sigh, I sat opposite him and realized I was white. "You trying to psych me out? You always play white."

He beamed a loaded grin at me. "I changed since we last met, Star."

"Apparently. Since when did you work for the mafia?"

"Since Aurora Valentini took me in off the streets."

"Off the *streets*?" I blinked at him. "Does Cin know?"

He pursed his lips. "No. I don't want her to know either. I don't take charity."

"So you'll take charity from the Sicilian mafia but not from a friend?"

He narrowed his eyes at me. "Is this how you want this meeting to go?"

"No." I gritted my teeth. "What's going on, Chadwick?"

"I got myself a job. One I don't hate. Seems like you did too if you're friendly with the Irish. Or is that emerald on your finger not an engagement ring?"

"It is an engagement ring," I stated proudly. "And nobody *hires* me. I choose who I work with."

"Not everyone is as lucky as you."

"Lucky? You think we don't all have unpleasant histories?" I sneered at him. "I ended up in a fucking trafficker's nest, and you landed on the streets when there were people who'd have your back stateside if you'd just have asked.

"The government might not support us, but we make our own friends, don't we?"

He cut his gaze to the ground. "I was in a bad place, Star."

"So? That's what friends are for. You had our backs in the sandbox; we'd have had yours at home."

"Not everyone's like you. Maybe I forgot that. It'd been some time since we last caught up. And when I said I was in a bad place, I meant it. Got off my meds and shit."

"You're back on them?"

"I am."

Relief filtered through me. "Good. That's what I like to hear." I picked up a pawn and studied the piece—it was the same we'd used back when we'd been in Baghdad together. "It's good to see you, Chadwick."

"You always did ride people's asses when you liked them," he teased.

"Exactly. That's how you know we're friends."

"Good to see you too, Star."

I didn't bother demurring: "What are you doing with the Sicilians?"

"Like I told you, Aurora took me in and she realized what I can do—"

"She took *you* in?"

"There's no funny business. Hunter De Laurentiis is her husband."

"I know. But why you? In particular, I mean? When you said she realized what you can do, does she know what you've done?"

"Does she know what I did for Uncle Sam? Sure. Does she know what I did off the books? No. That's why it's called *off the books*."

"You didn't tell her?"

"No. Of course not. But she probably read between the lines anyway. She's canny like that." He shot me a look loaded with warning. "Aurora's good people. The streets around her base are riddled with the homeless and she took us in, gave us food, put a roof over our heads, gave us a place to wash ourselves and our clothes—"

"She gave you the basics to allow you to pick your lives up again."

He nodded. "Good people, see?"

"I see." I wouldn't have expected that of Aurora either. Not when she exuded 'stone-cold bitch' vibes. "So you got a promotion?"

"I did."

"Do I wanna know how?"

He smirked at me, and Jesus, it was good to see that smirk. "Nope. Anyways, are we playing?"

"We're playing. I'm glad you've found your feet, Chad."

"Me too, to be honest. When I said I was in a bad place, I meant it."

"You willing to work with me?"

"In what way? I won't betray Aurora, Star."

"Not asking you to. If you didn't realize at the Summit, we're allies."

Snickering, he shook his head. "You and your prickly ass attitude, I swear. You reverse psychology the fuck out of people."

"That's not a verb."

"It is for you. But yeah, if you don't expect me to feed intel from the Sicilians back to the Irish, I'll work with you."

"You're going to let Aurora know?"

His gaze was measured as he took in the first move I made on the chessboard. "Yes."

I hummed. "Interesting."

We played for a while, and I scoped him out, trying to see if he'd changed his strategy. I was unsurprised to learn that he had. I figured I had too. He was more cautious; I was less. Fitting considering our pasts. They shaped us, after all.

"You still talk to Cin?"

I thought about what Conor, Troy, Cin, and I had gotten up to recently. "I still talk to her, yeah."

"Don't tell her you saw me," he said as he made a questionable move on the board.

Taking his knight, I replied, "If you think I'm getting on her bad side because of you, you're mistaken."

He hissed under his breath. More at my comment than at the piece I took. "You already texted her about our meeting, didn't you?"

"Yup. You're lucky she's busy or she'd have been here herself."

His mouth tightened.

"Never understood why you fought it, to be honest."

"Fought what?"

His growl used to do shit to my insides. I guessed that was the power of Conor if he could make a hunk like Chad unappealing.

"You and Cin would be perfect together."

"Creed liked her."

"They weren't dating," I pointed out, unsurprised that I took his rook when he wasn't focusing on the game.

And it wasn't a lie.

Fucking while in the sandbox did not a relationship make.

"Bro code."

I sniffed. "That's dumb. He shouldn't stop you from dating her. You heard from him?"

"He's overseas."

"You kept in touch with him but not us?"

"It's different between us."

"Why?"

"Just is."

I huffed out a sigh. "If she kicks your ass, I'm going to watch."

"And enjoy?"

"You bet."

He arched a brow at me. "You gonna tell me what happened to you in this 'trafficker's nest?'"

"If you want to know."

"Of course I do."

So, I blew out a breath and shared the sorry state of my past with him.

The passage of time hadn't changed our bond.

But I'd still sic Cin on him.

FOUR POLITICIANS ARRESTED IN THE NETHERLANDS—SUSPECTED TIES TO 'SPARROWS'

DUTCH NATIONAL POLICE, under the guidance of Interpol's Special Trafficking Unit, arrest four politicians in the ongoing investigation into the 'Sparrows' organization, citing 'corruption' and 'fraud.'

43

TEXT CHAT

CIN: *Well?! How did it go?*

Star: *It went okay. He was living on the streets for a while, Cin.*

Cin: *Jesus H. Christ! What the fuck did he do that for?*

Star: *Said he went off his meds.*

Cin: *So he went and lived on the streets? I have a goddamn apartment in the city. He could have lived there.*

Star: *You know how men are.*

Cin: *Moronic?*

Star: *Lol. Yeah.*

Cin: *Don't make it seem like you understand his logic.*

Star: *I don't. I gave him hell. But you can't change what's already done.*

Cin: *Is he still cute?*

Star sends picture

Star: *Sneaked this when he grabbed a hot dog.*

Cin: *Wow. He's hotter.*

Star: *Lol. Thought you'd think that.*

Star sends picture

Cin: *Why didn't you lead with that one? My God, that ASS!!!*

Star: *Tell me you didn't wolf whistle!*

Cin: *Haha, you know me too well.*

Star: *Even I have to admit he has a fine ass. Shame he IS an ass.*

Cin: *He just needs me to whip him into shape.*

Star: *LOL. Is that what he needs?*

Cin: *;)*

Cin: *Did he ask about me?*

Star: *He did.*

Cin: *And Creed?*

Star: *Nuh huh. You need to speak with him yourself.*

Cin: *Give me his number and I will. I've tried to get in touch with him before but I could never find him.*

Cin: *Man, I need to tap that ass.*

Star: *You're leaving upstate New York soon, right?*

Cin: *Yeah, probably heading to New Mexico if you don't need me.*

Star: *Got a job?*

Cin: *Two, actually. Man and wife. Haha. It'd be hilarious if it wasn't reality.*

Star: *There's a story.*

Cin: *They're getting divorced. She wants his watches; he wants her shoes—not sure why he wants the shoes. I didn't ask—so instead of giving each other what they want, they're gonna splatter each other's brains out and I'm not averse to taking their money which is currently sitting pretty in escrow.*

Star: *Ahh, the Ledger. Your best friend.*

Cin: *Made by one of yours.*

Star: *Yup. Not sure if Hunter considers me a friend anymore though. He's still pissed at me. Haven't heard from him in months.*

Cin: *What did you do again?*

Star: *Kinda helped his grandfather die.*

Cin: *Yeah, people get real weird about shit like that.*

Star: *IKR? I guess I get it. Even if it was his grandfather's idea.*

Cin: *This is why snipers should only be friends with snipers.*

Star: *Not a bad idea. You know Conor's brother? Eoghan? He has PTSD issues.*

Cin: *Him, you, me, and Chadwick lol.*

Star: *Yeah. Wanna talk about it?*

Cin: *Talk? Are you being serious?*

Star: *Deadly.*

Cin: *What kind of talk?*

Star: *I dunno. Like, if you've had a bad day or something…*

Cin: *You want me to share?*

Star: *Yeah.*

Cin: *Why?*

Star: *I dunno. He doesn't seem to be doing great.*

Cin: *So, this is for him?*

Star: *It is, but what with him and Chadwick, it got me to thinking that we probably need it too.*

Cin: *Hmm.*

Star: *Not like we can talk to shrinks, right?*

Cin: *No.*

Star: *I was thinking a poker game or something.*

Cin: *I'm more interested. What are the stakes?*

Star: *God knows. Only just thought of it.*

Cin adds Troy to the chat

Troy: *Sup?*

Cin: *You still play poker, right?*

Troy: *Duh.*

Star: *How's Lyra?*

Troy: *Hates her new school. But she saw Katina in the library and that made her feel better.*

Star: *Why?*

Troy: *Dunno. Guess she figures she's not alone.*

Cin: *Still can't believe how swaaanky your new digs are.*

Troy: *Me neither. Didn't ask for them but won't say no. Not when Lyra's safer here.*

Cin: *Best way. Are you settling in?*

Troy: *I don't like being so high up, but what can you do?*

Star: *You got an emergency route out of there planned?*

Troy: *Two. You?*

Star: *Three. But one involves a helicopter.*

Troy: *Knowing Conor, he's crazy enough about you to have one stationed up there at all times if it'll reassure you.*

Cin: *She's not wrong.*

Star: *If I promised to teach him how to fly it, then he'd probably be down...*

Troy: *Fucker's rich enough. Get him spending those dollars.*

Star: *He isn't into FinDom lol.*

Troy: *Nah, him and that glittery jizz are just a sap for you. Anyway, why have you hit me up? Talking to either of you wasn't on my list of things to do today.*

Cin: *You're as friendly as always.*

Star: *You have trauma issues, Troy. I'm thinking of starting a poker game with ex-servicemen and women. Do you want in?*

Troy: *What are the stakes?*

Cin: *Good sign that you're not arguing about having trauma issues. *coughs* Or that you're fucked in the head.*

Cin: *How much do you want to lose?*

Troy: *Fuck off. I'm a much better player than you.*

Star: *She's good, Troy. Improved since the last time you played her.*

Troy: *How do you know?*

Cin: *We play online sometimes.*

Troy: *You two are fucking weirdos. How about two k?*

Cin: *That's all?*

Troy: *Some of us have kids.*

Cin: *Don't make it seem like you don't have money. That security system in your house was worth a small fortune.*

Troy: *Yeah, and it's not as if it's an investment that'll accrue interest. That was a quarter-million dollars I'll never get back.*

Star: *I'm fine with 2k. Makes it enough to be interesting.*

Troy: *Okay, I'm down. Gimme the particulars nearer the time and I'll make it happen.*

Cin: *Cool. I'd better get going. Got shit to do, people to kill.*

Star: **snorts**

Troy: *Speak later.*

Star: *Happy snipering.*

44

CONOR

THOUGH I WAS sweaty from my workout, I pressed a kiss to Star's shoulder and waited for her to take the box in my hands.

"What's this?" she asked.

"Something to make you happy, and seeing as you're about to eat with family, you could probably wear it too."

Laughing, she untied the ribbon on the box and smirked. "Flannel PJs?"

"I got a matching set for me and one for Katina as well."

Her eyes gleamed. "We're definitely wearing these tonight. Aidan will show up in Brioni, Camden in vintage Gucci, and Savannah in her designer *du jour*. We have to break glass ceilings."

"Not sure we can do that in a penthouse. Aren't we too high up?"

"You have to start somewhere." She peered at her watch then grabbed my arm and started dragging me toward the bedrooms. "We have enough time to change. You go and get ready and I'll give these to Kat."

"Nah, I gave her set to her earlier. Hers have polar bears on them. I just got us regular plaid."

With a shake of her head, she chuckled. "You're one of a kind, Conor. You know that?"

"I mean, I try."

Still needing to clean up after my workout, I pulled out the new PJs that I'd actually *physically* bought—hadn't just ordered them online—and headed into the shower.

After washing up, I changed, just in time to hear the doorbell.

Knowing it'd be the food, I left that with Star and went to our office to check how my 3D printer was progressing, then I scanned my emails and made sure some programs were still running.

A half-hour later, Star called out, "Conor, Savannah just texted to let me know they're on their way up."

The doorbell sounded again. I stretched then shut my computer down for the night, smiled at the new picture frame on my desk of Kat and me on the Staten Island Ferry, and moved into the hall to greet my brother, Savannah, and Camden—the reason for the dinner.

I caught them just in time to hear Savannah grumble, "I spent thirty grand on your new wardrobe, Star, and you wear pajamas to meet with us?"

"We're among family, aren't we? I'm jealous I didn't think of it," Camden, Savannah's brother, joked as he hauled Star into him. "God, it's good to see you. When Savannah told me that you wanted to meet up, I was so freakin' happy—"

"Star?! The polar bears are winking!" Katina chuckled as she pulled out her pajama sweatshirt as she ambled down the hall. Kat flashed a glance at the door, then she blanched. She dropped the hem of her sweatshirt. Gulped. Blushed. Then rubbed her eyes. "Is that…" She peered at Savannah, and Aidan, then studied Camden. "Savannah," she whispered. "You're the best aunt ever!"

Savannah grinned as she shoved Camden in the shoulder. "Meet your number one fan in the whole universe, Camden."

Though he grinned back, he held out his hand for Kat. "It's a pleasure to meet you, Katina. It's an honor to meet my *numero uno* fan."

Kat gaped some more then, in a flurry of energy, barreled into Savannah. She squeezed her so hard, Savvie yelped, then she quickly grabbed Camden's hand and shook it up and down like she was the Hulk.

"Sir, I just need you to know that *Untold Promises* changed my life."

Star snorted, but Camden sent her a dead serious look and stated, "It changed mine too. I'm glad we had the same vibe from it."

Her eyes turned round and for a moment, I didn't know if she was going to melt into the ground or just fade to dust, but she only whispered, "I knew we were soul mates."

Chuckling, Star retorted, "What have we said about being a stalker, Katina? Come on, brat, let's stop freaking Camden out."

Kat nodded then drifted backward. "This is my house, Camden. *Mi casa es su casa,* okay?"

Aidan laughed as she darted toward her room, muttering about telling Juniper and Ginger. I'd thought they were a style of teabag from Starbucks for a week until Star told me they were her new frenemies at school.

"You're still trying to hide from the paps? It's that bad, Camden?" Star asked, breaking into my train of thought as she beckoned everyone into the apartment and guided them into the living room.

Determined to focus, I heard Camden admit, "This time of year always sucks."

"If you want to stay with us, I don't think Conor would mind," she offered, shooting me a glance.

I hitched a shoulder. "Kat said it—*mi casa es su casa,* Camden. We have plenty of room here."

He shot me a sheepish grin. "Thanks, but it's okay. I'm staying at the Langham. It's just that I was saying to Aidan how difficult it was to get out of the hotel with the press haunting my every waking move."

"The offer's there," I said amicably, earning a kiss from Star as she clapped her hands together.

"Do we want something to drink first or food?"

"Food!" Savannah barked. "I'm hungry."

Aidan and Camden laughed but Star just rolled her eyes and snagged Camden's and Savannah's hands to tug them forward. The move was borderline juvenile and it made me happy to see.

She'd settled into the penthouse as if there'd never been a day where she wasn't here. Mostly, I wished that there *hadn't* been a time when she hadn't been here, but hell, I had her now.

Leaving the three to walk ahead, I stayed behind with Aidan. "Why's this time of year hard?"

"I don't know," he answered with a frown. "But I *do* know he's a gambling addict. Got the shit kicked out of him two Christmases ago by some two-bit bookie."

I hitched a shoulder. "If Camden's finding it tough right now, then maybe him hanging around Savannah will help? You know how close-knit they are."

"Close-knit and argumentative as fuck. I totally understand why Ma used to knock our heads together when we were kids. They never shut the hell up."

"Is that why you tried to dump him on my door?"

"How do you know that was my endgame?"

"You didn't offer to let him stay with you."

"I like the guy but the pair of them together drive me insane."

Chuckling, I walked with him toward the dining room where the trio had already started digging into the food that Star had ordered.

Spying the dozen-plus cardboard takeout boxes, I laughed when I saw she'd gone for broke and had ordered Italian, Chinese, Korean, *and* steak.

"For me, I assume?" I teased, grabbing the steak and dumping it on a dish without waiting for an answer.

"You're turning into one-hundred-percent prime rib," she joked.

"You need to diversify your diet, Conor. You know red meat isn't great for you, don't you?" Savannah chided, pointing at me with her chopstick.

I grunted but it was Star who said, "Nag your own husband, Vana."

"You're not married yet," Savannah pointed out.

She jerked the neckline of her top down, revealing the phoenix with my name interspersed amid the ephemeral lines. "See that? I'm as good as married."

"You're not a brother in the MC."

Star sniffed. "Honorary brother."

"Since when?"

"I don't know. I'm guessing since I got my ass blown up for the club."

Camden's brows lifted. "Your ass got blown up at a club?"

"No. An MC is a motorcycle club, Camden," Savannah explained.

"I've watched *Sons of Anarchy* like a normal person," he argued. "But since when do you know an MC, Star?"

"Since I've been living with one."

Camden shook his head. "I'm the rocker but you're the rebel."

"Let's not tell your fans that, huh?" Star derided, slurping down some noodles.

Camden flashed a glance at her now-covered tits. "Does that really mean you're married?"

"It does in the land of the Sinners' MC."

Aidan, having grabbed some fettucini Alfredo, asked, "When did you get that, Star?"

"Recently."

He sighed. "When?"

"A short time ago."

Aidan mocked, "I guess that's me told," to which Savannah laughed and bumped fists with Star. The look he shot me was pointed. "By someone other than you. Thanks for the update, Kid."

I ignored him. Cut off some prime rib. Blinked at him. "It wasn't about anyone other than Star and me."

Aidan grunted.

"You didn't tell Mom and Dad about... *this*?" Camden asked, breaking into our stare-off.

"Why would I?" Star countered, forking up some Pad Thai. "We all know how your mom feels about me."

"I don't," Aidan grumbled.

"I kind of do, actually," I countered. "Lorelei has a problem with Star because of Gerry, Star's dad."

"What happened with her dad?"

Star tilted her head to the side at me. "What happened with my dad?"

I hitched a shoulder. "Don't blame me. Savannah told me this time."

"Savannah," she snapped.

"What?! I'd just found out Mom is writing her goddamn memoir—"

"And you didn't lead with this conversation the first time we met up again?" Star bristled. "How am I only just learning about this? She can't publish anything without me signing off on it!"

Savannah sighed. "She felt it was a good time to write about her life."

"And that included her and Dagger and Gerry being in a menage."

Camden put down his forkful of Kung Pao chicken. "A thousand hours of therapy didn't block those memories out of my brain."

Savannah's nose wrinkled at the bridge. "Yeah, it was kind of a traumatizing time."

"Wait, your parents and Star's dad were in a threesome? As in, *living* in a threesome?" Aidan gaped at them.

"Yeah," Savannah muttered. "It was a weird time. They'd lost Casey, Star's mom, and he'd started using again."

"Started fucking everything that moved again too," Star said bitterly.

I rubbed her knee. I knew those memories remained a sore spot when she pressed her fingers to mine, knotted them together, and didn't let go.

"And you became a problem child," Camden retorted.

"Can't deny I got to be a problem. Whenever he used too much, I'd act out," she explained to Aidan. "I only behaved when he was clean. Then I realized *why* he was clean and…"

"She rebelled again," Camden answered for her. "I didn't hate it when they were together, but I didn't like finding them in—" He thrust another digit through the circle he made with his thumb and pointer finger then did some kind of movement that was more like origami than anything else. "—various positions."

Aidan plunked his elbows down on the table. "I can see Lorelei being into that, to be honest."

"Of course. She's all about sexual empowerment," Savannah agreed. "Did you know the last time I saw her she gave me a vibrator to gift to Victoria?"

Aidan burst out laughing. "No. I didn't know. Did you give it to her?"

"Sure. That's why I didn't tell you. You'd have told me not to."

He grimaced. "I'd have told you to keep your nose out. Not because I'm a prude—"

"Oh, I knew that already, babe," she chirped with a wink.

"—but because I don't need Eoghan coming to me telling me my wife is corrupting his sister-in-law."

"Like she'd tell Eoghan what I gave her," Savannah scoffed.

"She has a point," I said with a laugh.

"Has she used it?" Star queried. "She's a sweet girl but looks like she has a stick up her ass."

Savannah snorted. "I didn't ask her, dumbo. Just left it with her. It's there when she's ready and only she knows when that is. Mom just wanted her to be prepared."

"It's weird that Mom even thought about her sex life," Camden grumbled. "She's met her, what? Twice?"

"She's pulled back from her clients but I think she misses it."

Star frowned. "She's not working as a therapist anymore?"

Savvie bit her lip. "Nope."

"Why not?"

"She says she wants to devote her time to her memoir."

A sharp scowl flashed across Aidan's brow at something she said, but he simply focused on his pasta before he reached for a slice of garlic bread.

Someone wasn't thinking about getting laid tonight.

I heaved a sigh at the notion of this meal triggering an argument, but I guessed it meant the siblings would have to get together more often.

I was pretty sure regular catchups were why my brothers and I didn't argue that much, just bickered.

As everyone settled into their meal and Katina popped her head in for dessert, I realized Star had grabbed her a pizza that she'd been eating in the living room she'd staked as her own.

That was when I knew Katina was capable of being *shy*. Camden was why, of course. It sucked meeting your idols—I'd know. I was sure I was going to die when I'd met Savannah and Camden's father, Dagger.

Here, Kat had a golden opportunity to eat with Camden himself, to ask him whatever she wanted, but she was too busy hiding out in her living room.

When she anxiously toed the rug beneath the dinner table, blushing as she peeked at Camden, hovering over cookie dough ice cream as she informed Savannah about my French braiding skills when Savvie had told her how pretty she looked—which had Aidan shooting me a bewildered glance—I experienced the weirdest feeling.

It wasn't bad, just weird.

Just *happy*.

So fucking happy.

And it was unusual.

But good.

Fantastic, even.

My family and Aidan's were tangled together and I loved it. I loved that this was my future.

I loved that this was an unexpected blessing.

In my life, I'd experienced too few of those.

Like she knew where my mind was, Star squeezed my hand. Our knotted fingers remained clasped.

As they always would.

PRESIDENT DAVIDSON FOCUSES ON THE 'SPARROWS' IN THE FIRST CAUCUS OF HIS RE-ELECTION CAMPAIGN

PRESIDENT DAVIDSON DECLARES the opposition 'unfit to rule' while two congresswomen seek bail for Sparrow-related crimes and various senators are being investigated for ties to the New World Sparrows.

When asked about rumors of his stepping down, Davidson declared that his loyalty was to the people of the USA who, in this time of corruption and greed, needed a steady hand at the wheel.

STAR

Star Sullivan

Vana: I wish we'd never eaten at your damn place.

Me: Why?

Vana: Aidan won't stop asking about Camden.

Me: Conor's asked me about him too. I just said he's a recovering addict.

Me: He was okay that night.

Vana: I caught him betting in the kitchen.

Me: Ah, shit.

Vana: And he smelled of weed when he came up.

Me: Double shit.

Vana: Camden would say it's okay to open up with Aidan about everything, but he's got so many issues that it's knowing where to start. Aidan would probably suggest rehab and that won't work.

Me: If it was possible to fix people, I'd like to fix him.

Vana: We could always neuter him.

Me: LOL. Not sure how he'd feel about that.

Vana: Maybe he'd get himself under some semblance of control.

Me: You just huffed then, didn't you?

Vana: Maybe. Did you know the last time he went to rehab, one of his stalkers broke into the facility?

Me: Jesus. Your family is so fucking unlucky.

Vana: YOU are our family too. Stop excluding yourself.

Vana: I'm not the only one who's going to regret our dinner.

Me: Why?

Vana: He told Mom about it.

Me: So?

Vana: She wants to see you.

Me: Then she can go fuck herself lol.

Vana: She might like that though.

Me: Hahahahahaha.

Vana: :P

Vana: Don't expect to get out of this lol.

Me: I'd like to see your dad.

Vana: They come together as a pair.

Me: I GTG.

Vana: No, what a surprise lol.

Me: Not because of the conversation. I'm waiting for someone. They showed up. TTYL.

Vana: Okay. TTYL. BTW the last of the articles goes live today. All those politicians' dirty secrets are out in the open.

Me: Good. Lay low on the writing front for a while. I'm shifting focus to the Interpol department handling the Sparrows and this charity Rachel has started. You okay with covering society events?

Vana: Duh.

THOUGH I KNEW she'd continued the conversation, my focus was elsewhere.

When Priestley O'Reilly pushed the front door to her building open, I was there, shoving alongside her. My phone slipping into my coat pocket as I finished talking to Savannah and concentrated on my real reason for being out in the goddamn cold on a side street just off Ninth Avenue in Hell's Kitchen.

Having staked out her routine for the last couple days, I knew she took her baby to the kid's grandmother and went to hot yoga. Then, she spent the day doing dick knew what in her apartment before picking up the baby around nine, sometimes later.

When I pressed my hands into her back and pushed her over, she yelped as she went flying.

The second she was on the floor, I dropped down, dug my knee into the center of her back, and asked, "Comfortable?"

"Help me up, dammit! Who the fuck—"

She shrieked in pain as I grabbed her hair and slammed her face into the floor.

"I don't think I will," I informed her, ignoring her squeals. "Not until I'm ready." Digging the boniest part of my knee into her spine, I whispered, "I'm going to help you up and then we're going somewhere together."

She ceased her struggles but started sobbing. "Who are you?" she whimpered, terror and pain leaching into every word. "Are you with the Five Points?"

"Why? Been expecting a visit from them?" I added more pressure. "Wonder why."

Letting go for a fraction of a second, wanting her to experience hope, I robbed it from her by jerking her arm behind her back, not stopping until it snapped at the shoulder.

As she screamed, I peered around the hall and nodded at the doorman who'd rushed out from behind his desk.

Though he'd known to expect me, he gulped before staggering back a couple steps, his eyes drifting behind me.

Not needing to know who'd be there waiting, I jerked Priestley up by her dislocated arm so she'd pass out from the pain.

Thankfully, the cries of agony swiftly drew to a halt.

As soon as they did, the outer door opened and Brennan's man, Forrest, strode in.

"Yo, Harry, how ya doing?"

"I-I'm okay, Forrest," Harry stuttered. "Everything all right?"

"Sure, sure. Just business."

Harry flicked a look between me and Priestley. "She's a mom."

"She's a traitor. Should have thought of her kid before she betrayed the Points," I informed him coolly.

"That right, Forrest?"

"That's right, Harry. You know what to do when the cops come calling?"

"Tell them nothing then phone you," he rasped anxiously.

"You got that right." He raised two fingers to his temple in a salute.

"Speak later, buddy." When Harry hovered, Forrest chided, "Go on, Harry. You go back to your desk."

Hunching his shoulders, Harry disappeared, and Forrest helped me prop up Priestley.

Together, we walked to the waiting SUV as if she hadn't been beaten into unconsciousness but was sick and in need of urgent care.

Ha. She'd get that. *At the end of my fist.*

"Where's Brennan?" I asked as I shoved her into the back seat and climbed in behind her.

"Waiting at the Hole," Bagpipes answered from behind the steering wheel.

I jerked my chin up in understanding, aware that was Brennan's center of operations on the border between Brooklyn and Queens.

When Forrest climbed into the passenger seat, Bagpipes took off, and we made our way to the peculiar dead zone that had always fascinated me.

"Is it true there's an unofficial graveyard in the Hole?" I asked once we crossed the East River and made it into Flushing, cutting into their argument about whether the Bruins could beat the Maple Leafs.

"It's not exactly a graveyard," Forrest answered. "Ain't no headstones."

I snorted. "I'd never have guessed."

He beamed a grin at me. "Aidan Sr. and his da used to dump bodies there. That's half the reason it's a dead zone, I think. Brennan never said but I'm pretty sure that the O'Donnellys own this area, or part of it, and they kept it off-grid. It's the only reason why the city wouldn't have developed this neighborhood."

That made sense, especially when I caught sight of the dump that Brennan called 'the office.'

When we drove over a series of massive potholes that were flooded with groundwater, they jostled the SUV, rocking Priestley from side to side.

As her dislocated arm collided with the floor of the vehicle, she groaned and began to stir.

Putting extra pressure on her shoulder, I spat, "The only escape you're going to get is when you're unconscious so if I were you, I'd stay fucking quiet."

Soft whimpers whispered from her but she kept it low on the volume levels until we made it to Brennan's HQ.

"Oh, my God, is this the Hole?" she moaned as I hauled her out of the SUV a few minutes later.

I grabbed her bad arm and tugged, which had her dropping to her knees on the mud-strewn parking lot with a scream of pain.

Dirt splattered everywhere, grimy water from the puddles too. Her once-pristine outfit was marred by myriad stains, and her cheeks were coated in filth—the only clean parts were the tracks where her tears coursed.

"You can either walk to the door or you can be dragged by your arm," I told her blandly as I took in her pathetic figure. "The choice is yours."

"Why are you doing this? Wasn't killing my husband *enough*?" she screamed.

I huffed out a laugh. "It's funny how you two were perfect for each other. He was a fucking traitor and you're a treacherous cunt.

"Now make a decision."

She sniffled. "I'll walk."

Forrest and Bagpipes shot each other looks but said nothing as I towed her into the weird building that was Brennan's base, which appeared to be some kind of brothel from the forties. Bright red and brocade. Bizarre and oddly fancy for a place to torture people.

Forrest guided me to a back room where there were cattle hooks on the ceiling. The weird front had calmed her down, lulled her into a false sense of security as we wandered through rooms decorated in that strangely ornate way, but when she saw the easy-to-clean slaughter-house, that was when she started struggling.

One tug on her arm was enough to keep her under control, though.

Luckily for her, she didn't have a high pain threshold because there were plenty of worse things I could have done to her. *Would* have done, too, if she wasn't such an easy mark.

Shoving her onto a lone seat in the center of the barren space, I watched her clutch at her arm as she peered at me through panda eyes.

"I have a son," she cried, shoulders quaking with her sobs. "He needs his mommy."

"It's okay," I told her. "He's with his grandmother. She can raise him. And when she dies, if he needs a home, I'll take him in. I'm surprisingly good with messed-up kids.

"Though I'm thinking he's too young for you to have fucked him up with poison about how crappy the O'Donnellys are. Lucky for you."

Her mouth wobbled but she surged off her seat in a pathetic attempt at an attack. "You can't have my baby!"

As she came at me, I stuck out my foot, sent her flying, then I dropped to my knees next to her on the ground, stuck my fingers in her nose, and snapped it.

When she howled, I shoved my fist under her chin, snapped her mouth shut, and snarled, "I told you to stop with the screaming. Your *baby* barely sees you, Priestley. I don't think he'll miss you too much when you're gone."

Back to whimpering, she tried to roll onto her side and started sobbing. The moment I let go, she cried, "Why? Why? Why?"

"You talked."

"I didn't! I didn't!"

Forrest cleared his throat. "You sure about this?"

"You soft or something?" I snapped.

"Forrest ain't soft."

I peered at the doorway and found the head honcho himself staring at me.

Arching a brow at Brennan, I demanded, "You got a problem?"

"No. Just checking in on the situation."

"Brennan!" Priestley cried, sitting up and turning to him with beseeching eyes.

I kicked her in the face and watched as, howling in pain, she returned to her fetal position of earlier.

He frowned, his discomfort clear. "You got any answers yet?"

"This is why you don't send a man to deal with a woman. Bitches are your weakness. You need to watch that." I wagged my finger at him then shoved Priestley onto her back when she bobbed up again. "You want a quick death, Priestley?"

"I don't want to die," she pleaded.

"It's going to happen today." As she sobbed, I continued over her noise, "You signed your own death warrant when you sold Conor out."

"I didn't, I didn't!"

"You fucking did. The person who told me wouldn't have lied to me." *Not unless Anton wanted another fork through his palm.* "He told me you shared intel with Sheridan Reinier."

"Danny?" Priestley whispered.

"Sheridan Reinier," I corrected. "Not Danny."

With her good hand, she grabbed my arm and sat straighter. "You know him? Where is he? Is he okay?"

Totally confused, I shot Brennan a look. He was just as bewildered as I was because Priestley had stopped sounding terrified for herself and was starting to sound worried for the prick whose eternal resting place was a metal coffin.

Well, until he was moved so some other schmuck could spend his last days in the shipping container.

"Who is he to you?"

She ducked her head between hunched shoulders. "He's my boyfriend."

"Your boyfriend?" I repeated.

"He's gone missing." She sniffled before she glowered at Brennan. "Did the O'Donnellys have him killed as well?"

"Explain this to me," I demanded, ignoring her question. "You told him shit about the Five Points during pillow talk?"

Priestley sniffed. "What? I'm not allowed to talk to my man about the bastards who killed my husband?"

"Not sure you're in a position to snipe at us when you got over Callum so quickly," Brennan rumbled. "And I know for a fact that Finn has been giving you cash, so it's not like you need—"

"You gave her cash?" I blurted out, shaking my head. "Jesus, you are fucking pussies for bitches."

"She hadn't done anything wrong by that point," Brennan snapped. "And she has a kid."

"She's got two arms and legs as well. There are things called *a* job. She spends her days at home alone with Callum's mom looking after the kid. Lazy bitch.

"You weren't such a 'mommy' then, were you? What were you— Reinier's sugar baby?" I scoffed, kicking her in her bad shoulder until she was sobbing on the ground again. "You sold out the people who were literally putting food on your fucking table, you stupid cunt."

"I didn't! I didn't!"

"You did, you lying bitch. You can tell me what you said or you can enjoy an extended stay here. The choice is yours."

"I didn't say anything," she screamed, her face turning red hot.

"Maybe she didn't—"

"Shut the fuck up," I snarled at Forrest, who jumped back in surprise. "She did. The word of the person who told me is *sacrosanct.* This cunt's isn't. She sold your people out. Her husband sold your people out. She's a fucking traitor. If you can't handle this, leave it to someone who goddamn can."

Blanching, Forrest hunched his shoulders. "She seems convincing."

"Because she's got a pussy, you believe her? You should know not to trust something that bleeds once a month and doesn't die," I sneered.

"By that logic, we can't trust you," Brennan retorted.

"You can trust me because I'd die for Conor and Conor would do anything for his family. That's how you can trust me. You're fucking lucky. Not many people get that kind of grace from me." I narrowed my eyes at the unlikely trio. "You three can head on out and leave this to someone who she can't bat her eyelashes at and convince she's innocent." When none of them made a move, I barked, "Get the fuck out."

"You heard the lady," Brennan rumbled, directing Forrest and Bagpipes with a jerk of his chin. He slouched back against the wall though.

"Are you sure, Bren?" Forrest inquired, edgy with nerves as he kept on glancing at Priestley.

"I'm sure. Leave the psycho and the traitor with me," he said with a sigh.

As they traipsed out, I whispered to Priestley, "I'm going to rip your fingernails off. Are you ready for that? Every time you don't answer a question, that's your punishment."

Her gaze darted over to Brennan—it was loaded with a plea. I snapped a glare at him but found he was staring straight ahead, his eyes unfocused.

Though I heaved an inward sigh, I saw the change in Priestley when she realized that her best chance of getting out of here with her head attached had walked out of the back room.

The change was immediate.

Satisfying too.

Men were led by their dicks.

"You can't do this to me," she hissed, that 'lost little girl' look fading from her expression to be replaced with that of the stone-cold bitch she was.

"Where did your tears go?" I mocked.

"You can't treat me like this. I'm a Five Pointer's wife!"

"I think it's unwise to use that as an argument," Brennan retorted. "Seeing as your ties to the Five Points are through two traitors."

Two?

"Her father-in-law," he said, answering my silent question.

Priestley growled, "You have to stop her, Brennan. She's going to hurt me and I haven't done anything wrong."

"Do you know who Danny is?" I queried, getting up from my standing position to peer down at her.

"He's a pencil pusher," she dismissed.

I angled my head to the side as I studied her, knowing full well that she was a consummate liar. "What's your son's name?"

She reared back in surprise. "What?"

"You heard me. What's his name?"

"Niall. Are you going to hurt him too?"

For the first time, I saw genuine concern in her expression.

Hmm.

"Your mother's name?"

"Sandra." She swallowed. "She's dead. You can't get to her anymore."

"Shut up, Priestley. Answer the questions she asks," Brennan retorted.

"Where did you meet Danny?"

"At a bar."

"Who approached who?"

"I-I approached him."

"Classy," Brennan retorted.

"Callum was *murdered* over a year ago."

"Yeah? And you didn't know where he was for the most part," he snarled. "No body, no death certificate."

Before he could piss me off by calling her a whore—the double standards with these mobsters were annoying—I demanded, "What was Danny's job?"

"He was some kind of pencil pusher! I'm telling you I don't know that much about him!"

There.

Just the faintest of flickers beside her mouth—right at the corner.

"You're lying."

I pulled out a sapphire nail file, which she studied with flared eyes as she started wriggling backward on her ass.

As if that would stop me.

"I'm not!"

"You are," I rasped, kicking my booted foot against her dislocated shoulder.

When she screeched and fell back, I grabbed her 'good' hand, holding it firm as she struggled despite the pain, then I popped the tip of the file beneath her thumbnail.

As I levered against it, she released an agonized scream that made her wails of before look mild in comparison.

"No lying," I said simply when her acrylic and real nail were on the ground.

She stared at me with wild, dazed eyes, her hand cradled against her chest as blood gently spurted from the wound, dribbling down her jacket.

Bewilderedly, she whispered, "He worked for some kind of agency."

"A modeling agency?" I mocked.

Staring down at her nail-less thumb, she whispered, "No. He was in law enforcement."

"Did you know when you approached him?"

Her mouth trembled. "I did. I'd heard him talking on the phone outside."

"What made you approach him? Revenge?"

"No!"

Lie.

"Liar," I rumbled, jerking the nail file at her until she was scrabbling away from me, dragging her ass against the ground.

As I chased her, she cried, "No! It wasn't revenge!"

"What was it, then?"

"I heard him talking about Conor—" She flashed both Brennan and I desperate looks. "—on the phone with someone called Smythe. H-He said…"

"What did he say?" I questioned when she let the words fade.

"They were laughing," she whispered. "About getting rid of him. I was going to help! Going to help save him—"

I couldn't stop my chuckle from falling. "Two lies. Two nails, Priestley."

She started sobbing before I got anywhere near her. This time, I didn't have to kick her shoulder to incapacitate her. Brennan was there. His foot was on her chest as he held her down, snarling, "You knew someone was going to come after Conor and didn't warn us? That was your one fucking chance to get back in our good books, bitch."

Priestley was too busy screaming as I tore off two more nails.

When she fainted from the pain, I stared at Brennan triumphantly. "Still think she should be saved because she's a girl?"

His mouth was taut and there was a raging fire in his eyes at the danger she could have spared Conor from.

I had my answer.

SEC WADES INTO SPARROWS INVESTIGATIONS

FALKEN FINANCES SHUT down by the SEC under the guidance of Interpol's Special Trafficking Unit amid the deepening investigation into the 'Sparrows' organization and its ties.

46

CONOR

SOMEONE SAVED MY LIFE TONIGHT - ELTON JOHN

Conor O'Donnelly

"SHE'S GOT CANCER."

I arched a brow at Ma as I guided her around our fourth apartment viewing. "Is it going to kill her?"

"They've got it under control for the moment." Ma studied me, more interested in my question regarding Dotty O'Reilly's current status healthwise than the property. "Why are you asking?"

"Because Priestley isn't going to be around for much longer."

Understatement.

Priestley was lucky to have lived this long after the Summit. It was only because we'd been busy that Star hadn't dealt with her yet.

She blinked at me. "What has she done?"

"Betrayed us."

Her lips pursed but my phone buzzed, and I smiled as I got a text message from the woman of the hour.

> Star: Someone Saved My Life Tonight - Elton John.

> Star: Fitting considering what I'm doing, but it just came to me and made me think of you.

Me: That's true love. And it's truer love that my rock-loving ass is going to tune into Elton John.

Star: :P

Me: I'll listen later. Still with Ma. She dead?

Star: Soon.

Star: <3

Me: <3

"Love looks good on you, son."

Ma's soft statement had me glancing at her.

Unsure of how to answer that, I just frowned. "Thanks?"

"It wasn't an insult. It was a compliment! You're happy?"

My lips curved. "Very."

"I'm glad to hear it." She heaved a sigh. "All my boys are attached. Never thought I'd see the day."

"Who do you think would hold out the longest?"

"You."

The immediacy of her answer had me grumbling, "Thanks again, Ma!"

Her chuckle was unapologetic. "You were always such an odd duck, son. Knew it would take someone special to put up with you. That's why you have so few friends."

"Charming. And I *had* a friend." Until he betrayed me. My family. My faction.

Friends sucked.

She patted my shoulder. "I loved you so I knew someone else would."

"You're trying to make it better but you're making it worse," I grouched, shoving my phone into my pocket. "Do you like this place?"

"I like that it's in your building." She glanced around. "It's nicer than Eoghan's and Brennan's."

"They're pretty similar."

"They're not," was her droll retort. "How many square feet is this?"

"Four thousand."

"That's ample." She nodded as she stared around the bare-bones apartment which had been emptied yesterday after I'd decided she'd be better off here anyway. The tenants hadn't been happy, but I didn't give much of a damn. "I'll take this one."

I knew my ma too well.

"Good. I'll speak with the agent and get you moved in... Next month?"

She peered around. "Just needs some paint."

I'd believe *that* when ET did phone home.

"What about the kitchen?"

Tapping her finger against her bottom lip, she mused, "Yes, it's too modern. *But* I like that it has two ovens. Leave it for now. I can stay with you or Aidan when I decide what I want for—"

"No, Ma. Get it done now. If you need out of the house sooner or want to work on the property once you're moved in, then you'll need to stay in a hotel in the city."

"Why can't I stay with you?" she demanded.

"Because we have families! And right now, Savannah and Aidan are dealing with some stuff and they have construction going on next door so they're grouchy, and Star and Kat only just moved in with me! We're still settling into our routines."

She huffed. "I could help with babysitting."

"Why would you want to move in with us when you want your own space anyway?"

Quiet reigned for a moment, then she released a sigh. "I miss the noise, Conor. Your da wasn't always there, but when he was, there was never a peaceful moment. I'm not used to there being no chaos.

"It's okay though. You're right. I'll move into a hotel and make a decision about the kitchen..." She frowned, but it was more to herself. "Do you think Inessa would like to help me?"

This was when I wished her and Aoife's relationship was as strong as it once was.

I wasn't about to be guilt-tripped into agreeing for her to move into Aidan's apartment or mine just so she could make age-long decisions over a kitchen.

That path led to her being a permanent 'roommate,' and I was *not* signing up for that. I loved my ma but living in the same building was close enough for me.

"Savannah probably would. She might draw Star in."

"Would that be a problem for you?" she asked. When that had me frowning, she clarified, "If Star helped me and Savannah with the kitchen."

"Why would it?"

"I don't know. You said it like it could be a bad thing."

"Not for me. Maybe for you. Star isn't like your other daughters-in-law."

Christ, I wasn't even sure if the word 'backsplash' meant something non-torture-related to Star.

Ma hooted. "You don't think I realized that already?" Patting my arm, she said, "You underestimate me, son."

"Do I? Ma, she's never going to say things that don't put you on edge."

"You mean her telling me that her father's and Dagger's band used to lick cocaine out of groupies' assholes was just a preview?"

My lips twisted as I tried not to laugh. "Yeah. Although I think they were technically snorting—" At her arch look, I cleared my throat. "I meant, what with your recent obsession with Our Lady, I know that kind of talk isn't very popular with you now."

"Ah. So you meant don't ask Savannah if you don't want her to bring Star along?"

"Yes."

She hummed. "Do you know your da used to speak in his sleep?"

"I didn't know that." I grimaced. "What did he talk about?"

"Things I shouldn't have known. Worse things than ass-crack coke-snorting." She patted my arm again. "Don't worry, son. We'll make it out of a kitchen consultation alive. That's all that matters, isn't it?"

Grinning, I tugged her into a hug. "It is."

When she embraced me back, both of us just stood there, not moving, just hugging. It was weird but nice, and then she mumbled, "Haven't done this in a while, son."

"We haven't," I agreed, surprise lacing the words. "I didn't realize."

"I did. I thought you were mad at me."

Was I?

Huh.

Maybe?

Knowing she knew about my abuse and hadn't raised the subject with me was... *rough.*

It wasn't that I needed to discuss it with her, but that she didn't bring it up left me both on edge that she could drop the conversation like the bomb it was at any given moment and irritated that she couldn't care enough to ask about that time, to ask what the ramifications of it were on me.

It probably took me longer than it should to say, "No. I'm not mad at you." I kissed the crown of her head, meaning it because life was too fucking short for grudges. If I had a problem with her not talking about the abuse I'd endured, then conversation was a two-way street. "You can always ask me, Ma. Hugs come for free."

She sighed against my shirt. "Thank you for finding this apartment for me."

"You're welcome. I hope you're happy here. Is a room going to be for Uncle Paddy?"

"Maybe. Will your brothers have a problem with that?"

"Do you care if they do?"

She paused. "I suppose you're right. I don't."

"Well, then." I shrugged. "Life's short, Ma. Be happy. I think Da would want that for you."

"I think he would too, but it's strange. I don't like Paddy in that way. I just enjoy being around him."

"Is it the beer gut?"

She huffed out a laugh. "What was it Savannah called your father?"

"Ah, a silver fox."

"Yes, I was definitely married to one of those. I suppose it spoils you. But Paddy's good to be around and he's at a loss too. We've both let our families down—"

"Sounds like a recipe for miserable conversations."

"No, you're wrong. It's nice. We're not perfect and we accept that about each other."

I squeezed her. "Have you tried apologizing to Aoife?"

"No. What's the point? There's no forgiving what I did." She swallowed. "Does she miss me?"

"I don't know."

"Then why did you ask?"

I sucked down some air. "Star let me down and did some bad... things. She said sorry and I told her it wasn't enough, that she had to atone. Sometimes, you don't give up, you find a solution and a way of saying sorry."

She reared back. "Is that what you think I should do with Aoife? I tried before, but she lost it—"

"Then try again." I thought about her strange obsession with Our Lady and mused, "If you made it about religion, Ma, then no wonder she freaked. Instead of making it about the church, you need to make it about her. About the woman you love like a daughter.

"I think that's the only option you have open to you if you don't want to live like *this*."

Her eyes rounded and she released a shaky breath. "She won't let me near her, though. Neither will Finn. You know, ten years ago, I would have said that Finn not speaking to me would have broken my heart, but losing them *both* is what's broken me.

"I'm not saying I don't deserve it, but I wish..." She sighed and then shot me a lopsided smile. "Wishes don't come true for people who've done what I have."

"It's not about wishing. It's about working for Aoife's forgiveness." I rolled my eyes as she shook her head in disagreement. "Anyway, how's it feel to be back in the city?"

"Good. I think it will be better for me than being all the way upstate for the time being."

"You don't want to sell the estate?"

"No. I might spend summers there. The winters are too lonely."

I pressed a kiss to her cheek. "Whatever you need, whatever makes you happy, we'll figure out a way."

"You're a good boy, Conor."

I winked at her. "That's not what Star says."

47

CONOR

Conor O'Donnelly

WITH A BORED TONE, Eoghan drawled, "Why am I here again?"

"Because if I have to suffer, then you two dipshits can as well."

My lips twitched. "It's not that bad when they aren't playing."

Eoghan frowned. "That makes no sense."

"You haven't seen them play," I retorted.

"They're atrocious," Declan confirmed, shoving his hands into his pockets as he stared at the stadium around him. "I can't believe you're making me do this."

"Hey, I'm not making you do anything," I retorted.

"Technically, that's a lie," Eoghan demurred. "Aren't you the one who told Aidan about PSN?"

"I still think that sounds like a treatment for erectile dysfunction."

"Maybe if it was PNS," I said with a chuckle. "Otherwise, that's a Freudian slip if ever I heard one. You need to talk about some bedroom problems, little bro?"

"Fuck off. The only problem I have are you fuckers trying to mess with my life. How the hell is it that the only brother who doesn't like sports, the only one of us who was relieved not to have to fake it anymore now that Da's dead, is the one who has to talk about goddamn soccer on a sports network?!"

"Life isn't fair," Eoghan concurred.

"He's right. Your life is so hard, Dec."

He scowled at us both. "I'd prefer it if you sounded more genuine."

I grinned. "Have you heard yourself?"

"Whining like a little bitch," Eoghan agreed as he scanned his notifications.

Declan huffed. "You're not the ones on the brink of making complete asses of themselves while discussing shit you have zero interest in to people who actually know what they're talking about!"

"That's true," Eoghan said. "But hey, Con, we get to watch the humiliation live."

"That's why I woke you up. Knew you'd get a kick out of it."

"I'm glad my misery will put a smile on your face," Dec groused, but he sounded less sincere than before. More hopeful. Not about the misery, but about the smile on Eoghan's face.

He'd been more of a miserable ass than usual.

Before either of us could reply, the TV staff, who'd been setting up around us, approached Declan.

As they shuffled him in front of the cameras, I elbowed Eoghan in the side. "Hey, did you know this place has the same groundskeeper as the Yankees?"

"You say that like it's a good thing!"

His aghast tone had me snickering. "It's the only good thing about this team. Oh, and they have the highest-grossing concession stand in the MLS."

"We overpaid, didn't we?"

"Probably." I hitched a shoulder. "This presidential election campaign is going to be expensive."

He snorted as we moved so we were positioned beside the cameras.

The assistants side-eyed us nervously but didn't say anything when we remained quiet.

Only until they went live and Declan was broadcasting around the nation.

Without planning it, that was when Eoghan and I attacked.

Sure, it was juvenile, but if you couldn't be a dick around your brothers, then when could you?

As we pulled faces at him like ten-year-olds, his smile grew tighter and tighter as he talked about shit none of us were interested in to people who, as he'd said, knew their stuff.

Twenty minutes later, once the interview was over, he moved from behind the cameras and immediately dove at Eoghan.

As the two of them started to fight, I grabbed Dec, yelling, "Run for your life, Eoghan!"

He snorted but loped down the field while I retreated the other way, leaving Dec to decide who he was aiming for.

When he tried to mow me down, Eoghan was there, like a ninja, and to the bemusement of the camera crew, we got into a fistfight.

By the end, Declan favored his right side, I was limping, and only Eoghan came away untouched.

He was, however, beaming.

Declan and I grimaced at each other, silently agreeing that it was worthwhile.

"Next time you have to do one of these interviews," he said happily. "I'll be a part of your cheer team, Dec."

"So generous of you," he said with a sniff, rubbing his hip where he'd gone down heavily after I shoved him off me.

As we bundled into Dec's SUV, he muttered, "Aela'll kill me if I bruise up."

"Ma never gave us shit unless it was on the face," Eoghan pointed out.

"Our women are not Ma. She was a lot more forgiving about shit that should have been impossible to forgive."

Dec frowned. "She also had six boys to raise."

"So? You telling me if Shay got into a fight that you wouldn't care so long as his face wasn't fucked up."

"No. But Shay doesn't have five brothers."

"That means dick," I dismissed. "I'm not talking smack about her, just saying that it's not a bad thing to have women who care is all."

"Meaning Star will care?"

From the back seat, I peered at Eoghan. "What's that supposed to mean?"

He shrugged. "She's just as likely to come back with bruises. They're stock in trade for us."

Us.

Ex-ninjas.

"I'd want to know who bruised her."

"Is this how we know we've grown up?"

Eoghan chuckled. "Declan, we just got into a fight in front of people in your stadium."

"Our stadium. Don't make out like it's mine."

I slapped him on the shoulder. "On the paperwork, it is, bud."

"Where did I go wrong in life?"

"I think it's too late to ask yourself that question," Eoghan drawled.

With a laugh, I stated, "I think so too."

"What is this? 'Give Declan Shit' Day?" He huffed. "I'm not inviting you to any more live interviews. Pulling faces at me like that, asswipes."

When I saw a Duane Reade, I asked, "Pull over, would you?"

"Why?"

"Need something."

"What do you need from a drugstore?" Eoghan inquired.

"Why do you ask like that? You can buy anything in those stores."

"We just don't buy stuff, do we?" Declan answered, turning to look at me once he'd parked.

"From how full our apartments are, I can safely say that's not true."

Eoghan frowned. "Yeah, but… not regular stuff."

"You think toothpaste just miraculously appears in the bathroom, huh?"

"No, I thought my housekeeper bought it," was Eoghan's retort.

"Never understood why you don't have one of those, Con."

"Don't like people in my space. It's enough for someone to come in once a week. Star's the same. I offered to get a housekeeper but she said no."

"Then what are you buying?"

"Tampons."

Eoghan raised a brow. "Tampons."

"Yeah. You heard of them?" I mocked.

"I've heard of them. Just… why are you buying them?"

"Because Star asked me to get some."

"I gotta see this," Declan muttered, climbing out of the car once I did.

When Eoghan joined us inside the store, I heaved a sigh. "We're taking this juvenile shit one step too far."

Declan shrugged as he picked up some Swedish Fish and tossed the bag in his hand.

Eoghan pointed. "They're over there."

As we approached the aisle, I whistled under my breath.

"Damn, there are a lot of different products for this," Declan muttered.

Eoghan picked up two boxes of tampons. "How do you know which ones to pick?"

"I don't know. She just said tampons."

"Inessa would have been more specific, so maybe Star doesn't care?"

"When did she start?"

My lips twitched. "Yesterday. I came onto her and she told me to get friendly with my right hand again."

Declan chuckled. "Wait a couple days. She'll be horny as fuck."

"Not every woman's the same. Inessa would claw out my eyes if I tried to touch her."

I studied him. "She suits you."

His smile was smug. "I know."

"I haven't figured out which option Star is yet." I rubbed my chin. "Don't feel like getting my balls handed to me on a platter, though. I think I'll wait for her to make the first move."

"There won't be *any* moves if you don't buy her some of these." Declan stared at the aisle. "Why do you think they have so many of these when they do the same thing?"

"I mean, different thicknesses, that makes sense," I countered.

"Tampon saved my life once." Declan and I shot Eoghan a look. "What?! It did. Tampons were used in 'Nam first, ya know. Stopped me bleeding out in Venezuela."

"Was it a super plus or just a plus that stopped the bleed though?" Declan retorted with a smirk.

Eoghan chuckled. "I don't know. I just stuck it in and plugged it up."

"That's way too much like Carrie for my taste."

With a snigger, Declan strolled down the aisle. "Organic! They have organic ones. What the hell's organic about a tampon?"

"Maybe it doesn't have plastic in?" I asked, snatching the box from his grasp. "I don't think it's good to put plastic up there, do you?"

"Cocks go in and babies go out so no."

"Eloquent, Eoghan. Very eloquent."

"True, ain't it?"

Though I rolled my eyes, I grabbed one of the ultra, the super plus, the super, the regular, and the light—just to be on the safe side.

And if my sweetest sister-in-law could turn feral during her period, then who the hell knew what Star would become...

"That reminds me," I muttered. "I need to buy hot chocolate."

48

TEXT CHAT

KAT: *I made this group chat because it's efficient :)*

Conor: *Efficient for whom?*

Star: *Her.*

Maverick: *Lol.*

Alessa: *Kati? What is wrong?*

Kat: *I mean, nothing's wrong. In fact, in my opinion, everything is right. But the school doesn't agree and that's backward of them.*

Star: *Stop prevaricating. Get on with it.*

Kat: *I picked a bad time, didn't I? You're always grouchy when you do that bleeding thing.*

Star: *You know the name of it.*

Kat: *I just didn't want to embarrass you because there are boys here.*

Star: *The boys know what a period is and won't blush. And if you didn't want to embarrass me then you shouldn't have brought up the bleeding thing.*

Star: *Now, get on with it. What have you done this time and whose arm do I need to break?*

Kat: *Conor, get out the hot chocolate.*

Conor: *It's on hand. Now, Star's right. Get on with it lol.*

Kat: *No arms need to be broken, but I may or may not have detention. It totally wasn't my fault though.*

Conor: *And it was easier to tell us all at once?*

Kat: *Sure was. I can take initiative and can streamline efficiently.*

Maverick: *Are you trying to tell us you got in trouble at school or settling in for a job interview?*

Alessa: *What did you do?*

Kat: *I spat on someone.*

Conor: *Did they deserve it?*

Alessa: *Conor!*

Kat: *They did deserve it, Conor. Yes. I'm glad you asked that question.*

Conor: *Feel free to take the floor and justify your saliva landing on someone.*

Alessa: *Are you trying to make the rest of us look bad?*

Conor: *;0) Who, me?*

Star: *Lol.*

Maverick: *What did you do, brat?*

Kat: *Hey, I resent the implication that I'm a brat. I was defending someone's honor.*

Conor: *Whose honor?*

Star: *You got my attention.*

Maverick: *The next time she's with us, Alessa, she'll be even worse. These two are as bad as each other.*

Kat: *This kid was picking on the lunch lady in the cafeteria. He said she was on 'minimum wage' and that she didn't have the right to tell him what to do.*

Conor: *I think we're lucky you didn't smack him.*

Star: *You spit on the kid, right? Not the lunch lady?*

Kat: *Star!*

Star: *I know you too well.*

Kat: *Not well enough. As if I'd spit on Mrs. Reisz. She's so nice.*

Conor: *What did you spit on that belonged to the little bastard?*

Alessa: *They're not going to punish her for using spit as a weapon, are they?*

Maverick: *I doubt it. You need to calm down, babe. I know you're reading up on this shit but it's just a schoolyard prank.*

Alessa: *Saliva transmits diseases, Maverick. You're lucky, Katina, that you only got a detention.*

Kat: *I don't think the principal likes the kid either. Even if his dad has this big business in the city and gave the school a library.*

Conor: *We can give them a laboratory if you want, Kat?*

Kat: *Oooh, is that an option? Can you upgrade the gym?*

Conor: *If you want.*

Alessa: *Is this your idea of a punishment?*

Kat: *Alessa! I was totally in the right.*

Conor: *Wouldn't say 'totally.' Alessa has a point. If we encourage spit, what's next?*

Star: *How about this... Kat, if you don't work on your impulse control, the only place you can practice cartwheels is in the gym.*

Kat: *WHAT?! That's so unreasonable. How am I supposed to get better?*

Star: *You get better at the gym.*

Kat: *It's not like I can practice in a yard anymore.*

Alessa: *You can practice when you visit here.*

Kat: *But that's every other weekend. What about every day?*

Conor: *We have a massive terrace.*

Kat: *I could fall off the side.*

Conor: *How could you? There are walls and glass barriers!*

Star: *She has a point. If there's a way to fall off the side of a building this high, she'd discover it.*

Maverick: *Wait. What's the actual punishment here? No cartwheels unless she's in school? That doesn't sound like much of a deterrent.*

Alessa: *I agree.*

Kat: *I was sticking up for the underdog. Isn't that what the Green Berets taught you to do, Maverick?*

Maverick: *Nice try, kid.*

Kat: *:**

Star: *They did, actually.*

Maverick: *I know. But that doesn't mean she's getting out of it. You have to stick up for the underdog without getting caught, Kati.*

Alessa: *JAMESON! That is not the point here. The point is you can't go around spitting at people.*

Star: *Some people need to be spat on.*

Maverick: *I agree.*

Alessa: *You're all animals.*

Conor: *I resent that.*

Star: *Okay, no cartwheels outside of the gym and no Switch for a week. How about that, Alessa?*

Alessa: *I think that's as good an outcome as you're capable of giving, Star.*

Kat: *That's horrible. I was doing a nice thing!*

Conor: *For the lunch lady.*

Star: *Where did you spit on the kid, anyway?*

Kat: *Got him right in the eye. Teehee.*

Conor: *I can tell you're stricken with guilt.*

Kat: *What does stricken mean?*

Conor: *It means plagued with it. Burdened by it.*

Kat: *Oh, yes. I am. Very much so. And next time, I promise I won't get caught.*

Maverick: *Not that there'll be a next time...*

Kat: *Right. Of course, there won't. I'll do better, Alessa, I swear.*

Alessa: *Why don't I believe you?*

Star: *Because you're a smart woman.*

Alessa: *Sigh. I want more than a promise of doing better, Katina. You've been given a wonderful opportunity at that school. I have to go through a special course just to get a general education certificate so that I can go to college.*

Alessa: *You're very lucky, and if you get suspended or expelled for behaving like an animal, then think about how disrespectful it is to Star, for paying your fees, and to me, who can never have an opportunity like you're throwing away.*

Kat: *I'm sorry, Lessie. <3 I never thought of it that way. I promise*

I won't be reckless again. Thank you for everything. xoxoxoxoxo I'll try to be a good girl from now on. <3

Star: *And try to get that B in English up to an A, yeah? Otherwise, I'll never hear the end of it from Savannah.*

Kat: *I'll try. <3 <3 <3*

Star: *Good girl. So... five days of no Switch. ;P*

Maverick: *I see what you did there. Soft touch. Still, I agree.*

Maverick: *That's a fitting punishment. ;)*

49

CONOR

Conor O'Donnelly

WHILE DATE NIGHTS with Star always ended with a bang, they were definitely outside of my comfort zone.

The ones that I didn't plan, at any rate.

The first with her at the wheel was a soccer match, the second, a nightclub when I goddamn loathed techno music, and then there was tonight.

We were attending the opera.

The fucking opera.

My rock-loving self was going to watch *Carmen* at the Met when I'd prefer to stick pins in my eyes.

The woman had better know how much I goddamn loved her.

I wasn't about to argue, not after surviving our first period together with my head intact, and especially not knowing how the date would end, but still, *the fucking opera?*

When I tugged on my bow tie for the twentieth time since she'd collected me from the Saturns' stadium where my brothers and I had been talking strategy for the last few hours, she grabbed my hand, dragged it to my side, then quipped, "You're worse than Kat on school picture day."

My nose crinkled. "When was the last time I wore a tux, do you think?"

"Oh, I don't know. Your communion?"

I grinned. "I'm not that bad. I think it was Eoghan's wedding. Savannah might have been a bridezilla but she didn't make me wear a bow tie for more than the photos."

"And now she's earned your undying loyalty?" The twinkle in her eye told me she wasn't unhappy about that.

"I like her. She's a freak so I'm comfortable with her. Plus, she makes Aidan happy."

Her gloved fingers swiped across my jawline. Some men might have preferred the silk against their skin, but I preferred Star's calluses. She wore her history in her hands, on her palms, and I preferred her at her most raw.

"You're a sucker for family."

The tender touch and the mocking words were discordant, but I smirked anyway. "And you like me so that means you're a sucker too."

She snorted. "The logic is far-reaching but I'll accept it."

When she shifted in her seat, I said nothing, well aware that in these moments leading up to our 'dates,' she turned inward. Becoming somber.

It made sense. The past and present were colliding for her, and that required some mental skulduggery on her part.

I'd have left her to her process, knowing full well that it was integral to her healing, but even seeing her in a fucking cocktail dress with killer heels wasn't worth this torture.

I growled under my breath a final time as I dragged the ends of the bow tie and freed myself from its chokehold.

"I've felt more comfortable garrotes," I grumbled.

"Do I want to know how you know how 'comfortable' a garrote is?"

"Da left things around the house that he shouldn't have," was my retort as I tugged on my collar. Which, now that I thought about it... "My shirt's tighter."

"And?"

"It's not the bow tie. It's the shirt!" Jerking my neck to the side, I heaved a sigh. "This is your fault."

"How is it my fault?" she spluttered.

I stuck my hand in front of her face and started counting. "One, I'm happy."

"And that's a bad thing?"

I ignored her. "Two, I'm eating regularly."

"I repeat, that's a bad thing?"

"Three, Kat always wants to eat junk food after gym class. Ergo, all your fault."

She sniffed and shoved my hand away. "You're not gaining weight."

"My shirt is too small."

"No, it fits. You were skinny before. Now you have meat on top of the muscle."

My brow puckered. "I wasn't skinny."

"You didn't eat for hours," she argued. "Then, you'd eat a steak and apple pie in ten minutes! That's not healthy. That's binge eating."

"I take it back about liking Savannah. This is her fault, isn't it?"

A soft laugh drifted from her. "No, it's not actually, but she did make me realize you eat like a bougie college student. And when you're hacking, you live off Coke and candy, Conor."

"There's nothing wrong with that. It's not cocaine. Anyway, you live off candy too."

"I do. But I eat green things as side dishes."

"Only because of Kat. She'd never let you get away with making her eat green things if you didn't too."

"Exactly. That's the compromise of being a parent."

I blinked. "Negotiation?"

"Yup. You're still new to the game so you're rusty. But you'll get used to it."

As Craig, one of my crew, drove us toward Fifth Avenue, I asked, "Okay, so when she wants hot dogs—"

"You make her drink water. Or milk. Or juice. No soda. And later, you make sure she eats something healthy." She shrugged. "It's not like you need to know this. I mean, I handle it."

"No, I'm…" I coughed. "I mean, I want to know. I need to know. That's what being a dad is, right? Being responsible?"

Her head tilted to the side and the lights from the traffic illuminated her expression. "She told me about your conversation."

"Which one? We talk a lot."

If I sounded proud, so be it. Much like her mother, Kat was a tough nut to crack, but I'd cracked that shell which meant I knew too much about Camden and the ins and outs of floor work in gymnastics.

"About wanting to call me Mom and, once we're hitched, you Dad."

"She hasn't called you that yet, has she?"

"No." She peeped at me. "Thank you for letting her open up with you."

"You don't have to thank me for that," I grumbled, unfastening my top button for good measure.

"I think you'll find that I do. I never talked to you about being her father figure, just kind of threw you into the ring, and you've shown up more than I could have anticipated."

"I already told you that I knew you came as a package, Star, and I never wanted anything else." I cleared my throat. "I couldn't imagine myself having kids, so I feel pretty blessed, to be honest."

"Why not?"

"They're a lot of responsibility, they're fragile and easy to break, and the psychoses you can impart on them…" I whistled under my breath.

"So, it was less about you and more about them?"

I shrugged.

"Even before we met in person, I knew you had it in you to be a great father."

"Why?"

"Because of how important family is to you. Your main goal in life is to keep your siblings alive—"

"That just means I'm a neurotic wreck," I dismissed.

"If you were a regular Joe whose brothers worked in white-collar jobs, sure. But they're not. So you're not. You're appropriately and adequately anxious about their welfare."

I snorted. "Thanks, I think?"

She chuckled. "No 'I think' about it. It's the truth. But that was before we met, and now, just seeing you with her has confirmed it."

She stunned me by reaching forward and pressing her lips to mine in a soft kiss.

In fact, it was softer than soft. It was loving and loaded with (entirely unnecessary) gratitude. It was gentle and warm and everything my abrasively abrupt Star usually wasn't.

"In the future—" I whispered against her mouth as she began to pull back. "—you can thank me like that every time."

When she chuckled, we settled in for the ride. Her hand knotted with mine.

Ten minutes later, and knowing we were approaching Midtown, I asked, "Truth time?"

She swallowed. "I'd tried to run off the week before. I was beaten black and blue and he made me attend with no makeup."

My eyes flashed at that. "Are you being serious? Did nobody say anything?"

"It was a power move on his part. *That's how rich I am.*" She huffed out a laugh. "I was grateful for the money once he was dead. Do you want to know why he bought me?"

Fuck, what a question.

I cleared my throat. "Hit me with it."

"I sprained his dick."

"You, what?" I couldn't stop myself from laughing. "You go, girl."

"He was into that." My laughter faded as she continued, "He'd anger me until I reacted. He'd starve me if I wouldn't obey. Then, when I grew too compliant or if I was just so fucking lost that I didn't care if I never ate or slept again, he'd give me a whisper of a chance at hope."

"He let you think you could escape?"

"I fell for it. Every. Fucking. Time."

"You were desperate."

"I was." Her fingers separated from mine and they drifted along my chin. "I'm desperate for other things now."

I arched a brow. "Orgasms?"

She smirked. "What can I say? You've made a believer out of me."

Sensing the change in her, and needing to taste that cocky smirk, I slipped my hand behind her nape and dragged her into me.

Her lips parted again in a silent request for a deeper kiss, which I was eager to give, eager to free her from the taint of that fucker, eager to help her take back control over this part of her past.

She groaned as I thrust my tongue against hers, taking everything she had to give and returning it threefold, needing her to understand that I was more than just 'all in.'

She goddamn owned me.

As much as she was mine, I was fucking hers.

When she groaned, deep and low in her throat, I felt it inside my bones.

With a tender trail of my finger, one that was in sharp relief to the hunger of my kiss, I traced the sweetheart neckline of her dress and followed it to its natural end. Soft goosebumps on the tops of her breasts made an appearance as she reacted viscerally to my touch.

In a flurry of activity, she surprised me by dragging her skirts to the side, swooping them over her arm so she had more freedom of movement.

As she straddled me, her mouth retreated so she could mutter against my lips, "This was supposed to happen in the opera box, but fuck that. I want you. *Now.*"

That in itself was proof of healing, but I didn't say that, didn't even have a chance to think it because she was pulling down the neckline of her dress and her tits were spilling out.

I studied her delicious curves in the twinkling street lamps that provided us with a faint illumination through the tinted back windows.

"You are so fucking beautiful," I rumbled, dropping kisses along the soft swells before nipping here and there in the run-up to the main event.

When my lips found her nipple, I tugged the tip between my teeth, rolling it over the edges, then I lashed it with my tongue.

A shaky sigh rushed from her as her nails dragged over my scalp. She hauled me deeper into her, snapping, "Don't tease me, Conor!"

Smugly, I tested the resilience of her nipples with a soft bite. Meanwhile, my hands were busy. I slipped one along the inner length of her thigh until I found the outer edge of the crotch of her panties.

As she hissed in response to my bite, I nipped harder, enjoying how her hiss morphed into a long, low moan when my fingers stroked the fabric that shielded her.

Sliding my thumb over her clit, rubbing it back and forth, her knees tightened around my thighs and she wriggled farther down my lap.

"Now, Conor, now," she rasped with no small amount of urgency.

I plucked at the crotch of her panties, pulling it away from her pussy and stroking my thumb down the line of her slit.

As her slippery juices coated the digit, I groaned around her nipple, biting down when I thrust it inside her and felt her inner muscles clench down hungrily in response.

Her nails dug into my scalp one final time before they were between us, sliding over my tuxedo jacket, over the starched front of my studded shirt, and down to the fly.

When she went straight for the zipper, not even bothering to cup me, I grinned in delight as she freed me from the cage of my pants.

After gracing me with a single stroke of my cock, she decided that enough was enough because, before I had the chance to savor her touch, she was bucking onto her knees, dislodging my mouth from her tit, and moving ever nearer so that when she seated herself on my lap again, my dick fell against her slit.

That was my cue to take control.

With one hand holding her panties to the side, I rubbed the tip of my dick over her clit, rasping, "Rock your hips, my Star." With a soft cry, she obeyed, and I whispered, "You have no idea how gorgeous you are. You light up my fucking life and you don't even know it, my beautiful, beautiful girl."

The rocking of her hips increased in its pace until she was

breathing heavily. Her arms settled on my shoulders for better traction, and I felt her working her way up, and up, and up.

She was close.

I knew she was.

It was getting easier for her to come, more proof of her healing.

"I am so goddamn proud of you," I whispered as I tilted her chin down so I could kiss her again.

As I swallowed her moan, I let my dick trace down her slit and encouraged her to pause as I fed the tip into her. When she took me, slowly, inch by inch, we groaned into each other's mouths.

Gravity helped settle her around me, as did the natural rocking of the car as we drove over a pothole. Thanking fuck for how goddamn slow traffic was in Manhattan, I gripped her outer thighs and encouraged her to ride me.

She was frantic—all jerky, rocky movements as she tried to find her release. Then, I ran the outer edge of my thumb over her clit and she bucked on top of me, stilling, freezing, *imploding* around me.

The suddenness stunned me, but I urged her on, not for myself, just so that she could ride out the pleasure, wanting it to flood her, needing it to overwhelm her. Needing to give that to her when she gave me so fucking much, more than she even knew.

When her pussy stopped clutching at me, that was when I moved faster. Bucking from underneath, taking my own pleasure now that hers was complete.

As I exploded into her, she cupped my face and started kissing me. Her hunger for me as powerful as ever.

Coming down was painful but only because the high was so sharp, so fucking sweet.

When she sagged into me and started dotting kisses on my forehead, at the corners of my mouth, and on my chin, I whispered, "What are you doing?"

"Showing you."

My brows lifted. "What are you showing me?"

But even as I asked the question, I already knew the answer.

"How much I love you."

Slipping my arms around her waist, I hugged her hard, burying my face into her chest, loving her and needing her and feeling so fucking happy that I didn't even care about the tux or *Carmen* or two hours of opera torture anymore.

With her tits smothering me, I mumbled, "I'll wear the bow tie."

Her laughter was soft, tinkling. So unlike Star that it was as if I had another woman on my lap. But it wasn't. It was her.

Mine.

Always fucking mine.

"How do you manage to make everything better?" she whispered, her fingers stroking over my hair.

Another woman and I'd have retreated. *Cringed.* Instead, I burrowed into her touch. "I don't."

"Lies."

"Do you have a game plan for the aftermath of this?"

"I'm wearing panties, plus my skirt is long and black and lined."

"I don't want to ruin the dress. I haven't even seen you in it. Plus, it'll be my pants that are ruined, not your skirts."

"Not ruined. Maybe it'll make it better."

I laughed. "Depends on what your idea of fashion is, I guess."

"You could set a trend." Her nose nuzzled into mine. "Do you care if people know what we've been doing?"

"Not really."

"Then, what's the problem?"

"No problem," I said with a sigh as she snagged my white handkerchief from my top pocket and quickly shimmied me out of her then pressed the folded fabric between her legs, tucking her panties back into place.

"There, no stains," she crowed as she zipped me up.

When she didn't shuffle off my lap, I settled my hands tighter around her waist and asked, "How do you feel?"

"Like I had an orgasm."

"You know what I mean," I chided softly, tracing soft kisses along the sinews of her throat.

"You don't normally ask."

"You don't normally jump on me *before* you hit the scene of the crime."

"Fair," she mumbled, arching her throat to the side to give me better access.

"It always surprises me how you were mistreated in public."

"Because I didn't act out? Didn't rebel to liberate myself?"

"Partially that, but partially the fact that no one helped you."

"I didn't have a label on my forehead that said 'sex slave,'" she countered. "And it wasn't like that."

"What was it like?" I questioned gently.

"Do we have to talk about this?"

"I think it'd be good for you. Good for me too. Katina is starting to see a shrink, but we never bothered to find ourselves one. Maybe we can be that for each other." Oddly nervous, I hitched a shoulder. "Just an idea."

"You won't like what you hear."

"Do you think you'll enjoy hearing why I disliked having my hair pulled before you?"

She tensed. "No."

"We both have parts of our pasts that will be painful to share, but that doesn't mean we shouldn't talk about them *if* we need to talk about them."

"I'm sorry I keep stroking your hair."

I clucked my tongue. "I didn't say that to make you self-conscious. I meant it when I said *before* you."

"Why am I different? And don't say because I'm your penguin."

"Because you're my person, Star. The one I'll always let in when I lock everyone else out."

She took her sweet time before saying anything, as if weighing the meaning of what I had just told her.

Eventually, she mumbled, "When I was with Hans, among other passive-aggressive moves, he'd control me through food."

I stilled. "What? He starved you?"

"Gave me food for good behavior. Denied me food for bad. I was so accustomed to having my appetite controlled that it was a miracle he managed to get me pregnant in the first place.

"For the first year or so, I was *always* underweight. To the point where I was skin and bones."

Hatred for her fucker of an ex-husband filled me. "If I could electrocute him to death, I would."

"But then, you'd have denied me the fun of stringing him up," she said lightly, her fingers automatically moving toward my head where I knew she was going to play with my hair. She paused, though, as if she remembered…

I snagged her hand in mine and plunked it on my head. "*You* can play with my hair. No one else. Only you."

She swallowed. "Are you sure?"

"Of course."

"Did he force you to…"

"Blow him? Yeah. Used to pull on my hair until I did as I was told." My tone was free from bitterness, mostly because I'd come to terms with what had happened a long time ago. Well, as much as a person could. "You've never triggered me," I told her candidly.

"I'm glad," she whispered, hugging me to her.

"Me too," I said, leaning up to kiss her. "What happened at the opera?"

"He used to like offering me freedom."

My brow furrowed as I thought about the dates we'd been on. "What does that mean?" I asked when I couldn't make sense of what she said.

"It means when we were in public, he'd fuck me over or beside balconies so that I could throw myself over if I wanted."

"That was his idea of freedom?" I rumbled.

Death.

That had been how he'd told her that was her only way out.

"Trust me, some days, it felt like it could be."

"What stopped you?"

"I wish I knew. Sometimes, it was sheer obstinacy. Killing myself felt too much like letting him win."

"Thank Christ for your obstinate self."

She chuckled.

"We didn't fuck in the opera box," I pointed out.

"We didn't, but I didn't need to either. I wanted you here, *now*. That felt liberating too."

"I'm glad."

"Me too." Star cleared her throat. "Who'd have thought the O'Donnellys had a box at the opera?"

"You can thank Declan for that." I cupped her chin and angled her head down. As I brushed my lips over hers, I whispered, "Thank you for sharing that with me."

She swallowed. "Thank you for listening."

So long as she was the one doing the talking, I'd always listen. But only time would prove that to someone who'd gone through what she had, and in my mind, we had forever.

Somehow, not even that felt long enough.

50

CONOR

Conor O'Donnelly

WHEN WE MADE it to the opera house, my brows arched in surprise and I tipped my chin toward the steps that would lead us to the balconies.

"What is it?" she asked, peering around.

"Hunter DeLaurentiis is over there. Did you know he'd be attending tonight?"

She scoffed. "No. But I appreciate how highly you rate my ability to machinate."

"Is that a word?"

"It is in my dictionary."

My lips twitched. "The last time I saw him was at Saverina's christening. He wasn't pleased with you."

"Understatement. Another friendship burned," she mumbled with a sigh, shooting a wistful glance his way.

"You can make it up to him," I said as I guided her toward the same staircase where DeLaurentiis was leading his wife.

"I don't have enough time in my day for all the atoning I've got to do." Her expression turned sour. "I don't know how your da got anything done when he had to repent for so much."

I chuckled. "Da's idea of repenting came with a price tag."

"I don't suppose you're open to that too?"

"Nope," I said cheerfully. "You have to mean it."

She grumbled, "Typical." Her gaze darted over to DeLaurentiis. "Never told you how he saved my ass in Lebanon, did I?"

"No."

I let my hand settle on the exposed ball of her shoulder. She looked divine in a very un-Star-like frothy confection with several bouncy skirts that danced around her calves and a sweetheart neckline that cupped tits I'd already savored once tonight.

The dress might not have been something I figured she'd wear, but the boots—Doc Martens—definitely were.

I wouldn't have been surprised if she had a gun or a knife strapped somewhere I hadn't felt up yet.

Though the notion intrigued me, I dipped my head to better hear her when she said, "Managed to break out of the compound where I was being held. He was hiking in the area. Fed me, treated my wounds, and got beaten for his pains by the guards who were hunting me down."

"Go and talk to him."

"And say what? Sorry I conspired with your grandfather to get his ass killed?" Her brow furrowed. "Speaking of… Crayon."

"Crayon?"

For whatever reason, where she'd hesitated before, that stirred her into action. She grabbed a firm hold of my hand and dragged me toward DeLaurentiis.

Before I knew what the hell was happening, she had a hold on DeLaurentiis's arm, forcibly turned him around, and demanded, "What have you done with Crayon?"

DeLaurentiis, surprised at first, glowered down at Star the moment he realized who was doing the tugging. "What do you want?"

"Watch the tone, DeLaurentiis," I warned, causing him to arch a brow at me.

"You found what you were looking for, then?"

"Not like you don't know that already," Star argued. "I met Aurora at the Summit." She dipped her chin at DeLaurentiis's bride. "I'm sure she kept you in the loop."

"She did. I made the choice not to reach out."

Star narrowed her eyes. "Figured that for myself. What have you done with Crayon?"

"The man who murdered my grandfather? With *your* help?"

"Yeah. He's a friend."

"Typical," DeLaurentiis scoffed. "He's a friend but you only just remembered him—"

"DeLaurentiis," I snapped. "I understand that you're angry with her, and I know better than anyone what she's capable of, but watch your fucking tone.

"I'm sure you wouldn't appreciate it if I talked down to Ms. Valentini."

DeLaurentiis merely glowered at me then, to Star, drawled, "Crayon is working with the Camorra now."

"He's alive and well?"

"He's earning himself quite a salary," Valentini mused, placing a hand on DeLaurentiis's forearm and gently squeezing.

Star frowned. "You're paying him?"

"He's very skilled at what he does."

"You must have coerced him into—"

"That's between Crayon and the Camorra, Star. It has nothing to do with you," DeLaurentiis retorted.

She released a breath. "He was doing you a favor."

"I know. I don't have to like it, though, do I?"

"No use blaming Star when it was your grandfather's plan," I argued, squeezing her shoulder and encouraging her to back into me for support.

DeLaurentiis eyed her up and down. "I heard what happened to Ovianar."

Shit.

Star immediately tensed.

"It's dangerous being your friend," Valentini concurred.

From the outside looking in, Star appeared as staunch as ever, but I felt her sag, ever so faintly, into me.

"Isn't it dangerous being friends with any of us?" I countered, annoyed at their dismissal of her. "And there's no denying the lengths she'll go to for those she considers her people."

"It was Alberto's plan," Star whispered. "I just helped coordinate."

"He should have asked *me*," DeLaurentiis snarled, looming over her, his usually affable features puckering with rage.

And hurt.

As well as grief.

I understood. How couldn't I? But nothing was simple with Star.

Nothing.

"He couldn't ask you. Couldn't involve you. Why would he when I was there? You'd never have been able to do what had to be done, Hunter."

"You don't know what I'm capable of," he argued.

"You're not capable of arranging your grandfather's murder," she snapped, bristling. "And that's not a fucking insult. That's a compliment. I wish I didn't have it in me to..." She sighed. Broke off. "Hunter, without you, I wouldn't be here today. I wouldn't almost be at the end of the road with the Sparrows. Thank you for that.

"I understand if you can't stand to be around me, and I understand if you can never forgive me, but know I'm grateful for what you've done for me in the past and I hope, one day, you can find it in you to know that when or if you're backed into a corner, I'll be there, trying to figure a way to get you out."

With that, she grabbed my arm again and pushed us toward the box Declan owned.

When we made it in there, hidden behind the curtains, she turned into me and buried her face in my chest.

Her shoulders didn't shake, and I didn't feel tears through my shirt, but her arms enveloped me in a crushing hug that I returned.

I knew it wouldn't always be easy being Star's soft place to land, but that didn't mean it wasn't worthwhile.

I had one of the most well-connected, deadliest women in the world in my arms, calling me her fiancé, sharing a home with me, allowing me to raise her child with her…

If anyone was lucky, it was me.

51

STAR

Star Sullivan

RACHEL GRITTED HER TEETH. "Why are you so truculent?"

"What this mean?"

Alessa, as Ukrainian as Amara, hitched a shoulder. "Don't ask me."

I shot Amara a glance. "It means I'm a difficult pain in the ass."

"*Tak*. This why I like you. I also am difficult."

Rachel grunted. "I know. But you have an excuse."

"What excuse?" Alessa questioned, evidently curious as to the First Lady of the MC's logic.

"The same one you have—English isn't your first language."

I smirked at Rachel. "You just can't stand that I have ideas that will work."

"You've never been involved in something like this before. How do you know it'll work?"

"Because people hate those galas you're oh, so famous for."

"Uh, *no*, they don't. They're a legitimate tax write off and the women get to wear their jewels and brag to their friends about who they're banging. This is a tried and tested method of raising funds for the new foundation."

I rubbed a finger down my nose, making sure she knew that I was flipping her the bird.

"You might find it boring, Star," Alessa said kindly, "but maybe it's something rich Americans like doing."

"Star was rich American. Father rock star, no?" Amara demanded.

I snorted. "Yeah. Why won't you just let me fund the charity, Rachel? Then we don't have to answer to any-fucking-one."

"Apart from *you*. I'd prefer to owe Lucifer a favor."

That had me cackling. "Good one."

"I mean it."

"I know you do."

"Plus, we need more than your fortune if we're going to make a difference." Rachel sucked in a breath, her Type-A ass straightening the many items of stationery she'd brought with her to the meeting room.

AKA her dining room.

"Rach?" Rex, her Old Man, hollered from down the stairs. "Where are you? Got a kid that needs feeding and I tried but she prefers you."

Rachel's nose crinkled. "I'm so sorry, ladies."

"You don't have to apologize," was Alessa's kind retort. "Sommer needs to eat and we're all friends here."

Amara either didn't agree or didn't care. "What about Lily? She rich. Bottomless is her bank account, no?" she queried. "Anyway, she your assistant. Why she no here?"

Lily Lancaster was not only Rachel's assistant, but she was the daughter of the one-time Sparrows' money man—Donavan Lancaster.

On top of that, she was the Old Lady of the MC's Road Captain, Link, and Kat and I had lived at her house until we'd moved out. Alessa and Maverick still lived in her pool house.

She was also a darling.

And if I said that, it meant she was pretty much ready for canonization.

"I'm in the dining room," Rachel belatedly called out to Rex. "Lily isn't here because I have her working on other projects right now. I can't hit her up for cash every time I—"

"Just wait. I will. Especially if it means I don't have to attend a fucking gala," I retorted, earning myself a cool glare from Rachel.

Alessa started cooing over the baby the moment Rex ambled through the door.

Amara, as disinterested as I, stared at her nails.

A flustered Rachel took Sommer, and Rex pressed a hand to her shoulder, squeezing gently. "No rush, babe."

Sommer didn't agree as she immediately started fussing.

"You can feed her here. I've seen more interesting tits than yours before, Rachel," I said easily, rocking back in my chair, waiting for her to glower at me.

Something had triggered Rachel's anxiety this morning—she'd been persnickety since we showed up—and she and I had a difficult relationship at the best of times. Today, I was being a pain just so she had somewhere to focus her annoyance.

Anxiety was a bitch, and it was new for the lawyer who made ice look warm and cozy on a good day to be showing her emotions. I figured Rex thawing her out was messing with her mojo.

On cue, Rachel *did* glower at me, but she worked some magic with her shirt and Sommer disappeared beneath it.

Rex, his hand still on Rachel's shoulder, pulled some other kind of magic stunt because one second, she was sitting on the chair, and the next, she was perched on his lap while *he* sat on the chair.

The moment she rested against him, she released a sigh.

It'd be sweet if I was into that shit.

"What are you guys arguing about? I could hear you bickering upstairs."

"I not bicker."

Rex frowned. "You're a natural bickerer."

"Is this insult?" Amara, scowling, asked me.

"Nah. It's not a curse word or anything. More like he's saying you're *truculent* too."

That had Rex chuckling when Amara pursed her lips and glowered at him before she pointed to herself. "I being nice."

"She is actually," Rachel confirmed with a sigh as she stroked a hand over Sommer's head while she nursed. "Star's being the pain."

"Hey, I brought up the anonymous tip line," I retorted. "That's a great way to get help to those who need it."

"I thought you were struggling to nurse," Alessa said softly, changing the subject because the tip line was what had triggered our argument in the first place—I wanted to fund it, and Rachel wanted to organize a gala for it.

"I tried that trick you showed me," Rachel answered. "I don't have enough milk to feed her, but it's kind of soothing—"

"I don't need to know this," I muttered.

"Stop being such dude," Amara sniped. "Nothing naturaller than baby fed from mother."

"There's you told," Rex mocked, earning a squint from me.

Defiantly, Rachel drawled, "Star's pissy because she's holding a grudge."

"Grudge? What is grudge?"

"Like that movie," Alessa whispered. "The one that made me cry."

"You always cry in movies," Amara dismissed.

"A grudge is when you're mad at someone for holding something over you," I explained.

As if on cue, Amara stared above my head.

"Not literally, Amara," I retorted, folding my arms across my chest. "Anyway, I don't have a grudge."

"Bullshit. You do," Rachel countered in a light voice so as not to disturb Sommer.

"Why would you have a grudge against Rachel, Star?" Alessa asked.

My jaw worked because I knew where Rachel was heading and I didn't want to discuss it.

"I don't want to talk about this," was my flat retort. "The tip line and our disagreement about funding has nothing—"

"You don't want to talk about blackmailing rape victims? Gee, I wonder why."

Even Rex stilled at the dichotomy of Rachel's singsong tone and her actual words.

I gritted my teeth. "Not cool, Rachel. Not cool. That was between us when we were at war with the Sparrows.

"With the leadership in tangles and their means of communication in disarray, it might as well be a whole new world for them."

"Who did you blackmail?" Alessa demanded.

"I don't need to justify my actions," I countered.

Rex peered at me. "Seems cold even for you, Star."

"You have to do what you have to do, Rex. You saying you haven't pulled stunts just as bad in your time?"

His clenched jaw told me that he'd shut the fuck up and wouldn't judge my ass.

Good.

It wasn't like he was a fucking angel.

"Who did you blackmail?" Alessa snapped, her soft voice hardening.

Because it was her, I actually answered, "I have no reason to explain myself when I was *in the middle of a war.* But the daughter of a bank president who gave me access to Sparrows' bank accounts from inside his own bank and others he had access to as a board member in some Swiss accounts." I tipped up my chin. "Rachel gave me permission to do it, so you can turn that judgmental look onto her too."

Rachel sniffed.

Amara frowned. "You needed permission? What are you? Toddler?"

"What?" Rex stopped snickering when I glared at him. "It was funny. It's not like you're the kind of woman who usually asks for permission."

"I had to ask because Rachel told me she'd have Kat taken from me—"

Alessa gasped. "You wouldn't!"

"No. You're her next of kin, Alessa. You'd have been given custody of her," Rachel soothed.

It gratified me when she appeared as if she regretted opening that particular can of worms too.

"Who would take her?" Amara queried, her expression puzzled. "She brat. No one want her."

"I take exception to that," I grumbled, even though I couldn't deny Kat *was* a brat. That was what made her interesting.

"Star doesn't exactly have a legal claim to Katina. You know, what with kidnapping her and crossing state lines—"

"Kidnapping?" Amara muttered, more puzzled than ever. "How do you kidnap someone who is your daughter?"

Rachel heaved a sigh. "Ohio, the state, fostered Katina into Star's care. She wasn't supposed to bring her to New Jersey without express approval. Ergo, she kidnapped Katina. There are probably all kinds of alerts open on Kat's head."

"There won't be for long," I sniped. "I'm dealing with it."

"Dealing with it? The only way you can deal with that is to pull shady moves," Rachel retorted.

I growled under my breath. "Why the fuck did you bring me in on this foundation if you disapprove of everything I've done?!"

"Because you should be involved. No one has worked harder to help the victims than you, but you're so fucking difficult as usual that you're impossible to work with," Rachel spat, which made Sommer burble a wail as she stopped nursing.

She was the only reason I didn't storm to my feet or slam my hands against the table in annoyance.

Gritting my teeth, I bit out, "Two words. Pot. Kettle."

Rachel narrowed her eyes at me. "You're the ornery one."

"Hate to break it to you, Rach, but you're not exactly a teddy bear." I sniffed. "We need to find a common ground if we're going to work together."

"Bring Lily in. She's a natural peacemaker. Plus, she's rich as fuck and will donate," was Rex's pragmatic answer.

He wasn't wrong about her being 'rich as fuck'—Lily had a piggy bank full of *billions*, not just a few paltry million like me. Or Rex, and probably Rachel, for that matter. In fact, now that I thought about it, Amara and Alessa had *also* received a couple million from Lily as unofficial compensation for what her father and brother had put them through when they were enslaved by them.

I was literally surrounded by millionaires.

"That's not a bad idea," I muttered, concocting a plan to have Lily and I fund the tip line because, whatever Rachel thought, we needed that in place. Stat.

"First my idea," Amara groused.

"We do work well together," Rachel mused. "Tiff would be good too. She and Lily bounce off each other."

"Hell, while we're at it, why don't we make it a whole Old Ladies' project?" I queried. "It's not like Giulia, Indy, and Stone don't have something to bring to the party."

Rex hitched a shoulder. "Sounds smart to me."

Rachel pursed her lips. "You can deal with Giulia."

I grinned. "You afwaid of a wittle Old Lady, Rachel?"

Her eyes promised me hell which was creepy considering she was stroking Sommer's head lovingly. "No, but you're the same level of annoying so you two can pair off."

Rex laughed. "She's not wrong."

Though I huffed, I couldn't argue. Amara nodded. "Is good idea. Your brains not just in your balls, Rex."

"Why, thank you, Amara," he said pleasantly. "Always nice to get a compliment from you." In an undertone, he muttered, "Instead of another fucking dog." As if their new pup heard his species being taken in vain, Alfonso started barking in the backyard.

"Or kittens," I added.

"I have new ones," Amara offered, tone eager. "If you want more. A rabbit too."

"No! Two are enough. And where the fuck did you get a rabbit from?"

After that, the incendiary meeting defused some with the presence of Rex and Sommer. Once we agreed that bringing in the Old Ladies was a great idea, I ceded to the fact that a gala would bring international attention to our foundation which was what we needed.

As well as cash.

Lots and lots of cash.

What with safe houses and the legal costs of helping victims gain citizenship if they wanted to stay here in the States. Never mind chartering jets to get them back to their home countries if they preferred that option, plus the funds to help the women once they *were* back home, not just with shelter and food, but therapy too because fuck if they didn't need that—it all cost a fortune.

As we headed out, Rex caught me before I could leave. I tipped my chin at Alessa who I'd brought over to Rachel's house and was returning to Lily's home.

"Wait for me in the car," I told her, passing her the keys.

As she disappeared with a sullen glare, I arched a brow at Rex. "If this is about me giving Rachel shit—"

"Nah, you drive her crazy but she likes it. Says it keeps her sharp."

"Huh."

His lips twisted. "You remember when we brought Donavan Lancaster over to the States?"

"Ya mean after he fled to Asia and we hauled his ass back from Cambodia?"

"Yup. A guy helped us—"

Watching Amara walk back to the clubhouse, I angled my chin up and gave him the side-eye. "I remember, Rex. I never forget a favor."

His Adam's apple bobbed. "His sister…"

My mouth tightened. "Was a Sparrows' victim."

"*Was?*"

"Yeah. Was."

"Dammit to hell. Did you tell the—"

"Of course, I informed the family. What do you take me for?"

"Steel wanted to know, so I'll fill him in." He cupped my shoulder. "Not sure how you get as much done as you do, but fuck if I'm not grateful for it." A sigh escaped him. "We live in a cruel world, Lodestar."

There was no arguing with that. "And it's getting crueler."

"I hoped that… after he helped us…"

"I think we need to face facts that we're not always going to be able to deliver happy endings." *God, that was hard to get out.* My throat felt raw, as if salt had grazed the lining of my voice box and was scratching it with every word I uttered. "I'd better get out of here."

Nodding, Rex did the weirdest thing—he drew me into him and squeezed me in a hug. "I shouldn't have judged you in there. I'm sorry, Star."

I relented just enough to hug him in return. "Don't worry about it." When he patted me on the back again, I told him, "Can tell you've picked up daughters along the way. You're turning sentimental in your old age."

He winked at me. "You think that's an insult, but I know otherwise. Drive safely back to the city, ya hear me?"

"I hear you."

With a final hug, we parted, and from the dead silence in the car when I jumped behind the wheel, I knew I was in for a frosty ride over to Lily's place.

Heaving a sigh, I muttered, "Alessa, I've done worse shit over the years than blackmail someone, and I'd do worse still to take down the Sparrows."

"Does Conor know?"

That had me scowling at her as I pulled off Rachel's driveway. "Do you think he'd toss me out if he did? He knows what I'm capable of."

"That means he doesn't know."

"What's your problem, Alessa?"

"I'd want to know if Maverick was capable of hurting people who'd already been—"

"Fuck off, Alessa," I snapped, taken aback by her judgmental tone despite the fact I'd been forewarned by her reaction in Rachel's dining room. "You think that's the worst any of us have done? Jesus Christ, we were both soldiers. You think it's okay to kill people?"

"No, but—"

"No. *No buts.* Don't you dare judge me when I'm the goddamn reason one of the largest human trafficking rings in the world has imploded. You want me to tell Conor? I'll tell him. In my time.

"Now, I don't want to talk to you. This whole meeting was a

headache and I have enough shit of my own to handle without adding to the mess."

She didn't reply and I didn't expect her to.

When we pulled up outside the gates of Lily's home, I drawled, "Go on, Ms. Innocent. You get your pious, self-righteous ass inside and tell Maverick what a cunt I am for doing what had to be done to get the answers we needed to take down a centuries-old secret fucking society."

She shot me a stony look but jumped out of my ride.

I reversed and shot off down the street, relieved when I was on the highway and heading back to Manhattan.

There was only one problem.

It was pretty fucking big too.

If easy, happy-go-lucky Alessa could react like that, how would Conor?

I wanted to be confident in him, wanted to think he'd accept that I did what had to be done to finish the job, but…

No matter what I'd said to Alessa, there was *always* a 'but.'

Especially when taking his past into consideration.

With my eyes locked on the city skyline in the distance, I whispered under my breath, "Fuck."

CONGRESSWOMEN DENIED BAIL

CONGRESSWOMEN YEATS and O'Hark denied bail!

Interpol's Special Trafficking Unit declares this a victory in the fight against the 'Sparrows.'

52

CONOR
TIRED OF YOU - FOO FIGHTERS

Conor O'Donnelly

TWO WEEKS LATER

"SHE'S IN?"

"She is. Moved in yesterday," Savannah confirmed, her voice bleating from the speaker of Star's phone. "You should have helped me with the kitchen."

"Why? You like shopping. I don't. Plus, she knows you. She doesn't know me."

"She's your mother-in-law too," Savannah argued. "How can she get to know you if you don't spend time together? It's not like we're best buds."

"Bullshit. You know you cream your panties every time Magdalena 'wife of Irish Mobster Aidan O'Donnelly Sr.' talks to you."

"Firstly, *ew*. And secondly—"

"No secondly. You've been spending too much time with teenagers if you can say 'ew' without cringing."

"Why do I like you again?"

"I'm not sure," Star mused. "Either way, kitchens are your purview. Not mine." She paused. "Bathrooms and living rooms too. If she needs a computer, then *maybe* I'll help. But she has a son for that so go talk to Conor."

"I don't think you're going to convince her of anything, Savannah," I drawled, watching as Star arched a brow at me from the counter as I strolled into the kitchen after deciding it was time to break that conversation up before it devolved into an argument.

Aidan thought Savannah and Camden bickered but that was nothing on these two.

Star wiggled the coffee pot, prompting me to mouth, "Thanks."

As she stretched to reach for one of the mugs in the cupboard so she could pour me some—revealing, in the process, a luscious sliver of CK panties that made me want to twang the waistband—she told Savannah, "Don't you think we're better off staying out of each other's way?"

"That's not how family works," I answered before my sister-in-law could.

Her expression turned pained. "Is this part of that atonement thing?"

"If you want it to be, it is." I smirked when she rolled her eyes, sensing that I was joking. "Teasing aside, you don't have to like Ma. I don't expect you to spend time with her. I only ask for your Sundays."

"Such a sacrifice," she retorted with a wink as I sidled up to her, my hand settling on the curve of her hip after I retrieved something from my pocket. There, I drew the wrapper along the tender flesh until she grinned and snagged the Baby Ruth from my grasp.

"You're only arguing about this because if you do it, then you know I'll expect you to talk to Mom," Savannah grouched.

"Lorelei and I have nothing to say to each other." She tore open the candy. "And it's not just that."

"Not just what?"

"I struggle with knowing what Magdalena and Aidan Sr. did, or didn't do, to their sons."

Her words came as no surprise to me. Some days, that was a struggle for me as well.

Savannah clearly understood her predicament because she didn't immediately reply. Then, slowly, she verbalized, "Parents are humans. Humans make mistakes. I think if you spoke to Lena, she'd be the first to admit that she made mistakes. That there are things she wishes she'd done differently."

"She does," I confirmed, leaning beside Star. "I know there's plenty she regrets."

Star's brow furrowed. "What do you want from me?" She tore off some of the Baby Ruth, chewing with consternation.

I shot her a smile. "Nothing."

"To help out when I ask you to come along," Savannah muttered, thinking the question was aimed at her. "Oh, that reminds me. She wanted you to fix something for her in the bathroom, Conor."

"Since when am I the handyman?"

"Since Aidan got out of it by saying he had to meet with someone about a ball."

"A ball?" Star repeated. "Like a ball with dancing or a soccer ball?"

"Soccer. Declan and he were arguing about players last night. He's trying to get someone called Paco Perez to play for the Saturns. He's with Paris or Madrid." She hummed disinterestedly. "Maybe even Berlin."

"Informative as always, Savannah," Star drawled.

"Hey, it's soccer. What do you want from me?" Savannah mocked, throwing Star's words back at her.

"To pick a capital city and stick with it."

I smirked into my coffee cup. "He plays for a team in Berlin."

"This is your master plan, isn't it?" Savannah queried.

"It is, but I'm mostly dealing with statistics. Thank God. I'm leaving the meetings to my brothers. I have to get some perks from time to time."

When our doorbell rang, I flicked to the app on my phone to see who was there and arched a brow when I found Eoghan hovering in front of the camera—glower fixed firmly in place.

"What do you want?" I questioned, though I knew his exact reason for being here. Didn't stop me from giving him shit: "You're taking this *Peaky Blinders* thing too far."

Eoghan grunted. "You gonna let me in or do I have to buzz Aidan?"

"Let him up, Conor. Don't forget Troy and Dead To Me are on their way too. Chadwick as well."

"The guy who's Aurora Valentini's guard?"

"Yeah, him."

Savannah sniffed. "I don't like her."

"She's ultra-intelligent and doesn't bullshit. I like her."

"She and Jen have only just started getting along."

"And?"

"How are Jen and Paddy doing?" I queried, sensing another brewing argument. "Paddy's been AWOL from Sunday dinner the past few weeks."

"Been visiting with her. As far as I can tell, they're doing good. Paddy loves Saverina. It's a relief, to be honest, considering I set them up to meet. I thought I was going to blow shit with Jen again, but I didn't. Thank fuck."

"Ah, yes. Star told me about that mess."

"You told him?" Savannah groused.

"You never said it was a secret," Star retorted easily, uncaring if Savannah was pissed or not.

That right there was how they proved they were sisters—that was the kind of stunt siblings pulled and got away with.

When the buzzer rang again, I huffed. "You're doing this on purpose. You could have arranged this for a couple hours later, dammit."

"I'm not! This was the only time everyone could get together and *you* offered to take Kat to her class so I could do this. Did you braid her hair?"

"I did. It's wonky."

"Stop being a perfectionist," she retorted. "You'll have done a better goddamn job than I would have."

"Can't argue with that," I sniped, which made her chuckle.

"Anyway, before you have to leave, there's something in the—"

"Who's leaving and where? Hello, I am here, you know?" Savannah grumbled.

"I can easily hang up the phone," was Star's pleasant retort.

"Katina has a gymnastics class, Savannah. Star is meeting up with Eoghan and some other ex-servicemen and women while I'm out."

"Why?"

"Veterans Anonymous."

"AKA, poker. Five card draw, to be precise."

"Oooh, can I come up? I can beat all your asses. Plus, I've done stuff that means I'm practically a soldier."

Star's lips twitched. "If you feel like losing your stake, then feel free, Vana."

I clucked my tongue—she only used that nickname when shit was going down *or* she was in her feelings. "Now, now, children. Play nice."

"I'll be up in five minutes," Savannah snarled.

"I *am* playing nice," Star answered even though Savannah had hung up, reaching over to tug on my collar as she leaned on tiptoe and pressed her lips to mine.

When she sighed into the kiss, I breathed her in, absorbing everything she had to give which was a surprising amount considering how closed off she could be sometimes.

"Eww, man, you two keep kissing all the time," Kat groused. "You have guests, and *I* had to open the door!"

"Never get between a man and his woman, Kat," Eoghan rumbled, meaning I had time for one last tug of my teeth to her bottom lip—she'd feel that during the game. "Especially when it involves kissing."

As I pressed a final, parting kiss to her mouth, Kat queried, "Why, Eoghan?"

"There's a lot of meaning that goes into a kiss. It's a 'hello' and a 'goodbye.' It's a silent 'I'll miss you.' It can also mean 'I love you' when you're in a situation where you're not comfortable sharing that truth verbally with other people around."

Kat watched Eoghan as he rested his forearms on the island

counter. When she mimicked him, I almost snorted. "That's a lot to say when you're swapping mouth juice."

"Mouth juice?" Star laughed.

Kat giggled. "I'm not wrong, though, am I?"

We shared a glance and chuckled. "No," Star concurred. "You're not wrong. Neither is Eoghan. A kiss is a secret language that—"

"—you're not allowed to learn until you're at least thirty," I chimed in.

"More like when I hit middle school. I know who I'm going to kiss too."

"I don't need to hear this," Star muttered. "You're already enough trouble as it is without throwing hormones into the mix."

"Maybe it'll calm her down," I said with a wink. "It made Eoghan more zen."

My younger brother snickered, the grimness in his expression lightening for once. "It did actually."

"Kat isn't a boy," Star remarked.

"No, boys have cooties."

"Until they're in middle school?" I teased.

She graced me with a severe nod. "Yes."

Eoghan snorted while Star heaved a sigh. I just grinned. Then the door buzzer rang again—my app revealed Troy and Dead To Me were there, bickering as always.

"We'll leave you to the poker game but next time, I want to play too," I warned.

"Me three," Kat sang.

"Until you can afford the stakes, you can't play," Star retorted. "By the way, I put something in the refrigerator for you."

Warily, I asked, "What?"

Her cheeks turned pink. "Some snacks."

Better than a head.

"For Kat?"

"Both of you."

Eoghan cast a glance between us. "She's looking after you, Conor. Say 'thank you.'"

"Thank you," I parroted. "I can buy food—"

"Take the snacks and go, Kid," Eoghan retorted, shoving me in the shoulder.

"She doesn't need to feed me," I grumbled at him.

"It's a woman thing. Inessa does it to me all the time." To Katina, he explained, "It's like a kiss but for when you leave."

Kat frowned. "I'd prefer a kiss to raw veggies. Star's snacks are boring. She sticks hummus in a box with some carrot sticks and thinks that's supposed to fill a person." Kat tugged on Star's hand. "Can't we grab hot dogs afterward?"

"You'll have to ask Conor. Politely."

Kat batted her eyes at me.

"We can grab hotdogs." I cleared my throat. "After we eat the carrot sticks and hummus."

It was worth Kat's *boo* for the shy smile Star shot at me.

Before we headed out of the kitchen, I collected the boxes from the refrigerator—confirmed that there were a bunch of crudités and what appeared to be ranch dressing and hummus in two small containers—then gave Star another kiss farewell because I couldn't resist as Kat hugged her around the middle.

As we walked down the hall, with me trying to avoid Stimpy's urge to trip me up as he wove a path between my feet, I tugged on the tail of Kat's braid. "We'll leave soon, kiddo. You ready to go?"

"Yep. Just need my bag."

She ducked into her room and collected her gym bag.

As I watched her navigate the chaos of the space, my gaze drifted over her stuff.

She'd settled in but it still seemed temporary, which put me on edge.

It wasn't *hers*.

Sure, she'd staked a claim with the addition of a bunch of pink shit, and dotted here and there were the 3D-printed frames I was making her, ones with photos Star had sent me upon request, and Ren and Stimpy's bed was here too, but even Da had let us have *Teenage*

Mutant Ninja Turtle-green walls or, in Eoghan's case, *Superman*-catsuit blue.

Together, we headed to the door once I snagged the bright-pink tote she used for class and fisted it in my hand—kid's stuff was tiny, so tiny that it made me question if I'd ever been that freakin' small.

At the door, we met with Savannah and Chadwick; the former looked like there was an upcoming grudge match, but the latter didn't appear to want to be here.

After we let them in, gave our farewells, and walked toward the elevator, I asked, "Do you want to change your bedroom, Kat?"

She bounced on her toes, already buzzing for the upcoming class. A gentle hand on her shoulder stopped her from doing a handstand against the elevator doors.

"Change what, Conor?" she chirped.

"Everything. The colors, the furniture. It's still too much like a guest room with your things in it."

The bouncing stopped. "Can it be pink?"

"It can be pink." Then, I realized whom I was talking to—Star's daughter. "How much pink? Give me a percentage here."

"Ninety-nine percent pink."

"That's a lot of pink. Don't you think you'll get pink fatigue?"

"No such thing."

"I disagree. If you have ice cream for breakfast, lunch, and dinner, do you think you'd like it by dinnertime?"

"No one does that, Conor, silly."

"I've done it. So I know the answer."

She squinted at me. "Which ice cream meal is best?"

"Breakfast, because by dinner time, you're sick of a good thing. Plus, it feels naughty so it tastes better."

Kat pondered that as we made it to the garage.

When we were in my Mini Cooper, she queried, "How much pink *wouldn't* be pink fatigue?"

As I turned onto the road, I calculated, "Seventy percent."

"Why?"

"Because it's more than half, so that appeases your pink-loving soul, but there's thirty percent that lets you go wild and keeps the pink fresh. That's a good amount."

"I'll think about it," was the only confirmation I got.

This kid, I swear. By nurture alone, Star had crafted her mini-me.

"Can I have a coat rack tree too?"

My heart literally pinged in my chest. "Kat, it isn't a coat rack."

"Sure it is. We put our coats on it, don't we?"

"Yes, but we're not supposed to."

"Why do I put my coat on it then?"

"Why do you do cartwheels inside the house? Tornado Tina."

She giggled at the nickname but then, her laughter faded. "Can I have a coat rack tree so that I don't have to spoil your tree?"

I shot her a grin. "Sure you can. I'm surprised I didn't think of that myself."

Unless…

She beamed a smile at me.

Nah.

I hadn't just been…

No.

I narrowed my eyes at her. "You knew the tree wasn't a coat rack."

"Nuh-huh."

"Did your mom put you up to this?"

"My—" She blinked. "Mom." Just when I thought she was drifting into a dissociative state, she sighed. "No. Mom didn't."

Because I figured she was testing it on her tongue, I left her alone, mostly as it was cute listening to her repeat the word under her breath.

As I drove us to her school where the gym session was located, I played some songs. It was only when she started singing along to one that I realized Star must have listened to *noxxious* in her time. Otherwise, Kat wouldn't know the lyrics.

The thought had me hiding a smile. *And* sending her a song.

Me: Tired Of You - Foo Fighters

Star: Should I be offended?

Me: Just listen to the damn song.

An hour later, I was sitting eating crudités and ranch dip, watching Kat do some weird shit in the air, when a woman sat down beside me.

"I always forget to bring snacks," she said with a sigh before she turned to me and shot me a smile. "My name's Ali Hart."

I recognized that last name. "I think your kid is the kid my…" What did I call her? "…daughter…" Not entirely the truth, but it was good enough for me. Plus, I liked how it sounded. "…spat on because he was being rude to one of the cafeteria staff?"

Cheeks flushing, Ali Hart released a nervous laugh. "That's water under the bridge. Just a misunderstanding."

I frowned at her and turned to the side, angling away from her so she knew I didn't want to talk.

Returning to my carrot stick, I held it between my teeth so I could clap when Kat proved that, in the gym, she was hot shit on the mat— seemed as if she were only deadly when there were antiques in the vicinity.

"She's good," Ali praised, sidling closer. "I know coach is saying she wants Katina to come for extra classes."

"How do you know that?"

"Charles told me."

"Why does Charles know?" I asked suspiciously.

She gave a tinkling, *read annoying*, laugh. "I think he has a little crush on her."

"How cliché of him," I mumbled under my breath.

Her hand landed on my arm. "I'm sorry. I didn't hear that."

When her tits brushed my bicep, I sighed with annoyance at the come-on. "Look, I'm not—"

But I didn't need to defend my honor.

Not with Kat around.

"Hey! Get off my dad," she shouted.

From across the gym.

So loud that everyone heard.

And everyone twisted around to find out *why* she was hollering like this was a football game.

Ali turned bright red but she cleared her throat and bustled away as quickly as she'd attempted to worm her way in.

I shot Kat a thumbs-up, but she was too busy glowering at Ali to see it, and it was then that it hit me what she'd said.

Dad.

I knew she'd call me Conor after this class was over, but using that particular label had been her initial instinct.

This time, when I dunked a carrot stick into hummus, I was grinning like a loon, and once we were ready to leave, I didn't just get us hot dogs—I got us pizza and cannolis because that's what dads should do after gym class.

At least, that's what *this* dad did after gym class, and who the fuck else mattered?

53

STAR

Star Sullivan

AS WE SETTLED around the poker table I'd set up in our den, I knew Savannah's presence would be an issue for Eoghan, but it hadn't stopped me from allowing her to join, mostly because he needed to get over himself.

We were all fucked up—Savannah too.

No, she hadn't killed someone—or many someones—but she'd seen people die and she'd coped with more than most civilians ever did in her relatively short life.

As a result, I didn't push him when he played quietly, but neither did I let him off the hook.

After dealing the cards, I peered over my hand and took a look at the group around us.

Cin was studying Chadwick like he was a brownie and she'd been dieting for a year. Troy kept eying Eoghan—he was cute in his *Peaky Blinders* get-up, but I thought it was more to do with her sizing him up for the kill. Savannah was scowling at me and her cards which was totally a bluff—I knew her tells better than she did.

"I have to share something with Conor."

As an opening line, it wasn't as smooth as it should be, but it was weighing on my conscience nonetheless and that was supposed to be the point of these meetings.

At least, that was what I'd figured from watching *The Queen's Gambit* with Conor.

Eoghan arched a brow. "What do you have to tell him?"

"That doesn't matter."

"It'd help if we knew—"

I sniffed at Savannah. "I'm not telling you without telling him first." A yowl from the kitchen told me the hellcats were fighting.

I didn't bother getting up to umpire, knowing that Ren would high-tail it out of there in a few.

"How bad is it?" Cin queried, dragging her eyes from Chadwick's bulging biceps.

"I mean, I guess it's bad? It's not the worst thing I've ever done though."

Troy harrumphed. "Guess that doesn't mean much." She perused her cards and then Eoghan—in that order—before folding her hand. "Not with you, at any rate."

"Why don't you want to tell him?" Savannah demanded.

"Because I think it might make him mad."

She tossed down a twenty-dollar chip. "You'll get used to it. Some-times, you might even like it."

"I don't need to know about you and my brother's sex life," Eoghan grumbled, throwing a chip into the center of the green baize too.

Savannah cackled. "If you can't stand the heat, get out of the kitchen. Anyway, don't pretend as if you're innocent.

"Inessa might be more close-mouthed than a mime, but she blushes like the rest of us."

A wicked glint made an appearance in Eoghan's eyes. "I'll have to reward her for keeping her mouth shut, then."

"Make it emeralds. Diamonds are so insipid against her blonde hair."

Eoghan looked like he wanted to argue, but he apparently saw the sense in Savannah's logic. "Fine," he said with a huff. To me, he asked,

"You scared he'll push you away if you tell him whatever it is that'll make him mad?"

Uneasiness settled inside my soul as I started calling bets. "I don't like that I'm concerned he'll do that."

"Because it makes you feel weak?" Troy asked.

The question was surprisingly insightful, even more so coming from Troy. "Yeah. I wouldn't have cared before. Now, I care. It sucks."

Ren, hissing, raced out of the kitchen as expected.

What wasn't expected?

When he dive-bombed onto my shoulder after bouncing on the sofa.

I managed to catch him before he could fall off and skid onto the baize.

"You love him," Savannah retorted, fiddling with her chips as she eyed my hold on the cat with an amused eye. "Love makes you all kinds of out of sorts. Just take it as a good sign."

"Especially with you, seeing as you don't normally care about hurting people's feelings," Chadwick rumbled, his voice low and gritty.

Dumping Ren on my lap, I cast a look at Cin, just to make sure she hadn't melted into a puddle on the floor as I sniped, "I don't have to tell him."

"If you think you should, then do it. Makes no sense not to," Savannah said with a light shrug.

"I disagree." Troy tossed her cards onto the table. "I wouldn't tell him anything. Best way." Ah, there was the Troy I knew well.

"This isn't an op. I love him, Troy."

She sniffed. "Even more reason not to tell him. I love my bees. Didn't stop me from letting Harrow's Bees keep them."

"Harrow's who?" Savannah sputtered.

"Never mind. Give me a show of hands who thinks I should tell him and who thinks I shouldn't."

Savannah, Dead To Me, and Chadwick raised their hands for 'should.' Troy and, shockingly, Eoghan, raised their hands for 'shouldn't.'

I arched a brow at Eoghan. "Thought you'd want me to be open and honest with him."

"If it'll break his heart, why would I want that?"

Would it break his heart?

Or would it lessen the faith he had in me? A faith that was on shaky grounds because of the stunts I routinely pulled…?

He often said that he didn't want me to change. I took that to mean he didn't care if I showed up to a party with shitkickers on my feet instead of stilettos or if I wore jeans to a funeral. He didn't need me to coddle his ma or to keep my nose out of the Five Points.

No, he accepted me.

There was no denying that.

In some ways, with the atonement he asked for, what he wanted was harder. Change, for him, required me including him. It meant a molecular shift in how I dealt with business. But, when it boiled down to it, I had to accept that there was no point in being a part of his life if I wasn't open to that.

So, I guessed I had my answer, didn't I?

Rubbing my eyes, I muttered, "I think it's time for somebody else to share. Whose turn is it?"

"There's this man who wants me but he won't ask me out on a date because his friend *used* to want me," Cin drawled, tossing a chip down and staring pointedly at Chadwick as she did. "A friend who I texted recently and who hasn't texted me back… What do I do to pull his head out of his ass?"

I hid a smirk but Eoghan groaned. "Is this going to be about our love lives?"

"It's going to be about whatever we need, I guess. If that means you need advice on which jewels to buy your wife, Eoghan, then that's what it'll be."

Though he rolled his eyes, he muttered, "Why can't you have both of them?"

Savannah arched a brow. "See, there's my kind of thinking. Why wouldn't Hermione go for Harry *and* Draco? It just doesn't make any sense."

"Are you talking about a throuple?" Cin crooned. "That's my favorite dynamic."

Chadwick, though his ears were burning, cleared his throat. "It's for kids, Cin."

"Boring," she dismissed.

"Who the hell are Hermione, Harry, and Draco?" Troy demanded.

"Lyra's not old enough yet to have read *Harry Potter*," I grumbled to Troy as Ren started purring as he began kneading my lap. "Unfortunately for me, Kat is."

"I like it. It's sweet," Savannah chimed in. "I wish she hadn't ended up with Ron and that they'd fucked on screen. But hey, it's for teens."

"Because teens never fuck," Eoghan mocked.

Chadwick rumbled out a laugh. "Ever. Abstinence is the only way."

"Said the bird to the bee," Savannah sang as she shoved her chips into the middle of the table then, with a pretty smile, chirped, "All in."

My lips twitched as the rest of the table groused when the majority folded. Only Chad stayed in for the hand.

Ten minutes later, when I peeked at Savannah's cards before I shuffled them back into the pack, I had to hide my surprise.

My sister from another mister had definitely become better at bluffing—I guessed that was what happened when you became the queen of the Five Points.

54

TEXT CHAT

Star: You're going to have to stop me from wanting to strangle Rachel.

Lily: She's not that bad.

Star: If she talks about this fucking gala one more time at a meeting, I'll scream.

Lily: Scream, then. Lol. She'll know you're angry if you scream. Let it out. Holding stuff back only builds resentment.

Star: You've been listening to Tiff, haven't you?

Lily: Helped her study for her finals last semester, and now I read her textbooks for fun.

Star: For fun? Jesus H. Christ.

Lily: It's interesting.

Star: Riiiiiight.

Lily: You and Rachel are both control freaks.
That's why you don't get along. You're not
happy sharing the throne of queen bee with
someone else.

Star: I don't think I'm queen bee.

Lily: Hmm. If you say so lol.

Star: I do!

Lily: Think you're queen bee?

Star: Grr. 'Say so.'

Lily: :P By the way, I heard back from Juneau
News.

Star: Oh?

Lily: The tip line will be featured in their daily
periodicals as well as in ad campaigns on,
say, TVGM.

Star: That's fantastic! Well done, Lily.

Lily: :) We've been working on this together.

Star: Yeah, but I wanted to kick the head of
Juneau News in the balls during that meeting.
You schmoozed him.

Lily: Don't tell Link. He gets mad when I flirt
with other guys.

Star: Can't blame him when it makes them
putty in your hands.

Lily: Haha, it didn't!

Star: It did. He wouldn't have done anything
for me but look at what he did for you.

Lily: I'm paying him!

Star: Yeah, but those kinds of features and slots would cost a hell of a lot more.

Lily: It's for charity.

Star: Suuuure, charity begins at home with those news corporation cunts. Anyway, that's fantastic news. The more people who know about the tip line, the more we can help.

Star: Fuck, this is like a load off my freakin' chest. We're finally getting somewhere.

Lily: We are! I'm just happy to be a part of this. Thank you for not just taking my money lol and letting me help.

Star: Need all the help I can get, Lily. Not only with the funds, but with your schmoozing skills. We're going to make a real difference. I can feel it.

Lily: Me too. :*

Star: Thank you for everything. Seriously. I mean every word.

Lily: Stop! You're making me blush!

Star: Then Link isn't doing a great job in killing that blush reflex. :P

Lily: Oh, trust me, he does a wonderful job. ;) Speaking of… GTG.

Star: Hahahaha.

55

STAR

MAKE THIS GO ON FOREVER - SNOW PATROL

Star Sullivan

A WEEK LATER

"EAT."

Conor frowned at me, then at the bowl of soup in my hands. "I've eaten."

"When?"

"A couple hours ago," he mumbled, his gaze drifting to his computer.

"It wasn't," I argued, half wondering when *this* had become a thing —me caring enough to pester a dude about his eating habits. "You ate breakfast before I went to Kat's school to deal with those little fuckers who keep stealing her shit and that was five hours ago—"

"Wait." His eyes flared wide. "You didn't deal with them personally, did you?"

I sniffed. "It'd have been more effective but no. Kat asked me not to break their arms this time."

"Good. That school has ex-presidents' grandkids for pupils. There's probably Secret Service crawling all over it. I'll bust your ass outta jail but I'd prefer not to have to."

"Don't care if they're related to George Washington himself. You think I have a problem with getting in the face of an ex-POTUS' grand-brat if they're being horrible to Kat?"

"No, but even though we have an in with Davidson, I'd rather not piss off the Secret Service—"

"There are ECD in their ranks."

"I know." He shook his head tiredly. "It'd be nice if people could stop having an agenda."

"Like you don't," I couldn't help myself from teasing. "Look, I made this. So you have to eat it."

Conor stared at it. "*You* made it? Or did Panera?"

"Me. I made it."

"From a packet?"

"Nope. With real shit."

"Real shit. I hope you're not talking literally. I knew I shouldn't have introduced you to pop culture."

I hooted. "You think I stole that idea from *The Help*? That was pie and this isn't curried so you'd taste it if it was shit." Spooning up some of my concoction, I sampled the simple vegetable soup for myself. "See? No feces were harmed in the making of this meal. Plus, I like you so I'm less prone to punish you."

Still suspicious, he asked, "What flavor is it?"

"Jesus H. Christ, Conor. Eat the damn soup."

When I pushed the bowl in front of him, he took the spoon and ate some.

Brows lifted, he declared, "It's good."

"I can cook. When I want to. I survived a desert storm, Conor. Without MREs. Trust me when I say Dead To Me and Grail were *not* doing the cooking."

He smirked. "And you wanted to cook. For me. I'm honored." His gaze turned distant. "And horny."

"I'll accept both statuses."

"Is this why you brought soup?"

I snorted. "Horny wasn't the end goal, more like you had to be hungry and weren't moving from your desk any time soon."

"It's this match-fixing business. It's fascinating."

My lips twitched. "That's what you're doing?"

"Uh huh. I'm working on two pieces of software that deal with predicting outcomes. The first one is for targeting serial assailants in murder or sexual assault cases."

I pursed my lips in thought. "That program you started developing for your da? That takes stats and enables you to figure out the likelihood of the next place of an attack as well as their neighborhood?"

"You remembered!"

"Of course I did. It's fascinating. And creepy. Like *Minority Report* without Tom Cruise."

He grinned around his soup spoon. "Yeah, apart from we're not the government."

"I thought you'd have stopped working on that now that he's dead."

"How can I stop?" He grimaced, his expression so pained that I had to reach out and grab his hand. "You're giving back by working with Rachel on this charity, and this is my chosen method."

"True." I rubbed my fingers over his then knotted ours together. "What's the second project?"

"Making software that predicts match outcomes."

Sensibly, 'predict' came with air quotes.

I grinned. "Similar coding structure I'd imagine, only with different inputs?"

"Yeah," he concurred, going into a basic rundown of how he was creating the system. "This way, we'll be able to manipulate other teams and force wins so that the Saturns surf toward the top of the league."

"While making a lot of money gambling and taking bets on those games?"

He winked.

"Declan's taking to his new job as club president?"

"Not really."

"It's only because it's soccer," I grouched. "If it were any other sport, you'd be all over it."

"I can't argue with that," he agreed, making me shake my head with a sigh.

"The Saturns are playing this weekend. I was going to take Kat..."

His nose crinkled. "That's a silent command to come as well, isn't it?"

I shot him a winsome smile. "I'll make you more soup."

"If we stop for apple pie at Aoife's bakery first, then we have a deal."

"I thought she'd stopped baking it to make something more interesting now that she's gone viral again?"

"She always bakes it for me," he preened.

Snorting, I watched him eat then asked, "You ready for our appointment later on?"

His gaze flickered to the clock. "It's online, isn't it?"

"Unless you feel like time-traveling back to earlier this morning so we could catch a flight to Lyon, sure."

"You're extra snarky today."

I folded my arms against my chest. "You worked all night."

"Are you pouting?" he inquired, peering at me like I was a bug through a microscope.

"I am." And I wasn't ashamed of it.

"You worked all night too."

"Only because you did."

"Okay?"

"I like sleeping with you."

His grin turned cocky. "Sweeter words have I yet to hear. My woman likes sleeping with me. Do I get a gold star?"

"You can get a black eye if you'd prefer?"

"Nah, I'll take the gold star."

"And I meant *sleeping*. Not fucking. Though I like that too." I cleared my throat. "With you."

I wasn't sure I'd ever want to do that again with anyone else. Just the thought made me want to puke.

"You used to be the best I'd never had," he said softly, trying to grab my hand then yanking my arm when I wouldn't unfold it from my chest before pressing his lips to my knuckles. "Now you're just the best."

"'Just?'"

He winked. "You know what I mean."

I hid a grin. "I know what you mean."

"We'll sleep tonight. In bed. So you don't have to make soup instead."

It wasn't *instead*. It was *because of*.

I was *not* a nurturer. It wasn't in me to be like that. But Conor... ah, hell, I wanted to make sure he was okay.

In fact, it was becoming a *need*.

So many people had been taken from me.

My mom, then my dad thanks to Jorgmundgander's sweep-up process, then family I hadn't even known were fighting in my corner...

I needed Conor to be all right.

I had to keep him alive.

Not that I could tell him that. He seemed to appreciate my unique way of thinking, but this whole 'thing' was some freaky shit even I couldn't find any logic in.

I didn't think he'd get it if I said, 'Please don't die, Conor.'

It didn't have the same ring as, 'I love you.'

"Hey," he chided as if he knew I'd spaced out, his fingers reaching for my chin. "The soup's delicious. Thank you."

"I'm glad you're enjoying it," I said simply.

"I am, but I like that you made it for me." A gleam lit up his eyes. "If you ever feel the need to bake, you could always..."

"Bake you an apple pie?" I hooted. "Not sure I should try to compete with Aoife. Making soup isn't exactly baking."

"A man can never have too much apple pie in his life," he intoned piously.

"I have no idea how you stay so ripped with all the shit you eat." I'd yet to see any signs of weight gain, even if he complained his shirt collars were tighter than before I came into his life.

"Good genes. And I'll tell Aoife you called her apple pie shit. Just in time for the upcoming afternoon tea," he teased, surprising me with his awareness of that.

Although, on second thought, I shouldn't have been surprised. Conor seemed to have a preternatural awareness of all things family.

I refused to admit that I turned to mush inside at the idea that he considered Kat and me family too.

"I told Savannah I'm not going."

He snickered. "It's cute that you think that will deter her."

My lips twitched—he had a point. "Worked the last two times."

"She was busy writing articles then."

"True. When she's not so busy, she's always more dangerous." I tapped my chin. "Though I'm not convinced she's not that blogger. *I told you so.*"

His brows lifted. "Never heard of them."

"You are so tunnel-visioned sometimes—it's unreal."

"Definitely extra snarky," he repeated, licking his spoon clean as he finished up his soup. "How are you doing?"

"I'm fine."

"You're a control freak who's making soup because we didn't sleep together. I hardly think you're fine when your years-long project to take down the Sparrows is now in the hands of the authorities."

"Want to know the truth?"

"No, baby. Please lie to me."

I flipped him the bird. "It's nice."

"What is?"

"The notion of passing it over to people my grandfather hand-picked to make justice happen."

"You vetted them too *and* had some kicked off the team," he pointed out.

"We did that together," I dismissed, though he was right.

Ultimately, two officers had been removed from the team upon my request.

One, because his uncle's cousin's wife had ties to the Triads on mainland China, and the other because she'd worked on organized crime for the last ten years and her arrest rate was shady—I couldn't prove she was on the take, but I'd gone with my gut feeling and had her removed anyway.

"So, it's nice to hand over the responsibility is what you're saying?" he asked, brows high. "But, wait, you said *the notion.* What does that mean?"

I bit my lip. "I'm antsy."

"About?"

"Waiting for the other shoe to drop."

"Which other shoe?" Clarity had his eyes widening. "You're still fixating on the shit Reinier said?"

"Yeah." I blew out a breath. "You're probably the only person I'd admit that to though."

"It's not a bad thing to go with your gut, but I don't know how to help you when we're gaining more and more access to the Sparrows' operations and we've come across *nada* about that."

"Guess this is a good time to tell you I've had the Sinners put out feelers, then?"

"Why didn't you tell me before?" he grumbled.

"Because I sound crazy. Reinier's making me paranoid and I hate that."

"You've been hiding it."

"Not particularly." This time, I sucked in a breath. "Regardless, you know I've been slipping into the department's files, making sure they're staying on track, reading their reports, and, so far, all the red notices are achieving what I hoped they would. But you're right— nothing on organ trafficking."

His gaze narrowed upon me. "You're saying good things but your vibe is off."

"I feel like that. I've been anxious since that last meeting with Rachel," I admitted, threading my fingers together and toying with them.

"You should have said something," he groused. "Why didn't—" His gaze cut to the left at the sound of yet another fight between Ren and Stimpy, who snarled at each other like they weren't cat and cat but cat and *dog.* As Stimpy careened into the room, Ren chasing him, he sighed. "Cats are a lot easier to deal with when they're made of glitter."

I couldn't disagree.

Even if I thought that glittery cat statue of his was weird as fuck.

His hand snagged mine, putting a stop to my fidgeting, as he asked, "Why didn't you say you were feeling anxious?"

"Because…" Swallowing, I peered at him. "It's not just anxiety. I'm scared."

His lips parted, then he spluttered, "Of what? *Me?*"

"Of your reaction," I mumbled, staring down at our joined hands. "I-I was dismissive at first but then it's built up in my head."

"Then you'd better hit me with it. Da always told us that confession was good for the soul," he said dryly.

Having never felt the need to confess before, I didn't know.

I sure as fuck didn't know where to start—that was why I'd taken ages to bring this to his attention in the first place.

"Last year, I did a job for the Valentinis."

His head tilted to the side. "I remember. They gave you a laptop from that rapist asshole and that's how we found out where Liam and that Triad kid were being held by their kidnappers."

"Yeah." I cleared my throat. "That's right."

His gaze was expectant. "And?"

"There was a list on there—"

"That's how you got insight into some Sparrows' bank accounts, right? I don't remember what you were hunting for, just that that was the outcome," he said drolly.

"I'm a bad person."

He blinked. "I'm not a good one."

"No, but you'd never do something like this. I knew it was a horrible thing to do. There's no redeeming—"

"Is this about our atonement deal? Because you're doing a great job," he encouraged, and it was so positive, his expression was so proud as he tried to egg me on to speak, that it made me sick to my stomach.

"Back when we're talking, things were different. Not as hopeful. We were still looking for a way to bring the Sparrows down.

"That's why I needed to do it. It was an act born of desperation, but I'd have followed through with it if Rachel hadn't put a stop to it."

"Hadn't put a stop to what?" he inquired.

I didn't answer that. "Rachel said if I went ahead with my plan, she'd work it so the 'right' people knew I had Kat which would get my ass busted for kidnapping a minor."

"We need to talk to your grandfather about making that charge disappear."

I swallowed. "Already have."

"It's gone?"

I nodded.

"Good. Now, that was a pretty solid threat. Why did she use that against you?"

"Damian Headley wasn't just the mastermind behind a kidnapping ring. He wasn't just a serial date rapist. He was also a blackmailer." I stared down at my boots. "Some of the women had *very* high-powered fathers."

A blanket of silence settled over us.

"One of the fathers was a bank president, right?"

His flat tone had me swallowing because I knew he was piecing together what had happened.

"Yeah. Headley had footage of his victims."

"That's what Rachel meant. She was talking about you blackmailing someone. The day after the siege at Troy's."

I bowed my head. "Yeah."

"*I* was a rape victim."

I kept my gaze on my boots. "And you think I'm not?"

That didn't appease his anger. "Someone could have done that to me. Hell, *to* us. I, I mean, *we* could have been… No one deserves that." I could hear the ire in his voice shifting, morphing.

Then, there was more silence.

Dead. Stark. Roiling silence.

Until: "I can't look at you right now."

And the prophecy came true…

He was leaving.

Fuck, he was leaving.

When his chair rolled back, and he got to his feet and walked out of the room, I didn't chase after him, didn't try to defend myself when he knew *who* I was and what I was capable of.

Instead of justifying myself, I closed my eyes and sought calm.

He had every right to be angry, to be disappointed even.

I just…

I liked *this*.

Us.

The idea of breaking it was paralyzing.

That was why, an hour later, I hadn't moved away from his desk. I just remained in that spot, fixed in place, staring out onto the cityscape ahead.

He probably wanted me to leave.

It was his place, after all.

Yet movement was beyond me.

When he returned, I half-expected him to rail at me for still being there. Only, he didn't. He said nothing. Didn't look at me. Didn't touch me.

I sucked in a breath, taking note that it was easier to do that now he was here.

Without a word, he logged back onto his computer, hit his mouse a few times, and the sound of his fingers tapping on the keyboard let me know he was going to work and he wasn't going to talk to me.

Then, however long later, the annoying bubble sound from a Skype call rang and I turned around even though it was the last thing I wanted, knowing the meeting had started.

Even that was hard.

My hips felt stiff, and my waist too. God, it was like I'd aged twenty years.

Spying a bunch of people on the monitor, I knew I needed to concentrate when I couldn't put faces to names, but I didn't have it in me to give a damn.

My grandfather was there, as was the head of the 'Anti-Human

Trafficking' Department and his top-ranking detectives. Six of whom had already helped agencies the world over make dozens of arrests.

The meeting went on around me, and I didn't even care that I spaced out. Conor's anger was a living entity. It went deeper than disappointment. It was worse—*this was tangled with hurt.*

I'd often sought ways to push people away in my life. That I'd done this without him in mind, when the last thing I wanted was for him not to be my partner, hell, my penguin, was the ultimate of ironies.

I probably deserved it too.

I was a terrible human being and—

"Star? What do you think?"

I jerked at my grandfather's question and studied him blankly.

"I don't understand why we're getting them involved anyway, Anton," a woman called Hoyt retorted, simultaneously covering up my hesitancy and infuriating me enough to break me out of my stupor.

"And who the hell are you to dictate whether or not we *should* be involved," I snapped, "when you were all sitting on your asses while this trafficking bullshit went ahead under most law enforcement agencies' noses?"

Anton sent me an amused look. "Whatever your thoughts, you can't deny it's unusual to confer with people such as yourself and Conor, Star."

I lifted a shoulder. "No more unusual than to confer with you."

"Ah, but that's where you're wrong. I'm an honorary member of Interpol's General Assembly."

Conor's surprise was clear. "You are?"

"I am. Since last year."

"That was fortunate timing, wasn't it?"

"Very," Anton confirmed with a small smirk.

Hoyt sniped, "It's time to leave this to the officials."

"Is it when you're still depending on intel that Conor and I are providing you? Anyway, *Hoyt,*" I snarled her name like it was a curse. "You're only on this team because I vetted you first."

"*You* vetted *me?*"

Her screech would have satisfied me if I'd been in a better mood. "I deemed you clean enough to work this case, unlike Johnson and Batesman who I didn't. Don't make me wonder why you'd be questioning our presence on this team when we're still key sources of intel."

She gaped at me until she sputtered, "My record is pristine."

"No one is pristine," Anton drawled, making Hoyt straighten her shoulders at the silent reprimand. "Star and Conor's presence on the team, despite their backgrounds, is vital to ongoing operations. If you have issues with their help, I don't want to hear anything about it unless it's to resign your post in the department. Have I made myself clear?"

He received a bunch of shrugs and grunts for his pains from Ingridsdottir, Schmidt, and Deschamps, but Hoyt's was definitely the most vinegar-laced.

"Anyway, Star, we were discussing the best way to deal with the FBI who isn't cooperating with our red notices. They claim we procured our evidence illegally."

"That's ridiculous. Other agencies aren't fighting this," I retorted. "They're just grateful for the intel."

"The FBI isn't clean of the Sparrows' taint," Conor said flatly.

Wasn't that the truth.

I knew for a fact the Five Points had uncovered a Sparrow in the FBI—Caroline Dunbar.

"We can't trust that they'll act neutrally," one of the cops, Aaron Goldstein, agreed, nodding at Conor's statement.

Conor had brought him in during my 'absence' when Aidan's game plan had been to tear down the NWS by planting law enforcement officers with known Sparrows, who'd work to gain their trust, and who would eventually be inducted into the organization.

That plan hadn't gone swimmingly.

Dead To Me had told me she'd taken out Senator McClure on Conor's orders because Goldstein had uncovered the sex slave he was holding in his fucking basement.

"Act neutrally?" I repeated with a scoff. "You can't trust they're not Sparrows more like. While you can't compel a law agency to make an arrest, you can shame them into it.

"Of the recent arrests that have been made, is there anywhere they refused to act but, say, the DEA didn't?"

Goldstein cleared his throat. "Most of our groundwork has been on the European side of things. Stopping the trafficking in its tracks.

"The SEC has been cooperating and we've made ground with the Washington DC Police Department as well as the DEA and Homeland, but with the Feds blocking us, things are slower in the US than we'd like."

Shit, I *had* spaced out if I'd missed that part of the conversation.

"Throw an unknown Sparrow under the bus and use that as proof the Feds need to clean house," I rasped, well aware that Conor shot me a sharp look.

"Meaning you 'know' of an unknown Sparrow?" Goldstein queried.

"If I give you this intel—"

"They're a dirty cop who turned rat to the Five Points?"

"Yes," Conor grumbled, nodding at Anton's insight.

Clearly, he wasn't happy about burning the insider connection, but I knew the Irish had the FBI director in their pocket, and if Dunbar's arrest shamed the Feds into cooperating, well, *good*.

Goldstein shrugged. "They must have left a trail."

"Undoubtedly. Do I have your agreement you won't bring the Five Points into this?"

"This is why we don't work with known mobsters," Hoyt mumbled.

"That's a load of crap," I retorted. "You take the intel where you can find it and be grateful for what you're given. In this instance, a way to bring the FBI to heel."

"The name, Conor?" Goldstein asked, pen poised over a notepad.

"Caroline Dunbar. She works out of the—"

"I know her," Goldstein interrupted, interest gleaming in his eyes. "She's got a missing finger, doesn't she?"

"Something like that."

"Why isn't Davidson wading into this and whispering in the director of National Intelligence's ear? He can make the FBI behave, can't he?" I demanded, peering at Conor.

He blinked at me. Nodded.

That was it.

Fuck.

That was his way of telling me he'd speak with his da's old friend, the director of the FBI, and get him to stop being so fucking stubborn.

"Once we prove their ranks are sullied, I'm sure we'll be in a better position," Anton said easily.

"So, we'll reconvene after the FBI are under control?" I queried.

"Yes, we can—"

Nodding, I got to my feet and, without waiting for a reply, wandered out of the office and headed into the bathroom off our suite.

There, I ran the shower and started stripping off.

Once I was naked, I headed inside the cubicle. Tipping my face against the spray, I ignored the sound of my cell phone ringing and washed up from the sweat of cooking soup and the *colder* sweat of confessing an unsavory truth to Conor.

When that was done, I tucked the towel around me and moved into our bedroom, only to find Conor there, lying on the bed, staring at the ceiling.

Though I didn't exactly ignore him, I made for the walk-in closet where my stuff took up over half of the space now thanks to Savannah and her shopping spree.

As I dragged on some sweats and a tank, I returned to the bedroom and was about to leave when he darted upright and grabbed my hand on my way past the bed. "Where are you going?"

My heart stuttered.

Did he want me out?

"Back to the office," I said, hating how hesitant I sounded. "There's a brothel in Queens that was staffed by Sparrows' victims."

"How did you find out about them?"

"That idea I had to have an anonymous tip line came through." I didn't even have it in me to be smug.

"What are you going to do with the women who are working in the brothel?"

"Rachel's conferred with some women's shelters to get them out of there, but it's not going to be enough for long. We need our own shelters.

"We're planning the gala with that in mind now. She says that it isn't sustainable for Lily Lancaster or me to fund everything."

He grunted. "She has a point but that's a lot slower route."

"I know. She hasn't turned our cash down yet, but we're waiting for the facilities to get the appropriate licenses from the city."

"Goddamn bureaucracy."

"I've tried to grease the wheels as much as I can, but we're to blame for how slow shit is right now. The government is whacked up on a local, state, and federal level because of our exposés."

"Fuck."

That about summed it up.

"She allowed Lily and me to fund the tip line. That was a battle but it was worth fighting." Biting my lip, I asked, "Do you want me to sleep in another bedroom tonight?"

His gaze narrowed upon me. "Is that what you want?"

No. "I know I upset you."

"I think that's natural. Considering my past."

"Yeah."

"It's hard to be frustrated with a loose cannon for being a loose cannon. Especially when I can imagine your mindset when you went through with this plan."

"I did what I had to."

"I know." He blew out a breath. "Your resilience is something I love. Your strength too. But your propensity for utilizing collateral damage for your own gain is worrying.

"It's not like you can say you're a different woman now, not when this happened so recently, and it's not as if I don't fucking love *this* woman.

"Aside from bringing me into your team, I don't want you to change, Star. But I'm allowed to be mad, just as you are, and we can need space without it meaning that one of us has to sleep on the couch."

When he tugged me onto the bed, I turned away from him and stared at the wall opposite where there was this weird piece of glass that, if you hit a button, would turn fogged or transparent so we could watch each other showering.

He had a lot of random shit in this apartment.

Anything from rooms that were thematic to interior design inspired by comics.

He was lucky I didn't give a fuck what a room looked like so long as functionality was there.

"It also means that homemade soup won't fix anything."

"The soup wasn't to butter you up," I said flatly. "It was just to feed you. I don't like it when you don't eat or don't sleep. It makes me worry."

His hand smoothed down my arm and he grabbed my fingers, tugging me backward until we were lying flat, him down his half of the bed, me with my head resting on his abs.

Both of us stared at the ceiling for what was probably several lifetimes before the urge to make another confession hit me: "I can't be ashamed of what I've done to destroy these bastards. I did what no one else could. *Me*. I worked on this when people thought *sparrows* were just a breed of fucking birds.

"This was my fight. For years. I was alone. I had no one to rely on. Then I had you and you helped but I was still spearheading this. I had to use whatever resources were open to me to bring them down. I was incapable of doing anything else.

"Do I wish there'd been another way? Of course. But I had to fight fire with fire and the only kind of..." I decided to use his favorite word. "...*atonement* I can get is by doing whatever I can to bring the Sparrows' victims home.

"I'm not going to change, Conor—whether you needed me to or not. I will always do whatever I have to for the people who matter to me. That includes you now.

"I'm willing to do the dirtiest shit imaginable to keep you safe. You've no idea what I'm capable of. You think you do, but I'm warning you here, now, that if you can't handle *this*, you can't handle my worst."

A raging silence followed my words, but he didn't let go of my hand. Didn't shove me away. Didn't tell me I was a hideous person—I already knew that anyway.

When the silence continued, when it pierced my heart, when it ruptured my soul, when I realized I'd been a fool to let him in, I started to sit up.

Then, he whispered, "I can handle your worst. Just don't expect me to laugh and joke about it."

"You think I laugh and joke about what I've done? If there *is* a hell, Conor, then I'm fucked because one day, I'll be sitting beside Belyaev, Foundry, Smythe, DeLaCroix, and Reinier, just waiting for the devil to make us pay for the sins we've committed."

More silence.

God, it was so cacophonous that it hurt my ears.

Then, a heavy sigh. "I love you, Star. Nothing's going to stop that. Not your worst. Hell, not even your best. Understood?"

Trying not to take that to heart, I bit my lip. "Don't say that if you don't mean it because if you don't, then I'll walk out the goddamn door right this second and head back to West Orange."

He sat up, slipped his hand around my throat, and tilted my face toward him. "Stop talking about fucking leaving me," he snarled, his actions in direct contrast to the force of his words. "You. Are. Mine. Do you understand that?"

Then, before I could answer, our mouths were colliding, teeth almost clashing as he nipped my bottom lip so he could thrust our tongues together.

For a moment, I froze, totally unused to him like this, but the fire in him surged into me, swallowing me whole and sucking me down into the pit that was the want and the love I had for him. That was the love and the want he felt for me.

My hands slid around his shoulders, fingers digging into the muscles there as I held him close, needing him to be nearer, craving him to be *in* me. No barriers. Nothing between us.

I tugged at his tee, dragging it against his torso, raking it up his abs so that I could pull it over his head.

When he refused to stop kissing me, I settled with hooking it under his arms and letting my fingers explore his lean muscles.

As I delved between us, I toyed with his fly until I managed to unfasten the button of his jeans and could slide my hand into the pocket of space before I reached the bulge that was his dick.

With panting breaths, I let him tongue fuck me as I focused on shaping him and then jerking him off. His pre-cum made my palm slick and the immediacy of his response never failed to reassure any insecurities I might have had.

With a groan, he pulled back an inch, breathing just as heavily as I was, then he snagged a hold of my bottom lip with his teeth, nipped gently, then whispered, "You do not get to leave me."

"I do if I'm not wanted for who and what I am," I retorted with a panting breath.

His hand covered mine. "Does it feel like I don't want you? Does it feel like you repulse me?"

It didn't. But men's bodies weren't the most trustworthy monitor of *anything*.

Still, this was Conor.

He'd let me stroke his hair, had held me as I had a nightmare, and knew almost all of my secrets and hadn't run yet.

This was what acceptance felt like—*it wasn't always going to be easy.*

My hand tightened around his cock until he grabbed one of the straps of my tank and urged it down my shoulders. He did the same with the second until my tits were hanging in the hammock the neckline made, and he bowed his head and pressed his mouth to one.

I dragged my nails along his scalp as he sucked on my nipple, biting it hard enough for me to hiss before he tongued the part he'd bitten which made me jolt in surprise.

Pleasure sizzled around those nerve endings.

My fingers clutched at his hair as my hips rocked when the zing of sensation zipped between my nipple and my clit.

"Oh, fuck," I breathed. "That felt good."

He growled against my skin, making me moan as he sucked, interspersing bites with sucks, and then his hand dropped down, flexing beneath the waistband of my sweats and finding soft skin beneath.

When I parted my legs, I groaned as he aimed for my clit and found it.

With that direct stimulation, I started riding his hand, my fingers digging into his scalp as I held him in place. It bewildered me how wet I'd become until I realized this was angry sex.

Conor-and-Star-style.

The thought made me react like I'd been stuck with a cattle prod. Well, not one of his. A *standard* issue one.

I leaned down so I could nip the upper curve of his ear then bit down until he hissed and relinquished his hold on my nipple. That was when I tugged his head back and thrust my tongue into his mouth before kicking up a leg so I could straddle him.

He stopped me, even as he was fighting for control of the kiss, and dragged down my sweats so that I was bare. I didn't argue, relieved to be free from the confines, then shifted over him so I was straddling his lap.

When he reached over to the nightstand, I frowned but then blinked when I saw the fancy wrapping.

"What is this?"

"Your belated Christmas gift," he rasped.

"You're giving me this now?" I complained.

"You'll be grateful," he countered, panting. "Open it."

Breathing heavily and unhappy with the distraction, I snagged the bow and tore it apart. The four sides of the box parted to reveal a slimline vibrator, thick as a bullet, as long as the barrel of a revolver.

When I studied it, he rumbled, "Body-safe silicone. Bluetooth capabilities. Rechargeable. Same vibration capacity as a plugged-in

Hitachi." When I squinted at him with disbelief, he snorted. "Try it for yourself if you think I'm bullshitting."

I heard the taunt and knew he meant every word.

I sucked in a breath, braced myself because this was Conor and he never made false promises, then hit the slight bump of the 'on/off' button.

It buzzed.

"Holy shit," I whispered, feeling the vibrations ricochet through my hand.

It was a deep, thuddy pulse that I *needed* to experience where it was meant to be experienced.

Slipping it between us, I gently rubbed it around my clit, and I was pretty certain I saw God and all the saints when I did.

"Oh, fuck," I bit off, rocking forward and pushing my forehead against his. "Oh, Conor. I-I—" Words eluded me as the intense buzz made me yelp when I finally made it to my clit.

My head rocked back in response and he attacked my throat, sucking on my pulse, leaving yet another hickey for me to smirk at in the morning.

When he fucked a finger into me, I cried out as he pushed back against the front wall of my cunt.

The immediacy of my orgasm was *devastating*.

It was like my entire body caved in, imploding around those nonstop vibrations as he fucked me with his fingers then tugged the vibrator from my weak grasp and slipped that inside.

More devastation left a trail in his creation's wake as the intensity shot me higher, pummeling me with a pleasure so deep that it made every muscle in my body quiver in response.

Because it always took me so long to get off, I started crying when he grabbed a hold of my hips and hauled me deeper into him because this was short and sharp and everything in between and it was heaven and hell combined.

As he rubbed his cock around my clit, he bit off a curse. "Fuck, that feels good," he mumbled against my throat, the gentle vibrations rioting with the violent ones down below.

Then he took it away.

Left me.

I felt the barrenness of the space.

Felt the loss of the vibrations—

A sharp, piercing scream escaped me as he held it to my clit, and pressed his dick to my cunt, and thrust up into me with less care than usual, but fuck if I gave a damn.

I needed him.

I felt so goddamn empty and my pussy was pulsing around nothing. Being full gave me something to hold onto.

I sank down on him, just enjoying the sensation of fullness, but it only made the vibrations more intense.

A choppy wail rushed from my lips as his hands grabbed my ass and he started moving me on top of him, urging me to ride him.

My brain and body were both flying high as I began, but I paused halfway because another freakin' orgasm was there, right there.

"Conor!" I screamed, coming so hard and so fast that I knew my heart was going to explode if I didn't turn off this machine *now*. My thumb hovered over the button, but he shoved my hand away, not giving me any reprieve.

As I pulsed around him, I knew the vibrations were strong enough for him to feel deep inside. He ground out a curse then growled as he came, my pussy milking him for every drop of cum as I climaxed a-goddamn-gain, his fingers digging into my ass as he continued urging me to ride him, not stopping until both of us were wrung out. Then, and only then, did he reach for the vibrator. Then, and only then, did he switch it off.

I sagged against him and did the unthinkable—I burst into tears.

Never in my fucking life had I…

My brain blue-screened.

I couldn't…

What the—

"Shh, shhh," he rumbled against my ear, stroking his hand over my hair, soothing me, gentling me. "It's okay. You were so beautiful, Star. So fucking beautiful."

"It felt… I couldn't…" I garbled out more nonsense words.

"Shh, shh," he whispered, rolling back onto the sheets and drawing the corner of one blanket over us.

As he cuddled me into him, he kept on murmuring the sweetest of words, words I didn't deserve. God…

"I don't deserve you," I sobbed. "I'm a horrible person and you're not."

"I'm capable of horrible things too," he replied softly, his hand continuing that slow, long stroke as he soothed me when I was the one who should be soothing him. "But maybe, together, we can do something better? We can *be* better. Or we can at least try…"

I bit my lip. "I killed Priestley."

"I know you did."

"Brennan told you?"

"No. Ma said that Niall was with Callum's mother now. Full time. I read between the lines." His throat bobbed. "I trust that she deserved it?"

"She did," I whispered. "Some people need to die, Conor. Forrest and Bagpipes, hell, even Brennan softened up because she had a pussy. But I fucking *knew* she was scum. She turned." I clicked my fingers. "Just like that and just for me. How can I not… How could I stop? She was dangerous. She'd have made that kid hate the O'Do—" I broke off. "—*us,* too."

He pressed a kiss to my temple and, slowly, as if he were allowing the words to form organically, murmured, "I've never needed you to be anything other than yourself. I think I forgot that today. I'm sorry, Star, and I'm grateful that you do the dirty work to protect the people you love."

I pressed my forehead against his chest. "Even if that dirty work makes you hate me?"

"I could never hate you."

"You say that now."

"I say it and I mean it. Just… the only thing you could ever do to make me hate you is to leave me." His arms tightened around me. "And to take Kat away. Don't do that. Please."

I closed my eyes and hugged him as tightly as he hugged me.

"Never," I whispered. "No more leaving. I swear."

That was the easiest promise I'd ever made in my whole life.

CONOR

Conor O'Donnelly

AS I LAY IN BED, Star cuddled into my side, my gaze fixed on the ceiling, I listened to the silence of the apartment.

With Katina still in school, waiting to be picked up by my driver, Craig, the place was how it used to be.

Dead.

There was no denying that Star brought life to the penthouse. That she brought life to *me* too.

A few weeks ago, I'd defended her to Hunter DeLaurentiis, and now, I was in the position of defending her to myself.

She wasn't an easy person to love, but when *she* loved, there was no denying that you were welcomed into a unique club with incredibly few members.

That didn't make it any easier to accept what she was willing to do to achieve her goals, but the only option was not to be with her anymore and that wasn't going to happen.

She was mine. Even the bullshit moves she was capable of, as hard and as difficult as they were, didn't change that.

"I can feel you thinking. You're not going to rage quit me, are you?"

Her whisper had me tilting my head down as I contemplated her pensive expression.

In their time, my brothers had done worse shit than Star did on the regular, but I had never questioned my love for them.

Why was I questioning my love for her?

That was a dumb question because I wasn't.

I'd had a hair-trigger reaction and that wasn't on her—it was on me.

Needing to erase her worry, I whispered the only thing that mattered, "I love you."

I couldn't imagine that it was easy for Aoife to love Finn after the lies he'd told her. I couldn't believe that Ma had found it easy to forgive Da when his actions led to her kidnapping and gang rape.

So, no, love didn't have to be easy.

She released a soft breath. "I love you too. Is that enough?"

"I'm allowed to disapprove. Just like you can disapprove of the stunts that I pull. We have to work together to get over the bumps in the road."

"We do," she whispered.

"No rage-quitting allowed."

"I've never been in a long-term relationship before where forever is the end goal."

"You think I have?" I let my fingers move in a circle, the tips brushing her skin, soothing us both I hoped. "This is new for us. We're bound to fuck up."

She swallowed. "I don't want you to leave either."

"I'm not going anywhere."

"That means you have to eat right."

I stilled. "What?"

"You have to eat right. I don't want you to die."

Because I was at a loss, I asked, "What makes you think I'm going to die? I mean, everyone dies, but..." Flustered, I rumbled, "What do you mean?"

She peeped at me. "When I tell you that I love you, what I'm saying is, 'Please, don't die.'"

My brow furrowed as I took in her unusually open expression.

She meant it.

She goddamn meant it.

"I wish I could promise you that I won't," I said eventually, finding it hard to uncover the words that would make all this better when that was impossible…

I'd die one day.

That was the only certainty in my world—taxes sure as fuck weren't.

She burrowed her face against my chest, and her fingers somehow found the tattoo on my arm where she traced the letters as she whispered, "I know you must think I'm crazy."

"I mean, a little? But people in glass houses shouldn't throw stones."

That had her snickering.

She didn't reply though, just stayed quiet as I stroked my hand over her hair.

This softer side I got to see was a privilege few were afforded, I knew. And the fact that she wanted so many people dead apart from me was, I figured, a compliment.

Out of nowhere, two Tasmanian devils raced into the room, bringing with them meows as Ren bounced onto the bed and used it as a trampoline for his ultimate port of call.

Groaning, she turned her face into my chest. "Is he sitting in the light fixture?"

"He is." I peered at the menace who stared back at me unapologetically.

As for Stimpy, he settled against Star's back and started purring.

"How is this our life?" she whispered, sounding as bewildered as I felt.

But my lips curved. "It's good, though, isn't it?"

"You can say that after… today?"

The fact that I was smiling said it all.

Nothing would ever be normal with Star.

Thank fuck for that.

"I can say that after today," I confirmed softly. "Every part of you, from the soldier to the mother, is the love of my life, Star. I didn't forget that today and I won't ever forget that. Understood?"

She swallowed. "Understood."

Which was when all hell broke loose as Ren decided he needed to break shit up a little.

And he dive-bombed onto me from the light fixture.

Straight on my junk.

57

TEXT CHAT

Lodestar: Hey

Cruz: Hey. You okay? Need a body boiling?

Lodestar: Nah. Not this time. Though I appreciate your willingness to boil a body.

Cruz: Never work a day in your life if you love what you do.

Lodestar: I feel ya.

Cruz: So, no body. What's up?

Lodestar: I just wanted to loop you in on some shit that's going down with your mom.

Cruz: Caroline—what's she done now?

Lodestar: As we already knew, she's a Sparrow but the Feds uncovered that in an internal review. She'll likely be arrested soon. If you want to go see her, now would be the time to do it.

FIFTEEN MINUTES LATER

Lodestar: You okay, Cruz? Talk to me, bud.

Cruz: I'm fine.

Cruz: Appreciate the heads-up, but it wasn't necessary.

Lodestar: Like that, huh?

Cruz: Yeah, it's like that.

Cruz: Won't forget the solid you just did me though, Star.

Lodestar: Think nothing of it, man. Speak soon.

Cruz: Yeah, speak soon.

FORMER FBI AGENT IN STANDOFF THAT SENDS SHOCKWAVES THROUGH NYC

IN A SHOWDOWN *that shocked the city, FBI agent Caroline Dunbar turned a weapon on her colleagues and triggered a hostage situation. The newly uncovered Sparrow died at the scene.*

58

STAR

WISHING ON A STAR - ROSE ROYCE

Star Sullivan

WITH SAVANNAH SHOVING me forward like she was trying to get me to walk off a gangplank, I nearly fell into the hotel room.

"Go on, get in there," she groused, shoving me extra hard when I wriggled away from her.

"I'm in, I'm in," I argued with a huff, straightening before immediately groaning at the sight ahead of me.

House parties with the MC were one thing. Afternoon fucking tea with my sisters-in-law was a whole other ball of wax.

At the abruptness of our entry, conversation drifted to a halt.

Awkwardly waving at them, I slunk over to the table where they were seated with those stupid, multitiered plates with cakes, scones, and sandwiches in front of them.

I'd have killed for a steak.

Doing this with Tryn Bowen was bad enough. Savannah just wanted to torture me.

"I wondered when you'd show your face," Aoife drawled, her tone amused as she poured coffee into a china cup. "You look like you could use this."

I plunked my ass down in one of the tiny seats. "Yeah, I need it.

Savannah dragged me out of my apartment and brought me here. She's more terrifying than Al Qaeda."

Savannah shot me a smug smile. "I've been taking lessons from Aidan."

"They're working." I yawned. "Okay, so you can carry on talking. Just pretend I'm not here."

Aela stared at me over Cameron's head. "Not likely. This isn't school, you know? Attendance isn't mandatory."

Ouch.

Fuck me for being contrary, but Aela was growing on me more and more.

"Shut up, Aela," Savannah sniped. "These gatherings are a ritual."

"I thought it was a chance to bitch about our husbands. Apparently, I didn't get the memo."

I tipped my cup at her. "I'm here for the tea even if I'm drinking coffee."

Aela studied me with wary eyes—she didn't trust me yet.

Smart woman.

I found it interesting when Aoife reached over with a set of silver tongs and started loading up a dish which she proceeded to set in front of me.

Huh.

I wasn't sure why it surprised me that she was in charge here, but surprise me it did.

"Aela's right, Star. It isn't mandatory to come to afternoon tea if you're not interested. Saturday and Sunday dinner is enough familial obligation for one week for any sane woman."

Call me contradictory but... "It's not like it's every week."

Aoife chuckled. "I feel as if this is your idea of purgatory."

"I wouldn't go that far, but it's definitely not my usual scene. Doesn't mean it's bad, just means it's different." The glance I shot Aela was loaded with my defiance.

"That reminds me. I need to thank you, actually, Star," Inessa said, somewhat timidly.

I got the feeling I scared her.

My lips quirked up in a sharkish grin—loving Conor hadn't made me soft. "Why?"

"Eoghan was happy after he came back from your poker game."

"Glad to hear it. He won't always be happy though," I warned. "Sometimes, he might be angry. Sometimes, he might be sad. Hell, sometimes, he might not even want to come."

"I know, but this seems healthier than what he was doing before."

Camille's snort was delicate. "Burying his troubles and pretending they didn't exist while glowering at anyone in the vicinity who smiles at you?"

Inessa's lips twitched. "I don't mind that last part. I took him to a club with me and Lisandra two weeks ago. We didn't get hit on once. She complained but I loved it."

"Dancing with a two-feet wide barrier around you makes it so much easier. And less stinky. What is it with men who don't wear deodorant, huh?"

"They're lower forms of humanity," Savannah drawled, pinkie extended as she took a sip of her coffee.

Me being me, I snagged her finger in a mockery of a pinkie promise. "Since when do you drink coffee like you're the queen?"

"It's the china," Savannah said unapologetically. "It gives off different vibes than the 'My husband is a serial killer' mug Aela got me."

"I didn't get you anything. I made that for you, hag."

Savannah bared her teeth in a smile. "I can feel the love across the table."

"My heart's doing something right now, and it's not beating for you." Aela softened it with a wink though.

"What's this about Eoghan?" Aoife queried carefully, the only one who hadn't gotten distracted from the original theme of the conversation.

"Star started this little get-together for her ex-soldier buddies. It's a poker game and I whooped soldier ass," Savannah explained.

"Lies," I retorted.

"Why the hell were you there if it was for soldiers she served with?" Aela demanded.

"Because Star plays poker like a card shark—"

"And you don't?" I retorted.

"Exactly. It's not often I get to cut my teeth on a game with you."

"Who won?"

Savannah pouted at Camille. "She did, but I beat everyone else. Eoghan included."

I didn't bother bragging. "I'll teach you all I know, young grasshopper."

Savannah flipped me the bird. "You're kindness incarnate."

"I know. It's a weakness, really."

Aoife chuckled. "You two are more like sisters than you know."

"Oh, we know it," Savannah retorted. "No one else would put up with her ass if we weren't related."

"I feel this," Inessa teased, elbowing Camille in the side.

"Shut up, brat," was the older sister's response.

"Mostly, after that poker game, I'm just left reeling from how hot everyone is there. If I didn't have Aidan..." Savannah whistled. "I'm not sure who I'd have hit on."

"Let's see, the Consigliere's bodyguard, an assassin, a sniper, your sister, or your brother-in-law," I mocked, grabbing a red-velvet cupcake with buttercream and eating it in one bite.

Seriously, how small did they make this shit?

"He wouldn't be my brother-in-law if I wasn't with Aidan, now would he?"

"Hey, he's mine!" Inessa groused.

"And you're not a skank who steals other women's men," Aela pointed out.

Savannah pretended to wipe a tear from her eye. "That's the nicest thing you've ever said to me, Aela."

"You should invite Dagda next time."

My head whipped around so fast it probably would have recorded as speeding on a radar. "What?!"

Aoife was unapologetic in her madness. "He's probably as fucked up as the rest of you. Savannah included."

"Hey! I resent that."

"You were the one who admitted you and Aidan had sex after he hanged those traitors," Aoife said calmly.

I peered at my sister. "Under their swinging bodies?"

"No! Back at home, thank you very much."

While Aoife's nose crinkled, I shrugged. "You have to celebrate wins when and where you can."

"I'd appreciate the backup if you didn't make that even creepier. I can't see Conor wanting to fuck under the hanged corpses of traitors," Savannah drawled.

"He'd be down if I was down, I think. He's very..." A smile danced on my lips. "...open to new experiences."

I didn't realize it, but every single one of my sisters-in-law moved closer to the table at my words.

"My cousin tried to hook up with him at my wedding," Inessa said in a quiet voice.

My brow puckered. "Remind me to kill her."

"You can't kill everyone he's been with," Camille pointed out calmly, flicking a glance at her manicure. "What would be the sense in that?"

"Anyway," Inessa grumbled, "she said he was different."

"Different, how?" I argued. "He's got one dick and two balls like any man."

Inessa shrugged. "She just said he was different. And he never gave her his number. If I liked my cousin, I'd probably have been annoyed on her behalf."

"Which one?" Camille questioned.

"Klara."

"God, I used to hate her."

"She was so jealous I got Eoghan. I think that's why she went for Conor. But..." She cleared her throat. "I mean, something happened at our apartment when we got home and Conor had to focus on repairing our security system."

My nose crinkled. "I should probably apologize to you for that."

"What do you need to apologize for? It's not like…" Her eyes widened as she jerked to her feet. "*You* invited that woman, that *whore*, into our apartment?"

"I thought the O'Donnellys were the front for the Sparrows," I admitted with a shrug. "Plus, aCooooig needed his code rattled and his ego brought down a notch."

"I don't believe you! You ruined my wedding night!"

I frowned. "Conor told me once that you never even met Eoghan until the day of your wedding. Don't pretend like I wasn't doing you a favor.

"A woman deserves to know if her husband is bringing a side piece into the marriage bed."

"Wait, so, you did it to piss Conor off or to let Inessa know Eoghan had a girlfriend?" Camille questioned—I was starting to pick up on the fact that she was always the voice of reason in these matters.

I hitched a shoulder. "Both."

"You're clearly not sorry so why apologize?" Aela retorted.

"Because I didn't know I'd ever be sitting down for afternoon tea with my sister-in-law who I happened to…" I paused. "I didn't mean to hurt Inessa. Just Eoghan."

Savannah snorted at that, but her gaze was amused—she was used to me being the cat among the pigeons.

I figured she was mostly glad that, in this instance, she wasn't in any danger of getting bitten.

"Does Eoghan know?" Aoife inquired, her tone serene.

"He does, but I didn't apologize to him if that makes it any better," I directed at Inessa who Camille was gently trying to encourage to sit down again.

Aoife flashed a look between us. "I think we need to let bygones be bygones."

"When she says 'we,' she means 'you,' Inessa," Aela drawled.

Inessa huffed, but her gaze turned thoughtful. "Eoghan offered to change our furniture after that night."

That wasn't off topic. Much.

"Is that a good thing or a bad thing?" I asked warily.

"Good. And we came to an agreement as well after everything. I suppose..." Her brow furrowed. "It goes against the grain to say this, but I should thank you.

"Our honeymoon was odd and you probably helped because he was apologetic when, otherwise, he could have been... *difficult.*"

"Don't thank me," I said honestly. "I'm glad that my actions changed the course of things for you though."

She graced me with a regal nod, but her dislike of me had outweighed her fear.

I found that I didn't mind. Even if, moments before, I'd been amused by her anxiety around me.

Aoife, clearing her throat, remarked, "I learned that Lena has moved into your building, Star. Savannah."

"How did you find out?" Aela inquired as she jiggled Cameron on her knee.

"Overheard Finn and Aidan talking about it."

"I had to help her with her kitchen," Savannah said with a huff. "Star was useless, of course."

"Of course," I agreed easily, though my gaze darted between the women as I tried to figure out where Aoife was going with this.

First a mention of Dagda, now Lena?

I'd attended enough Saturday night dinners at her place to know that her MIL was not a topic of conversation to be discussed in front of Aoife.

"Why did she leave the estate?"

"Why didn't you ask Finn?" Inessa queried, her tone softer.

"Because we rarely talk about her. I know he doesn't want to hurt me but..." She sucked in a breath. "Finn hurts too. She's the only real mother he's ever had."

"Shame she's a murderous bitch," Aela grumbled as she resettled Cameron on her lap.

Aoife carefully placed her cup down on the table. "I don't think she's murderous. A bitch, yes, but not murderous. That implies she wants to go on a killing spree. Even I know the Lena of today isn't the Lena of… back then."

Aela frowned. "Is Finn still taking Jake to see her?"

"Yes. That's why Finn was discussing things with Aidan. He needed to know where to visit her."

"I've been around when he drops by," Savannah admitted.

Aoife cut her a look. "Why do you sound awkward?"

"Mostly because it is. Lena tries but Finn's quiet. Jake's… I'd say he's too young to figure out there's something going on between them."

Absently, Aoife reached up and rubbed her chest as if something were paining her.

"I can't get involved for obvious reasons," I admitted lightly, "but I know a gun-for-hire, Aoife. You almost had her over for dinner…"

"Why do I feel as if you don't say that to anyone you don't like?"

I beamed a grin at her. "You're catching on."

I *did* like Aoife.

She was a gentle soul who baked brilliant brownies and who, despite all odds, had found her place in the world even though said world was content to toss her under the bus a few dozen times.

"I-I don't want her dead," Aoife muttered.

"Who's the gun-for-hire?"

"I thought you liked your husband," Savannah teased Aela, who promptly flipped her the bird.

"I do. I was curious."

"Her name is Dead To Me," I answered easily. "You know her as Lucinda."

Aela's eyes widened. "She's a sniper? I thought she was a soldier."

"The two aren't mutually exclusive," I drawled.

"I don't want her dead," Aoife spat, tone sharper this time.

"Okay, Aoife, calm down," Inessa soothed. "We didn't think you did."

"Finn…" Her jaw worked before she released a breath. "Finn has tried very hard to make up for what he's done—"

"How's that going?" was Camille's gentle inquiry.

"It's going well." She rubbed her brow. "I feel as if there are two discordant parts of my marriage and I hate that.

"I love my husband. I-I'm not ashamed to admit that I don't want to be without him, no matter the mistakes he's made in the past, but this feels like…"

"A scab that won't heal," I said simply, taking a sip of coffee afterward.

"Yes," she replied, bobbing her head. "It's raw and deep and I hate it. I hate that it affects my life. I hate that none of you want to talk about her in front of me, and I hate that my brothers-in-law all tread warily around me. I hate that Finn acts as if he's dropped a bomb whenever he utters her name."

When the china cup in her hand cracked, we all jerked in surprise, but I was the one who snagged her hand, peered at it for cuts, and placed a napkin around the small slice in her palm—not a lot of damage considering the act.

"Keep pressure on that," I instructed.

Dazedly, she nodded. "T-Thank you."

"You have a lot of unresolved anger," I muttered. "Trust me. I'd know. I'm the queen of that."

"She is," Savannah agreed, but she'd moved around to Aoife's other side and was kneeling next to her. "What do you want to do, Aoife?"

"I want to go back in time. I want my mom to be alive. I want to not know what Lena did to her. I want to unlearn that Lena was a pawn…" She closed her eyes. "It's impossible, but it's holding me back and I hate that. I want to move forward. Onward. I-I want to wipe the slate clean.

"Last Thanksgiving and Christmas, we were alone for the first time and even though I knew Finn missed his brothers, he didn't complain. He was happy and he played with Jake and he was… perfect," she breathed. "It was weird. No bickering with Conor over the wishbone and no sniping when Brennan ate all of the honeyed parsnips because Lena makes the best in the world.

"No Aela and Declan pretending they hadn't made out in one of the bedrooms—"

"Hey! Like you don't do it—"

"No Lena making us wear those stupid hats from the crackers she has imported from the UK." She pressed her hand to her mouth. "I was lucky that you stood by us, that you didn't choose a side but fitted in around us and what happened, but I still want that back. I just don't know how to reconcile what I know with a path forward."

"You don't."

Aoife peered at me with glossy eyes. "I-I don't?"

I hitched a shoulder. "I don't like Lena. I think she's a meddling old coot who needs to retire to Boca Raton so she can leave the kids she fucked up to live their lives without her snooping around all the freakin' time." Around me, sharp gasps sounded, but I ignored them. "*However*, I don't think those fucked-up kids would like it if she became a snowbird. I think they need her for some weird reason. Conor, especially.

"With that being said, knowing that doesn't mean I have to like her. It doesn't mean I even have to endure her presence aside from on Sundays because that's the least I can do for the man I love."

Aoife blinked at me. "You're saying I should just go on Sundays for Finn's and Jake's sakes?"

"Nah. My past isn't your past, and we both know what I'd do to the people who wronged me." I showed her my teeth. "Lena would be dead and buried if she'd mowed down my mom. Whatever you're doing right now, is a lot healthier than what I'd do—"

"And more legal," Savannah muttered.

"—so whatever you decide to do is what you decide to do. You can want Sunday dinners and family time while barely acknowledging her."

"Wouldn't that be awkward?" she mumbled.

I grinned. "For who? You? Nah. Her? Sure."

Her eyes caught on mine then the words came out in a rush. "I miss her too."

"You do?" I grimaced. "What's to miss?"

Aoife swallowed. "She became like a second mom to me."

"That's just creepy."

Savannah nudged me to shut up.

"What? It is! Talk about a weird way to alleviate her own guilt." I shuddered. "And people say I'm a fucking mess. Anyway, no one can tell you what's right or wrong for you is what I'm saying.

"In my relationship," I admitted, "I'm the Finn and Conor is the Aoife."

"What?" Savannah spluttered around a laugh.

"It's true. I've done some unforgivable shit. Folks might think I don't deserve him, but the only option open to me is to do whatever I can to be worthy of him." I sucked in a breath. "It's hard and I can empathize with Finn because trying to make amends isn't easy, but that's how it should be.

"Have you decided on what Finn can do to atone?"

Aoife frowned. "No?"

I didn't think she meant for it to be a question, but it came out that way.

"Why not?"

"You have, Aoife. You wanted him to cut ties with Lena," Inessa prompted.

"Yeah, but that's not enough, is it? That's a knee-jerk reaction," I argued. "Atonement is proactive. Now, a couple months ago, I didn't believe in this atonement shit, but Conor's made me see the error of my ways."

"You're growing up," Savannah said with a fake sniffle.

I gave her the side-eye then returned my focus to Aoife. "He could have made me suffer and be miserable, but he didn't."

"What did he ask of you?" Aela queried, her tone cautious.

"I tend to think I can only do things myself," I admitted gruffly. "That I'm a team of one. He wanted me to change the way I think. He wanted me to include him. That was what he needed from me and I've done that. Do I fuck up? Sure. But did I open up to him too? Yes."

"Our relationship is different though," Aoife argued.

"Duh," I retorted. "But what do you want from him?"

A silence as powerful as a loaded gun slipped between us as the others waited with bated breath for Aoife to answer.

Eventually, when the sound of a pin dropping would have been as loud as an atomic bomb blast, she whispered, "To be his priority. Always. Above his family. Always. To take my side. No matter what. Over everyone and anyone, including his brothers."

"I-I think he does that now, doesn't he?" Inessa queried. "After everything, I mean?"

"Yes," she said softly, her eyes locking on mine though, not Inessa's. "He does."

"Okay, so maybe verbalize that to him—"

"I might have told him that in some variation."

"Men need reminders," Savannah tacked on. "Never does any harm to repeat something until it's set in stone."

"Very true," Aela agreed with a hard chuckle.

"So verbalize it again and then say you would like to give Sunday dinner a try with the family.

"And while I've no desire to help the old bitch, I'd like to suggest that you think about how you need Lena to atone too.

"Before you say she can't, I know that, but I think I'm the only one who'd find it entertaining if you blank Lena at her own dinner table."

"It wouldn't be fair to everyone, would it?"

"Nah, not really, but as I said before, that doesn't mean you have to make it easy on her.

"Did you know Conor used to have nightmares as a kid and she wouldn't comfort him back to sleep?" I sniffed. "I'll deal with her, but I won't sort out her fucking kitchen." If that was pointed at Savannah, then so be it.

She took the hit with an eye roll.

Aoife bit her lip. "I need to think about it."

"Be odd if you didn't." I patted her arm. "Your life's been in stasis since everything came out. Some things going forward, and others going backward. We both need to embrace the future because we can't do anything about the past."

"Wise words," Camille intoned gently as she held out a plate for me to take. Seeing as mine was still full, I shoved it at Aoife.

"Eat," I directed. "They might not be as good as yours but they're still good."

Her eyes were slightly dazed. "Thank you."

"No worries."

"No," she repeated, tone firmer, her hand reaching for my free one. As she squeezed, she said, "Thank you."

My lips quirked in a half-smile. "My pleasure."

"I-I have an apple pie over there for Conor," she mumbled.

"He'll appreciate that," I said softly, aware she was still reeling from the unintentionally emotional conversation we'd just had.

Nodding, she bowed her head and seemed to drift off from the conversation as other chats came into being around the table as we all, silently, agreed to let her come to terms with what had just been discussed.

Around ten minutes into the shift in conversation, I received a text from Conor with a new song. I popped an earbud in so I could listen to it. Rose Royce's "Wishing on a Star" was the opposite of his style but the title made me smile and the melody had me humming which was when I realized Aela was studying me.

When she saw I'd caught her watching me, she raised a brow and tipped her chin at Aoife before dipping it at me in silent thanks.

I bowed my head and returned my focus to the dish in front of me.

I might not like afternoon tea, but at least it came with cake.

SENATOR FITZGERALD COMMITS SUICIDE

SCOTT FITZGERALD, senator of Indiana, committed suicide last night and his body was found prior to his attempted arrest by the FBI as agencies around the nation investigate the Sparrows.

He is but one of the officials believed to have taken their lives to avoid justice.

Sheridan Reinier, Garry Smythe, and David Foundry are three others—their bodies have yet to be found, but their ties to the NWS, according to Interpol, run deep.

Fitzgerald leaves a wife and three daughters behind.

PART 4

The ocean does not apologize for its depth and the mountains do not seek forgiveness for the space they take and so, neither shall I.

    - Becca Lee

59

TEXT CHAT

THREE MONTHS LATER

Dead To Me: Are you stalking Temper?

Lodestar: I have better things to do with my time than stalk her.

Dead To Me: Hmm, that's a non-answer.

Lodestar: How is that a non-answer?

Dead To Me: It is. You have better things to do with your time, sure, but what about your money?

Lodestar: What's that supposed to mean?

Dead To Me: It means I know she betrayed you lol.

Lodestar: Then why ask?

Dead To Me: Because I want to know if it's you.

Lodestar: Me, what?

Dead To Me: Stalking Temper! She asked me yesterday if I was behind it and I was sad to say that I wasn't.

Lodestar: I'm paying someone.

Dead To Me: To stalk her?

Lodestar: I think she's full of her own shit lol. He's not 'stalking' her. He's following her.

Dead To Me: Wow. Splitting hairs much?

Lodestar: I don't trust her.

Dead To Me: We can agree on that. You think she's doing something behind our backs?

Lodestar: I just have a bad feeling.

Dead To Me: She's already proven she can't be trusted. So I can't blame you. Is there anything I can do?

Lodestar: Nah. I've had Eagle Eyes monitoring her for the last four months or so. If it freaks her out at the same time then all the better.

Dead To Me: Lol. If I ever question why we're friends, you do or say something like that and I remember.

Lodestar: Does that mean I'm predictable?

Dead To Me: The fact I figured you'd be behind Temper's panicked call this morning... Maybe? But also... you got a sniper in for a two-buck thief's job so... no?

Lodestar: :P The bitch deserves to be panicked.

Dead To Me: We both agree. Did you know she asked me for Creed's number?

Lodestar: What a bitch.

Dead To Me: Right?

Lodestar: I figured she was one of us, but now that I know otherwise, it's making me second-guess a lot about her. And being related to you isn't enough to make me forgive her.

Dead To Me: Hell, I'm the one with blood ties and I don't forgive the cunt either!

Dead To Me: What's Eagle Eyes' mission?

Lodestar: Just to monitor her.

Dead To Me: Expensive task. Not that I know you're short of funds or anything, but your gut must be screaming…

Lodestar: It is.

Dead To Me: About what in particular?

Lodestar: How did she know Muñoz was trying to take me out?

Dead To Me: Huh.

Dead To Me: There if you need me, Star. You know that, right?

Lodestar: Depending on it.

Dead To Me: You know, if we were regular women?

Lodestar: Yup.

Dead To Me: This is where we'd send each other hearts, isn't it?

Lodestar: :P Or xoxo

Dead To Me: Uh huh.

Lodestar: The thought's there?

Dead To Me: Sure is.

SHOCK WIN FOR THE NEW YORK SATURNS UNDER O'DONNELLY'S NEW MANAGEMENT

60

CONOR

Conor O'Donnelly

"I'M SO FUCKING MAD. Because you want Declan to go legitimate, we have to sell our art!" Aela hissed as she prodded her fork in the air at me and then Aidan and then Finn.

Clearly, we three were the bad guys in this scenario.

The thought made me hide a smirk.

"Which art?" Savannah inquired, nosy as ever.

"My secret stash," Declan said lazily as he stretched, reached out his arm, and hooked it over his bristling wife's shoulder. "The stolen shit."

Aidan groused, "You should have gotten rid of that sooner. The Saturns have just started winning since you transferred in that player from Berlin."

"That wasn't the point of this diatribe," Aela muttered.

"Thought you'd want him to be legit," Star stated. "For Shay's sake."

"I do. But I'm a hypocrite and I like having a Manet in my bedroom."

"You have a Manet in your bedroom?" Inessa queried.

"How the hell did you get that, Dec?" Eoghan demanded after he spooned up some of Aoife's cheese and broccoli soup.

"I have shady connections," he admitted without an ounce of shame.

"You need to get rid of them," Finn said.

"No, he doesn't. Shady connections for us are law enforcement agencies! The more shady connections we have, the better."

Dec tipped his glass at me. "Fair point, Con. Still, I'm with Aela that it sucks to have to get rid of our art."

"Can't you keep it? It's not like people go into your bedroom. Unless you're swingers." Star's brows lifted hopefully. "Are you? That'd make you more interesting for sure."

Aela squinted at her. "Just as you were starting to get on my good side."

Star just grinned before tucking into her meal.

"It's hidden behind a safe," Declan added. "We only open it up when we're going to sleep in there."

"That's not weird," I muttered.

"Weird but security conscious," he argued.

"I say keep it," Brennan mused. "We're not going to get rid of our less-than-legal pasts overnight. Might as well enjoy them and cover them up—"

"Secrets don't die. They outlive us all," was Star's unusually serious tone. "If you keep that Manet now, Seamus will have to handle its disposal when you're worm food. That'll be much more awkward if he's a politician."

Brennan shot her a dour glance. "They're not exactly in their dotage."

"Neither was my mom and she died when I was a kid."

I glowered at Brennan then mimicked Declan and curved my arm around Star to tug her into me.

"It's okay, Conor. I'm not upset." Her hand settled on my thigh and she squeezed me gently there. "Just saying if you're going for broke, make it clean."

Aela huffed but the conversation trickled down so we heard Inessa telling Aoife, "I swear to God, it gave me blue eyeballs, Aoife. How you can read that crusty vajayjay stuff is—"

"Blue eyeballs?" I drawled with a laugh. "What are you reading?"

Inessa's cheeks blushed. "Nothing."

"Ha, doesn't sound like that to me," Eoghan teased, leaning over to smack a kiss on her cheek.

Aoife prodded the air with her fork. "Stop teasing her. Be grateful that we read what we do because you reap the benefits."

Finn chuckled. "She's right, Eoghan. Shut up."

At that, Aoife kissed Finn—on the mouth.

None of us knew what had happened, and Finn wasn't willing to talk about it, but three or so months ago, shit had changed between them.

Out of nowhere, they weren't sitting at the heads of the table for Saturday night dinner anymore. No, they were sitting in the middle of a new glass table that was longer than the other one, with us all clustered around them, the heads no longer set with cutlery.

Weird, but it was their house and we didn't question it.

Then, crazier still, Aoife, Finn, and Jake showed up at Ma's apartment for Sunday dinner. While their relationship remained strained, it was better than not having them there at all.

Finn had started smiling more, had stopped looking like he was walking on eggshells, and then, when Aidan asked him to reschedule a trip he'd booked for his family to Denver for some book convention Aoife wanted to attend, Finn had refused.

Small steps, but I thought Star had something to do with it because when I'd told her about Aidan's expression at Finn's refusal, she'd smirked.

Now, my woman smirked a lot, but that was a special kind of smirk. One that was smug and happy at the same time.

I dipped my head down and whispered, "I don't know what you did to fix them but thank you."

She arched a brow at me. "I didn't do anything."

"If you say so."

"I do." She tucked into her dinner without taking credit for getting involved, but she didn't stop me when I hugged her to my side.

But I knew how she rolled.

She hadn't said anything either when I'd lost a week in my office with work and had dropped ten pounds. Then Ma started popping up in our apartment with food. Food I was hard-wired to want to gorge on.

Star rarely said anything—*she acted.*

"Conor told us that you got the adoption papers through today, Star?"

She angled her head at Aidan and then peered at the second, smaller table that was set up in the next room where Katina, Shay, and Victoria had taken to sitting so they could watch TV at the same time. "I did."

My older brother hid a smile. "It wasn't an accusation."

"Hmm."

"Did you get the whole 'kidnapping of a minor' thing cleared up too?" Aela asked, surprising me with the fact she knew about that.

Since Star had started attending afternoon tea with the other women, I knew she'd grown closer to them.

"I didn't. Grandfather did."

That was new too.

Anton had morphed into 'Grandfather' when he'd visited the city to tell her Kathy Harridan, her burned ID, was no longer wanted in Ohio for kidnapping a child.

"Interesting," Finn mused. "His power is definitely terrifying…"

"And he only abuses it for family," I teased. "Something we can all get behind."

Aidan touched his napkin to his lips. "I respect a man who'll go to the ends of the earth for his kin."

"That's why you've got the ECD causing problems for the British on the borders with Northern Ireland?" Aoife asked coolly. When Aidan arched a brow at her, she continued, "Dagda told me. He's happier since you had him move back to Ireland, so I have to thank you for that. I won't thank you, however, if you get him killed."

I took a sip of wine. "I still don't understand how that helps the US."

Aidan shrugged. "Doubt it does. I don't expect Kuznetsov to tell me his whole game plan so long as he helps us down the road with Seamus."

Most of my brothers stared at Star as if she could explain. Star just hitched a shoulder. "Grandfather has good intentions. For the most part."

"Helpful," Finn retorted.

"When did I ever say that I'd try to be helpful?" was her smartass reply.

Finn rolled his eyes.

"Are you looking forward to tomorrow, Savannah?" Camille asked.

"I am. I know there'll be an argument, but I haven't eaten with the folks for a while." Savvie tossed a glower at Star who was keeping quiet. "Star's promised that she won't cause trouble."

"It's Conor who'll cause trouble. Drooling into his food instead of talking like a regular human being," Brennan mocked. "Still can't get over that crush on *noxxious,* can you, Kid?"

I flipped him the bird. "It'll be fine."

"You're meeting your idol as a son-in-law this time," Eoghan mused, but he was hiding a grin. Jackass. "That's a lot of pressure."

"Never meet your heroes," Declan agreed.

"Just try not to show me up," Aidan retorted.

I huffed. "Thanks for the vote of confidence!"

"I know how you got the last time you met Dagger. I wasn't sure if you were going to cry, collapse, or come in your pants!"

"Aidan!" Aoife hissed. "The kids will hear!"

He shrugged unapologetically.

"You're going to miss dinner with Lena?" Inessa inquired, obviously trying to change the subject to something more manageable. "All of you? I'm surprised she didn't invite Lorelei and Dagger over so that she wouldn't have to do without her precious boys for a day."

"She offered," Aidan said dismissively. "I told her what I keep on telling her—our wives also have families."

Because I was sitting so close to Star, I noticed the faintest tension emanating from her limbs. She kept it hidden, though, not just throughout the rest of the meal but all the way home too.

Only after we tucked Katina in bed did I confront her about it.

"We don't have to go tomorrow if you don't want to. We both know how you love Ma's company," I drawled.

Though she smirked, she didn't look up from the computer where I knew she was multitasking between coordinating an event that was being held at the Four Seasons for the ATRF—the Anti-Trafficking Relief Fund—speaking with Goldstein regarding a Sparrow who'd only ever spoken to his compatriots in a code she'd broken this weekend, and slowly gaslighting Temper Black into believing that the Brothers were trying to have her eradicated.

All in all, it was a slow week for my fiancée.

"Your ma's sole redeeming quality is her ability in the kitchen."

I snorted. "Not the love she has for her family?"

"Nope," she said, popping the P. "Just what she can do with some beef and potatoes."

"We both know you're dreading seeing Lorelei tomorrow."

She sniffed. "I dread the upcoming apocalypse from over-dependence on fossil fuels, Conor O'Donnelly. I do not dread seeing the woman who helped raise me."

"Methinks the lady doth protest too much."

"You would." She glanced at me. "You working on your spreadsheets?"

"You make it sound like a seventh-grade project," I grumbled with a pout.

She chuckled. "Trying to predict the future is definitely something you think you can do at that age."

"I'm not trying to predict the future. Patterns are everywhere. Particularly in Italy where match-fixing is done as a fine art."

"You settled on next season's purchases?"

"In the process of doing so. We need to attract mid-level names from the upper leagues of the sport over in Europe. It's hard when the team is worth shit."

"It's doing better now," she argued.

"Yeah, but not Real Madrid or Paris St. Germain good." I hitched a shoulder. "It's a work in progress. Speaking of, I was thinking about inviting the Kensington FC chairman to your gala."

"Why?"

"Alain Brentner has a good striker we want to buy but he's holding out."

"So?"

"*So*, he's the son of Juniper Brentner, which will bring a nice glossy sheen to the event because she's still a Hollywood A-lister, and I'd like to lean on him."

"Lean on him. Ha. Rachel will kill you if you commit a crime at her prissy gala."

"I'm not scared of her."

She smiled. "You're scared of me though, aren't you?"

"When you're armed, yes." I grinned at her. "But you're not armed around the house."

"A pencil can be deadly in the wrong hands. This you know."

"Yeah, but you're not going to stab me with a pencil."

"No, I don't need to. With the amount of apple pie you eat, you'll give yourself cyanide poisoning."

"That's if you crush apple seeds. I don't eat apple seeds. Just apples."

"Semantics."

"Big semantics. Huge ones. So?"

"So?"

"Do you want to invite Alain Brentner to the gala?"

"Translation: Please invite Alain Brentner. What did he do anyway?"

"Insider trading."

"Got proof?"

"Rock solid."

"Brentner's an industrialist too, isn't he?"

"Yeah. But the insider trading was within Kensington FC."

She yawned. "Fascinating. I'll invite him. But you have to blackmail him when I'm there. I'll need some entertainment. This gala is looking set to be boring as fuck."

My lips twitched. "Whatever floats your boat."

Because that had been surprisingly easy to convince her of, I strode over to her desk, moved behind her chair, and rested my hands on her shoulders.

As I rubbed her there, she arched her neck, letting me get deeper into the crevices where the knots in her muscles told a story of their own.

"Maybe I *am* nervous about tomorrow," she admitted with a grumble.

"No. You don't say," I mocked.

She sniffed.

My fingers trailed over her throat, trickling over her front to settle over her lower belly. "Did you charge it?"

"Of course."

"I need to work on a better battery life." I sighed. "I also need to convert one of the spare rooms because I can't have Kat coming across this shit."

"I think you should establish a sex toy line."

"Nah, America's not ready for a president to have an uncle in the sex toy business."

"Shortsighted. There'd be a lot less violence if people had more orgasms."

"I can't argue with that." I leaned down and pressed a kiss to the nook between shoulder and throat. "Where is it?"

"In my desk drawer," she whispered.

"Use it. It'll calm you down."

She gulped but didn't argue other than to say, "I'm not stressed about tomorrow. I said I'm nervous." Her hand curved around the handle on the drawer and she tugged it open, retrieving the toy I'd made for her alone. "You never told me why it took you so long to make this."

"Had issues with the motor. It kept burning out, so I had to make one."

"You should have been an engineer."

"Maybe. It's not my calling," I dismissed even though I knew my smarts fired her up.

Snagging the toy from her fingers, I flicked it on then ghosted it over her breasts.

Her throat held me in thrall so I continued tasting that area, wanting to leave a thousand marks dusting her skin so she knew she belonged to me, that I belonged to her.

Her head lolled to the side as I teased her nipples then traced circles over her abdomen until she was squirming against the chair, the mechanism rocking back against me as she arched and wriggled, her legs parting to allow me between them.

Moving my lips against her ear, I whispered, "Wider."

She released a keening sound then lifted a leg and lodged her heel against her pussy. Angling her thigh to the side, she sobbed as I slipped the vibrator behind the waistband of her PJ bottoms.

Aware that she'd be bare beneath, I moved lower, lower, waiting for her soft cry as the vibrations began to make themselves known.

"Conor, please," she whined, and that plea went straight to my dick. "Please, please."

I moved the tip of the vibrator around her clit.

I'd studied the favorites on the market and had reasoned that an edge was necessary for extra pressure; that was why I'd shaped it like a lipstick but with a wider, more slanted head. I burrowed that sharper tip against her clit before laying the whole thing flat against her most sensitive spot for maximum sensation.

A breathy moan escaped her as her hands moved around to clasp me around my nape. Once she started rocking her hips faster, I slid the vibrator down, using her arousal as lube.

When I pressed the tip inside her, her short, sharp scream had me hiding a smirk in her throat.

Sucking down hard in time with her pulse, I circled the tip around her slit and thrust into her, only shallowly, letting the mouth of her cunt absorb most of the vibrations.

Fingers scrabbling at my hair, mouth releasing gasping breaths, she came. Wailing my name.

Heaven had a sound.

I chuckled against her throat, pulling back to study the purple marks I'd left behind, then retreated to let the vibrator find her clit.

After a few seconds of that treatment, her leg lifted, mimicking the other's position so she looked as if she were sitting in a lotus position, and both snapped together as she groaned her way through another orgasm.

"Fuck, Conor, fuck," she moaned.

I alternated a couple more times between her slit and clit, not stopping until she'd come a third time and was panting like she'd run a mile, "S-Stop, C-Conor, p-please." Then, and only then, did I switch off the device.

She jerked in response to the loss of vibrations then stumbled to her feet.

Within seconds, her PJ bottoms were on the floor and she was bent over the desk. I needed no further invitation, but I didn't give her what she wanted.

Instead, I dropped to my knees and buried my face in her cunt.

"No, no, no, no," she sobbed as I slurped my way through her juices, only to focus on her clit, sucking down hard on the hyper-sensitized nub.

As I ate her out, encouraging her to come a fourth time, though it was slower than the others, she angled back, fingers hanging on to the edge of the desk, the motions panicked as if she didn't know what to do with so much pleasure.

My cock ached like a fucker, but only then did I get to my feet. Twisting her around so we were face-to-face, I stared into her dazed, half-blind eyes and propped her against the surface.

Freeing my dick, I let it fall against her slit. The pressure had her arms giving way.

"I love you, Star," I rasped as the head of my dick found her gate.

"L-Love you, C-Conor," she slurred, her eyes falling closed as I thrust into her slick cunt, the muscles weakly clinging to me as if they were as exhausted as she appeared.

She hummed when I filled her then pressed her fingers to her belly. "Feel so good," she confessed with a sigh.

"I want one more," I whispered.

Her face screwed up as I reached for the vibrator again, but she didn't stop me, especially when I pressed it into the space between my dick and balls. As I turned it on, my head rocked back in immediate response.

"Oh, f-fuck," she cried, her other hand coming up to grip her hair. "I-I… C-Conor," she said brokenly. "So close. So close. It hurts so good. So close."

Her exhausted pussy clutched at me, drawing me impossibly deeper, urging me to cum as the inexorable vibrations drove me to hell and back.

I tipped my head forward again and glued my eyes to hers as I slowly thrust into her.

A pained wail escaped her as I retreated.

A choked sob was let loose when I filled her.

It was to that melody that I worked us both to release.

It was slow. Achingly slow.

My muscles trembled, sweat beading along the length of my spine as if I were working out. My entire being tensed in anticipation as I moved ever nearer to the end.

Then she screamed and I quickly bowed over her, covering her mouth with mine to shut her up. The change in position, the shift in pressure, had us both losing it.

I hissed out a long breath as my entire being seemed to be suffused by a darkness so pure, the only light was her—gleaming like the star she was in the endless universe that was the surfeit of pleasure she gifted me with.

As I shuddered through it, she clawed at my shoulders, nails digging deep enough that I knew my back would have been shredded if I weren't wearing a tee.

The vibrator's battery conked out at long last, making the throbbing silence even more powerful as the final jerking pulls of her pussy on my cock drained me of everything I was.

When I sagged into her, she groaned as she tried to hug me but ended up leaning her limbs against me as if that were all she was capable of.

I didn't complain.

I felt like a bowl of limp noodles too.

Burrowing my face between her tits, I mumbled, "Mine."

She breathed, "Mine."

I smiled.

Sucked in air that was stained with sex.

Closed my eyes.

Home.

I was home.

61

STAR

Star Sullivan

WHEN I TOOK a seat at the dinner table, my lower body protested the move.

I wasn't exactly ready for one of those inflatable ring things, but goddammit, my ass felt as if I'd been doing deadlifts/squats/lunges on repeat for the last twelve hours.

The orgasms had been worth it, though, and they came with an added benefit—I was less worried by Lorelei's passive aggressiveness and more focused on the aches in my muscles.

"Star?"

I blinked at Savannah. "What?"

"Pass the dinner rolls?" she drawled, but her eyes were spitting at me. I just had no idea what she was spitting.

The problem was, the bread was here and she was there and that meant reaching over to give her the rolls.

For how my ass and inner thighs ached, she might as well have been in the Gobi Desert.

Conor, seeming to sense my predicament, acted like a gentleman and did the deed for me. Then, in an aside, he murmured, "Dagger asked what you've been up to the last couple years."

Oh.

That was why Savannah had been glaring at me—she'd thought I was blanking her dad.

That had me turning to the head of the table to find her father shooting me a wary smile.

Ah, Dagger, ever the peacemaker.

"I've been focused on bringing down the organization that enslaved me, Dagger. It hasn't been a picnic."

To give him his due, he didn't cringe away from my answer. "I think you should speak with Lorelei's publisher. The world needs to read your story."

"Why? Do we want to make the world manically depressed? Mine has a happy ending, but ninety-eight percent of the women like me didn't have a happy ending in sight until I escaped." I glanced at Lorelei. "I'd appreciate reading an advanced copy of the manuscript before you send it to the publisher."

Savannah's mother studied me over her wine glass, and while I saw the dislike she had for me in her eyes, she surprised me by stating, "That's only fair."

"A biography would be good exposure for the charity," Savannah mused, her tone thoughtful. "I could write it for you."

I sighed—no matter what I said, she'd tell Rachel, who'd never shut the fuck up until I did it.

Allowing these two harridans to meet to discuss the upcoming gala and the coverage Rachel wanted Vana to write in her new column in the *City Times* was the stupidest thing I'd ever done.

"If she doesn't want to revisit it on the page, you shouldn't pressure her, Savvie," Aidan stated.

Savannah just hummed, which told me she was going to ignore Aidan no matter what he said. "Where's Misha, Aspen?"

Aspen narrowed her eyes. "Why are you asking, Savannah?"

Like a cat poised to strike a mouse, Savannah pinned Aspen to the ground. "We've brought our significant others. I was just wondering why you didn't bring the Forgotten Boy with you."

"The what?" Lorelei queried, her confusion genuine.

"Forgotten Boy, Mom," Savannah chirped.

"Is that like a *Peter Pan* thing?"

I hid a snort but Aspen took control of the situation surprisingly fast. "Mom, it's nothing. Misha and I had a fight."

"I warned him not to hurt you," Aidan rumbled as he stared down at the pastry rose on his plate like it was a puzzle in need of solving. "Just give me the word, and I'll break his balls."

"You mean bust them."

"I know what I said, Savannah."

"Just use your fingers, Aidan," Lorelei encouraged, mimicking how the, well, whatever it was should be eaten.

"To break Misha's balls or to eat the canapé?"

As Lorelei scowled at her eldest daughter, Aspen argued, "Misha didn't hurt me. His balls don't need to be busted or broken. Anyway, can we not talk about this right now, please?"

I picked up my own appetizer, took a bite, and sighed in delight at the harissa-infused meatball. "This is delicious, Lorelei. Thank you."

The other woman didn't look at me, just nodded. "You're welcome."

"I don't understand why this is so awkward." Camden skewered his mom with a glower. "It's Star. *Star.* Why are you making it weird? It wasn't like that when Vana, Star, and I got together."

"*I* don't understand why we weren't invited," Paris muttered.

Aspen sniffed. "Just another instance of us being excluded."

I rolled my eyes. "Don't be brats."

As the twins turned toward me and began bickering, I almost missed Aidan telling Conor, "Need to speak with you later."

"Sure. Whatever."

"We are *so* not brats! You hurt our feelings," Aspen declared, sounding exactly like Vana—I'd tell her that later. It was sure to piss her off.

"How could we do that?" Camden retorted. "We didn't invite cameras to the get-together, Paris. You didn't miss out on a scoop for your stupid reality TV show which is all you care about now anyway."

"No one takes us seriously in this family," Aspen spat.

"For good reason," Savannah drawled. "All *your* wins are achieved on *our* backs."

Paris hissed under her breath. "That's not fair, Savannah."

"Did you, or did you not, ask me to write about the show in my column?"

"You're our sister! It's the least you can do!"

"Paris, I didn't ask Camden or Dad for scoops when I was starting out," Savannah ground out. "I worked my way up on my own. Sometimes, being a nepotism baby is the hardest thing you can be because you expect everyone else to do you a favor."

"Savannah," Lorelei chided.

"What? It's true," Savannah retorted. I noticed her cheeks turn pink when Aidan…

Aidan did *something* with his hand on her knee.

I didn't think even Savannah was kinky enough to want to be fingered at her family dinner table though, so I assumed he was trying to calm her down.

Savannah didn't get along great with her sisters at the best of times, but something was definitely going on here…

Bubbling away beneath the surface.

"Your sisters are trying to find their way. Not everyone is as focused as you and your brother," Lorelei said with a sigh, clearly trying to play the role of peacemaker.

"We're plenty focused," Aspen reasoned. "Just because we're not trying to bring down a secret society or have won more Grammys than anyone else in the universe doesn't mean our project isn't worthwhile."

Because I'd heard this argument when they were kids and were trying to use Dagger's name to sell Girl Scout cookies, I didn't take much notice, just shot Conor a glance to see how he was taking this.

Meals with his family were a lot less fraught with sibling rivalry…

That was when I saw he was blindly eating his appetizer, his gaze flickering between the 'kids' as if this were a sitcom and he was glued to the screen.

My lips twitched—trust him to be fascinated.

I didn't know if it was because this was Dagger's family and he was eating at one of his idols' tables or if it was because this was new territory for him.

Knowing Conor, it was probably both.

"Your project is important, but maybe Savannah's right, Aspen. I can't keep going on that damn show."

"But Daddy!" Paris whined. "You promised!"

He heaved a sigh. "I did promise."

I chuckled. "You haven't changed, Dagger."

He cut me a look. "We've all changed, Star."

As our gazes tangled and held, I tipped up my chin while he pursed his lips.

That the first 'reprimand' came from him was a surprise.

"Where's Katina?" Savannah queried quickly, changing the subject.

"With Aoife for Sunday dinner with Ma," Conor answered, just as quickly.

Not unlike sharks, they scented blood.

"Who's dragging who along for the visit?" Savannah teased.

I snorted because as much as Aoife had taken my words to heart, she still found it tough to hang out with Lena—for good reason.

"I'd have liked to meet her. Savannah's told me a lot about her," Dagger said, his voice gruff. "She sounds as if she's a cheeky little thing."

I hummed. "She is. I didn't feel comfortable bringing her for this first meeting."

"Understandable," Camden grumbled. "If the atmosphere in here is anything to go by. I just don't understand why you wouldn't reach out sooner."

"Because I had different priorities." My focus settled on him, but I shot him a smile. "Now, my priorities are more family-oriented."

Camden huffed as he sank back in his seat. "Good."

"You're barely around anymore, Camden," Paris groused. "You can't judge Star when you're worse than she is."

"What's that supposed to mean?"

"Paris's right," Aspen defended. "You're always a no-show whenever we call."

"Because you turn up with cameras! Is it so weird to think that I don't want one in my face when I'm not working?"

She sniffed. "Last week, we wanted to meet up for lunch. You said no."

"Because, I repeat, you bring cameras with you wherever you go."

"We promised we wouldn't," she bickered.

"Camden, if they promised, then you should have met up with them!" Lorelei scolded.

"That's a promise they never keep," Camden muttered. "Anyway, I wasn't in the city. I was in Florida."

Dagger's brows lifted. "You were using the studio?"

"They have a studio in Florida?" Conor whispered in my ear.

Dagger, overhearing the question, chuckled. "It's a private one, Conor. On my estate. Camden uses it more than I do these days."

"Most people want rehashes of the same old *noxxious* tracks rather than new material. Never been the same without Gerry's songwriting."

Overwhelmed at being the center of his idol's focus, Conor gaped at Dagger for a full thirty seconds.

"Conor, stop being weird," Aidan clipped, slouching back in his seat. "Talk to Dagger. He's a regular human being before he's a guitarist."

As I chuckled, hero worship filtered into Conor's expression. *God, he was so fucking cute.* "But he's Dagger Daniels."

"Who you've met before," Savannah remarked, sounding more amused than she had at any point throughout this interminable meal.

"Yeah, but, he's Dagger fu—" Conor sucked in a breath and shot Lorelei an apologetic smile. "Sorry. Didn't mean to swear at the table."

Lorelei laughed. "Your mom keeps her children in better line than I can."

"No," Savannah argued. "They swear around Lena. He's just trying to impress Dad."

When Conor glowered at her, she stuck out her tongue and grinned when Aidan kissed her cheek.

"You'll get used to who I am, Conor," was Dagger's friendly retort. "Like Aidan said, I'm just a guy who plays guitar."

"For one of the bands that got me through my childhood," Conor quipped.

I squeezed his knee and shared a look with Aidan. It was probably the first time Aidan and I ever really had a moment, so it was both strange and... *nice*.

Ugh.

Was this my life now?

Describing emotional connections as 'nice?'

Before I could vomit in my mouth, Lorelei mused, "Let the boy crush on your rock god self some more, Dagger. It's always good for your ego after you go on the girls' show."

Dagger's nose crinkled. "That's demoralizing."

"Our audience loves you, Dad," Paris trilled.

"They love him a little too much," Lorelei said lightly, an odd combination of annoyance and amusement lilting her tone.

"What happens on set?" I queried, curious enough to ask him.

"Girls as young as Paris and Aspen come on to me like I'm not happily married," he said with a huff.

Savannah chuckled. "That's because most 'rock gods' would enjoy having girlfriends as young as their daughters."

"Ew," Aspen said with a shudder.

"*You* don't need to get your leg over an old man to make money," Savannah retorted.

"Savannah!" Dagger barked, his tone tougher than usual.

She merely arched a brow at him. "Tell me I'm lying. Nepotism babies—"

"Savvie, I'm sensing a lot of unresolved tension building between you and your sisters," Lorelei stated as she picked up one of the savory pastries on her plate.

Savannah sniffed. "No unresolved tension here."

"We only asked if we could talk about Camden's addiction problems on our show, Mom," Paris whined, making me shoot a concerned glance at Camden who, unsurprisingly, had tensed up like he'd been shot.

For the first time, Lorelei's calm demeanor quivered. "You wanted to feature Camden's addictions on your reality TV show?"

"I don't understand why it's such a secret. Everyone already knows about that stalker who broke into his rehab facility—"

"That's the exact goddamn reason *you* should understand, Aspen," Lorelei snapped.

Camden's chair scraped against the dining room floor, but Savannah grabbed his hand and dragged him to a halt. "Over my dead body will they talk about my problems on a fucking TV show!"

"You should have brought this to us, Savannah," Dagger growled, his eyes growing narrower as he pinned his twin daughters in place with a stare. "Of all the insensitive... You know how delicate a topic this is for our family. You know how your brother and I struggle every goddamn day, and you think our addictions are—"

"Fodder," Savannah supplied when he hesitated.

"*Fodder,*" Dagger agreed, "for your show?"

Apparently sensing she'd gone too far, Paris swallowed. "We didn't mean any harm by it."

"To even ask was to mean harm. I'm just grateful you broached the subject with me first," Savannah snapped.

Lorelei carefully replaced her cutlery on the table. "I understand how difficult it is for you to find your place in this world. You're the daughters of a man who's internationally renowned, you're the siblings of a star who puts your father's career in the shade, and Savannah's reputation in her field is just as solid as Camden's.

"But you've used your family enough to find your footing. No more, girls. No more. We've humored you long enough. Your father has been more than generous with his time, but if your show is still performing poorly, then that's something you'll have to face without leveraging us anymore."

"But Mom—"

Lorelei whipped her head to the side. "No, Paris. No. Our family has been through enough tragedy as it is. I won't compound that by letting you try to weasel your way into getting what you want. How could you even think we'd—" A sob bleated through her words, freezing them forever on her tongue. "—after all the problems we've had because of drugs and gambling and alcohol!"

"Lorelei," Dagger rasped, jerking to his feet and moving around the table to reach her side. His hand fixed on her shoulder the moment he was at her back, and something about the picture they made had me sucking in a breath.

This was love.

What they had.

They'd survived several tragedies and they were still standing.

Still there, fighting together, persevering, and striving.

My hand blindly sought Conor's, and though he didn't realize the epiphany I'd just had, his fingers knotted with mine immediately. Like always, he squeezed twice. Just two pulses, but they were our code.

I love you.

God, I wanted what Lorelei and Dagger had—with Conor.

No one else.

Suddenly, it made sense to me why I'd never needed another guy for anything but fucking and why I'd used men for sex and had abused their eagerness to screw me to get what I wanted.

I'd been waiting.

For my Dagger.

But someone who was uniquely meant for me.

Conor O'Donnelly.

"Look what you've done," Savannah spat at her twin sisters, breaking into my epiphanic moment.

Paris doubled down on that by releasing a sob and shooting away from the table, Aspen scuttling after her, leaving us in their wake.

Lorelei had turned her face into Dagger's belly, but I still heard her loud and clear when, in the deafening aftermath, she hissed, "I bet that makes you happy, Star. Seeing our family torn apart—"

"Mom!" Savannah and Camden argued at the same time.

"Lorelei," Dagger chided, but he continued petting her hair as if she were a dog that needed stroking to calm her down.

"That's uncalled for," Conor rumbled.

My brow furrowed at the blatantly unfair accusation. "Not particularly," was all I said, reaching for my glass of wine with my free hand. "I take no joy in your misery, Lorelei. Not when I've always considered your family to be mine too."

She sniffed and turned her angry gaze on me. "If that's the truth, then why is this the first time I've heard from you in years?"

"Serving overseas and then being undercover in the CIA wasn't conducive to weekly phone calls with my father's girlfriend," I murmured, aware my words had more of a bite than before. "Then there was the little problem of being locked up in a cage in Lebanon—my owner didn't allow me to make phone calls back home either.

"And, afterward, when I was bought and was forced to fuck for food, Lorelei, you weren't my priority then, either.

"And if you're asking why I haven't called in the years since I escaped captivity, then that's probably because I've been focused on bringing down a global trafficking-slash-terrorist organization that has infiltrated every government on the planet.

"Throw in the fact that I knew you'd give me this welcome, it's safe to say I didn't feel like reaching out.

"And, hell, phones and emails work *both* ways. I don't remember you reaching out to me."

To punctuate my speech, I let go of Conor's hand, placed the wine glass beside the table setting, picked up my cutlery, and carefully settled a bite of chicken in my mouth.

As I chewed, Dagger staggered around the table and took a seat where Paris had been. Once he swiveled to look at me, his hand moved to my shoulder. "That really happened to you, Star?" he rasped, his tired eyes crinkling at the corners in concern.

"No, Dad, she just thought she'd make it up," Camden snapped.

Dagger blinked. "I-I didn't realize. I just thought you were like Casey."

Curiosity had me asking, "And how was my mom?"

He swallowed. "Flighty. Never able to settle. It's one of the reasons we were so often on tour when you were youngsters."

"I used to think she was encouraging your dad to tour because of the money we earned. The record company got the bulk of the royalties from record sales, but the band picked up the lion's share for ticket sales," Lorelei admitted, her voice low as she studied me as if I were a freak at the circus.

I speared her with a glower and jabbed a finger in the air. "*That* is not why I told you what happened to me. I don't need your pity, Lorelei."

She licked her lips but graced me with a soft nod. Her background in psychology was doing us both a favor at that point.

Conor cleared his throat. "You were saying you were working in your studio in Florida, Camden?"

I shot him a grateful smile for changing the subject even as my mind was ticking—Mom had wanted to tour for reasons that were shaped like the Brotherhood...

As Camden nodded, answering, "Making new music," I was typing under the table:

> Me: When my mom first got with my dad,
> what was her mission?

The story went, after all, that they met at the US Embassy in Madrid.

That wasn't the coincidence the Daniels believed it to be...

"I didn't think you'd be able to get much work done," Dagger admitted. "The neighboring estate has been getting noisier and noisier. I wish I'd never built the studio on the west plot."

"It was quiet over there, actually. No parties."

"I thought you'd be the first to attend."

Camden flipped Vana the bird. "I don't like it over there. Haven't gone to one since the early days."

"You attended a party on the neighboring estate?" Dagger clarified, his shoulders still hunched as he plunked one elbow on the table.

"Only the one. The women..." He pulled a face. "I'm ninety-nine percent certain they were drugged. I didn't realize at first because most of the attendees were high, but safe to say, it skeeved me out enough to get the hell away from there and to never go back."

"And you didn't report it?!" Lorelei demanded, her hands slamming against the table, making the cutlery and glassware rattle.

Anton: If memory serves, it was related to the Lockerbie bombing. noxxious were on a world tour. The dates were, shall we say, opportune. Why?

Me: No reason. Just curious.

Hmm.

"Who could I report it to?" Camden argued, bringing my focus back to our conversation. "I did call the cops but they said they sent a patrol car to investigate.

"They never stopped the party, though, and haven't intervened since. The parties haven't been as frequent as they used to be anyway. There wasn't even a single one while I was down there.

"I just figured the owner had stopped visiting." He chewed on the inside of his cheek. "I wasn't disturbed by any noise. Got a new album partially written. Music is always a proactive way to process my… struggles." His nose crinkled. "But, fuck, after Star's admission, I'm feeling fucking petty for struggling, period."

My shoulders straightened. "Why?"

"Why? Because I'm a poor little rich boy who can't deal with the bright lights he sought out years ago. What you went through, Star, was hell. Absolute fucking hell."

The sound of a chair scraping startled me enough to have me hunting for the source of the noise.

When I saw it was Lorelei, when I watched her round the table, when I realized she was approaching me, I froze.

Then, she leaned over me and dragged me into her arms.

For a moment, I didn't understand what the hell was going on.

Then, she whispered, "I'm sorry, Star. So sorry."

My mouth trembled.

Once.

Before I tightened it.

Before I let myself be hugged.

Before I experienced the loving embrace of a woman who'd been a surrogate mother to me my whole childhood.

Acceptance felt strange.

But good.

It was like I could breathe easier. As if my shoulders weren't as weighed down as they'd been just five minutes earlier.

Over Lorelei's shoulder, I saw Savannah watching me, tears in her eyes.

Somehow, that made this real.

62

CONOR

Conor O'Donnelly

"WHAT ARE YOU WORKING ON?" I asked as I propped my chin on Star's shoulder a few hours later.

Her browser had a bunch of tabs open, over a hundred plus. How the fuck she worked like that I had no idea.

"A hunch."

My brows lifted. "What kind of hunch?"

I didn't just glance over the tabs this time, but at the content.

"Something that was said today at the dinner table triggered…" At her hesitation, I pressed a kiss to her shoulder in gentle encouragement. She sighed. "I'm checking bank statements."

"Whose?"

"Reinier's."

"Thought you'd gone through those?"

"I did. I'm just double-checking my work."

"Are you keeping something from me, Star?" I asked lightly.

She turned her head and pressed a kiss to my cheek. "No. I know I'm wasting my time but I have to check. Why waste yours too?"

"Tell me what the hunch is."

"You'll think I'm insane."

"I do anyway. I am too. We can be insane together."

That had her snorting but she didn't immediately answer.

Brain ticking, I tried to figure out what might have her instincts tripping. "Is it related to Temper Black and Eagle Eyes?"

"Nah. He's still stalking her. Though I am trying to figure out how she knew about Muñoz stalking me."

I hid an amused grin at how blasé her tone was. "Belyaev?"

"No. Not really. Asswipe. Kat had a nightmare about him last night."

"I heard her cries." And they'd fucking killed something inside me, especially when she'd asked to sleep next to Star. Her confidence was such that you could forget she was a little girl sometimes.

Until a nightmare struck.

I thought back to today's dinner when I'd seen her messaging Anton under the table. "What did your grandfather have to say at dinner?"

"You saw that?"

I chuckled. "Of course I did. I'm preternaturally aware of you, Star. Duh."

Warmth gleamed in her eyes—she liked hearing that. Not that she'd admit it.

"I asked what Mom's original mission was when she got with Dad."

"Which was?"

"Related to the Lockerbie bombing." She tensed. "Allegedly."

"Huh. Interesting." Then, a thought occurred to me. "That's where Eoghan said he was sent for training—Lockerbie." When her mouth tightened, I asked, "Coincidence?"

"No such thing."

My brow furrowed. "But if Jorgmundgander had her killed... Why..."

"More questions. No answers," she rasped.

Sensing and empathizing with her frustration, I decided to change the subject somewhat and processed everything we'd learned today. "This is about the estate next to Dagger's?" A single nod was her answer. "You think the drugged women at the party were Sparrows' victims?"

"No way of knowing for sure. I checked who the estate belongs to, and it's owned by 'Bright Holdings.' The directors are tucked behind a bunch of bullshit Belizean laws that protect shadow corps." Her sniff of disapproval was followed by a tug on her bottom lip between her teeth. "Do you know how much a body is worth on the black market?"

"Ah. We're back to organ harvesting?" When she hitched her shoulder, I sighed. "It's around half a million, isn't it?"

This time, her glance was less hesitant and more appreciative. "You researched this."

"Of course I did. It was worrying you so I checked it out, but we've scoured every aspect of the Sparrows' comms platform and tore it apart for Interpol," I pointed out. "Nowhere there did they talk about that. Nowhere were there any references to harvesting the women they sold for their organs. No money to follow, Star. So if—"

"Don't you think that's weird?" she blurted out.

"I think if they've hidden that from us, there's plenty of other shit we haven't uncovered yet. Was there anything in Bear's motel room?"

"No. Nothing. Not in all the files he left behind either." For a second, she looked guilty. "I've scoured them twice. It's an itch I can't scratch." She rubbed at her forehead. "Maybe that's why Reinier brought it up—to drive me insane."

"You could ask your grandfather. Or his *Pauks*?"

"The Brotherhood fed Bear's investigation."

"How do you know?"

"Steganography. Bear stored a lot of info on some random pictures. The code led me to the *Pauks*. I was sure that I told you."

"I've slept since then. Not a lot, but some," was my sheepish retort.

She hummed. "If the *Pauks* knew anything, it'd have been in Bear's motel room. Ergo, Anton and his *Pauks* know dick."

When she stared blankly ahead, I questioned gently, "Hey, where's your head at?"

"There's a massive market for this," she rasped. "As far as I can tell, it's mostly the Mexican cartels who are peddling this particular ware…"

"But?"

"Why would you run such an extensive trafficking system without having that as a sideline? There had to be pregnancies that resulted from their brothels and, I mean, I hate to go there, but kids…"

"They could be harvested for organs too," I said with a grimace.

"Girls die all the time, right?" At my disgust, she continued, "Might as well not let the meat go to waste. Those fucking asswipes.

"What corrupt millionaire wouldn't pay a small fortune to arrange an illegal organ donation for their sick child?" That made my grimace deepen but she forged ahead. "This just doesn't make any sense. They've been doing this for decades." She sucked in a breath. "It's a circle that feeds itself."

Why did that bring back the image of Jorgmundgander?

"Do you know what else doesn't make sense?" I asked as a thought occurred to me. "Something that you should ask your grandfather."

"What?"

"How his *Pauks* and Bear got on the same team."

"Huh. You're right. That *is* weird. What put him on their radar and vice versa—" Her cell rang and when she saw the Caller ID, a frown flashed across her brow as she put the call on speaker. "Maverick?"

"Dost Mohamet Khan."

When Star blanched—her features immediately turning pinched and pale—I settled a hand on her shoulder and curved my arm around her to support her.

"How do you know that name?" she rasped.

"You've heard of it?"

"How do you know it, Maverick?" she barked.

He heaved a tired sigh. "I had a flashback."

"To when?"

I didn't know much about Maverick's condition, but I knew that his PTSD and CTE had him flashing back to periods of his life that were doused in trauma.

"That day in Kembesh." His swallow was audible. "But Nic told me to ask Eagle Eyes about Dost Mohamet Khan. I don't remember that conversation. I genuinely don't. But it was so fucking real, Star. Nic was there—right goddamn there."

"Who's Nic?" I asked her softly.

"Maverick's CO, also his partner at the time. He died in Kembesh. It was a minor battle but a disaster all round. The US covered up what happened to the battalion that defended an outpost there.

"They had to deal with an ambush on their own and had no military *or* medical support."

"Jesus."

She pulled a face in agreement. "I was at the battle, so was Eoghan. But not in the middle of it all. Most of the fighting was around the outpost, but there were skirmishes along the border.

"We probably wouldn't have survived if we had been in the thick of it. Maverick was one of the lucky ones."

"Yeah," Maverick choked out. "I feel fucking lucky."

"Hey," she argued. "You made it out to see another day. That's more than Nic did."

Maverick fell silent, whether that was because he was chastened or because he was speechless—I had no way of knowing.

Star pierced the silence with, "Eagle Eyes is a sniper, Maverick."

"Yeah, he's with the Hell's Rebels' MC down in Texas."

"Why would he know anything about what happened in Kembesh? Why would Nic put you on his radar?"

"He was in Kembesh too," Maverick clipped.

"Who was?" I asked.

Star shot me a look. "Eagle Eyes."

"Don't you think it's strange how so many of you were in this battle?" I questioned, unease settling in my gut like a lead weight.

"It's a small world over there," she said, shrugging.

"Who's Dost Mohamet Khan, Star? How do you know him?" Maverick demanded.

"He was the man who enslaved me. My first owner."

Sucking in a breath, I pressed my hand to her nape and gently squeezed once, twice, wanting to reassure her that I was here for her.

"You told me that you were assigned to a museum to protect their antiquities," Maverick rumbled slowly. "And you were taken because you were hunting down a double agent? That wasn't a lie?"

"No. But I lied to you about the country. It wasn't Iraq, but Afghanistan."

"For fuck's sake, Star. Why lie?"

"Because we always keep something back, don't we?" she mumbled guiltily, her gaze clashing with mine. She looked so miserable that I had to squeeze her nape again. Just to reassure her that I knew she was trying.

Sometimes, in this fucking life, especially in *her* life, that was all you *could* do.

"What's going on, Star? What the hell is happening?"

"I don't know," she admitted. "I can tell you Khan's dead if that helps?"

Maverick was quiet for a moment. "You killed him?"

"The first time I picked up a gun after I got free, he was in my crosshairs. Luckily for me, he traveled to the UK and made it easy for me to take him out."

My jaw worked. "What the hell was he doing traveling to the UK?"

"He was a Sparrow," she drawled. "That meant he got away with trafficking. Probably genocide too. Until me."

Pain loaded down Maverick's every word as he confessed, "I've tried to get in touch with Eagle Eyes but he isn't answering."

"No, he's on a job for me."

"What kind of job?"

She cleared her throat. "He's tracking Temperance Black."

"Cin's cousin?"

"Yeah. Her."

"What's she done?"

"She's a Brother."

"Thought they were the good guys?"

Star sighed. "What's a good guy these days?"

"Whoa, that's a philosophical debate in the making," I said, reeling her in. "Can you contact Eagle Eyes and get him to speak with Maverick?"

"I guess. I don't know why he wouldn't be picking up your call though, Mav." She pursed her lips. "Leave it with me. I'll update you tomorrow."

"Alessa said you're meeting with Rachel tomorrow?"

"I am. At her place. Is she still not talking to me?"

Maverick didn't answer.

I squeezed Star's shoulder again because we both knew what that meant.

"I'll drop Kat off at Rach's place tomorrow for the weekend, okay? Let Alessa know she can collect her from there."

"Not sure when I became your go-between but I'll tell her."

Star huffed out a laugh. "You became that the day you met me."

"And what an inauspicious day that was for my meeting with the Antichrist."

Rolling her eyes, Star rumbled, "You can't see it but I'm flipping you the bird."

"Use it for better things, like emailing Eagle Eyes and getting him to call me ASAP."

When he hung up, I leaned my ass against her desk and stared down at her. "What was going on in Kembesh?"

She blinked up at me. "Why do you assume I know?"

I scoffed. "Don't give me the innocent eyes. We both know they're wasted on me."

She smirked. "That's why I like you the best though."

"You're full of charm and BS."

Rather than be annoyed, she looked even more like the cat who'd eaten the canary at my wording as she rocked back in her seat. "Kembesh borders Pakistan and a bunch of ex-Soviet states. Weapons flowed into Taliban forces there. That's why the US established an outpost in that area. *That* and it's where Dost Mohamet Khan used to live before the place was destroyed during the battle. Officially, his title was 'government administrator' for that region."

"Unofficially?"

"Thick as thieves with the Taliban." She sniffed. "Sparrows too."

"When you said that you thought a CIA agent had turned, you thought they were working with the Taliban?"

She hesitated. "I'm not sure. I just knew someone was dirty."

"Didn't you have any suspicions?"

"No. We were a big team back in those days and it was constantly fluctuating. Looking back, I figure that's how they stayed under the radar. It's only because I'm so paranoid that I realized something was going on."

"What would be the gain for a double agent?"

"The Taliban was looting their own artifacts and there were foreigners stationed there during the war that smuggled them out of the country. That added up to a *lot* of money being made."

"Funding the war," I stated, folding my arms across my chest.

"Partly."

"And the two-timing fucker was a Sparrow?"

She flung her hands wide. "Why wouldn't they be? Seems to me like you get any semblance of power in this fucking world and you get a choice—you wanna suck Brother or Sparrow ass?"

Despite the seriousness of the situation, I chuckled. "At least the Brothers are—"

"What?" she demanded before I could finish that sentence. "What are they? For all we know they're as bad as the Sparrows."

My brows lifted. "Star, come on. I thought you accepted—"

"I did," she muttered, interrupting again. "But I'm telling you something's not right, Conor. This organ trafficking shit…" She sucked in a breath. "Never mind what Reinier said about Anton."

I tensed. "Reinier was dying. He'd have said anything to get under your skin."

"He said I'd be a fool to trust my grandfather. He said he had information about him."

"Where?"

"His estate in Florida. He claimed it was a secret. I thought he was lying to save his ass."

"And now you don't? I thought you trusted Anton."

"Do you want to know what has never sat right with me?" she rasped.

"What?"

"A couple of things. Firstly, Mom."

"What about her?"

"That she died. That he was powerful and she died and that he didn't try to take me away from Dad, that he didn't try to groom me as his next-in-line. He's already offered me his position once he's gone."

"He had Aleks at that point," I said cautiously. "Maybe he wanted a son as his heir."

"See, your da was insane and the shit he did was bad, but I can't deny that he was, in his way, a family man.

"If anyone had targeted his kids, they'd have died. Horribly. If they'd succeeded in killing his kids, then they'd probably have lived longer just to be tortured.

"I can get behind that mentality. It's what I'd do for Kat. Anton had to know Dagda killed Mom. He had to know it was a Jorgmundgander sting." She rubbed her chin. "I just can't help but feel as if he led us down a gnarly path and because we were so busy being stuck in the middle of it, we couldn't see past the noses on our faces.

"Why didn't he stop it? Why didn't he do something to save her?"

Wishing I had an answer for her, I rasped, "I don't know, Star."

And I didn't, but that didn't take away from the sorry truth of the situation—*she was right.*

Everything intensified from the center of a crisis. Looking outward and gaining perspective when bullets were being fired was next to impossible.

Even, it seemed, for someone of her experience.

"Then," she continued grimly, "there's the fact that I just can *not* have been that goddamn hard to find."

"He said Aleks was seeking info on you and that's why he was murdered," I reasoned.

"That's what Anton said. But Reinier…"

"It all comes back to him?"

"I wish it didn't, but it does. The way he talked about Anton, it was like they knew each other, Conor. He said something along the lines of 'That old bastard—more faces than Janus himself.'"

"And you agree?"

"I do."

"He was trying to save his ass. Wouldn't he have sold Anton out worse than that?"

She conceded that with a nod. "Maybe. But he was more interested in trying to buy me off with blackmail material."

"He said nothing else?"

Sheepishness whispered into her expression. "He was mostly begging not to die and for the pain to stop. He forgot his own name after a few blasts of that cattle prod of yours, never mind Anton's."

"What did you ask him today?"

"I wanted to know about Mom's original mission. He said he 'thought' it was related to the Lockerbie incident. Is that something you'd forget? When it's your flesh and blood?"

"I don't know, Star. We wouldn't, but we're not him."

"No, we're not," she concurred. "And that's what makes me not trust him. We had tunnel vision. We were given a directive and we fulfilled our objective and we didn't question because why would we?

"But now, with distance and time, I've got a lot of unanswered questions, and there's danger in asking the wrong person the wrong thing."

I pondered her words. "What's the wrong thing?"

"Are the Brothers as knee-deep in the shit as the Sparrows are? Are they just better at hiding in the shadows?"

Hell.

"You think that's a possibility?"

"I don't have concrete answers. Not without further investigating and…" Her gaze settled on mine, loaded down with her concern and indecision. "I want to live. I want to be with you, Conor. I want to raise Katina. I want to be happy. I want *us* to be happy." She lifted her hands and used them to rub at her eyes. They were dry, though, when she next looked at me. "Is that so much to ask?"

"No, it's not, baby," I told her softly, even as I knew Star didn't have it in her not to seek the truth.

It was a toxic trait we both shared.

As I gently rubbed her shoulder, she whispered, "If I wait until he's dead, which can't be that far out, and if I suck up to him, pretend, then I can slip into his role and dismantle the Brothers from the inside."

The hopefulness in her words had my lips twitching. "You and Aidan are more alike than you know."

"I needed *that* insult after today."

I had to chuckle. "Reinier'll be dead by now."

"Without a doubt. And who orchestrated his death? Who's covering it up?"

"The Brothers," I said slowly.

"Anton knew who Reinier was. It's bullshit that he didn't know Smythe and Foundry were involved too." She gritted her teeth. "Ever since Reinier mentioned goddamn organ harvesting, this has been eating away at me."

"You should have been open with me from the start," I retorted grumpily.

But she shook her head. "I'm paranoid, Conor. In fact, I make someone with paranoia look trusting. That's why I didn't tell you." She worked her jaw. "There comes a point where you start thinking the shadows aren't just a trick of the light, they're where the monsters hide in plain sight."

Softly, I reasoned, "That makes sense."

"I hide it from Kat because I don't want to terrify her, but it's different with you." Her expression was beseeching. "You might think I'm crazy. Legitimately crazy." Her hand grabbed mine, fingers clutching at me with a desperation that made me hurt for her. "I can keep a lid on it for the most part, but this... I thought I could. But I can't. And you deserve better than some rabid fuckwit who spends her days covered in aluminum foil so the listening station on the moon can't overhear us talking."

"We're a team, Star," I informed her. "That means if you start using aluminum as a fashion accessory..."

She swallowed.

"…then I start wearing it too."

Her eyes closed on a silent sob of relief.

I leaned forward and pressed a kiss to her trembling mouth. "We're back at the beginning, aren't we?"

She slipped her arms around my waist. "But we're worse off."

"At least we're together," I rasped. "And that's how this has to go, Star. Together, you hear me?"

She nodded against my belly. "Together."

Blindly, I stared ahead at my center of operations where I protected my brothers from jail sentences and where I kept Acuig Corp. one step ahead of the SEC and ensured the Five Points ruled the roost that was NYC.

This office was where I played with electricity and where I'd monitored, hacked, and surveilled more people than the Feds likely had since their inception.

This was my base.

Star had made it my home.

I cupped the back of her head and, with a tenderness only she brought out in me, stroked her nape. "Anton has to trust us."

"Agreed. He can't suspect that we think he's scum."

Such a way with words…

"He's still coming for the first gala, isn't he?" I asked.

"Supposed to arrive in the city this Friday."

"Do you have any idea where Reinier's secret estate is? Other than what Camden had to say about a party house next door to the Daniels' place?"

"No."

"Keep searching." I sucked in a breath as the realization struck… "If you need to put pressure on that bank president, do it."

"Even though…"

"Even though his daughter was a victim and didn't deserve to be blackmailed?" I blew out the breath I'd just sucked in. "This is bigger than one person, Star. I get that. Explore every possible avenue first, but that's endgame material. Understood?"

"Understood." She rocked her head back. "I wish things could be simpler."

"My life has never been simple, Star," I told her, trailing my fingertip along the curve of her cheekbone. "But until you came along, I wasn't happy. I'd rather be in this with you than living a simpler life without you."

She tugged her bottom lip between her teeth. "Maybe you're the crazy one."

"I think aluminum foil suits me rather well," I concurred, which earned me a small smile.

"What did Aidan want at dinner?"

I blinked as my mind rewound to the meal at Dagger and Lorelei's place. "We never got around to speaking... Not after Lorelei apologized to you." Leaning down again, I kissed the tip of her nose. "We're going to make a brighter future for ourselves, Star. Away from the shadows of our pasts, okay?"

While she nodded, for the first time in our relationship, she looked at me to make this situation better.

It was there, in the desperate hope that tightened her brow and in her beseeching stare. It made me determined to give her the peace she fucking deserved after what she'd been through.

"I promise, Star, once this is over, we can live our lives in PJs and camp out with Kat at gymnastics practice and hack into her school computer system to make sure she gets straight As."

Her smile was tremulous but it was there. "You promise?"

"I do and I *never* break a promise."

Some of the usual cocksureness returned to her expression and, suddenly, all was right with my world again...

Now I just had to fulfill my goddamn purpose on this fucking planet—helping my woman bring down the bad guys.

Who, for once, weren't my brothers.

Yay for fucking me.

63

TEXT CHAT

LODESTAR: *Yo, how goes it with Temper?*

Eagle Eyes: *Same old, same old.*

Lodestar: *Any change in her routine?*

Eagle Eyes: *Nope. Not since she became the deputy director, at any rate.*

Eagle Eyes: *You getting sick of paying me to watch this boring bitch?*

Lodestar: *Nah. I figure I'm building your kid's college fund.*

Eagle Eyes: *My kid? How the fuck did you know Ama is pregnant?*

Lodestar: *:P You shouldn't ask stupid questions.*

Eagle Eyes: *Touché. No one else knows. We're keeping it close to our chests. Keys and Saint haven't told anyone either.*

Lodestar: *Must be real awkward with so much family. They never talk about that shit in the poly books.*

Eagle Eyes: *It is what it is. Since when do you read books on polyamory?*

Lodestar: *Since my sisters-in-law introed me to the world of smut. It's an eye-opener, lemme tell you.*

Eagle Eyes: *I know. Ama's just as bad. Or do I mean good? :P*

Lodestar: *You mean good, hah.*

Lodestar: *I won't say dick about the sprog, anyway, lol.*

Eagle Eyes: *Just FYI, I ain't a charity case, Star. I'm perfectly capable of making deposits into my kid's college fund. If they even want to go to goddamn university.*

Lodestar: *Whoa, calm down, bro.*

Eagle Eyes: *I'm calm, I'm calm. What's up?*

Lodestar: *You heard of someone called Dost Mohamed Khan?*

Eagle Eyes: *DMK, sure. Blew his brains out on a top-secret mission.*

Lodestar: *That's impossible.*

Eagle Eyes: *Nah. Watched his skull shatter through my scope… No surviving that.*

Lodestar: *I killed a Dost Mohamed Khan in London. A few years back. We can't both have killed the same fucking man!*

Eagle Eyes: *Sure we can.*

Lodestar: *What?! O.O*

Eagle Eyes: *DMK was a patrilineal name.*

Lodestar: *Meaning there are a fuck ton of men called that?*

Eagle Eyes: *Yup. But they're specific to a certain family in the Kembesh region in Afghanistan.*

Lodestar: *This is going to give me a headache.*

Eagle Eyes: *Look at it this way, they were all Taliban. Whoever you killed, he deserved to die.*

Lodestar: *Nothing is ever that simple.*

Lodestar: *Why would a soldier, dying on the field, tell his boyfriend to ask you about him?*

Eagle Eyes: *Huh. I don't know. Which 'field' did he die on?*

Eagle Eyes: *I mean, the DMKs (that's what we called 'em) were asswipes. They were the dicks who got some mustard gas from their ancient armory and sprayed it over the battlefields of Kamor.*

Lodestar: *Dude, that was THEM?*

Eagle Eyes: *Yeah. One fam. I'm telling ya. All. Fuckin'. Douches. This is strictly on the DL, btw, Lodestar.*

Lodestar: *Figured that out myself. What was your mission? Take out the leader?*

Eagle Eyes: *Great-Grandpa DMK, yup. Alleged ties to Bin Laden himself and, they say, friends with a bunch of oligarchs in Russia. They were the ones who fed guns through Pakistan into Afghanistan.*

Lodestar: *Russian oligarchs?*

Eagle Eyes: *Yup. You know they had their mitts all over Afghanistan.*

Lodestar: *You remember the names of those Russians?*

Eagle Eyes: *Jesus, we're talking intel from years back, Star. If I remember, I'll let you know, K?*

Lodestar: *For sure. Appreciate that.*

Eagle Eyes: *As for the soldier telling his partner to ask me about DMK, I can only think it's because Kembesh was the gateway for Russian arms. Who was the brother?*

Lodestar: *Dominic Ellis.*

Eagle Eyes: *Ah, shit. Good man. Fucking brilliant soldier. I loved being attached to his squadron. You said Nic told his partner? Maverick, right? They tried to cover it up, but Nic's PTSD was fucking horrific by the time Kembesh hit. TBH, I loved the man but it'd have been either enemy fire or his own bullet. That's how fucked he was.*

Lodestar: *It's criminal that the higher-ups didn't let him retire.*

Eagle Eyes: *Too good at what he did. Plus, what he didn't know about the local topography wasn't worth knowing. Honestly, he was like a mountain goat.*

Eagle Eyes: *Back then, we were losing ground, not gaining it. Nic was key to some of the terrain we won back. Then, he died and the clusterfuck that was Kembesh got covered up.*

Eagle Eyes: *Swear to fuck, whoever served and fought there each has a different story to tell.*

Lodestar: *I've noticed that. Not totally unusual. The only thing anyone can agree on is that backup was non-existent.*

Eagle Eyes: *I wouldn't tell anyone else this, because they'd think I was crazy, but I always said the whole thing was a setup anyway.*

Lodestar: *You're talking to someone who's the right kind of crazy to listen.*

Eagle Eyes: *Figured as much.*

Eagle Eyes: *I always thought it was to burn the DMKs.*

Lodestar: *What made you think that?*

Eagle Eyes: *I got my mission. On the day of the battle.*

Lodestar: *No way!*

Eagle Eyes: *Yup. Didn't know it'd be so fucking whacked but I managed.*

Lodestar: *Good job. Why would the battle have been to cover up your mission?*

Eagle Eyes: *Here's where you'll think I'm crazy. Don't blame you because this is all conjecture and shit I've picked up over the years, but I think they were the only ones who knew about the Russian connection.*

Eagle Eyes: *The names of the oligarchs, I mean.*

Lodestar: *What makes you think the US would go to that extent to shield some Russians?*

Eagle Eyes: *You can still ask that after everything that's come out with the Sparrows?*

Lodestar: *Fuck.*

Lodestar: *Double fuck.*

Eagle Eyes: *Yeah, that sums it up. Anyway, if I think of the names, I'll let you know. You sure you still want me to hang out with Temper?*

Lodestar: *Definitely. Stick close.*

Eagle Eyes: *Will do.*

Lodestar: *Do me a solid and get in touch with Maverick? I'll forward you his details in a sec. He's been trying to get in touch with you about this.*

Eagle Eyes: *Sure thing. Nothing to tell him, mind.*

Lodestar: *Tell him what you told me. It'll stop him from thinking he's going nuts.*

Eagle Eyes: *Got it.*

64

CONOR

Conor O'Donnelly

"COME IN, PADDY!" I yelled as the door opened once I unlocked it on the app on my phone.

Returning my attention to the milkshake I was making Kat, I watched with a smile as she played on the floor with Ren and Stimpy.

I liked my diamanté cat statue but only the real deal made her laugh so that made them worth the ten pairs of socks they'd destroyed, my *Star Trek* couch they'd shredded to fuck, and the weird stench of cat litter that permeated the guest bath.

I guessed that was how I knew how much love I had for my kid— the destruction was worth the giggles.

As I spooned too many scoops of ice cream into the blender, Paddy walked in, looking like a disheveled and plumper version of my da.

I was gradually getting accustomed to how disconcerting that was. I didn't remember that being a thing when he was younger, or maybe it was just me implanting that imagery over him.

Either way, I waved a hand at the blender. "Want a milkshake?"

He scratched his chin. "I'd prefer a beer."

I tipped my head at Kat. "Nope."

Though he heaved a sigh, he nodded. "What flavors you got?"

"I ain't a freakin' ice cream parlor, Paddy. I have vanilla, vanilla, and vanilla."

Kat popped up at my side. "There's cookie dough in the fridge." She beamed at me and Paddy shared some of that smile by proxy. "Hi, Uncle Paddy!" she chirped. "How's your back?"

"Umm, my back?"

"Grandma Lena was saying to Aunty Savannah that you've got a big zit on it."

My brows lifted. "How the hell does she know you've got a zit on your back?"

Paddy flushed. "I showed it to her."

"Why?"

He pulled on his collar. "I thought it was shingles."

"Shingles?" I repeated blandly.

"I get them every couple years." He scowled at me. "What is this, the Inquisition?"

"What's the Inquisition, Conor?"

"It's where these douches asked a lot of questions and did some bad stuff to people who didn't deserve it to force them to answer. And it happened for centuries, too."

"Did the douches kill them?" she asked solemnly.

"They did."

"Then, I think that's hyperbolic of you, Uncle Paddy."

"Hyper-what? I don't have high blood sugar, kid."

Katina peeked at me, silently asking, 'Is this guy for real?'

"Not everyone's reading at your level, Kat."

"But he's old."

"Hey!" Paddy huffed. "Why is it when I come anywhere near you, the sprog, or Star, I leave with a complex?"

"She's right. You are a drama queen. How's the zit?"

"It's fine," he grumbled. "Thank you for asking."

"What's with the bruise?" I queried, staring at his chin.

He scratched his nose. "Your mom's still a dead shot with an Idaho potato."

My brows lifted. "What did you do to deserve it?"

"Do you wanna know?"

"No." Eying him, I grimaced as I blitzed the ice cream and poured the milkshake into a glass for Kat, directing, "Don't put it on the floor. If the cats get into it, you can clean up their diarrhea."

Her mouth rounded. "But I'm a kid."

"So? Kids can clean up messes too."

"That's not fair."

"How is it not fair? Just don't put the glass on the floor so they can't spill it over and drink it, please."

Her brow furrowed. "But I'm playing on the floor."

"Then you need to get up off the floor and you need to drink it before getting back down on the floor. Simple."

Paddy scratched his chin. "She always like this?"

I smoothed a hand over Kat's hair. "Yup."

"In my day, we didn't let kids answer back."

"That's why in my day, so many adults are effed in the head," was my pleasant retort. "Me included."

"I know what 'effed' means, Dad," Kat called out as she wandered back to the cats and put the damn glass on the table.

Score two for me.

"She's calling you 'Dad?'"

If I preened, so be it. "She is. Sometimes. I never know when but it's always a pleasant surprise if she does."

He hummed. "Interesting. Looks good on you. You've always had a way with kids."

"How would you know?"

"Saw you with Declan and Eoghan."

"They don't count."

"They were kids. Brothers or not!" He studied me. "Your ma mentioned she's in therapy."

Not willing to discuss that with her in the room, I sniffed. "What are you doing here?"

"Can't a godfather just come for a visit?"

"Maybe. But you're a special type of godfather."

"My complex is increasing in size."

"So's the net worth of Acuig Corp." I arched a brow at him. "Vanilla with or without cookie dough?"

He blinked at the change of topic. "Just vanilla, please."

"Fine. So, what's going on?"

"Nothing."

"Nothing?"

"Nothing, I swear." He even raised his hands. "Not like I had to go far. I'm in the same building as you now."

I still didn't believe him.

He huffed again. "I guess I just wanted to visit and Liam told me that everything's settled with the Rabid Wolves too so I had to thank you."

"You don't need to thank me. He's family." I thought about the basket of candy he'd sent me six or so weeks ago. "Plus, I'm not running out of junk food any time soon since he sent me a treasure trunk of the stuff. That's thanks enough."

He shook his head with a soft laugh. "You're the best of us, Conor, do you know that?"

"Hardly. Anyway, I'm glad his problems are settled. Is… everything else under control?"

"He says so. Got himself into the NHLPA Player's Assistance Program." He hitched a shoulder. "Doesn't share much with me for obvious reasons."

Tilting my head at him, I asked, "Do you want us to buy a hockey team in the city?"

"What? So he could play here?" He frowned. "You'd do that for me?"

"Family. Remember?" That was all I said before I blitzed his drink too, but I split his between an extra glass so I could share.

As he accepted the milkshake, he stared down into the concoction, muttering, "He wouldn't thank you for the suggestion. I was a shitty da, Conor."

"Don't you want to make up for it?"

"I do, but I doubt he'll let me."

"Don't you think he should be around family? Just in case his situation deteriorates?"

He palmed his chin. "I mean, sure, I guess. But you can't just buy an ice hockey team, Conor."

"Why not? We bought a shitty soccer team. Why not add a great ice hockey team to the portfolio?"

Paddy chuckled then took a sip of his drink. "This is good."

"She likes it with coconut milk. Always makes it taste better."

"Huh. Didn't know you could milk a coconut."

I sighed. "You need to borrow books from Kat, Paddy."

Because my godfather had inherited all the good nature from my grandmother and my da none of it, he laughed, deep from his belly. "You might be right there, Kid." When I just chuckled, he peered at me. "You're tired."

"It's been a busy couple of days."

"Lena told me about this gala Star's planning. She's excited about the dress she's bought."

"You taking her?"

He looked at me over his glass. "Would you have a problem with that?"

"No."

"Maybe, then."

"You got a tux?"

"From Aidan's wedding."

"It still fits?"

His smile was sheepish as he patted his beer gut. "Your ma's food's too good."

"Get yourself to our tailor and tell him it's urgent. Put it on my account." I took a sip of my own milkshake, sighing at how good it tasted. "You remember where it is."

"Can't do that, son. It'd be cheeky."

"So would flashing everyone at the gala if your buttons burst."

He hooted. "Fair, fair. Okay, I'll go today. Thank you, Conor."

"My pleasure." I angled my head at him. "Think about it, huh?"

"The ice hockey team?" He grimaced. "I mean, there's a big difference between a suit and a whole team, Con. Don't you reckon that's a bit excessive?"

"We're buying respectability and legitimacy, Paddy. It's not like they come cheap."

My godfather pondered that but he just said, "You look like you need to get some sleep. Want me to watch the kid while you nap?"

"You'd do that?"

"Sure. She's playing with two cats, not knives. Even I can keep her from slicing herself up."

"Is that supposed to reassure me? She's my kid, Paddy."

"I can tell. Watching you argue with her was like watching you argue with Lena when you were a boy. Your da wouldn't get it."

"Da was an asshole."

"Blood or bust," he agreed with a moue of distaste. "I ain't my brother, Conor."

"I know."

"I was a shitty da, but not like he was. I didn't make Liam do anything he didn't want to do."

"What went wrong then?"

"I was depressed a lot. You live in your family's pocket as long as we do, being without them is hard. Pretending to be dead, existing without a real identity, it took its toll.

"Now, I ain't explaining it away, ain't saying I didn't fuck up because I did. But I shouldn't have had a kid with how my head was screwed on, but his ma insisted, and now, I'm glad she did because he's a good man. A little lost since what went down, but who could blame him?"

"Don't you think bringing him into the fold would help him find himself?"

"He's not like us. He's an only child. Not used to a big family. It might make him feel worse."

"Or it could make him feel better." I tipped my milkshake at him. "Don't let her into the office unless Star's here, and don't let her play with the katanas in my living room—"

"What the hell's a katana?"

"A sword."

"You got a sword in your apartment with a kid around?" he spluttered.

"It was a gift from Declan," I mumbled. "It's up high and locked in a glass case so she shouldn't be able to reach it, but don't fall asleep with her around. She's worse than a magpie."

Paddy tugged on his shirt collar. "I dunno, Kid. Shay is normal. I watched him a few times but he didn't try to play with swords or nothing."

"That's because Kat's more fun than him." I chuckled. "It's okay. We're going to go watch a movie together until Star comes and picks her up. They're going to visit Kat's sister. So, if I doze off, just elbow me if she wanders away from the TV. Think you can handle that?"

He rubbed his hands together. "Sure can. You got any of that Disney shit? Used to love watching it with Liam."

That almost had me choking on my milkshake. "*You* like Disney?"

"Some of those movies are fuckin' strange, Con. Chicks getting kissed by fellas when they're dead, dads being tossed over cliffs by a back-stabbing sibling, pricks with hooks trying to kill a group of kids—"

I raised a hand. "I totally get why you like it now." Shaking my head at him, I asked, "*Peter Pan*, *The Lion King*, or *Snow White*, Kat?"

She stopped teasing Ren while Stimpy clawed his way up her shirt. "If you fall asleep, then you owe me some cake after gym class as well as a hot dog."

I smirked at her, and even knowing I'd lose the deal, I still held out my hand. "We have ourselves an agreement."

65

STAR

LATER THAT AFTERNOON

Star Sullivan

"I'M TELLING YOU, Star, if you don't stop canceling the goddamn ice sculptures for the gala, I will attack you with one when they show up at the event hall!" Rachel growled, her tone discordant with the way she was gently sweeping from side to side to get Sommer to burp.

"Why does it have to be ice? Do you know what a waste of money that is? The statues will literally be water by the time the event is over."

"Yeah, but it's fancy, and the whole place has a winter wonderland theme."

"So use fake snow," I snarled. "That's wintry—"

The doorbell rang.

Giulia whistled. "Saved by the bell. You two are fucking intense when you're arguing. That's me saying that. *Me.* I'm more attitude than tits and since Samael, my tits are massive. You two need to take a chill pill."

"She right. Chill pill. Where we buy?" Amara demanded, slamming her hands on the table. "Very stressful this is listening argue to you."

"Wow, that was more garbled than usual," Tiffany said kindly. "Is everything okay, Amara?"

"No. Stressed. They argue. Too much." Amara scowled at me. "She want ice. Give ice. She ice lady, *tak*?"

Rachel sniffed. "Yes. I want ice. Give me ice, Star."

The doorbell sounded again.

Because I needed a time-out, I got up and strolled away from the table. "Ice melts, Rachel. What you'll end up with once the night is over is an expensive bucket of water. But if you feel like wasting funds that could go elsewhere, you know, like the dozens of shelters we're establishing…"

I didn't finish because her growl of exasperation told me my point had been successfully rammed home.

With a smug smile, I swaggered over to the door where I found a diminutive woman standing on the stoop as I spied her through the peephole.

Her hands, tucked in old-fashioned but well-kept leather gloves, pleated nervously around the handle of her purse as she hovered there in a coat that had seen better days but which had once been of good quality too.

The whole shabby/quality thing made me think she'd fallen on hard times.

As I tugged open the door, I asked, "Who are you?"

Bright spots of color peeped into being on her cheeks. "I'm looking for Rachel Laker. Is that you?"

"Why are you looking for her?"

Her shoulders quivered. "That's between me and her."

The mousy vibe grabbed my curiosity. "You been hurt by some asshole who needs to die?"

The woman reared back. "Excuse me?"

"Stop scaring my clients," Rachel snapped, shoving me in the side as she hissed, "Who said you could open my door for me?"

"You had a baby attached to you." I sniffed. "I thought I was being helpful."

"Even when you're dead, you won't be helpful. You'll somehow manage to orchestrate things from beyond the grave," she muttered before pinning the stranger with a professional smile and holding out her hand. "I apologize for the unorthodox start. My name's Rachel. And you are?"

"I'm Maria." She bit her lip. "Bear told me to come to you when… I mean, Bear suggested you'd be able to help me."

"You're his ex-partner?" Rachel inquired.

My nose crinkled. "You're Kendra's mother? *You?*"

The last time I'd seen that hag, she'd been licking pool balls that some other clubwhore had popped out of their ass for the entertainment of the unattached MC brothers.

I didn't think Maria was an ass-to-mouth kinda woman.

"For my sins, yes. Not that I've heard from her in years."

Rachel beckoned Maria inside. "Bear did tell me that there might come a time when you'd be in need of my services."

"I-I can't afford—"

"He covered my fees, but even so, I'd do this for free. Rex, Bear's son, is my partner." Her smile turned a little less forced. "He's also the father of my daughters."

"Bear would have made a wonderful grandfather," Maria said wistfully as she stepped inside the hall.

"Yes, he would've. He made an impact as a father, that's for sure. I can't imagine the impression he'd have made on my daughters had he been given the chance." Rachel held out her arm. "If you'd like to come with me? Star, you can head back to the meeting."

"Star?" Maria demanded, twisting on her heel with more force than at any other point of the conversation. "Are you Star Sullivan?"

My brows lifted at her suddenly assertive tone.

There was no way in fuck I was heading back to that meeting when this looked set to be more interesting, but it seemed I didn't need to argue with Rachel to get myself an in.

"That's my name. How do you know it?"

"Bear. He gave me something to give to you."

Fascinating.

I shot Rachel a smug smile. "I'll just head into your office with you then."

Her eyes narrowed, but she refrained from sighing and merely stepped away. Maria followed, and I brought up the rear.

As we walked into Rachel's anal-retentively neat study, I plunked myself down on the sofa in front of her desk, sprawling comfortably as Maria headed for the visitor's seat where she perched on the edge of the chair, her knees tucked together, hands on her lap where she was holding her purse.

I was starting to get the feeling that Maria had been raised in a convent.

"How can I help, Maria?" Rachel asked kindly as she seated herself behind her desk. "Bear informed me that there might come a day when you'd seek out my services but he never actually shared what you might need from me."

Anxiously, Maria tucked a hair behind her ear. Not that the hair had strayed from her neat chignon.

Seriously, where the fuck had Kendra come from? Maybe she was proof that incubi *did* exist?

"Bear left me a key if you recall."

"I do," Rachel confirmed. "To a safety deposit box."

"I fell ill earlier this year. As a result, I lost my job. I had no intention of ever retrieving whatever he left for me, mostly because it felt like I'd be opening Pandora's box. I had no idea what it could be and, as much as I loved him, Bear was the biggest mistake of my life. I compromised my morals for him; I became something I vowed I'd never…" She swallowed. "I said to myself that I'd only open the box if I was desperate, and I never imagined that day would come because I'd have to be on the brink of homelessness before that would happen."

"You came close to losing your house?" I asked quietly.

Nervously, she nodded. "My boss retired and he was replaced by this corporate youngster with a bank balance for a heart. When he eventually fired me, he refused to write me a recommendation.

"I was too weak to wait tables so I tried to…" She sighed. "You don't need to know what I've done to make ends meet, but I realized how ridiculous I was being when Bear would have provided for me."

Her smile turned wistful as she opened the zipper on her purse and curled something around her fingers. "He always did."

That was when she revealed a chain of rubies to our astonished eyes.

Peering at the jewels, Rachel queried, "May I?"

"Of course. Bear thought that you'd be able to help me sell them."

"Me?" Rachel repeated as she lifted the chain to the light. "I'm not a fence. I don't have—"

"You're friends with the Valentinis," I finished for her, piecing Bear's intentions together faster than Rachel did.

"You think these are the rubies they're seeking?" she asked, staring down at the antique settings.

"Why else would Bear think you could sell them for Maria?"

She blinked. "Good point."

Maria released a relieved breath. "You can find a buyer for me?"

"If they're authentic, then yes."

"Bear said they weren't fakes," was Maria's worried retort.

"No, I don't doubt that Bear would... I mean, the person I'm thinking of is looking for a certain item." Rachel waved a hand. "If they don't want to buy the rubies, then I'm sure there's someone in my client list—"

"List of crooks, more like," I muttered, earning myself a glower from her.

"—who'd be more than interested in a piece of this quality." Rachel studied the chain and then glanced at Maria. "I'll get in touch with the family I'm thinking of now. One of them is my best friend. She'll give you a more than fair price if it's the piece they're seeking."

"I don't know what a fair price is," Maria admitted.

"I'm sure Rachel knows someone who can appraise it on your behalf."

Rachel nodded. "I can think of a few people. Can you stay in West Orange for a few days so we can make arrangements?"

Maria shook her head. "I promised myself that I'd never stay around here again and I meant it. I'll head to Verona. It's cheaper there anyway."

"Maria, I'll gladly fund your trip—"

"I don't take charity." Maria grimaced at the rubies. "Usually."

"You can pay her back with the funds from the sale," I said simply. "Don't stay in Verona. Go to the city. You might as well. Any appraiser will be there anyway and so is Aurora Valentini."

"I can't afford to!"

Getting to my feet, I snagged the rubies from Rachel's grip and evaluated the stones. "These are worth a couple million, Maria. You can afford a suite at the Plaza if you want." I studied the chain which was too long to be a bracelet but too short to be a necklace. The gems were cool to the touch as I inquired, "Why did you wish to speak with me?"

Maria reached into her purse again and, this time, she retrieved a letter and a larger envelope, one that was packed full and sealed with a strip of Scotch tape.

Both had my name on them.

"I appreciate the courier service," I said cheerfully, though there was something weird about getting mail from a dead man.

"I apologize for taking so long to deliver them to you," Maria admitted rawly. "Bear seemed to think I'd open the safety deposit box as soon as I received the key."

I hitched a shoulder. "Better late than never. Thanks."

I wiggled the packets at her then retreated to the sofa, leaving Rachel and Maria to sort out their business.

Retrieving a letter from the envelope, I shifted focus from their conversation and concentrated on what could be Bear's final words.

As I read, I could feel my heart rate start to increase until, by the end, sweat had beaded on my brow.

Bear hadn't expected to be in a coma before his death.

He'd expected me to get this letter *years* ago and if I had, it'd have...

Christ, it'd have changed everything.

With shaking hands, I reached for my cell.

There was only one thing to do.

Me: Eagle Eyes, I need you to bring Temper
Black to me.

Me: Immediately.

Me: Will send coordinates for retrieval as
soon as I have them.

Eagle Eyes: On it.

Then, I snapped a picture of the letter and uploaded it into my chat with Rex.

Me: Figured you'd want to know. Bear sent
me a letter.

Rex: What?

Me: Read it.

Rex: Thanks, Star.

Me: I'd want to know if there was one last
letter floating around from my mom or dad.

TEN MINUTES LATER

Rex: Holy shit

Me: Yeah, that's about how I'm feeling
right now.

Rex: You need us, we're there.

Me: Appreciate that but I've got this.

Rex: Reel them in, Star.

66

CONOR

Conor O'Donnelly

AT FIRST, when Star called, I thought she was hyperventilating.

I could only hear the sounds of heavy breathing in my ear.

Then, I managed to make out, "Need. Helicopter."

My brows lifted. "Star, I need you to calm down. Do you hear me?"

"Running," she gasped.

"Where to?" I muttered. "Did I hear you right? You need a helicopter?"

"Land it in the yard of the Sinners' clubhouse. We need to get to DC and then to the Catskills."

Though I was confused as fuck, I picked up another cell and made the call for a pilot. Once that was arranged, I told her, "He's collecting me, then you. You'll fly us to DC for obvious reasons. He should be here in thirty minutes."

Abruptly, the sounds of thudding came to a halt. "Then I can stop running," she groaned.

"Why were you running in the first place?" I sat up straighter in my desk chair. "Is someone chasing you?"

"No one would be dumb enough for that. Plus, I wouldn't run. I'd just kick their asses then and there," she grumbled, her breathing slowly becoming more regulated. "I had to leave my SUV at the bottom of the MC's road."

"Why?"

"It was blocked by a truck."

"Prime came calling, huh?"

She snorted. "I don't think the club was repeating their dog food subscription. Although, with how many animals they have around, who the fuck knows?" A massive sigh sounded in my ear then, more to herself than to me, she rasped, "No need to freak out now that we're dealing with this."

I heard the sound of stomping. "What's going on?"

"Heading back up the road to the compound so I can hitch a ride with your helicopter."

"Our helicopter," I corrected as I started to gather a few pieces of kit together.

"What are you doing?"

"Getting some of my shit in order—"

"Go into our bedroom. Check the cabinet in the walk-in closet, the one that's nearest the window."

"Why?"

"Because there's a go bag in there. One for each of us. They're black duffle bags."

"A 'go bag?'" I questioned blankly. "What the hell's that?"

"The clue's in the title, Conor. Jesus H. Christ. It's what we need for a mission."

My mouth rounded. "How long—"

"When did I make them up? The day I moved in."

This woman.

Shaking my head, I muttered, "You going to tell me what's got you riled up? Or why we need a go bag today? Are Rachel and you arguing again?"

"Of course, but this isn't related to that. Someone came to her door during the meeting—Bear's ex."

"Rex's dad? Didn't know he had an ex. Thought his wife passed away."

"She did. But he had an affair and knocked her up. Anyway, when he died, turns out he gave her a safety deposit key. In the box, there were some rubies and some letters. Those were addressed to me." She sucked in a breath. "You know how you were asking the other night about the link between the *Pauks* and Bear?"

"Uh huh," I murmured as I went to retrieve our go bags. Then, realization struck. "He told you in the letters?"

"Temperance fucking Black," she snarled.

"What?" I gaped at nothing. "*She's* the connection?"

"Apparently. He said she approached him and offered to work with him years ago."

"Must have been with the Brothers' approval," I said uneasily.

"I've told Eagle Eyes to bring her in. We'll get more answers out of her."

Finding the duffle bags, I hauled them over my shoulder and returned to our office.

"What else did Bear send you? You said there were two letters."

"There were." She cleared her throat. "Our suspicions were correct."

I stilled. Then my door buzzer sounded.

"Who's that?" she demanded.

Checking out the cameras, I murmured, "Aidan." My chin tipped forward when I saw Brennan beside him. "Bren, too."

She released a breath. "Thank fuck."

"Your grandfather might like to think he's all-seeing and all-knowing, but he isn't," I retorted. "He's not due in the city until Friday. Remember?"

"After what Eagle Eyes shared with us last night, you still think that?"

I grimaced. "To be honest, I'm not sure what I think about any of this. I just know we're in the middle of a shitstorm and nothing is making much sense."

I released the door so my brothers could walk in and yelled, "I'm in my office."

"No shit, Sherlock," Aidan drawled as he strolled in, a cross between James Bond and a walking advertisement for tailored suits.

Brennan, as always, looked like a bruiser. You could dress him up in Brioni, but fuck, you couldn't take away from the fact he was the fists of our family.

"What do you want?"

"To speak with you, moron," Brennan grumbled.

Aidan perched his ass on Star's desk and folded his arms across his chest. "I wanted to talk yesterday but after everything with... *every-thing,* it didn't seem the appropriate time."

I put Star on speaker. "We're listening."

Aidan cast a wary glance at my cell. "You won't like what I have to say, Star."

"It's that kind of day, Aidan. Hit us with it."

"I think your grandfather is losing his shit."

My brow furrowed. "Why in particular?"

"At first, I could okay this beef he has with the English. Don't particularly feel Irish, not like Da, but to honor our ancestors, why the hell not?

"So, I got the ECD to target wherever he wanted to wreak havoc. On the border with Northern Ireland, ships brought in cargo from the UK to the Republic. I had them screw with trucking logistics, fuck with that embassy's security so he could listen in—"

"You didn't tell me about that, Conor," Star growled.

My nose crinkled. "Aidan asked. What was I supposed to do? Say no?"

"Erm, no, you were supposed to share. Isn't that the crux of this whole teamwork crap you keep spouting?"

"I only knew about the embassy security. Not the rest of—"

"Before this triggers a full-on domestic squabble," Brennan sniped, "let's deal with what matters here?"

"Get on with it then," she spat.

"I think he's trying to overthrow the fucking Irish government," Aidan stated, agitatedly stroking a hand through his hair.

"You can't *think* that. Where's your evidence?"

"How about that he told me to station the bulk of the ECD's numbers outside the Stormont Estate?"

My brow furrowed. "He wants to lay siege to Northern Ireland's parliamentary buildings?"

Tensely, Aidan admitted, "I'm thinking so. I mean, his influence will be pivotal in getting Shay where we need him to be, but I'm not about to go to jail for conspiracy to bring down a fucking government! That price is too high, even for goddamn me."

Star was silent for a moment, then she croaked, "What the hell is his endgame?"

I pinned my brother with a stare. "Do you know?"

With a shrug, he said, "I just figured he was building up Russia's power in Europe."

"And you were okay with that?" Star snarled.

Flicking a look at Brennan, his expression didn't give anything away as Aidan replied, "Not entirely, but you're the ones who put me on his fucking radar! Everything comes at a cost. I figured this was the price you were willing to pay."

Scrubbing a hand over my face, I muttered, "You should have discussed this with us."

"I'm the head of the ECD. Not you. Not Brennan, Declan, Finn, or Eoghan." He pursed his lips. "Anyway, I *have* come to you to discuss this. This is a crisis point.

"What he's asked of me before have been petty political disruptions. This is the first time he's requested something with such monumental repercussions."

"He was probably building up in increments, trying to see how far you'd go," Star mumbled wearily.

"Unluckily for him," Aidan clipped, "I'm not Da."

"Who, ironically, he didn't like." I blew out a breath as I slumped down in my chair. "We can't allow him to—"

"When's the planned attack?" Star interrupted.

"In two weeks' time."

"He won't be a problem by that point. Democracy might not be perfect, but it's better than a fucking autocracy," she grated.

Aidan, Brennan, and I shared a look between us, but I was the one who asked, "Star?"

"You know what I have to do, Conor."

"We'll do it together, Star," I assured her, wanting her to know that I had her back.

"He once told me that he and his father tried to assassinate Stalin." She barked out a bitter laugh. "Seems like I'll be following in his footsteps of taking down megalomaniacs."

Aidan cleared his throat. "You have my backing if that's any consolation."

"She's going to kill her grandfather, Aidan," I grumbled. "She doesn't need your approval."

"Calm down, Conor," Brennan retorted. "We all know she's got the biggest balls out of the four of us."

Star didn't comment, didn't even snicker, just asked, "When's the helicopter's ETA?"

67

STAR

Star Sullivan

I'D WANTED to trust him.

I really had.

Mostly, I was annoyed at myself for *wanting* to even try.

It seemed nuts to think I'd warned him about becoming the next Stalin, and here he was, already crazy enough that he thought he could… Hell, I didn't even know what he intended to do.

Fuck with Britain, and Northern Ireland, then wage a war against them on the European Union's behalf?

Maybe Aidan was right and he was trying to shore up the 'motherland's' powers?

All it took was a spark in the right place to fuck with the delicate nature of the world stage… Why not start a war while he was in full despot mode?

I had no way of knowing his game plan, but whatever his logic, I was an American soldier to my core. I fought for freedom, not goddamn dictators.

As every instinct in my body pinged to life, outright screaming that I'd been dumb to trust him, a fucking *fool*, a helicopter landed in the Sinners' backyard.

That was when my grandfather answered my message.

Me: Remember you told me that Belyaev died of a heart attack in his hotel room in Cincinnati? Who gave you the bad intel?

Anton: Why do you ask me now?

Me: It just occurred to me that you never told me who was behind it.

Anton: Yes, well, it's an uncomfortable situation.

Me: Why?

Anton: You are friendly with her.

Me: Who?

Anton: Temperance Black.

Me: That goddamn bitch. Why is she still alive?

Anton: Because she's your friend.

If I hadn't already smelled the bullshit from a mile away, I did now.

Still, he'd walked into the trap I'd set, a trap that might not have worked but did, and which meant I could handle Temper without causing any raised eyebrows in the Brotherhood.

Me: I'll deal with her for you.

Anton: I'd appreciate that.

With the go-ahead, I sent D a message.

Me: Temper's a traitor.

Cin: What kind of traitor?

Me: The worst kind.

Cin: She's too self-righteous to be a traitor.

Me: Trust me, she fucking isn't.

Me: I'm about to pick her up. You want in?

Cin: Sure. But... I need to know what she's done, Star.

Me: Remember Kembesh?

Cin: How could I forget that fuckfest?

Me: She's the reason there were no medevacs that day. No backup. She sabotaged a fleet of Chinooks.

Cin: Are you fucking kidding me? How the hell do you know that?

Me: Got a letter from Bear.

Cin: Rex's dad?

Me: Yeah. He's a solid source, D. But you can always ask her yourself...

Cin: I'll send coordinates.

Me: Send them fast. My helicopter just showed up.

As I tucked my phone into my pocket, I switched focus and watched as Sinners rushed out of their clubhouse to see what was going on, yelling until they realized the helicopter was for me.

The pilot jumped down onto the marshy turf, peering around the space awkwardly until I pointed at Hawk and shouted, "Hawk, take him back to the city and I'll owe you one."

Hawk, ever the generous grouch, merely hitched a shoulder in agreement and the guy jogged over to him.

Now that I knew the Sinners wouldn't eat the pilot for breakfast, I leaped into the helicopter, quickly grabbed Conor's hand in greeting, then got myself situated for the trip.

Along the way to DC, Conor coordinated on my behalf and we picked up D who, fortuitously or not, was in Hoboken doing only God knew what with God knew whom.

We'd been friends for too long for me to even consider asking her for details.

A short while later, when we touched base in DC, Eagle Eyes was standing in a small park on the outskirts of the district, an ominously still trash bag at his feet, phone tilted horizontally as he played a game.

Only when the helicopter landed did he look up from the screen and beam a grin at me.

"I remembered the Russians' names!"

After the day I'd had, I braced myself because I had a feeling I knew who they'd be.

"They wouldn't happen to be Kuznetsov and Belyaev, would they?"

Eagle Eyes pouted. "How did you know?"

While I clamped down on the urge to scream, D was the one who rumbled, "We've been suckered."

Christ, understatement.

My grandfather had been pivotal in arming the fucking Taliban against the Americans.

If he was capable of that, what *wasn't* he capable of?

Conor slipped behind me and settled a hand on the small of my back. "We weren't to know. He gave us everything we asked for, so why wouldn't we trust him?"

"Because we're not total noobs on the job?" D grouched, shooting a disgruntled look at me. "At least we know who's on our side and who isn't."

"Small consolation," I ground out, as pissed as she was.

I'd shit the bed. Big time. Fuck, there was no bigger fail than this.

"I think I'm missing a piece of the puzzle here," Eagle Eyes mumbled, gaze darting between the three of us.

"It doesn't matter. I appreciate the intel and I appreciate you getting Black here to me now.

"Final payment will clear within forty-eight hours."

He nodded. "Appreciate that."

"Congrats on the sprog, Eagle Eyes," D chirped.

He glowered at me but I just shrugged. "You asked me not to tell your mother-in-law. Not Dead To Me."

"I figured that was obvious," he groused before he booted the limp form on the ground.

Temper didn't even groan when she rolled down the slight incline toward the idle helicopter.

"She's unconscious?"

"Yup. Drugged. Should be waking up in two or so hours. Do I wanna know what she's done, Star?"

"Betrayed me. Too many times to be forgiven," I said flatly.

Betrayed our country.

Betrayed our people.

Betrayed everything we fought for.

God damn her zealous ass.

D cursed under her breath. "I'm ashamed to call her fucking family."

Seeming to sense that was all the info he'd gain, he shrugged. "Godspeed the lot of you." With a salute, he backed off then started sprinting toward the street.

As he left, Conor approached Temperance and hauled her dead-weight onto his shoulder.

The sleek move had D whistling under her breath. "Didn't know he had it in him."

Her mood shifted more than the weather in Vermont. Mine wasn't so swift. I didn't even have it in me to joke that I was a lucky lady. All I could think about was Anton. What he'd done. His sins.

Fuck, his crimes against humanity.

She clapped me on the back, jerking me from my thoughts. "You got a plan?"

"When don't I?"

D chuckled. "True. Okay, then it's showtime!"

I grabbed her arm. "You sure you're going to be okay with…"

"Torturing her?" She smirked at me, but I knew her well enough to read her expression, to see the hurt and the betrayal buried beneath. "She called Creed. Chad told me. Said I was okay with her reaching out."

Knowing her 'unusual' feelings for both men, I mused, "Never did like her. That was before I learned she was a traitor."

"Me neither." Her smile was weak. "So, this'll be fun."

As Conor dumped Temper on the floor of the helicopter, we followed him and climbed aboard.

Five minutes later, we were in the air, and after a quick gas stop at a private airfield, and ninety minutes solid of flying, we were in the Catskills.

My mood didn't improve any, but listening to Conor and D chat over the radio had a way of putting me in a less horrified mindset.

Part of me was processing having a genocidal warmonger as a blood relative, Kat too; the other part of me had accepted a long time ago that I was a monster in sheep's clothing, but I'd found someone in my family tree who made me look like a fucking saint.

Silver lining?

It was either that or put a bullet in my head, and I'd already promised Conor that I wouldn't leave him.

As I landed the helicopter in the clearing, it was obvious to see that the Brotherhood hadn't been by recently.

D peered at the pits we'd dug for Foundry and Smythe who were no longer 'there,' but a few bones remained in residence. "I guess we can confirm that Kuznetsov doesn't suspect anything or this place would be crawling with Feds who'd pin the crimes on us."

"He wants me as his heir," I rasped.

D chuckled. "You don't have it in you to be Dr. Evil."

"Thanks. I think."

"It's a compliment."

Annoyed, I retorted, "You were angry with me for letting myself be conned by him earlier."

She sniffed. "I just realized that he offered you everything you could possibly want. As much as we like to think that we're not, we're only human.

"If someone offered me my heart's desire, how could I say no? Especially when the stakes were so high."

My throat felt thick as I croaked out, "Thank you, D. I'm sorry I dragged you into this."

She punched me in the bicep. "Don't get sappy. No apology necessary. Walked into a hail of bullets for you before, Star, and haven't brought it up that you got your ass imprisoned by a geriatric megalomaniac, either. By comparison, this is nothing."

I'd done the same for her and would do worse still to protect her—that was how deep our friendship ran.

It must have been exhaustion from the day's events that made me want to laugh *and* cry at her words.

"You know," she mused, toeing her boot over the remnants of the two Sparrows. "I don't want to be alive when it happens, but I think this is a good way to go out."

"Being kibble for wild animals?" Conor sputtered.

"Yeah. Seems natural."

Grateful for the less sentimental direction in our conversation, I hid a snort at Conor's horrified look. "Less talking, more action."

As I watched him set up the piece of tech that killed any and all incoming and outgoing signals into the area, D queried, "Why are we even here?"

"Seems a shame not to grace Temper with the same fate as she gifted Reinier," I said simply.

D high-fived me. "I like the way you think."

"You don't hold much loyalty for family, do you?" Conor asked.

"Some family you make, you're not born with." She hooked her arm around my neck. "Star's not blood, but she might as well be. Then, throw in the fact that Temper's chasing after my man, she's fair game."

"Don't ask, Conor," I quipped when he seemed set to pepper her with questions.

Releasing her hold on me, D loped over to the shipping container with the key I handed her and Conor's super-bright flashlight.

"Get ready for a stink," she warned cheerfully.

I grimaced when the scent of death immediately flooded the clearing. Not even a brisk wind swept it away, and the coffin flies that buzzed out didn't travel far either.

D popped her head into the container and shouted, "This is both gross and cool, Star. You need to come and look."

"I'm assuming you're not excited about the corpse?" I mocked as I stepped into the container with my go bag in hand.

By comparison to what I'd smelled in Afghanistan after a battle, this was practically pleasant, but I still withdrew a jar of Vaporub from my gear and swiped it under my nose.

"Jesus Christ," Conor rumbled from behind me, immediately spinning on his heel and heading outside.

Though I knew she pricked her ears for the sounds of him vomiting because I saw the disappointment flash over her expression, D still teased, "I'll tell Troy, Conor. She'll go back to calling you Glitter—"

When Conor stepped inside, he had Temper over his shoulder. "Fuck off, *Lucinda.*"

After he dumped Temper, I tossed the jar of Vaporub at him. "Heads-up, love."

He grabbed it, swiped it under his nose, but still gagged while D, totally unoffended with his banter, chuckled and waved a hand at the wall. "Reinier was an artist with a grudge."

I hummed at the mural of dried shit then stared at the corpse which was, no nicer way to describe it, seeping. "He can't have survived long after I dealt with him."

"So this was his last message," Conor mused around a retch as he bowed over, hands on his knees as the virulent stench seemed to grow stronger now that fresh air was streaming and not trickling into the container.

D and I shared a look but didn't comment.

If anything, I wished I were like him and wasn't accustomed to these kinds of horrors.

"Maybe apply some more?" I suggested.

He waved a hand over his head. "Don't worry about me. Nothing to see here."

D snorted but mused, "Reinier's penmanship could do with some work but it's definitely an address."

"He claimed he had an estate in Florida." I studied the address. "Can you look it up for me, Conor?"

"Yeah," he choked.

"Go stand by the door," D ordered.

He didn't argue.

Once he was over there, he said, "Tell me the address then I'll disengage the signal blocker. Don't speak until I have the location pinpointed. I'll tell you when the blocker is re-engaged." D nodded her understanding as I called out the address. After a short pause, he stated, "Okay. We're free to talk. The address is in the Keys."

"That's our next port of call then," I rasped.

"Nuh-uh," D argued, grabbing my arm as I made to move toward the door. "I think it's time you told us what this Bear guy said in his letter."

With a shrug, because I had nothing to hide, I shoved my hand in my coat pocket and retrieved the note so I could pass it to her.

Star,

> *We've never had the opportunity to meet but I know you've been fighting the Sparrows for longer than I have, and seeing as I know my time is near, I figure I should pass the baton onto you.*

> *We're both fighters in this hidden war and I salute you for your sacrifices. That's how the Sparrows get you—by those sacrifices—and I can't imagine what you've had to endure because what they did to me was hell. Living hell.*

> *I truly wish you well in your fight and I hope you won't stop until they're no more. Until we're free from their taint.*

Because wherever they establish a nest, they poison paradise.

To help, Rex, my boy, should have shown you the motel room I've been working out of. Everything I know about the Sparrows is in there, and I hope it can be of some use to you.

But there's info that isn't safe to be left in that room.

I first came across a second secret society called the 'United Brotherhood' via a woman who went by the name Temperance Black. She approached me and offered me intel.

My case against the Sparrows had stalled. I'd bought this docket of information from a dark website nine or so months before, managed to get hacked in the process, and lost the docket as well as everything I'd uncovered about the NWS over the years.

(After that, I took printouts of everything. That's what you'll find in my motel room.)

So, by that point, I was depressed as well as desperate for anything that'd help me move forward with my investigation, and I dove in too deep.

Looking back, she promised me the earth, and, in some instances, she gave it to me.

But everything comes with a price.

I trusted her.

I was a fool to do so.

If you ever meet her, back the fuck away.

She's one of them.

The United Brotherhood is as corrupt as the New World Sparrows. When I uncovered details about the leaders—a bunch of amoral motherfuckers I've yet to have the misfortune of researching, by the way—it was purely by chance.

I didn't know who they were, and when I approached Temper about them, she was quick to reassure me that they're the 'good guys.'

They're not.

I realized where I'd heard one of the names from—Kuznetsov.

Whispers abound of this asshole close to the border with Mexico—the shit he deals in makes me wish the Sparrows were more *powerful than the Brotherhood.*

Organ harvesting, fentanyl-running, child exploitation, arms-dealing (and we're not talking AKs here, but uranium, for God's sake,) you name it, he's got his hands in that pie.

The more I investigated Kuznetsov, the more I uncovered the links between the Sparrows and the Brotherhood.

They might be separate entities, just like two siblings are, but they're from the same family.

That was when I knew I didn't have long left.

Temper was supportive when I was working to take down the Sparrows, but after what would become our final meeting, I knew I'd pushed things too far.

There's a Sinner who's like a son to me. Name's Maverick. I know you know him. He served in a battle in Kembesh. I believe you were also deployed there at the time.

I happened to uncover intel from a veteran who was living on the streets in Houston who claimed 'someone' had paid him to help them ambush a fleet of Chinooks that would have been pivotal in the battle.

At first, I thought it was bullshit. Then, I asked him who that 'someone' was. The name Black is a common one, but fuck if it didn't make me look at her differently.

I asked her if she was behind the lack of medical support in that battle which had taken too many of our men, and I knew it was her no matter if she denied it.

Because I didn't feel like dying, I pretended to accept her bull-shit story.

That was the beginning of the end.

We returned to business as usual, then I came across this Sparrow called Bogdan Belyaev who I learned sourced the women they ran as sex slaves in the Baltics. That fella, Kuznetsov, dealt with the logistics of getting them over here.

*Which was when I learned there were two Kuznetsov guys.
A father and son. A team.*

*That's how I know these assholes were in this together. How I
knew the Brotherhood was as bad as the Sparrows.*

*So, I went on the hunt for more information. Spoke with a cop
on the take in Cincinnati. He told me that it's known among
'certain' officers Belyaev and Kuznetsov Jr. perished in car
crashes,* but *their death certificates showed they both died
of heart attacks at the same fucking time of day as the other.*

*I brought it up to her; she dismissed it. I shouldn't have pushed,
but I was angry, and fool that I was, I didn't let up until it
was too late.*

I might be wrong, but I'm tying up loose ends just in case.

Do not trust a CIA operative by the name of Temperance Black.

Do not trust the United Brotherhood.

*My motel room is as up-to-date as I can make it. However, I've
tried to keep most things Brotherhood-related out of there.
What I have, you can find in the envelope attached.*

*I hope you can do what I couldn't—take down the Brothers and
the Sparrows—our world will surely be a better place
without them.*

*We never met, Star, but a seeker of answers knows a fellow soul
even from afar.*

*I'm a Satan's Sinner to my core—so if God can't help you get
the job done, maybe the man downstairs can.*

Wishing you success in your investigation,

Bear

WHEN D STOPPED READING, she turned to me, saw my clenched
hands, and rumbled, "You can leave Temper with me."

"Sweet fuck, I can *taste* that stench." Conor coughed around a
splutter as he pinched his nose and strode deeper into the container.

"She's awake," he rasped, surprising me by grabbing the plastic bag and tearing into it. When his booted foot landed on Temper's throat, D and I shared a glance. "Black," Conor greeted, sounding only partially nasal.

The stench *was* getting stronger with every passing moment.

Sluggishly, Temper slapped at his feet, her body wriggling in an attempt to escape.

"The moment I met you," Conor ground out, loading more pressure on her throat, "I knew you were trouble. As for the moment I heard of the Brotherhood, I knew they were asswipes, pretending their shit didn't stink, pretentious and self-righteous. Nothing worse than someone claiming they're perfect when they make pond scum seem saintly."

"N-Not! Wrong woman. Wrong. Woman," she croaked.

He released her then snagged her hair in his fist and dragged her over to a chair.

This time, the look D and I shared was bemused.

"Damn, this is hot," she whispered.

"You should have seen him torture that Byrne guy."

She folded her arms across her chest. "He's yours. I can only drool from afar."

Though I snorted, I didn't argue.

She was fucking right.

He *was* mine.

All goddamn mine.

As Temper shrieked and cried out, Conor hauled her onto the chair. By that point, she was a shaking mess.

"What are you doing?" she cried, the words still faintly slurred.

"How did you know Muñoz was hunting Star?"

Her head rolled on her shoulder but she started snickering until Conor backhanded her. "*That's* what you're asking?"

"What should he be asking?" I queried, stepping closer to Temper.

Her eyes peeped open. "Funny when you try to stop something from happening and you make it happen anyway."

"Stop with the bullshit, Temper," D growled. "Answer the question."

"Own flesh gonna kill me. What would Uncle Gene say?"

"He'd say you're a traitorous cunt."

"Doubt it." Temper groaned. "He likes me. Never liked you. Everyone always likes me, Lucinda. You're the one everybody hates."

"She's wrong," Conor groused. "I like you, D."

D sniffed. "I like you too, Conor. We vibe."

"Can anyone join this 'vibe' party?" I mocked, but I nudged D in the side too.

"Throat. Hurts."

"Well, let's try to take your mind off that." Conor kicked the chair with his foot so she tipped backward.

Right onto Reinier.

"Oh, my God! It fucking touched me!" she cried, scuttling over the floor, away from the rotting corpse, like the spider I supposed she was.

That was when I had a 'eureka' moment.

Alessa had told me that the Kuznetsovs were like spiders. That they had webs in every corner of a person's house.

A pauk in English was a spider.

Why had that only registered now?

With my mind elsewhere, D proved she was focused on her target. Her hand slid out to snag Temper in her hold. The moment she had a grip on her wrist, Temper was shrieking and clutching the now-broken joint to her chest. "Answer Conor's question. Or I'll stop playing nice."

"I knew Star wouldn't forgive me for betraying her! I-I figured that would make her cut me some slack," she growled.

"You put Muñoz on her tail?"

She sniffed. "He owed me one."

"He was a Sparrow."

A burst of laughter fell from her. "You've no idea, have you? None at all."

"Do you know how I killed Reinier, Temper?"

She grimaced at the corpse. "I can smell it. Electricity."

"I have the same toy in my go bag." As she tensed, I nodded.

"Exactly. You don't want to fuck me around. You want to answer what I ask or I will make sure that you suffer—"

"We're sisters-in-arms! We served together!"

"And I should never have trusted you as far as I could throw you." My problem here was that she was as indoctrinated as I was from breaking under force. Faced with that, I knew I had to lean on her passions, of which she had many. "I thought you were all about America. All about serving the Land of the Free."

"Yeah, your self-righteous ass used to be the only decent thing about you. Now I'm learning that's a lie too," D grumbled. When Temper didn't reply, D yanked on her hair. "Answer us."

"I am not dirty. I serve the people. I act for the people. I protect the people," she spat.

"You're more deluded than I first thought," Conor rumbled.

"Deluded? More like deranged. Anyway, cut the bullshit, Temper. What happened? How did you get involved in this mess?" D demanded.

"Mom got sick and Kuznetsov promised he'd help us. Plus, he told me I'd get a promotion." Spite flashed over her expression. "At long fucking last."

"D? Is that true about her mother?"

She rasped, "Shelly needed an organ transplant. A new liver."

"Guess we know how she got one of those." I blew out a breath as Conor and I shared a look. "Why did the Sparrows kill Belyaev and Kuznetsov?"

Temper's smile was like the dawning sunlight in the morning. I didn't know until now that that could be sickening.

Then D broke her nose and she stopped smiling—thank fuck.

"Don't forget, Temper, I'm the only one who ever made you cry," she gibed.

Temper drew away. "DeLaCroix wanted to hurt Kuznetsov."

"Anton or Aleks?" I asked.

"Anton," she rasped, shooting me a hate-filled glance. "The Brothers have always been more powerful. DeLaCroix got too big for his station." Her laughter was faintly manic. "Look who showed him."

"You slipped him the cyanide?"

"Ten points to you." She whistled. "Been helping out with a little sniper problem we've been having too. Got so many running around, they're becoming a hindrance." Before I could wonder why she admitted to that, Temper cackled. "I've almost killed you twice, D. Family ties stopped me."

"*You* are the reason so many snipers have been killed over the last couple of years?" D shouted, kicking Temper in the gut until she was coughing blood. "I can promise you this. Family ties *won't* stop me."

"You're Anton's pitbull, huh?" Conor rumbled softly. "Who he sends in to fix his problems?"

She bared her teeth—they were bloodstained, one had even worked loose, revealing a gap that made her whistle with each breath. "Sounds about right. Been serving him for a long time. He trusts me." God, she sounded *proud* of being trusted by a fucking genocidal maniac. "I'm the reason he's in charge of—"

She stopped before she finished the sentence. But I figured I knew what she was going to say.

Since I'd waded into Anton's life, he'd become the head of the Brotherhood without a council to keep him in check.

And, no matter what he was promising me with the Sparrows, that didn't mean he couldn't bring their trade under the Brotherhood's umbrella.

Christ, maybe that had been the end goal all along?

"Oh, yeah, he trusts you so much that he sold you out to me. Told me you were the one who gave him bad intel on Belyaev's death. Told me you were the one who said Belyaev died in a hotel room in Cincinnati and not in a road accident. Some trust he has in you," I sneered, "when he sanctions your death."

She coughed up some blood and let it spatter on the floor. "He's wrong. H-He must have made a mistake. I never told him that.

"The Belyaevs and Kuznetsovs have been close friends for decades. Anton took Bogdan's loss personally so he must have gotten things muddled. He'd lost his heir too. Made things worse. Yeah, that has to be it. That's why he's mistaken. I could clear it up if—"

"Wasn't my mom an heir?"

Her laughter was, in a word, *manic*. "You can fry me until I sizzle like bacon, Star, but that's the one thing I'll keep from you. I'll never tell you what happened to her. It's too damn satisfying knowing the truth will haunt you until the day you die."

"Bitch," Conor growled, kicking her in the gut and watching as she curled up in a ball on the floor to protect her torso.

"Conor," I appeased. "It's all right."

His nostrils flared but he backed off.

"That's it, little boy. Let the women talk," Temper taunted until D was pressing her knee onto her sternum and placing her whole weight on the other woman's chest.

As his hands balled into fists at his sides, I stared at the woman who was *willing* me to never have any peace. Who was never going to let my mom's memory be at rest.

Jaw clenched, I stated, "Reinier is the reason I was enslaved."

"If you say so," Temper slurred.

I gritted my teeth. "Anton told me Aleks was searching for me."

"Why seek out something you know where to find?"

That news had nausea swirling around my gut.

So, he *had* known my whereabouts.

"Why did you bring Bear into it?" Conor demanded.

When she didn't answer, D moved aside and I grabbed her already broken nose, then twisted it.

"Don't ask me how the old bastard did it, but the only reason he was on our radar was because he'd managed to infiltrate a meeting of our council. He thought they were Sparrows." She sniffed. "I was told to keep an eye on him, to help him, even. The Sparrows have been dying a long death, Star. Your input was minimal." She swallowed. "Anton really sold me out?"

"He did."

"I-I don't believe you."

Not willing to waste time on this, I opened the conversation with Anton, turned my phone so she could see the screen, and let her read the message thread.

Her eyes widened. "You faked that!"

"Why the hell would I?"

"You're just not as important as you like to think you are," D rumbled.

Chuckling in agreement, I informed her, "Cin's right. You're expendable."

"He made me the deputy director of the CIA!"

"And? Clearly, he's got someone else ready to jump into the position. You're nothing to him, Temper. You mean dick to him."

"SHUT UP!" she screamed, surging upward, fists raised.

I saw her coming from a mile away. So did Conor. He was there first. He grabbed a hold of her hair again, slammed her face into the floor, and didn't stop until she was a bloodied mess.

"Conor," I soothed. "Let her go."

His face was red with exertion, but he stopped at my request. Breathing heavily, he retreated.

Conor, I knew, was slow to commit violence unless someone had hurt a person he loved.

If I left him alone with her, I knew Temper would die at his hands today.

Torture wasn't everyone's idea of a love language, but it was mine.

Temper rolled to the side and spat out blood-stained saliva. "You won't kill me. You can't. I'm one of you."

D choked out a bitter laugh. "You're trash. That's what you are."

Before they could start arguing, I rumbled, "Bear wrote me a letter." She stiffened. "Said he had reason to believe that you fucked with a bunch of Chinooks so there was no support for the battle of Kembesh."

I didn't even need her to answer—I saw it in her expression.

She *had*.

I stormed over to her and kicked her in the head. "*You* were the double agent. I fucking knew someone was over there, screwing shit up, but I didn't know it was you."

"You'd be amazed how much you failed to notice," she jeered even as she tried to shield herself from my attack.

Twisting her arm behind her back, I hauled her next to Reinier's corpse and shoved her face into his guts which were split open from cuts and sores that had festered and torn apart.

"Why would you betray our brothers-in-arms like that? Is it because of Dost Mohamet Khan? Is that why?" She shrieked and heaved and retched until I dragged her away from the mess of empty pupae from the coffin flies in Reinier's putrefying flesh so that I could hurl at her, "Answer me!"

"I don't know who that is."

"Bullshit!" I rammed her face back into the corpse. "Tell me, Temperance. Fucking tell me."

"YES," she screamed, spitting out gore and pupae. "The Brotherhood was sending arms across the Pakistani border into Afghanistan. Dost Mohamet Khan was the only one who knew about our involvement. He was the go-between—"

"All these years, I believed you were a fucking zealot. A patriot so short-sighted that..." D's mouth worked. "How could you, Temper? How fucking could you?"

"Because she *is* a zealot," Conor growled. "But her morals are for hire."

With that, I shoved her face back into Reinier's guts. As she passed out with a mouthful and a noseful of Reinier's rotting flesh, I turned to Conor who asked, "We head to the Floridian estate, then what?"

I sucked in a breath that was soaked with the flavor of death. "Then we make moves to take over the Brotherhood."

"You make it sound so simple," D drawled.

"He's an old man. How hard can he be to kill?"

She fist-bumped me. "You deal with one treacherous old fuck and I'll deal with this young one. Then we meet in the middle?"

"No." I swiped at my hands with a wet wipe I retrieved from my go bag. "I think I'll need you over in Europe."

I reached for my cell as a thought occurred to me.

Me: What drug did you use on her?

> Eagle Eyes: Sodium thiopental. You're
> welcome lol.

Truth serum.

Mostly bullshit, but the anesthetic *did* lower inhibitions and made people chatty. That explained a lot.

"Star?"

I blinked at D. "What?"

"Europe?"

"Europe," I confirmed.

She huffed. "Informative."

"D?"

"Yup."

"When you're done with Temper, do *not* start a fire."

She sniffed. "Spoilsport."

"Arsonist."

"You see, you think that's an insult..."

"I know it is." I arched a brow at her. "Agreed? We don't need emergency services flying over here when a wildfire starts, and we sure as fuck don't need them snooping around our kill zone, now do we?"

"No, I guess not," she said with a huff. "You want me to clean up the place, though? Just in case Kuznetsov catches wind that you're onto him and he uses this crime scene against you?"

"We have people we can send in to do that," Conor informed her.

"Make her suffer, D."

"She betrayed us, Star. Don't you worry—" D drawled as she cracked her knuckles. "—I will."

68

CONOR

THE JOURNEY down to the Keys required a second pit stop for gas. That was when Star asked Savannah where Dagger's estate was so she could land the helicopter there.

Which, of course, was when we had our confirmation that the Daniels' neighbors were, in fact, Sparrows because that was the address Reinier had smeared onto the wall before his death.

During the flight, and wired, I got to work.

Firstly, I sent the worm Star had gifted me crawling through several top-secret databases, wanting to make sure that the case files on Smythe, Reinier, and Foundry were all slowly edging out of detectives' interests.

They were.

Secondly, I reasoned that if Anton wanted to frame us with their murders, he would have used his *Pauks* to store the intel, so I hacked into one of their known online playgrounds and set some Trojan horses as traps so that one of the team would let me in. Hopefully before doomsday.

Finally, I crashed into Reinier's security system before we even crossed into his estate, and we 'borrowed' one of the Daniels' SUVs to tear down a hole in a border fence.

When we made it over to the main house, it was dark and the lights weren't on—nobody was home.

The building was surrounded by a pool which was still well-maintained as was the rest of the property.

"We need to lie low with the flashlights," I told her. "The gated community has security patrols."

Though she nodded her understanding, she was quiet as she picked the locks on the back door.

Hell, she'd been quiet ever since takeoff in the Catskills.

Whether she wanted to admit it or not, she liked Anton.

It wasn't as if I could blame her—*I'd come to like him too.*

It was weird to think that a tyrant could be pleasant.

Having lived with one for so long, it was dichotomous to what I knew of them, but Anton was clearly a better actor than Da.

As we moved throughout the massive edifice, quietly scanning each room for signs of an office, she eventually said, "Do you know what hurts the most?"

She'd been silent for so long that her words startled me.

"It all hurts, Star," I tried to reassure her. "You were starting to trust him."

"Maybe I was to a certain extent. I wouldn't have introduced him to Lyra if I didn't think he was on our side, but when you're undercover in the CIA, you pick up different levels of trust. He breached a few of those levels, sure, but I was always wary."

"Sure you were," I scoffed.

"No, I mean it," she stated, not even a hint to her tone that she was being argumentative. "There's a reason he hasn't met Kat yet. So much didn't add up but this does." She sucked in a breath. "What hurts the most is that I'll probably never find out what happened to my mom. Why did she have to die? Why didn't he save her?"

"Why didn't he save Aleks too?" I tacked on gently.

"Heirs usually matter," she muttered, bewilderment coating the words. "I don't understand his logic."

"We don't have to. We just need to take him down."

I wanted to comfort her, but I knew in this there was no comfort to be found. The only thing that would make any of this better for her were answers. That was always her cure-all.

We were birds of a feather in that.

"What do you think we'll find here?"

"Bear's packet of information revealed enough to confirm that Temper needs to die, the Brothers *are* engaged in everything he said they were, and that I was right to kill Princes Edward and Ludwig and Ke Jintao.

"But I'm hoping that, here, we'll find the means of bringing down the Brotherhood. Reinier said he had billions of dollars' worth of blackmail material on clients, friends, and politicians.

"Everyone he came into contact with.

"It's not enough just to eradicate the world of the remaining Kuznetsov. We need to tear down his empire too." As the heavy nature of her words tumbled around us, she released a sad sigh then tucked her hand in my own. "Thank you, Conor."

"What for?"

"This. Being here. I don't have to be alone again."

I squeezed her fingers. "You think I don't feel the same way?"

"We're birds of a feather, aren't we?" she whispered, unknowingly mirroring my thoughts.

Tugging her closer, I rested my chin on the crown of her head for a couple of seconds. "We are."

Ten minutes later, we found Reinier's office.

That was when she got a text message.

Cin: The bitch died earlier than planned.

Star: You wanted to draw it out?

Cin: Wanted to keep at her with the questions. No success. I think she had a heart attack.

Star: Likely. Eagle Eyes used sodium thiopental on her.

Cin: That explains it. Shit.

Star: Did she answer any of your questions?

Cin: Said that she'd prefer to die than serve under you.

Star: She knew Anton wanted me for his heir?

Cin: Apparently. I got angry when she started talking about how she was the one who told Reinier you were suspicious of her. Thought you were going to rat her out as the double agent.

Star: I wasn't. I didn't even know she was in the same area as me.

Star: That means the working ties between the Sparrows and Brothers are closer than we imagined.

Cin: I'm so fucking sorry, Star.

Star: Not your fault.

Cin: I lost my shit when she started talking about how she was glad you had to suffer. Fuck, she kept her eye on you, Star. She told me about Hans.

Cin: I don't even have the words to talk about this.

Star: We DON'T need to talk about it. He's dead. I killed him. That's all you need to know.

Star: Was anything said about my mom?

Cin: No. But you knew she wouldn't say dick. The cunt.

Star: Fuck.

Cin: Sorry, Star. I really goddamn tried.

> Star: Thanks, Cin. I know you did. I'll pick you up on the way back.

> Cin: Nah, I feel like a hike.

> Star: You sure?

> Cin: Yup. Gotta clear my head so I can figure out what to tell my folks about their favorite niece's disappearance. She wasn't lying about them preferring her over me.

> Star: :/ Good luck.

> Cin: I'll need it.

"If he was bringing the Sparrows under the Brotherhood umbrella, unifying it like it was before the Sparrows branched out," I mused, "then how did he think he'd get you to go ahead with it? As his heir, I mean."

Tiredly, she sighed. "I have no idea and I'm not sure I want to know." She rubbed her temple. "But unification sounds like something an egomaniac would strive for, don't you think?"

I hummed, but a half-hour later, I was struggling to break into Reinier's safe, and my mind was elsewhere.

When I finally cracked the code, Star sucked in a sharp breath that was loaded with dread as she dragged the door open.

Not even we could have expected to uncover what we did though.

A jail cell wasn't good enough for the likes of Kuznetsov.

Some men needed to burn. Luckily for the world, we weren't afraid to light the match on his funeral pyre.

69

POSSE TEXT CHAT
THREE DAYS LATER

LODESTAR: *How's Cruz?*

Indy: *Could be better. I know you looped him in before that shit went down with his mom. Thanks for that, Star. From one Old Lady to another. :P*

Lodestar: *Don't mention it. Really. Please. Lol.*

Indy: *No, I will. It matters. Thank. You.*

Lily: *Just take the gratitude, Star.*

Tiffany: *My professor would have a lot to say about your inability to accept gratitude, Lodestar.*

Amara: *I say she pain in ass.*

Rachel: *You would lol.*

Giulia: *I don't think it's that.*

Giulia: *There's a reason I made you an honorary member of the Posse, Star.*

Giulia: *Cruz is Star's family. Who doesn't look out for family?*

Stone: *Cunts?*

Indy: *LOL. So, I rescind my thanks, Lodestar. You're just not a cunt now.*

Lodestar: *I prefer that.*

Lily: *Of course, you would.*

Lodestar: *Are you rolling your eyes at me?*

Rachel: *She's rolling her eyes at you.*

Lodestar: *You're all together?*

Lily: *Jealous? :P*

Rachel: *Missing West Orange?*

Lodestar: *If you could see me, you'd see the two birds I have pointing your way.*

Lily: *I'm at work. Rachel and I are discussing this year's FAST gala.*

Rachel: *Which, thank Christ, you have nothing to do with organizing.*

Lodestar: *The feeling is mutual, Rachel. I'll be glad when this is all over and I don't have to talk about table settings, charity auction lots, or ball gowns for another year.*

Stone: *I'm not sure why you two don't get along better. You're both Type-A control freaks.*

Tiffany: *There can only be one alpha in any pack.*

Giulia: *No offense, Tiff, but you don't need a fancy psych degree to figure that one out.*

Tiffany: *Charming!*

Lodestar: *Someone got out of bed on the wrong side this morning.*

Giulia: *Nah. My nipples feel like they're going to fall off.*

Lodestar: *TMI*

Lodestar: *But, I'll bite. Why?*

Giulia: *Samael got a tooth.*

Lodestar: *Did you know that babies are born with all their adult teeth in their skulls?*

Amara: *Tak, we have all seen the photo on Facebook.*

Lodestar: *Amara is clearly not impressed.*

Amara: *How cats?*

Lodestar: *Ren and Stimpy are fine.*

Lily: *Thought they were Crepe and Suzette.*

Lodestar: *Nah. They're calamitous AF. Ren and Stimpy are more befitting. Kiddo can call them whatever she wants but they answer to Ren and Stimpy now lol.*

Amara: *Got a pretty dog. You want?*

Lodestar: *No!*

Stone: *You're quiet, Alessa. Everything okay?*

Lodestar: *She's still mad at me.*

Lily: *I think being mad at Star for being Star is futile. *shrugs**

Lodestar: *I agree.*

Amara: *Not nice what did but think is worth it. Sparrows need die.*

Lodestar: *I definitely agree.*

Alessa: *Yes, well, I'm finding it hard to accept.*

Giulia: *Don't be like that, Alessa. You don't even know what I've done since I became Nyx's Old Lady. I'm not proud of it or ashamed of it. Just like you shouldn't be ashamed of what you've done to be here, at this point in your life.*

Lodestar: *Wow, philosophical stuff. Having sore nipples is obviously good for you, Giulia.*

Giulia: *Fuck off. I'm trying to defend you. Don't give me shit.*

Lodestar: *I'm not! Just saying it how I see it.*

Lodestar: *Anyway, Alessa's entitled to be mad. I know she'll forgive me in time, and I have plenty of that now. :)*

Stone: *That right, Alessa? You just need time? Or do we need to arrange some kind of intervention?*

Lodestar: *Dear God, no.*

Alessa: *Time heals all wounds, no?*

Lodestar: *Some more than others.*

Alessa: *On this, we can agree.*

CIA DEPUTY DIRECTOR LATEST MISSING PERSON

TEMPERANCE BLACK, the current deputy director of the CIA, has been declared as a missing person by the MPDC.

Rumors in DC claim that she is but one of many officials who have decided it is simpler to go 'missing' than to face the repercussions of their ties to the NWS.

The question is… was the president aware of these potential ties when he nominated her?

70

CONOR

FIVE DAYS LATER

Conor O'Donnelly

"CONOR! WHERE THE HELL IS EOGHAN?"

I smiled at my sister-in-law. "He said he was going to be running late."

Inessa scowled at me. "Why didn't he tell *me* that?"

"Probably because he figured I'd let you know."

"I know you're not married yet, Conor, but you should know that communication is key, and using your brother as a messenger isn't better than a cellphone."

"Don't be too hard on him, Inessa. He's doing me a favor."

That had curiosity filtering into her gaze. "He's been better since Star started those poker games."

"He has, hasn't he?"

"Drinking less," she confirmed. "Happier. Still has his days. I can't walk into a park without him seeking out sniper's nests, but generally, he's more upbeat than before. This favor of yours…"

"Won't hurt his progress."

She hummed. "I'll hold you to that."

I grabbed her hand and raised it to my mouth so I could kiss her knuckles. "You look beautiful, by the way."

"The real tragedy is that this dress is being wasted on my brother-in-law and not my husband," she grumbled. "How long is this favor going to take— Wait. This is why he had Brennan pick me up, isn't it? Dammit, he isn't coming at all, is he?"

"Unlikely," I admitted.

"What a jackass move. I swear, you O'Donnelly brothers think you can get away with murder because you're all so damn pretty."

My lips curved into a grin. "I'm not sure that's why we get away with the stunts we pull."

"Maybe not with the cops, but definitely with your wives." She stacked her hands on her hips. "Brennan told Camille to tell you that he and Declan are dealing with some soccer person."

"That's the president of a very important soccer club, Inessa," I chided.

"If you say so." She sniffed dismissively. "I suppose we're both messengers for our in-laws tonight."

"You're better at it than me though." I winked at her. "Lisandra's here, isn't she? I seem to remember Star mentioning something about you enjoying dancing with her…"

A twinkle gleamed in her eye. "I see where you're going. I think I will take this as an opportunity to dance and get drunk with Camille and Lisandra.

"The best part is Brennan will keep all the men two feet away and I don't have to deal with his angry growls tonight, Camille can!" Before I could utter a word, she patted my cheek. "Best brother-in-law ever."

As she waltzed off, I called out, "Save that for Brennan later."

Without turning back, she waved a hand in the air, evidently on the hunt for Lisandra and Camille now that she had a game plan for the evening.

Though Eoghan *was* doing Star and me a favor, I smirked because Inessa deserved to let her hair down for a night and Eoghan was a jackass for leaving it to me to tell her he wasn't going to make the gala.

With a glance around the massive event hall, I knew Star would be happy to hear that I agreed with most of her decorative choices. She'd ultimately won the 'no ice sculpture' argument as well as the other fight for more 'environmentally friendly' options.

Each of the tables had a pruned herb bush in the center, for exam-ple, which should have been both ridiculous and hilarious but was actually damn smart because the air was scented with their perfume and it added to the aura of the so-called 'winter wonderland' theme, especially as what appeared to be powdered sugar frosted the leaves.

Massive snowflakes hung overhead—no cheap tchotchke either. These gleamed with crystals that I knew a place called Swavski or something had donated to the cause.

And with the white dress code and the sparkle of the women's gems, the place *felt* frosty. Ice sculptures or not.

Snagging a canapé that was shaped into a small mound and topped with goat's cheese—white was an unfortunate theme with the food too —I accepted a glass of white wine as I cast a glance over the busy party and hunted down my woman.

I'd arrived late because Star had to show her face here while I had to work behind the scenes.

We'd spent the past week preparing to crash the *Pauks'* servers and said crash was due to happen in less than twenty minutes, which meant engaging with Anton was imperative before he figured out what we'd done.

Which, essentially, was destroy the drone footage he had of Star, Dead To Me, Troy, and me in the Catskills with three missing VIPs.

The asswipe *had* collected evidence on us.

Yet another reason of, oh, around ten thousand, that he needed to be erased.

I was hoping that once we were in the *Pauks'* database, we'd have more of a rundown of who was a Brother, but the timing was key.

Scanning the crowd, I eventually found Star hovering beside the table we'd been allotted, her gaze on her phone.

Heading over to her after I sank back the wine and left the glass on a server's tray, I slid an arm around her waist.

Beneath the silk, there was boning that was hell-sent to fuck with my head and my dick as it supported her tits while letting her natural curves shine through.

"Did I tell you how beautiful you look tonight?" I crooned.

"Twice. You can tell me a third time if you want though. I won't complain."

While I chuckled, I pressed a kiss to her temple. "You picked this dress to drive me insane, didn't you?"

"I do most things with the aim of driving you insane, Conor. You need to accept this if we're going to continue our relationship to its natural end."

"What's the natural end?"

"When we're worm food."

"That's my kind of marriage," I said approvingly.

"You can take the Catholic out of the boy but not the boy out of the Catholic."

"That makes no grammatical sense."

"I'm still right."

I groused, "Actually, it has nothing to do with Catholicism. I just feel like arguing with you until I die. I'm weird like that."

"Apparently." She peeked at me over her shoulder. "At least someone appreciates this travesty of a dress."

"Travesty?" I clutched at my heart. "Harsh, Star. Harsh. I'm taking it that Savannah picked it?"

She harrumphed. *That* was answer enough.

The halter neck exposed the length of her spine, and above her ass, there was a big bow that my hands longed to pull apart. Unfortunately for me, that wasn't going to happen tonight.

I knew nothing about fashion design, but I had eyes and the cut of the silk made it so that it sat flush to her curves. It swooped around her feet, revealing shining silver peep toes. I shouldn't find it endearing that her toenails were bare but I did.

Savannah could drag her into the dress, but never could Star be dragged to the salon though.

It *was* a travesty, however, that I couldn't fuck her in it, but there were worse travesties in need of handling on our agenda.

"All set?" I asked her when her attention shifted to her phone.

She hummed. "Kat was just telling me that Shay is a great babysitter."

"So long as she's focused on his pretty face and not the thirty-strong security team the kids have on them..."

"Oh, she's completely unaware of the guards," she assured me. "Grail is waiting in the wings. She told me that he's arrived but I haven't seen him yet." She leaned into me, her spine touching my chest, giving me her weight in more ways than one. Star didn't lean on anyone. *Just me.* "I'm doing the right thing, aren't I, Conor?"

"I think we can officially say that no geriatric is safe around you," I said lightly, "but yes."

"I didn't kill Dagda," she mumbled, and was that...? Yes, it was. A soft blush danced on the arcs of her cheeks. "And the majority of the old people in Manhattan are safe."

"For the moment," I teased, brushing another kiss to her temple.

"It always stuns me that you can joke about this stuff."

"Prefer me to cry?"

"No. But, how come you don't want Dagda to atone too?"

"Are you pouting?" I snorted at the mention of the fucker who was simultaneously the man who'd killed my father and Aidan's new deputy in the ECD. "It's not like he's in Aruba, Star. He's based in a country where it is always raining. A perpetual storm cloud over his head can be my retribution."

"Some people enjoy the rain."

"It isn't a tropical island. It's *Ireland.*"

"Blasphemy."

My lips twitched. "I suppose. If you're Irish. Which neither of us is."

That stunned a chuckle out of her and had her pulling away from my hold. "Your da just turned in his grave."

"That he did." I settled my chin on her shoulder. "I miss Da but I know that he was sick, and he'd have been a terrible patient. I find comfort in that. Plus, Dagda is at our beck and call. It's not a small thing to have a man of his skills on our payroll. It gives Eoghan some slack too."

"Not tonight."

"Nope. Not tonight."

I pressed a hand to her belly and encouraged her to lean her weight on me once again. "I love you."

She sighed. "I don't deserve you."

"At least you know that."

Her snicker made me grin. "Charming."

"I keep it real, Star. That's my job in your life."

"Oh, *that's* your job."

"Uh huh. It's why you want me to stick around until we're worm food."

She clicked her fingers. "You caught me—"

"Star! Conor!"

Anton's voice acted like a bath in liquid nitrogen as it came from about forty feet across the room. The tension infected her limbs until she was frozen solid. At least, it felt that way. From the outside looking in, she didn't react.

At all.

Then—

"Oh, God," she choked out.

"What is it?"

"That…" Her spine straightened. "When I first saw the picture of him that Bear had put in his motel room for me to find, I thought I recognized him."

"What?" I muttered, whispering the words in her ear. "You recognized Anton? From where?"

"I didn't know. And when I saw him at his place in Moscow, he didn't register so I reckoned I was mistaken." She swallowed. "But I saw him. At a party I attended with Hans."

I stiffened. "Are you shitting me?"

"I'm not. I wish I were." She gulped. "He was wearing that same red velvet smoking jacket. Fuck, he's—"

"Anton," I greeted as he neared, knowing I had to give her time to compose herself. "How are you? How is everything?"

Anton, unaware that Star's silence was loaded, discussed how his stay in New York had passed and what he'd done during the days he'd whiled away with Lyra. "I just wish," he finished, "that I'd been able to spend some time with you, Star. I'd like to meet Kat before I have to leave."

"It's been..." She swallowed. "...*busy*. You know, what with the gala... Thank you for your donation."

With every word she uttered, I felt her mask solidify until her speech had returned to its regular cadence and her expression was relaxed.

The only person who'd be able to tell a difference was me because she was like a block of ice in my arms.

To compound matters, Anton leaned into her and pressed a kiss to her cheek. Thankfully, her mask was so in place that she didn't even flinch.

Her innate strength would never fail to astonish me.

"Of course," Anton drawled. "It's a worthy cause."

My hand tightened on her hip.

Worthy cause, my ass.

"I see you fought and won to keep from having ice sculptures at the gala," Anton quipped, his tone amused.

"Do you know the carbon footprint of those things?" She tutted. "I don't know what Rachel was thinking."

"I'm assuming the foliage was your idea?" he queried, peering at a massive bush of basil that had been pruned into the shape of a spade—the card variety, not the garden implement—and which had the same frosting as the other bushes.

"It was. It ties in with the food. I thought it was clever."

Anton hummed. "You'll never be a party planner, dear, but that's not what you are, is it? Your talents lie elsewhere."

Star's smile was lazy and disconcertingly authentic. "I don't know. I might consider a career change."

"Please, don't," I joked around a fake laugh. "You've been a stressy pain in the ass in the run-up to this party."

Anton chuckled. "Your mother was just the same. Hated dressing the part."

At this, Star's mask showed the first signs of crumbling.

I could literally feel her longing for more information about her mother. Knew that she wanted it desperately.

Scraps…

That was all she had left of the woman who'd brought her into this world.

Because of *this* man.

The one who could dole them out and who was the reason for them.

"She did?" Star questioned, her tone shaky.

Anton's smile seemed sincere, but hell, he'd fooled me since the start. I wasn't about to trust my judgment. "She loathed parties. Preferred guarding the events rather than attending. Aleks was far more sociable. He was the one who smoothed the path for me, while Galena protected it."

Star swallowed. "I wish I'd gotten the chance to know her better. The real her."

"I doubt she played a role with you, child," Anton demurred.

"She was the life and soul of every party we ever attended as a family," Star admitted, tone raw.

I beckoned over a server and reached for a champagne glass. Passing it to her, I watched as she took a deep swig then snagged one for myself. Anton did the same, slowly sipping his as he mused, "People change, Star."

"Not *that* much," she snapped before sucking in a deep breath. "It doesn't matter."

"Of course it does. I wish you'd had more time with her too," Anton countered, taking a long sip of his champagne. His nose wrinkled when he reached the base. "You should have told me the vintages you'd be serving would be swill, Star. I'd have donated better wines to the event."

She hitched a shoulder. "It's organic."

Warily eyeing the flute, Anton snorted. "Of course it is. Everything is organic or vegetarian nowadays. No wonder nothing tastes as it once did." He released a soft chuckle. "Since Chernobyl, all wine has radioactive matter in it, did you know that? They say it doesn't affect the taste, but I say they don't have a wine cellar that isn't tainted."

I lived like Bruce Wayne without the Batman sideline so I wasn't exactly 'in touch,' but Jesus wept, in that one statement alone, he proved he was so out of touch he might as well have lived in the Antarctic.

"Tell me about her?" Star rasped, entirely uninterested in his snobbish tastes in wine and more focused on her mother.

"Now?"

"Yes. It's not as if this event is more entertaining than anything you could have to say." She peered at me. "It's okay if you want to mingle."

Tenderly, I chucked her under the chin while my fingers on her hips squeezed her there. Twice. "I think I can cope with not having to talk to people I'm not interested in. Anyway, I'd like to learn more about your mother too."

Anton shrugged. "For all that Galena loathed parties, she was a social creature. Plenty of friends as she was growing up."

"Are they still alive?"

He frowned. "I assume so. If they haven't perished from illness. There's a room in the house in Uvala Lapad that contains all Galena's personal effects."

She jerked like she'd been hit with a bullet. "Why didn't you show me?"

"Our last interaction there involved you stabbing me in the hand with a dinner fork, Star. I wasn't entirely sure if you'd maintain our bargain or not.

"That room is a private sanctuary of mine. Aleks' too. I wasn't going to share it with someone who could have betrayed me."

"I can understand that." She pursed her lips. "What's in the room?"

"Mostly her childhood things. Before she left for the US and to…"

"Con my father into falling in love with her?"

Anton reached for a handkerchief in his pocket and began dabbing his top lip. "Yes, I suppose. Your candidness will never cease surprising me, child.

"Regardless, she moved the furnishings of her apartment into one of my properties. Since her death, I brought her things with me to whichever home became my main address."

"Aleks' too?"

"Yes. Unofficial shrines, I suppose. It's the Orthodox Russian in me. Even if I haven't practiced for many years." He tilted his head to the side. "Is it hot in here?"

"No. I told them specifically to maintain a seventy-two-degree temperature."

"Why?" I asked. "Or is this because of Kat's global warming presentation too?"

"Global warming presentation?" Anton choked out a laugh. "Is this why you disagreed with the ice sculptures?"

"There is no planet B," Star said simply. "I'd like her not to have to live under a dome or to have to relocate to a colony on Mars."

Anton patted his forehead. "You know I agree with you, but at least she'll have the funds with which to make such costly endeavors. She's still Belyaev's heir. I'm sure that as much as the man favored male children, he'd have left her well cared for."

"I never thought of that. She costs me a fortune in broken laptops. She needs to start paying her way."

"I know you're intent on bankrupting yourself with funding the foundation but I think we can afford more computers," I teased.

"Not with the bill for that private school we just got," she mocked.

Anton's chuckle was weak as he slurred, "I'm certain it's—" The sibilant hiss was extended until he stuttered, "—h-hot in here."

"Honestly, it isn't. I'm actually cold," I answered.

"Don't be a wimp. Anton's probably hot because he's Russian. They have baths in ice water lakes."

"They also drink a lot of vodka before, during, and after said soak," I argued. "Isn't that right, Anton?"

But Anton wasn't listening.

He staggered back, his hip bumping into the table beside him.

"Anton?" Star cried, leaping forward to grab his arms and prop him up. "Are you okay?"

"Call—" He sucked in a sharp breath but his head rolled on his neck before he could finish the sentence.

There were a few shrieks from the women around us who witnessed Anton's collapse, but with my aid, Star propped him upright, and once I'd looped his arm around my shoulder and she'd huddled into his waist, together, we retreated from the event hall.

Along the way, I saw Aidan watching us.

He tipped his glass at me.

STAR

WON'T - TANERÉLLE

Star Sullivan

THE SETUP WASN'T primitive by any stretch of the imagination, but when Anton's eyes slowly blinked open and he looked around the hospital room, I knew he'd be aware that something was 'up.'

A man like him used private hospitals that made the Plaza seem inelegant.

Still dressed in my gown, I stood. "He's awake, Conor."

The hum of his fingers on his keyboard ceased. "Good. That's a relief."

It wasn't a lie.

There was no antidote for tetrodotoxin, but if treated swiftly enough, survival wasn't unusual.

Not that I intended for him to survive.

Straightening, I perched on the side of his bed and reached for his hand. "The interesting thing about tetrodotoxin, Anton, is that a fatal dose can trigger symptoms in under twenty minutes. Not that your dose was wholly fatal.

"Why would I deny myself the pleasure of ending your sorry life?"

His blurry eyes flared wide at that, jerking from left to right, and his hands clutched at the sheets, but there was no moving when the breathing tube that was keeping his airways open pinned him in place.

That was the only flaw in my plan.

To keep him alive, he needed the breathing tube.

And, that tube stopped him from talking when what I wanted more than his death were his final words.

"Are you looking for your guards, Anton?" I chuckled. "The Five Points took care of them for me."

"The least we could do to help such a… *worthy cause*," Conor quipped.

"I suppose you're wondering why you're here." My lips tightened. "I don't think I'll ever know what you did to my mother. There's so much bullshit surrounding her life and death that I can't see the forest for the trees.

"Maybe you don't even remember anymore. Maybe she mattered so little to you that you filed it as 'unimportant' in your head, but I set myself on this journey for her.

"Along the way, my resolve and belief in her faltered. However, that doesn't change my origin story, as it were.

"Back then, I was young and foolish. I thought that following in her footsteps would give me answers, but I should have realized how idiotic that was." Though I chuckled, it was sad. "There's an irony to the fact that the one man who could give me those answers is the one I'm killing, but you see, my need for resolution can't supersede the need this world has for you to die."

Though his head flopped from side to side, I could see the awareness in his eyes—this was it.

The end.

Just… not yet.

Perching beside him, I reached down and stroked a finger over the many, many scars on his chest. "I don't suppose you'd have long left anyway. Not just because you're almost ninety, but organ donations are never quite as good as the real thing.

"Not that these organs *were* donated, were they? Not freely." I trailed a hand over his arm. "What even is there to transplant here? A new carpal tunnel?" I hummed when I saw the question in his eyes.

"Yeah, I figured out what the Brotherhood is. The other side of the same coin.

"The Brotherhood and the Sparrows *are* Janus, aren't they? The god with two faces. The god of beginnings and endings." I smiled at him and it was genuine and wide and loaded with my happiness as I stated, "I can't wait to disband the Brotherhood, Anton. I can't wait to tear down the thing you've spent your lifetime cultivating. I can't wait for the Kuznetsov legacy to die out."

His fingers twitched and I translated that faint movement with ease.

"I'm not a Kuznetsov," I said with a chuckle. "I'm a Sullivan. I'm a Daniels. I'm a *noxxious* brat because they're my family. *You* are not. *You,* in fact, are nothing. The moment I cremate your body is the moment I'll eradicate you and everything you stand for." I patted his cheek. "Brick by brick, I'll demolish the Brotherhood, just like we did the Sparrows, but I won't let them know your name. You won't even have infamy. You'll just be a shadow, much as you've always been.

"Still, maybe there's one consolation, Anton," I reasoned as I stood. "Maybe I have the heart of a Kuznetsov. You made me into this, after all. You fabricated the person standing here.

"I quite enjoy the symmetry of you beginning my journey and me ending yours. And why would I just switch off your breathing tube when this is so much more befitting a man of your history?" With that, I slipped my hands around his throat and whispered, "Do you see your death in my eyes? Eyes that I inherited from you?" My grip tightened. "You won't hurt another soul, Anton. That'll be my legacy.

"Yours is one of blood and pain and misery and horror. You're a warmonger. You made me into that too but I'm choosing peace." My hands squeezed harder. *Harder.* "Funny how peace comes with the price of murder."

As I choked the life out of him, as I watched it drain from his bulging eyes, as his skin turned purple and blood vessels burst, as the machine started to beep, as the alarms sounded, no one came running.

Why would they?

He'd only survived so I could kill him with my bare hands.

These last, final moments were unnecessary. A waste of medication. A waste of an emergency team's time. But they weren't a waste to me.

This, after all, was the only closure I'd *ever* get.

As he took his final breath, I sucked down the deepest inhalation I'd experienced in over a decade.

Abruptly, the alarms disengaged and the machines stopped their functions.

Conor moved behind me, his hands settling on my wrists as he carefully pried mine away from my grandfather's throat, informing me, "Everything's ready for the next phase."

I blinked and allowed my arms to relax as he shuffled me away from the corpse. Then, he tugged me into him, holding me in a tight embrace that I didn't know, until he graced me with it, was the only thing likely to keep me together.

"He needed to die, Star," he whispered in my ear. "We'll find the answers you need some other way, hmm?"

My fingers tightened around nothing, then as I clutched at him, I rasped, "He'll be the last person I ever kill, Conor, with these hands."

"If you say so," he appeased, his tone soothing.

"I do."

He hummed. "Are you ready? They're waiting."

For a moment, I felt lightheaded. That was when I realized I was holding my breath. "Can I do this?"

"Of course, you can." He chuckled. "There isn't a doubt in my mind that you're the one person who *could* handle this."

My fingers reached for his and I knotted them together. "No. *We* will handle this."

"Together," he said with no small amount of satisfaction.

"Together," I repeated before I bolstered myself and studied Anton's still form. "You turned off the alarms?"

"I did." He sighed. "You know, when Da died, it was surreal to think this powerhouse, whether it was for good or bad, was gone. All that insanity housed within a skin suit."

I coughed out a hoarse laugh. "That's one way of thinking about it."

"You can mourn what should have been," he whispered in my ear.

"Do you?"

"No matter what I thought of Da, there was no denying that I never could have told him about Father McKenna. He'd never have believed me. Not back then. I don't think he'd have believed me *now*. He betrayed me a long time ago in that sense. Didn't mean I didn't love him."

"I don't love Anton," I croaked.

"Maybe you loved the idea of him. He was your grandfather."

"He made Hitler look warm and cuddly, Conor." I tipped up my chin. "I spent ninety-nine percent of my life without a grandfather. I'll survive. Anyway, I'm ready."

Though he nodded, I heard him sigh again.

Together, we left Anton's bedside and moved over to the workstation he'd set up.

Within the same mall that they'd used as a hospital black site for Dagda, it was impossible to tell if it was day or night. Only when I saw the monitor did I realize how long we'd been here.

"I'm lucky you spoil me," I said flatly.

"Spoil you?"

I peered at him. "Black-site hospitals for dying men don't come cheap."

"It was cheap at the price. Closure is expensive."

That had me swallowing. "I wish you'd gotten that."

"Me too."

"I wish I hadn't hurt you."

"Me too," he repeated. "But there's going to be a long time between now and us being worm food, and the truth is, Star, no one on this planet can make me happy like you can. You're as unique as the entity you're named after.

"The things you've done aren't ideal, much as there are things I've done that aren't ideal either, but we see past that. You are who I love. Who I want to be with. Who I want by my side. That's more than enough—it's fucking everything."

His words had a small shiver rushing down my spine. "I used to have a mantra."

"'I will not bend. I will not break,'" he quoted back at me. "I know. You whisper it in your sleep."

"I do?"

"Uh huh. You don't have any secrets from me, Star," he teased.

"I'm glad," I told him, meaning it. "I-I think it's time for a new one though."

"Hmm?" The look he shot me was quizzical. "A new mantra?"

"Teamwork makes the dream work."

His laughter had me hiding a smile. "I like that one."

"Thought you might." I turned into him. "I'm not great with words, not like you. I-I can't say s-such lovely things. I don't have it in me. But what I can say is that you are my person, Conor." I stared straight at him. "You make me want to be someone who is deserving of you. You make me want to be happy. You make me want peace. *You*. Not Kat, not Vana. You. I want to live, Conor," I rasped, aware that tears were flooding my eyes. "I want to live with *you*. Can we do that? Can we live?"

His smile was gentle as he cupped my cheek. "I can't wait. We've got a lot to do, Star. We've got a lot of life to live. You sure you're ready for that?"

"'I was born ready.'"

"You know what? I think you were."

He smirked and united our mouths in a soft, tender kiss that had me closing my eyes with how perfect it was.

How perfect *he* was.

Those impossible-to-explain citrus notes that always reminded me of him surrounded me, drowning me in his scent. As I sucked it down, breathed him in, and found comfort in his arms, I forgot for a moment what was about to happen.

That was the power of this man.

"Does this mean I've earned atonement?" I whispered, staring into his eyes and drowning in them.

"You have." He smiled before gracing me with another gentle kiss.

"Now, as the woman who chopped off the head of the snake that eats itself," he rumbled against my lips, "your work today is *not* done. You've still got some Is to dot and Ts to cross...

"No matter how long that takes, we handle this together, and in between, we can still live, baby. We can still have more than we had yesterday."

With a shaky nod, believing in him, I stared at him and put on the mask I never needed to use when we were alone.

He chucked me under the chin and surprised me by gently pressing down on the wings of my phoenix tattoo that peeped out from beneath my sweetheart neckline. "Hello, Lodestar."

"Hello, aCoooooig," I greeted before I turned to the monitor and took a seat in front of it.

There, waiting for me on mute, were the faces of the Interpol team who I'd used to bring down the Sparrows.

Goldstein, Hoyt, as well as Ingridsdottir, Schmidt, and Deschamps.

Hoyt, as always, was scowling. "Why were we commanded to attend this meeting?"

Calmly, I studied her. "In our Brothers we trust."

Her eyes widened then she, Ingridsdottir, and Deschamps replied, "In our Brothers we trust."

The second the last word drifted from their lips, Goldstein demanded, "What the hell?" Then, his features pinched as red blossomed on each of the Brothers' foreheads, then their skulls fractured, blood spurting where a sniper's bullet blew their brains out.

"WHAT THE FUCK?!" Schmidt screamed as the other top members of the squad collapsed, some falling forward, others backward.

"Conor," Goldstein snarled, jerking to his feet. "You—"

"The New World Sparrows," I stated, speaking over him, "and the United Brotherhood were the two faces of the same coin, Aaron.

"Anton, with the dismantling of the Sparrows, became the head of that unified group, but tonight, he suffered a heart attack. *I* am the new leader, and together, we're going to disassemble the power source, much as we have with the Sparrows."

His mouth gaped like a goldfish. "Y-You, what? I don't… Conor?"

Conor, as calm as I, rested a hand on my shoulder. "She's right, Goldstein. The Sparrows are choir boys in comparison to the Brotherhood."

"You want to take them down?" Schmidt rasped.

"I do. I want their bones dusting the floor. I want their blood shed and their asses rotting in jail cells. We're not going to stop until their networks are infiltrated and infected and infested until they're no more. Do you understand?

"As of now, you are the two members of the team who we officially know are not Brothers.

"Interpol is riddled with Brothers so we'll keep Anton's passing a secret, but I expect you to uncover the parasites in your department.

"Anton hand-picked you all, and though I investigated each and every one of you, Hoyt, Ingridsdottir, and Deschamps were squeaky clean on paper. The only way to uncover them is to use that motto."

Though his features were still pinched and pale, Goldstein frowned. "We'll burn that route quickly."

"Then we burn it quickly. We just need to figure out who's who in the team. Fast."

"You can't kill them all," he argued, terror leaching into his expression.

"This is a cull," I said quietly. "We will do what needs to be done to eradicate this threat to our society. Do you understand, Aaron?"

He swallowed. "Is there a sniper on me?"

"Yes. Schmidt, too."

"If you're going to purge Interpol, what makes you any better than the Sparrows or this Brotherhood?"

I smiled at him. "I never promised to be better than them. But I *am* promising to do what needs to be done to make our world a better place.

"The Brothers were into child trafficking, Aaron. Organ harvesting. That's the tip of the iceberg. I've got thousands of terabytes of information, some paper files too, on exactly what they've done and are involved in.

"I know Conor picked you because you have an unusual sense of justice—"

"It still ends with the bad guys rotting in prison. Not an early grave."

"It does, and we share that desire, but this is a unique circumstance. You can be the face of this investigation, Aaron. You can be the one who is celebrated as taking down these monsters. You can be the next secretary general of Interpol if you so choose—"

"Or, like Hoyt, Deschamps, and Ingridsdottir, I can die?" His demand was bitter.

I shrugged but before I could answer, "I'll do it," Schmidt interrupted. "I'll be the face—"

"Fuck off," Goldstein snarled. "I'm your superior."

"If he's willing to do what needs to be done, he can be the last man standing in your team," was my simple retort.

Goldstein's nostrils flared. "How are you going to cover up their deaths?"

"I blame the Sparrows, of course."

"You're just as corrupt—"

"'An ideal form of government is democracy tempered with assassination.'" When that Mark Twain quote went over his head, I sighed. "You're mistaking me for someone who claimed to be *good*, Aaron," I sniped, my patience broken at long last. "I'm not a white hat. I'll never be entirely clean. I'll always exist in the shadows."

"Because that's what it takes," Conor interrupted, his palm settling on my shoulder. "You can't bring these bastards down by riding in on a white horse, sword in one hand, shield in the other, Goldstein.

"If you ever want our world to be less corrupt, then you're going to have to get your hands dirty like the rest of us."

He swallowed, but I knew that he saw the truth of Conor's words in the resignation in his expression. "What's our first move?"

I smiled at him. "Good decision. Smart."

And that was when I underlined the words 'The End' on this part of my life.

Some endings were beginnings, after all.

One lay on the bed to our left; one sat on the monitor in front of us.

It was fitting, however, that Conor was at my back.

That was where he'd always be.

God, how I loved him.

How blessed I was to have him.

My man. My love.

My everything.

72

TEXT CHAT

GRAIL

21:34 Bitter grapes served

ACOOOOOIG

04:44 Target eliminated

THE WHISTLER

04:54 Target eliminated

DEAD TO ME

04:54 Target eliminated

EAGLE EYES

04:54 Target eliminated

DAGDA

05:14 Target secured

TROY

05:14 Target secured

LODESTAR

05:15 Mission complete

PART 5

Maybe it's time for the fighter to be fought for, for
the holder to be held, and for the lover to be loved.
- Madalina

ACUIG CORP. PURCHASES NEW YORK
LIBERTIES AND ANNOUNCES THE NHL
TEAM WILL NOW BE KNOWN AS THE
NEW YORK STARS.

73

STAR

I WANT IT ALL - CAMERON GRAY

Star Sullivan

SEVERAL MONTHS LATER

UPSTATE, NEW YORK

"FUCK," he rasped in my ear as I rode him.

His hands dug into my ass as he helped me maintain the pace which had started to falter as my orgasm approached.

"You going to come for me, Star?"

I whimpered.

"You are, aren't you? I want to feel you come around my cock, my naughty girl."

I shuddered.

"Give it to me," he demanded, one of his hands sliding around to thumb my slit from behind.

"Oh, Christ," I rasped, surprised by how good that extra pressure felt.

Jerking upright, I slapped my hands on his chest.

My head tipped back as I allowed the sensations to flood me, shutting out the world to focus on the here and the now.

The new position let me grind down on my clit, and each and every time, I got smacked in the face with just how damn good this felt.

That was when I—

God.

Slightly cool.

Silicone.

My head flipped forward in response, but it was too late.

That goddamn toy was on my clit already.

My eyes closed in response as the vibrations sizzled through my system.

"God, your pussy clamps down around me so fucking beautifully when I tease you with this, baby. You like that, huh?"

"Too... much," I croaked out, but I didn't move away from the vibe, nor did I slap his hand aside.

Instead, I hovered there, just waiting, waiting. Enjoying. Suffering. Needing...

When he twisted us around so I was on my back, I didn't argue. I didn't have the words to argue.

I just lay there, feeling him start to thrust into me as the vibrator worked its magic.

My eyes popped open the first time he hit home.

"God, Conor, my... I... You—"

"I know, naughty girl. It's too good," he teased, licking my earlobe before sucking on it.

I shivered at the move.

He pulled the vibrator away.

I glowered at him. "What are you doing?"

"If it's too much then—"

Huffing, I snagged the damn thing from his grasp and muttered, "You just go back to doing what you're doing and leave this to me."

"It's enough to emasculate a man."

I sniffed. "There's no fun in using this alone. Now, get busy."

Though he chuckled, he complied. I shuddered as he retreated then fucked hard into me.

The growl that escaped me was pure hunger.

Goddamn, that felt good.

I'd tried the toy without him there but it wasn't as much fun as having him fill me. But with a face, a body, and a cock like Conor's, why would it be better without him in the freakin' room?

As he sped up, the vibrations worked their torturous magic and I came around him, clutching at his shaft, back arching, offering myself up to him on the altar of release.

When he tugged on one of my nipples, I released a hissed breath. "F-Fuck, Conor—"

"You like that, huh, baby?" he grated out.

"I do. Christ, I do." My feet moved higher on his body so I could dig my heels into his ass.

As he pumped faster into me, I could feel how close he was. Moving the vibrator so that it was rubbing against the side of his shaft, I wasn't surprised when, barely a few seconds later, he was coming, his head tipped back, throat corded with the strain that came with orgasms.

Pulling the toy away, I switched it off and tossed it on the bed.

Only our heavy breathing dulled the silence of our room, then he collapsed on me and twisted us over again. When he tucked me inside the sheet, I didn't bother moving.

"We have to get up soon."

"Not yet," he complained.

I peered at the clock on the nightstand. "In a half hour."

He groaned. "Why was this a good idea again?"

"Because Troy wanted to throw Lyra a pool party for her birthday and she hasn't made any friends in school apart from Kat yet. So, where better than here?"

Here was Aidan's estate upstate.

"Plus, Savannah loves her."

"I know. I listened to them talk about Enid Blyton last night. It was… disturbing."

"Why was it?" I asked, amused.

"Because Lyra was talking and Savannah knew way too much about kids' books."

I snorted but said, "I'm glad Liam made it."

"I'm surprised. Didn't think he would. He's still pissed about the trade."

"Not sure how he can be pissed when his new team outplays the old team. Men are so irrational."

"I hope you're not including me in that."

"You're many things, sweetheart, but irrational ain't one of them."

"Now it's my turn to have heartburn."

For a second, I just blinked at him. Then I realized what he meant. "Huh."

"Huh?"

I smiled. "I've gotten used to the heartburn."

"Is that good or bad?"

"Good. When you say that sweet shit, it doesn't feel weird in my chest anymore. It's just… my new normal."

His grin wasn't cocky, not like it could have been. Instead, it was warm. Heartfelt. Fuck, it went deeper than that.

It was *home*.

He was home.

The last couple months since Anton's death had been a race against time to clear out the Brothers in Interpol.

In that time, we'd grown closer than ever. I mean, it wasn't as if I hadn't recognized that. But it was only now that I felt it. Deep in my fucking bones.

Leaning down to press a kiss to his lips, I whispered, "I love you, Conor."

"I never get tired of hearing that," he mumbled. "I love you too, baby."

Closing my eyes, I pushed my face into his throat, enjoying how, in his arms, I was allowed to be me. Not the hacker, or the spy, or the soldier. Just me. I could be weak. I could be vulnerable. I could even be fragile.

He accepted every inch of me.

Squeezing him, I muttered, "I think we should stay here all day."

"Tough. You dragged my ass up here so we're going to have fun."

"And you say *I'm* the contrary one."

He slapped my butt. "Imagine what Lyra would think if you didn't show your face, hmm?"

I grimaced. "Good point. She's only just started to look brighter, hasn't she?"

"I think Anton made more of an impact than we anticipated."

"I wish I'd known. I'd never have introduced them if I had even a hint…" Regret settled heavily in my soul for that miscalculation.

"Don't beat yourself up over this, Star. The bastard would have died sooner or later."

With a final squeeze, I clambered off him and then stood beside the bed. Grabbing his hand and knotting our fingers together, I asked, "Shower?"

"How could I refuse an invitation like that?"

An hour later, I retreated to the kitchen and found Aoife organizing things with the expertise of a general in the middle of a siege.

Moving toward one of the three islands in the kitchen, I stood there and muttered, "It's disturbing how good you are at this."

She arched a brow at me. "Disturbing good seeing as I'm arranging all this and you didn't need to talk to a stranger to get it done?"

"That is very sound logic. Disturbing *great*. I need to get you a gift. What do you want?"

"You already gave me a gift."

"I did?" My brow furrowed. "Oh. Dagda."

"Yes, the fact he's still alive," she drawled as she iced Lyra's birthday cake. "And… Dad."

I hummed. "I didn't know if he was going to step down. I've cursed him a couple times—"

"A day. For the past six months," Conor tacked on as he drifted into the kitchen, squeezing my waist with one hand before heading for the fridge.

Along the way, he kissed Aoife on the cheek then withdrew a bottle of juice which he tossed at me.

"You make me sound obsessive," I teased.

He winked at me as he got some water for himself. "Nah. That's not possible."

Whistling as he left the kitchen, I watched him go, muttering under my breath, "It's not fair to be that hot all the time."

Aoife snorted. "I'd like to tell you that you get used to it, but you don't."

"What? Them being hot?"

She nodded then glanced at our sister-in-law who'd just shown up. "Camille, am I right?"

Camille patted down her hair. "Excuse me?"

Aoife stared at her knowingly. "You don't get used to them being hot."

"I'd say your agreement is non-verbal from the state of your lipstick," I joked.

Her eyes flared wide before she walked over to the stove, grabbed one of the copper pots dangling from above it, and stared at her mouth in the reflection. She shot me a glower. "There's nothing wrong with my lipstick."

I smirked. "Made you look."

She huffed but began patting her hair again. "And no, you don't get used to them being hot." She licked her lips. "Or the things they do."

"Fan Camille down, Aoife. She's overheated."

Aoife chuckled. "Leave her alone. She's young and in love."

"And we aren't?"

"We're in love but we're not young."

"That makes me feel ancient. I'm like eight years older than you."

She just snorted as she finished doing some special icing thing that made the frosting look like roses for Lyra's *Beauty and the Beast*-themed cake.

"You spoke to him?"

"Who?" Aoife inquired.

"Your dad. Duh."

Camille stopped patting her hair to study Aoife who just shrugged. "Once or twice."

"You didn't know he was going to step down?"

"No. Found out with everyone else on CNN yesterday," she drawled, but the lack of hurt was feigned.

Davidson was fucked up.

"You know, when I spoke with him, he cared, Aoife," I said gingerly.

That made her sniff her disdain. "He cares about the wrong things. That's always been his problem."

Camille and I shared a glance, then Camille teased, "Aoife, is that a hickey I see?"

My lips twitched as Aoife blushed. "No."

"Yes, it is. And you tried to use concealer. How sweet."

"Mostly because I knew you'd give me crap for it," she groused.

"I'm technically giving you crap for the concealer, not the hickey." She sighed dreamily. "I love it when Brennan leaves love bites on me."

"I'm going before I vomit in my mouth," I declared, disappearing with the juice bottle in my hand, leaving those two to cackle like hens in the kitchen.

As I stepped toward the patio, I found Brennan staring onto the pool.

Though Eoghan and I shared a similar history, I found myself gravitating to Brennan at these types of events.

I figured it was because he was a grump 365 days a year and I could respect that level of consistency. In turn, I thought he respected my appreciation of his grouchiness.

Over the last half-year, and with so many of these fucking family events that they celebrated almost every goddamn week, we'd grown closer.

As close as two miseries could grow, at any rate.

"I'd offer you some juice but I don't know where your mouth's been."

He smirked at me. "Exactly where it's supposed to have been."

"But did you wash it afterward? That's the real question."

He just arched a brow at me.

"Gross. You can't do that when you have kids," I pointed out.

His brows arched higher. "Why the hell not?"

"You're seriously asking me why you can't walk around with your wife's pussy juice on your face when there are little people in the vicinity?"

"People have sex after they have kids. Which we're not having yet, by the way."

Was it just me or did he sound grumpier about that than usual?

"They have sex, but they clean up too. Clean up, locked doors, and music. Or the sprogs think you're crying."

"That sounds like the voice of experience talking."

"It is. I had Jake and Kat thinking Conor made me cry for weeks after the fact."

He rolled his eyes. "Conor told me Kat asked him if she can be an O'Donnelly."

I grinned. "He's proud."

"He is." He grabbed the OJ bottle from my grip and poured it into his mouth from a height. "There, so I don't offend your sensibilities," he mocked once he'd swallowed.

I sniffed.

"I'm surprised she didn't ask to be a Sullivan."

"Why would she when she knows I'll be an O'Donnelly eventually?"

"You're not stringing him along?"

I groaned. "We're not back to you being protective, are we?"

"I'm just watching out for my kid brother," he retorted, giving me the side-eye.

"Why would I be stringing him along?"

"Because he's helping you with your 'mission.'"

This time, it was *me* giving *him* the side-eye, and mine was loaded with stink. "You're not ruining my day, Brennan O'Donnelly. I just realized that your brother stopped giving me heartburn and I'm not letting you spoil my epiphany."

"Heartburn?" he repeated, his brow puckering. "He gave you heartburn?"

I wafted a hand. "Never mind."

"Hell, no. I'm curious now. Why does he give you heartburn?"

"I said he'd *stopped* giving it to me."

"Why did he give it to you in the first place?"

"Because he always knows how to say the right thing and it's so beautiful it hurts. But I've gotten used to it. So now there's no hurt, just…" I mumbled into the bottle. "…good feelings."

"Good feelings. Damn, Kid must have some patience."

"Why must I?"

I twisted around and found Conor standing in the doorway. He must have gone back to the kitchen because he had two croissants in his hand. As he strolled over to me, I wasn't surprised that one had ham and cheese in it—my preference.

"Because she's a piece of work, that's why."

"Your brother is wearing Eau de Camille," I countered.

Conor's nose crinkled. "Jesus, Brennan, there are kids around."

"So? They don't come near me."

"That's because you frighten them all away," I retorted.

Brennan snickered. "You say that as if it's a bad thing. I'll like children that come out of Camille. That's it. The rest, I'll tolerate."

"You can't just tolerate your nieces and nephews," Conor pointed out.

"I'll go to war for them, but I don't have to like them," Brennan argued. "And you can't make me change my mind about that."

Conor shook his head. "You gonna kiss your mother with that mouth? Ma just arrived with Paddy."

He cursed under his breath but scurried off to clean up.

"Momma's boy," I called out, earning myself the bird he flipped my way.

Conor curved his arm around my shoulder. "Did he give you a rough time?"

"No more than usual."

"I don't know why you seek him out."

"I like him."

"I don't get it. I like him but I have to."

"You don't have to."

"I do. He's Brennan."

"There's no logic there."

He shrugged. "Brennan would help me when I had nightmares. He'd take a beating from Da so I didn't get into trouble. He'd kill someone for me if I asked. So yeah, I have to."

"Which is why I like him. Because even without *knowing* that, my gut clued me in. He gives me a hard time because he loves you. He's just fucking bad at showing it."

Conor's grin was lopsided. "He is, isn't he?"

We shared that grin before we turned our attention back to the pool.

Lyra was sitting under a parasol, patiently allowing Troy to apply sunscreen while Kat sneaked behind her and dive-bombed into the water, soaking them both through.

"Goddammit, Katina!" she yelled as she spun around to glower at my daughter. "How many times do I have to tell you? Lyra burns—"

Lyra didn't hang around. She dive-bombed into the pool too and landed a few feet away from Kat.

Troy somehow managed to spot me through the window and, glowering, she raised a hand, pointed two fingers at her eyes, then pointed them at me.

"Did she just do that?"

I snorted. "She thinks she's De Niro."

"She's scarier than him in *Taxi Driver*."

"Give her a mohawk and sure, I can see it."

"Your daughter's a menace," Savannah declared as she stepped into the room from the French doors that led onto the pool area.

"Of course she is. She's mine."

"You always know how to make an entrance, Savvie," Conor praised affectionately.

Dressed in a cotton cape and wearing a massive sun hat, big shades, and a bright-blue bikini, Vana was definitely dramatically attired.

"She got my hat wet. I was more impressive without the floppy hat."

I rolled my eyes. "I'll buy you a new one."

"That's hardly the point." She strode over to the pair of us. "Lyra's a sweetheart."

"In comparison to my menace?"

"You said it. Not me. Did you hear about that brothel in Queens that got raided—"

"Oh, no," Conor argued. "No shop talk. We're allowed two days off, Savannah!"

She sniffed. "The news cycle stops for no man. You two are boring."

"Aoife's in the kitchen. She'll listen to you," I called after her, smirking as she unknowingly mimicked Brennan and flipped me the bird from behind.

"I'm glad the brothel got shut down."

"Me too." I looked at him. "You found it."

"You got it shut down."

Together, we grinned. "Teamwork makes the dream work."

HOMEGROWN BRAND SET TO BECOME HOUSEHOLD NAME

ELLIE'S BAKERY becomes the fastest-growing chain in the food industry with the acquisition of fifty new storefronts in the tristate area to open in the next year.

Several more restaurants are planned along the East Coast.

Ellie's Bakery, which has experienced shocking growth thanks to multiple viral blogs and videos about their infamous brownies, is looking set to become a household name.

74

TEXT CHAT

Conor: The parameters of the bet have shifted.

Star: Which bet?

Conor: THE bet.

Star: Narrow it down.

Conor: The 'Kat'll be a cheerleader' bet.

Star: Ah, fuck.

Conor: She got the offer.

Star: And?

Conor: She didn't turn it down.

Star: FUCK.

Conor: Ha. HA! Validation is mine. Vindication too.

Star: Pfft. So, what? I won't bust your code for a year. Big deal. *sniffs*

Conor: Nah, I've changed the parameters of the bet, remember?

Star: You can't do that!

Conor: Sure, I can. You'll like this one. You can ram through my code whenever you want so long as, when it snows, it's your turn to do a snow angel.

Star: That's it?

Conor: Nope.

Star: Wait…

Star: You don't mean…

Conor: I do. I really fucking do.

Conor: Naked snow angel time! And I'm taking pictures.

Star: Double fuck! This is the better deal and it STILL sucks.

Conor: *blows kiss*

Star: Fuck off.

Conor: ;)

Star: You suck!

Conor: I'll lick later.

Star: Gah. Go away. I'm going to crack that prediction software you're working on.

Conor: Lol. Please do. You might make it work. ;)

EX-CIA DIRECTOR REVEALED TO BE ONE-TIME LEADER OF NWS

SHERIDAN REINIER MIGHT STILL BE MISSING, but his legacy remains as fresh as ever.

Interpol's Special Trafficking Unit has revealed that a secret Floridian estate housed thousands of terabytes of data regarding New World Sparrow activity that have seen a record number of red notices being published—over eight thousand in the past three months alone.

With new insights revealed into how the secret organization worked, the sheer magnitude of their global influence is still being calculated. Experts say it might be decades before we fully understand their reach.

75

TEXT CHAT

CONOR: *So, I think I've figured it out.*

Star: *What? You've been working on Reinier's files, haven't you?*

Conor: *Yeah. Firstly, Anton did have slaves. I'm sorry, babe.*

Star: *I figured as much. Bastard.*

Conor: *He got rid of them during your stay at Uvala Lapad.*

Star: *He killed them?*

Conor: *Yeah.*

Star: *Christ. What a monster.*

Conor: *The bastard keeps on surprising me. I thought his trying to start another World War was bad enough.*

Conor: *But, that's not all.*

Conor: *Reinier has a whole file on Sparrow operations within Jorgmundgander.*

Star: *My mom?!*

Conor: *No. Your father's murder was documented. I'm sorry, baby. Some of his meds were tampered with.*

Star: *I want to see the reports when I get back.*

Conor: *Of course. Hey, I love you.*

Star: *I love you too. I will NOT break down. I fucking won't. I won't. Tell me what else you've uncovered.*

Conor: *I know why Bogdan Belyaev and Aleks Kuznetsov were killed.*

Star: *Why?*

Conor: *Belyaev and Kuznetsov (Anton) were planning a takeover of the Sparrows. Belyaev would run the Sparrows, and Kuznetsov (Aleks) would head the Brotherhood. So, the other leaders took them out.*

Star: *I'm surprised Anton wanted to share the pie.*

Conor: *Temperance wasn't wrong when she said their families go WAY back. When Anton spoke of Aleks, I used to wonder why, if he was so all-fired GOOD, he was friends with a fucker who murdered his wife.*

Conor: *Anyway, the interactions are odd. Bear had it right when he said the Brothers and the Sparrows are like siblings. They bickered a whole hell of a lot.*

Conor: *I looked at DeLaCroix's emails at the time, and he was crowing to Smythe about beating Anton at his own game.*

Star: *Jesus. If Reinier has files on all Jorgmundgander operations that were at the behest of the Sparrows, then does that mean Anton was lying about Reinier killing Mom?*

Conor: *I have to think so. We'll get there, baby. We'll get you the answers you need.*

Star: *I'm starting to lose hope, Conor. I thought I could deal without knowing but fuck, it hurts so badly.*

Conor: *I know. But there are millions of files to work through. Somewhere, we'll find out what happened to her. I won't stop until you know the truth.*

Star: *I love you. Thank YOU.*

Conor: *You don't have to thank me. How goes the book launch?*

Star: *I'm hating every minute of it.*

Conor: *It must be so hard being a bestselling author. :P*

Star: *Savannah wrote it.*

Conor: *Speaking of memoirs, I read Lorelei's autobiography yesterday.*

Star: *Ugh. I couldn't get past the first chapter. I didn't need to know so much about my dad.*

Conor: *Lol, yeah, she got... graphic.*

Star: *Bleugh.*

Conor: *Surprised you let her publish it.*

Star: *Fuck it. If it makes her happy, then it makes her happy.*

Star: *You'll never guess what Savannah told me today.*

Conor: *?*

Star: *She's going to write kids' books.*

Conor: *Are you for real? LMAO.*

Star: *I mean it. She was dead serious too. Says that Lyra's inspired her.*

Conor: *I'm offended on our daughter's behalf.*

Star: *ROFL. Me too! Bahahaha. We won't tell Kat, eh?*

Conor: *Definitely not. We'll never hear the end of it.*

Conor: *BTW, thank you for my 'I'm a spy's perfect boyfriend' mug lol.*

Conor sends photo

Star: *Hahaha. You're welcome. :**

Star: *Oh, Savannah wanted me to tell you that the Israelis are coming to instruct the Five Points next month.*

Conor: *Yeah, Aidan said. Why's she telling me via you too?*

Star: *Fuck knows how Savannah's mind works. She's even crazier now that she's pregnant.*

Conor: *Lol. True.*

Conor: *Go back to your launch. It'll be over soon and you're making the foundation a fortune.*

Star: *That's the only bearable part of all this. *sighs**

Star: *:**

Conor: *<3*

CHAPTER SEVENTY-SIX

STAR,

I'm sure you have zero interest in communicating with me after what I did to your mother, but I owe you a debt of gratitude and Aoife was telling me this week about how little closure you've gotten with everything that happened to your mom.

I've been following you in the press, watching you and Conor O'Donnelly strip the world of scum, and I read about that shooting incident in DC where you were targeted...

The papers said it was a close call. I asked Aoife and she said it was closer than close.

It got me thinking—they never tell you that old age makes you introspective—and here I am, writing you a letter at three AM.

Look, these may just be rumors, and as Jorgmundgander operatives, we definitely weren't given all the details, but the Jorgmundgander base was up in Scotland. A place called Lockerbie. Does the name ring any bells? If it doesn't, in 1988, there was a bombing up there in a plane. Random place for that kind of shit to happen, don't you agree?

The whole thing was a tragedy, as things in this line of business often are.

Back in '88, I heard about it and pinned it on the New World Sparrows. It was one of many reasons why I started getting, shall we say, incendiary.

Barely ten years later, I was approached by Jorgmundgander while rotting away in a prison cell, running the ECD from there with help from some guards who were allies, and I figured it was a way to keep on taking down Sparrows and it'd enable me to run the ECD better.

I enlisted, never realizing I was signing my fucking soul away to the people who orchestrated worse acts of violence against the public than Hitler or Mussolini could ever come up with.

Anyway, I didn't send this to salvage my conscience. I'm already fucked when I meet Peter at his pearly gates. What I wanted to tell you was a story.

You ask any Jorgmundgander operative and they'll tell you that training includes learning of anecdotes about past missions that went awry or variants on that—they're shaped like exercises but they're warnings.

So, one day during training, when I'm starting to realize what I signed up for, they talked about this ex-operative who 'tried' to stop a sanctioned bombing that, allegedly, was supposed to trigger political strife between an African nation and the West.

The ex-operative failed, of course, and the bombing went ahead and people died as, and I quote, people are wont to do.

I never thought much of it afterward. There were more stories, worse than that, and I started my time as an operative for them, getting kills under my belt and days knocked off my sentence. I'd sold my soul to the fucking devil, but it was helping me work with the ECD, coordinate attacks on the English and the Sparrows and such, so I carried on.

A death was a day knocked off my sentence; sometimes a kill was important enough to earn myself a week.

Deaths became time served and that was my one focus.

I always knew why I'd been approached, not just because of my skills, but because the US has never not had an interest in liberating Ireland.

Just like they remained puppeteers in the nations who were in

England's empire that wanted independence. It's all been a key part of destabilizing Britain's imperial rule.

As we stand, I'm not sure who was supposed to benefit. Maybe no one. Maybe everyone. Maybe just the Sparrows and these godforsaken Brothers.

After decades of war, we're no further along than we were in the forties, so only time will tell who's the winner here.

As far as I can see, we're all just goddamn losers in a game no one asked us to play.

Anyway, one day, I'm waiting to kill this diplomat, and the Jorgmundgander official assigned to my task force got drunk and put on the radio.

It was a nighttime special for noxxious *fans, of which he was one. The drunker he got, the more loose his tongue became, and he started bragging about how he'd fucked Gerry Sullivan's wife back when she worked with the snakes.*

I dismissed it as nonsense at first—the talk of someone who'd downed too many beers. But we'd been staking out this particular embassy for forty-seven hours, waiting for this diplomat, so I peppered him with questions, my partner did too, both of us wanting to see how far he'd take the bullshit.

Casey Sullivan, he shared, hadn't always been called that.

She'd been Galena back when he knew her.

There'd been rumors she was related to someone in the top ranks, but nepotism hadn't played a role in her recruitment—she'd been one of the best with a kill record almost as good as mine.

Then, the Lockerbie bombing happened.

The agent claimed 'Galena' had spent years trying to stop it. When she realized there was still a green light on the bombing, she ran to America, he said. Started using an old handle and took up with the CIA. Got with Gerry fucking Sullivan. Married him. Had a kid.

He even said that he was sure a tip-off to the authorities about the threat came from her.

His story was ludicrous.

Goddamn insane, but I was bored.

Then, the following day, that agent died.

Suddenly, his story didn't seem so ludicrous.

I wasn't so bored.

A couple of weeks later, I'm staring down the barrel of a gun and Casey Sullivan's in my sights.

You can take this however you want. You can believe it or you don't have to. At first, I didn't. But then, Faraday died of 'natural causes,' a guy who popped vitamins and worked out religiously, who got drunk on two bottles of beer and ate bags of iceberg goddamn lettuce as a snack. Heart attack, they said when I asked.

Heart. Attack.

I never saw my partner again and figured he shared Faraday's gossip with the top brass. Not that it got him anywhere. He was on the end of my scope a month after your mom. If my rep wasn't what it is, I don't doubt they'd have killed me off too.

Not that they didn't try in New York, but that was another sin. Christ, I've committed so many that they're difficult to keep track of.

Maybe this brings you closure, maybe it doesn't. I figured you'd want to know—I would. Should have told you that day we met at the black-site hospital, but you know how it goes—we don't share; we hoard intel.

Aoife's not letting me get away with that, and seeing as you've been so good with her and seeing how she considers you to be one of her best friends, I wanted to share what I knew.

Your mom wasn't a good person if she worked for Jorgmundgander, but she tried to stop a bombing where two hundred and seventy inno-cent people were killed. I think that makes her a hero, especially as she paid for it with her life.

I doubt that's any consolation to you, Star, but it would be to me.

All the best,

Dagda

NEW INSIGHTS REVEALED INTO LOCKERBIE BOMBING

WITH THE LATEST revelations into the United Brotherhood's and New World Sparrows' activities, the depths of their depravity should come as no surprise.

The Lockerbie bombing, it has been revealed, could have been prevented.

A tip-off was sent to multiple agencies warning of a potential strike against the doomed flight.

Worst of all, the tip-off was sent from CIA agent, Casey Sullivan, wife of *noxxious* band leader, Gerry Sullivan. It is unknown how Mrs. Sullivan was aware of the threat to the Pan Am flight, but her death was, until recently, also shrouded in mystery.

While Interpol's Special Trafficking Unit has confirmed that Mrs. Sullivan was murdered, they have not said by whom. Leaked documents sent to the *City Times* uncovered a NATO-run military operation by the code name Jorgmundgander which both organizations used as their own personal armies and who targeted Mrs. Sullivan in a direct attack.

Sullivan, it appears, fell out with the leadership of Operation: Jorgmundgander over the terrorist attack and parted ways with them. The timing of her death, years after the bombing, remains a mystery.

Sullivan, who also went by the name 'Galena Kuznetsov,' has a muddied past with ties to both the United Brotherhood and Jorgmundgander. She is the mother of Star Sullivan, who, the *City Times* can reveal, is a key source of intel for Interpol's STU.

Our journalists are working around the clock to investigate the leak which consists of tens of thousands of documents.

ACUIG CORP. DOMINATES SPORTS LEAGUES

WITH THE NEW YORK Saturns having taken home the CONCACAF Champions League Cup and the New York Stars heading for this year's Stanley Cup Final, is there anything the real estate mogul can't do? Which major sporting league is next for Acuig?

77

CONOR

SEVEN YEARS LATER

Conor O'Donnelly

"YOU LOOK GORGEOUS," Camille declared, sniffling as she finished touching up Kat's makeup.

"You do," Aoife agreed as she stopped doing this twisting thing with her hair that put it in a better braid than I'd ever been able to achieve.

I didn't want to stare in the mirror.

If I did, I'd see my little girl.

All.

Grown.

Up.

When the fuck had that happened?

How had seven years spun by like the blink of a goddamn eye?

How was this her debutante ball? How was it that I'd had to teach her to dance the cotillion?

I scratched my jaw from the sidelines, watching as her aunts got her ready for the big event while Star and I sat together, seeing our little girl become a woman before our very eyes.

"I knew Camille would get the makeup right."

Star had to referee over which of her sisters-in-law would 'do'

Kat's face for the big day. She'd offered to get a professional in, but that had caused more of an argument.

I wasn't sure if I wanted to know how she'd picked the winner. As each of my brothers' wives aside from Savannah had given birth to boys, I figured they'd clashed over this moment because Third, our nickname for baby Aidan, wasn't going to be ready for this occasion for another thirteen years.

"I'm not looking," I grumbled. "If I don't look then she's still ten."

Star snorted as she pressed a kiss to my cheek. "Think about your ma having to care for all the grandkids tonight. That should make you laugh."

"She thought it was bad having six sons. Ten grandkids." I whistled under my breath. "Thank God Paddy's with her. It'll stop her from pulling out her hair."

"You just have to love how, out of all of them, Third's the worst."

I shuddered. "The terrible twos were nothing in comparison to the terrifying threes."

She nodded. "How did she even get on the kitchen counter yesterday?"

"Probably bribed one of the boys into lifting her up," I said with a grimace. "It's a good thing you saw her trying to grab the handle of that knife."

"You need eyes in the back of your head with Daniels' kids. You think she's bad, you should have been around for Aspen and Paris. Jesus Christ, it's no wonder Dagger went prematurely gray."

"Two of them," I breathed, eyes widening with horror. "At once."

"Exactly."

"Daddy, what do you think?"

My heart stopped at that title.

It always did.

But especially at a moment like this, when she was nervous and excited at the same time.

'Daddy' had come after a year of us being a family. It had morphed into 'Dad' when she was a teenager. That we'd reverted to Daddy broke my heart even more.

It wasn't right that she was growing up.

God, all my kids were going to do this to me, weren't they?

I turned to stare at her and tried to brace myself for the fallout, but there was no bracing big enough for this.

"You look beautiful, Katty," I choked out, using the nickname so that I didn't totally crumple into a ball of misery and joy.

She giggled. "Katty? Really?"

"Really," I teased, helping Star off my lap so that I could stride over to our daughter and tug her into a hug. In her ear, I whispered, "You're going to be the belle of the ball."

"Don't tell Lyra that. She'll be jealous when it's her turn next year. You know she's all about being Belle."

I chuckled. "You know what I mean." I squeezed her. "You okay?"

"Nervous, but happy."

"That's all right then. I schooled Seamus myself. He'll be here soon with your corsage, and he's got it down pat on how to present you so you can trust him to know what to do if you get nervous and forget." Or I'd beat the shit out of him. "So just relax and have fun, okay?"

"I will."

As I pulled away, I reached into my pocket and retrieved a box. She beamed a grin at me. "Thank you, Daddy."

"You don't know what's in it yet," I pointed out.

She shrugged. "Doesn't matter. You picked it so I know it's given with love."

That had me blowing out a breath.

Somehow, the precocious kid who knocked shit over without trying had become a thoughtful, intelligent, kind young woman, capable of breaking her father with a few words.

Silently, I handed her the box and as usual, Star's timing was perfect because she slipped her arm around my waist.

"From both of us," I croaked.

Star smiled up at me, her hand finding mine before she knotted our fingers together. "Love you," she whispered.

"Love you too," I mouthed.

"Oh, they're beautiful," Kat cried, unaware of the exchange.

I smiled at her as I cupped her cheek and pressed a kiss to the other one. "Just like you." I gave a squeeze to Star's fingers. "Ready?"

She bit her lip and handed Kat another jewelry box. "This was my mom's, baby. We found it amid her things. I want you to have it."

Kat's eyes were wide, tears rimming her lashes as she opened the box to reveal a large diamond pendant that was surrounded by tiny sapphires.

There'd been many such pieces in Galena's room at the Uvala Lapad palace, many trinkets that we'd brought back to the States once Star inherited Anton's vast wealth, but out of them all, this was the one she'd earmarked for Kat from the beginning.

As I fastened the chain around her neck, I pressed a kiss to her temple. "Now, I have to see to something. I want your second dance, do you hear me?"

She nodded as she fumbled to put on the diamond earrings.

Star shot me a questioning look but I ignored it as I headed toward the door. She grabbed me at the last minute and tugged on the back of my tuxedo jacket.

"What 'something' do you have to see to?" she inquired.

I blinked at her. "I'm just going to threaten Seamus within an inch of his life not to let any boy around her longer than fifteen seconds."

A smile danced on her lips. "I think he likes her."

"I know he does," I said grimly. "That's why I know he's the best man for the job."

"We want him to be president. He can't go around beating up boys for flirting with our daughter."

I sniffed. "Who says he can't?"

78

———————

SEAMUS
TWO YEARS LATER

"STOP IT," Katina groused at my side. "This isn't funny."

"It's kind of funny," I teased, knocking into her with my elbow.

"It isn't," she argued. "It's in bad taste."

I smirked at the *Harry Potter* meme. "You need to lighten up."

"Today's a somber occasion," she argued.

"Didn't stop you from wearing pink."

She huffed. "A pink scarf. Everything else is black."

I tried not to think about what *else* could be black.

Or, fuck, *pink.*

I didn't need to be getting a boner in front of a crowd of millions.

Especially not because of my cousin.

God, that sounded so bad.

But she wasn't really my cousin.

What the fuck was it with me?

Did I get a kick out of the taboo or something?

First Victoria, now Katina.

Never mind Aunt Inessa.

I'd worry I was sick if my shrink hadn't told me it was perfectly normal. The trouble was, it didn't feel perfectly normal.

Not the way she made me smile.

Not the way she made me happy.

Not the way her obsession with pink always made me snort.

Not the way I wanted to hold her and to kiss her brow, to help her when she had one of her darker days.

I sometimes thought that was what made us so perfect for each other—we knew what real evil was. We could be each other's soft place to land. We both had shrinks, we both had goals, and we both wanted to accomplish more than what our parents had achieved.

The only trouble?

She saw me as a friend.

A fucking friend.

I released a breath as she stepped out of the car, trying not to stare at her ass and how her skirt pulled taut around her hips.

"If she catches you looking, she'll kill you."

I smirked at Kat's brother, Niall, the only one in the family who seemed to recognize my less-than-friendly feelings for Kat. "She won't catch me."

"You make it *so* obvious," he retorted. "Girls are gross anyway. Kat's grosser than them all. Pink sucks."

"You'll change your mind about girls when you're my age," I promised him. "You ready for this?"

"Have to be, don't I?" he grumbled, tugging on his necktie as Kat leaned into the back of the limo again and helped her younger siblings out.

There was fourteen-year-old Benjamim who'd been saved from a child brothel in Rio de Janeiro, then there was six-year-old Enzo, who they'd managed to spare from death when a now-jailed tycoon had paid for his lungs and heart in a transplant that would've saved his kid while using Enzo like his body was an organ store.

Minnie, the only one in the car with Star and Conor, was a baby. Her mom had killed herself a few months after Minnie's birth, unable to deal with what had happened to her as Sparrow chattel, unable to cope with bearing her rapist's child.

Each of Star and Conor's sons and daughters was born of or into tragedy, but here, they were normal.

Here, they were annoyed at having to wear suits and were grouching at being awoken at six to get ready for the ceremony.

Having promised to help Kat with her younger siblings—for obvious reasons—I dragged Enzo and Niall out onto the sidewalk and straightened up their ties and jackets as Benjamim did the same with his own suit.

"You just have to smile when a camera pops up in your face. Don't say a word," I ordered.

"And don't touch anything," Kat prompted. "Don't fidget either. Just stand still and don't get into trouble."

Enzo giggled. "I'm a good boy."

"No, Enzo, you're not. I love you and I love that you and Third are our bringers of chaos, but today, you need to be good. This is bigger than all of us. Mom has worked for decades for this moment, ya hear me? She's earned this."

"Hey, so'd Conor," I argued.

Kat sniffed. "I love my dad, but he didn't know anything until Mom came along."

"Girl power," Niall said with a sigh.

"Exactly," Kat chirped. "We're the best, Niall. Remember that now and it will save you lots of problems in the future."

Though I snorted, I saw the other cars were parked, my family already on the sidewalk. "Right, are we good to go?"

"I think I need the bathroom," Enzo whined.

"Jesus," Kat grumbled, pinching the bridge of her nose. "I took you *twice* before we got here. Do you really have to go?"

His bottom lip popped out from between his teeth. "Maybe?"

"How about you make a decision now, kiddo," I quipped, "and if you decide not to drive Kat and me crazy, then we promise we'll take you to the movies tonight."

"Can I pick what we go see?"

"Duh." I didn't care what we watched. Not if Kat was there. It was a win-win for me.

Enzo grinned, revealing a space where his teeth were missing. "I don't need the bathroom."

"Magic," I drawled.

"Enzo, when you smile, keep your mouth closed. We have to look perfect for Mom."

That had me blinking at her. "Star never said you had to look perfect."

I'd know. I was there, listening into their conversation when she'd asked Kat to help with the younger kids. Kat was only on edge because of something else Star had shared with her.

Apparently, she had a large legacy from her father and a living aunt from his side of her bloodline too…

I had no idea why that knowledge upset her, but it had, and she'd been acting like a dragonfly had burrowed into her ear and taken it hostage ever since.

"No, she just asked us to look decent," Kat agreed. "So, look decent we will. Right?"

Niall sniffed. "You're worse than Lenin."

"I'm not," Kat argued, straightening her shoulders and then grabbing Enzo's hand. "And I regret telling you about him now." To me, she ordered, "You get Niall."

"I'm not holding his hand! I'm not a kid," Niall cried.

"Don't worry, dude," I soothed, clamping my fingers on his shoulder. "That better?"

"Much better," Niall said with a sniff, glowering at his sister who surprised us both by sticking out her tongue at him.

I hid a grin at the move because *that* was Kat. Not this uptight Type-A chick that was dealing with *something* since Star had dumped the news of her inheritance and her aunt on her last night.

Why she'd waited until this moment to share that with her kid, I didn't know. Maybe it was because Kat was starting college in the fall, or maybe she just figured it was time—who the fuck knew how Star's mind worked?

What I did know was that Kat was dealing with the aftermath of these revelations and me being the moron who was head over fucking heels for her, I wanted to help.

Even if that only meant corralling the demon spawns that were her siblings.

As guards gathered around us and aides began to lead us toward a stage, we stayed in a pretty tight formation, which was a miracle considering how many of us were here.

The whole O'Donnelly clan numbered over two dozen now with all the kids.

To be honest, I was lucky I didn't have to keep control of my siblings because if Kat thought Enzo was a bringer of chaos, that was nothing on my freakin' brother, Dermot.

Even Aidan the Third was behaving, and she was a fucking nightmare worthy of Savannah and Aidan Jr.'s DNA.

Of course, with any family event of ours, there had to be drama.

When the guards suddenly shouted, "GET DOWN! SHOOTER!" and we were shoved onto the ground, men piling on top of us and the kids to keep us safe, I heaved an impatient sigh. Even Enzo, the youngest of our group, yawned.

This was life as an O'Donnelly, after all.

Especially this new version that was the hybrid Irish Mob/sports team owner/renowned kids' books author/baker/face that smashed a thousand Sparrow and Brotherhood ships.

Around us, the mania of an active shooting situation blared to life, but to the kids, Kat and I played 'I Spy,' which wasn't fun when your vision was limited to two feet on the ground but it kept them occupied until security contained the sniper.

Fifteen minutes later, Lucinda popped up, brushing us all down and making us presentable again.

"Who was it, Cin? Are they in custody?"

She tutted. "I'm not Cin anymore, Seamus. I'm Lucinda."

Kat snorted. "What a difference a name *doesn't* make."

"I work with your mom now."

"And?" Kat arched a brow at her. "Let me guess, you handled the shooter."

Cin preened. "I can't help it that I have an eye for these things."

"That's why Star hired you, isn't it?" I questioned in a low voice. "It has nothing to do with you being a great assistant—"

"—or the only person who'll deal with her without wanting to strangle her," Kat finished.

Cin smirked. "You can't put words in my mouth. Anyway, the shooter is in a body bag and so he should be for disturbing this momentous occasion. Now, the crowd is ready—"

"You mean to tell me that you didn't clear out the audience?" Kat shrieked.

"Why bother? They weren't targeting the audience."

"So reassuring, Cin."

She sniffed at her. "Come on. We gotta get this ball rolling."

"Are people still trying to kill us?" Enzo asked as he tugged on my hand.

Kat and I shared a glance. "You don't need to worry about that," I told him.

"I'm not worried. I'm asking a question," he replied, sounding far too serious for a six-year-old.

But I knew how that worked.

Hadn't I watched my grandparents be slaughtered when I was around the same age as him?

This life… this world… No matter what Star promised, there was no cleaning it up entirely.

The urge to make a real difference had me in a chokehold.

Not for the first time, either.

"We'll never let anyone kill us, Enzo," Kat reassured him. "That's not the O'Donnelly way, is it?"

He blinked but he agreed, "No, it's not."

"Your mom is untouchable anyway," Cin quipped.

I stared in the distance, seeking out my aunt, and found her soothing Minnie on her hip. Uncle Conor was making faces at the baby, and as much as it always was with the two of them, hell, my parents and aunts and uncles as well, it was like the world didn't exist when they were together.

Everyone else faded into nothingness.

Maybe not their kids, but that level of connection, the unity, the *love*, it was something I'd been raised with and something I craved.

Nervously, I studied Kat and saw a wistful expression on her face as well.

Did she feel it too?

"Come on, troubles," Cin chirped, breaking into the moment. "Let's get this show on the road."

Kat surprised me by slipping her hand into mine and squeezing it tight. As our fingers knotted, she peered at me. "Good to go?"

My heart stuttered. "Good to go."

As if the last twenty minutes hadn't happened, the O'Donnelly brood strolled down a short path that led to a stage where over five hundred people were seated, most of them press which explained why they hadn't run off—they were covering the event. Cameras were broadcasting it around the world and tomorrow's papers would be plastered with it too.

As a clan, we made it onto the stage, moving into pre-arranged positions. In the middle, Star's parents, Lorelei and Dagger Daniels, stood pride of place.

For the first time, I wasn't with Kat but had to return to my parents' and siblings' sides.

That didn't mean I wasn't looking at her.

Maybe Niall wasn't the only one who'd noticed my crush on Kat… I knew Uncle Conor had helped arrange the security for the stage and had worked with Cin to ensure our safety. He was probably why I could stare straight at her instead of being out in the cold.

Did that mean he didn't mind?

To a round of applause, Star walked toward a podium once some boring diplomat introduced her to the crowd.

Christ, I needed to focus. Not think about Kat. And whether her overprotective father might approve of me having feelings for her…

"It's taken nine years of striving, of fighting, of international cooperation, of governments uniting together with sanctions to fight the toxicity that has infected this world for over four hundred years, but here we are, still standing.

"Even today, they tried to stop us, but this is the proof we needed to show you that our fight isn't over. It will never truly be over.

"Today, however, isn't about the New World Sparrows or the United Brotherhood." She waved a hand and more people climbed onto the stage: Aaron Goldstein as well as the Satans' Sinners' MC's Old Ladies who worked with Star on her foundation. "It's about remembrance."

Behind us, the odd black wall that had blocked the audience from seeing behind us cascaded to the floor, revealing a labyrinthine path forged from walls that were inscribed with names.

Millions of them.

"Today, we celebrate the lives of those who didn't make it. We beg forgiveness for failing them, and we promise them we'll never allow their deaths to have been in vain.

"May this monument stand forever as a global apology to the women, men, and children who endured and who found peace in death.

"May this monument stand as a thank you to the people who served on the side of justice and died in the act of duty.

"May this monument prove that we stand united against authoritarianism, that democracy is as Abraham Lincoln himself said, 'A government of the people, by the people, and *for* the people.'"

At the second massive round of applause in less than ten minutes, Uncle Conor moved behind her, Minnie on his hip—as always, presenting a united front.

While the audience opened up for questions that peppered Aunt Star about her new role as a UN ambassador, I zoned out, more curious over Kat's pained expression as she angled herself so she was looking back at the monument.

Did she know how beautiful she was?

Did she know how gracious and graceful?

How couldn't she know how badly I wanted to kiss her? How badly I wanted to turn that freakin' frown upside down?

As I studied her, a reporter asked, "What's next for you, Ms. Sullivan?"

"There isn't a 'next.' That implies this is over. It is *not* over.

More names will be added to the monument as and when we uncover those we failed. More arrests will be made and more governments will topple as crooked officials are revealed through our investigations.

"This monument exists because two million women deserve to be remembered."

"But personally, Ms. Sullivan? There are rumors—"

"There are *always* rumors." Star smiled at the crowd, a special smile that hadn't existed before. That was a new mask. A PR mask that had come into being when she'd become the face of the ATRF foundation and had been revealed, by a tabloid, to be one of the key sources of intel for Aaron Goldstein's Special Trafficking Unit. A move I still wasn't sure was a leak Conor had orchestrated or not, but I figured it was likely. "The rumors of a split are *not* true. I've decided to make an honest man out of my fiancé." When Conor's brows lifted, she chuckled. "See? Even he didn't know that. You are *not* invited to my wedding; it will most definitely be a family affair.

"But it's time. Nine years, he's waited for me, and I know he'll wait a lifetime, but the longer this investigation carries on, the more I realize that there will never be a definite end point to it. *That* was what I was waiting for.

"There is centuries' worth of corruption to unravel, and together, Conor and I, as well as the team at Interpol, will work to bring justice to those we failed, while the ATRF will work to ensure that the victims have a safe place to land."

As the journalists applauded, I was close enough to Conor to hear him mutter, "I'll hold you to that promise, seeing as you skipped out on the tequila. I'm rather looking forward to being an honest man."

"Teamwork makes the dream work," she told him, turning into him as the cameras flashed, her cameo-beringed hand settling on his chest, her nose nuzzling Minnie's.

None of us knew that *that* shot would be the one featured on the front pages in the morning.

None of us knew that that shot would, panned wide with the monument in the background and the clan surrounding them, be used in the history books and that kids, years down the line, would have to reason in their essays why that was such a powerful image.

Why it was a declaration of love and intent.

Why it represented the fight for democracy and liberty for all.

No, to us, that was just Conor and Star.

Our uncle and aunt, mother and father, brother and sister-in-law.

As they made history together, I turned to Kat and found her watching me.

I smiled.

She smiled back.

AUTHOR NOTE

Well, there we have it.

I hope your heart feels full. I hope you enjoyed it. I hope it made you happy.

<3

Don't forget the second FILTHY TRUTH hits 500 reviews, I'll be dropping a bonus scene in my Diva reader group!

You can join here to read it when it happens: www.facebook.com/groups/SerenaAkeroydsDivas

PLUS...

If you need more of the Feckers, then there's Filthy Sinner which is dropping on the 24th January! You can preorder it here: www.book s2read.com/FilthySinnerSerenaAkeroyd

AND...

As I'm sure you gathered, I have a lot of ideas for this universe. While this chapter might be closing, it isn't over. The next faction on the agenda is... THE FORGOTTEN BOYS!

You can preorder the first book in the series here: https://book s2read.com/BratvaOneSerenaAkeroyd

FINALLY...

I'm so pleased to announce that I'll be co-authoring a project with Cassandra Robbins!! A character from her Disciples will be falling for a Fecker!! Can you guess who?!

You can preorder here: www.books2read.com/FilthyDisciple

Much love to you all,

Serena

xoxo

THE CROSSOVER READING ORDER
WITH THE SINNERS & VALENTINIS

FILTHY
FILTHY SINNER
NYX
LINK
FILTHY RICH
SIN
STEEL
FILTHY DARK
CRUZ
MAVERICK
FILTHY SEX
HAWK
FILTHY HOT
STORM
THE DON
THE LADY
FILTHY SECRET
REX
RACHEL
FILTHY KING

<u>FILTHY DISCIPLE</u>
<u>THE CONSIGLIERE</u>
<u>THE ORACLE</u>
<u>LODESTAR</u>
<u>SILENCED</u>
<u>END GAME</u>
<u>FILTHY RICHER</u>

FREE BOOK!

Don't forget to grab your free e-Book!
Secrets & Lies is now free!

Meg's love life was missing a spark until she discovered her need to be dominated. When her fiancé shared the same kink, she thought all her birthdays had come at once, and then she came to learn their relationship was one big fat lie.

Gabe has loved Meg for years, watching her from afar, and always wishing he'd been the one to date her first and not his brother. When he has the chance to have Meg in his bed—even better, tied to it—it's an opportunity he can't refuse.

With disastrous consequences.

Can Gabe make Meg realize she's the one woman he's always wanted? But once secrets and lies have wormed their way into a relationship, is it impossible to establish the firm base of trust needed between lovers, and more importantly, between sub and Sir…?

This story features orgasm control in a BDSM setting.
Secrets & Lies is now free!

CONNECT WITH SERENA

For the latest updates, be sure to check out my website!
But if you'd like to hang out with me and get to know me better, then
I'd love to see you in my Diva reader's group where you can find out
all the gossip on new releases as and when they happen. You can join
here: www.facebook.com/groups/SerenaAkeroydsDivas. Or you can
always PM or email me. I love to hear from you guys: serenaakeroyd@
gmail.com.

ABOUT THE AUTHOR

I'm a romance novelaholic and I won't touch a book unless I know there's a happy ending. This addiction is what made me craft stories that suit my voracious need for raunchy romance. I love twists and unexpected turns, and my novels all contain sexy guys, dark humor, and hot AF love scenes.

I write MF, menage, and reverse harem (also known as why choose romance,) in both contemporary and paranormal. Some of my stories are darker than others, but I can promise you one thing, you will always get the happy ending your heart needs!